9 Historical Romances
Promise Love Fulfilled
at Christmastime

the Christmas
BRIDES
COLLECTION

Kelly Eileen Hake, Kristin Billerbeck,
Lauralee Bliss, Irene B. Brand, Lynn A. Coleman,
Vickie McDonough, Tamela Hancock Murray,
Colleen L. Reece, Therese Stenzel

BARBOUR BOOKS
An Imprint of Barbour Publishing, Inc.

Jamestown Bride Ship © 2007 by Irene B. Brand
Navidad de los Suenos © 1999 by Kristin Billerbeck
'Til Death Do Us Part © 2009 by Lauralee Bliss
Courage of the Heart © 2009 by Tamela Hancock Murray
The Snow Storm © 2002 by Lynn A. Coleman
An Irish Bride for Christmas © 2008 by Vickie McDonough
Little Dutch Bride © 2008 by Kelly Eileen Hake
An English Bride Goes West © 2008 by Therese Stenzel
Angels in the Snow © 2000 by Colleen L. Reece

Print ISBN 978-1-63058-154-1

eBook Editions:
Adobe Digital Edition (.epub) 978-1-63058-564-8
Kindle and MobiPocket Edition (.prc) 978-1-63058-565-5

Cover Image: RonTech2000 / GettyImages

Published by Barbour Books, an imprint of Barbour Publishing, Inc., P.O. Box 719, Uhrichsville, Ohio 44683, www.barbourbooks.com

Our mission is to publish and distribute inspirational products offering exceptional value and biblical encouragement to the masses.

 Member of the
Evangelical Christian
Publishers Association

Printed in the United States of America.

Table of Contents

Jamestown Bride Ship by Irene B. Brand 5

Navidad de los Suenos by Kristin Billerbeck 53

'Til Death Do Us Part by Lauralee Bliss 105

Courage of the Heart by Tamela Hancock Murray 153

The Snow Storm by Lynn A. Coleman. 203

An Irish Bride for Christmas by Vickie McDonough 255

Little Dutch Bride by Kelly Eileen Hake 305

An English Bride Goes West by Therese Stenzel 351

Angels in the Snow by Colleen L. Reece. 399

Jamestown Bride Ship

by Irene B. Brand

Dedication

In memory of Dr. Herschel Heath, Dr. Charles Moffat,
and Dr. Elizabeth Cometti, my history professors at Marshall University,
who made a profound impression on my life and helped
prepare me for a writing career in historical fiction.

Chapter 1

Jamestown, Virginia Colony, 1620

Susanna Carter could hardly believe that she had survived the long sea voyage to Virginia. When Captain Trent bellowed from the quarterdeck that the colony was in sight, she left her cabin and hurried on deck as fast as her weak legs would carry her. She had lost count of the days they'd been on the voyage, but it seemed a lifetime since she had left London. The days on shipboard had been frightening enough, but after the ship left the Atlantic and moved slowly up the James River, the thick forests bordering the river had reminded Susanna of huge giants ready to pounce on their victims.

The sails were furled, the progress of the *Warwick* slowed to a crawl, and waves splashed against the tree-lined riverbanks. Susanna leaned against the bulwarks and stared in dismay and disappointment. Surely this village of squalid huts couldn't be Jamestown—England's prized possession in America! Advertisements had circulated in London for several years claiming that the New World offered opportunities for a life surpassing anything to be found at home.

As she turned her weary head and slowly surveyed the area, Susanna wondered if she had made a wise decision when she left London. Jamestown was the most woebegone place she had ever seen. She saw nothing except a fort constructed with tall, wooden posts enclosing a few houses and a church, with several homes and other buildings outside the palisade. It seemed incredible that she had endured weeks of seasickness, hunger, and every discomfort imaginable to reach the Virginia colony—a place she hadn't wanted to visit in the first place.

And regardless of her grandmother's plans, it would be a *visit*, and a short one at that. She touched the soft leather bag hanging inside her garments, which contained enough coins to pay her return fare to England. Even if Grandmother no longer wanted her, Susanna didn't doubt that her maternal uncle would be happy to give her a home.

In spite of her disappointment in Virginia, after a rough ocean crossing, Susanna was pleased to see something besides water and trees. She welcomed a few days of respite from the rigors of sea travel.

Ada Beemer, a friend Susanna had made on the voyage, joined her. "Are you feeling any better?"

"Not much, but at least I haven't been sick at my stomach since we left the Atlantic and sailed into Chesapeake Bay."

"Have you eaten anything?"

"I tried some cold gruel this morning, but I'm not sure it's going to stay down."

"It's good you didn't eat any of the pork. In spite of the thick salt packing, it's rancid now. I can hardly force it into my mouth."

Looking to the left, Susanna saw a large group of women surging toward the bow of the ship. Women were so scarce in the colony that for the past two years, the Virginia Company in England had recruited women to travel to the New World as brides for the colonists. The *Warwick* carried fifty potential brides, and Susanna scanned their faces, which mirrored a wide range of emotions—excitement. . .fear. . .resignation. . . hope. . .determination.

Riveting her attention on Ada, one of the prospective brides, Susanna tried to judge her friend's feelings, but her face revealed nothing. "Aren't you scared? Apprehensive of what's waiting for you?"

With a brave little smile, Ada admitted, "Of course I am. But whatever's waiting for me in Virginia can't be any worse than my life would have been if I'd stayed in England. When my father gambled away his inheritance and then took his own life, our whole family could have ended up in debtors' prison. My mother's brother was kind enough to settle our debts and give us a home, but there are three children younger than I, and I wouldn't add to his burden. Coming to America seemed to be my only option."

"Well, at least you had someone who wanted you. Grandmother lost all patience with me when I refused to marry the second man she chose for me." Bitterly Susanna added, "And treating me like a criminal, she transported me to Jamestown to live with my aunt."

Ada laughed softly. "But adults always arrange marriages. Why did you expect anything else?"

"I expected to marry someone I can love. My parents were devoted to each other, and that's the kind of marriage I want."

"The kind of love you're seeking is very rare in marriages. I hope I can learn to love the man I marry, but if not, I'll try to respect him."

"Aren't you taking a terrible risk? The man who chooses you might be a terrible person."

Ada shrugged her shoulders. "That's a chance I took when I made my decision. The men were screened by representatives of the Company, even as most of us were. But some of these women are convicts, and the English authorities are shipping them to Virginia to get rid of them. The settlers are taking a risk, too."

"From what I've heard of London's poor, many people are put in jail simply because they had to steal to feed their families."

Nodding, Ada agreed. "That's true, and that's why I've been kind to those women. But I pray that everybody finds the right mate. The two chaperones who sailed with us will talk to the men before they're allowed to approach us and will refuse anyone they consider unacceptable."

"The chaperones will be returning to England, won't they?"

"Yes, they're supposed to go home," Ada said, her eyes twinkling merrily. "But with women so scarce in this colony, they might decide to stay."

Observing the stern face of the stout, middle-aged woman who was beckoning Ada to join the other brides, Susanna doubted that she would stay behind. Which suited Susanna's purposes, for it would be impossible for her to return on the *Warwick* without another female on board. As strict as the chaperones had been with their charges, Susanna knew they would provide all the respectability she needed.

With a deep sigh, Ada said, "I'll soon learn what my future is. And I'm selfish enough to wish you *would* stay in Jamestown. I'd like to know that you're on the same side of the Atlantic I am, but I understand how you feel."

"You've been a good companion. I don't believe I would have lived through the voyage if you hadn't befriended me. I pray that God will lead you to the right husband," Susanna said.

"I believe He will. I'll try to let you know how I fare."

"Until the *Warwick* returns to England, I'll be with my aunt, Eliza Wilde, and her husband, Lester, but I don't know where they live." Gazing again at the few buildings, she added, "The settlement is small, so we shouldn't have much trouble finding each other."

Susanna returned to the tiny cabin where she had slept, picked up a small chest, and returned to the deck. The ship's captain, an acquaintance of her family, would see that her larger trunks were delivered to the Wilde home.

The ship was gliding closer toward the bank, and even that small movement nauseated Susanna. She clutched her stomach, which was sore to the touch. Whether from lack of strength or because she'd lost her land legs after so many weeks at sea, she felt dizzy, and her stomach heaved. Determined not to lose the food she'd eaten earlier, she turned her attention to her destination.

Although this colony had been established for several years, it seemed to Susanna that there weren't enough houses for the more than one thousand inhabitants reported to be living here. But Captain Trent had told her that some settlers lived in outlying districts. Above the squeaking of the ship's timbers and the snapping of the rigging, she heard him barking orders at the sailors.

The ship listed sharply to the left when it nudged roughly into the long wharf that jutted out into the river. When it righted itself, Susanna lost her balance. She grabbed at the bulwark and didn't fall, but the nausea returned. Without time to return for the pan she had used in the cabin, she leaned over the rail and lost her breakfast into the muddy water of the river.

Hearing loud laughter, she looked up to see several men looking her way, amused at her distress. Anger overriding her embarrassment, Susanna stared at them with a haughty expression meaning, "How dare you laugh at a woman of quality," a glance her grandmother would have approved. The men looked away quickly.

She scanned the large crowd waiting on the riverbank to see how many others had witnessed her distress, but most of them were looking toward the women waiting to disembark. The ship stopped, and two sailors jumped out to tie it to palings on the wharf.

Susanna's gaze rested briefly on the compassionate gray eyes of a handsome man standing close to the ship, who must have noticed that she was ill. Thankful for his apparent sympathy, she nodded to him but turned away when Captain Trent approached.

"Miss Carter, as soon as the other women get off, I'll take you to your family. I'll send your trunks later on in the day." He carried a small chest, but he leaned over and picked up the one at her feet. "Stay close beside me," he said. "I don't want these men to think *you* are a prospective bride."

Susanna made an effort to stay beside him, but her legs seemed to have a mind of their own, defying her efforts to move forward. Determined, she forced one foot after the other until she reached the wharf, which didn't have a rail for her to hold. The water swirling beneath the narrow wooden structure brought back her dizziness. She looked toward the captain for help, but he had his hands full already. Unable to control her legs and sensing that she was falling, she uttered a weak cry.

The *Warwick* was already in sight when Joshua Deane left the forest path. He wended his way among the wattle-and-daub structures of Jamestown, dismounted, and tied his horse to the hitching post in front of the stockade. When he shipped his hogsheads of tobacco several months ago, he had stipulated that the tobacco be exchanged for household items and seeds. He hoped this ship had brought them.

A ship's arrival was always a time of rejoicing, but he was surprised at the size of the crowd, as well as the excitement. As the ship neared the shore, Joshua noted the large number of women standing near the bow. Suddenly realizing the reason for the men's eagerness, he chuckled softly. The importation of wives was probably one of the best things the Virginia Company had done for the colonists. By experience, Joshua knew how lonely a man could get without female companionship, but he wasn't desperate enough to wed a complete stranger even if other considerations weren't involved.

Speaking to the colonists he knew, Joshua worked his way slowly toward the river. He reached the bank just as the ship nudged into the wharf. Three men beside him laughed uproariously, and he followed their pointing fingers. A woman, hardly more than a girl, leaned over the side of the ship, losing her dinner. He turned angrily on the three men who found her predicament amusing, but she didn't need his help. Imperiously, she lifted her head and stared scornfully at the men until, shamefaced, they looked away. Her eyes shifted to his, and she must have realized that he hadn't shared their amusement, for she inclined her head toward him. She looked away, but Joshua was concerned about her, for she looked as if she were going to faint.

A man approached the woman, and when Joshua saw that it was Captain Trent, he knew she was in safe hands. Eager to have a word with the captain about his shipment, Joshua worked his way toward the wharf, where several sailors held the prospective grooms at bay. They formed a path allowing the women to make their way unhindered up the bank and into the meetinghouse.

Joshua wended his way toward the captain just as the woman swooned. The captain saw her stumble, but before he could drop the chests he carried, Joshua leaped forward and caught her, swinging her upward into his arms before she fell into the shallow water.

"Thank you," the captain said. "That was quick thinking." He wagged his head sympathetically. "Poor girl! She's been sick most of the trip, but I thought she looked better today or I'd have been watching her more closely."

Joshua nodded toward the church. "Shall I take her up there with the other women?"

"No, she's not one of the brides. Her name is Susanna Carter, and she's come to visit her aunt, Eliza Wilde. Her grandmother, Lady Carter, put her in my custody to assure her safe delivery. I'm glad you caught her. I wouldn't want to get in bad with a family of quality!"

"I know where the Wildes live. I'll carry her there. It's only a short distance."

Susanna stirred in Joshua's arms and opened her eyes. Her eyes shifted from him to Captain Trent, who peered anxiously at her.

"Oh! What happened?"

"You almost fell off the wharf. Mr. Deane caught you. Are you strong enough to walk to your aunt's home? It's not far."

"I think so. I'm sorry I've been such a nuisance to you."

"After several weeks at sea, it takes awhile to learn how to walk on land again," Joshua warned. "With your permission, I'll carry you."

Susanna's eyes looked like black satin as she studied his face. Seemingly satisfied, she said, "Thank you. I am tired, and I don't believe I can walk."

Her lids slipped down over her eyes as she settled more comfortably into his arms. Joshua tightened his grip, feeling a strange sense of possession as he walked up the bank. Susanna's small, embroidered white cap had loosened, freeing her thick auburn hair to fall over her shoulders. A stiff breeze from the James twirled some of the loose tendrils around Joshua's face. He gazed at the dark lashes that swept across her delicately carved cheekbones. She was very pale, and he sensed that several weeks of seasickness had caused her smooth skin to lose color. Still, considering the sweetly curled lips set in an oval face and arching eyebrows just a shade darker than her hair, Joshua thought she was the most beautiful woman he'd ever seen.

So intent was he on his appraisal of Susanna, Joshua had forgotten the captain's presence. He looked up quickly when the captain said, "I've got two crates for you on the ship."

"I'm glad to hear that. I thought a ship was due, and I hoped it was bringing my supplies. I came on horseback today, but I'll bring a cart tomorrow to haul them to the plantation."

"That's soon enough. Your boxes are far down in the hold. It will take awhile to get everything unloaded."

Joshua had thought Susanna must be asleep for she hadn't moved, but without opening her eyes, she said, "When will you be leaving the colony, Captain?"

"A week or more. Why? You planning to go back? Your grandmother indicated that you were going to live in the colony."

She opened her eyes and gazed at the captain, and Joshua noted another facial feature—her determined chin. "That is *her* idea. Please don't leave without seeing me," she said.

The captain cast a puzzled look at Joshua, who had noticed that Susanna hadn't answered the captain's question.

Susanna lifted her upward curving eyelashes, and she managed a small smile. "Are we almost there?" she asked.

"Yes."

"Then please let me try to stand. I'd prefer that Aunt Eliza doesn't think that I'm unable to walk. She doesn't even know I'm paying her a visit, and I don't want her to think I'll be a burden to her."

Joshua looked at the captain uneasily.

"That might be best," the captain agreed. "But take it easy, Miss Carter."

Still holding her securely, Joshua set Susanna on her feet.

"Lean on Joshua until you're sure you can stand," the captain advised.

Susanna staggered slightly when her feet touched the ground, and Joshua tightened his hold. When her legs seemed to support her, she took one tentative step and then another. "I believe I'll be all right," she said, looking up at Joshua. "Thank you. I won't delay you any longer."

"We're almost to the house. I'll walk along behind you, and if you have trouble, I'll be here to help."

She accepted his help with a slight smile, and although Joshua could tell it was an effort, she walked with determination. He admired her slender body and straight back, as well as her courage. The cap fell to the ground, and her auburn hair swayed around her shoulders. He picked up the cap and handed it to her.

Although all the Jamestown houses were similar in construction, the Wilde home was larger than most of them. Huge logs shaped the oblong structure covered with a sod roof. Walls were made of smaller branches, which were daubed with thick clay found in the river marshes. Smoke drifted upward from a stone chimney. A narrow porch ran the length of the home.

As Captain Trent stepped up to the front door, Susanna leaned against a post for support.

"I'll leave you now," Joshua said.

"Thank you again."

He walked away, but he glanced back just as Eliza Wilde opened the door. He took one more glance at Susanna before he forced himself to look away. Five years ago he had made up his mind that there was no place for a woman in his life. What was there about Susanna Carter that made him question if he had made the right decision?

Chapter 2

While she waited for the door to open, Susanna realized that all of her trembling wasn't caused by seasickness and fatigue. What if Aunt Eliza didn't welcome her? She was a long way from home to find out that she wasn't wanted in Jamestown either. She remembered her uncle as a large, brusque man. What if Uncle Lester didn't want an uninvited houseguest? If she wasn't physically able to go home on the *Warwick*, would she be forced to marry one of these strangers in Jamestown just to have a roof over her head?

She glanced toward Joshua Deane's straight, well-built body and his long, easy stride as he walked away. Remembering his large, gentle hands as he'd carried her, she contemplated for a moment that marriage to *him* might be all right. But was he even now hurrying away to choose one of her shipmates for his bride? Or perhaps he already had a wife.

Her musings ended when the door opened and a tall, angular woman stepped out on the porch. After five years, Susanna had almost forgotten what Eliza Wilde looked like, but happy memories with this favorite aunt revived immediately.

Eliza shifted her eyes from Susanna to Captain Trent, then back again to Susanna, recognition slowly dawning in her eyes.

"Brought you a guest," Captain Trent said.

Eliza stepped closer to Susanna, disbelief in her dark eyes. "Susanna? Is it really you?"

"Yes. I'm sorry to come without an invitation."

"Why, child, you're welcome. I've never been so happy to see anyone."

Tears filled Susanna's eyes as Eliza pulled her into a tight hug. "Come inside out of the cold. You, too, Captain, and tell me why I've been so blessed." As she closed the door behind them, Eliza asked in a startled voice, "Has Mother died? Is that why you've come to me?"

"No, she's all right. . .but she doesn't want me to stay with her anymore." Susanna managed a small, tentative smile. "We don't get along very well."

Eliza stepped back from Susanna. "And I can see why! You're too beautiful—she was afraid you'd steal some of *her* admirers! What else did you do to anger her?"

"I turned down the men she wanted me to marry."

"And I'll bet they were twice as old as you and ugly as a rhinoceros but with plenty of money."

"Yes," Susanna answered and laughed softly, recalling her two suitors and how well Aunt Eliza had described them.

"Cap," Eliza said, "excuse us for airing our family problems before you. Sit down, both of you, and I'll get you a noggin of tea. I keep water hot all the time."

"I can't stop now, Eliza. I've got unloading to do."

"Then come later on in the week for a meal."

Captain Trent took a letter from the chest he carried. "Lady Carter sent this to you."

Eliza made a face. "Full of instructions on what I'm to do with Susanna, I'll wager." She tossed the letter on a chest. "I'll read it later."

Shaking hands with Susanna, the captain said, "One of the men will fetch your trunks up later on today."

Eliza closed the door behind the captain and turned to Susanna again. "I can't believe it's really *you*. If I have my way, I'm going to keep you here."

Motioning to her grandmother's letter, Susanna made a face. "I'm sure the letter will explain that's what grandmother intends, but I'm expecting this to be a short visit. If I'm feeling better, I'm returning to England when the *Warwick* sails. Uncle Felton will take me in."

"We'll talk about that later," Eliza said, and she patted a bench close to the fireplace, which Susanna sank onto wearily. "How about a cup of tea for you?"

"Tea! In Jamestown? It's a rarity in London. I've tasted it only once."

Laughing, Eliza said, "We don't have India tea either. It's sassafras tea— something we got from the Indians. It's used for medicinal purposes more than for general drinking, but when I'm tired, a hot cup of it makes me feel better."

Eliza took a pewter cup from a corner cupboard, lifted a heavy iron kettle from the crane hanging over the coals in the fireplace, and filled the cup. She handed the tea to Susanna, and she wrapped her hands around the warm cup. "Lester likes a cup of this every night for supper."

"Where is Uncle Lester?"

"In his workshop behind the house. His carpentry skills have come in handy here in the New World. He makes furniture, and because very few settlers bring household items with them, he has a thriving business."

Susanna sniffed the herbal tea and took a tentative taste. It wasn't distasteful, and she sipped it slowly.

While Eliza talked about their five years in the Jamestown colony, Susanna looked around the large room. A huge fireplace dominated one wall. A musket and a harquebus hung over the mantelpiece, which had been hewn from a huge tree trunk. A powder horn hung nearby. An iron crane, projecting over the coals, held several iron pots exuding tantalizing scents. The tea settled Susanna's stomach, and the food actually smelled appetizing. A pair of boards had been nailed together to form a table that stood on a trestle in the center of the room, surrounded by several benches and stools. A bedstead, covered with colorful quilts, was built into the wall. It was a small but comfortable home, Susanna decided, but apprehensively, she looked for another bed.

Interrupting her aunt, she said, "Is this your only room?"

"Yes, except for a little storeroom where Lester can sleep. Until we make other arrangements, you can sleep in the bed with me."

"Oh, no! I'll sleep in the storeroom. I shouldn't have come!"

"Don't be concerned about it," Eliza said. "As soon as you finish your tea, you must go to bed and rest. In a day or two, you'll feel fine, and we'll find a place for you to sleep." She motioned toward a ladderlike stairway beside the front door. "The loft is a nice warm place. We can fix a bed for you up there. Want some more tea?"

"No, thank you, but it was very good."

Eliza took the cup and set it on the table. She poured water from an iron pot into a wooden bowl and laid out some linen cloths and a square bar of soap. "While you take a good wash, I'll go tell Lester we have company. I don't s'pose you have any clean clothes in your chest, so I'll lay out one of my night-gowns. A good sleep will do wonders for you." She fastened shutters over the two small windows, which left the room in semidarkness, and pointed to a white sheet hanging on a rope beside the bed. "Pull that curtain when you get into bed."

Tears shimmered in Susanna's eyes when Eliza hugged her again and kissed her forehead. "Since God didn't favor us with any children, it will be wonderful to have some of my own kindred to share our bed and board."

As she washed away the stench of the long sea voyage, tears streamed down Susanna's face. The kindness of Joshua Deane and the obvious pleasure of Aunt Eliza to have her visit had made her arrival in Jamestown more pleasant than she could have imagined.

She wrapped her body in the voluminous nightgown, climbed into the high bedstead, and pulled the curtain. She tucked the bag of coins under the pillow. The mattress was filled with straw, but it was more comfortable than the damp cot she'd been sleeping on. It seemed strange to lie down without the shifting motion of the ship beneath her, but her eyelids felt heavy.

Susanna's last conscious thought was about Joshua, wondering if she would see him again before she left Virginia. . . .

※

Susanna sat up in bed and yawned, happy to be feeling like her old self again. She opened the curtain. Sunrays filtered into the room through the windows covered with oiled paper. She swung her feet over the side of the bed.

Eliza sat on a stool by the fireplace, sewing, and she turned at the movement. "Good morning," she said pleasantly. "You look better."

"I feel like a human again, and I'm even hungry. I don't remember much about the past day or two, but I think I went through the motions of eating."

"You've been here two days, and you've been out of bed a few times. But you would eat a small amount and fall asleep at the table," Eliza said, her face crinkling into a smile. "But you've been drinking a lot of water, and I thought that was better for you than food."

Susanna made a face. "After the first month, the water on board tasted terrible." Noticing her trunks beside the bed, Susanna said, "Good. I can have clean garments now."

"I washed the ones you were wearing when you arrived."

"You shouldn't have done that," Susanna protested. "I don't want to make extra work for you."

Lester, a large man with a full-moon face, stepped into the room. His blue eyes brightened when he saw that Susanna was awake. "Welcome to Jamestown and our home, niece. We talked a bit yesterday, but I don't think you were alert enough to know what we were saying."

Laughing, she said, "No. . . Everything is hazy, so we'll have to start over."

"Wrap a blanket around you and come to the table," Eliza said. "We'll have breakfast so Lester can go to work."

Breakfast consisted of porridge made from peas and beans, a hunk of dark wheaten bread, and sassafras tea. The food tasted strange to Susanna, but she could have eaten more than she did. Hesitating to risk more sickness by over-eating, she settled for small portions.

While Susanna changed into fresh garments behind the curtain, Eliza washed the breakfast utensils. "You should unpack your trunk today and hang your clothes on the pegs behind the bed. But before you do that, we might as well discuss what Mother had to say in her letter."

Susanna sat in the only chair in the room before the fireplace, while Eliza settled down on a nearby bench. "Mother writes that she's expecting you to stay with me, yet you said when you arrived that you intend to return to England on the *Warwick*. As you must realize, this places me in a predicament."

"I know, and I'm sorry, but although Grandmother is my guardian, I'm not content to let her dominate my life completely. What exactly did she write?"

"She asked me to give you a home until I could arrange a suitable marriage for you. But what puzzles me—if you intend to go back to England, why did you come in the first place?"

"Because Uncle Felton was in Scotland, and I had no one else to go to. Living with Grandmother had become impossible. Besides, I wouldn't insist on staying with her when she wanted me to leave. I believe I'm courageous, but not to the extent of trying to live on my own in London."

"God forbid that you would have tried that! But unless you step beyond the pale of society, what else can you do except marry? So why not marry and settle down here?"

Susanna shook her head, and she couldn't hide the discouragement that overwhelmed her. "It's not that I object to marriage so much. . .I'd just like to feel some emotion for the man I marry. Grandmother's only concern was that

I marry someone with money and prestige. I don't believe that's the kind of marriage God had in mind when He said that a man should leave his parents and stay close to his wife, and that the two of them would be as one."

Eliza's eyebrows lifted and her mouth twisted humorously. "Well, well! I hadn't expected such biblical insight from someone reared in my mother's home."

Susanna felt her face flushing. "My last tutor was a devout Christian. He studied at Oxford University where he had an opportunity to read a Geneva Bible. He copied passages from that Bible, and he had me memorize them. Grandmother didn't know or she probably would have let him go, for she seldom went to worship. I'm thankful that God worked through my tutor to teach me how important faith is in my life. If I hadn't already trusted God as my protector, I wouldn't have lived through this voyage."

"We, too, have become more dedicated in our faith since we came to America," Eliza said. "We face danger every day, never knowing when the Indians will attack our settlement. And there's so much disease! Lester and I turn each day over to God. Otherwise, we couldn't bear the frustration. The first preacher who came to Jamestown brought a Geneva Bible with him, and it's still in the meetinghouse. But now there's a copy of the King James Bible, which the preacher uses most often in his sermons."

"Yes, that's the translation used in most English churches now. My tutor thought the day would come when every home would have a copy of the Bible. Wouldn't that be wonderful?"

"It would, indeed," Eliza agreed. "But we've strayed from the subject. I wish I could persuade you to forget about returning to England with Captain Trent. Several ships come to Jamestown each year now—you can always go home later if you don't like it here. So why not give the colony a chance?"

Susanna shook her head. "There's nothing here for me."

"But what is there for you in England? Have you considered that it might have been God's will for you to come to America? I know it takes courage to carve a new home out of the wilderness. But an eighteen-year-old girl who would set out on a sea voyage to an unknown land rather than bow to her grandmother's wishes has to be courageous. Jamestown needs people like you."

Susanna didn't answer, but as Eliza turned toward the fireplace to check a simmering pot, she considered her decision. *Should* she take a look at Jamestown before she made up her mind?

Chapter 3

Within a week, Susanna had walked with Eliza several times around the settlement. Despite an agitated protest from her aunt, Susanna had moved into the storeroom to sleep. The room was cold, but after she made her bed there, Eliza kept the door open all the time so heat from the fireplace could penetrate the room. The first night she slept on the floor on a pile of blankets was a miserable experience, but Lester solved that problem by building a wooden cot for her.

Although minus a few pounds, her health had improved remarkably, and she was barraged with suitors. As soon as the unattached men of the colony learned that she was no longer ill, there was a steady stream of callers at the Wilde home.

Uncle Lester had turned out to be quite a tease, and he thought it hilarious that Susanna was besieged with eligible men. Finally, she accused, "I believe you're inviting these men to see me."

He laughed uproariously. "I'll admit it. I want you to stay with us."

"I warn you, Uncle Lester. When the next man shows up, I'm going to lock myself in the storeroom and you can entertain him."

"It's cold in there."

"Nonetheless, I mean it."

"I agree with Susanna, husband," Eliza said. "I want to keep her with us, too, but if she doesn't have a little peace, we'll drive her away."

Lester threw up his hands. "All right, I'll discourage any more visitors. But be honest with me, girl—haven't you seen one man that has stirred your heart a little?"

Susanna lowered her eyelids. How could she answer? None of the men who had called at the Wilde home had touched her heart, but she couldn't forget Joshua, and she wondered why he hadn't come to see her. She chose her words thoughtfully so she wouldn't be lying but would still prevent a statement that would make Uncle Lester suspect her feelings for Joshua.

"All of the men who've come this week have seemed nice enough, but marriage is for life, Uncle. I don't know any of these men, but you do. Which one do *you* think would make a suitable husband for me?"

Eliza seemed amused at Susanna's statement. "There!" she crowed. "She's put you on the spot. Serves you right for meddling."

Lester stirred in his chair, and his face flushed.

Hoping to add to his discomfiture, Susanna teased, "I really think you're tired of having me in the house, and like my grandmother, you want to get rid of me."

He jumped as if he'd been stung. "That's not it a'tall!" He looked reproachfully at his wife when she joined in Susanna's laughter. "There are several settlers who might make you a good man, but I'll mention two. Aaron Waller is probably your best choice—or Philemon Sommer."

Lester stared defiantly at Eliza, as if expecting her to disagree with him.

"Aaron Waller?" Susanna had seen so many strangers that it was hard to put faces and names together. But she finally placed Waller as a well-dressed man with a lean face, long, prominent nose, and wavy blond hair. "Isn't he that *old* man?"

"He's not as old as I am! Besides, he's a nobleman with some wealth. He has a nice home on his plantation and even has servants, so you wouldn't have to do the housework."

With a frown in his direction, Eliza said, "And he also has two grown children who are almost as old as our niece. Besides, he talks continuously about how rich he is and what famous ancestors he has."

Irritated, Lester said, "Well, if you don't like him, what's wrong with Philemon Sommer?"

"I remember him," Susanna said. "He's a very shy young man, but he seems like a good sort of fellow."

"Everybody likes him, for he's trustworthy and easy to get along with. He's a cooper and works hard. I think he'll be going a long way in the colony. You could do worse."

"No doubt you're right, but I won't marry him. And although I don't appreciate your matchmaking, I would like for you to do a favor for me. Will you out find who Ada Beemer married? She was one of the brides on the ship with me, and I'd like to see her. I hope she found a good husband."

"I'll ask around," Lester promised. "But it could be that she married someone who lives away from town."

Because Susanna knew that many of the settlers had taken up land outside the settlement, she didn't expect any immediate news, so she was surprised when Lester came in for supper that evening and said, "I found the lady. She's living in the settlement, married to Eli Derby. He's a good man—never misses Sunday meeting. He makes a decent living by cutting trees and shaping them into fairly good lumber."

"Ada will probably be at church tomorrow," Eliza said. "Do you feel able to attend? I should warn you that the preacher gets carried away sometimes, and we could be there a few hours."

"I want to go. I feel as healthy as I ever did. It was the rough seas that caused all the trouble."

"Another reason for you to stay in Jamestown," Lester said. "Why would you take another sea voyage and be sick again? I was seasick most of the time when I came over, and when I set my feet on the solid earth again, I vowed I was staying in America, either dead or alive."

He stared hopefully at Susanna, but when she didn't encourage him, he shrugged his shoulders in defeat and promised, "I won't meddle anymore."

~~~

The building was crowded. The benches were uncomfortable. The room was cold. But when Susanna lifted her voice with the other worshippers in the meetinghouse on Sunday morning, she sang as fervently as she had when she'd joined her tutor and the housekeeper as they worshipped in London's Chapel of St. John.

> *"Thou the all-holy, Thou supreme in might.*
> *Thou dost give peace, Thy presence maketh right;*
> *Thou with Thy favor all things dost enfold,*
> *With Thine all-kindness free from harm wilt hold."*

As she continued singing the hymn that had been used in worship since the twelfth century, Susanna's troubled spirit found peace. While all heads were bowed in prayer, she whispered, "God, flood my soul with the assurance that Your presence does make everything right. It doesn't matter whether I'm in England or in Virginia; You can keep me safe from harm. Father, increase my faith and help me make the right decision. Should I stay in Jamestown or go home?"

Susanna raised her eyes to find Joshua Deane watching her. He was leaning against the wall, and she wondered if he had placed himself so he could watch her. One corner of his mouth lifted into a slight smile. He smiled with his lips, but not his eyes, but still she sensed that the attraction she felt for him was not one-sided. Unlike those other men whom she'd met the past few days, she wanted to see more of Joshua. All through the long sermon, her thoughts kept returning to him.

After the benediction, Susanna leaned close to her aunt. "Joshua Deane is here. Why don't you ask him to eat with us?"

Eliza regarded her niece with an appraising glance, whispering, "I'll invite him, but you're barking up the wrong tree."

Not wanting Joshua to suspect that she had initiated the invitation, Susanna didn't accompany her aunt when she approached Joshua. Instead, she searched the congregation to see if Ada was present. Susanna spotted her friend several feet away and waved to her.

With a word to the man at her side, Ada hurried toward Susanna. They clasped hands, and Ada said, "You look so much better. I've been worried about you."

"My health is almost back to normal." Looking deep into Ada's eyes, Susanna asked, "How are things with you?"

"Good! I've got a lot to learn about living here, but I'm sure I have a good husband. Come and meet him."

Susanna walked beside Ada to her companion, a small man with a pleasant countenance, gentle brown eyes, and long, black hair tied back with a leather thong. "Eli, this is my friend, Susanna. I told you about meeting her on the ship."

He bowed slightly. "It's a pleasure to meet you, ma'am. I didn't have an easy time on my voyage over either, so I know what you went through. Welcome to the colony."

"Are you going to sail home with Captain Trent?" Ada asked quietly as the congregation filed out of the building.

"I don't know. My aunt and uncle are eager to have me stay here. If only everyone would stop trying to find a husband for me, I wouldn't mind waiting for the next ship so I could be sure I'm strong enough to start another ocean journey."

A smile trembled on Ada's lips, and she said softly, "Come to see us. I'll not do any matchmaking."

"Where do you live?"

"I'll show you." They walked outside the stockade, and Ada pointed to a small house at the edge of the forest. "That's our home," she said, and Susanna noted the pride in her voice.

"I'll come sometime this week."

Ada and Eli walked away, and Susanna waited for her family. As the churchgoers passed by, she recognized a few of the women she had met on the ship, most of them with men noticeably older than they were. Eliza had explained that the mortality rate among women was extremely high in the colonies, especially during childbirth, and that some of the settlers were widowers with children who needed a mother.

Before Eliza joined her, Susanna saw Joshua mounting his horse and riding away. Her gaze followed him.

"Turned me down," Eliza whispered when she stepped to Susanna's side. "I'm not surprised. I need to talk with you about Mr. Deane."

Someone called her name, and Susanna turned to see Aaron Waller approaching with a girl and a boy, probably in their late teens. Although most of the people in Jamestown wore drab garments without any ornamentation, the Waller children were dressed in the latest London fashions. Obviously, when he bragged about his wealth, Aaron was telling the truth.

Acting as if he were doing her a favor, Aaron said, "I want you to meet my daughter, Margaret, and my son, Abraham." Susanna shook hands with them, but hostility blazed from their eyes. Even if she had been interested in their father, their attitudes would have discouraged her.

"You're invited to be a guest in our home whenever it's convenient for you," Aaron said, but Susanna was spared an answer when Captain Trent hailed her.

She turned toward him.

"Miss Trent, it's a pleasure to see you in such fine fettle."

"I'm feeling much better. When will you start back to England?"

"I wanted to talk to you about that. There's a leak in the hold that has to be repaired which will delay our departure. Are you still considering a return to England, or has one of the settlers persuaded you to stay here?"

Aaron, who had overheard their conversation, said, "What's this? You're returning to England?"

Although annoyed, Susanna said, "That's my intention, and nothing so far has happened to make me change my mind."

Ignoring Waller, the captain said, "Since we've waited this long, I may delay our departure until after Christmas."

"But you must come to my plantation for a weekend visit before you return to England," Waller insisted.

"Thank you, but my future is unsettled, and I can't accept the invitation."

Eliza, who had silently witnessed this exchange said, "Gentlemen, please excuse us. My niece is still recuperating, and it's time she went home for a rest."

⊷⊷⊷

Riding away from the settlement, Joshua was angry with himself for turning down Eliza's invitation. Instead of saying a blunt, "No, thank you," he should have answered civilly. He could have offered the excuse of another engagement, which was true, for he intended to stop at a sick neighbor's to take care of his animals and cut some wood. But he could have done that after they had eaten.

Since the day he had seen Susanna on the ship, Joshua had thought of her often. And judging from the look of gladness he'd seen in her eyes when she looked at him during worship, he was foolish enough to believe she had thought of him, too. Was it possible that she had asked Eliza to invite him to eat with them? He groaned aloud. If so, what must she think of him?

Many times during the past years, as he'd worked hard to claim his plantation from the wilderness and had built a comfortable home, he wondered why he had bothered. He intended to remain single, so why did it matter whether he made a success of this New World venture? Only to himself did Joshua ever admit that he was lonely. Because his first marriage had ended in such a disaster didn't mean that it would happen again. Why should he deny himself the pleasures of a wife and family because of fear?

When he had set out for the Virginia colony, he had compared himself to Abraham—the biblical patriarch who had made several long journeys before he arrived in the land God had promised him. Abraham had had plenty of problems, but his faith in God hadn't wavered, believing that what God had promised He would fulfill. Joshua had that kind of faith once, but he had lost it. Was God speaking to him again? Calling him to put the past behind him and step out in faith to start another life? His decision would be easier if he knew whether God was also preparing Susanna Carter to share his life.

Chapter 4

Plodding the short distance from the meetinghouse to the Wilde home, Susanna's heart seemed as heavy as her feet. She had been exhilarated when the worship service ended, but now weariness had overcome her.

She glanced upward and noticed that Eliza watched her with concern in her eyes.

"Did he give any reason for refusing?"

"He said, 'No, thank you,' and walked away."

When they entered the house, Susanna said, "I'm going to rest awhile." She picked up a quilt from the bed, saying, "I'll lie down in the storeroom. You and Uncle Lester go ahead and eat. I'll have something later."

When a knock sounded on the outside door, Susanna said, "I'll see who it is."

Susanna took a sharp breath when she opened the heavy door. Joshua stood on the threshold. She stared at him, speechless.

"Who is it?" Eliza asked, tying an apron around her waist.

Susanna stepped backward and motioned for Joshua to enter.

"Mrs. Wilde," he said, "I was too hasty in turning down your invitation. I'm committed to stop at a neighbor's and help with his work, but I decided I could do that after dinner. That is, if the invitation still stands."

"Of course it does. I'm just ready to set the food on the table. Take his coat, Susanna."

Distracted by his presence, Susanna remained tongue-tied as she laid the quilt on the bed and hung Joshua's coat on a wooden peg. She was thankful when Lester entered the cabin.

Ending an uncomfortable moment, he said, "Glad to have you share our food and drink, Joshua. Wife, if we've got time, I'll take him to the shop and show him the progress I'm making on his furniture."

Eliza nodded assent. "I'll be dishing up the food while Susanna sets the table, so don't take long."

"Let's go out the back door," Lester said, and the two men left the house.

Susanna went to the cupboard and lifted out the pewter plates and spoons. "Why do you think he came back?" she asked.

With a deep sigh, Eliza said, "It's beyond me to figure out how a man's mind works. Does it matter a lot to you that he did return?"

"It doesn't matter so much that he *did* return, but I would like to know *why* he changed his mind."

Susanna had gotten her emotions under control when the men returned, and she entered the conversation, hoping that she wasn't betraying the confused thoughts and feelings that still surged through her. The roast duck, sweet potatoes, and corn bread her aunt had prepared could have been tasteless for all she knew. She found Joshua's presence across the table disturbing, although she occasionally forced herself to meet his eyes. Most of the time she observed him through lowered lashes, keenly aware that he watched her with a clear, unfaltering gaze.

They were almost finished when someone pounded on the door. "Come in," Lester shouted.

A boy opened the door and stepped inside. "Mrs. Wilde, my pa's got a fever and he's thrashin' around in bed. Ma wants you to help."

"Right away," Eliza said, getting up from the table and taking off her apron. "You come with me, Lester. I may need your help. Joshua, please excuse us for a short time. You and Susanna finish your meal. We'll be at the house across the street."

With some unease, Susanna watched her aunt and uncle leave the house. A tense silence seemed to envelop the room until she said, "Would you like another serving of sweet potatoes?"

"No, thank you. I'll finish this piece of corn bread and that will be all I need."

She sipped on a noggin of milk until Joshua laid his spoon aside and pushed his plate away from him. "This was a fine meal. Eliza is a better cook than I am," he added, a humorous glint in his eyes.

"Why don't you take a seat closer to the fire? I'll put the plates and spoons in a pan of water and wash them later." But he helped her carry the utensils to the basin, and she spread a cloth over the food on the table.

She pointed to a rough straight-back chair, covered with one of Eliza's quilts. "In spite of all the pretty furniture Uncle Lester makes now, he won't give up that chair. It was the first one he made when they came to the colony, and he's attached to it. I think you'll find it comfortable."

He waited until she was seated on a three-legged stool with her back to the fireplace before he sat down. "You look very well. You must be over your illness," he said, as his eyes swept over her approvingly.

"As soon as I got off the ship, the nausea stopped. I slept for a few days then started eating Aunt Eliza's nourishing food. I regained my strength rapidly."

He eyed her speculatively. "The day you arrived, you indicated you might sail with Captain Trent when he returns to England."

With a slight smile, she said, "From what he said this morning, that may not be for a few weeks. I haven't made definite plans. My aunt and uncle are urging me to stay in Virginia."

"Perhaps I shouldn't ask, but why did you make the trip in the first place if you're going back so soon?"

She explained briefly that her grandmother had forced her into coming to Jamestown. "She had her own social life, and I was a hindrance to her." Susanna stopped short of mentioning that the biggest argument was because she wouldn't get married. To forestall further questions, she queried, "I'm interested in hearing about your plantation."

"When I first came to Virginia, I rented land from the Virginia Company, but two years ago, a provision was made whereby the company would give a man fifty acres for each person he brought to Virginia. I imported enough indentured servants to be awarded three hundred acres, but I've only had time to clear a hundred acres or so. My major crop is tobacco. Part of my land lies along the James River, and I bring my tobacco to Jamestown on a barge where it's transferred to ships and shipped to England. I exchange it for supplies or livestock to improve my holdings."

"And you prefer living here rather than in England?"

"Yes, I do. I was the youngest of four sons, and I didn't think I could move forward at home. The New World gave me a chance and I took it." He stood up, with what appeared briefly to be a reluctant look on his face. "It's been a pleasure to visit with you, but I must leave now. My neighbor may have several things to be done."

"I'm pleased that you could share a meal with us. I think often of how you helped me on the day I arrived in Jamestown."

"I've thought of it, too," he said. "It was an unusual meeting."

Flustered by the gentle softness of his voice, Susanna took his coat from the peg, and Joshua shrugged into it.

He paused before retrieving his hat. "I live about fifteen miles from the village. If you would be interested in seeing my plantation, I could bring my cart and take you for a visit. Or would you prefer to go on horseback?"

"Horseback would be fine, although I haven't ridden much since I had a pony as a child."

"I'll bring a gentle horse."

Without any idea what the social customs were in the colony, Susanna hesitated for a moment. "Then I would like to visit your plantation, with Aunt Eliza's permission, of course."

"I'll come into Jamestown Tuesday morning and bring an extra horse and ask your aunt's approval. I have two families living on the plantation—one of the women cooks for me sometimes. I'm sure she will prepare a meal for us."

"I'll look forward to it."

Joshua picked up his hat from a bench as the door opened and Eliza entered. Shivering, she rushed to the fireplace. "The wind is cold. Even if the house is just across the street, I should have worn a shawl."

"How is your neighbor?" Joshua inquired.

"His condition isn't critical. He's had a high fever for several days and started talking out of his head this morning, which alarmed his wife. After he drank some herbal tea, he settled down, but Lester is staying until he goes to sleep. Must you leave so soon?"

"Yes. But I would like to come back Tuesday morning and escort Miss Susanna to see my plantation. With your permission, of course."

Eliza's eyebrows pulled together, and perhaps trying to assess Susanna's wishes, she scanned her niece's face with keenly observant eyes. "You're sure you're up to a long ride in the cold weather?"

"Yes. I'll rest most of the day tomorrow."

"Then, by all means, go. I want you to learn more about our colony." With a hearty laugh, she said to Joshua, "You see, Lester and I are trying to persuade her to stay with us."

"So she told me." He stepped out on the porch and pulled his wide-brimmed hat low over his ears. "I'll be here Tuesday."

After closing the door behind Joshua, Eliza stirred the coals, added more wood, backed up to the blaze, and lifted her skirts.

Susanna sat on the stool she'd occupied earlier. "What did you mean this morning when you said you'd have to talk to me about Joshua?"

Eliza pulled a bench closer to the fire and sat down. A thoughtful smile curving her mouth, she questioned, "Why, of all the men you've seen, have you fixed your interest on Joshua Deane?"

"I don't have the least idea," she answered, with a trace of laughter in her voice. "I suppose Grandmother would call it contrariness. And really, I can't say I've fixed my interest on him, but I've thought of him often since our eyes first connected at the wharf. Don't you approve of Joshua?"

"Of course—there's not a finer man in this whole colony. But he's not interested in getting married. He's a widower, and before you get any further involved, you need to know how his wife died."

Terrible images built in Susanna's mind. Her concern must have shown in her expression, for Eliza hurried to explain, "Oh, Joshua didn't have anything to do with her death, except he may blame himself for not being more watchful of her. You see, about two years after they moved to Virginia, both she and their son were killed in a native uprising while Joshua was away overnight. All of their buildings were destroyed. Joshua was heard to say after their deaths that he would never sacrifice another family to the rigors of colonial life. I didn't hear him say that, mind you, but I believe it's his opinion, for I've not known him to be attracted to any woman—that is, until you came."

"My interest in him probably stems from the help he gave me when I was so sick, but there is some spark between us. Enough attraction, at least, that I'd be foolish not to explore its possibilities."

"I agree that you should see more of him, but I wanted you to know the obstacles you face. Nothing would please me more than to see you wed to Joshua."

"I'm glad you approve. Let me help you wash the plates and utensils. I haven't done any work since I've been here."

Grinning, Eliza said, "Have you ever done any housework?"

She shook her head. "You know we had servants, and Grandmother would have been appalled if I'd offered to help. But I don't intend for you to wait on me, so you can teach me how to be a housekeeper."

"Which you'll need to know if you stay in the colony. But as long as you're a guest, you don't have to work." She picked up a long piece of wood and made another notch on it to indicate the passing of another day. "This year has gone by fast. It's only a short time until Christmas and the beginning of a new year."

"How do you celebrate Christmas in Jamestown?"

"There's not many festivities that day. We have a service at the meeting-house, and I prepare a big meal. But on New Year's Day, there's a lot of revelry—shooting contests, races, and things like that. I do hope you will at least be here for all of the fun."

Susanna found herself hoping that she might still be in Jamestown at that time, also, but the celebration had little to do with her reason why.

Chapter 5

Susanna had never given much thought to choosing clothing because her maid usually laid out her garments each morning. Since she'd arrived in Jamestown, she had chosen the simple dresses and petticoats she'd worn on shipboard. But considering the ride with Joshua to be a special occasion, she searched through her trunks. She'd been so opposed to coming to Virginia that she hadn't paid any attention to what her maid had packed.

The first trunk she opened contained summer garments, so she pushed it aside. From the other trunk, she selected a cotton petticoat, a linen chemise, and a rust-red dress with an open-fronted skirt which exposed an underskirt of dark gray. For warmth she chose a black cloak and a matching hood.

Unaccustomed to styling her own hair, Susanna asked Eliza to help her. Her aunt brushed Susanna's auburn hair briskly and pulled it back tightly from the forehead to the back of her head, leaving a fringe of bunched curls along the sides.

Although the air was still cold when Joshua called for Susanna, the sun was shining and Uncle Lester predicted a fair day. The horse Joshua brought for her was a small, dapple-gray mount. As he helped her into the sidesaddle, Susanna wondered if the saddle had belonged to his wife. As if he was reading her mind, Joshua said, "I borrowed the saddle from my tenant's wife. She rides this horse when she and her husband come into the settlement, so the horse is accustomed to ladies' skirts. You'll be perfectly safe."

Riding side by side, they followed a narrow, northwest trail out of the settlement. Numerous acres had been cleared for the village, but only a small portion of the area had buildings. The rest of the clearing had been planted with corn and other grain and vegetables, for the stalks were still standing. Soon the forest closed in around them, and with Joshua leading the way, they rode single file.

Most of the trees had lost their leaves, but the barren limbs spread out over the trail blocking the sunlight. In midsummer when foliage was on the trees, Susanna imagined that the trail would be semidark throughout the day. Recalling tales she'd heard of native uprisings and how they attacked from the forest, a nervous tingle spread through her body. But Joshua looked back from time to time and smiled, which was reassuring. Had there been any danger, she was confident he wouldn't have invited her to go with him.

After a few miles, the trail widened, and Joshua slowed his horse so she could ride beside him. "I've never seen so many trees in my life," Susanna said.

"Thick forests cover most of this peninsula, and we don't have the kind of tools we need to clear acres of land. We girdle the trees, and when they die, we plant around them. The forest soil is fertile and produces good crops."

"I don't know what you mean by girdling."

"It's a method used in England. We cut a notch about a foot wide in the bark all around the tree and peel off the bark. This causes the trees to die, and even though the trunks continue to stand for a few years, it doesn't hinder growth. After they completely decay, we dig the roots from the ground and burn them. It's a slow process, but there isn't any easier way to clear the land."

"I can understand now why the explorers called America a *new land*. At home, so many people have lost hope, but in spite of the difficulties they've had, everyone I've met in Jamestown is optimistic about the future. Has Virginia lived up to what you expected? Are you sorry you emigrated?"

The moment the words escaped her lips, Susanna wished she could recall them. A bleak expression crossed his face.

"I'm sorry—I shouldn't have asked that."

His eyes were speculative when he looked at her. "Eliza has told you about my family?"

"Not much, but enough to know that you may have regrets."

"For months after they were killed, I was miserable, blaming myself for their deaths, wishing I had never brought them to this dangerous place. But I eventually realized that people die young in England, too. I left home because I thought I could make a better life for my family in Virginia. My wife was willing to come with me—it isn't as though I forced her to do so. After several miserable months, I finally realized I had to put their deaths behind me and continue to do what I'd come to this country to achieve. I've been satisfied, but not particularly happy. Still, I haven't let that stand in my way of creating a home in the wilderness." Joshua spoke with the certainty of a man who would never be content with an unfulfilled dream.

"I'm torn between conflicting emotions, too," Susanna said. "I lost my parents several years ago, and I've felt as if I'm a nuisance to my grandmother. My aunt and uncle want me to stay here. I like much of what I hear about the New World, but it's a big choice to make."

The trail narrowed again, which made conversation difficult, and when Susanna's eyes grew weary of the wide expanse of barren trees and the leaf-littered trail, she concentrated on her companion. His powerful shoulders were covered with a black woolen coat, he wore a wide-brimmed hat, and his knee-high boots came to the cuffs of his breeches. He glanced often from side to side, and she knew that he was alert to any kind of danger they might encounter. She felt safe with Joshua—a security she hadn't experienced since her parents had died. But was this reason enough to stay in the New World, especially if Joshua didn't want her to stay?

As they neared his home, Joshua was beset with a nervous tension that was not habitual for him. Why was it so important for Susanna to like his home?

When they left the main trail and turned toward the area where his holdings were located, he slowed his horse until she rode beside him. They climbed a small hill, and he said, "We're almost there. I hope the ride hasn't been tiring for you."

"A little," she admitted, "because I probably haven't ridden for a year or more. But everything has been interesting—so unlike anything I've ever seen at home."

"You can rest before we start back. I told Eliza we wouldn't return until late afternoon."

They came out into a clearing, and Joshua halted his horse to give Susanna an overall view of his home. He watched her expression anxiously, as she surveyed the ten-acre clearing marked by trunks of girdled trees, two tenant houses, a barn and stable, fields of tobacco stubble, pasture fields for his horses and cattle, the rail fence that kept his livestock out of the cultivated fields, and lastly his home that overlooked the James River two miles away. To add to the pastoral scene, a herd of white-tailed deer grazed at the edge of the forest.

After several minutes, she turned and looked directly at him, and her eyes glowed with enjoyment and pleasure. "I have never seen a more beautiful place. Most of my life has been spent in London. I didn't know such natural beauty could be found anywhere."

Because of her pleasure in his home, Joshua experienced an air of calm and self-confidence, knowing for certain that he had reached the place to which God had directed him. Like Abraham, he had followed God's leading into the promised land.

He briefly touched Susanna's gloved hands as they rested on the pommel of her saddle. "Your approval means a lot to me. Let's go on to the house, so you can rest."

As they neared the buildings, Susanna said, "This is the first brick home I've seen in Virginia."

"My first house, similar to those in Jamestown, was destroyed by fire. The local kiln turns out good bricks, so I decided to build a more durable structure than my first home had been."

Stopping in front of the one-story house, which faced the river, he lifted her down from the saddle and tied the horses to a hitching post. "I built only one large room at first, but I've recently added a bedchamber. Lester is making the furniture for that room."

He opened a wide, heavy door and ushered her into the interior of his home, which was similar in size and furnishings to the Wilde dwelling. A woman, who was working at the fireplace, turned to face them.

"This is Mary Stevens. Mary, meet Miss Susanna Carter from London."

A stocky woman with a ruddy complexion and graying hair, Mary dipped into a slight curtsy. "Pleased to meet you, ma'am. Would you like some refreshment now? I have some mint tea ready."

"Yes, please. I am thirsty."

Joshua helped remove her coat and shawl and laid them on a bed built into the wall. "Sit and enjoy your tea while I take the horses to the stable. They'll get their food before we do. I'll return soon."

Mary brought a mug of tea to the table and a small piece of cake. "I'd not want to spoil your appetite, but a cup of tea goes better with a little something sweet. We pick the leaves from native plants in summer and dry them. Be there anything else I can fetch you?"

"Nothing more. Do you do all of Mr. Deane's cooking?"

"No, ma'am. He fixes most of his vittles. I just help out when he has company."

"How long have you been in Virginia?"

"Two years. My man and me, we be indentured servants."

"What are your terms?"

"Mr. Deane paid to bring us over—two hundred pounds of tobacco for the both of us. But we had to promise to work for him seven years to pay back our fare. When that time is up, we're free to take up land of our own."

"That seems like a fair arrangement."

"I guess so, but the time seems to pass immortal slow. It's almost like being a slave."

"Except that you have hope of being free."

"Yes'um—that's why we took the chance. Mr. Deane is good to us. Though it's smaller, our house is as good as this one. And he gives my man a day each week to work on a field of his own. The sale of our tobacco so far has brought enough to buy a pig, and by the time we're free, we'll have some more livestock to take to the fifty acres of land we're supposed to be given. We could have done worse."

"I pray that you'll continue to prosper."

"Thank you."

A blast of cold air heralded Joshua's return. He hung his coat and hat on a peg behind the door and held his hands toward the warmth of the fireplace. "What have you prepared for us?"

"A pot of succotash, corn bread, and a squash pie. Ought I to serve it now?"

"If Miss Carter is ready."

"I'm hungry, and the food smells good."

"You can put the food on the table," Joshua said, "and we can serve ourselves."

Thoughtfully, Susanna watched as Mary dipped the mixture of corn and beans into a large wooden bowl and cut the corn bread from an iron skillet and placed it on a trencher. She carried the two containers to the table, then took a pewter platter from the mantel and put the pie on it. Susanna had already learned that there were few servants in Jamestown—the woman of the house took care of the household chores. Unmarried men usually did their own housework, as Joshua had done since his wife's death. Prior to coming to Jamestown, Susanna had never done any work in the kitchen. Could she ever learn to be a housewife?

"If that's all, Mr. Deane, I'll go home," Mary said.

He nodded. "Thanks for helping."

Joshua pulled out a bench for Susanna, sat to her left, and bowed his head in a brief prayer of thanks for the food.

Dipping the succotash into pewter bowls, he explained, "Mary has two little ones, but her husband, John, watched them while she prepared our food."

"Is hiring indentured servants satisfactory?"

"It has been for me because I hired men with families, who are likely to stay put. Sometimes single men will run away to live with the natives."

"That surprises me. I thought they were hostile."

"There are always a few renegades who hate the English and are dangerous. But if it hadn't been for the help of the natives, the first group of settlers in Virginia thirteen years ago would all have died. This area was populated by thousands of Algonquin Indians, who lived in two hundred villages governed by Chief Powhatan. They taught the settlers how to farm."

"When I knew I was being exiled to America, I talked to my tutor about the colony. He explained that most of the first group of settlers perished because none of them were farmers, and that was about the only way to make a living here."

"All of them would have died if the natives hadn't provided food. Later, when John Rolfe married an Algonquin maiden, a pact was made with her father, Powhatan, and we've had peace for a few years. But it's an uneasy truce because the natives don't like Europeans taking their land. I can't say that I blame them. We have about a thousand settlers in Virginia now and less than a hundred live in Jamestown—we keep taking land that the natives claim. I'm always alert for an Indian attack."

"Uncle Lester said that many of the men who came in 1607 expected to find gold just as the Spanish had farther south."

Nodding, Joshua said, "That's true, but there is no gold in this region, which disappointed the men who weren't willing to do manual labor."

After they finished their meal, Susanna insisted on helping Joshua wash their utensils. Although she tried to put into practice the few things she'd learned from Eliza, her hands were soon smarting from the strong soap, and she handled the bowls and spoons awkwardly. Embarrassed at her ineptness, she wondered if Joshua realized how inexperienced she was as a homemaker.

"We'll start back to Jamestown soon," he said when they'd finished. "But let me show you the bedchamber I've added. One of my servants has some carpentry skill, and he did most of the building."

Almost as big as the main room, the bedchamber had no furniture. There was one window with a glass pane, which Joshua explained was made in Jamestown. "It's not high-quality glass but preferable to the oiled paper over the windows in the other room."

He pointed out the beamed ceilings that had been carved from trees cut on his own property. "Instead of attaching a bed to the wall, I'm having Lester make a bedstead, as well as some other furniture." He noticed when Susanna shivered slightly, and he pointed to a small fireplace in one corner of the room. "I'll keep a fire going when I start to sleep in here."

"You have a very comfortable house. It seems to me you've done very well."

He closed the door behind them as they went into the other room. "It's a slow process, though, and I'm not a patient man," he admitted with a slow smile. "It seems as if I've been struggling for years to build a house. My plans are to have an even larger home before I'm an old man."

"How old are you now?"

"Thirty, my last birthday." Susanna quickly calculated that there was a twelve-year difference in their ages.

"Perhaps we should start back now, so I can escort you into Jamestown and have time to return before nightfall." He held her coat. "You can wait here in the house while I bring the horses or walk with me to the stable."

After buttoning the coat, she put on her hood. "The walk will be good. My joints are already a bit stiff from the morning ride."

As they walked, she commented on the vast clearing, and Joshua explained, "We have to provide a broad expanse so we won't be subject to a surprise attack. The natives prefer to do their fighting from the protection of the forest."

She shivered, knowing that it wasn't caused by the cold wind wafting upward from the river. Rather, she was startled to think how frightening to be inside the buildings and have enemies attacking from all sides.

Although Susanna didn't know a whit about farming, she sensed that Joshua was a good husbandman of his property as he proudly showed her around his land. Her respect for him had increased greatly during this visit.

She was tired, and the trail seemed endless before they reached Jamestown. When they arrived at the Wildes', she invited him to come inside.

But he said, "Not today. Make my excuses to Eliza."

"Thanks for sharing this day with me," she said simply. "I had a wonderful time."

He took her hand and pressed his lips against her gloved fingers. "No more than I did. Your approval of my plantation caused me to like it even more. I hope you decide to stay in Jamestown so this won't be your last visit."

Susanna stood on the porch and watched him ride away until he was out of sight. This day had left her with much to think about. Did she have a future in Jamestown?

❧❧❧

Joshua's mind was made up. Since his wife's death, he'd had no desire to marry, but spending a day with Susanna had made him conscious of how fond he'd become of her. He didn't doubt that their mutual attraction to one another was of God. Should he speak to Lester, or should he allow some time to pass before he made a move? But if Captain Trent should make a sudden decision to return to England, she might go out of his life as quickly as she had come into it.

Thinking that Susanna might leave the colony before he saw her again unnerved Joshua, and he knew he must move quickly. But how soon? If her feelings weren't as involved as his, he didn't want to scare her away.

Chapter 6

Curious about the kind of furniture her uncle was making for Joshua, the next morning Susanna wrapped a shawl around her shoulders and ran across the short distance to his shop. He was smoothing a large board with a plane, and he didn't see her immediately.

When he looked up, he said, "You've come for a visit, have you? Better be careful or I'll put you to work."

"I'd like that. I'm not much help to Aunt Eliza. What can I do?"

He peered curiously at her. "Do you mean it?"

"Yes."

"This is dirty work, and we don't want your pretty brown dress to be soiled. Wear an old dress tomorrow, and I'll find something for you to do."

"Do you have time to explain what you're making now?"

Pleased, he said, "I'll take time. I'm making a bed, chest, and night table for Joshua Deane. I bought a big log from Eli Derby. He sawed it into lumber for me, and I've done the smoothing and shaping myself."

"Joshua mentioned that you were making some furniture for him. I'd like to see it."

"This chest is his. It's finished except for putting oil on it. It's a pretty piece, if I do say so myself." He ran his hands over the smooth surface of a plain chest made with six cedar boards nailed together, secured with a latch and wooden pegs. A long drawer at the bottom of the chest opened with knobs which were shaped like claws. "The top part is four feet by twenty inches, and it's two feet deep. It has an eight-inch drawer."

He pointed out the headboard, footboard, and railings of the bed, also in cedar, which had already been oiled, giving Susanna an idea of what the finished product would look like. She sniffed the clean, aromatic scent of the cedar, thinking how pleasant Joshua's bedchamber would be.

"I'll finish the chest today. Then I'll start on the night table. It's the smallest, but it will take more time."

"Maybe I could put oil on the chest."

"That would be a help, but it's a hard job," he warned. Holding up a wide slab of lumber, he added, "I'll make the table tomorrow out of cedar, but I'll use small oak limbs for the legs—they're sturdier than sawed lumber."

Lester showed her some tops he was making for the kids in the settlement for Christmas. "You can oil these, too, if you want to."

"I'll plan on doing that tomorrow. I'm going to see Ada Derby this afternoon."

"Have a nice visit, and I look forward to having you work with me tomorrow."

Susanna noticed the big smile on his face as she turned to leave. She was pleased that she had been able to bring her uncle a little pleasure for all he and Aunt Eliza had done for her.

≈≈≈

The custom in Jamestown was to eat only two meals daily, so Susanna figured that midday was a good time to pay a visit. Marveling that she could move around the little settlement without a chaperone, she walked toward the fort and found the house Ada had pointed out to her.

"Oh, come in," Ada said when she came to the door. "I'm so happy to see you. I've been lonely today. Let's sit close to the fire."

Ada's home wasn't as big as the Wilde house, nor was it furnished as well. Except for a few benches, the table, and a bed, furniture was nonexistent. Pots and pans hung from the rafters. Only one window, covered with oil paper, provided light in the room. A large fireplace covered one wall of the dwelling, however, and it was cozy.

"I've been baking this morning," Ada said. She put a bran muffin on a wooden plate and gave it to Susanna.

Susanna nibbled off a section of the pastry and complimented Ada on being a good cook. As she continued to enjoy the muffin, Susanna asked, "Why have you been lonely?"

Ada sat beside her on the bench. "Thinking about home. My mother and father were happy together, and we had such jolly times. That is, until my father inherited some money and gambled it all away. Although I knew when I left that I'd never see any of them again, it seems so final now that I'm actually settled in Virginia."

Hesitantly, Susanna asked, "Are you sorry you came?"

Blushing, Ada said, "I miss my family, but I'm not sorry I've become Eli's wife. I'm sure I couldn't have found a better man in England. He's a hard worker, and he has great plans for the future. I'm fond of him," she added, and her face reddened.

"Then you believe it's possible to love a person after such a short time?"

Ada nodded. "It happened to us—there was an immediate attraction when we first met. You can't imagine how much I dreaded marrying someone I didn't know, but I'm sure we'll have a happy marriage." She looked curiously at Susanna. "Why do you ask? I hear you've had lots of men calling on you. Do you have a fondness for one of them?"

"I'm not sure. I'm not ready to name him, but there is one who interests me. He's a fine man, and my aunt speaks highly of him. But I don't know if I think enough of him to give up my ties to England. And I don't know if he would want me to stay."

"You said you'd lived with your grandmother. Is she your only relative?"

"I have some aunts and uncles in England, but I've always liked Aunt Eliza best."

"Then it would work out all right for you to live here."

Since she was unsure of her feelings for Joshua, Susanna tried to think of another subject. She noticed a lute hanging on the wall. "Does your husband play the lute?"

"He plays every evening. It rests him after a long day at work."

"According to Aunt Eliza, there isn't much celebration of Christmas here except a church service. But wouldn't it be nice if we could have some special music? Maybe you and I could sing while Eli plays for us."

"He's shy, but I'll ask him."

"Come by for a visit and let me know."

When Susanna returned to the Wilde house, Aunt Eliza was entertaining Aaron Waller. Susanna wasn't glad to see him, but she displayed the good manners she'd been taught.

He stayed for a long time, and before he left, he again issued another invitation for Susanna to visit his home. She turned him down firmly, hoping to avoid other invitations.

After she closed the door behind Aaron, she turned toward Eliza in distress. "Do you think I'm wrong to discourage him so firmly?"

"No, I don't. I feel sorry for the unmarried men of the settlement, for I know they're lonely, but that's no reason for you to sacrifice yourself by marrying someone you don't even like."

"That's the way I feel about it," Susanna said, relieved that her aunt shared her opinion. "No one except Joshua has stirred one bit of emotion in my heart, and I won't lead other men on by flirting with them."

"And you—" Eliza stopped abruptly in the middle of the sentence and rushed to open the door. The church bell was ringing. "Oh, my!" Eliza exclaimed, her hand at her throat.

"What is it?"

"When the bell rings like that, it's either very good news or very bad news. A ship could have been sighted, or it could be that the Indians are attacking." She threw a coat around her shoulders. "Get your coat. We'll go see."

As they ran down the street, a man stuck his head out of the door of his house, shouting, "Indians! Indians! Get to the fort."

"You rustle on inside," Eliza urged. "I'm not going without Lester. His hearing's none too good, and he might not have heard the warning."

Susanna obeyed her aunt, but she stopped at the fort's entrance and watched until she saw Eliza and Lester hurrying toward safety.

Inside the fort was chaos. Frightened women huddled in the middle of the area, clutching their children, most of whom were crying or looking around wildly, fear in their eyes. Men huddled in groups, some waving their arms excitedly, a few of them talking and shouting, others seemed stunned into silence.

Pulling at the collar of her dress, Susanna struggled to catch her breath. She wondered how long she would have to stay inside this place. She had never liked being in crowds. She was thankful that her grandmother had arranged a private cabin for her on the *Warwick* and spared her from spending weeks in constant company of a large group of women.

"Susanna!"

She turned at the sound of her name and spied Ada hurrying toward her. "Do you know what's going on?"

Susanna shook her head. "Aunt Eliza and I headed this way as soon as she heard the bell ringing. A man said that the natives are attacking but that's all we heard."

"Eli is circulating among the men, and he'll let me know when he can."

Eliza joined them. "Don't worry until we find out what has happened. We've had false alarms before. Some people are just naturally skittish and see an Indian behind every bush. Let's find a place to sit down—maybe inside the church. We need to be praying anyway."

"I'll tell Eli where we are, so he won't worry about me," Ada said.

As they watched her approach Eli, Susanna said, "I'm happy her marriage is working out so well."

Smiling, Eliza said, "Eli is a good man, and I'm pleased he and Ada got together. Not all of the marriages work out. One woman stabbed her husband to death a few nights ago, and the leaders of the colony have put her in irons to send her back to England when the *Warwick* sails. Another man has been beating his wife, so he's been locked up."

"Then this wife experiment hasn't been successful?"

"Oh, I think it has, but you can't expect 100 percent success. God's own Word said that man shouldn't live alone. It's His plan for us to live together in families. It's my opinion that the colony wouldn't have survived if the women hadn't come."

Several men and women were inside the church, but unlike the tension that had prevailed outside, Susanna sensed a calmness of spirit among those who had gathered for prayer. She sat beside Eliza on a bench near the back of the small building, clasped her hands, and looked toward the front of the church, where a crude wooden cross hung from the arched ceiling.

Looking at the cross and remembering what had happened on a similar cross hundreds of years before, Susanna had the overwhelming conviction that she was in the place God wanted her to be. She bowed her head, first asking God to forgive the ill feelings she had harbored against her grandmother. Silently she prayed, *God, maybe she did me a favor to send me to this unknown land. If You have a purpose for my life here, guide me to know what it is.* Her thoughts turned to Joshua. Although she had looked over the crowd of men inside the palisade, she hadn't seen him and that concerned her. *God, protect him if he's in danger.*

When Susanna raised her head, Ada, who had sat down beside Susanna while she had prayed, whispered, "Eli said the preacher will make an announcement as soon as they can sort out truth from rumor. He'll call us if the preacher speaks outside, but he thinks he'll come inside the church."

In the front of the room a man started softly singing a song that English children particularly liked, and soon others joined in. As they sang about the ships sailing to Bethlehem, Susanna said quietly to Eliza, "Is there room in this fort for all the inhabitants of Jamestown?"

Grimly, she answered, "During an Indian attack, you'd be surprised how many people can crowd in here. Not only the people in the village but from the outlying plantations, too. It's bedlam. Usually, we're forted up only a short time, but once we were sequestered for a week, and I thought I'd lose my mind. I told Lester then that I'd not come inside again, but whenever there's a scare, we always head this way."

"I've been wondering about Joshua. Will he take refuge in the village?"

"Not likely. He's got a brick house, hasn't he?" When Susanna nodded, Eliza continued, "He was living in a daub-and-wattle house when his family was killed. I figure that's the reason he built a sturdier home."

"His tenant houses are made out of brick, too, and his house *is* sturdy. I'll try not to worry about him."

The preacher came into the building, followed by others, until all the seats were filled and men stood around the walls. He didn't have to call for silence, for everyone seemed tense and eager to know what to expect.

"We've ruled out a general attack by the natives, but there is some bad news," he said. "A family who lived on the edge of the wilderness has been killed, but it apparently occurred a few days ago. This seems to be an isolated incident, for which we're thankful."

Susanna held her breath until he gave the name of the family.

"Let's thank God for our safety. The leaders of the colony have already dispatched some soldiers and other citizens to investigate what has happened."

After the pastor prayed, a man asked, "Then it's safe for us to return to our homes?"

"The head of each household can make that decision. If you want my opinion, I'd say that those who live in the village would be as safe at home as you have been. Those who live outside on plantations may want to stay here until the search party returns with a definite answer about what has happened."

Joshua was unaware of the Indian scare until the soldiers stopped by his plantation to learn if he'd had any trouble. He volunteered to go with them, leaving his tenants to guard his property.

When they arrived at the small clearing and saw the mass slaughter of the family, Joshua's mind flashed to the scene on his property when he had returned from an overnight hunting trip and found his wife and son dead and his buildings burned. His stomach roiled, he felt dizzy, his ears rang, and he staggered toward a tree and leaned against it for support. He forced himself to open his eyes and look at the destruction around him. The house had been burned, and the man, his wife, and three children had been slaughtered.

One of the soldiers came to Joshua and placed his hand on his shoulder. "If I'd known what we would find here, I wouldn't have asked you to come with us. Why don't you go back home, Joshua? We'll take care of this."

Joshua straightened his shoulders and shook his head. "I'll stay. Everyone here has had someone die in this colony. I suppose it's the price we pay to settle a new world. But it's a bitter price, my friend."

"I know. If you think you're up to it, come and look over the victims. I don't think the natives are responsible."

"What?"

Steeling himself to look at the bodies of the slain where they were lying, Joshua walked around the area. "I see what you mean. They've been killed in Indian fashion, but there are no moccasin tracks."

"The outbuildings were burned, and the cattle driven off, but the house is still standing and none of the furnishings taken."

"So it's Englishmen who have done this."

"That's my opinion," the soldier said. "There has been some stealing in other places, and I'm laying the deed to a couple of runaway servants. As soon as we bury the dead, we're going after them. I figure they're not far away and probably saved the house to live in it at night."

"I'll help bury the dead and then go back to my home to tell my servants that the crisis is apparently over. We will be on our guard, because those men are liable to attack again."

As Joshua helped bury the five victims, he felt as if he were digging a grave for his own dreams and aspirations. Again he had been reminded that this country was too harsh for gentlewomen, especially one like Susanna. His hopes of bringing her to the plantation as his wife were as dead as this slaughtered family.

Chapter 7

When Lester came in for supper on the third day after the scare, he immediately said, "This crisis is over. The Benson family was murdered, but no one else."

"Thank God for that," Eliza said. "But who's to know when the Indians will strike again?"

As he washed his hands, Lester said, "It wasn't natives, but a couple of runaway servants. The soldiers discovered them and hanged them. I am thankful the matter is over and we are all safe."

As they bowed their heads and Lester prayed a blessing over their food, Susanna added her own silent thanks that Joshua had been spared. She had missed seeing him, but to convince herself that all was well with him, she had spent the days of waiting embroidering monogrammed handkerchiefs to give him for Christmas.

While she helped Lester in the shop, putting oil on the furniture he had made for Joshua, she had looked up expectantly whenever the door opened, but two days passed and Joshua didn't come.

She made plans with Ada and Eli to practice the music to sing at the Christmas service. Susanna had asked to borrow a hymnal from the preacher at the church. Although he refused to let her have a good hymnal, he loaned her a few sheets from an old book.

When Ada and Eli arrived for their first practice, Susanna invited them to sit around the table, and she spread the pages out so they could see them.

"Eli can't sing and play, too, and I'm not very brave," Ada said. "I don't think I can stand before the congregation and sing unless there's more than the two of us." She glanced toward Eliza. "Why don't you sing, too?"

"Lester is a better singer than I am, and I don't see any reason why we can't help out. That is, if we know the songs."

"I looked through these sheets and found a few familiar songs," Susanna said. "We can probably find one or two that we all know."

"I'll sing with you in the meetinghouse," Lester said, "if you'll promise to go caroling with me afterward. One of the highlights of my boyhood was when the carolers came on Christmas Day. My mother always had a treat of shortbread or some other pastry for them. As I got older, I joined the singers. It would bring back good memories to do that again."

"We could go caroling as soon as the meeting ends," Eli said, as he plucked the eleven strings of his lute with the thumb and fingers of his right hand.

Susanna read the titles of the hymns she'd found, and they finally agreed on two that all of them knew. "Let's try 'Good Christian Men, Rejoice' first and then 'The Coventry Carol.'"

After they had practiced for a long while, Eli pulled out his watch. "We'd better be getting home, wife. I have a lot of work to do tomorrow."

"We only have two more evenings to practice, but we'll make it," Eliza said.

The following day, Susanna couldn't seem to concentrate on any task. When her aunt asked repeatedly if anything was wrong, Susanna just shrugged her shoulders. She realized, however, that she wasn't hiding her unhappiness from Eliza, for she often found her aunt looking at her with sympathy.

Finally, Eliza sighed loudly and said, "I'm sorry, Susanna, but I tried to warn you against Joshua. He buried his heart with his wife and son."

Susanna could hold back her feelings no longer. "But he's seemed interested in me."

"I know he has. I may be wrong."

"Perhaps he's afraid to leave the plantation after what happened to the Benson family." Eliza didn't reply but continued to knit, the clacking needles blending with the crackling coals in the fireplace.

Susanna finally added, "Apparently you don't believe that's the reason."

"No, I don't, but I'm willing to be proven wrong. Lester is taking Joshua's furniture to him tomorrow morning. Why don't you go with him?"

"Wouldn't that seem a little forward?"

Eliza laid aside her knitting and walked toward the fireplace, saying matter-of-factly, "In England, it wouldn't be acceptable, but we aren't as restricted in our behavior in Virginia. If you want to know why he has stopped seeing you, go and ask him."

"Very well, I'll do that. . .if Uncle Lester doesn't mind."

"He'll welcome your company. I'll send Joshua a loaf of my bread, which will bake overnight in the oven and be ready by morning."

As Lester drove the cart pulled by two horses toward their destination, the trail through the forest seemed even smaller than it had on Susanna's first journey to Joshua's home. She shuddered in the crisp, frosty air, and she could see her breath like fog before her face, but after a few miles the sun shone through the leafless trees. She sat on a narrow seat, rubbing shoulders with her uncle, who took up more than half the room. She repeatedly looked over her shoulder to be sure that the canvas still covered Joshua's furniture.

"Ho, the house!" Lester called when he pulled the horses to a halt as they arrived at their destination.

Joshua opened the door and stepped out. He smiled with what appeared to be pleasure when he saw Susanna, but his expression immediately stilled and grew serious.

"Brought your furniture," Lester said. "I thought it could be your Christmas present, even if you are paying for it."

"Good day, Susanna," Joshua said, extending his arms to help her from the cart. But after that first pleased glance, he hadn't looked directly at her. "Go on inside to the fire while I help Lester unload."

Without answering, Susanna went into the house to open and close the door as they carried in the furniture. When they brought in the last piece, Susanna followed them into the bedroom. The pinkish cedar furniture blended with the white oak wall paneling. Briefly, she contemplated little touches that would make the room more homelike. She decided upon a coverlet for the bed with a bright cushion or two, a bowl on the chest, and a tiered candlestick holder on the table beside the bed. But given the coolness of Joshua's reception, she didn't think she would ever have the opportunity to decorate this room. However, she wanted to know one way or another.

The bedroom was cold, and Joshua shut the door behind them when all the furniture was in place. They returned to the main room. "I'll drive your horses to the stable and feed them some grain," he said to Lester.

"Thank you," Lester said, "but I brought grain along with me. You can wait inside, niece, until the horses have eaten."

Joshua started to follow Lester outdoors, but Susanna said, "Could you stay a minute?"

He closed the door and turned to face her. His eyes met hers for a moment and they darkened with emotion, but he looked away.

"I've missed seeing you," she said.

"Yes, I've missed you, too."

She waited.

"But I've been busy working the plantation."

"Along with a loaf of bread, Aunt Eliza sent an invitation for you to share Christmas dinner with us."

He paused, and Susanna's heart hammered in her chest. Would he ever answer?

"Thank her for the invitation, but I won't be able to come."

Fighting back tears, she buttoned her coat and tied her hood more securely. As she brushed by him on her way to the door, Joshua caught her arm. "I have a reason for refusing. I've already invited my tenants and their families to share the holiday with me in this house."

"I'll tell Aunt Eliza." She tried to free her arm, but he still held her.

"I think you know how I feel about you, and I thought I had put the past behind me. But when I saw the slaughter of the Benson family, the past became the present, and I knew I couldn't risk another family. It isn't that I don't care!"

She shrugged off his detaining hand, smothered a sob, and answered him in a cold voice that reminded Susanna of her grandmother. "It's your decision.

Aunt Eliza told me that you'd buried your heart with your family, and I believe it. But I wanted to find out for myself."

"Susanna," he pleaded, but she swept by him and out the door. Although she had humbled herself to come here today and confront him, she still had enough pride left that she wouldn't let him see how much his words had hurt.

Lester was checking the harnesses on the horses, but he gave her a hand into the cart. While Joshua paid him for the furniture he'd built, Susanna kept her eyes ahead. She didn't want him to see her tears, and she didn't look back as they drove away. Had she been wrong in thinking it was God's will for her to come to Virginia?

⮞⬥⮜

Joshua watched until Lester and Susanna were out of sight, wondering why any man in his right mind would turn down a future with her. He had been devoted to his wife, but theirs had been an arranged marriage, and he had never sensed the emotional feelings for her he had experienced when he held Susanna in his arms and carried her to the Wilde house.

After completing the day's tasks, Joshua sat before the fire for a long time. Over and over in his mind he seemed to hear the words of Jesus to His disciples, "O ye of little faith." If Jesus were sitting with him now, would He be saying the same thing to him?

Joshua acknowledged that he lacked the faith to trust God for the future. Regardless of what happened to him *or* Susanna, if she became his wife, they could be happy during the time God gave them together. He knew he loved her, and he believed she loved him, too. And he would like to have a family. Each day as he worked long hours in the fields, he often wondered why he worked so hard. It seemed futile to build up a plantation when he had no progeny to inherit it.

He rehearsed in his mind several Bible references concerning marriage, and two in particular seemed to speak to him. In the beginning of time, *"The* Lord *God said, It is not good that the man should be alone; I will make him an help meet for him."* And the writer of the book of Hebrews had asserted that *"Marriage is honourable in all."*

When he retired to the bedroom and went to sleep for the first time in his new bed, Joshua's mind was made up. He would spend the holidays with his tenants and their families as planned, but the day after Christmas would find him in Jamestown, on his knees, asking Susanna to marry him.

⮞⬥⮜

The next day Susanna went looking for Captain Trent and found him in his tiny office on the *Warwick.* "Have you set a sailing date yet?" she asked.

"The day after Christmas."

"Uncle Lester thought the weather might keep you here all winter."

"It might have if I took a northerly route, but I aim to head south and hope to avoid stormy weather. I don't anticipate any problems." He peered keenly at her, his brown eyes speculative and concerned. "You aimin' to sail with me?"

The moneybag hanging around her waist felt as if it weighed a ton—it weighed on her conscience more than that. She had been angry with her grandmother when she'd stolen the coins, and it hadn't bothered her conscience, for she considered it part of the inheritance from her father, which her grandmother controlled. But she couldn't use the stolen money for her fare. She would take it back to Grandmother and ask forgiveness.

Realizing that the captain was peering at her with troubled eyes, she said, "Yes, I want to sail with you, but I don't have any money." From her pocket, she took her mother's gold brooch and a diamond-studded gold ring that had belonged to her father. "I know they're worth more than one hundred and twenty pounds of tobacco, and that's the price the settlers paid to bring their brides. Is this enough to pay my fare?"

Captain Trent bent his head and scanned the two items. "Money enough and to spare. But, Miss Susanna, I don't like to take your valuables."

"I don't want to lose them, either," she said, putting them back in her pocket, "but I must leave Jamestown, and I have nothing else to barter. I'll be ready to go on the twenty-sixth of December. That is, if there will be other women on the boat."

"The two chaperones are returning on the ship. You'll be safe enough."

Susanna's steps lagged as she left the riverbank and walked to the Wilde home. As always, her aunt was busy with household chores, and Susanna fleetingly wondered why she'd ever considered becoming a colonial housewife. At best, it was a life of drudgery. No doubt her uncle would arrange a suitable marriage for her in England, and she could live a life of ease. But why did this thought leave her with an inexplicable feeling of emptiness?

Unable to think of any easy way to break the news, Susanna squared her shoulders and entered the house. When Eliza looked up from her mending, Susanna said, "I've made arrangements to leave with Captain Trent the day after Christmas."

Eliza stared at her as if the words didn't register for a moment. Then she gave a cry of despair and said, "Don't leave us. You were made for the New World."

Cynically, Susanna answered, "No. If I stay here, I'll eventually give up and marry one of the colonists—for I can't continue to live in your home indefinitely."

Perhaps it was obvious to Eliza that her mind was made up, for her eyes filled with tears of frustration. "So be it."

"I'll not be using Grandmother's money. I'll take it back to her."

"But—but how will you pay your fare?"

Susanna took the jewelry from her pocket. "Captain Trent will take these in exchange for my passage."

"Susanna! Those are family heirlooms. You should keep them."

"I have no other way to pay my fare."

Shaking her head, Eliza said, "I pray that you won't live to regret this decision."

Chapter 8

Christmas Day dawned much like one would have in England. There was a slight mist in the air, a cold wind blew off the river, and fog hovered so low that it seemed as if the clouds had descended on the village. Walking to church with her aunt and uncle, the dampness penetrated Susanna's whole body and she shivered. Her mood was as dreary as the weather. Since the day her grandmother had given the ultimatum that she had to immigrate to Virginia, Susanna had planned her return to England. Tomorrow morning, she would finally have her way when she boarded the *Warwick*.

She knelt with the others when the service began, but although she prayed earnestly for God's guidance in her life, she received no satisfactory relief for her troubled spirit.

Perhaps knowing that the worshippers wanted to seek their own hearths during the raw weather, the preacher's message was shorter than usual. When the quartet prepared to sing, Lester said, "These songs are familiar ones, so join in with us if you know the words."

Eli plucked the strings of the lute to introduce their songs, and Susanna's spirits lifted during their presentation as her thoughts were transported to the little village of Bethlehem the night Jesus was born.

They sang the first lines of "Good Christian Men, Rejoice" before the congregation joined in. Susanna was pleased that they'd chosen songs that were meaningful to all of them.

When the service was over, they strolled through the village, singing songs that spoke of the coming of Jesus into the world to save all mankind. Despite her breaking heart, as she raised her voice in praise, Susanna received the assurance that God would work His will in her life—in His time, not hers.

The day that Susanna had looked to and dreaded finally arrived. Hoping until the last minute that she would see Joshua to give him the six monogrammed handkerchiefs she had made, before she left the Wilde home, she handed them to Eliza. "Please give these to Joshua the next time you see him. He may not want them," she said bitterly, "but I don't want them either."

"I feel in my heart that you're making a mistake to leave. Please wait for another ship. Some men are slow to change their minds. Joshua may come around yet."

Lester had tied Susanna's trunks on his wheelbarrow, and he waited outside. Opening the door, he said, "We should leave. The captain won't want to be delayed."

Susanna took one sweeping glance, trying to memorize every detail of the room where she had felt so much warmth and welcome. Then, with Eliza weeping beside her, they started toward the wharf. Captain Trent had announced his intention to leave by midmorning, and when they arrived at the riverbank, Susanna decided that all the colonists must have turned out to watch the ship leave.

Ada and Eli detached themselves from the larger group and hurried toward her. "I just can't believe you're leaving," Ada said. "I'll miss you."

"I've been proud to know you, miss," Eli said. "It would have been a pleasure to have you for a neighbor."

Susanna shook her head and swallowed the lump in her throat. "It wasn't meant to be."

"You didn't stay long enough to find out," Eliza hissed in her ear, even yet unwilling to accept her niece's departure.

But Susanna didn't believe she had much choice. She didn't want anyone except Joshua, and he wouldn't marry her. Maybe when she returned to England and went to live with Uncle Felton, she would find someone who would fill the void in her heart.

A wagon approached hauling several barrels of tobacco, and Captain Trent called, "Stand aside, ladies and gents, until we get these barrels aboard, and then we'll set sail."

Obviously he was jubilant at the prospect of going to sea. Noticing Susanna, he stepped to her side. "Then you've decided to travel with me?"

She nodded and handed him a small bag holding the jewels for her fare. Two sailors shouldered her trunks and carried them onto the ship.

A bugle sounded and soldiers marched from the fort with the woman prisoner, who walked along with her head held high as if she felt no remorse for the crime she'd committed. Susanna felt sorry for the woman, because life was difficult for the people who lived in London's hovels—most of them didn't have an opportunity to live decent lives. Too bad this woman, too, couldn't have found a home in Virginia.

Everybody had boarded except Susanna, and Captain Trent said, "Are you ready, miss?"

She nodded assent, for her throat was too tight for words. She threw herself into Eliza's arms, and Lester put his big arms around both of them.

"It is still not too late to change your mind," he said. "You can have a home with us as long as you want to stay."

"I know," she murmured. Not since her parents died had Susanna experienced such love as she'd received from her aunt and uncle. It was hard to leave them. She turned from them, blinking away her tears and trying to smile.

"Wait!"

Susanna heard the shout and turned toward the sound of a horse galloping down the bank. It was Joshua!

"Praise God from whom all blessings flow!" Lester shouted, taking off his wide-brimmed hat and tossing it high in the air.

Just before he reached the gangplank, Joshua threw the reins to a bystander, leaped from the saddle, and ran toward the ship, his arms outstretched. With a glad cry, Susanna ran to meet him.

He hugged her tightly for a few moments, then held her away from him and searched her face. "Surely you aren't leaving!"

"I have no reason to stay."

"You soon will have," he said. Dropping to one knee before her, Joshua kissed her hand. "I love you, Susanna Carter. I want to marry you. Please stay and be my helpmeet. We can build a beautiful life together in Virginia. I know we can."

Her eyes very bright and with a tender expression on her face, Susanna caressed his uplifted face. "I know we can, too, for I love you, Joshua. I've known for many days that you were my reason for coming to Virginia."

She tugged on his hand, and he stood beside her. To the cheers of the settlers, Joshua gathered Susanna into his arms and kissed her.

Flustered, Susanna pulled away from him. "I thought you didn't want me," she murmured.

He reached for her again but turned when Lester and Eliza crowded close to them.

Lester pumped Joshua's hand. "Boy," he said, chuckling, "you just about missed the boat."

Eliza tucked her moist handkerchief into her coat, and her smile was tender as she bent over to kiss Susanna.

"Hey!" Captain Trent shouted as he bounded down the gangplank. "Does this mean I'm going to lose a passenger?"

Susanna turned in his direction. "Yes, Captain. Joshua said the words to keep me here. I'm going to marry him."

The captain handed her the leather bag holding her jewelry. "Then you don't owe me any passage fare. I hate to lose the money, but I'm happy you're staying. You two were made for each other."

Quietly, she said, "And will you do a favor for me?" She unfastened the bag of coins from her waist. "Will you see that my grandmother gets this? It's a bag of coins I took from her, intending to use the money to pay my way home."

He pointed to the bag of jewelry she held. "But why did you give me these jewels?"

"The jewelry was mine, but even though the coins could have been taken from my inheritance, when it came right down to it, I couldn't steal from her. I pray that she'll forgive me."

"I'll have a word with Lady Carter and tell her what a fine man you're getting."

"Thank you. I'll write a letter to her eventually, but I don't want to delay your departure. May God be with you as you journey!"

Susanna placed her hand in Joshua's and smiled at him. "I have found my home here in Virginia—the one God planned for me."

Epilogue

A week later, Susanna and Joshua stood hand in hand in front of the fireplace in the Wilde home. Ada and Eli stood beside them. Eliza and Lester sat on a nearby bench, holding hands, looking as happy as if the wedding were their own. The room was crowded with as many well-wishers as the room could hold.

Susanna wore a white wool dress she had brought with her from England. It had a long pointed bodice with full short sleeves and a voluminous skirt gathered at the back. She fingered the pearl chain with an ivory cross pendant that had belonged to Joshua's mother. Eliza had placed a lace cap on her head.

Susanna slid a sideways glance toward Joshua, who looked handsome in a dark blue doublet and a white shirt with a lace ruff at his neck. His gray breeches met his white stockings at the knees, and he wore a pair of buckled shoes he'd recently imported from England.

The smell of pine branches permeated the room and mingled with the scent of food Eliza had worked for days to prepare for the wedding feast. The church bell pealed for several minutes to mark the beginning of the ceremony.

The minister stood before them, and in a reverent tone began the traditional service accepted by the church. After a short prayer, he read passages from the Bible dealing with marriage.

The ceremony was short, but Susanna was breathless with joy and awe when she took her vows. It was inconceivable that after such a short time in Virginia, she was actually getting married. She remembered her arrival at Jamestown and how miserable she had been until she had met Joshua. Her life hadn't been the same since, and she silently thanked God that it wasn't her grandmother's dominance but His will and wisdom that had brought her to the New World.

Their vows taken, smiling broadly, the minister declared them man and wife.

Susanna's lips found their way instinctively to Joshua's, and when their lips met, she felt transported on a soft and wispy cloud of emotion. "I love you," she whispered softly through half-parted lips. His grasp tightened, and he kissed her again to seal the vows they had made for eternity.

Navidad de los Suenos

by Kristin Billerbeck

Chapter 1

Rancho de Arguello, The California Territory, 1844

I sabella giggled as she hung the last of the drying peppers in the scorching summer heat. She danced a fandango to celebrate the finishing gesture. Her older sister shook her head at the precocious young beauty. Isabella had been named for her striking looks. She was blessed with lustrous, silken black hair and full, warm brown eyes that complemented her sun-drenched skin. Her loveliness was renowned throughout the territory, but her grown-up appearance hid a tender and naive young heart.

As Isabella's parents watched their vivacious daughter from their sprawling, adobe home, they discussed her future in serious tones.

"You see, my dear? She is far too young for marriage. She still giggles like a child," Señora Arguello argued.

"She is seventeen. The rancheros have been lining up for marriage since she was ten years old. A beauty like Isabella can only benefit from marriage; remaining here will simply lead to trouble." Señor Jose Arguello shook his head. "She will mature in her wifely role. It is time, Ramona. It is probably past time. The priest will come at Christmas and she will be married. Why wait another year? We can certainly use the cattle her marriage will bring."

"Yes, Señor." Ramona Arguello relented uneasily. "But whom shall she marry? She has had so many offers, yet I've never seen a man who caused her heart to stir." Señora dropped her head sadly, her faded black hair falling forward around her worn complexion.

"Don't talk to me of such fancy of heart stirrings. I am the patriarch of the rancho, and as such, I will choose for my daughter the man whom I see fit. Just as your father did," Señor Arguello added firmly.

Señora Arguello remained undeterred. "But, I loved you, Jose," she pleaded with her husband. "Isabella is not in love."

"She will have better than love. I am offering her to Antonio Fremont for a thousand cattle," Señor Arguello revealed.

His wife inhaled deeply, her hand slapping her chest in surprise. "A thousand cattle! Oh, Jose, no. Not even for a thousand cattle. He is nearly thirty years older and he's already buried two wives! Surely you can find her someone more suitable."

"Are you questioning my judgment?" Señor Arguello charged, his eyes growing thin.

"Of course not, Señor. I—I just. . ." Señora Arguello bowed to the determination of her husband. "I will make arrangements for her dress and the celebration." She walked despondently from the room and the conversation.

Señor Arguello turned to the nearby window. "Isabella!" he snapped impatiently.

Isabella stopped her lighthearted play and grew solemn. "Yes, Papa?" But it wasn't long before her high spirits reappeared. "Papa, look at the peppers. Are they not beautiful this year? I can't remember when they had more color," she pressed excitedly.

Her father's demeanor appeared to soften momentarily before his scowl returned. "Your mama needs to see you immediately."

Isabella lifted her full, ruffled skirt and dashed into the dim house to her parent's private room. The occasions when Isabella entered the quarters were rare, so she knew her mother had something important to tell her. Isabella found her mother sitting with her head bowed. She caught her mother surreptitiously wiping her eyes before looking up at Isabella.

"Mama, are you feeling okay? Papa says you must see me. Did you see the peppers are all hung?" the young woman chattered persistently. The golden brown of Isabella's bare shoulders glistened under the midday candlelight used against the darkness within the whitewashed adobe walls. Señora Arguello straightened her back and ceased weeping.

"Yes, my darling. Your father and I have decided it is time for a rancho and a family of your own. Your father has made arrangements with Antonio Fremont. You are to be married this Navidad, when the priest comes to visit and celebrate the birth of our Savior. Your papa will make sure Pastor Sola is here as well."

Isabella fell to her knees, nearly fainting at the news. She felt dizzy and sickened, yet she knew to argue her case was pointless. Arrangements had been made, and to question her father's authority, especially after he had given his word to Señor Fremont, could only lead to disaster.

She remembered the bedraggled, old character who came to the annual cattle counts. She pictured with clarity his oversized belly and the hungry eyes that scrutinized her as if to devour her very soul. She shuddered at the image of marriage to such a man. She was very nearly ill by simply being in the same room with him and his foul smell of drink. Now she would be forced to share a home with the surly ranchero.

"Isabella?" her mother questioned. "Did you hear me?"

"Yes, Mama," was all Isabella could manage to say.

"Señor Fremont is a fine man. He is the wealthiest Califorñio in the territory. You will have dresses of fine Spanish lace for everyday wear. You can plan fiestas and rodeos that last for weeks on end. There are no limits with such a man. You will be the envy of every señorita on the rancho," Señora Arguello said enthusiastically, but her downcast eyes gave her true feelings away.

Isabella knew her mother didn't approve of Antonio Fremont. It was obvious by the tears she'd shed and the desperate attempts to convince Isabella that her new life wouldn't be so desolate.

Isabella closed her eyes in agony. She felt physically weak that she would be leaving the only home she'd ever known to live with a ranchero older than her father. Such was the way of life on the ranchos. Women lived in complete submission first to their father's authority and then to their husband's. She let out a deep sigh. "Yes, Mama, Spanish lace."

"You will own more cattle than any woman in the territory," her mother added brightly.

"The Bible says better a dry morsel, and quietness therewith, than an house full of sacrifices with strife," Isabella quoted.

"It is your duty to make sure your home is without strife, Isabella," her mother reprimanded.

"Of course, Mama. I'm sorry. May I be excused, please?"

Señora Arguello nodded, and Isabella curtsied in deference, then ran to the patio and fell to her knees in desperate prayer. *Oh Lord, why of all men must I marry him? Lord, You have ordained each and every day of my life. Please find a different path for me. Please. I beg You, Lord. Anyone but him, anyone!*

"Isabella?" Victoria, her older sister, blocked the last of the sun from Isabella's view. Tears welled up in Victoria's eyes. "I'm so sorry." Her words let loose a wave of tears and the sisters instinctively embraced.

"Oh Victoria, how can they do this to me? Does Papa care nothing for me?" Isabella cried.

"He cares greatly for you, Isabella," Victoria responded softly. "He has betrothed you to the richest man in all of California. As far as Papa's concerned, that is the best. The other rancheros have been trying to betroth their daughters to him for some time now. Papa would only allow you to marry a true Californio. Born and bred on God's land."

"Why did you get to choose your husband, Victoria?" Isabella protested, tears streaming freely.

"Because I am not beautiful, Isabella," Victoria answered gently and plainly, wiping her sister's tears away.

Isabella's eyes widened. "Of course you are. Who told you such nonsense?"

"My sweet sister." Victoria caressed her again before pulling away and looking directly into Isabella's deep, brown eyes. "You see only what you want in those you love. I appreciate that you find me beautiful, and I know in your virtuous way you believe it with all your heart. But the commotion you cause at the annual rodeo shows the difference between you and me. Father has been planning your marriage for a long time, Isabella. I'm sure he knows what he's doing."

Isabella shook her head violently and stood up, her dress whirling wildly. "No, not you." She pointed a long, slender finger at her only sibling. "I can take the lying from Mama because she must support Papa, but I know you can't possibly approve of my marrying that—that squalid, old man!"

Victoria remained silent at the accusation, its truth apparent.

Chapter 2

Fall descended upon the tranquil valley of Rancho de Arguello. With the new season, the golden hills transformed to a lush green, providing a natural background for the great oaks that dotted the landscape. The cattle roamed freely, enjoying the fresh grass and freedom from the arid heat of summer.

Isabella's exuberant personality had all but disappeared along with the summer's hot season, and fall did not bring its return. She went about her daily activities with a melancholy she had never before exhibited. She walked instead of danced, spoke instead of sang, and wept instead of laughed.

"She has not been the same since I told her," Señora Arguello observed to her husband, lifting the curtain to watch her daughter outside.

"The old Isabella will return when she realizes what I have done for her. She is simply maturing," Señor Arguello answered.

"She is wilting," Isabella's mother replied. "She's not devious enough to act in such a manner on purpose. Isabella would never hurt one of us intentionally."

"Is that an accusation, Señora Arguello? Are you insinuating that I have hurt my daughter?" The señor's voice was harsh, but his sad eyes told of his own questioning heart.

"Of course not, Señor." Señora Arguello held up her palms, adamantly denying the allegation. "I only meant—"

"I hope so. Preacher Sola will be here tomorrow," Señor Arguello interrupted. "He will talk some sense into her. He's always had such an easy way with Isabella, with her keen interest in spiritual matters. They seem to understand one another." He paused, staring off into the distance. "Yes, it will all be better when Preacher Sola arrives."

"I hope so. Preacher Sola is such a kind, godly man. The first Protestant I ever met," Señora Arguello mused. "I was beside myself when Isabella disappeared that morning. Only three years old and out somewhere on the rancho by herself." The woman's lips trembled at the memory. "She faced certain death out there all alone. I praise God every day for that circuit-riding preacher and his odd ways. Without him, our daughter would not be getting married this Christmas."

"Even so," Señor Arguello hastily added, "he comes here as my guest, not to take part in the ceremony. No Califorñio marriage would be blessed without the Catholic priest from the mission performing the ceremony."

"Of course, dear."

Just then, the pounding of horses' hooves sounded against the road leading to the adobe house, and Isabella sprang to life, dropping her sewing on the patio and running headlong toward the horsemen.

"Preacher Sola!" she squealed excitedly. "Preacher Sola!" She lost her sandal along the way but kept running regardless. Soon, she was within the circle of men, their Bibles readily apparent on each leather horse pack. She stood beneath the churchmen, but with the noon autumn sun glaring down into her eyes, she couldn't find her beloved Señor Sola.

She shaded her eyes with a graceful, slim hand and searched again. Before her eyes could scan all the men, they were stopped cold by the finest man she had ever seen. He looked to be Spanish, with his unruly, dark brown hair and deeply set eyes that seemed darker than coal. His facial features were aristocratic, giving the impression of noble birth, perhaps Spanish gentility. His shoulders were broad, and his legs extended well down the horse's sides. Isabella could not take her eyes from his. The stranger seemed to hold her with an intense, unseen force. At last, he spoke.

"You must be Isabella," he said softly with a respect usually not extended to women on the rancho. She was so awestruck by his courtesy that she could only nod in reply, her mouth falling open.

"Isabella, Preacher Sola has told me so much about you." The stranger jumped down from his horse, and Isabella stood frozen under his warm gaze. She felt so small beneath his towering frame, and she was awe-struck by his shaven jawline. She had never before seen a mature man without facial hair, except for the Indians. The straight lines of his features were mesmerizing.

When Isabella remained silent, he spoke again. "Señor Sola says you are his special girl. I must say, I was expecting a girl of about three by his descriptions. He still sees you as a child, Isabella. Preacher Sola was heartbroken that he could not be here for your wedding ceremony. He sent me in his absence, to let you know his heart would be here."

Isabella woke from her dreamlike state, and she frantically looked among the men once again. "Preacher Sola is not here?" she repeated fearfully.

"No, Señorita. Señor Sola's health is failing, and he was unable to make the trip. I am the new preacher on this riding circuit. My name is Juan Carlos Vega." He bowed before her and gently kissed her hand. She felt her knees weaken and pondered the strange new sensation this man caused within her stomach.

The other churchmen led Juan Carlos's horse away, leaving him alone with Isabella on the plain.

"I'm sorry you're disappointed, Isabella. We would not allow Señor Sola to join us. He would have come anyway if he hadn't been assured of your happiness surrounding your impending marriage."

Isabella tossed her head from side to side, her long dark hair reflecting the afternoon sun. She couldn't believe what she was hearing. All her hopes rested upon Preacher Sola. She needed him. This handsome stranger would never convince her father to break his vow. She finally had words. "I don't know who you are, but I need Preacher Sola. It is vital that he come. I have so many questions about the Bible and my upcoming marriage. He must be here to interpret. No one on the rancho reads."

"I read, Señorita," he replied calmly. "I would be happy to translate for you. Did you have a particular passage in mind or an area troubling you?" He whispered to imply the strictest confidence.

Isabella was transfixed by the magnificence of the stranger's face. She heard nothing of his words. His eyes were gentle and trustworthy, and his expression, genuine and concerned. Her troubles evaporated, and suddenly she had the strangest thought. She didn't want to discuss Antonio Fremont or her disastrous marriage. She wanted to reach up and softly kiss Juan Carlos Vega. She felt the heat rise in her cheeks.

Juan Carlos walked with her to the patio and sat down, taking her hand. "I understand your disappointment that Pastor Sola is not here, but what I don't understand is the sadness in your eyes. Your tears are not from a young woman in love, are they?"

She shook her head. Something about Juan made her trust him instinctively. Perhaps it was that he was her only hope against her father's promise, but she poured out her heart. "Antonio Fremont, my betrothed. He is a vile man, but Papa thinks because of his wealth he is the best choice for me. He has already had two wives. Am I not worthy enough to be a first wife? Because he owns the most cattle, must he own me too?" She threw her hand to her heart. "Oh, I know I sound ungrateful, but you have not met this man. I need to know what the Bible says about honoring your father and your mother and when that honor may be broken. For I know what the Bible says about a wife's submission, and I am not ready to take such a vow with Antonio Fremont."

"I think you know what the Bible says, my child. You just don't want to listen to it," his low voice answered tenderly. " 'Honour thy father and thy mother.' Not just when you want to, but always. I must believe your father wants and is doing what's best for you. Pastor Sola speaks so highly of your father."

She shook her head again. "No, there's another verse. The one about being equally yoked, like the oxen that pull the cowskins. How can I be equally yoked to such a man, who does not have the fear of God within him?"

"You raise a very good point, but I think your father has spoken. From what I understand, a ranchero is not generally given to changing his mind, especially when it means relenting to a señorita."

Isabella fell to her knees at the feet of the handsome preacher. "Oh please, Señor Vega, I beg you. Please find the scripture I refer to and talk with Papa. If you do not do this, what will I do? I have been endlessly praying to my heavenly Father. I would rather die than marry Señor Fremont."

"I will do what I can, Isabella." The use of her Christian name by his deep voice stirred her heart. She looked at him, and their eyes locked. Not the eyes of a preacher, but the eyes of a man. A man with emotions and sympathy for her plight, and perhaps something else. He rose quickly and left her on her knees in the bright afternoon light. Isabella watched him walk away, wondering at her breathlessness.

Chapter 3

Isabella tossed her dress carelessly into her bota, her traveling bag made from cowhide. Her sister watched the commotion in disbelief. "Isabella, where can you possibly go? Father will only find out where you are and be angrier than ever. Not to mention your reputation will be ruined and no one will marry you," Victoria added. "Why don't you come stay with Raul and me in the outer adobe for a while? It will get your mind off your marriage until the fiesta."

"No, Victoria. I will not marry that man. I must go. There is no other way. Señor Vega is not willing to fight for me. And Papa will not respect the word of a Protestant other than Pastor Sola. Pastor Sola shall not come this Navidad. I'd rather work the fields like an Indian or tend to the tanning vats than marry Antonio Fremont. Look me in the eye and tell me you wouldn't run, too." A moment passed. "You can't do it, can you?"

"Where will you possibly go? I will worry."

"I will run to the mission church. Perhaps I can enter the convent."

"They will not accept such a woman as you. You are of noble Californio birth, not a Spaniard or Mexican as the nuns are," Victoria argued. "Isabella, you have never even been off the rancho, you have no idea what awaits you out there. The smugglers, the whalers, the sailors, it is simply not safe!"

"God will guard me, and He cares not of my nationality if I want to serve Him. Good-bye, dear sister. I love you. Do not tell them of my plans, only that I will find work and be safe." Isabella kissed her sister and ran into the darkness of the night with only the full moon to guide her steps.

Isabella walked for over an hour, and the chill of the night began to nip at her core. She pulled her shawl tighter and braced against the cold breeze that carried the coldness of the far-off ocean fog. It would take her nearly two days to reach the edge of her father's land, but she trudged on, knowing her journey was necessary. She must get to the neighboring rancho and the mission that operated upon it.

She had packed dried beef and planned to drink from the small creek she followed. As the night became darker, Isabella found herself wishing she had taken a horse. It would not have been missed until morning, but it would have made her tracks much easier to follow.

She heard a twig snap, and she automatically stopped in her tracks. Looking around her, she could see nothing in the darkness. She stepped as quietly as possible and hid beneath an oak tree, hoping the animal or wayward soul would pass without noticing her. Frozen in her fear for hours on end, Isabella eventually fell asleep under the great tree.

She woke to morning's first light and wiped her eyes, closing them tightly at first to shield them from the bright morning sun. Its heat felt so good, but the dew on the golden grasses reminded her of her chill. Her whole body ached from walking. Isabella was used to being catered to, not undergoing strenuous exercise, and she wondered if she were truly up to the task of working for a living. Suddenly, her newfound independence didn't seem as hopeful an idea as it had the night before in the warmth of the adobe.

Her stomach grumbled, and she grimaced at the thought of dried beef rather than fresh eggs prepared by the servants. She ate the beef heartily, though with a scowl on her face at its salty taste. She continued to walk while she ate, knowing she'd lost too much time by falling asleep. Isabella was so engrossed in her own thoughts that it was a great surprise when she heard men murmuring nearby.

She stopped chewing and looked around her, hoping she would just find a wayward cow and that the speech she'd heard was as much a part of her imagination as the twig snapping had been the night before. After a moment, she knew her ears were not deceiving her. She ran to hide behind the closest tree, but in the open grassy flatlands that proved impossible, and she was seen immediately in a whirl of black.

One of the men yelled, "It's a woman, over there!"

She heard the loud gallop of horses closing in on her and knew her dash was pointless. Papa would be so angry, she thought, *if* he ever found out what happened to her. She stood in the field, closed her eyes, and murmured a small prayer, bracing herself for whatever lay ahead.

Suddenly, Isabella was swept upon a horse and into the hands of a man. She felt like a child in the large man's arm, and fear gripped her, her heart beating so loudly she couldn't hear another sound, not even the horse's hooves hitting the ground. She trembled. Looking down at the rushing ground alongside her, she closed her eyes tightly again, unwilling to believe what was happening. She let out a deep breath and opened her eyes, seeing only the black leather gloves that held the reins and her waist in a firm grip. *Oh, what have I done? Papa, I'm so sorry.*

She swallowed hard at the sight of a long, silver blade at her side. In one swift movement, invisible to her eyes, the sword was lifted high above them and they were forging ahead under the glistening blade. She watched its sunfilled reflection until it blinded her, forcing her to shield her eyes with her free hand. They galloped toward the group of horsemen, but the assembly seemed to be running from them, not leading them.

Recognition seized her, and she jerked her head around and saw the noble face of Juan Carlos Vega, smiling knowingly down upon her. He kicked the horse with a yell, spurring them closer to the band of horsemen. Isabella turned her face into his chest and held tightly to his black jacket, never more joyous to see anyone in her life. Suddenly the riders split up and tore in two different directions while a designated rider turned to face them. Isabella prayed at the sight of the stranger forging ever closer, fear mounting once again. When he was within several feet of them, the man stopped the horse and jumped from his mount, pulling out his own saber in invitation to Juan Carlos. The man was short and stocky, with full muttonchops and a scraggly beard. He held death in his eyes, and Isabella feared for Juan Carlos and the trouble she had led them both into.

Her rescuer took her hands from his coat and roughly handed her the reins with his free hand. He bolted from the horse easily, leaving her to handle the trotting horse herself. Isabella thanked God that she was an excellent horse-woman and steered the horse away from where it might be spooked, wishing she could just keep running and get home to safety. When she was a fair distance away, she heard the clanking of metal and turned to see Juan Carlos in a danger-ous dance of sword fighting.

"Oh Father, please protect him," she whispered.

Juan Carlos kept his eyes on his opponent and circled the man. Suddenly the swordsman lunged at Juan, and the fighting began again. Isabella had watched many sword fights during the annual rodeo when vaqueros showed off their many cowboy skills, but never before had she witnessed a true duel. Juan's technique seemed beyond compare to that which she had witnessed, perhaps because the others were staged. She wanted to turn away, but her interest was too keen, her mind too anxious, the outcome too important.

Juan Carlos moved the sword like a dancer, thoroughly in touch with his partner, blocking each jab his opponent made with a graceful, muscular arm. Juan Carlos seemed to know where the man would strike and almost casually deflected any attempts on his life. The sound of steel against steel rang into Isabella's ears, and she shuddered at the constant noise, praying it would end soon with Juan Carlos still easily in control.

Fatigue began to overtake the bearded man, but Juan Carlos held the saber high in the air, as though its great weight had no impact on his muscular frame. Suddenly Juan Carlos lunged unexpectedly and swooped the sword away from his opponent. Isabella began to gallop closer, but when the man picked up his sword and came at Juan again, she pulled the reins back. The opponent lifted his sword once again but dropped it from the overwhelming weight, too tired to fight any longer. Juan Carlos stepped on the blade, keeping it firmly upon the ground.

"You are on Arguello property. Are you aware of this?" he asked sternly.

"Just kill me swiftly," the man begged.

"I will not kill you. I am a man of God. You are trespassing with the intent to rustle cattle, no?" he asked.

"Yes," the man admitted.

"Take your pistol and your blade and get off this land. The next man that finds you may not be as forgiving as I." Juan Carlos lifted his foot and allowed the sword to be raised.

The man scrambled to get off the ground and ran to his horse, galloping away as if in fear for his life. Isabella was mystified by this man of God, as he called himself, and turned to Juan Carlos questioningly. His skills with a sword were certainly nothing like those displayed by the men at a rodeo. Juan Carlos held a subtle mastery over his sword, as one who used his talent often. He ran to her, breathless from his battle, and caught his horse by the reins. Placing his sword back into its sheath, he looked at her with the same intense brown eyes that had made her powerless the day before.

"Why did they not use their guns?" Isabella asked innocently.

"The noise would have alerted your father to rustlers. Most likely, they don't ride as well as your father's vaqueros, and they would have all been killed. Are you well, my child?"

"I'm not a child!" she exclaimed as she brushed off her skirt.

"A figure of speech. No need to be offended," he said as he tightened the reins on the horse. His eyes never met her own, but she could see he held back his smile.

"Where did you learn to fight like that? Certainly Pastor Sola did not teach you that." She watched him suspiciously.

He laughed, his brown eyes seeming to delight in her question. "You are a perceptive one, no?" He mounted his horse, and suddenly she felt his warmth against her back. Her fiery spirit left her as she basked in the protection of his arms. "Let's get you home," her rescuer declared. "You might still make breakfast."

"I'm not going home!" she said defiantly. "I will take care of myself." She remembered her plight once again and knew Juan Carlos's arms would not protect her back at the adobe from her papa's wrath. She squirmed to get loose of his embrace.

"You will take care of yourself," he said incredulously. "And how will you ward off the next group of rustlers that comes your way? There's no way to hide in this flatland until you reach the hills." She felt his arm leave her as he pointed toward the horizon.

"You just let me worry about that." She tried once again to jump from the horse, but his strong grasp of her waist made escape impossible. Her struggle was in vain against his bigger size, and she sighed miserably. She knew she should have been grateful for his timely heroics, but she held only contempt when he led the horse back to Rancho de Arguello.

"I will not let you run to danger," he said evenly. "Pastor Sola would never forgive me."

"You don't understand," Isabella protested. "You're sending me into danger. The way home is the path to destruction! By God's own Word, 'Enter ye in at the strait gate: for wide is the gate, and broad is the way, that leadeth to destruction.' You see? It would be too easy for me to marry such a man and live in wealth. God has chosen another way for me. It must be true. I want to serve Him, but how can I do so when I'm married to Antonio Fremont?"

To her surprise, he stopped the horse and dismounted, helping her gently from the saddle. He tethered the horse near the creek and sat on a flat rock at the water's edge, lifting his arm for her to join him. Men gave little attention to what women had to say in Isabella's experience. Yet Juan Carlos heard her, and by stopping the horse he was actually acknowledging her in a way she'd never known.

Chapter 4

The creek ran peacefully behind them, its gentle trickle allowing Isabella to become lost in Juan Carlos's deep brown eyes. Her thoughts were broken by his deep voice.

"Pastor Sola said you knew your scripture well. He was starting to teach you to read last time?" Juan Carlos asked. Pastor Sola was the only other man who had ever spoken to Isabella without giving her an order. She felt herself instantly drawn to Juan's interest.

"I know my letters, but I still struggle with the words." Her voice trailed off in discouragement. "Papa says there's no need to read, especially for a lady. So I practice in secret." She shrugged.

"Isabella," he said softly. "Isabella, it is a very dangerous world out there. Your papa is right to give you away in marriage. This way he knows you will be safe." He cupped his hand around her face, and she felt herself starting to cry. "You are trying to choose your own path, when God has already directed your circumstances through your papa's ordination. Marrying Señor Fremont will keep you safe. Life in California off the rancho is a very different place. A violent place." He didn't look at her for a reply.

Isabella shook her head. "No, Juan Carlos. You have no idea what you're asking of me. Please find the scripture that will release me. If Papa fears the wrath of God, perhaps I will be free. Pastor Sola would not have just given me away to a heathen like Antonio Fremont. Why should I suffer because you have come instead of him?"

"Isabella, you must honor your papa's word. It is one of the Ten Commandments."

"Am I bound by the law when I live under the cross?" Isabella squared her shoulders.

A look of wonder crossed Juan Carlos's face, and slowly a smile presented itself. "You know your scriptures *quite* well, Isabella. Better than any woman I've met on the circuit. It is a rare quality indeed."

"I will learn more as I get better at reading. Help me, Juan Carlos. Take me to the convent."

Juan shook his head. "God will bring you other blessings, if your marriage isn't to be one of them." The bubbling creek echoed behind them, and Isabella thought how beautiful her papa's land was. She would be so sorry to leave it, but she would indeed leave it. The horse turned, and Isabella was blinded once again by the molded, elaborate, silver handle of Juan Carlos's sword.

"Where did you get that sword?" she inquired, transfixed by its elegant design.

"My father gave it to me. He was a Spaniard. Mexico issued him land near Mission Carmel for his work in the territory. He died before he ever got to settle there." Juan Carlos looked so strong, it felt odd to hear him talk in such a melancholy tone.

"I'm sorry. How old were you when he died?"

"Sixteen, just a year younger than you are now." His brown eyes looked to the brook.

"You made it without getting married." She lifted her chin confidently. "Why shouldn't I give my life to God and avoid marriage altogether?"

"Isabella." He shook his head, a sly smile lifting the corner of his straight mouth. "It is different, and you know it. I am a man, and I haven't always been a man of God. I once lived by the sword instead of the Word. And if you leave the safety of your father's way for you, you will live by the sword, too. Living in darkness with God is far better than life without Him. You must trust me on this. A beautiful woman like you is not safe alone in the territory. You need a husband." His tone left little room for argument.

Nothing he'd said registered except that he thought her beautiful. She had been told such nonsense since she was a child, but never had it meant anything to her until uttered by the dashing, sword-fighting Juan Carlos Vega. She looked at him with renewed interest. Perhaps she did need a husband after all. A believing husband her father just might approve of. A Spanish nobleman was nothing next to the birthrights of a Califorñio, but perhaps Pastor Sola's blessing might convince her papa otherwise. Isabella's mind reeled with the possibilities.

Suddenly a high-pitched squealing came toward them. Juan Carlos's eyes popped open wide, and he flew to his feet. "Get on the horse now!" he shouted, and Isabella did as she was told without hesitation. Before she could turn around to see the intruder on their quiet moment, Juan Carlos was behind her, giving the horse a start. They pulled into a full gallop within seconds and left the wild boar that chased them in the dust.

The aggressive boar had accomplished one thing. Isabella was headed toward home without further delay. The rancho came into view, and she couldn't believe she'd walked all that way and was mere minutes from her adobe. "No wonder you laughed at me," she said quietly. "I was such a short way from home that I never would have made it to the mission church." She ached that Juan Carlos knew just how foolish she'd been, ached at knowing her valiant escape effort had been so pathetic.

"No one is laughing at you, Señorita." She thought she felt Juan Carlos close his arms a little tighter around her, but it was probably wishful thinking. Her girlish ways would only be an amusement to such a fine man of noble birth. A man who listened to her thoughts. It seemed a dream to have the character of her beloved Pastor Sola dwell inside a man who looked like Juan

Carlos Vega. Of course, it was no more than the dream. She was engaged to be married to a Califorñio. *As it should be,* she thought sadly.

"Isabella!" Her father's stern voice called out to her from the adobe. Her entire family came running toward the horse, and she wished she might crawl under a rock. "Isabella, in your room immediately. Your mother will be along shortly."

She looked to Juan Carlos and noticed he tried to ignore the reprimand, but it was ludicrous to think he'd missed it. She was but a child to him. Any thoughts to the contrary were in vain.

She sat in her darkened room, opening the curtain slightly when her sister came in to soothe her. "Isabella, I am glad you did not get far. I would have been sick with worry. Juan Carlos is a good man. He offered to go searching for you early this morning. He whispered something to Papa and so he was allowed to go alone."

"He is a fine man, Victoria. He is a true hero. He rescued me from a band of cattle rustlers, then he had a sword fight like a Spanish conquistador, then he pulled me out of harm's way from an angry boar."

Victoria giggled, "Oh Isabella, your imagination. It is good to have you home." Victoria patted her arm condescendingly. "Mama will be here soon. I must see to the servants and dinner."

Just then Señora Arguello came into the room, and Victoria left them alone. "Isabella." The señora stroked her daughter's cheek and pulled her into a warm embrace. "I'm sorry Señor Fremont is not who you would have picked, but you must never betray your father again, do you understand?" Señora Arguello pulled away. "He will lose authority with the Indians and vaqueros, and that could be dangerous for us all. There's no telling what might have happened to you out there alone," her mother added ominously, and Isabella kept her adventures quiet this time. "Now I'll arrange for you to bathe. Antonio is coming tonight for dinner. I've laid out your best lace gown."

"Mama, why must I marry a wealthy man? Cannot a poor man who loves the Lord take care of me?"

"Isabella, this is far too hard for us women to understand, but your papa says the Americans are coming and our wealth is more important than ever to maintain the territory. The Mexicans want control of this land, the Spaniards want control, and now the Americans as well. The Californios have worked hard to remain under Mexican rule while still being independent. Papa says it is only because of our wealth that we maintain that rule. Your marrying Antonio Fremont helps us all, you understand that?"

Señora Arguello gave her daughter a loving smile, and Isabella simply nodded in agreement.

"It is a hard thing for a ranchero to have no sons, but a blessing indeed to have such a daughter that would bring in so many cattle," Isabella's mother continued.

Isabella ached at the notion that the value of her life could be measured with cattle. They were such big, stupid animals. Who cared how many cows she was worth? Pastor Sola didn't. And perhaps Juan Carlos Vega didn't either.

Later that day Isabella dressed in her finest, but she didn't feel like dancing or celebrating, not with the knowledge that Señor Fremont would be arriving for dinner. As the sun began to descend, she walked along the patio, taking in the beautiful orange and pink sunset that lit the clear winter sky.

"It's kind of dark to be out alone, isn't it, little one?" Juan Carlos appeared from the shadows, his Bible in his hand.

He seemed to come from a dream, and Isabella did not want to let him out of her sight. His handsome, chiseled features held her. She walked toward him, as though drawn by his eyes. Without another word, Juan Carlos swept her into his arms and led her in a contradanza, a dignified dance from Spain.

"My mama taught me this dance." He closed his eyes momentarily. He hummed an accompaniment, and Isabella giggled with enjoyment, relishing every sensation he sent her body soaring into. *This is how a woman should feel about the man she marries,* she thought dreamily.

Too swiftly his joyful humming ceased, and Isabella opened her wide, brown eyes. "We are finished?" she asked, disappointed.

His tone was fatherly, reserved. "Isabella, I want you to be kind to Señor Fremont tonight. It is very important to your father. . .and to me," he added.

Isabella could only nod. Being nice to Señor Fremont was the last thing on her mind. She wanted to become lost in an elegant dance again, to forget she was marrying another. Life had been so simple until she was asked to grow up so suddenly.

"Make your papa proud. Do what he asks of you. Let us go in now." He took her arm, looking straight ahead, avoiding her admiring eyes.

"Wait." She stepped in front of him and looked at him fiercely, trying to ascertain whether the feelings between them were only hers. She caught his deep-set brown eyes. Instantly she knew: Juan Carlos did not think her a child after all. The recognition set her stomach aflutter, and for the first time since her engagement, she felt hope.

"Let us go," he said again by way of excuse.

"No," she pleaded. Juan Carlos was about to kiss her. She may have been naive about many things, but this she was sure about. He gazed at her a moment longer but remained stoic and immobile. She finally reached up and kissed him timidly, softly. His eyes closed, and he returned her kiss sweetly before breaking from her embrace, holding her at the shoulders.

"Isabella, you are a betrothed woman and that kiss is for your husband and no other," he said firmly, a stern look replacing the smiling brown eyes.

She nodded. "Very well then. I suppose you must marry me now." She crossed her arms.

"Isabella, even if I were in a position to marry you, which I am not, your father would never allow it. I am a Spaniard, not a Califorñio, and if you knew of my past, you would understand how impossible such an idea is. You are to marry Antonio Fremont, though it pains me to say it. It is what's best. Any ideas to the contrary are mere folly."

"Because you were born a Spanish nobleman, you were baptized a Catholic, so my papa should not object to you, is that not true?" she challenged.

"Isabella, your family awaits. Honor your father and your mother."

She watched him walk purposefully into the adobe, his broad shoulders straight with resolution. His defiance only made her more certain that she would never marry Antonio Fremont, for she loved the preacher, Juan Carlos Vega.

Chapter 5

Juan Carlos sat at the edge of the great table opposite the man who would marry Isabella. Everything she had told him about Señor Fremont reverberated in his ears with vivid clarity. Although Señor Arguello did not serve hard drink, the coarse ranchero had brought his own and was drunk by the main course of the meal. The foul words he flung easily disgusted Juan Carlos, and the vulgar way he eyed Isabella made Juan Carlos want to take to the sword once again.

Juan Carlos knew Señor Arguello loved his daughter, and he saw in the older man's eyes fear. Fear that his daughter would suffer for his mistake.

With clenched teeth, Juan Carlos forced himself to keep his eyes from Isabella. In her exquisite, Spanish cream lace gown, her beauty was legendary; but if others saw what Juan Carlos felt, the preacher would have no credibility with Isabella's father. Juan Carlos planned to appeal to the ranchero for Isabella's freedom, and any feelings of his own would definitely harm his chances for success.

No matter how many cattle Isabella was worth, her papa had to see that Señor Fremont was an abhorrent choice for a husband. Getting a ranchero to admit his wrong and change his word, however, was not going to be easy. In the California Territory, a man's reputation was as important as the number of cattle he owned.

"Isabella, come sit on my lap, my dear." Señor Fremont pulled away from the table, screeching his chair against the planked floor, and reached around his abundant belly to pat his round legs. His speech was slurred from drink, and he looked as though he was having a difficult time holding his head up.

Juan Carlos waited for Señor Arguello to protect his daughter, but the father remained silent. No admonition escaped his mouth. Isabella was obviously frozen with fear, and she remained seated, seeming to ignore the plea from her intended, offering him more water instead.

When Señor Arguello motioned for Isabella to move over to their guest, Juan Carlos stood up angrily. "I must protest. Isabella is not married yet, and therefore, in the eyes of God, this is sinful. Would you ask Isabella to sin before the very preacher who saved her life as a child? As I sit here in Pastor Sola's absence, I ask that you not do so in front of me." Juan Carlos looked at Señor Fremont, and the man threw out an arm in disgust.

"Sit down, Isabella. The preacher is right," Señor Arguello commanded, a look of discomfort crossing his brow. Isabella sighed with relief and mouthed "thank you" to Juan Carlos.

After the meal, Antonio Fremont bedded down for the night, too intoxicated to stay awake any longer. Isabella quickly scurried into her room, anxious to get away.

"Señor, may I have a word with you." Juan Carlos pulled Señor Arguello aside, anxious to share the scripture that would release Isabella from such a disastrous marriage. They walked into the crisp night air and sat under the stars. "The Bible says a man is to love his wife as Christ loves the church. A man like Antonio Fremont is not capable of such a love. He does not walk in the way of our Lord—that much is obvious."

The night was dark and the torches were snuffed out for the evening, so Juan Carlos could not see a reaction and prayed silently his words would be taken well.

"Why do you talk to me of love?" Señor Arguello replied. "I love my daughter enough to give her to the wealthiest Californio in the territory. Any father would be proud to call Antonio Fremont his son. A thousand cattle she is worth."

"She is worth far more than that. The Bible says that a virtuous wife is worth far above rubies."

"I will be the wealthiest Californio when Isabella is married. You cannot put a price on that!" Señor Arguello stated proudly, lifting his chin.

"You have put a price on it: Isabella." Immediately, Juan Carlos regretted his words.

"Pastor Sola would never come into my adobe with such insolence. What gives you the right to question me? You, a Spaniard," Señor Arguello said before he spit in contempt. "Worse yet, a Spaniard without a birthright, who travels the territory with nothing to call his own except a Bible. Isabella is a woman and she'll do what she's told."

"You are acting in greed, not Christian love, and it is my duty as a man of God to tell you so. You have the right to do as you see fit, but I must preach the Word as God has given it. Just as Nathaniel once did to David."

"And what would your Book tell me to do, preacher? Give my daughter to a man of God without a single steer to call his own?" Señor Arguello asked accusingly. "Just because you are handsome, you think yourself a worthy husband for my daughter? You. . .a Spaniard. You all think yourselves superior to us! Well, I'll have none of that. Isabella will marry a Californio as she was born to do."

Juan Carlos tried to hide his shock. He had mentioned nothing of his feelings, yet Señor Arguello knew what his thoughts were. Isabella's father must have recognized his jealousy during the evening meal. Either that or Señor Arguello had seen so many men fall victim to Isabella's innocent charms, he just assumed Juan Carlos was not immune. And he was not.

Juan Carlos took a deep breath. He had nothing to lose now. "If you did give Isabella to me, I would care for her like no other man, certainly unlike Antonio Fremont."

"I've seen your sword, Juan Carlos. I know you've lived by the knife—it's obvious by the condition of your blade. You haven't always been a man of God. Why should I believe you're one now and not just some poor man making cow eyes at my daughter to gain my herds?"

"Pastor Sola, for one thing. Do you think he would send someone who might harm his precious Isabella? He thinks of her as the daughter he never had. I can't give you an assurance that you would believe. I can only ask you to look at my heart and judge my actions. I will tell you that if I had a mind to take Isabella for my own, we'd be gone without a trace. But as I've said, I've given up that life. And I'm trusting you will come to see that I am now a man of God. I say these words in honor and respect, Señor. I would never seek to harm Isabella or her family." With those words, Juan Carlos turned on his heel and left Isabella's father alone in the night air.

❧

"He threatened me. The man of God threatened me!" Jose Arguello paced the floor of his room. "He comes into my adobe and questions my authority. He will be off this property tomorrow. No Spaniard is going to threaten my daughter's future of wealth." He pointed to the wooden floor. "He had the audacity to suggest I give her to him, a common beggar." Isabella's father let out a short laugh.

"Jose, maybe you're overreacting," Señora Arguello said hesitantly. "He does have a point—Señor Fremont committed several of the seven deadly sins just while sitting at the dinner table. He blatantly dismisses the commandments of our Lord, and he is so old, Señor. Juan Carlos is just telling you his observations. You needn't kill the messenger."

"You see, now you are questioning me. This Juan Carlos has done enough damage. I want him off the rancho tomorrow, and I'll have every vaquero behind him to insure he goes."

"But Juan, think of Isabella. She is beside herself without Pastor Sola here. Wouldn't it be wise to have the young preacher here at least until the priest arrives?"

"She will adjust," Jose said sharply.

❧

Isabella listened at the door of her parent's bedroom. All hope within her died. If Antonio Fremont's heathen behavior hadn't convinced her father, nothing would. She had to run again, but this time she wouldn't go alone. She would go with Preacher Juan Carlos Vega, with or without his assistance.

She tiptoed up the hallway and knocked quietly on Juan Carlos's door. He had a candle lit, and his Bible lay open on his cot. He opened his mouth, but Isabella cut him off in a whisper. "I must speak with you. Meet me at the stable."

She hurried outside and ran across the expanse to the horses' stalls. She found an empty one and huddled down in the hay to wait. It wasn't long before Juan Carlos called her name.

"I'm here," she said quietly, and he came toward her with a candle, which he blew out when he came closer. She couldn't even make out his form in the pitch black of night, but she could feel his warmth and hear his labored breathing from running the distance to the structure.

"Juan Carlos, my papa is unrelenting. I will have to marry Antonio Fremont if I stay." Her mouth felt so dry from nervousness. All her life everything had been taken care of for her, but now she felt she must act on her own or suffer the consequences. She drew in a deep breath for courage. "Tomorrow my papa will see to it that you are thrown off Rancho de Arguello, and I beg you to take me with you. I will do anything," she said breathlessly. "I would even—"

"Shh," he said. "Pray Isabella. Believe in the Lord your God and not in me. Call on Him. I am but a man and a weak one at that. The Lord has sent me to do His work, and already I find I am tempted beyond measure by your beauty. Isabella, I wish I could protect you, but I cannot. You must ask God. If I helped you, it would be as a man, not as a preacher, and I cannot go against your father's word because it would break my vow to God."

"I don't care how you help me. Just help me," she pleaded.

He found her face with his hands and held her ever so gently, kissing her softly on the forehead. She knew his kiss meant good-bye, and she grew more anxious than ever.

"Would you leave me to this fate? To have Antonio Fremont take me as his wife?" she asked desperately, hoping for a reaction.

"Antonio Fremont is not in the wrong, Isabella, I am. Is Antonio Fremont standing here kissing another man's fiancée in the dark of the night? Is he telling her with words and actions how he loves her when he knows she belongs to another?"

"I will never belong to another," she whispered through her tears.

"You already do, Isabella." He reached down and smoothed her cheek and walked out into the night.

Isabella felt more desolate than ever and chased him frantically, grasping his shoulder. "I know you were a smuggler. You could have me off Papa's property without a trace. We could leave tonight. Why won't you help me?"

"Where did you hear this?" he demanded.

"I heard the rustlers fighting over who would battle you. They knew of you. . .feared you. You were apparently quite renowned," she said accusingly.

"Isabella, I left that life behind when I joined God's army. Let this go and marry Antonio Fremont. I will not help you escape." He said with finality, "You are better off in the life you've known. God will provide." His voice trailed off, and he resolutely turned his back and was gone.

Chapter 6

The next morning the fiesta celebration of Isabella's engagement began bright and early with a hearty breakfast of steak and eggs. Although the California winter chill was brisk, the warm sun allowed for the meal out on the patio. Juan Carlos sat across from Isabella but refused to look at her. He said the prayer over the morning meal and quietly ate his breakfast.

At the close of the meal, Señor Arguello stood up to speak. "I'm sorry to announce that Señor Vega will not be staying for the wedding celebration. The preacher is very busy this time of year and has other commitments." He turned to Juan Carlos. "Preacher Vega, I have prepared a cart of cowhides for you to take to Preacher Sola in payment for your trip. Please give him our best and let him know how much we've missed him."

With the announcement, Juan Carlos nodded, rose, and said his excuses. Isabella felt like a caged animal and stood abruptly. "I will see that the servants have sent the proper provisions."

Isabella raced to grab her packed bota, then quietly snuck it into the cowhide cart. She pretended to go to speak with the stable chief but instead ducked into the oxcart and hid under the dried leather skins. She felt the cart lifted as it was hitched to a team of horses rather than oxen to speed their travel. About an hour later, she heard Juan Carlos's gentle voice, and her heart quickened.

"Señora, I am sorry I must leave on such a harsh note. Please give Señor my best and relay my sincerest apologies if I have offended him. May I see Isabella before I leave? I'd like to tell her good-bye."

For a moment Isabella felt guilty about deceiving those she loved. How she would miss her mama and papa and especially her sister. But one thought of Antonio Fremont, and she knew what she had to do.

She heard her mother's quiet voice. "You would be more than welcome to say good-bye to Isabella, but I'm afraid she is off pouting somewhere. No one has seen her since breakfast. No need to worry. She is probably by the creek sulking. This has been a very trying time for her. Marriage is not an easy step. The servants will bring her back, and I will relay your greetings. You have been most kind to us, Señor. I'm sorry you must leave."

"You are most kind, and I will pray, Señora."

"Si," Isabella heard her mother say sadly.

Isabella soon felt a sharp tug on the wagon, and she tensed, praying she would not be discovered until she was well off her papa's property.

Hours passed, and Isabella grew hot under the cowhides, lifting them often to allow more air to circulate in the cart. She gulped deep breaths of fresh air but finally grew tired of pressing against the heavy hides. As more time passed, Isabella started to feel dizzy, and the darkness under the pelts invaded her head. She felt the horses slowing just before the blackness overwhelmed her.

"Juan Carlos Vega! Back to your old ways, I see. There must be a hundred California banknotes in that cart." Brigadier General Manuel Torena in full Mexican regalia circled Juan Carlos's horse, smiling smugly at the preacher. "I knew your conversion was just a ploy. Once a thief, always a thief!"

Juan Carlos held his chin high, watching his old nemesis cautiously. "I am a man of God, General. These skins are a gift from Señor Jose Arguello for Preacher Sola's ministry."

"No Califorñio would give such a generous gift to a Protestant minister!" The general dismounted and motioned for his horsemen to do the same. "Search the cowskins!" he shouted. "Juan Carlos Vega does not simply smuggle pelts. He's got other provisions in there, I know it. Search!" he repeated with urgency, and the uniformed soldiers scrambled to carry out the order.

The men lifted the leathers, tossing them carelessly on the muddy soil of the road. Soon, one of the men screamed excitedly, "Murderer!" The soldier looked at Juan Carlos accusingly. "He's got a dead woman back here. And what's worse, she's a Califorñio! Look at her gown."

The soldier lifted Isabella's limp body out of the oxcart, and Juan Carlos felt the blood rush from his face.

"Isabella!" He jumped from his horse and ran to her. The soldier held a gun to Juan Carlos, but the preacher stared at the man with fire in his eyes. "Call him off, General!" he cried.

Juan Carlos's successful fighting reputation had not diminished, and the general motioned for his man to move.

"Isabella, my sweet. Wake up, my darling," Juan Carlos whispered as he held her seemingly lifeless body. He looked up at the men who had accompanied him on his journey. "Get some water!"

Isabella's raven tresses fell around her pale face. The red lips, once so full, so moist, were now colorless and dry, and her great brown eyes appeared sunken.

One of his horsemen brought a canteen forward, and Juan Carlos sprinkled the liquid into Isabella's mouth while he prayed over her. "Dear heavenly Father, restore her, Lord, restore her." He rocked her gently while the horseman took the canteen and let several drops of water fall into her open mouth. Soon, Isabella's pink tongue licked the drops, and eventually her eyes fluttered opened.

"Juan Carlos, where am I?" she asked. "Are we off Papa's rancho?" Isabella then noticed the soldiers, and she tried to sit up quickly but fell back wearily into Juan Carlos's arms.

"You're near Monterey," he answered softly. "You became dehydrated under the cowskins." He was furious with her for sneaking away. She might have been killed had they not been discovered by the general, but he kept his anger in check. It would not help his case with the general, and more importantly, it would do nothing for the frightened woman he loved. The sight of her filled him with an overwhelming instinct to shield and protect her. He would never let anyone harm her.

The general came beside his horse and removed Juan Carlos's sword. "Confiscate his gun!" he yelled, and the soldiers searched Juan Carlos roughly for a weapon the preacher no longer carried.

A soldier lifted Isabella to her feet while the general tied Juan Carlos's hands together with a vaquero's horse rope. Isabella cried in fear, "What are you doing to Preacher Vega?"

"Your Preacher Vega is smuggler, Juan Carlos Vega. He is no man of God, and now we can add kidnapping a Californio to his crimes. You will surely hang this time, Vega!"

"No!" Isabella protested. "I stowed away in the oxcart. The cowskins are a gift from my papa to Preacher Sola. I wanted to get away from my betrothed. I never meant to bring harm upon Preacher Vega!" Isabella struggled to be free from the man who held her, but he only smiled with dry amusement at her effort. "Juan Carlos did not even know I was with them. You must ask my papa! Surely, you will hang, General, if they find you killed an untried man of the cloth. You, not even a Californio!" she spat out viciously.

Juan Carlos marveled at her intelligence. Discerning that the general was a Mexican national and not a native Californio was one thing, but using that knowledge against him was amazing for an innocent young woman who'd spent her entire life on a sheltered rancho. She had obviously listened well to her father's prejudices and politics. The Californios, while under Mexican rule, considered themselves above their ancestors' nations. They were in every sense pure Californios. They wanted no part of Mexico or Spain.

The general paused for a moment, trying to decide whether Juan Carlos's fate might also affect his own. "You will spend the night in prison until we verify your story," he said to Juan Carlos. "The señorita will stay with my wife until we have proper guards to return her to her rancho. No false moves, Vega, or the lady may pay the price, *comprende?*"

Juan Carlos clenched his teeth, knowing the general was just cruel enough to harm Isabella and blame him. For now, there was nothing he could do but pray.

❧❦❧

Isabella bit back sobs as she watched Juan Carlos walk the remaining distance to Monterey with his hands tied behind his back. Every so often, the general would kick the preacher to speed his pace, and Juan Carlos would grimace in pain. The rest of Juan Carlos's circuit-riding preachers were set free without the cowskins, which the general had confiscated.

The blue sea of Monterey glistened under the foggy sky, and Isabella marveled at the enormous schooner in the beautiful bay. The port was a hub-bub of activity—soldiers marched in unison, shoremen worked the docks—but the busy trading post stopped all activity as the general passed by with his prisoner. Much to Isabella's dismay, they paid no mind to Juan Carlos, but they studied her with eager eyes. Isabella caught her breath and bit her lower lip nervously. A woman was obviously a rare sight in Monterey.

She could see in Juan Carlos's eyes that he wished to protect her, and his inability to do so only seemed to frustrate him more. Isabella cringed at the trouble she had brought to the man she supposedly loved. Her selfish actions had only succeeded in harming those she cared for: Pastor Sola would not get his California banknotes to support his ministers, her papa would not get the cattle as part of her marriage agreement, and worst of all, Juan Carlos might hang for her sins.

"Isabella, all will be well. Just pray, my love. God's plan will be for the good, no matter what that plan includes, do you understand?" Juan Carlos asked her when they arrived at the general's mansion. It was just like Juan Carlos to think of her when he was in danger.

"They will have to kill me first before they let you hang!" she shouted.

"Isabella." He let his head drop. "God's will be done, my dear. Go back home and marry Antonio Fremont."

"Antonio Fremont? She is betrothed to Señor Fremont?" the general inquired uneasily.

"Si, that's right, the richest ranchero in the territory, and she belongs to him, so it is in your best interest to get her home safely," Juan Carlos warned, and Isabella could see the general's face go ashen.

The general's home was a lovely two-story adobe on the shores of the bay. It was furnished with inlaid tables from China, camphor-wood chests, and embroidered silk bedspreads; but for all its wealth, the home was devoid of any warmth. Isabella felt this lack as soon as she walked into the general's lavish quarters. His wife Martina met them in the foyer.

"This here's Fremont's betrothed," the general told her roughly. "Take care of her or our post will be in serious jeopardy," he shouted, just before he ripped Juan Carlos from Isabella's sight.

"Trust in God!" she heard him yell behind the closed door.

Martina Torena studied Isabella suspiciously. "So, you are Antonio Fremont's choice," she said slowly as she crossed her arms and walked around the young woman. "What brings you to Monterey alone? Surely you are not here for a gown, for no decent ranchero would allow his daughter to roam the streets of Monterey without guards. You are running away, no?"

"No," Isabella lied. "I wanted to go to Preacher Sola, and I knew that Juan Carlos Vega could get me there, so I snuck into the cowskins." Martina's eyes thinned, the woman's disbelief apparent.

"I do not like pretty women in my home. You will tease my husband and ruin my marriage. I do not have a son yet, so I will not stand for your presence here. If the general does not find a way back for you by tomorrow, you will go alone, understood?" Señora Torena's dark eyes seemed to drill right through Isabella.

"Yes, Señora," Isabella replied meekly.

"Very well. The upstairs bedroom at the end of the hall is yours. See that you stay there and out of my husband's sight. Your meals will be brought to you."

Isabella scrambled upstairs, anxious to be free of this jealous wife. At the rodeo, women talked about her, but Isabella had always been protected from other women's jealous actions by her father's status. Here, she held no such power, and should she say something out of line, Juan Carlos's fate might be worse.

Hours passed for Isabella in her darkened chambers. She prayed, pleading that the Lord would be with Juan Carlos and that he would be freed from the false charges. "Dear Lord, do not let Juan Carlos suffer for my selfishness. I have acted on my own power, not trusting You to work all things together for good—even my papa's plans to marry me to Señor Fremont. I have struggled against only You, Lord, and I beg for Your forgiveness. I will marry Antonio without further delay, and while I have no right to ask You any favors, please spare the life of Juan Carlos. Oh, to have his blood on my hands is more than I can bear." She buried her tear-drenched face in her hands.

Just then the great wooden door opened from the hallway. A young Indian servant came in carrying a tray of fish. She shut the thick door forcefully behind her. "Juan Carlos Vega will come for you tonight. Listen at the door of the balcony." She pointed to a door in the back of the room. "He will not wait long."

"How do you know this?" Isabella asked desperately.

The servant ignored the question, obviously worried over being missed. "The general will visit the cantina tonight. You will only have a short time to escape. I must go," she said fearfully.

"Wait," Isabella pleaded.

"I am a believer. Go with God," the servant answered soothingly, holding Isabella's hand in her own.

The door swung open violently. "What is going on here?" Señora Torena's cold, evil stare froze Isabella in place. The older woman held a rod in her arms, lightly beating her hand with it.

Isabella squared her shoulders. "Your servant has not shown me proper respect as a Californio," she said haughtily, knowing that if the young woman proved to be a friend of Isabella's, she would suffer severe consequences.

"Ha! You impertinent. You are in the home of Brigadier General Torena, a Mexican national by birth, and I myself am a Califorñio. Your native status means nothing in Monterey, and it means nothing to me. Rosa, go!" she shouted to the maid as an afterthought.

The young Indian scurried from the room, anxious to escape the rod. Señora Martina Torena continued to beat the rod in her hand as she glared down on Isabella.

"Do you mean to harm me?" Isabella inquired uneasily.

Martina ignored her question. "Why will you marry Señor Fremont? He is old enough to be your grandpapa. He has children older than you."

"My papa has chosen him for me," she answered honestly, wishing she had submitted to that fact days earlier.

"Antonio does not love you," Señora Torena said viciously. "You are like an imported treasure, beautiful and useless. You are not worthy to marry him."

Isabella tilted her head, trying to understand why a complete stranger would sling such hateful words at her. "How—how do you know if Antonio loves me or not?" she asked nervously. Of course Antonio didn't love her—he didn't even know her. She was but an ornament to him. Why Señora Torena would trouble herself with such details was a mystery.

Señora Torena threw her head back and laughed harshly. Without a word, she turned and strode from the room, slamming the door with a vengeance behind her.

Isabella was left alone with her cold fish platter and her questions.

Chapter 7

Isabella's room was pitch black and she was never offered a candle, but she was too nervous to do anything but wait for the expected knock. Although her door was unlocked to the second-story balcony, her captors knew she would never venture out into the rough port city alone. She was far safer in the cold, dark room of her enemy. She prayed all evening that Rosa's words were true, that Juan Carlos would indeed rescue her.

The noise from the drinking establishments began to fill her room—a low rumble at first, then an outlandish roar as the night lengthened. A small knock sounded at her balcony door, and she bolted upright from her chair. She whispered through the door. "Who is it?"

"It is me, Isabella. Open quickly."

Recognizing the voice she had hoped so desperately to hear, Isabella opened the door as quietly as possible. Immediately her room was overwhelmed by the whoops and obnoxious laughter that filled the street. It sounded as though the entire town was immersed in criminal activity. At the sight of Juan Carlos, however, Isabella was tempted to forget all about her submission to her father's marriage plans. Even in the light of the feeble moonlight and city torches, Juan Carlos exuded strength and confidence. His regal profile and smooth, sun-blessed skin made him the ultimate knight in shining armor.

Although she was on the second floor, the low ceilings of the first floor made reaching her balcony a mere step up from his horse for a tall nobleman like Juan Carlos. He didn't wait for her to speak. He simply lifted her easily into his strong arms, arms she had grown so accustomed to in their short acquaintance.

"Hang on to my neck," he whispered as he climbed over the low, spindly wooden banister of the balcony and transferred them onto his faithful horse. With a quiet kick to the horse's sides, they were galloping like the wind into the thick, damp night. They rode past the mariachi bands in the taverns. Soon the lights from the city streets thinned, and he slowed the horse's pace to an easy canter.

In the blackness of the starry night and free from the darkened prison of Monterey, Isabella relaxed against Juan Carlos, letting out her first relaxed breath of the long day. "We are free," she stated simply.

"No, Isabella, you are free. I will go back to Monterey to pay the consequences for my past choices."

"No, Juan Carlos!" She turned to face him. "They will let you hang. Why did you steal me away if you were only going to run back into danger? Surely, this will make things worse for you!"

"I am a preacher. I must obey the law. And I have been arrested," he reminded her.

"But you have made it worse for yourself by taking me away in the night. Why?" She stared angrily into his eyes.

"You are trouble to the general, and I was afraid his wife might harm you," he answered without looking at her. Instead, he steered the horse along the dirt path that led back to the rancho.

"The general's wife. Why should she care about me? Just because I stir her ridiculous jealousy?" Isabella crossed her arms, leaning against Juan Carlos again. She could not fathom why he would take such a chance.

He spoke evenly. "Señora Torena, the general's wife, was in love with Antonio Fremont, your husband-to-be."

Isabella gasped, sitting upright once again.

"He made her no offer of marriage, and she finally married the general after waiting a year for a proposal that never came. Her family disowned her for not marrying a true Califorñio, and I was worried she'd take her vengeance out on you."

Isabella shuddered at the thought of the cold, dark eyes that belonged to the general's wife. Suddenly the woman's chilling stares made sense—the hostility, the jealousy. She turned on the horse to speak directly to Juan Carlos. "I won't let you go back to Monterey. You can live in the stables; the Indians will help you."

Juan Carlos laughed. "Isabella, I am a former smuggler. If I wanted to run, I assure you, no one would ever find me, but I don't want to run. I want to preach the Word of God, and perhaps His will is for me to do that in prison, as Paul did."

"How can you just accept such a fate? Will you not even try to save yourself?" Isabella was incredulous. She had always thought she lived for God, but Juan Carlos defied her beliefs. He was willing to give up his freedom for his faith—freedom that would have been his if she hadn't struggled so stubbornly for her own.

"It is not my job to save myself, Isabella. It is God's. You have tried to save yourself instead of letting God work His wonders for you. And here you are in the middle of the cold night on a horse with a former thief. You must trust in God, not just when times are good, but when they seem impossible. Only then will you see the true nature of God."

Isabella sighed. "But we could run together. I could go back to Pastor Sola's church and take care of him. Or I could just follow you." She felt like such a simpleton. She was so weak, weak and foolish. Only moments before she had been promising God that she would submit to her papa's wishes, and now she was throwing herself at a man who didn't want her.

"It is folly to covet what I cannot have," Juan Carlos said.

"Then you do have feelings for me?" she asked timidly.

She felt his warm breath alongside her ear and heard him whispering, "The first time I laid eyes on you, you pierced my heart to its very core. The look of joy you held in your sparkling eyes, so quickly replaced by sadness when you realized Pastor Sola was not with us. I will never forget that moment, Isabella. For it was then that I felt I had known you for a lifetime, that you would always be with me in my heart." He gallantly struck his arm over his chest, and she closed her eyes, treasuring his tender words.

"Then how can you ask me to marry another, when you feel as I do?" she questioned.

"You need only look at the trouble you brought upon yourself today, my little one. You are a Califorñio, I am a Spaniard. You know a life of luxury that I only knew as a child. . .and when I stole for it. God asks us to submit to Him. He asks us to honor our parents. You can only do that by marrying the man your papa has chosen for you. If you love me, you will honor your papa. I will have you home by morning, before the adobe rises, and you will go on with your life."

"You think I can just go on, knowing I have destroyed your chances for an honest life?"

"Isabella, you have nothing to feel guilty about. You made your choices, and I have made mine. I am not being punished for your sins, but for my own. When my father died, I made my choice. I entered a pirate ship of my own volition. I stole cargo from whaling ships, cowskins from rancheros, and jewelry from wealthy travelers."

"Then how did you come to know God if not from your parents?"

"My mother was Catholic and loved God with all her heart. But when she died shortly after my father, the church could not help me. They were too burdened with the needs of the local Indians. I had to go my own way. And I did, until Pastor Sola found me on a ship and told me of Jesus again. I had forgotten," he said softly. "I knew then I would turn my life over to God."

"So Pastor Sola saved both our lives," Isabella said.

"I suppose he did."

She felt herself relax once again, praying for God's mercy.

"Shh." Juan Carlos sat upright, and Isabella turned to watch him look around them. "Someone is following us. We're going to have to make a run for it. Hang on. Yah!"

The horse bolted into a full run, and Isabella suddenly heard the hooves that were indeed behind them. The chase escalated, and Juan Carlos's horse increased his speed. Isabella had never known a horse could go so quickly, and being in the darkness only magnified the effect.

She closed her eyes tightly, almost waiting to strike a tree, but the horse just kept running in the darkness with Juan Carlos guiding them safely. The wind whipped through her hair and she felt frozen to the bone, yet the horse raced on, swiftly and gracefully. They ran for what seemed like an eternity, but eventually Juan Carlos slowed the pace and steered them into a grove of trees, making the darkness even blacker. Suddenly a cabin appeared in the thick stand of trees.

"What is this place?" she whispered breathlessly.

"It's a smuggler's cabin. We'll be safe here until morning." He dismounted from the horse and took her frozen hands in his own. "Don't be afraid, Isabella, they'll never find us here."

Juan Carlos lit a fire in the hearth and read from his Bible by its light. After he had selected several passages, he stood. "I'll be outside just in case there's trouble. Get some sleep, Isabella. Tomorrow's a big day."

Chapter 8

The dawn was just breaking in the tranquil valley as Rancho de Arguello came into view. Isabella felt her heart in her throat at the sight of it. She was thankful for the familiarity and the safety it represented but fearful for her future and for that of Juan Carlos. Her papa's anger would not be silent, and this time she would pay a heavy toll for her rebellious actions.

She climbed off the horse, knowing it was the last time she would ever be in the comfort of Juan Carlos's arms, and she stared up at him longingly. "Juan Carlos, I—"

"Isabella, I must go. Your papa will not be kind if he finds me on his property. You are safe, and that's all that matters to me. I love you, Isabella. Pray, sweet one."

He spurred the black steed, and Isabella watched as the man she loved rode into the morning light. She fell to her knees on the grassy knoll near the adobe, sobbing for all she was losing.

"Isabella?" Victoria grabbed her and picked her up from the dirt. "Oh, Isabella, it's all right."

Isabella leaned into her older sister and continued to cry. "They'll hang him, sister."

"They won't hang him. Papa will see to it," Victoria said to comfort her.

"The general hates him. He will surely hang, and it will be my fault. My foolishness, my selfishness," she wailed. "It will be as though I made the noose myself."

"No, Isabella, no. Papa would never let that happen. Pastor Sola trusted Señor Vega, and Papa will always ensure Pastor Sola is taken care of."

"Victoria, leave us." Señor Arguello stood in the winter sun, a severe frown on his worn face.

Isabella looked up to him fearfully. "Papa, I'm sorry."

"Sorry! Isabella, it is a miracle you are alive. Where have you been all night?"

"I've been in Monterey. I snuck into Señor Vega's oxcart under the skins. Señor Vega was arrested by General Torena and taken away. Juan Carlos came for me in the middle of the night and returned me here, then went back to Monterey for his punishment."

Isabella's papa came down beside her and sat on the hard ground. She stared at him awkwardly, unsure of what to think of his uncharacteristic warmth. "Juan Carlos is a Spaniard, you know," he explained gently. "And

Spaniards think less of Californios."

"Juan Carlos doesn't. He says we are all equal in Christ, and why would he have placed himself in danger to rescue me?"

"Yes, I admit I was wrong about Señor Vega. Only a decent man would have brought you back to us without alerting the Mexican soldiers. Not only are you safe, but your reputation is intact, thanks to Juan Carlos's restraint. He should be rewarded for his efforts," Señor Arguello said as if to convince himself.

"Papa, I was wrong to leave, to not listen to you. Juan Carlos told me that, and now I must beg something of you, Papa. Though I know I am in no position to ask for favors, I only ask that you would send word to Monterey and see that Juan Carlos's life is spared for his valiant rescue of me."

"Isabella, that is not an easy favor to grant." Señor Arguello stood, and she also got up. "The Mexican guards and the Californios already have a strained relationship. Juan Carlos was a thief before he became a preacher. He stole the hides and tallow that we work so hard for. If he is executed, it will be of his own doing." Señor Arguello looked disappointed.

"But Papa, he has changed," Isabella argued.

"I know he has, or he would have never brought you back to me," her father admitted. "I will do what I can, but your wedding is in one week and the preparations must be made. He is a Spaniard, a former nobleman of some kind. And the Mexicans don't want war, so his life should be spared. I will look into his release, Isabella. I will do what I can."

"I will help Mama immediately, Papa. And I will never disappoint you again, Papa. I'm sorry." She looked at him with sad brown eyes, and for a moment, she thought she saw tears in her rugged papa's eyes. How could she have ever questioned her papa's love? Yes, he held fast to the patriarchal system in place on the ranchos. And yes, his word was law, but there was a gentleness about her father. A warmth she'd never seen in the other rancheros.

He nodded in reply. Then, for the first time in her life, Isabella felt her father hug her, awkwardly at first, then tighter. She stood stiff in his embrace, unsure of how to react, but eventually she fell into his hug. Her throat tightened with emotion.

❦

Isabella helped her mother drape white muslin cloth from the rafters of the patio. Wispy, white material flowed in the afternoon breeze, and her mother placed handmade, faux flowers elegantly around the circumference of the adobe. The entire home was awash with a festive air, and as the Indians prepared the ingredients for the baked goods for the party, Isabella found herself becoming less anxious over her wedding. She faced it with a certain resignation, knowing that if her father was able to spare Juan Carlos from punishment, she could endure a marriage with Señor Fremont. During her prayer times, God had spoken to her, telling her not to be anxious, and strangely, she wasn't.

Visitors began arriving the following day for the week-long festivities, and Isabella was assigned to insuring their comfort until her wedding. Although it was customary for the bride to remain idle, Isabella's papa thought it best for her to keep busy. She watched her papa load up an oxcart full of cowskins and ride toward Monterey. Never before had she had so much respect for her papa. It was unheard of for a ranchero to deliver his own cowskins, but Señor Arguello obviously loved her enough to see to Juan Carlos's release on his own.

The sound of lowing permeated the ranch, and Isabella looked outside to see a huge herd of cattle being rounded into the grazing lands. Their deep calls shattered all sense of quietness and peace. "That's what I'm worth," she said solemnly. "All those cows."

"Isabella!" her mama chastised.

"I'm sorry, Mama. I didn't mean it disrespectfully. It's just ominous to see my payment coming toward the adobe. I'm grateful for what you and Papa have done for me, really I am," Isabella said truthfully.

"I know you are, darling. You know, most women have to take the cows with them. If it wasn't for your beauty, you'd cost your papa quite a few California banknotes."

"I know. I'm glad Papa will get so many cattle."

"Your papa loves you so, Isabella. When you were gone, he cried like a baby." Isabella's mother held her hand.

"He did?" Isabella was stunned. Her papa was not given to showing emotions, and to know that he had actually shed tears filled her with an unidentifiable feeling.

"Yes, he did. It hurts him so much that you do not like Antonio Fremont, but he fears for your future if you stay here on the rancho. You must have a place of your own. Our land will go to Victoria's husband. Do you see now why your papa has promised you to Señor Fremont? It is not to make him wealthier. It is to insure your future."

"I know that now, Mama. I'm sorry I was so spoiled, so selfish. I will tell Papa immediately when he gets back," Isabella promised.

"He already knows, sweet. He would never say so, but he was hurt deeply when you ran away. He's only doing what's best for you, and sometimes that is painful."

"I know, Mama. Thank you." Isabella reached over and planted a swift kiss on her mother's cheek. "I'll go make sure the guests have everything they need."

Chapter 9

Isabella could hear her intended's obnoxious laughter from the other room. Luckily, Californio tradition prevented her from seeing him, and she didn't have to worry about being near him until the wedding day. She cringed at the thought of looking at him through the ceremony, but she would not be ungrateful again. And if she had to stare at him lovingly for her parents' sake, she would, no matter how much acting it took.

Isabella waited patiently for her papa's return, creating more fake flowers for the trellis over the patio; but when the darkness began to descend upon the landscape, keeping her hands occupied no longer soothed her mind. Just as the last of the sun slipped past the top of the mountain, Isabella saw her papa approaching. She ran to him, desperate for news and thankful for his safe return.

"Papa, Papa!"

He dismounted and looked at her sadly. "I'm sorry, my dear. There's no word. The general would not give me any information, but Juan Carlos was not at the jail. I asked several witnesses, and they said he had been taken away. Isabella, I'm sorry. No one knew where they took him."

Isabella broke down. "Papa, I love him. You don't think they'll kill him?" she inquired frantically.

"Shh. You must not say such things. Señor Fremont may hear. Juan Carlos is still a Spanish citizen, so most likely they shipped him back to his country, safe and sound. Whatever happens, it is no longer your concern," he said firmly.

But Isabella thought her father seemed preoccupied with something, something he didn't dare share with her. She thought she saw fear in his eyes.

"Papa, thank you for going to Monterey. I'm sorry I haven't been more grateful. I love you, Papa."

Her father was clearly uncomfortable at her emotional outburst. "Go help your mama," he ordered, dismissing her.

"Papa," she continued tentatively. "I trust you." Then she turned on her heels and ran into the house.

Isabella took out the family Bible and stared at it determinedly. She practiced the words she knew, looking for them within the great book. "Jee-sus," she pronounced cautiously. "God. Luv."

The next morning at daybreak, her papa galloped away on his favorite mare. Isabella couldn't imagine where her father might be headed on such an important day as the beginning of her wedding celebration, but she dismissed it, thinking he was probably just checking on the vaqueros' morning rounds.

When he didn't return by the next afternoon, Señora Arguello was calming the gathering of well-wishers, assuring them her husband would return by the evening to give his daughter away in marriage. Isabella spent her day in prayer, preparing to meet the end of life as she knew it on her familiar rancho. Soon she would be Señora Antonio Fremont and have a rancho of her own. She solemnly prayed to her heavenly Father, still beseeching Him to intervene, but outwardly accepting her fate.

"Mama?" Isabella spoke to her mother. Señora Arguello jumped with alarm. "Mama, where is Papa?"

"He'll be here," she said sternly, wringing her hands nervously.

"Mama, it will be nightfall soon. The guests are beginning to wonder at his disappearance. He should be here to entertain our guests," Isabella said.

"Isabella, is this your rancho?"

"No, Mama, I just—"

"Then don't question your papa again, do you understand? I would think you would have learned by now that your papa knows what he's doing," Isabella's mother snapped uncharacteristically.

"Mama, I'm sorry." Her mother's reaction frightened Isabella.

Señora Arguello put a palm up. "I don't want to hear that again, Isabella. If you are going to be a wife, you are going to have to learn your proper role. This questioning attitude must disappear. Instead of saying I'm sorry all the time, why don't you learn how to keep your mouth in check?"

"Yes, Mama. I'm sor—"

"Go check and see if the Indians are done with the cake," Señora Arguello ordered.

"Yes, Mama, I'll see to it right now." Isabella curtsied and ran into the house. She knew the cake was fine, so she simply went to her room. Victoria was there, packing Isabella's trunk.

"That's the last of it. Mama made you a fine trousseau, but I'm afraid the gowns are nothing compared to what you will be able to afford as the owner of California's biggest rancho. Papa says you can see the ocean on one side of your rancho and the great hills on the other and that everything in between belongs to Señor Fremont."

"Is that a fact?" Isabella said absently.

"Isabella, if you're still dreaming of that Spanish preacher, it's best to start thinking of your own husband. God will not honor such deceitful behavior," Victoria reprimanded.

"I'm not thinking of Juan Carlos, Victoria. I'm thinking of Papa. Where could he be on my wedding day? When he has become the most important Califorñio in all the territory, what could be more important than giving his daughter away?"

"I don't know, Isabella, but I'm sure as women, it's none of our concern."

"Victoria, Mama is not here, so you do not need to pretend you're not worried. Papa loves a good fiesta. Something is wrong. We must pray."

"You're right." The two women got down on their knees and held hands.

"Dear Father in heaven, we are so worried about our papa, and we know You know where he is. Please keep him safe. Lord, we just ask that You would bring him back soon and that You watch over him."

"Yes, Father, we pray that whatever Papa is doing, You are with him," Victoria added.

"Amen," they said in unison.

Chapter 10

The sun was nearly over the lowest peak when they heard the loud gallop of several horses. Anxiously looking out the small portal, Isabella saw her papa leading several men in Mexican uniform. "Soldiers!" she announced frightfully.

"Where?" Victoria came to the opening and gasped. "What could they want with Papa?"

Isabella drew in a sharp breath. "The woman with them! That's Señora Torena, the woman who was so vile to me in Monterey."

"Isabella, look! Pastor Vega is with them."

"Juan Carlos is here," she whispered numbly, her breath momentarily forgotten. She let it out with a deep sigh. "He's safe, oh thank the dear Lord, he is safe. Let us go!" Isabella said excitedly.

"No! We must wait for Papa. This can only mean trouble, and we have no place in it. Perhaps the soldiers are taking Juan Carlos away." Victoria's words reminded Isabella of Juan Carlos's troubles.

"Perhaps they are here for someone else," she answered hopefully. "Perhaps they are here for the ceremony."

"Isabella, Juan Carlos has been arrested. He will not be set free without a trial of the Mexican officials."

"What would Señora Torena be doing here?" Isabella looked at the darkened eyes that had frightened her so deeply days before, and she shuddered. "It cannot be anything good," Isabella admitted.

"No, it cannot. There must be a hundred soldiers with them."

"Perhaps I will not have to marry Señor Fremont after all," Isabella said brightly.

"What would the general's wife being here have to do with you marrying Señor Fremont? Isabella, I thought you had submitted wholly to this marriage."

Isabella opened her mouth to tell her sister that Señora Torena was once in love with Antonio Fremont, but she slapped it shut when she realized Juan Carlos had told her that information in confidence. It was not meant as idle gossip. "I am committed. I will do whatever Papa asks of me. He promised me he would help Juan Carlos, and it seems he has. I can ask nothing more."

It wasn't long before their mama came in to get them. "Girls, come now! Your father wants you on the patio."

"But, Mama, Señor Fremont will see me before the wedding," Isabella reluctantly reminded her. But her true fear was that Juan Carlos would watch her marry another. How could she look into the eyes of the man she loved and say "I do" to another?

"Your papa says to come," Señora Arguello replied firmly. "Now is not the time to argue tradition."

They walked swiftly to the outdoor patio, throwing on their shawls to protect them from the crisp night air. Isabella caught Juan Carlos's eye, and he smiled warmly at her, giving her more confidence. He didn't look frightened but curious as to why they were assembled. She returned a shy smile, and he winked at her. She felt her heart skip a beat and looked away from the warm, brown eyes she'd thought she'd never see again. *Thank You, God. Now I know he is safe.*

Señora Torena's eyes thinned at the sight of Isabella in her wedding gown, and Isabella felt all the fear from Monterey invade her body. She trembled under the icy glances the señora gave her, and she felt herself shiver. Pulling her shawl tightly around her shoulders, she focused on her papa, who cleared his throat.

"Senors and Senoras, I know that you have come here today expecting a wedding, but there will not be one," Señor Arguello announced to astonished eyes and collective gasps. "We will celebrate the Navidad in three days as usual, and I hope that you will all stay with us for the celebration. Father Pico has agreed to stay on with us."

Señor Fremont looked the most surprised of all. "What is the meaning of this? I have paid you a fair dowry, and now you deny me my bride!" He grabbed Isabella harshly, and she felt his fingers dig into her arm.

Señora Torena shouted angrily, "She does not love you, you fool! Let go of her. She is young enough to be your granddaughter! I have come to save you the humiliation of another child bride! You have destroyed my reputation, so there is nothing to stop me from telling you what an old fool you are. Everyone's thinking it, but no one is brave enough to tell you. I have nothing left to lose, Antonio. Nothing!" The vengeance in Señora Torena's voice was nothing like Isabella had ever heard. There must have been a great deal of pain for her to ride out to the rancho just to make such a scene.

"You will let go of my daughter now!" Señor Arguello stepped forward, but the soldiers came instead, rescuing Isabella from Señor Fremont's tight grip. Her papa continued to speak. "Amigos, I have a very sad announcement to make today. One that pains me greatly. It seems one of our own, a Califorñio, has become a traitor."

Another gasp erupted from the gathering, and Isabella felt herself swoon. She would not marry Señor Fremont today. Did anything else matter?

"Dare you insult a Califorñio in front of outsiders?" a ranchero yelled, upset over the Mexican army's presence.

"Mexico has domain over this land, whether we like it or not. Mexico granted us our land, and Mexico enforces its boundaries. It is the law whether we like it or not," Señor Arguello reminded them. "Without Mexico's militia, we are powerless to defend our land, do you deny that?"

"Who do you bring charges against?" Juan Carlos asked, shifting the conversation.

"Señor Antonio Fremont!" Señor Arguello pointed at the man he had supposedly given Isabella to, and a scowl of hatred overtook the older ranchero's eyes. Señor Arguello continued his charges. "He has stolen land from us. Without a thought or care should Spain come to retrieve its land from all of us, defeating Mexico's armies."

"Lies!" Señor Fremont pointed an accusing finger at his attacker.

Señor Arguello held up a portfolio of papers. "I hold here the original *disuenos*, the maps drawn by the Mexican government. I think you'll see how our land grants compare with what we hold today." He threw the maps on a table, and the assembly studied the boundaries carefully. Though none of them could read, they knew their land well enough to know the maps gave them substantially more land than they actually held in their possession.

"What is the meaning of this?" a ranchero inquired.

"Señor Fremont and General Torena. They have redrawn the maps. Years ago, when General Torena took possession of the territory as a brigadier general, he wanted a wife of Californio birth to insure his future in the post. Señor Fremont traded his intended, Señora Torena, for the original maps. Señor Fremont got the land intended for Señor Juan Carlos Vega's father, as well as some of our own property. In trade, General Torena received thousands of California banknotes a year and a Californio bride, Señora Torena. These men stole the grant. They have used their power to confiscate the land. Our land. Juan Carlos, please."

Señor Arguello held his hand out, beckoning the preacher to look at the map. "Your papa's land is here, swallowed up by Señor Fremont and his holdings. I have the deed in my pocket." He patted his heart. "It will be yours once again."

Señor Fremont started to run, but he was stopped easily by the mass of soldiers, who tied up his hands and threw him to the ground.

Señora Torena's evil, haughty grin filled her face. "You should have never underestimated me, Antonio. I might have lived my entire life silent, but when you chose to mock me by marrying this child. . .I found the maps!"

"Where is General Torena?" Señor Fremont asked. "He can verify my story."

"He's gone, Antonio," Señora Torena answered. "He ran to Mexico, and he won't be back to pay the price. You'll pay it alone. I warned him because he treated me well." She let out a long, loud laugh.

Juan Carlos traced his father's land with his finger, confusion reigning on his face.

"Juan Carlos!" Isabella could not help herself. She ran to his side to comfort him. "Juan Carlos, you are free!" She broke into a sob. In the flash of a moment, her marriage to Antonio Fremont was off and Juan Carlos was an officially recognized Californio by the Mexican government.

He rubbed his temples roughly, then looked to the Mexican soldiers. "What does this mean?" he asked the leader.

The soldier took the papers from Señor Arguello and studied them thoroughly before answering. "Señorita is right. You are free." He handed the papers to Juan Carlos, clicked his heels, and led away his men and their prisoner, Señor Antonio Fremont. "We will camp on the rancho until first light."

"*Gracias,* Lieutenant," Señor Arguello answered.

The fiesta band took a cue and began strumming their guitars and playing their horns. All other sounds and the gossip were drowned out by the cheery tunes, though no one felt like dancing or celebrating. Each ranchero was anxious to get a closer look at the map to see where he had been cheated. Juan Carlos seemed numb, and Isabella thought perhaps he was best left alone for a while. She moved away from him slowly, realizing no one thought her action the least bit curious since they were so involved in their own problems. Once she knew she wouldn't be missed, she exited the patio, running for her favorite quiet place.

Juan Carlos watched Isabella flee from the gathering, and he cringed at his callous self-concern when she'd just been humiliated in front of the rancheros. He was just so overwhelmed. He assessed his father's land carefully. It was all there, the fertile coastland property his Spaniard father had been assessed to keep a Spanish presence in the California territory. He'd just been given his life back, but he had no idea what to do with it.

Now that Isabella, his true love, was free, could he marry her? Would her papa allow such a marriage? His property made him an official Californio by Mexico's account, but the Californios were a tightly woven bunch. Would they ever accept him as their own? Certainly there were many men willing to pay for Isabella's hand in marriage. Payment with cattle he didn't own. He needed to pray, but first he needed to find Isabella and comfort her torn heart. She had been on the verge of a huge cliff, ready to jump into a marriage she clearly didn't want, and suddenly her impending marriage ceremony—the reason everyone had gathered—was dropped like a hot branding iron, without a thought to her feelings.

He found her on the back patio in tears. "Isabella?"

She looked up, then away. A lone torch caused the tears on her cheeks to glisten.

"I thought this was what you wanted? To be free from Señor Fremont."

"It is, but I am so overwhelmed. Papa told me nothing of his suspicions until all our family and neighbors were standing there. Just yesterday Papa was telling me Señor Fremont would take care of me, and today, I have no idea what will become of me."

A young ranchero came and announced his presence with a cough. "Ahem. Preacher Vega, would you mind if I spoke with Isabella alone?"

Juan Carlos felt his jaw clench at the sight of a young suitor already. "Yes, I would mind, Señor. The señorita is in need of prayer and counseling, young man. Please, your conversation can wait."

The young ranchero gave him a vicious look before sulking away.

"You see, there are many men who will willingly take Señor Fremont's place." *I am willing to take Señor Fremont's place*, he thought.

Her tears flowed freely. "How can you say such a thing to me? Do you think I kiss men freely? You still think of me as a child when I love you as a woman!" She ran into the adobe and left him alone to contemplate his poorly chosen words. He had tried to ease her pain and instead increased it. How foolish he'd been. Of course he loved her. Why hadn't he just said that?

Isabella sat in her darkened room alone, weeping for her broken pride. She had finally relented to marrying the old, squalid ranchero when her father released her at the most embarrassing opportunity, her wedding celebration. Everyone on the neighboring ranchos now knew she was discarded material. Of course men wanted to marry her anyway, but she had nothing to do with that. It was that cursed beauty they said she possessed, something she had nothing to do with. *It is a curse,* she thought. *Juan Carlos will never own the cattle to marry me, and so I will be offered to the highest bidder once again. Just like the cattle auction at the annual rodeo.*

Although her pride was wounded by being jilted on her wedding day, it was really Juan Carlos's words that hurt the most. He'd been given enough land to acquire cattle, and she had thought he would at least try to ask for her hand. Even if her papa wouldn't give her to him, the young preacher could have at least tried. His apathy told her his true feelings. Any man who truly loved her would have taken a chance to make her his bride. As she sat sobbing, a knock sounded at the door. She took her sleeve and wiped her eyes.

"Yes?" she tried to say as calmly as possible.

"Isabella, it's Victoria." Her sister opened the door, and the light from the candle she held lit her face. "Juan Carlos is on the patio. He wants to speak with you."

"No," she sniffled.

"Isabella, he's leaving tonight. It may be the last time you see him. After all he's done for you, you owe him a decent good-bye," Victoria reprimanded. "Get your shawl on and get out on the patio, or I shall let him into your room." The expression on Victoria's well-lit face told Isabella her sister was not bluffing. "You keep saying everyone treats you like a child. Well quit acting like one!"

Isabella rose and grabbed her shawl quickly. Just that morning, she had feared for his very life, prayed for his safety, and tonight she was angry because he didn't return her love. What a child she had been! Her sister was right. She dashed to the patio and found Juan Carlos under the bright torchlight.

He looked up, his deep brown eyes showing his sympathy. "I'm sorry, Isabella." He came to her and took her hand. His touch sent a familiar shock through her frame.

"No, it is I who should be sorry. This morning I prayed to God for your safety, and I am so grateful that He has answered my prayer. To ask for more is greedy. God has granted me my wish. You are safe, and I am free of Señor Fremont."

He brushed her long hair behind her shoulder with the back of his hand. "This morning I was a criminal and this evening I am a ranchero. It is too much to comprehend." His jaw tensed. "I just wanted to be a preacher. Yet, He has given me this land, and I don't know why. I do know that I love you, Isabella. You must believe that."

"But you will leave anyway, and you will not take me with you, will you?"

He tipped her chin and pleaded to her with his eyes, but she turned away.

"I must go," he said quietly. "I must find the general. He has disappeared, and I can track him. He's not a simple man. He will not be able to live outside the city and its delights for long."

"No!" she said fearfully. "Let someone else go. You are a Califorñio now. This is not your concern!"

"It is." He forced her gaze to his once again. "The general needs to be in prison for his deeds. I can put him there, and I must. To ignore it is to allow evil to reign."

"No, it's the Mexican army's problem, not yours!" she pleaded.

"I will return, Isabella. Count on it." With those words, he strode away from the adobe.

He would return, Isabella realized, but in all likelihood, she would already be married, sold for the greatest number of cattle.

Chapter 11

Christmas morning held no joy for Isabella. The house was awash with eucalyptus wreaths and pyracantha berries in celebration, but the day seemed desolate to her. The priest would come from the mission to say Christmas Mass that very evening, and her papa would most likely announce her engagement. But to whom? That remained the question.

Victoria brought in Isabella's gown for the evening's religious ceremony. Her wedding gown had been cleaned and pressed by the Indian servants, leaving no hint to its history. Looking upon the glorious Spanish lace creation, Isabella could only think of Juan Carlos. Where was he? It had been three days, and no word of the general's whereabouts had been sent to the rancheros staying at Rancho de Arguello.

"Isabella, look at your gown. The Indians have sewn a red sash on it. Isn't it the most beautiful thing you've ever laid eyes on?" Victoria asked cheerfully.

"Yes, it's wonderful," Isabella agreed. She stood and picked up the dress. "I have been in prayer for three days for Juan Carlos, but I must trust in the Lord. That is one reason He sent His Son—so that we could be free of this bondage of worry," Isabella proclaimed. "I have trusted in myself alone, and Papa chastised me for it rightly."

"Isabella, you are back!" her sister said in delight, hugging her tightly.

"Let us go string pyracantha berries in the grand room. Mama will love it! The room will sparkle with the bright color." Isabella grabbed her sister's hand, and they dashed out to the patio to collect the berries.

Once outside, Isabella giggled in between renditions of their favorite Spanish hymns. For the first time in months, she felt wrapped in the arms of her Lord, trusting in Him fully. Her papa's stern voice brought her from her reverie.

"Isabella!" he said sharply.

"Yes, Papa?" She stood up straight. This was it. Her papa had probably promised her to another ranchero and had come to give her the name of the man who would become her husband.

"Come here, my child. Victoria, go see if your mother needs anything. Your husband will be off the range soon enough."

"Yes, Papa." She curtsied and ran for the adobe.

"Isabella, you said when you returned from your. . . trip to Monterey that you trusted me. Is that true?" he asked.

"Yes, Papa. You saved Juan Carlos from the gallows, even when you

thought you couldn't. And you saved me from marriage to Señor Fremont."
She said the name with distaste.

"Isabella, you must find a husband, you know this?"

"Yes, Papa, I know this," she agreed.

"And you will trust my judgment from here on out, correct? No running away, no childish tantrums." He crossed his arms.

"Papa, I—"

"Isabella, when I make a decision for you, I make it because I know things you cannot know. Do you understand that?" he asked sternly.

"Of course, but—"

He pointed at her. "When you ran away, it was only by the grace of God you were kept safe. Juan Carlos was a thief and a smuggler, but he had the good sense to bring you home untouched."

"Juan Carlos is a man of God, Papa!" she answered excitedly. "And he is a ranchero now, a Califorñio by all accounts," she reminded him.

"He was born in Spain. The other rancheros will always see him as a Spaniard."

She knew to argue was pointless. Her father's mind regarding Juan Carlos was clearly made up. "Why did you rescue him if you think him no better than a common thief?"

"He is the one who told me of the true *disuenos,* the maps from Mexico. He obviously didn't know of his own holdings, or he would not have been in prison. When I remembered Señora Torena, I knew she'd be eager to take her revenge upon Antonio Fremont."

"Papa, don't you see? Juan Carlos gave you back your land. He is no longer a smuggler."

Her father's tone was without emotion. "Juan Carlos is a good man, but he has no holdings, Señorita. Now, before we discuss your wedding plans, I must have your word that you will trust me from the beginning this time. No more waiting until the last minute to listen to my plans for you."

"Yes, Papa, I will marry whom you choose without question," she promised.

⨏⨪⨏

That evening the celebrants gathered for the annual Christmas service and the priest read from the scriptures about Christ's birth and the road it offered back to heaven. The words offered Isabella hope and gave her a confidence that she hadn't possessed before her trial of obedience. She bowed low and took communion with heartfelt repentance and overflowing thankfulness.

Afterward, her papa made an announcement. "Friends and neighbors, what a great deal we have to be thankful for this Christmas evening. My daughter has been delivered from a disastrous marriage, and she has obediently offered to marry the man I have chosen for her."

Isabella's heart beat rapidly at her father's proclamation. He was going to announce her fiancé's name to the entire group before she was aware of the name herself. She steeled herself for the name, trying to slow her rapid breathing and prepare for whatever name he announced. She turned all the possibilities over in her head, hoping for the lesser of several evils.

"And tonight, in honor of my daughter's faithful compliance to the future I have selected for her, I ask you all to celebrate in the wedding of my youngest child this very evening."

Isabella dropped to the floor in a heap, and when she awoke, her mama was fanning her with an imported, fluted fan. "Isabella, get up," she whispered through clenched teeth.

Isabella rose flushed and swallowed the huge lump in her throat. The priest waited at the makeshift altar, and her papa held out his arm to walk her down the short aisle. Her sister came to her side and threw a lace veil over her face, and before she knew it, Isabella was being escorted down the aisle to the strains of the Spanish bridal march. Her weakened legs struggled to make the ten short steps. She had passed out cold before her papa had announced her betrothed and so had no idea who she was marrying.

From the side door of the adobe, she saw Juan Carlos enter, and she blinked several times to make sure she wasn't seeing things. She looked to her father questioningly, and a twinkle touched his eyes. "You see, my dear," he whispered. "You should trust your papa."

Juan Carlos reached for her willingly and led her before the priest, securely wrapping his muscular arm around her waist. His touch sent her soaring with excitement, still unable to fathom if it were real or if she were in a sweet dream. Isabella looked back at her father for confirmation, and he smiled and winked, taking her mother into his own arms.

Isabella faced the man she loved, the man who had made her believe she was more than a whimsical child who delighted in the simple pleasures on the rancho. He had opened her eyes to new sights and adventures, and she relished the idea of a lifetime with such a man. She didn't know where they would live, how they would make a living, or if they would even settle into one place, but neither did she care. She would willingly travel the world to be at the side of a man like Juan Carlos Vega.

The priest began the ceremony, and Juan Carlos smiled down at her, his straight jaw clean-shaven and brushed with the scent of eucalyptus oil. She inhaled deeply to make sure she was awake and felt invigorated by the masculine, woodsy scent.

"Do you, Juan Carlos Vega, nobleman of Spain and recognized Californio, take this woman, Isabella Arguello, to be your lawfully wedded wife? To love, honor, and cherish as long as you both shall live?"

"I do," he answered through a smile, his brown eyes mere slivers in their joy.

"Do you, Isabella Arguello, daughter of Californio Jose Arguello, take this man, Juan Carlos Vega, to be your lawfully wedded husband? To have and to hold, to honor and obey, as long as you both shall live?"

Isabella couldn't prevent a small giggle from escaping. "I do!" she said happily.

"Then, by the power vested in me by the holy church, I now pronounce you man and wife." The priest finished by announcing to the people witnessing the ceremony, "May I present to you, Señor and Señora Juan Carlos Vega."

The solemn congregation let out a holler, and the mariachi band broke into a bright fandango. The festivities had begun, and the crowds gathered around them to wish them the best.

Isabella was overwhelmed by the well-wishers, and she searched the room desperately for her papa. Seeing him across the room, she looked to her new husband. "Juan Carlos, I must speak with my papa," she whispered. He nodded knowingly, and she dashed through the crowds, smiling at all the congratulatory remarks.

At last she reached her father's side. "Papa, I don't understand. How is it that Juan Carlos should be my husband?"

"He owned the most cattle," her papa said simply.

"But he owns no cattle!" she answered in further confusion.

"This morning he owned no cattle, this evening he is the proud holder of five thousand head of cattle. He will make a fine son-in-law." Her papa grinned. "He is a true Califorñio as a land-grant holder, which insures the future of the territory. And he was baptized Catholic according to church records. He is everything I planned for you."

"Papa, where did Juan Carlos get five thousand cattle?"

"I gave them to him," he said simply.

"Papa, why? You say you could get another thousand cattle for my marriage, but you chose to give up five thousand more for me. I don't understand." She shook her head.

"Someday when you have children of your own, you will. I love you, Isabella. Be a good wife."

"I will," she promised.

He kissed her on the cheek. "Go find your husband. And do not question his authority as you questioned mine."

"Of course not, Papa."

"Go, Isabella, go and live your Navidad de sueños, your Christmas of dreams. I would do anything to give you the gift of your heart, and God has made it possible."

Chapter 12

The fiesta lasted late into the night until at last Isabella had her husband alone on the patio. "Oh, Juan Carlos, I cannot believe you are truly my husband." She looked at the fire's bright reflection in her exquisitely carved gold band. "This ring is a masterpiece. I have never seen real gold before. Where did you get it?"

"In Monterey, after I had the general arrested," he announced proudly. "One day when Pastor Sola and I were on the mission field, we stopped to make soup from wild onions in the fields. When I pulled an onion from the earth, that gold nugget on your finger was attached to the roots. I had it made into a ring as soon as your papa said yes to my proposal a few days ago."

"My papa said yes a few days ago?" She looked at him incredulously.

"I knew months ago," he whispered, kissing her softly behind her ear. "When I saw you, I knew some how, some way, God would make you mine. I felt it the first moment our eyes locked. Your papa was determined to get those maps and make our wish come true. And he knew just how to do it. It is true what they say of a woman scorned." He brushed her lips gently with a kiss. "Let us go."

"Go? Where would we go? It's the middle of the night," she asked, not caring if he took her to Spain itself.

"I have prepared a honeymoon suite worthy of my bride." He bowed before her.

His talk of travel sparked her curiosity. "Will you continue to preach?" she asked, suddenly realizing that she had no idea what the future held.

"Of course I will," he said, kissing her cheek.

"Will you be a ranchero?"

"I suppose if I own five thousand cattle, I will be," he said, tracing her lips with his finger.

"Juan Carlos, you are not answering me."

"Yes, I am. You just want to know more than is necessary. Do you believe I will take care of you?"

"Always."

"Do you believe I will make sure you are fed, clothed, and given shelter each and every night?"

"Absolutely."

"Then what more do you need to know?"

"Nothing," she admitted.

"Good, let us go." He helped her upon his horse, and he wrapped his Spanish cape around them both, surrounding her with his warmth.

"Where are we going?"

"Tsk, tsk. Will you never learn?" He held back his smile, but she could hear it in his voice.

Once again, the horse was in full gallop with only the moon and stars to light their path. She closed her eyes and allowed the wind to whip against her face, its cold sting fruitless against her rejoicing, warm heart. She snuggled closer to Juan Carlos, not caring where he led her or even if their ride would end. How could their destination possibly have any effect on her mood? She had been granted her fondest wish on Christ's birthday.

The horse seemed to know its route and slowed to a quiet, gentle pace under a blanket of starlight. Isabella kept silently thanking God, praising Him for the gift and miracle of Juan Carlos Vega, her husband.

It seemed mere seconds before they arrived at the smuggler's cabin where they had spent the night after escaping Monterey—he on the outside of the cabin, and she on the inside. Juan Carlos once again helped her from the horse.

"My lady." He gallantly held out his arm and invited her to open the door. Once she did, she gasped in surprise. "Oh, Juan Carlos!" she exclaimed, bringing her hand to her mouth. In place of the cold, sparse, dirty redwood cabin she'd visited earlier was an immaculate cozy honeymoon cottage. An elegant, carved bed from Spain dominated the little room, and candles were set everywhere. A roaring fire was lit in the fireplace. Eucalyptus petals were strewn on the bed and floor, giving an inviting, earthy scent.

"How did you do all this? Who started the fire? What—?"

He put a finger to her lips. "Shh. I can't tell you all my secrets." He took her by the hand. "Now I have one more gift for you to wish you a *Feliz Navidad*."

She shook her head violently. "No, Juan Carlos. I think my heart may burst if I receive something else. God has been so good. My papa has given me in marriage to the only man I will ever love and the cattle to start our own rancho, and best of all, I am Señora Juan Carlos Vega." She threw her hand to her heart and giggled.

He laughed at her and placed a kiss on her forehead. "These pearls were my mama's. I became a thief before parting with these, and while I'm not proud of my sins, I am glad their beauty will hang on the long, beautiful neck of my beloved Isabella."

She fingered the string of pearls gingerly. "Oh Juan, I have never seen anything so beautiful. They shimmer!"

"Like your eyes, my darling. You deserve nothing less, but before you think you will live the same life of luxury you are accustomed to, you must know of my plans for the Rancho de Carmel and the cattle your papa has entrusted us with."

"We will not live there?" she asked in shock.

"God has called me to preach. We shall leave the management of the rancho to Pastor Sola, and while we are young enough, we will travel the California Territory and tell of God's miracles."

"Together?" she asked. She had never heard of a woman on the preaching circuit.

"I would have it no other way. The money from the cattle will allow us to travel freely, and Pastor Sola can retire comfortably at the rancho. I will teach you to read, and we can travel until we have children," he said softly.

Isabella felt a blush rise in her cheeks. She nodded in agreement. "It's perfect." As Juan Carlos stopped her words with a kiss, Isabella felt a warmth she had never known. Although she had lived on the rancho her entire life, it was on this night in an abandoned smuggler's cabin that she knew she was truly home. And though her future might be uncertain, she knew she would always be in God's hands, where she belonged.

'Til Death Do Us Part

by Lauralee Bliss

Chapter 1

*T*o have and to hold, from this day forward, until death do us part. Leah Woods clearly recalled the words spoken at her sister Mary's wedding when she gazed into the eyes of her beloved. Now, as she stood in the parlor among their family and friends, staring at the one she loved, she knew she, too, would soon share those immortal words of a lifelong commitment. At age twenty-three, Leah was old compared to her friends and relatives who had already wed. Her sister had married at age eighteen, her mother at seventeen. But Leah made the decision to wait on the Lord to give her the man with whom she would spend her life until death separated them.

Now he stood before her—handsome with a head of ebony-colored hair and deep brown eyes—full of wisdom and faith, a man after God's own heart. Seth Madison. Her beloved. And nothing would tear them apart. Not the whispers that circulated on the streets of a pending battle, dark and foreboding whispers that seemed to grow with each passing day. No, she would have her dream come true, her marriage covenant with Seth when the New Year dawned, despite this conflict between the States.

And today we celebrate our engagement. Thank You, Lord! Please don't let anything take this happiness from my heart. Leah shook her head as if she suddenly waged war against some unspoken doubt. She refused to believe anything but thoughts of peace and love. No dwelling on rumors of war or of armies ready to bear down on their town of Fredericksburg nestled beside the Rappahannock River. No thoughts of bullets flying or shells exploding, bringing with them shattered lives. Nothing but life. Life forever. *Oh, please, dear Lord, let it happen!*

"Leah?" Concern filled Seth's voice. His dark eyebrows narrowed over his eyes the color of molasses. His finger gently swept her cheek. He drew back to examine the tip that glistened in the light of the oil lamp. "What's the matter?"

What was this he swept from her cheek? A tear of happiness? Or something else? Leah touched her face. She didn't even know the tear had escaped during her thoughts. She tried to smile but it felt forced. *Oh, please, dear Lord! Don't let my faith falter. Not now. We will see ourselves married, even in the midst of this war.* Her spirit hesitated. *Won't we?*

"You're worried about the war?"

His question mirrored her fear. She shifted her gaze to meet his and saw his concern.

"God will protect us," he said softly. "Don't fear the future."

"I'm not afraid." She straightened her shoulders, deftly wiping the stray tears from her face. "I—I'm happy. Happy that our heart's desire, our wedding, will happen whether the war comes here or not."

"I'm afraid the war is coming here, sooner than we think." Leah's father held a newspaper in hand, the very paper that he read day and night as if it were a holy writ. He shook it before them. "In fact, I've seen both the Yankees and men from our army roaming about the countryside."

"But why would the Yankees come here?" asked Mary, Leah's sister, who came forward. She waved her fan furiously, as if the words were annoying flies. "We're not Richmond, after all. Everyone says they want Richmond."

Leah's father frowned. "Yes, but our town is still a prize for the enemy. Think of our location—by the river and on a main road leading to Richmond. They believe if they take our town, it will put them that much closer to our capital."

"The Yankees will never succeed," said another guest, a friend of the family.

Soon a chorus of men's voices entered the conversation, various cousins and the like, all of whom had come to celebrate the engagement but now were caught up in the latest news.

"One Southern gentleman is still worth ten Yankee hirelings."

"We'll show them."

"Let them come! We'll teach them whose land this is."

"We'll whip 'em for sure."

Leah turned aside, wondering how this dreadful talk of war could have disrupted the joy of announcing their engagement to family and friends. A strange fervor suddenly gripped them all. And to her dismay, Seth seemed drawn into the conversation as he added his opinion. Everything had turned to this tale of death and destruction. Couldn't Seth relish the fact of their pending union? That in a few weeks she and Seth would celebrate their wedding with a beautiful ceremony, a good meal, and a fine waltz? That they would be Mr. and Mrs. Madison? But the war tugged at Seth as it did all the men of the land. There seemed to be no way to avoid it.

All at once, Seth came to his feet. His quick movement jarred Leah from the conversation. "Leah, I have to go now. I didn't realize how late it was. I'm sorry."

"I don't understand. Where are you going?"

"Leah, it's that time of day, remember? I have my duties to tend to." She saw him swipe his hat and coat from the rack.

Leah blew out a sigh, which drew a look of surprise from Seth. She tried to compose herself. "Oh yes, of course. I thought maybe you were. . ." She hesitated.

"I was going to join the war everyone is talking about?" He smiled, took her hand, and led her to a small room off the parlor. "And don't fret. I have no plans to join the conflict. My father needs help managing the store. And especially now that I'm engaged to the most beautiful woman a man could ever hope for. But before I go, will you give me a kiss farewell?" He smiled in such a way that she couldn't help but return it. He bent over her for a kiss. She enjoyed the strength of his arms around her. His masculine aroma awakened her senses.

"How long will you be gone this time?"

"I have only a few duties. It shouldn't take long, I promise." He gently tilted her chin until their eyes met. "Don't worry. I'll return by dusk tomorrow, and we'll have time to take our evening walk and look at the stars."

"I would like that very much," she said with a slight laugh. His kiss once more brought warmth to her being.

He released her then and retreated. "Any more kisses like that and I will never be able to see to my duties."

"Good. I—I would rather you stay here. All this talk of the Yankees coming. You haven't eaten either. There are the fine pastries and even a roast duck. And our guests are still here. Can't you see to these duties another day?"

He chuckled. "I'm not paid to eat but to work. How else will I be able to afford a fine house and other things for you—like that hat with the feather you saw in my father's shop window the other day?"

Leah would give up the hat and more if he would remain by her side. She leaned against the doorway leading to the parlor, looking on as he made his way to the door. He turned once more and waved. She did the same, watching the door shut behind him. How she wished she could dismiss the foreboding welling within. She glanced at the grandfather clock in the hallway, ticking away to the next hour. The hands would move painfully slow, all the way around the circle of Roman numerals, until the hour of twilight came once more and he would return. Then she would hurry to her cloak, grab hold of his strong arm, and allow him to lead her beside the homes of Fredericksburg to the meadow beyond. And the conversation would be about their wedding. Not news of any war. Only love.

"Hurry home to me," she whispered.

⋙⋘

Seth tugged down his hat as he walked along the street toward the town livery, trying not to dwell on the look he'd seen in Leah's eyes. How she wanted him to stay, especially on this day when they announced their intention to marry at the dawn of a new year. But he couldn't relinquish his responsibilities, even if the lure of Leah proved almost irresistible. He had a job to do.

The family he worked for, the Greens, was particular about who they hired and who knew their business. Seth's father would rather he learned the duties of a storekeeper besides the bookkeeping skills, but he was glad for this work on behalf of the Greens. They paid him well for the little effort required.

It made him feel even richer when he soon realized he'd be able to purchase the fine home he had seen on the distant horizon, and one Mr. Green was helping him acquire. It was a handsome brick structure surrounded by vast acreage, a home Leah was sure to love.

A chill swept over him, brought about by a sudden burst of wind. He buttoned up his coat the rest of the way before reaching the stable. Mounting his brown bay, Armistead, he made haste for the main road leading westward out of town. Though the air was cold, he felt an unusual chill of uncertainty. Was it only his imagination or did the air reek of uneasiness?

Many wagons clogged the road, driven by worried travelers. He rode past one with a husband and wife astride the wagon seat, their children peering out from behind the white canvas. Instantly he recognized them. Seth reined in his mount to walk beside the wagon. "Where are you headed, Mr. Whitaker?"

"Didn't you hear the news, Seth? The Yankees are coming! You'd best leave now with your family while there's still time."

"It's only rumors they may be coming. They haven't yet crossed the river."

"General Lee already has his forces over there on Marye's Heights. Just as sure as I'm speaking, those Yanks will be here soon, trying to chase them away. And our town lies right in the middle of it all. We aren't waiting for them, either. We're heading for our kin near Baltimore."

Seth glanced behind him to the buildings of Fredericksburg and the drab brown of the surrounding hillsides. "Have any of the Yankees been spotted in town?"

"They're still laying those bridges across the river. They'll be here soon. Gotta go now, and you best be going, too. Good-bye." The man urged the horses forward with a swift flick of the reins.

Seth watched him leave before wheeling about in the saddle to view the town where his beloved awaited his return. Perhaps he should heed the man's warning and fetch Leah out of harm's way. "I will," he promised aloud, "just as soon as I accomplish my duties for the Green family. It won't take long." He inhaled a sharp breath. *It can't take long. God, save us from whatever the future brings.*

The ride was marred by thoughts of Mr. Whitaker's warning concerning the enemy massing on the banks of the Rappahannock, their own troops lining the hills beyond, and the town of Fredericksburg and Leah caught in between. Would their troops protect the town from the Yankee invaders? He had seen only a few soldiers in their butternut coats walking about Fredericksburg, and most of them were young lads. The main force had long since abandoned the town. No wonder people such as the Whitakers were leaving in haste before the enemy invaded.

He nudged the horse to a swift gallop. He felt the need to hurry, even as his heart began to match the frantic pacing of his worry. He must complete these duties as quickly as possible.

Darkness had fallen when he arrived at Greenwood. All seemed quiet, to his relief. At least the war had not seemed to make it to this place, set near the Wilderness Run, a quiet and serene home much like one he hoped to own one day. As was his custom, he alerted the overseer to his presence and found a place with him in one of the small outbuildings for the night.

"Did you hear about the Yankees?" the man asked, pouring Seth some coffee. Coffee these days was rare, and Seth enjoyed the aroma before indulging.

"Everyone says they're coming soon, but I haven't seen any. Many folks are already leaving Fredericksburg."

"Well, I know Mrs. Green will be mighty glad to see you."

Seth knew she would, too. She often commented, "I'm so thankful to have a Christian man helping at my place." Seth was glad for the responsibility and, of course, the extra money he was making.

The following day after breakfast with the overseer, Seth went to work checking on the stock, seeing to his overseer's job, surveying the storehouse of provisions for the coming winter, and even mending some dilapidated fencing he'd noticed the last time he was here. When everything was in order, he ventured to the main house to be greeted by Mrs. Green.

"Mr. Madison, I'm so surprised you came out here. Have you heard any news of the war? How do you fare with the battle coming to Fredericksburg, of all places? I never thought the war would be in our own backyard. It's just terrible."

"Honestly, I'd like to return to Fredericksburg as soon as possible, Mrs. Green," he said, trying to contain the anxiety in his voice at the thought of Leah.

"I do hope my husband returns soon from Culpeper. I can't imagine him gone and the enemy ready to invade."

"I hope he comes back also, Mrs. Green. Have you received any news?"

"No news, I'm afraid." She tried to smile, but he could clearly see her concern. "I know you need to return to Leah quickly. And I've been meaning to ask you. Did you finally ask for Leah's hand? I only say that because I've seen it in your face for these many weeks. It's not like you can hide love." She chuckled.

"Why yes, in fact we announced our engagement just yesterday to friends and family."

"Oh, how wonderful. I cherished the day when my Betty found a good and honorable Christian man with whom to settle down. And now James is bravely serving his country in the army. I'm certain Leah's family is happy to have you become a part of the family. You're such a hard worker."

"I hope so. Have you heard from your daughter recently? I know you were worried about her and the grandchildren."

"We just received a letter, thank the Lord. She wants so much to visit, but

I told her to stay in Lexington where it's safe." She shook her head. "And she keeps asking about her husband James's home—the one they own on the hillside above Fredericksburg. I suppose with him away serving in the army, Betty feels it's her duty to know what's happened to it."

"I know of the place you speak," Seth said. Everyone in Fredericksburg knew of the Lacy house, a fine mansion and grounds on Stafford Heights, overlooking the Rappahannock River.

"She left the gardener there, Uncle Jack, to look after the place. But there has been no word from him in the longest time. And we know the Yankees have been on the grounds for months, using it as their headquarters and all." Mrs. Green shook her head. "They've probably taken everything. She fears the worst according to her last letter, wondering if there's anything of value left. I must say I am curious, too." She then straightened. "Oh, Mr. Madison, I know it's probably too much to ask. . ."

"I'd be honored to check on the status of the home for you and inquire of the gardener's health, if you wish."

"It is dangerous." She paused. "Especially with the Yankees coming and going. But. . .if you were to check on it, Mr. Madison, I'd pay you very well. Just to know how the house fares and what the Yankees may have done will ease our minds. But you must take great care."

"It's no trouble." It would be an easy task, he surmised, and one that would help him earn even more money for Leah's home.

"I'm indebted to you. You've been so good to us. Please give Leah my regards when you see her."

"I will." *And I'll do more than that when I see her. I'll kiss her wonderful lips and hold her close in my arms.*

Until he realized this additional task with the Lacy home meant he would not be back in time for their evening walk. He hoped Leah wouldn't be too disappointed. But the delight on her face when he presented her with the deed to their home would outweigh all the disappointments. Along with the look in her eyes and the gleeful lilt to her voice when he gave her the fine hat adorned with a feather for a Christmas gift. It would be worth it all in the end.

Seth felt the wind sweep his face as the horse galloped. He hoped to check on the Lacy mansion today, even with the fading daylight. But a glance at his pocket watch showed little time to spare. He decided he would make camp on the opposite side of the river, as close to the Lacy house as he could. He could make his observations and inquire about the gardener before dawn—a safer time anyway with the enemy in quarters. He would then be back in Fredericksburg in time to greet Leah and even enjoy breakfast with her and her family.

He decided to cross at Banks Ford, a place on the river with plenty of rocks and shallow water. He guided Armistead safely through the chilly waters and headed off into the woods. A cold wind brushed his face, carrying with it the faint odor of gunpowder. Anxiety once more crept up within him. He hurried on.

Suddenly a shot tore the bark off a tree to his right. He dismounted, hurrying Armistead to a hiding place in a thicket. His heart pounded in his chest, his palms wet with sweat as he watched and listened.

He heard a click in his ear.

"Hold it right there, Reb," a man snarled.

His pulse beat in his ears. Beads of sweat rolled down his temples. Slowly he raised his hands as men in blue advanced.

"What are you doing sneaking around this time of evening and on our side of the river?"

"I. . .I was heading to check on the Lacys' property," he said. "The Lacy house in Fredericksburg. Surely you've heard of it."

The sergeant looked him over and sniffed. "Riding in the dead of night to look over property, dressed in those fancy togs? Why, I've heard better tales told by a drunken soldier." He nudged his companion, who cackled. "What do you take us for?"

"He's a rebel spy, for sure," said the other. "Lee's sending spies to see what we're up to. He'd like nothing better than to find out when we're crossing the river so he can give us a taste of lead."

"Isn't that right?" the sergeant said, lifting his pistol higher. "You're a spy sent to scout out the Union position."

"No! My word of honor. I'm only here to check on the Lacy house on Stafford Heights. . ."

"A promise from some Reb means nothing. Now put your hands on your head and move out. And I can tell you, spies don't live to see the light of day."

Seth slowly put his hands on his head, even as he felt them tremble. *God help me*, he thought as they forced him back onto his mount and prodded him forward. They traveled until they arrived at the property of the Lacy home. Once there, they herded him into one of the stalls inside a stable.

"Please, I'm not a spy," he pleaded with the men. "I only work for the Greens. Their daughter Betty and her husband own this home. Let me explain. . ."

"Shut up, Reb. We're at war, in case you've forgotten. And you're the enemy." The heavy metal door rolled to a close before him. The clink of a padlock secured it.

Seth heard the shuffle of hooves and the whinny of horses in the other stalls, as if the animals were as anxious as he over this unfortunate turn of events. He wished then he had never agreed to do this task for Mrs. Green. He riffled his fingers through his hair. "God, what am I going to do?" Thoughts came fast and furious, like bullets unleashed in a fierce volley. *War is coming. The enemy is ready to invade. Leah is caught in Fredericksburg. And I'm accused of spying, which is a death sentence.* Asking for help seemed ludicrous, even if the plea came before the Judge of heaven and earth. Why would God help him? On this eve of battle, thousands of men's lives hung in the balance. Each soul pleaded for mercy and for deliverance.

He collapsed into the hay, shivering. He had never felt such hopelessness. . .or fear.

Chapter 2

He'll be back," Leah insisted, even as she twisted her handkerchief into so many knots, it became like a ball in her hands. She stood before the house, watching her father ready their meager belongings for the trip to Washington to stay with close friends who lived there. *Dear God, where could he be?*

"We can't wait any longer," said her father, tying down a chest in the wagon. "Help your mother finish packing, Leah, so we can leave. Time is growing short. The Yankees are starting to cross the river from the last report."

Leah looked up and down the streets of Fredericksburg. Townspeople raced by with fear written on their faces. Some pulled carts loaded with possessions. Others tried to drive their horses through the melee of people looking to escape the enemy bearing down on them. On all their lips was the word *invasion*.

Again she knotted her handkerchief. What could have become of Seth? Four days had passed, and no one had seen or heard from him. He had not returned that night for their walk—not that his absence was so unusual. Several times before, when Seth failed to appear after his duties, she tried not to worry. She calmed her anxiety by recalling several of those incidents, such as the day his horse became temporarily lame after stepping on a thorn, or when he made an unexpected visit to a sick friend. On those occasions, when Leah arrived at Seth's father's store to inquire of his absence, even Mr. Madison did not know his son's whereabouts. He would shake his head and bemoan Seth's preoccupation while wishing he were around to help run the store.

So what has kept Seth this time? She tugged her shawl tighter around herself to ward off the December chill. *Why must there be these trials, God?* She groaned, thinking of her hopes and dreams—her new engagement, the plans for Christmas, the upcoming wedding. Now she must think of leaving her home because of the war and worry over Seth's well-being.

She headed upstairs to the bedrooms and found her mother looking over her fine jewels in a wooden case. "Take this, Leah, and put it out in the wagon. I will not let the Yankees have any of it." She thrust the box into her hands. "There's no room but for two of your dresses in the trunk. Oh, I can't believe this is happening to us!"

Leah hurried to her room to see if anything of value remained. She looked but cared little about saving her belongings from the hands of the Yankee invaders. All she wanted was Seth. Again her heart wrestled with his absence. *Seth, how could you leave me at a time like this?* "Don't you love me?" she whispered, trying to keep her tears at bay. "Don't you care about us? What we will soon pledge to each other before the minister?" *Till death do us part...*

The words sent a chill coursing through her. Could he have been caught in crossfire and now be lying wounded on some dark road, pleading for help? Or maybe he was. . .dead. She shuddered and tried not to cry. At times she heard the crack of guns from nearby windows as Confederate sharpshooters did their best to raise havoc with the Yankee men building the makeshift bridges across the river. "No, dearest Lord," she said, refusing the fear that welled up within. She hastened out of the house and put the jewel box among the other boxes in the family wagon.

"Are you ready, Leah?" her father asked. "We must leave before it's too late. Go fetch your mother."

"I—I can't leave yet, Papa."

He whirled to stare at her. "What did you say?"

"I can't leave, not without Seth. I'm going to see Seth's family. I have to know what happened to him."

"But we must leave now! The Yankees are entering the town."

Panic assailed her at the thought of leaving Seth behind, not knowing what might have happened to him. "I can leave with Seth's family. I will be safe." She barely heard her father's frantic shouts as she took off down the street.

Leah weaved in and around the crowds that filled the street, some toting crying children, others laden down with possessions. A sudden explosion nearly knocked her off her feet. She screamed and hid in a doorway, watching smoke curl up from a damaged house down the street. Another explosion, like the sound of thunder, crashed nearby. *The Lord is my strength and refuge, my strong tower, and under His wings shall I find safety.* She tried to rein in her mounting fear, thinking instead of her quest. *Love conquers fear. Think of Seth. I must find Seth.*

She arrived at the general store, breathless, and found Seth's father loading the family's belongings into a spare wagon. "They'll steal everything for sure," he shouted to his assistant, "but it's better to be alive with nothing than dead from a Yankee bullet. Still, if I can spare some things, I will. Leave the rest in the Lord's hands."

"Mr. Madison, please!" Leah shouted above the commotion as the sound of another artillery shell burst nearby.

"Leah! What are you doing here? You must flee, child, before it's too late! The Yankees are crossing the river! Can't you hear the cannon?"

"Please, do you know where Seth is? I haven't seen or heard from him in several days."

Mr. Madison issued orders to his assistant, who rolled another barrel out of the store. "I don't know, Leah. No one has heard from him. I only pray he fled to safety."

"But he wouldn't leave me. I know he wouldn't. He'll come for me."

"Leah, please, we must go, and you should, too. Leave Seth in God's hands. We are all in God's hands. You're welcome to come with us. There's room in the wagon. Seth would want you to flee to safety."

Another shell screamed over the city, landing in the distance. The ground shook beneath their feet. "I—I can't leave, Mr. Madison. Not until I know what's happened to Seth."

"My dear, all you can do is pray. It's all any of us can do now."

Leah looked at him. She wanted to go with them as he urged and as she promised her father. But her heart yearned for Seth, to know he was all right. She feigned a need to return to her family's house and then quietly disappeared.

Leah stumbled back into the street where frantic crowds pushed by her. "Seth, where are you?" she murmured in despair. She hoped that somehow he would materialize out of the throng, his arms open wide to comfort her.

Instead she saw the haunted faces of people running to escape the coming onslaught. Terror filled their eyes. Some of the faces were stained black. The air stank with the odor of burning debris. She surveyed every one of them, praying a face might belong to Seth. Even if he were wounded, she would care for him night and day, never leaving his side. She would do anything to have him here with her. "Oh please, God, bring him back to me."

Another shell burst nearby. She shook, her hands breaking into a sweat. Fear ignited her voice in a startled cry. Her search turned to a flight for her life. She raced along the street to her family home, hoping her father might still be there. She flung open the door, calling for her family. Only the sound of commotion on the outside street met her ears. The windows rattled in their frames. The smell of burnt wood and gunpowder filled her nostrils. Running from room to room, she found each one empty.

She did the only thing she could do. She made her way to the cellar, the last place of refuge in the midst of the terror dominating Fredericksburg. "Seth. . . ," she whispered, cowering in a dark corner, "Seth, please come find me. Don't leave me like this with the Yankees coming. Help me."

⚜

Seth paced back and forth in the animal stall. At least the Federals had not harmed him, despite the accusations of him spying for the rebel cause. Likely, with the pending battle, he had been temporarily forgotten. But now he considered his predicament. If only he had not promised Mrs. Green he would come here. He should have realized the danger, but his quest for money had directed his heart. Thoughts of a fine home for Leah and even the beautiful hat with a blue bow to match her eyes outweighed common sense. Now it had come down to this.

He again tested the bars of his makeshift prison for the umpteenth time.

The days spent in this place were wearing him down. He must return to Leah and make certain she was safe, but there seemed to be no way out. The army would have their battle, and then he would be dealt with. By then, what would have happened? What would have become of Leah? Maybe she had already fled the area. Like the Whitakers, she had found safety elsewhere, with her family. He might never hear from or see her again.

Seth closed his eyes, regretting having left her the day of their engagement. He should have let the call of duty go and enjoyed a walk with Leah before this reign of fire and death came haunting them. But duty and the money beckoned to him. Duty first. Always first.

Suddenly he heard footsteps, and the sound of voices entered the barn. The doors to his makeshift cell parted. The two soldiers who had first accosted him by the river advanced, pistols drawn. "C'mon, Reb. The colonel wants to see you."

Seth eyed the men and the weapons trained on him. Stepping outside the barn, he squinted at the sunlight. Then he smelled the hot odor of battle. Before the stately home, cannons unleashed a fiery volley, sending a rain of destruction down on his town and, very possibly, on his Leah. Clouds of smoke rose in the distance. He envisioned the cries of the wounded, the fires ravaging the fine buildings, and Leah caught up in it all. He shuddered even as the men prodded him toward the main house.

The grounds surrounding the fine mansion were abuzz with military officers in blue, all talking at once. Other men waved signal flags and still others rode about the grounds on horses. No one paid him any attention with the fury of battle in their midst. Seth was marched into the house, up the stairs, and to a small room where he was left with his thoughts.

Time passed as a war raged within him as well as around him. Seth could only wonder how much longer he would feel the beat of his heart before death silenced it forever. How could he die and leave behind the one he loved? How could God call him home on the threshold of an engagement and their wedding? Not to mention the glad tidings of Christmas, which he and Leah enjoyed so much. He swallowed hard, remembering the smoke and the fires in Fredericksburg. There would be no Christmas this year. No freshly cut tree decorated with burning candles or the sound of laughter as presents were exchanged. No huge feast with a goose, apple stuffing, roasted chestnuts, and plum pudding. But he would gladly trade all those pleasant scenes just to be with Leah again. To look into her eyes, caress her flushed cheek and strands of silken hair, and feel the warmth of her soft lips.

A group of men burst into the room. From the military insignias on the uniforms, Seth could tell some were of a higher rank. No doubt the colonel the soldiers had mentioned stood among them.

"This is the spy for General Lee, sir," one of the men said. "Found him not far from the crossing a few days ago."

"I'm not a spy," Seth said in earnest. "I was hired by Mrs. Green to check on this place for her daughter. This is their home that you are now occupying."

"I suppose it's a coincidence, then, that you arrive here at the highest point of military activity?" the colonel remarked. "Surely you knew this place has been in Federal possession since last spring. And now we are engaged in battle with the enemy."

"I was just asked by the mother to check on the condition of the property and save some of their valuables if possible. Mrs. Green lives near Wilderness Run and can vouch for my words. If that gardener—Jack is his name—is still here, he can also tell you. Do you know of him?"

"I do not, and we have no time for such nonsense. We're in a battle here. And spies will be judged swiftly and soundly. Sergeant!"

The sergeant and his fellow comrade immediately flanked Seth. He felt the blood drain from his face. His legs became unsteady. "Sir, please, I beg you. I'm not a spy. Sir, I—I'm newly engaged to a fine woman in Fredericksburg. Why would I jeopardize my future to spy?"

"Many do such things while leaving their sweethearts behind. We're all sacrificing our lives for a cause. Others gladly spy if the price is right." He paused. "But I will say that you seem familiar with the terrain, knowing the places to ford the river. Do you know the area?"

"Yes, I know the area very well. I've lived here all my life."

The colonel paced before him. He whirled and stared as if searching the depths of Seth's soul. "Then we may be willing to negotiate."

"I don't understand."

"We are sending our troops across the pontoon bridge into harm's way. But we have need of information concerning the roads and other obstacles the men might face. It would be better to have that information now rather than sacrificing our men to obtain it, especially with rebel sharpshooters picking us off one by one." He pointed to a large map spread out across the desk.

Seth stared, unmoving, first at the man and then at the map. "I—I don't know what you are asking."

"It's quite simple, Mr. . . ?"

"Madison. Seth Madison."

"Mr. Madison. We need information on the terrain we face. Roads. Other favorable river crossings not in enemy hands. And information on the civilian population in Fredericksburg, militia units, et cetera, would be helpful. If you are willing to supply us with accurate information, you will surely live to enjoy your wedding day—that is, in the event that a stray bullet doesn't get you."

The glaring faces that bore down on him were like pistols ready to unleash their fearsome volley. For a moment, then, he saw Leah's tender face, her sweet smile, her hand outstretched to him. He saw his own hand reach for hers, drawing her close as they faced the minister who waited to marry them.

"If I don't wish to. . . ," he began, knowing well the answer.

"Then I'm afraid your sweetheart will bury you instead. And that would be most unfortunate. But be quick with your answer. We haven't time, and my men are awaiting their orders."

Suddenly the scene blurred, replaced by the image of Leah, dressed in black, her face in a handkerchief, prostrate over his grave, weeping. The loud weeping reached his ears, until he realized it was the scream of distant shells hurling through the sky, followed by a rumble like thunder. He looked at the men and saw war in all its cruelty. Not in wounds, death, and destruction. . .but in a way he never imagined in his worst nightmare.

God, help me.

Chapter 3

Leah huddled on the cold cellar ground, listening to the dreadful sounds of battle. She was thankful for the canned peaches and other provisions on the shelves that helped stave off her thirst and ease her hunger pains as time passed. The entire house quaked as shells exploded within the town. When that ended, a new sound began. The sound of invasion. Footsteps pounded on the ceiling above her. She heard furniture being dragged about, accompanied by the shouts of voices. For a moment she wondered if the battle was over and her parents had returned. That is, until the door to the cellar creaked open and light shone on the dark coats—blue uniform coats. She heard the words of men whose tongues betrayed their Northern roots.

"But there may be something good down there," one of the men said. "Let's go check it out."

"You heard the orders. We're supposed to be marching to meet up with the front lines. The battle is still going on, you know. As it is, the colonel is getting upset that we've been stealing. He isn't happy about the piano, either."

"They're Rebs, Charlie. They deserve everything they get."

Leah drew farther back into a recess, praying with all her might that the Yankee invaders wouldn't venture down the stairs. After a few more moments of bickering, the men closed the cellar door. Leah wiped her face with the handkerchief and sighed.

More dreadful sounds could be heard upstairs, plundering and laughing, until a strange quiet fell. She waited another two whole days before gathering her courage to venture out of her hiding place. One by one she climbed the steps, listening intently for any sound. When she heard none, she slowly cracked open the door. The sight made her throat close over with emotion and tears sting her eyes.

Splintered furniture lay scattered about. The piano was missing. Windows were smashed. A portion of wall to the front parlor was gone. She blinked back the tears, recalling the beautiful party her parents hosted only a week ago to announce her engagement to Seth. And then came the memory of his face so close to hers and his arms gripping her before he disappeared. Now everything was gone, torn away by the battle the men had talked about on the day of their engagement. A battle that had taken everything precious from her.

Just then, her gaze fell on the family Bible lying on the floor. Despite everything, she still had God's Word, which never ends. *For the mountains shall depart, and the hills be removed; but my kindness shall not depart from thee, neither*

121

shall the covenant of my peace be removed, saith the LORD *that hath mercy on thee.* She recalled well the scripture from Isaiah, a verse that gave strength to her weak heart. She managed to find a chair still in one piece and sank slowly into it, holding tight to the Bible. It was then she saw the stains on her skirt from her stay in the cellar. She pushed back strands of hair hanging in her face. What a sorry sight she must be. She ought to do something to make herself presentable.

"Oh, listen to me. As if anyone cares what I look like. Look at our home." Then she thought of Seth, missing now for over a week. "Look at us." She gazed at the ceiling and the broken chandelier hanging sadly from above. "I wouldn't care what Seth looked like. I only want to know he's safe. Oh dear Lord, I will surrender everything if You would bring him back to me." She held tightly to the Bible.

Just then a knock came. Despite the holes in the walls and the broken door that allowed anyone to enter, the caller stood on the front step, waiting for an answer. Leah came to her feet. *May it be Seth*, she prayed, peering through the damaged door. Instead she stepped back in horror. It was a man in blue. A Union soldier!

"Ma'am." He removed his cap.

Leah backed away, her hand over her heart. *Dear God, save me!* She looked to the cellar door. Too late to escape.

"Ma'am, I won't hurt you. Are you Miss Woods?"

She didn't know whether to answer him or not. He appeared quite young, perhaps the age of her cousin, who was fifteen. Suddenly she heard her voice say, "Yes, I'm Leah Woods. What do you want?" *Leah, why did you tell him your name? Have you lost your senses?*

He extended his hand through the hole in the door, gripping something. It appeared to be a letter.

Leah took it with trembling fingers. "Who's it from?"

"Your fiancé. Mr. Madison."

Leah could hardly breathe. "Seth!" She had the envelope opened before remembering her manners. She looked up to thank the courier, but he'd already vanished.

She managed to return to the chair. It was indeed a letter in Seth's handwriting.

My Beloved Leah,

I can only write a few words and pray this finds its way into your hands. I pray you are safe, wherever you are. I am alive and well. I cannot say where I am, but God has spared me. I pray every day that we will soon see each other.

I am forever yours,
Seth

She brought the letter to her lips, kissing the lines he had written. *The courier must know where he is!* She dashed to the door and looked out, hoping for a glimpse of the young man while questions plagued her. Why had a Union soldier brought her the note? Why did Seth give a note like this to the enemy? Was he a prisoner of the Federals? Maybe he had been treated poorly, barely able to survive his ordeal, but somehow managed to bribe a Yankee into delivering the note. Or maybe he had done the unthinkable. . .and joined them.

"No." Seth would never join the Yankee army. He loved this town, the people, and their state. But the questions remained. There were the ceaseless duties that Seth talked about. Duties that would bring them money, yes, but he never really explained them. Nor had she ever really asked. Now she wondered. Could they have been duties for the enemy?

"No. Not Seth. He would never do such a thing." She tried to dismiss it, even as she set to work picking up the mess created inside the Woods home. The task proved impossible with the onslaught of questions brought on by this note delivered via a Union soldier. Why didn't Seth say in his note where he was or what had happened to him? What was the real reason he left her the afternoon of their engagement? If only she could rejoice in the fact that he was alive and eager to come back to her. But now she only wanted to find out where he was and what he'd been doing.

Leah gazed once more out into the street. Instead of seeing the shattered homes, dead horses, or even their piano in the middle of the road, she searched for a man in blue. Any man in blue. She walked down the street then, looking around, hoping beyond hope the courier might still be lurking about.

The stench of death and the odor of smoldering fires soon overcame her. She covered her face with a handkerchief and stumbled along. Finally she came upon a few stragglers—men in ragged blue, tired from their ordeal but looking to gather a few of their comrades together before marching on. Leah didn't care about propriety, danger, or anything else. Love and hope were her pillars of strength. "Please, can you help me? I'm seeking the Yankee soldier who gave me this note."

They looked at her with red, sunken eyes. "Ma'am, we're heading back across the river to rejoin our units. Most everyone has left. And we've got to leave quickly."

"But one of your soldiers came to my door just a short time ago and gave me this note. It's from my fiancé, Seth Madison. I must know where he is."

He shrugged. "Ma'am, I don't know any man from our unit who would be giving a Southern woman such as yourself a note. You must be mistaken."

"But I have the note right here!" She waved it before his eyes.

They shook their heads and turned to march toward the pontoon bridge in the distance. Leah followed until she saw the bridge and the last fragment of the Union Army making their way across the Rappahannock River.

Then she heard a sound she never thought she would hear. The shout of victory. Whirling about, she saw the first units from the Army of Northern Virginia approaching. Men in their butternut coats returned with smiles on their faces, a gleeful lilt to their voices, with muskets waving in the air.

"We whooped 'em! We whooped 'em good!"

"Yippee! They're goin' back to Abe Lincoln to tell 'im to leave us be."

Their side had won the battle. But to Leah it was a shallow victory, for she still didn't know the future. She had seen her home destroyed and her dreams cast to the wind. If the sight of Fredericksburg and the absence of Seth meant anything, they had still lost.

She returned to her family's damaged home. Tears stung her eyes. She could do nothing but wait once more on the Lord for a miracle.

❧❦❧

"You've been a great help to us, Mr. Madison," the officer said as aides began rolling maps and burning papers in the fireplace. "Though I wish the outcome had been different." He wiped his face. "It's not easy suffering such a terrible defeat."

"I only wish this conflict would come to an end." Seth watched as the enemy bore litter after litter of the wounded into the Lacy home. Groans pierced the air. He could see now this place of military activity rapidly turning into a place of the dead and dying as the wounded were brought in from the battlefield.

"I do as well. I miss my family. I pray every day it ends. But I cannot turn away from my country. We can't be a divided nation. Somehow, someway, we must come together if we are to survive in this world."

"May it not be by the kind of intimidation I was forced to suffer, but rather by godly means."

The captain wheeled to stare at Seth. His lips turned downward into a scowl. "You forget that this is war, sir. The colonel needed your help. If not, more of my men would have died. Look at them."

Seth did not want to look at the dying. He only thought of what happened and rage filled him. "But you used my life and my bride-to-be's sorrow as the price, Captain."

"It no longer matters. You are free to go."

Seth felt no joy at these words of freedom, not after what happened. He picked up his worn hat and placed it on his head.

"I hope you find your fiancée well," the officer added.

He only nodded and headed out into the cold and blustery December day. The grass still sparkled from the ice that had fallen. His boots slipped as he walked along the path to see Union soldiers scurrying about and more wagons coming, bearing the wounded.

Then he saw him—Private Owen, the soldier he'd entrusted with his letter to Leah. He hurried forward, even as he slipped and slid on the icy road. "Did you see her, Private? Was she there or had she left Fredericksburg?"

The soldier paused. "I saw her."

"You did! Is—is she well? Please, tell me." He held out his hand.

The soldier nodded. "The house where she lives isn't in good shape, but she's well. She has your note."

Thank You, dear God, for keeping her safe. Seth thanked the man for his help.

The soldier held up the pocket watch Seth had given him in exchange for the errand. "Thank you for the watch. It'll make a fine Christmas present for my father."

Seth didn't tell the soldier that it was also his father's watch. He would have given away everything he owned to see the message safely delivered into Leah's hands. Now he was free to return home, but to what? He had heard of the devastation wrought upon the town from the Union invasion. He was not looking forward to witnessing it, especially after what had transpired.

He walked the road and across the bridge that would lead him back to Fredericksburg proper, heading for home—or what was left of it. The soldiers paid no attention but hurried in their companies to join up with the main body of the army. The battle was over, the war left to be fought another day. And now he must fight his own personal struggle. A war of his own making. To somehow justify the reason for living and not dying.

The smoking ruins before him wrenched his heart. Shells of fine homes stood before him. The sickness of shame filled his throat. His feet slowed. How could he return to this town? How would Leah or anyone ever accept him if they knew the truth? Yes, he'd loved her so much that it had driven him in his decision to assist the enemy. But he found no solace in it anymore. Only doubts and a restless spirit. His feet slowed even more. He took his time going back, though he should be running to embrace Leah.

Once he reached town, he saw the stunned townspeople staring at the destruction around them. The odor of death hung in the air. As he neared the Woods house, he saw their expensive piano in the street. It looked as if men had danced on the top, for it had caved in. Half the keys were missing. Leah loved that piano and often played and sang songs.

The emotion clogged his throat. He stopped in his tracks. How could he see her with this heavy burden in his heart? What words could he say? He began to pace about the street, wondering how to handle their meeting.

He didn't even hear the voice calling his name until he glanced up. The voice belonged to a friend of his father's, Mr. Perry.

"Seth, how are you? How is your family?"

"I–I'm not sure, Mr. Perry."

The man stared in confusion. "You just returned?"

"Yes. . .I just came back."

He nodded. "I hope your home is in better shape than ours. We have another hole blasted out in the front, right alongside the door. You'd think they would use the door instead of making a new one. Those no good Yankees made a mess of everything. But we're all alive, and I thank the good Lord for that. We can always rebuild a home."

Seth managed a nod. He finally went to the Woods home, but it was empty. Maybe she had gone looking for him. He decided to check at the family store, thinking she might be there. As he walked, he worried over what he might find. No doubt a store would be the first place the invaders would ravage.

As he expected, the place had been ransacked. The shelving contained but a few items, but at least the building itself was intact. Father would rebuild the business.

Then he saw a note left there on his father's desk, undisturbed.

Dear Son,

I pray God has kept you safe. If you see this, we are with my sister, your aunt Gracie, in the country. We will spend Christmas there as well. When you return, come find us and bring Leah, too, if you see her. We will send word to her family where they are staying in Washington.

Godspeed,
Father

Bring Leah. Dear, sweet Leah. He gazed out the window to the street beyond. How sick with worry she must be. After all, he had sent the note to her, telling her of his desire that they be reunited. How could he abandon her, despite what he'd done?

I won't abandon her. She needs me, and I need her. She wouldn't need to know what I did. I won't tell her or anyone. He tucked the note in his pocket. A surge of strength entered his feeble limbs. Having settled his quandary, the anxiety to see her now welled up. "Thank You, Lord," he whispered. *This will remain a secret between You and me. It's all I can do. Please now, help me find her so we can begin again.*

Chapter 4

Yes, ma'am, I sure did see him. Most definitively it was Seth."

Leah could barely breathe. "Where? When? Oh please, tell me everything, Mr. Perry."

Mr. Perry stood near her home, a grin on his face when he came bearing the news. "Just ran into him here an hour or two ago. Then saw him headin' for his pa's store."

Leah scolded herself for having left the house for even a moment. But she had to get away. She couldn't stand the sight of the ravaged place any longer. "Did he say anything? Like where he's been? Anything at all?" She had to contain herself from wanting to reach out, grab the older man, and visibly shake the words out of him.

"He didn't say much, miss. Looked kinda ragged, but so do we all. The war has taken away plenty, but it hasn't broken our spirit. We'll keep on fighting, and we'll drive the Yankees back up North where they belong. And don't you worry about your house. It will be all right. We'll help each other get through this."

Leah wasn't worried about the house any longer. Instead, she took off down the street, calling Seth's name. He was alive! Her beloved Seth was alive! The Lord had heard her prayer. He had brought deliverance to her through the storm of battle and had even sent Mr. Perry to tell her the good news. She cared little for the reminder of war in the smoking rubble of Fredericksburg. All she could think about was seeing Seth.

She ran all the way, breathless, until she arrived at the Madisons' store. "Seth! Oh, Seth!" Her voice echoed in the empty place. The only sound was a mouse skittering across the floor. "Seth! Oh, please answer." She refused to let despair overcome her. If God could bring Mr. Perry to her, bearing the good news, He would help her path cross with Seth's. She believed it with all her heart. Despite the ravages of war, the testing of her faith, the fear, and the doubts, God was faithful. He had heard her innermost cries and answered them. Now if only she could see Seth's face and feel his strong arms around her.

She turned, ready to go into the street once more. Suddenly he was there, standing in the doorway, framed by the light of the sun, like an angelic vision from on high. "Seth!" She rushed to him, nearly tripping over her feet.

His arms about her were warm. He buried his face in her hair, breathing deep as if savoring the moment. He said nothing, just held her tight. She didn't ask what he had gone through. He was here, uninjured, and safe in her embrace once more. They held each other for a long moment until she finally stepped back. "Oh, Seth, I was so worried. I ran into Mr. Perry. He told me he saw you. Oh, bless God, you're all right." She came and held him again. "We made it, didn't we? We both made it through this awful thing. Oh, I was never so scared in all my life. Alone in the cellar with the war going on and strangers in Father's house. And then—what they did to the home. But I'm so glad we know the Lord. He took care of us and kept us safe. It doesn't matter about our things or a house. What matters is that we have each other."

He only stared as if unable to speak the words. The words flowed freely from her lips, despite his strange silence. *He must be in shock by things too dreadful to say.* No matter. Her love would help bind his wounds. She would not force him to tell her what happened. War was a terrible thing, and he would confess when the time was right.

She took his hand in hers and brought it to her cheek. "Dear Seth, it's all right. You're safe from the enemy."

He withdrew his hand and thrust it into a pocket of his trousers. The move surprised her.

"It's all right. You don't have to tell me anything right now. I understand."

"Do you really understand, Leah?" His words were forceful, probing, as if he really wanted to know.

"Of course. The battle has done so much to everyone. We are all out of sorts right now, not knowing what to do or where to go. I'm sure seeing your father's store like this is hard, too. I know I grieved when I saw our home, but there's nothing to be done now. At least our families are safe. Mine has gone to Washington. And I did see your family off, Seth. I know they escaped the worst."

"Father left a note. They're at my aunt Gracie's where they'll be spending Christmas. They said, too, they're contacting your family by letter and hope to hear from them. We should go there and be with family. It makes no sense to stay here. There's nothing here."

Leah had been to his aunt's before. She had a fine brick home in the country far away, she was sure, from the scars of battle. Thoughts of a place of refuge to celebrate at least a little of the season filled her. Especially celebrating it with the one she loved and would soon marry. "Seth, let's go as soon as we can. I'm so tired of being scared. I want peace and rest. Don't you?"

"You don't know how much," he said, his voice soft.

She took up his hand, hoping her touch imparted reassurance. Thankfully, he did not pull away this time but even gave her hand a slight squeeze. It reassured her that everything would be all right with time. They were shaken, as everyone was, by the horror of war. But with Christmas, family, and the grace of God, things would soon be back to the way they were on the day of their engagement—with the feelings of love and a hope for the future.

She prayed.

✦

Leah and Seth spent time taking stock of the house and writing in a ledger what was left in the store to give an accurate account to Seth's father. Leah found a certain relief in being reunited with Seth again, but strangeness as well that she could not identify. Yet she was so glad to be with him, she abandoned her concern and relished the time spent with him.

Fredericksburg had become a grim reminder of the vestiges of war—smoldering buildings, wrecked supply wagons, and a few people with shovels assigned to the grisly task of burial. Leah tried to avoid staring at the difficult scenes and looked forward to leaving this place as soon as possible.

When they were ready to leave, they found a family heading west out of town and obtained a ride with them. Seth rode with the father on the wagon seat while Leah remained in the back with the two children. They spoke of the fire and the smoke they had seen and the men in blue who had come into their home.

"Papa took out his gun and tried to stop them," said the little girl. "They put him against the wall and took his gun. And then they saw us and said they wouldn't take anything."

Leah was amazed the Yankees had shown a change of heart. "They took things from our house," she said. "I could have used a dear child like you with me to keep the Yankees out of my family's home. Maybe I would still have my piano." She tried not to think about it.

The young girl laughed and scooted closer to Leah. She put an arm around the little girl. Thoughts of motherhood rose up within her. Oh, there was much to look forward to. She would put aside the losses they had all endured and think of what was to come. The wedding in January. Maybe God would bless them with children right away, like a darling girl.

When the wagon came to a stop, Seth appeared, offering his hand to Leah. "We can walk from here. It's not far."

"Good-bye," she told the girl before taking Seth's arm. "Oh, what a sweet thing she is. She told me how her father defended their home when the Yankees came to steal their belongings. But as soon as they saw the children, they put everything back and left. I guess there are some kindhearted men on the other side."

"They will stop at nothing to win," Seth said.

"Who? Our men?"

"No, the Federal Army. They will do whatever they can to win. And it doesn't matter how."

"I guess that's how it is in war. Both sides want to win, but only one can be the victor." She tugged on his arm. "Let's not talk about it right now, Seth. Let's talk about our wedding. Where shall we have it? We can't have it in Fredericksburg. Maybe your aunt Gracie will let us have it at her house. My parents would agree."

"I'm sure Aunt Gracie would be happy to have it there."

"We will ask her."

They lapsed into silence. Leah wanted to talk more about who to invite, the gathering, and where she might find a suitable dress. But Seth seemed lost in his thoughts. How she wished she knew what ailed him. What had he witnessed in the week he'd been gone from her? Had it been a nightmare for him as it was for her?

Leah put away these thoughts as they neared his aunt's home. Cheerful boughs of white pine decorated the windows, along with a wreath hanging on the front door. Candlelight glowed in the windows. What a pleasant sight to see after the sights of a war-torn Fredericksburg bearing the marks of torture.

When the door opened to their knock, Seth's mother trembled and clung to the doorframe. Tears spilled down her cheeks as she took hold of Seth. "My dear, dear son," she moaned. She then turned to Leah and gave her a warm embrace. "I'm so glad you both are safe. Oh, praise God." Mrs. Madison led the way to the drawing room where they took seats. "I'm surprised you didn't go with your family, Leah. We did hear from them and they are safe. They will return after Christmas."

Leah was glad for the news as she gazed about the cheerful room. A small Christmas tree stood on a table, decorated with berries and handmade ornaments. Garlands of fresh pine accented the fireplace mantel. The aroma of gingerbread scented the air. Leah breathed in the spicy scents of the season. Everything looked so warm and inviting, she nearly cried.

Seth's two sisters, Clara and Sylvia, immediately bustled in and asked about Fredericksburg and their home. Seth tried to speak but the words seemed caught in his throat. Instead he spoke in a whisper as he told them how the Yankees had taken pretty much everything in the store. The building was still intact.

The girls moaned their losses.

"We mustn't dwell on this," Mr. Madison interrupted. "We can replace possessions. What matters is that we're safe. God has been good to us." He smiled at Seth, who remained quiet, his fingers intertwined in his lap.

"I only wish we knew what's left," Clara pouted. "If I even have any more dresses."

"I only have two dresses myself," added Sylvia.

"I do have an account of the store's goods that are left. . ." Seth began, removing a paper from his pocket.

"We'll see to possessions later," Seth's father said. "Let's instead draw close to the throne of God's grace and find help in our time of need." He waved to the family who came and knelt to offer prayers of thanksgiving for their safety and for God's protection. He also said a prayer that Leah would soon be reunited with her family.

The families then enjoyed some fresh eggnog and gingerbread cookies. Sipping her eggnog, which tasted much better than the peaches she'd been eating from the cellar, Leah watched Seth. He sat still in his seat, his eyes drifting to various places—a painting on the wall, the fireplace, the Christmas tree. He did not seem to look at his family or even acknowledge them. It frightened her to see the conflict within him. Before the awful battle, he moved with care and confidence among their families and friends. He remained hopeful. Determined. And with a twinkle of joy in his eyes.

But this man before her was not the Seth Madison who had left her the night of their engagement party. This man was somber. Troubled. Covered in a storm cloud.

What was she to do?

❈❈❈

During the next week, as Christmas drew near, Seth realized the recent events in his life were disrupting his relationships. As much as he tried to keep it hidden, he feared the working of his inner soul betrayed him. He would have to do something before his family and his bride-to-be discovered he had aided the enemy. As it was, Leah had been giving him strange looks. His family did not seem to pay him much mind with the pending holiday celebration and all it entailed with making gifts, preparing food, and sharing stories.

But Leah's reaction concerned him the most. She knew him well—his dreams, his innermost thoughts. He fought to keep the secret sealed within but sensed she wanted to know what had transpired. She never questioned anything since his arrival back, but the silence was deafening, as reservations remained thick in the air.

Plagued by these thoughts, he rose from his bed one night and went down to the drawing room. It was a quiet and dark place but for a few glowing embers left in the fireplace—a far cry from the merriment shared earlier that evening when they all gathered before the fire. He took up the poker to stir the embers, added some wood, and watched new flames burst to life. He brought over a chair and looked on as the flames danced before him and cast shadows on the wall.

His hands clenched. If it weren't for the Yankees who had falsely arrested him, everything would be well. They were to blame for it all. The injustice overwhelmed him. He was only assisting the Green family as a favor that terrible day. And he was helping his marriage, too, by offering Leah a fine home as a way to establish themselves in the midst of wartime.

He then realized he had not seen the Greens since the battle. He must visit as soon as possible and tell them what he'd seen at the daughter's home, but not divulge anything else that occurred. He hoped Mrs. Green would settle the accounts with him as well. At least the money gained out of the venture might ease the guilt in his heart. And soothe Leah as well.

Seth turned in the midst of his contemplations and, to his dismay, found Leah hovering in the doorway. The firelight outlined her feminine form clad in a dress she had hastily put on. Her hair lay strewn about her shoulders as she made her way into the drawing room. "Can't sleep?"

He shrugged. "I haven't slept for days."

"I'm sorry. " She stood waiting. How he wanted to tell her everything, but he couldn't bring himself to do it. Finally she said, "It will pass, I'm sure. Who can sleep with these armies all around us and wondering what the future holds?"

"Yes, that's true."

She sighed. "At least we're safe. I'm so glad to receive another note from my family. But I do wonder what will happen to us. Our families' homes are damaged. Our belongings gone. Your father's livelihood is gone, too. How shall we live? What about us, Seth?"

"We will have money," he added before she had a chance to question him further. "I have good news to share. Remember those duties I had been tending to?"

She nodded.

"Well, I've been working these last few weeks for the Green family. For a time I helped the husband with his business. When he needed to return to Culpeper, I then helped Mrs. Green with various tasks. But then I was asked to check her daughter and son-in-law's house near Fredericksburg. And I made good money that I put away for us."

"So that's why you were so preoccupied lately? Are you worried that things have changed with them and these duties?"

"I need to return to Greenwood and find out where I stand with my work and the money they still owe me. Perhbps you would like to accompany me when I drive there to see them? I know we need to be back here for the evening, as my family always has a huge celebration on Christmas Eve."

"That would be fine, Seth. I would like to go driving with you and meet them."

He smiled, opening his arms wide. She immediately came to him. "I was so worried about you," she murmured. "Will you be able to tell me where you were during the battle?"

His arms fell away under the weight of her suggestion. "I was safe. I just couldn't return because of the shelling and the invasion. I so much wanted to, but I couldn't. Believe me."

"Why did a Yankee soldier give me your note? You must have been in contact with the enemy somehow."

He stiffened. "He. . .he wanted a pocket watch for Christmas. When a soldier has little else of value, a pocket watch makes a good convincer. And with the Federal troops in command of the town at the time, he seemed a logical choice to deliver the note."

She appeared to accept this part of the sordid tale; why burden her with the rest? He had kept himself alive to be with her at this moment. Though he hated what he was forced to do by sharing information with the enemy, he did it out of love. Only, why did the excuse seem immoral when it shouldn't?

Wasn't love enough? Or could it be that guilt was stronger?

Leah stepped back again to scrutinize him. "You look so tired, Seth. Please try to get some rest."

"I will. And Leah. . .I'm very glad we're together again."

"Oh, so am I. It was so hard when you were away. Sometimes I wanted to blame you for not returning as you promised. I knew it was in God's hands, that there was a reason. And God kept us both safe." She offered one of her radiant smiles before shuffling off to the stairs.

Would she be glad of their covenant if she knew what really happened at the Lacy house? He thrust the doubt aside but clung instead to two basic truths now—they were alive, and they were together. And nothing would tear them apart. He had sacrificed much to keep it that way.

He only prayed it wasn't too much. . . .

Chapter 5

Christmas Eve morning dawned sunny but cold when Leah appeared in front of the house, dressed in a heavy wool coat and a muff borrowed from Seth's aunt Gracie to keep her hands warm. She offered Seth her brightest smile after he gave her a woolen lap robe to shield her from the morning cold. When he took his place beside her on the wagon seat, Leah admired his aura of strength and the feel of his warmth. Behind the reins, he appeared in command of life rather than displaying the wandering of a confused heart. Hope surged within her.

At first, Leah worried when she didn't see Seth at breakfast—until his aunt told her how he had been up before dawn to prepare for their trip. Leah was thankful for this time they would have together. Maybe alone in the wagon, absent from family members, Seth would feel comfortable enough to tell her about the week he'd been away. She still yearned to know what had happened during that time. As it was, she was barely able to confide in him about the dreadful fears that plagued her during the shelling and shooting and then the sound of Yankees plundering the house. She wanted them to talk about that terrible time when they had been apart. To find comfort and healing in each other's company, which still seemed stiff and distant.

"Your aunt said you were up before dawn," Leah commented as he ushered the horses to the main road.

"Too much on my mind, I suppose."

Leah waited, hoping he would reveal the thoughts burdening him. Instead, she heard only the sound of hooves beating the ground, the creak of the wagon wheels, and the feel of the breeze on her face. "I'm so glad we found a safe place to celebrate Christmas. All during the bombardment and then with the enemy invading, when I was in the cellar for so many days, I thought about many things. Like Christmas last year. Remember that time, Seth? We shared our first kiss."

His fingers felt for hers within the muff. She relished his touch. "Of course I remember. You were so surprised, too. Even then I wanted to ask you to marry me, but the timing wasn't right. We had only known each other a few weeks. I thought maybe you'd consider me too forward."

"It was only a little kiss. A promise of a future event." She tucked the lap robe closer around her legs. "You do want to get married, don't you?"

"Of course I do. Whatever made you think I didn't?"

How could she tell him that his elusiveness since the battle unnerved her?

How would they share other difficulties that were certain to come up in a marriage if he couldn't confide his present concerns? She sighed, wishing she knew how to ask such things.

He drew the wagon to a stop beside the road, just as the brilliant golden hue of the sun appeared on the horizon. "I have something for you."

Leah straightened in her seat. Seth reached behind her into the wagon bed and brought out a large rectangular box.

"I'm glad I had Father set this aside before the Federals came through town and raided the store. I was going to wait until Christmas, but this seems as good a time as any, being Christmas Eve and all."

She lifted the box cover to reveal the hat with a feather she had admired for many weeks in the window of his father's store. "Oh, Seth!" she cooed.

"I thought you would like to wear it today, especially with the visit."

"Oh, yes." Leah took off her woolen cap and donned the hat with a blue ribbon that she tied beneath her chin. "How do I look?"

"Like a grand and beautiful belle of the South." He leaned over and gave her a kiss.

The sensation of his lips on hers sent tingles through her. "Oh, thank you, Seth. Everything is all right now, isn't it?"

He drew back. "What do you mean by that? Why shouldn't it be?"

She fiddled with the bow beneath her chin. "I don't know. It just seems like the war has changed you somehow. Almost as if you had fought in it."

Seth flicked the reins, and the wagon moved off.

"But you didn't fight in it, did you?" she pressed.

"We all fight different battles, Leah. There are battles with weapons that we don't see and hear. Even the Bible talks about other weapons—spiritual weapons that try to weaken our faith."

"Yes, that's true. Oh, Seth, if something's bothering you, I so much want to pray with you about it."

"I. . .I only wish I had been there for you during the battle, that you didn't have to suffer through it alone. I know you must think I abandoned you in your time of need. You don't know how much I wanted to be there. But I couldn't."

Leah remembered the many times she had questioned his activities, and yes, why he had not returned as he promised. "I know there were other times you weren't able to come home," she began slowly. "I'm sure there was a good reason." She waited, hoping he would elaborate.

He guided the wagon down several different paths off the main road until a fine home appeared, situated on a small knoll.

"The house is all right," he said in relief. "They didn't harm Greenwood."

"So this is Greenwood."

"Yes, the plantation where I once worked." He drove the wagon down the road. Several other carriages and wagons were there. Laughter could be heard echoing from inside the house. It seemed the family was entertaining for the holidays. Seth offered his hand, helping Leah from the wagon. She straightened her bonnet and took his arm as together they walked slowly toward the house.

"I feel strange intruding when they have guests," Leah murmured.

"They are fine people. You will like them very much. Mrs. Green asks about you all the time. She was delighted to hear we were getting married."

Leah offered a smile to the young girl who opened the door to their knock. When Seth gave his name, the girl disappeared.

She soon returned and shook her head. "I'm sorry, Mr. Madison, but the master won't see you."

The expectation on his face disintegrated into confusion. "What? But tell Mr. Green it's Seth Madison. The family hired me to. . ."

"I'm sorry, but the master says you aren't welcome."

Leah looked at the young maid and then at Seth. As the young woman began to shut the door, Seth held out his hand to keep it from closing. "Please. There must be some mistake. We had an arrangement. If I could talk to him. . .or Mrs. Green. . ."

Just then a tall man walked into the hallway. "Is he still here, Rosy?" came his booming voice.

"Yes, it's Mr. Madison, sir. He says you know him."

The man came forward. Seth extended his hand. "Mr. Green. It's good to see you again."

"I don't know how you dare show your face here, traitor," he said in a low voice.

Seth's hand fell limp to his side. "M–Mr. Green," his voice wavered.

"Get off my property now."

"Sir, I don't understand."

"Do you take me for a fool? Or anyone? Even your bride, perhaps? You should tell her the truth. And then find your own kind to be with, Yankee lover."

The door slammed in his face.

Leah's hand fell away from Seth's arm. She stepped back to stare at him and then at the closed door that bore the cheerful greenery of the season. Only now the greenery might as well be naked brown branches in the wind, scraping her flesh. "Seth. . ."

He refused to look at her but marched to the wagon.

She hurried after him. "Seth, please."

He climbed onto the seat and grabbed up the reins, looking as if he might leave her standing there. Instead he waited until she hoisted herself up to sit alongside him before he turned the wagon around.

"Seth. . ." Her hands began to sweat inside the muff. Her extremities trembled. Why had that man accused Seth of being a Yankee lover? It made no sense. None of this made sense. Her confusion only grew as Seth's silence persisted. "Seth, please. . .why did that man say such things? I thought you said this family knew you."

"I'd rather not talk about it right now."

Her doubts multiplied as she considered what had happened. A Yankee soldier did give her Seth's note that day at the house. There was Seth's unexplained absence at the height of the invasion. Could he have been working for the enemy all along? The same enemy that ruined their town and caused such grief? "No," she whispered. "Please, God, let it not be."

"So you believe him?" he suddenly challenged, his face rigid like stone, his eyes wide and staring. "You think I'm some Yankee lover?"

"Seth, I—I don't know who you are. Something is different about you. You haven't been the same since you left the night of our engagement. Was your duty to. . .to join the Yankees?"

"I did not join them," he said stoutly, "no matter what anyone says. My heart, my blood is Southern. I may not agree with everything the South stands for, like the issue of slavery. But I'm not fighting against our native state of Virginia, either."

"What cause are you fighting for?" she asked softly.

He hesitated. "I wish I knew. I thought I knew. But now I don't. The cause I wanted so badly to preserve, the one I gave my heart and soul for—our covenant together—seems lost. I think I've made the worst mistake of my life." With that he lapsed into silence.

Tears filled Leah's eyes. How could he think their upcoming marriage was now a mistake? She didn't know what to say throughout the rest of the painful trip home. He had all but given up on them and their promise of marriage. Instead of a Christmas filled with joy and goodwill, it might well be a Christmas of good-byes. The thought grieved her to no end.

◆◆◆

He drove in silence. Somehow the Greens had been made privy to the goings-on at the Lacy house. The mere thought made perspiration break out on his forehead, even with the cold December day. He thought he had done the right thing, remaining in the land of the living for Leah's sake, even if it meant sharing information with the enemy. He did it so Leah wouldn't grieve in some horrid black dress and thick veil covering her face like a storm cloud. But what did he have as a result? Hatred from those he once knew. And a bride-to-be who still grieved, even though he was alive. His sacrifice had been for nothing. It would have been better if he'd died a so-called spy.

He looked at Leah. She stared straight ahead, her hand clutching the ribbon that held in place the hat he'd given her. At least she had not taken it off and dashed it to the ground. Perhaps it was a symbol of what remained. A certain trust she stubbornly clung to, despite what she witnessed at Greenwood.

His hands tightened around the reins. How he wished he could erase this label of a traitor. Perhaps he should turn around and tell the Greens what happened at the Lacy house. Maybe they would understand if he explained the terrible decision he was forced to make in the seconds he had before he was led away to a Yankee noose. What sane decision could anyone make when placed in such a dire position?

Now, as he neared his aunt's home, he must somehow force himself to smile and be of good cheer with the Christmas festivities upon them. There was, after all, the joy of Christ's birth. But there was no such joy in his heart, only the sting of death, like the stark images of Fredericksburg after the battle.

Just then Leah's hand slowly curled around his, soft at first, and then strengthened into a squeeze of reassurance. He trembled and breathed a sigh of relief. The wagon drew to a stop.

"I'm sorry, Seth," her voice whispered like the drip of clover honey. "I shouldn't doubt you. I know I don't understand everything, but. . ."

He tightened his hand around hers. "Leah, I had to make a choice. A choice no man should ever have to make. The night of our engagement, I was on an errand for Mrs. Green, to check on her daughter and son-in-law's house, which is the Lacy house overlooking the river."

He paused then continued. "I had crossed the river en route to my duty when I was captured by several Union pickets. They told the men in charge I was a spy for General Lee. I tried to tell them I was hired to check on the condition of the Lacy property by Mrs. Green. No one believed me. They were going to hang me."

Leah's hand fell away. Her eyes grew wide and began to glisten. She shook her head.

"Suddenly the colonel gave me a choice. He said they would spare my life if I would give them information about Fredericksburg." He looked then at the horses bobbing their heads, the nostrils blowing clouds into the air. "They gave me only a few moments to choose. Life or death. All I could see was you dressed in black, weeping over my grave. And then I saw our wedding; both of us standing at the altar, speaking our vows. The choice was before me. Leah, I couldn't leave you a widow. I had to come back as I promised the night of our engagement."

"Seth. . . ," she whispered.

"So I made my choice. I gave them the information they wanted. I told them things that likely have left people suffering. Homeless and in pain. And other consequences, like Mr. Green labeling me a traitor. And he's right. I am a traitor."

"You're not a traitor." She grabbed his hand once more, cradling it against her cheek. "You did the only thing you could do to come home to me."

"Leah, I am." He caught his breath. "So I'm going to leave as soon as Christmas is over. I'll join up with the Army of Northern Virginia. And in the meantime, I'll pray that God gives you a good and godly Southern man to marry."

She released his hand. Her face reddened and her cheeks glistened as well as her eyes. "H–how can you say this to me? How can you give up on us like this?"

"Because I surrendered all that I am. And all that I could have been to you." He snapped the reins and the wagon moved off.

Silence encompassed the ride back to his aunt's home. For a time he considered the things he had said. The cause for which he had traded the information in the first place. Maybe by joining Lee's forces, he would find reconciliation. To be on the front lines, facing the enemy head-on—the enemy that had stolen his heart and spirit—would be the balm he needed. To die for the Confederate cause as he should have done at the Lacy house. Maybe that would right the wrong.

When they returned to his aunt's home, Leah helped herself down from the wagon and hurried inside without a word. He sat still in the wagon seat, silent, his eyes closed but his mind active with sights and sounds he wished he could block out forever.

He finally moved to take care of the horses, realizing he couldn't remain locked in the past. He must look to the future, whatever that future held. A part of him hoped that somehow Leah would be in it. That they would see their wedding day on the dawn of the New Year. That all of this had not been in vain. He did serve a God greater than any trouble—past, current, or future. He must have hope, somehow.

Seth could hear the sounds of laughter coming from the house. The Christmas Eve celebration was in full progress. Now he must put on a cheerful countenance and join in the celebration. He must get through the holiday festivity. Then he would give his family the news he had given Leah. He would join the cause and never look back.

Seth took off his hat and stepped inside to be met by the fragrant scents of apple cider, roasting chestnuts, and candles burning. His aunt Gracie bustled over to give him a mug of mulled cider. "Come now and join us," she urged with an acceptance that soaked into his very being. How he wanted to be a part of all this, if only he did not feel so isolated at the same time.

Sitting down, Seth sensed the family gazing at him in expectation. "So let's talk about your wedding!" Aunt Gracie began with a smile. "It would be fine if you all decided to have it here, you know."

"I hope your family will be agreeable, Leah," added Seth's mother. "We want both families to be a part. What do you think they would like?"

Seth could see the blank look on Leah's face. Her hand trembled slightly as she sipped on her cider. "I haven't really talked to them about it, with the battle and all, Mrs. Madison."

"They say they will be back after Christmas," said Mr. Madison. "It was in the letter we showed you a few days ago."

"Oh, that dreadful battle, tearing families apart," mourned Mrs. Madison. "I'm so glad we're all safe and together for Christmas. And I know you will soon be together with your family, too, Leah."

"Wherever did you end up during the battle, my boy?" Seth's father now inquired of him. "You were gone for many days. No one knew where you were."

Seth felt the heat in his face. All at once he blurted out, "I was captured by a Union picket line while trying to help the Greens with a request. I was held prisoner during the battle."

Everyone put down their mugs and stared. The cheerfulness of the evening had been snuffed out like a candle's flame. Only the ticking of the grandfather clock in the hall could be heard.

"I had no idea," Aunt Gracie began. "Why, it must have been terrible, Seth."

"I would rather not talk about it, if that's all right. Can we enjoy Christmas now that we're together?"

It was a hollow wish at best, especially with the stares he received. A cloud hung over the celebration. How he wished he could be transported in time to the engagement party, with the season bathed in love and expectation instead of fear and despair. But everything had changed because of the war. The cursed war. His fist clenched. He hated the war with every part of his being. The conflict brought death and destruction to the mind, body, and soul. Now it had left him with no bride and no future.

Chapter 6

Leah opened her eyes to greet another day. Slowly she came to her feet, took up a quilt to wrap around herself, and padded over to the window to gaze at the countryside. The sun's rays were just beginning to stream across the barren land. Today was Christmas Day. A day to remember the Savior's birth. And a day to be with loved ones near and dear to her heart. But once the merriment of the holiday abated, she would face the painful reality that Seth would be gone forever. She would be alone, without his love, without a future.

Tears blurred her vision. What could she do to stop the inevitable? The tentacles of guilt seemed to grip him, robbing everything, but most of all their love. What could she do to rid him of the guilt he bore? Even if she were to continue confessing her love to Seth and tell him she harbored no ill will for the decision he was forced to make, the words would be ignored. Even the Christmas present she had made for him, a shirt and handkerchief embroidered with his initials, would never do the work of healing.

She could do the only thing left to her. Slowly she dropped to her knees and bent her head. She poured out her grief and pain to the One ready to accept her pain and embrace her. The One who knew everything. The One who held them both in His hands. And the One who could mend their relationship that now lay in tatters.

Leah heard a rap on her door. She came to her feet, drying her eyes and trying to compose herself. "Yes?"

"It's Mrs. Winslow, dear. We'll be having our family breakfast soon. I hope you can join us."

Seth's dear aunt Gracie was at the door. "I'll be ready, thank you." What a blessing the woman had been during this time of trial. Leah didn't know what she would do without her. She hurried to the wardrobe and took out the dress Aunt Gracie had lent her for the holiday. Noting the blue lines crisscrossing the fabric, she then looked at the pretty hat Seth had bought for her with the matching blue ribbon and a feather. She so loved the color blue. Seth knew it was her favorite color. They had shared so much of their lives with each other. Their likes and dislikes. Hopes and dreams. His words of commitment flooded her thoughts. They had not been pure imagination but real. And she had the evidence to prove it.

At once, Leah went to fetch the note Seth had sent to her through the Union courier.

I am forever yours.

141

Her finger traced the words written by his hand. Words that came from the depths of his heart. She held the letter over her own heart, recalling the words they would speak to each other at the marriage ceremony. *Till death do us part.* "I know we have not yet said our vows, Seth," she told herself. "But the day we got engaged is the day we made a commitment to say those words. To not allow this war or anything else to come between us. To not be apart until God takes us to His heavenly home. And I won't let what happened to you that day at the Lacy house tear us apart. Dear God, that is my heartfelt prayer. Please remember us!"

She felt better after this confession of faith as she tied the bow that encircled the waist of the dress. She even smiled at her reflection in the mirror above the bureau. She would look and act beautiful. She would sweep Seth off his feet. And he would have no choice but to wed her in the end.

She drifted down the stairs to see the family gathered in the dining room. The delicious aroma of fresh coffee awakened her senses. "Good morning," she said brightly to everyone, but saved a radiant smile for Seth. He stared at her first then offered a greeting in return. She made certain to sit by him at the table. When grace was finished, Leah helped herself to the fresh crullers and spiced apples passed to her.

"I do love Christmas morning," she said happily. "It's such a special time. And I must show you what Seth gave me yesterday for my present. A beautiful bonnet from your store, Mr. Madison. I plan to wear it for our going-away trip after our marriage."

The family exchanged looks. Seth put his cup down on the saucer. She felt his hand gently nudge her elbow. She refused to acknowledge him but only continued with her head held high. "I'm so glad you're willing to open your home so we can marry, Mrs. Winslow. I think perhaps having the ceremony in the front parlor by the huge window would be lovely."

"Yes, yes, it would be," Aunt Gracie said slowly.

Mr. Madison's face grew redder. Mrs. Madison coughed in a handkerchief.

"But I thought the wedding was off," Clara announced.

Silence filled the room as everyone looked at each other.

Clara's eyes widened, and she slid down slightly in her seat. "I mean, isn't that what you said, Seth? At least I thought I heard you say that."

"He only meant that we must take time to prepare," Leah answered with an uneasy chuckle. "This war has interrupted so many lives and plans that have been made. The best thing we can do is go on with our plans. And we made many plans, didn't we, Seth?"

He looked puzzled and uncertain how to respond.

"We can't let the war take over our hearts, too, can we?" She felt her voice rise on the brink of desperation. She forced herself to remain calm. "We have to go on with living and with love. I won't let hate take over. I won't let the enemy win."

"Leah. . ." Seth stood and said to the family, "Please excuse us." He took hold of Leah's arm, escorting her from her chair. With swift steps he directed her into the parlor with the large picture window, the very place where they were to have their wedding. He closed the double doors, turned, and faced her with his arms crossed.

"Leah, why are you saying these things to the family? I thought I made my feelings clear yesterday. In fact, I told them the wedding is off."

"I don't care. You haven't confessed your true feelings, Seth. You've only told me about feelings that have been affected by the tragedy of this war. And I won't let that destroy what God has planned for us."

"But have you considered that this is part of God's plan? That He allowed these things to happen so He can direct our paths?"

"And you're saying our path no longer leads to marriage? That all this time of conversations and walks, of laughing and sharing our hopes and dreams, was for nothing? The occasion when we announced our engagement to family and friends was a simple delusion? And the note you wrote to me saying 'I am yours forever' was a lie?" She whirled, the tears coming fast and furious, despite her wish to keep them all bottled up within. She had tried to let faith rule the hour, but it was not to be. Not now and maybe not ever.

"Leah, we can't go through a closed door. . . ."

"I have not closed the door, Seth. I know you made an awful decision so you could return safely to me. If you shut that door, then everything you did to come back to me was for nothing. Don't you see?"

He stood still and silent. She saw his eyes shift back and forth as he considered her words.

"You're a man who plans and leads. Who considers everything. Who vowed to be mine forever. Now you want to throw it away?"

"I don't know. When I saw the anger in Mr. Green's face, I could feel the weight of the anger of the entire population of Fredericksburg. Maybe the whole South for what I've done. I can't carry that kind of burden."

"You aren't supposed to carry it, Seth. God's burdens are light. He helps us bear them. He didn't mean for you to carry them, especially alone."

"But I made them. And I know I can't carry them and burden you also."

"Can't you trust Him with this? Can't you let it all go?"

He turned his back to her. The response broke her heart. How she wished she could unwrap the joy of their love this Christmas morn. What a marvelous present it would be, far better than unwrapping any hat with a blue ribbon. But it seemed as if it would be a day of mourning once more. There was nothing more to say or do.

Leah hurried from the room and up the stairs. She shut the door. *O God, how I love him despite what has happened, but I must give our future to You. Dearest God, if our marriage is to happen, You must make it happen. You alone can mend the past and direct the future.*

But how, she didn't know.

Seth followed Leah partway up the stairs but soon retreated. He returned to the parlor and stared out the huge bay window. He had never felt so empty and lost. He had to admit his soul warmed to Leah's determination and abiding faith. In his heart he knew they were destined to wed. God had drawn them together for this moment in time. Now he must face the barrier keeping them apart—the guilt that Leah spoke of. His inability to rise above this terrible thing and claim victory over it. He must deal with the guilt or surrender in its wake.

Seth grabbed for his hat and strode outside. The cold air numbed him, but he took no notice of it. Instead, he saddled one of his aunt's horses. He didn't know what would happen once he arrived at his destination, but he would go anyway and pray for God's favor.

The ride took him a good hour. Not many people were on the road this time of day as everyone was at home celebrating Christmas. He knew better than to disturb the family at this time, but he had no choice. His Christmas was already disturbed beyond comprehension. He had to set things right, no matter the consequence.

After a lengthy ride, he entered the road that led to his destination. What if they refused to speak to him again? What if the master of the house pulled a gun on him and ordered him off his property? What if he had Seth arrested as a Yankee informer? Seth shook off the fear that sought to subdue him. He must go and see these people. They were the ones to confront with the illness in his heart. He must find a remedy with them or no remedy at all.

He guided the horse slowly up the road to the home at Greenwood. It appeared quiet, despite its being Christmas Day. He doubted the daughter, Betty, and her family had made the journey from Lexington to the celebration. He recalled how Mrs. Green had advised her to stay away because of the battle.

He came to the house and anchored the horse's reins to a tree. Just then he saw a dark-skinned man amble around the home from the barn area, carrying a bucket. The man stopped short when he saw Seth.

"Suh?" the man inquired.

Seth removed his hat. "I'm Seth Madison. I did some work for Mrs. Green."

"I know you." He then came over and cupped a hand around his mouth. "An' I saw what you dun, too. I shore did."

Uneasiness filled Seth. He took a step back. "I'm not sure what you mean."

"Ol' Jack here knows what happened at the Lacy house. You were there and Ol' Jack was there, too, you see. I dun saw it all."

Seth stared wide-eyed. "You're the gardener Mrs. Green called Uncle Jack, aren't you?"

"Yep, that's me alrighty. You didn't see me, nope. I was takin' care of the horses. But they had you in and out of the barn there at the house. I heard them braggin', them two soldiers, too. They say they wuz gonna hang you high. They would hang you with that picture of your sweetheart before your eyes, lessen you agreed to help them. 'Course I nevah believed the colonel would let them do all that. But they wuz desperate men. They wanted to win this here battle. They had to do what they were fixin' to do." He came up to Seth. "And you dun the right thing, helpin' them. You dun what you had to do. Ain't no shame for it."

"But it may have hurt a lot of people."

"Lookie here, what you dun told them didn't change nuthin'. They would've blown Fredericksburg to kingdom come anyway, with or without your help. So don't you go blamin' yourself for what happened, even if they says you's some Yankee lover."

"Yeah, a Yankee lover," he said grimly.

"Lookie here. Between you and me, I'm glad you did what you did. Them men in blue, they's fightin' for Abe Lincoln and to set me free to do what I wanna do and be who I wanna be. You talk about sufferin'? Think about what my brethren are sufferin'. And Mr. Lincoln there, he dun signed that there Emancipation Proclamation. And that's worth fightin' for."

Seth stared quietly.

"So why you here anyways? To talk to the massah?"

"Maybe it was to talk to a man like you."

"Humph. Many here don't think I'm some man like you say. They think we's just property. That's all we are."

"You're most certainly a man, Uncle Jack. And you're a man who can speak words of healing and wisdom to another man's soul. I don't believe in slavery. I never have. If what I did helped to free a man like you, I would feel better about it."

"You's right about that. You do what you do for lots of reasons, you know. For your sweetheart. And for me, too. Those men in blue. . .they ain't the enemy, you know. Nor the men in gray neither. Pride's the enemy. You gotta stand against the pride, Mr. Madison. Work for good, for your neighbor. That's the only way we're gonna win, if we're standing together, helpin' each other. Love your neighbor, like the Good Book says." He extended his hand then.

Seth grabbed hold of the man's hand and shook it. When he did, he felt the burden of his soul begin to lift. Praise filled his inner being. "Thank you, Uncle Jack. This has meant more to me than I can say."

"Should I go git Mr. Green there and tell him you're here?"

Seth backpedaled, releasing the man's hand. "No, no, that's all right. I think I found the answer I was looking for. Thank you." He wheeled then and took hold of the horse's reins, unwinding them from the tree trunk. "You don't need to tell them I was here, either."

Just then he saw a figure emerge from the house. It was a woman in a fancy dress. She waved frantically, calling out his name. To his astonishment, the woman was Mrs. Green.

"Oh, Seth, I'm so glad you came by. How are you?"

Seth was unsure what to say but told her he was well and wished her a pleasant Christmas Day.

"Yes, and the same to you." She hesitated at first. "I wanted to say that I'm ashamed for what happened yesterday. I told my husband I sent you to our daughter's house to make certain everything was all right—that I'd asked you to go, even though it was dangerous. And Uncle Jack told us what happened, how the terrible Yankees forced you to help them. Even using your poor sweetheart against you. My husband had no right to accuse you like he did. Can you ever forgive us?"

Seth stared in amazement at this announcement. "Of course, Mrs. Green. That's very kind of you."

"Kindness nothing. There was no kindness, and for that I feel ashamed." She handed him a small drawstring bag. "Here is the money we owe. You sacrificed so much to help us, and I'm indebted to you. I hope this money helps some. It's not Confederate notes either."

She offered a smile. Uncle Jack smiled also with his set of stained and missing teeth. To Seth, the smiles were sent from heaven above. A wave of relief flooded his soul.

Offering a farewell, he returned to his horse with a skip to his step and a ballad of thankfulness on his lips. This day was an answer to a heartfelt prayer and had been answered in a way he couldn't have begun to fathom. There was Mrs. Green's heartfelt apology, but most of all, there were Jack's words that rang true the more he thought about them. The so-called enemies were not enemies of blue and gray but squabbling brothers, spilling their blood over their rights and their lands. And what the colonel back at the Lacy house said was true, too. They must come together as a nation to survive. Seth didn't know how all this would end. He loved his state of Virginia and his family. But somehow they must be unified, working as one to make the United States strong once more.

But for now there was one union that occupied his thoughts—his promised union with Leah. The covenant he had made with her several weeks ago in the parlor of her father's house. They, too, must stand together as one, as they'd promised. To build a home and a future through the grace and mercy of God.

He prodded the horse. A biting wind ripped through his thin coat, but all he felt was warmth in the vision of Leah set before him. Dear, sweet Leah who accepted him no matter what had transpired. The love of his life and the one to whom he owed so much, more than any money or the hat with a blue ribbon. The perfect woman for him in every way. He would have no other.

Seth leaned forward, pressing his horse into a swift gallop, eager to see her beautiful face and share in this Christmas Day. But a sudden thought held back complete joy. What about the words he had spoken to her, of wanting to dissolve their engagement? What if she now refused him for the hurt he had caused? *God, please don't let me be too late. Please restore what has been foolishly taken away.*

Chapter 7

Leah tried to smile as she sat among the family, sharing the glad tidings of Christmas; but inwardly she felt miserable. She heard the family mutter, wondering where Seth had gone this day.

"Maybe he is off fetching some mysterious Christmas gift," Aunt Gracie said with a laugh.

"I only hope he comes back," Clara grumbled.

How Leah wished that were true. But blessings seemed hard to come by anymore. An engagement, after all, had been broken. She tried to muster courage on this Christmas Day by recalling the difficulties Jesus faced, even as a newborn when no one wanted to grant his mother a place in crowded Bethlehem. Then He, the King of creation, had to succumb to entering this fallen world in a place inhabited by animals. Surely God understood, and He would give her the strength to face whatever lay ahead.

"Come, Leah. There are some gifts for you."

Even though she felt apart from the gathering, Leah wiped away a lone tear and ventured forward. One by one, the family gave gifts to each other. Leah found a new fan and some mittens waiting for her under the tree. "How lovely, thank you," she said, again trying to force her lips into a smile.

"Don't worry about Seth," said Aunt Gracie. "Remember that one Christmas when he was younger and went out, only to come back with a milk cow tied to his saddle?"

"I remember that," said Mrs. Madison. "He'd bargained with some farmer on the outskirts of Fredericksburg and then forgot to get the animal until Christmas." Her smile faded away. "I'm sure the cow is gone along with everything else we left behind in Fredericksburg."

"But we have each other," Mr. Madison reminded his wife, giving her a warm embrace followed by a kiss. "And Leah, I know everything will work out between you and Seth. Time heals."

Leah couldn't help the tears that sparked in her eyes. She excused herself and wandered out to the hall. How confident she had been when this day began, filled with determination and faith. But how easily, too, it had faded away. She missed her family and wondered how they were this holiday. She missed her home and the way things were. But most of all, she missed Seth. And now she must release him to find his own path in life. But did she have the strength?

Suddenly she heard the door bang open in the rear of the home and someone shout a greeting. The family streamed into the kitchen area to hail the caller. Leah found her way to the gathering and saw Seth embracing his family. Suddenly their eyes met. In that gaze, she found a change. Hope rose within her.

"Where have you been? Sneaking around as usual?" quipped his sister. "Aunt Gracie has been trying to decide what gift you must be getting."

"And I'm sure it's a special one, too," Aunt Gracie said with a laugh. "Isn't it, Seth?"

"Maybe they are getting back together," Clara said wistfully.

"Come, come, I'm sure Seth would like to speak to Leah," Mr. Madison said, gesturing the family into the drawing room.

Leah stood silent, uncertain what to say. There was no gift Seth could give her this day but the gift of a changed heart. One that found God's mercy instead of being plagued by remorse. "Where did you go?" Leah managed to ask as her gaze fell to the wooden floor.

"Like Aunt Gracie said. To find a special gift."

"A gift?" She looked up, suddenly curious.

"I went seeking answers, Leah. I went back to Greenwood."

Shock radiated through her. "Back to the family that rejected you? But why?"

"I needed to find answers, and I did. The gardener was there, the same gentleman the Greens had sent to watch over the Lacy house and property. Uncle Jack knew what happened while I was held prisoner there. He offered encouragement to me, telling me that what I did helped him and his people a great deal. That there are different ways to look at this conflict, and not through our narrow vision." He paused. "I needed to see through his eyes, of one enslaved by others. And how there are men wanting to set him and others like him free. That perhaps my help to the Federals had not been in vain after all. Others appreciated it and looked on it as a gift."

Leah didn't know what to say but could clearly see that something had changed in Seth's troubled heart.

"Then as I was preparing to leave, Mrs. Green stopped me." He held up the bag. "She gave me the money they owed for my work. And she apologized for what her husband said yesterday. She'd heard what happened at the house and absolved me from any wrongdoing." He reached out and took her hand in his. "Leah, I felt like I was given Christmas gifts from on high today."

"I–I'm glad, Seth. Now you can do whatever God wills." She bit her lip, remembering his words earlier that morning, and tried hard not to weep. She turned, preparing to head back to the drawing room, when he touched her arm.

"Leah, I had to find redemption after what happened to me. And a way to renew the pledge we made that day in your family's home." He paused. "But maybe I'm too late to redeem it."

"Why?"

"I don't know. So much has happened between us. Can we still be together? Is it too late for you to marry me, Leah?"

"Is it too late?" She nearly laughed aloud at the absurdity of it. In an instant she rushed toward him. He dropped the bag of money on a nearby table to take her into his arms. "It's never too late, my dear Seth. And yes, of course I will marry you!"

He kissed her as if he had been away for years. And during this entire time, it might as well have been that long, the way she waited day and night for a miracle. Now they had witnessed the miracle of Christmas, a rebirth of love on the day when love was born and laid in a manger long ago.

"What will you do now?" she asked.

"We need to make plans for our wedding. And then I'll see what God wants me to do. I know I have done little with the conflict we are in. But maybe there is a place for me still."

"You mean you'll still join the army?"

"Maybe I can do something to help both sides. Even as Uncle Jack said, we must come together as a nation or be defeated. I know from working with the Greens that I can be of help, especially with my knowledge of the area and in various tasks. Maybe somehow I can be of use to both sides." He took her once more in his arms. "But right now I want to be of use to you. To be a good husband to you. And one day, a good father as well."

She giggled, nestling in his strong arms, enjoying his embrace. When they finally returned to the drawing room arm in arm, the family gazed at them with questions in their eyes. Seth told them what transpired at the Lacy house and then his encounter this day with the Green family. They sat in silence, listening intently to it all.

Finally Mr. Madison cleared his throat. "Well, son, I guess we've all learned quite a bit from this ordeal. I would say, too, that this makes Christmas even more meaningful, having gone through what you did."

"It also makes my engagement with Leah more meaningful, Father. How blessed I am to have a woman willing to stand by me, no matter what I may have done. One who never lost faith, even though it must have been torture for her to wait on God for an answer."

The look of adoration in Seth's eyes warmed Leah's heart. She smiled, and he smiled back.

"Then what are we waiting for?" said Aunt Gracie. "Let's plan the wedding!"

❧

". . .to have and to hold, from this day forward, until death do you part?"

Leah looked up lovingly into the dark eyes of Seth Madison. "I do," she said without reservation. She had already heard his equally fervent reply to the words that meant more to her than ever before. She barely heard the next words the minister spoke, sealing their marriage. Then Seth was bending over her, ready to give her a kiss in celebration.

Family and friends applauded and gathered around to offer congratulations. Leah clung to the arm of her new husband, thanking God, who had brought them through calamity to stand with joy as one. When she thought how close they had come to forfeiting their chance to be together, she nearly wept.

Leah hugged her mother and father. They had returned several weeks ago from Washington. Seth's mother dabbed at her eyes with a handkerchief before giving Leah a kiss on her cheek.

"I'm very glad you're a part of our family," she said. "There is no better woman for Seth."

"I will agree with that," Seth added, squeezing Leah's arm. "There's no one better to stand by my side and keep me on the straight and narrow."

"So what will you do now?" asked a cousin.

Leah looked to Seth, who considered the question. "I will be helping with supplies in the area," he said. "There are people in Fredericksburg who need to rebuild, and in order to get the money, farmers and other folks are hoping to sell goods to both armies. So I will help in negotiating the sales of food, dry goods, whatever I can."

"And I will supply Seth with food and dry goods—such as a new shirt and knitted socks," Leah added to the laughter of the families.

Suddenly she felt Seth's hand tug on her arm. She left the celebration to follow him into the hall.

"No. . .not again," she whispered.

"What do you mean by that?"

"The last time we wandered out into the hall after a special announcement, I didn't see you for days. You had your duties, if you remember."

"After the engagement, yes, I remember." He gathered her in his arms. "My dearest Leah, there is only one duty I must see to now. To honor you and love you and be there for you until death separates us, and we meet again in heaven." He then pulled out a piece of paper from his vest pocket. "But right now I have something to show you. . . ."

"It's a deed to a house! Oh, Seth, how did you ever manage it?"

"I had some help. A family was eager to move out of the area after the battle and was more than happy to let us have the house. We'll pay as we're able. So let's build our home together and make it a wonderful place for ourselves, our children, and our future."

Leah had never heard such wondrous words. Her spirit soared as she entered his tender embrace. "Oh yes, Seth. For now and evermore!"

Courage of the Heart

by Tamela Hancock Murray

Dedication

With special thanks to my uncle Grayson Bagley,
founding president of the Lunenburg County (Virginia) Historical Society.

I will hear what God the LORD will speak:
for he will speak peace unto his people, and to his saints:
but let them not turn again to folly.
PSALM 85:8 KJV

Chapter 1

The celebratory spirit of Christmas filled the Lambert family parlor. Pine branches decorated the mantel, holly sprigs accented brass candleholders, and evergreen wreaths with red bows hung on the inner and outer doors. Barry Birch's family never decorated with mistletoe, but Arabella Lambert's mother had hung a sprig in their hall doorway. The tangy scent of such winter greenery mixed with the heavy odor of logs burning in the fireplace. Barry looked at the face of his true love. Firelight flattered Arabella, though her beauty evidenced itself in the harshest sun.

He swallowed, though he had a good idea what her answer to his question would be.

With the blue eyes he loved so much, she studied him. "What is it, Barry?"

"You know me too good, don't you?" Unwilling to wait another moment, he dropped to one knee in front of her, observing the skirt of her green holiday dress before lifting his gaze to note her black hair and pink cheeks. She clasped her hands and brought them to her chest. A breath of anticipation escaped her lips.

"Arabella, will you do me the honor of becomin' my wife?"

Her blue-eyed gaze rested upon his face. The love in her rosy expression reassured him. "Yes, I will!"

He hadn't expected her to decline, yet relief that he'd received her official acceptance left him feeling lighter. He rose to his feet. "May—may I kiss you?"

The light in her eyes told him she didn't object to his request. "I reckon under the circumstances, one kiss would be all right."

When they embraced, the touch of her feminine form did not disappoint him. He brought his lips to hers, a moment he'd rehearsed in his dreams for years. As her body molded into his, he sensed that she, too, had dreamt of this moment. Her lips proved as soft as he'd imagined. Their gentle touch made him yearn for more, but he restrained himself. Such a refined woman deserved a gentleman in a fiancé. The memory of the kiss would linger in his mind always.

As she broke away, Arabella's downcast look told of her bashfulness at such bold affection, yet a little smile betrayed she wasn't displeased.

"You've just made this the most wonderful Christmas of my life," he said. "What do you say to us settin' a date of next Christmas for our weddin'? That'll give me a year to build us a house on the parcel of land Pa promised

155

me as a weddin' gift when the time came. And that time is now."

Her eyes shone. "That sounds perfect to me."

He nodded and swallowed. Would she feel the same way about marrying him if she knew his secret?

~∗~

Later, Barry rode his white steed, Friday, through the frigid winter night. Heading home to the Birch farm, he dreamt of his future with Arabella. Her pa had already approved the marriage. Barry's experience with livestock and coaxing vegetables out of reluctant mountain land assured they would eat. Selling the occasional load of firewood and lumber brought in enough money to buy a few items at the dry goods store.

The fact that he would inherit land also assured he could support Arabella and any children sent as blessings from the Lord. Barry favored the land Pa had promised for the house, with its flat piece that would make a fine yard. He enjoyed the view of the surrounding mountains. A plentiful underground source of water near where he planned to build the house would make a good well. Later, he'd inherit sixty acres from Pa in addition to the plot he'd agreed to give Barry as a wedding gift. Pa had the same agreement with Barry's two brothers, meaning the farm would remain in Birch hands for at least another generation.

Moments later, he secured Friday in the barn and then entered the home of his childhood—a white clapboard farmhouse—through the back door. Thanks to Ma, the kitchen always felt welcoming, greeting friends and family with the aroma of coffee she kept warm on the stove no matter what the season. Like the Lamberts, Ma's Christmas decorations consisted primarily of mountain greenery. The celebratory atmosphere lifted his spirits even higher.

Sitting at the oak table, Ma and Pa stopped their conversation to greet him. "How'd it go with Arabella?" Ma's eyes widened.

He puffed out his chest, unable to contain a display of happy pride. "She accepted."

"No surprise there." Pa rose from his seat and extended his hand for a congratulatory shake, then pulled him in for a loose embrace and a pat on the back. "She'd be a fool to turn down the best catch this side of the Mississippi."

Barry scoffed, "I wouldn't go that far."

Ma rose and embraced Barry, holding him longer than usual. "Did you set a date for the weddin'?"

"We're hopin' for a Christmas weddin'. That'll give me a year to build the house and dig the well on the northern tip. I hate the uncertainty of the South's secession. We're at war. I realize that means our plans might have to change."

"Like they changed for Silas." Ma sighed as she sat back down in her simple oak chair. "When he returns, he can marry his sweet Bridget."

"I pray he comes back soon, and this war will end, and that God won't take Silas out there on the battlefield. But if He does, we can take some consolation in the fact that at least Bridget won't be a widow. This war has already made far too many." Pa's lips turned downward.

"True." Barry recalled how two of the prettiest girls he knew had gone from carefree lasses to weary widows within the past six months. "I don't want Arabella to be another one."

"No one does." Pa's pensive expression had become a common sight since the war's inception. "I'm just hoping this conflict won't last much longer."

"I think the boys will be tired of fightin' soon enough." Ma nodded once for emphasis. "Our great Union will win easily and all will be back to normal."

"I don't know." Barry recalled the South's victory in Fredericksburg. "Robert E. Lee is a mighty fine general."

"Now I know you're not a Southern sympathizer." Ma's eyebrows shot up.

"Of course he's not, my dear." Pa made a shooing motion with his hand. "But no man can deny that the South has one of the best generals—if not the best—livin' today. I'm mighty afraid we're in for a longer fight than anyone expected. A long, bloody fight that'll tear this here great nation apart."

The thought of so much death, desolation to the land, and heartbreak for both sides left Barry depressed. He didn't want the war to last long enough for him to be called up to serve. One of the rich fellows he knew had hired a German immigrant to take his place, but even if Barry had such a sum of money to pay, he'd never ask that of another man.

"All this talk of war reminds me, son. You're quite a marksman. You'll appreciate this." Pa reached for a gun propped in the far corner. "Lookee here at what your uncle Martin gave me." Father's face lit up with a smile as he handed the new rifle to Barry.

Studying the smooth wooden stock and long metal barrel, Barry let out a low whistle. "This is one handsome weapon."

"That it is. A Henry rifle. Want to try it? We can go outside and shoot targets."

"Sure." He didn't mind shooting logs.

"You men have your fun." Ma's indulgent look reminded Barry of the many times she'd shown patience with his boyish antics over the years.

The two men donned wool coats against the chill and went outdoors. They passed the fence that marked the south field boundary. Barry noticed the cows munching. Soon they reached a wooded area. A pile of logs waited to be split. Pa set one bark-free log against a fallen tree about thirty paces ahead. He marked a small circle with some charcoal he carried with him. "You go first."

"Shouldn't you shoot it first since Uncle Martin gave it to you?'"

Pa winked. "Already did."

Barry chuckled. Eager to try the new gun, Barry loaded it then aimed. When he was ready, he took his best shot and hit the target.

"Bravo, my boy!"

Barry tried not to look too pleased when his father patted him on the back. With great skill, he loaded the gun and shot once more.

"You're a fine marksman, son. You'll be an asset to the war effort."

A lump formed in Barry's throat. "Why don't you take a shot?"

His father reset the targets and complied, easily hitting his marks.

"I'd say you're quite the marksman yourself." Barry grinned.

Father studied the pattern of hits. "If I were a young man, I'd take on them rebs in a minute. Just like your brother Silas. Why, he's out there on the battlefield now, doin' us proud."

Barry tried not to scowl. Father didn't have to remind him about Silas's impeccable war record. Already he'd earned one medal. No doubt he'd come home with more.

The terrible war had pitted father against son and brother against brother. Barry had never gotten on well with Silas in the first place. Everyone in the Birch and Lambert families supported the Union, so they weren't split on opinion. Yet the war, rather than uniting Silas and Barry in a cause, only made him feel more estranged from a brother he should have admired and respected.

The story of Cain and Abel came to mind: *And the LORD said unto Cain, Where is Abel thy brother? And he said, I know not: Am I my brother's keeper? And he said, What hast thou done? the voice of thy brother's blood crieth unto me from the ground.*

Barry thought about Silas, his brother by birth, and of his other brothers in the community of Christ and beyond. Barry still couldn't bear the thought of blood crying from the ground, even Southern blood. No matter how much he disagreed with the idea of them leaving the Union, they were part of the human family. Besides, Jesus said to forgive one another seventy times seven.

Pa's voice interrupted his musings. "You thinkin' about your brother?"

"Sort of." Barry searched for a way to avoid talking about Silas's accomplishments. "It's a shame he couldn't be here to celebrate Christmas with us, instead of freezin' on the battlefield with nothin' to eat but hardtack."

"Oh, I imagine the Union army came up with somethin' better than that on Christmas."

"That reminds me. We haven't had a letter from him lately, have we?"

Pa's tight jaw indicated he tried not to show concern. "I'm sure one will be comin' soon. Your ma's been writin' him ever' day. I'm sure he's just been too busy to write back. Maybe they sent him on a secret mission or somethin'."

Barry could hear desperation in Pa's suggestion. "Yeah. A secret mission." One that would keep his brother safe, he hoped.

Chapter 2

A few days later, Arabella watched Barry dismount Friday and tie the white horse to the hitching post in her yard. She wished she had worn a better housedress. The muslin one she had chosen for the day did nothing for her complexion, but it would have to do since her fiancé was on his way across the front yard. She consulted the hall mirror and noticed her dark hair, pulled back in loose ringlets, was none the worse for wear despite her vigorous attack on housework that day. For that much, she could be thankful.

Unwilling to look too eager by answering the door before Barry knocked, Arabella watched him step up to the porch, and a shiver raced up her spine. Hardly a moment went by when she didn't dream of him, seeing his image in her mind. She couldn't wait for the day when they could spend every hour together.

Finally, he knocked. She answered the door and greeted him. Once they were wed, she'd be sure to kiss him whenever they'd been apart, but to do so now seemed too forward.

Barry greeted her, and a wisp of light brown hair fell in front of his right eye. He swept it out of his face with a motion of his head, a habit he'd picked up since wearing his hair parted deeply to the side. "I know it hasn't been too long since we last saw one another, but I missed you mightily all the same."

"I missed you, too." She looked at him straight on before averting her eyes and motioning for him to enter. "So what have you been doing to fill up the time?"

"Huntin'. Pa and I went today. I bagged a doe."

She shut the door. "A doe." Barry always hated shooting a female. A buck would have made him more proud. "Your family will be eating well."

"You're right about that." He handed her a parcel wrapped in brown paper. "I brought you a shank so you can make your fine stew."

She brightened and took the package. "I'll be happy to make you all you want." Stew would be on the menu often once they married.

In a land where sportsmanship and hunting trophies were prized, she knew life couldn't be easy for such a gentle man. She remembered one day not so long ago when she witnessed him and his brother, Lance, fishing. Barry caught a bass and realized it was too small for him to keep. With a strong but gentle motion, he released the hook from the fish's mouth.

"Sorry I hurt you, little fella." With a frown, he threw the fish back into

159

the pond. Arabella couldn't imagine any other man having such feelings about a fish.

She remembered other times, seeing him flinch when he had to dress a fish or deer, or even a quail. But he considered hunting his duty since the meat supplemented the family's food supply. He didn't enjoy hunting for sport. Such notions weren't shared by most men she knew in this hardscrabble country. Though Barry was every inch a man, some ribbed him for being less than thrilled with killing wildlife.

Arabella didn't care who teased him. She'd stand by him no matter what.

"I'm lookin' forward to spring when I can plant my garden." Barry seemed to be apologizing for the necessity of hunting for food.

"Yes, you are so talented with your garden. I'll have to buy extra canning jars to put up all the food you'll grow for our family." An image of herself putting up vegetables came to mind. Canning was hot work that involved cooking large quantities of food in warm weather; but seeing colorful tomatoes, green beans, grape jam, strawberry preserves, and yellow corn preserved in clear jars lining the shelves, made families secure in the hard times of winter. The thought of making a home for him, whether the task be ironing shirts, beating rugs, or canning, gladdened her heart.

He smiled, warming her heart all the more. "Thinkin' about our new life together, and the love of the Lord we share, why, it gives me reason to live."

Such a proclamation made her feel inadequate but grateful. She beckoned him to follow her into the kitchen so she could store the meat. "I can think of nothing else. I pray this awful war ends before you're called to serve. And I pray every night for our brave troops."

"I want to be brave in your eyes." Regret tinged his voice as he followed her down the hall.

"You don't have to go to war for that. I'll always think of you as very manly."

"Do you mean that?"

They had reached the kitchen. She looked into his pale but lively brown eyes. "Why ever would I not?"

"Because. . .because. . ."

She couldn't remember a time when he seemed so at a loss to express himself. "Tell me." Her heart beat with fear. Was he sick? She set the meat on the table and drew near.

"There's somethin' I haven't told you. I—I should've told you sooner, but I didn't want to." He took her hand in his. "If you decide you don't want to marry me, I'll understand."

"Not marry you? I can't imagine anything that would make me change my mind."

"You might be sorry you said that after you hear what I have to say. I regret that I didn't tell you earlier; though since you know me well, this might not come as a surprise." He took in a breath. "It's just that I asked you to marry me, and I want you to go into it with your eyes wide open. I don't want to deceive you."

Fright clutched her gut. "Deceive me? How?"

"I'll never lie to you, Arabella, but the more this war drags on, the more I realize I might have to take a public stand that won't make me popular in these parts. You see, I'll never be the big war hero you want."

She let out a breath, releasing all fear with it. "Oh, is that all? I don't care about that. I think it's an honor just to serve. Don't feel you have to compete with Silas for medals. He always was cocksure, and I think you're better off not trying to best him."

Barry laughed, breaking the tension. "It's not Silas I'm worried about, although you're right, he's sure of himself. No, it's somethin' else. Somethin' about me."

She braced herself.

He studied the pine floor. "You see, I'm not at all happy about this war we're fightin'."

With a deliberate movement, she captured his gaze with hers. "I can't say I am, either. I don't reckon anybody's happy about it, except foolish boys looking for adventure. I'm afraid the realities of war set them straight right quick-like."

"I'm no longer a foolish boy, and I can promise I'm not lookin' for adventure. You see, I don't want to go to the war at all."

Arabella couldn't understand why he felt such conflict from a common-sense confession. "Well, nobody with a lick of sense really does."

He kept gazing at the floor. "I mean, I don't want to fight to the extent that I might have to deny goin' into the service."

She gasped in spite of herself. "Deny service? How can you say that, with our men dying every day for a cause that's right and good?" She wished she hadn't blurted out her thought. Now it was her turn to look away. "I'm sorry. I didn't mean that."

"Yes, you did, and you're right. It's just that, I can't bring myself to take aim and fire at another human, no matter what. I know it might sound silly to you, but there's a reason. A reason I haven't told anyone else about." He let out a sigh to fortify himself. "Do you remember my grandfather, Barnard Birch?"

She nodded. "He was a big man. Kind of scared me."

Barry chuckled. "He wasn't as scary as he looked. I was named after him, you know."

"I remember you mentioning that more than once." She smiled.

"He's the one who taught me how to shoot a gun. He was a great marksman. But when he gave me his trusted musket, he told me never to use a weapon to hurt another human. Ever. I promised him I wouldn't. That afternoon was the last we spent together. I—I can't break my promise to him. And

I have to say, I agree with how Grandpappy felt. I really don't want to take the life of another. No matter what side we're on, we're all members of the human family. And even without my promise to Grandpappy, I'd be hard pressed to harm another human. After all, the Bible says that we are to love our enemies." He swallowed. "If all this means you can't marry me, then I understand." His broken voice reflected a torn heart.

"Oh, Barry, if I were you, I wouldn't break my promise to my grandfather, either. I think you're very honorable to keep it. What you just told me makes me love you even more. I'll never give you up." Bold or not, she squeezed his hand. "I think you should tell your family about your promise. Maybe then they won't feel so bad about you not going."

"You might think that, but it's not so. Pa's ardent about his feelin's that we all need to join in the fight against the rebs. Even worse, he and Grandpappy didn't always see eye to eye on everything. He'd want me to disavow anything I said to Grandpappy." Barry sighed. "Like you said, refusin' to join the army's not a popular stance to take in this time and place. Everyone will think me a coward no matter what I say."

She could feel his distress. "No, you aren't a coward. At least, not in my book. And I'm willing to stand alongside you, and take whatever ridicule we'll have to endure, together."

He took in a soft breath. "You really mean that?"

"Yes, I do." Her strong tone bespoke her resolve.

Tension eased its way out of his expression, leaving him with the strong and straight features she loved so well. "Can I ask you somethin' else?"

"Anything."

"I think the less said about this, the better. I don't want you to lie, now. If somebody asks, I want you to tell them the truth about me."

"But you think it's best not to bring up the topic."

He nodded.

"I agree. The less said, the better."

"Thank you for understandin'. You'll be the perfect wife for me."

Nothing he could have said would have made her heart more glad.

Chapter 3

March 1863

The weather had just warmed enough for Barry and Arabella to picnic. Since their engagement, Arabella treasured her time with him even more, holding on to each precious moment as though it would be their last. While they didn't see each other every day, on Sundays they sat together in church. Sometimes Barry would hold her hand during the sermon. She cherished his warm touch.

As war raged, there looked to be no hope of the North winning so everyone could go home. Reports from the battlefields told of hardship, despair, and death. Arabella prayed each night for the Union soldiers, that they would defeat the rebs. Led by Saint Paul's letter to the Corinthians on Christian charity, she even brought herself to pray for the rebs, too. After all, they had families of their own. Surely they had fiancées, mothers, sisters, even children. Remembering Barry's words that both sides were members of the human family, Arabella clung to her prayers, and her hope.

Standing at the kitchen table, she placed lunch in a reed basket. She had prepared leftover beef with biscuits she had made the previous day. Sweet tea was stored in canning jars. She wrapped up a piece of cake for them both, although she had packed one smaller for herself than the slice she reserved for him.

Returning from his chores, Father noted her preparations. "Where you off to today, daughter?"

"On a picnic with Barry." Without thinking, she peered out the window and noticed spring sunshine. "We thought since the weather had broken, now would be a nice time to go."

His blue eyes, a trait he had passed on to her, twinkled. "Did you, now? You're not thinkin' of running off on us, are you?"

She concentrated on setting the cake in the basket. "No, sir. Just because Mary Lou married Jethro without telling you first, doesn't mean I'd do something so foolish."

Father's face clouded, making Arabella wish she hadn't reminded him about her sister's recent elopement. Jethro had long since departed for the battlefield, but not before ensconcing his wife with his parents. "She disappointed us, that's for certain."

Arabella had been disappointed in her, too. She'd always dreamed of being her sister's maid of honor, but that wouldn't be possible without a ceremony.

"Every day your mother cries, thinking Mary Lou might end up a war widow."

"I know, Father. There are too many war widows around us today."

"And a lot of 'em are girls who married in a hurry, without thinking through the consequences."

Though Father was too discreet to say so, Arabella knew some of the consequences he referred to were tangible. Recently, fatherless babies had become all too numerous among their friends and acquaintances.

"I promise I won't marry Barry without telling anyone."

Father rested his palms against the back of the chair, leaning into it. All traces of teasing had disappeared. His expression looked as serious as Pastor Thompson's when he laid a soldier to rest. "I want you to do me one better than that. I want you to promise me you won't marry him before this war ends."

Arabella remembered the most recent reports she'd heard about the war. No clear victor seemed likely to emerge soon. "Before the war ends? But who knows when that'll be?" Her heart beat faster.

"No one but the Lord Himself knows. Could be years."

She wondered if he heard himself talk. "Do you want me to stay unwed all that time?"

"No. I'd like the war to end, too." He leaned more into the chair. "I've been mighty upset by the whole situation. This fighting's a nightmare for this country. I don't want you to be one of the casualties."

"But. . ."

"I didn't want to mar your happiness the day you got engaged, so I held my tongue until now. But you must know I've been concerned about you. Promise me you won't marry before the war ends."

Arabella wished her father didn't feel the need to make such a drastic demand, but she knew he was motivated by fear—and a desire to protect her. "Surely the South will surrender soon. Maybe even before Barry's called to serve."

"You can sure pray for that. I know I do."

At that moment, Barry appeared at the back stoop. Spotting him before he opened the door, she took in a little breath. His presence always lifted her heart.

Unaware of the debate he'd interrupted, he greeted them with a blithe spirit. Arabella tried to mimic his mood. No need to spoil the day before they left the house. Father also acted as though he'd been discussing nothing more important than the sunshine, but she knew he depended on her to take his message to Barry.

After they left the house, they walked through the Lambert farm. The dewy scent of spring hung in the air. Trees were starting to bud, coming back to life after a long winter's nap. The day would have been perfect if not for her father's edict. He wanted to help her, she knew. Why did his love feel so harsh?

Courage of the Heart

Barry led her to the northern tip of the Birch farm, where he, with help from his pa and Barry's younger brother, Lance, had begun building their future home. Arabella loved seeing his progress. Every time she stopped by the site, a little more had been done. By this time, the foundation had been laid and she could visualize where the rooms would be.

"See there?" Barry pointed to a corner. "There's the parlor, and next to that is the dinin' room. In back is the kitchen. I have one bedroom on the bottom floor, just as you said you wanted. When we put up the second story, there'll be four more bedrooms."

She imagined the completed house. "It'll be awfully beautiful. I can't get over how big it's turning out to be."

"It might seem big now, but we'll fill it with children soon enough."

She blushed at the thought and took interest in grass growing nearby.

Barry set a clean brown horse blanket on a flat, grassy spot and motioned for her to sit. She kept her demeanor as ladylike as possible, situating her legs to one side and crossing them at the ankles. He followed suit, crossing his legs Indian style.

Glancing around, she recalled how years ago he had carved their initials together on a huge oak. The letters were still there, darkened with time. Arabella was glad the tree would be part of their front yard. Both of them loved their special place under that particular tree.

At midday, cottony clouds dotted the azure sky. In a moment of whimsy, Arabella could imagine angels playing harps as they floated in the sky, watching them picnic by their future home.

Barry broke into her thoughts. "You seem a million miles away."

"I reckon I am. I was thinking of angels."

He looked at the sky. "Do you think they're watchin' us?"

The way he reflected her thoughts made her feel close to him whenever they shared conversation. They were so in love with one another she couldn't imagine a moment of unhappiness with him. If only others wouldn't get in their way. "I wish I had an angel standing beside me now. I need some help for what I have to tell you."

A look of slight alarm and fear visited his features. "How so?"

She paused. "It's Father. He said we can't marry until after the war's over."

Barry's brow knitted. "That's a surprise. I thought your father was actually lookin' forward to the day we married. What changed his mind?"

"He didn't say we can never marry. He just said he doesn't want me to be a war widow."

"There's no danger of that, since I won't be fightin'." He frowned. "Oh, but you didn't tell him that."

"Of course I didn't. We agreed not to." Arabella brought her attention to the light lunch, but hunger eluded her.

He leaned on one elbow. "Maybe if we did, that would change things."

"I don't know. It might make things worse."

"I don't want to wait so long to marry you. You're the love of my life."

"Oh, Barry, you know I feel the same way about you. I've loved you forever."

He shifted upward and leaned toward her. When he took her hand in his, shivers ran up her back. "Then we'll have to find a way to be together forever, war or no war. I have a plan. Just you wait and see."

Arabella could only hope it would work.

Chapter 4

Barry got up from his milking stool and stretched. The occasional moo and familiar sound of the cows chewing their feed soothed him each day. Often he sang to the cows. They didn't mind that his voice wasn't good enough for the church choir. He ushered them back into the fenced field. Only after he had cleaned his tin bucket and stored the milk for future use did he seek out his father and brother in the south barn.

"Done milkin', Pa."

"Good, Barry. Why don't you help me and Lance finish up here in the barn? It won't take long."

Without protest, Barry took up a shovel. The animals needed constant attention and tending, but Barry didn't mind. He'd grown up on the farm and was accustomed to the work. The physical release felt rewarding. He didn't even mind the pungent, sweaty smell of the animals, and felt satisfaction in replenishing their stalls with fresh hay.

On the rare occasions he rode into Morgantown, he looked at the buildings and thought about the people who worked inside them. Feeling sorry for them, Barry couldn't imagine staying cooped up inside all day. He'd feel trapped.

He looked over at his younger brother. Lance wasn't so little anymore. He could pull his weight with the chores. That fact lightened Barry's load, but not for long. As soon as he married Arabella, he would have his own farm, and all the chores would be his—at least until they had sons large enough to help.

After vigorous work, he took a quick break to lean on the shovel and contemplate life. He thanked the Lord daily that helping with the farm had shielded him from serving in the Army of the Republic. So far, so good.

At that moment, his six-year-old sister, Rachel, ran into the barn. "Pa! Pa!"

He turned to acknowledge his little girl. Barry noticed she panted from exertion. "Silas is back!"

Barry's heart nearly stopped beating. His brother was back from the battlefield? But he wasn't supposed to return for at least another month.

Rachel's panting grew less pronounced. "They brought him in a wagon. The men were wearin' Union uniforms."

To Barry's mind, Rachel's report didn't sound right. "Where's Silas now?"

"In a chair!"

This time Barry was almost certain his heart stopped. "You mean, he's sittin' in the parlor chair?"

She shook her head. "No. He's in a chair that's got wheels. He says he gets to sit in it all the time."

"No!" Pa threw his shovel so hard it almost hit Friday in the knees. The horse jumped and squealed.

Normally Barry would have stopped to console his beloved horse, but Pa and Silas needed him more. He placed his hands on Pa's shoulders to calm him. "It might not be so bad, Pa. Let's go see Silas and find out."

"Bad? Is it bad, Pa?" Rachel's expression went from happy to distressed.

"God will take care of us no matter what our situation." Barry patted his little sister on the back. "Come on, let's go see him."

Pa and Barry rushed to the house. "I wish I hadn't missed the wagon," Pa lamented.

"I'm just glad they brought him home." Barry kept stride with Pa. Though older, Pa could move swiftly when he set his mind to it. "Maybe his condition's only temporary."

Walking by his pa, Barry felt mixed emotions. He wanted Silas home, but not at the price of a terrible wound. As they entered the house through the back door, Barry braced himself to see his brother. Nothing could have prepared him for the sight of Silas, once so tall and strong. Now he slouched in a wheelchair. The expression on his face looked stony, as though he didn't want to think about his present situation. Not that Barry could blame him.

Ma stood beside her dark-haired son, misty-eyed. Barry had never seen her so pale.

"Son! What have they done to you?" Pa embraced Silas, who returned the gesture. Barry let out an audible sigh of relief with the realization that his brother could still move his arms.

"Pa." Silas was unusually taciturn, even for him.

Barry went for an embrace. "Good to have you back, Silas. Home for good."

"Home for good." Silas sneered.

"You have so much to be thankful for. We have so much to be thankful for." Ma wiped her eyes with her everyday white cotton handkerchief. "So many of our brave men have died. But you're here, safe with us."

Silas snarled. "So much to be thankful for. Like the bullet that hit me in the back."

"But you're alive!" Ma reminded him.

"To live for what? I still feel pain. And Bridget won't want to marry me now."

"Hush," Ma said. "Don't think of such things."

"But Ma, I can't provide for her no more. I can't provide for nobody. I'm useless. Just a useless hunk o' flesh." Silas, the brother Barry had looked up to his whole life, cried.

Never talkative, Silas remained even more uncommunicative than usual the rest of the evening. Ma veered from too cheerful to tearful. The men tried to act as though nothing unusual had happened, with limited success. Rachel seemed confused and quiet.

After dinner, they had visitors. Bridget had brought Arabella along with her. Normally Barry would have been ecstatic to see her, but the pall over the Birch household kept any of them from gladness. All the same, he couldn't help but say a silent prayer to the Lord thanking Him for such a lovely woman.

Arabella and Bridget had been friends since childhood. Barry sensed that Bridget brought along her friend for support. As usual, word had traveled fast. Bridget's nervous attitude and Arabella's awkward greeting told him that everyone in town knew, not only that Silas had come home but that he'd been wounded.

After everyone exchanged greetings, Barry led the women to the study in the back of the house, where Silas had cloistered himself to read. He motioned for them to stay back while he approached his brother.

"Silas, you have visitors."

"I told you I want to be alone. Tell 'em to go away."

"You don't mean that." Barry turned to the women, who were still within earshot. "He doesn't mean that. He's overtired, that's all."

Bridget lifted her dainty chin and headed toward the den. "He'll see me."

Barry and Arabella hovered near the door. When Barry saw Bridget's eyes mist and her down-turned mouth quiver, he discerned the news for Silas wouldn't be good. Without a word, she flung herself on him, crossing her arms on his lap. She set her face in her arms and sobbed.

Silas stroked her hair, looking at her with the expression of a condemned man.

Barry took Arabella's hand and led her out of the room and into the front parlor. Arabella didn't protest.

"It's not so good for him, is it?" Standing by an upholstered rocker, Arabella dabbed her eyes with an embroidered white handkerchief.

"The doctors said there's no. . .no hope. . .for recovery." Discouraged, he plopped onto the black horsehair sofa in front of the fireplace.

"Then that means she won't marry him."

His heart hurt for his brother. "Did she say that?"

Arabella nodded and looked ashamed. "She told me outright on the way over here."

"Is there somebody else?" Barry felt ire rise in his chest.

"Not directly, but everybody knows there are plenty of men for Bridget."

The realization of what Arabella said took awhile to sink in for Barry. So Bridget could drop his brother, just like that. Sadness, anger, and sympathy visited him at once, leaving him not knowing how to feel.

"Oh, Barry, this is awful." Despite her strong statement, Arabella kept her voice soft enough so the others in the house, including his parents in the kitchen, wouldn't hear.

"I—I didn't think she'd leave him."

Arabella touched his forearm. "You're worried, aren't you? Worried that I'll do the same thing. Don't think like that. I don't care what happens; I'd never leave you."

No words formed on Barry's lips. Arabella's devotion had touched him too much.

❧❧❧

A few days later, Barry watched as Lance brought in a heap of wood, the aroma of oak mixing with the scent of Ma's venison roast. Lance threw it into the bin without complaint. The number of logs astonished Barry. Not so long ago, Lance would have struggled to carry half as many.

Pa nodded in approval. "Lance, you're growin' up. Growin' up fast."

Lance brought himself up to his full height and puffed out his chest. "Sure am, Pa. And I can't wait to have a big slice of that good venison, Ma. I'm mighty hungry."

Barry couldn't suppress a grin. Lance reminded Barry of himself at thirteen in both looks and demeanor.

Pa sniffed the air. "Yep, your ma sure does cook good. No wonder you've gotten so big, Lance. So what do you think? Do you think you're old enough to help me out here on the farm while Barry goes off to fight in the war?"

Barry's heart lurched.

"Fight in the war?" Ma stopped peeling a yam in midstroke. "Haven't we sacrificed enough? One of our sons is already a—a—cripple now."

"But think of the many other families who have sacrificed even more. And look at us. We still have Rachel and Lance."

"But—"

"I'm sorry, but I've made my decision. It's high time Barry went off and did his part." He eyed Barry. "Isn't that right, son?"

Barry wasn't sure what to say. "War is a serious business, Pa."

"Sure it is. We have Silas to prove that much. But now this family needs to do Silas proud. Show that his sacrifice was worth everything. As soon as we celebrate Lance's fourteenth birthday next week, I want you to sign up for the Union Army."

Chapter 5

The next Sunday, Arabella couldn't help but think about how glad she was that Bridget didn't go to their church. She'd hoped Bridget would change her mind about leaving Silas once she saw him, but her heart remained hard. Her dream that she and Bridget would be sisters-in-law was now nothing more than a memory. Bridget cried on the way home after she saw Silas in his broken condition. Surely seeing him unable to move, bound by a heavy chair even though he still sat upright and proud, had been a shock. But what good were her tears when she was abandoning the man she'd planned to marry?

Bridget wouldn't be alone long. But what about Silas? What did the future hold for him? Arabella had added Silas to her nightly prayers. She could understand, in a small way, Bridget's fear of marrying a man who could no longer walk. And she could understand Silas's fear and uncertainty about his own future. She prayed God would reveal His plan to them.

Barry's presence brightened her thoughts when she spotted him waiting for her at the church door, as was his custom. For her father's sake, she tried not to seem too eager when Barry was nearby. Sitting by him comforted her, but he seemed nervous. During worship, he didn't concentrate on singing, and, uncharacteristically for him, even missed a line. From time to time he squeezed her hand; but otherwise, she could sense he wasn't himself. By the time worship was over, she felt vexed.

After church, as soon as they had complimented the preacher on his sermon and bid him farewell, Barry took Arabella by the arm. She walked with him toward one of the large oak trees growing in a cluster beside the church. The other congregants, including their respective parents, were immersed in their own conversations. By the time they reached the tree, standing under its protective branches, her nerves had reached such a peak she couldn't even enjoy the spring breeze or the beauty of blooming dogwood trees.

He took her hands in his and faced her. "I have news, Arabella." His eyes caught the sunlight, showing his worry. He took in a breath.

She couldn't wait much longer. "What is it? Does it have something to do with Silas?"

"Not exactly." He paused. "You know how Lance'll be celebratin' his fourteenth birthday this Saturday?"

She nodded. "We're still planning to be at his party."

"Yep, the party's still takin' place. But now that Lance is older and gettin' stronger every day, Pa insists he can take care of the farm with him. In my place."

For the first time, Arabella felt a glimmer of hope. "Then the house can be built even faster, and the barn for the cows, too."

"I wish that's what it meant. But it isn't. You see, Pa insists that I sign up for military service next week."

Barry could see by her open mouth that Arabella didn't expect such a proclamation. "Next week? What's your father thinking, Barry? How many of his sons does he want to sacrifice?"

"As many as he has, it looks like."

"What will we do? You can't go." She touched his arm. "You haven't told your pa how you feel, have you?"

"No. And I don't want to. But it looks like I'll have to take a stand. And I'm goin' to do that at Lance's birthday party. Maybe with so many people around, Pa won't punch me in the gut."

"Barry! I wouldn't think he'd do that under the worst of circumstances."

"I don't reckon he will, but he's gonna be awful mad." Barry let out a breath. "All jestin' aside, everybody I hold in high regard will be at that party. I'd rather tell them all at once than to have people wonder about me. Let them know the truth, straight from my lips."

"It won't be easy to take such a public stand, but I admire you for it." She searched for words to encourage him. "But maybe you can ease your pa into it. Can't you talk to Silas? Surely he'd be willing to say something to him for you. I know you and Silas have never been the best of friends, but he is your brother, and surely he wouldn't wish you to be a cripple—or worse."

"I know, but I don't think I can depend on him. If anything, he respects me even less now. No, Arabella. I'm on my own."

"You're not on your own. You have the Lord. And you have me."

⤳⤳⤳

Lance's birthday arrived all too soon. Barry dreaded the party but remained patient as games were played and they ate Ma's special cake. Arabella hadn't left his side all evening. Even with her presence, Barry felt tense as he waited for Lance to finish his birthday treat.

Arabella squeezed his hand without anyone noticing. The end of the party was near, and people shifted in their seats in preparation for bidding farewell for the evening. The time had come.

Barry cleared his throat and stood in front of his chair. "I have an announcement to make."

Pa stood. "I know what it is, son, and I'm mighty proud of you for it."

Ma started to weep. "Did you have to spoil the party by reminding us?"

Pa patted Barry on the back, which was as affectionate as he ever got toward a son. "Don't pay your ma no mind. She understands what we men have to do."

Barry glanced at Arabella. Clear-eyed, she gave him a small nod of encouragement. "I know you think all us men have to join in the war effort, but good men can have a difference of opinion and still be good men."

"A difference of opinion?" Pa's hand fell away.

"That's right, Pa." He summoned his courage and looked his father in the eye. "I'm not servin' in the army."

Pa took a step away from Barry. "What's that you say?"

He summoned the courage to repeat his proclamation. "I said—I'm not servin' in the army."

"You mean, not right now." Pa's voice took on a tone of someone trying to understand the unknowable. "Maybe after you and Arabella wed."

"No, Pa. Not now, not ever."

Lance jumped from his spot on the floor, ignoring that a new slingshot fell from his lap. "Can I go in his place, Pa?"

"Of course not. You're too young." Pa's mouth formed an unrelenting line.

"Why don't you wanna go?" Lance cut his gaze to their wounded brother. "Is it because of Silas?"

Barry cringed. He couldn't help but look at his brother, broken, in a wheelchair. Silas stared at him, his mouth down-turned, his eyes expressionless. "I might as well tell you all now. I haven't told anybody but Arabella, but I made a promise to Grandpappy long ago that I'd never use my skill as a marksman to kill another human."

Pa harrumphed and crossed his arms. "Your grandpappy meant well, but he was soft. Too soft. And he couldn't foresee this terrible war."

Barry stood at his full height and faced his father. "Maybe so, but I agree with how he felt, and I plan to keep my promise to him. I just can't bring myself to kill another human, no matter how noble the cause. I'm sorry. I know that disappoints all of you. Some people might think refusin' to fight isn't manly, but I thought the least I could do was be man enough to face you all here today with my decision. I respect each of you, and I hope my stand won't cause you to think less of me, even if you disagree."

Arabella rose to her feet and stood by Barry's side. She surveyed everyone in the room: her parents, her future in-laws, their friends. "I'm not disappointed. Unionist, Confederate, pacifist. I don't care. I'll stand by you, no matter what."

Arabella's father stood, his face red. "Barry, don't you know I'm passionate about the Union cause?"

"Yes, sir. And I respect that. I want the Union to win, too."

"Then you should go and fight to help keep the states together, as one. As it should be."

Barry anticipated his future father-in-law might disagree with his position, but he hadn't expected such vitriol. "Yes, sir. I respect what you say. Every day I support the Union with my prayers. But I won't lift a weapon in anger against another human."

Mr. Lambert's face turned redder as he faced his daughter. "And you agree with this?"

She shrank in posture, but nodded.

"I do not, and I will not put up with such foolishness. I don't want you to be a widow. But I don't want you to marry no coward, either. I forbid you to marry him at all. Ever."

"Father, no!"

"Mr. Lambert. . ." Barry held up his hands to calm his future father-in-law.

Pa strode to Mr. Lambert and stood inches from him. Taller than Arabella's father, Pa's muscular build suggested he would win any fight between them. "Now lookee here, Lambert. Nobody gets to call my son a name, especially right here in my own house."

"I'll refrain from name-calling in the future." Mr. Lambert eyed his family, addressing his wife first. "Melanie, fetch my hat. Arabella, you're leaving with me."

"I don't want to, Father." She stood by her fiancé. "I want to stay here. With the man I plan to marry."

"No, you will go with me."

"Go with him, Arabella." Fighting his emotions, Barry clenched his fists by his sides. "You're livin' under your father's roof, and you must honor him as God commands."

Arabella looked at Barry, then back at her father.

"That's the first sensible thing he's said all day. Come with me, daughter."

Without further argument or discussion from any of the guests, the party broke up and everyone left with a much more somber spirit than they'd possessed when they arrived. Barry fought to keep from sprinting after Arabella, to beg her to run away and marry him that day; but he couldn't dishonor her in such a way. Since Arabella's sister had already eloped, he couldn't imagine she'd agree to such a wild scheme even if he asked. He took comfort in the fact she glanced at him with yearning before she left.

As soon as they shut the front door after the last guest departed, Lance scowled at Barry. "Thanks for ruinin' my party."

"I'm sorry, Lance. I didn't mean to. I didn't expect Mr. Lambert to explode like that."

The apology didn't take the frown off Lance's face. Not that Barry blamed his brother. He tried again. "There was no other time to take a stand. Pa was askin' me to sign up for military service next week. But I can't do that, you see."

"I'm mighty disappointed in you, son." The resignation in Pa's voice broke Barry's heart more than his initial anger. "I didn't want to say nothin' in front of the Lamberts, but you're lettin' down your family, and these great United States."

Barry cut his gaze to Ma. "Is that how you feel?"

Ma nodded, but she wouldn't allow her eyes to meet his. What could Barry expect? Ma would never say anything in disagreement with Pa. Barry didn't bother to ask Lance. He could see the disrespect in his younger brother's eyes. Rachel was still too small to understand adult concerns and looked confused by the whole discussion.

"Of course all of us think you should go," Pa said. "Especially with your brother havin' made such a sacrifice."

Barry could only look to his older brother for understanding. Perhaps Arabella had been right. Perhaps, since he knew firsthand the horrors of war and had suffered such a life-altering injury, he would support Barry's efforts to take a stand. "Silas?"

He didn't answer or meet Barry's gaze.

Barry walked to Silas's side and placed his hand on one of the chair's handles. "I respect and admire what you did, and I understand why you went. But do you think it will help the country for two Birch men to become broken over this senseless bloodletting?"

Barry expected his brother at least to give the question some thought, but Silas didn't hesitate with his answer. "Yes, I do think it'll help. The more rebs we can kill, the better. If we don't win, this country won't ever be the same."

"I want us to win, too."

"Do you now?" Silas snarled. "Do you want us to win enough to go and sacrifice everything? Maybe even your life? No one wants to lose his life in this war, Barry, but you're a coward to let others go and not go yourself."

Lance interrupted. "Silas is right. I know you think I'm a baby, Pa, but I'm not. I want to go. Let me go."

"No!" Pa's hard look almost made Barry wonder if he'd have to walk out and select a switch for himself to be whipped. "See what you've done, Barry? A boy wants to take your place."

"I won't let Lance take my place."

"You don't got nothin' to say about it. You're yeller, and that's not what a Birch is supposed to be. I hate you!" Lance ran upstairs.

Barry followed him to his room. Lance tried to shut the door before Barry could catch up to him, but he was too fast. "I need to talk to you."

"Leave me alone." Lance seemed to have a storm cloud over his head as he sat on the small maple bed and kicked his legs back and forth off the side.

"No. I have to talk to you."

Lance crossed his arms and stared at the unadorned pine wardrobe across the room. "I ain't listenin'."

"You think this is all fun and games, don't you? Like shootin' at targets."

He shook his head.

"You've got to understand that war is not a boy's game, but a man's sorrow.

Don't you see Silas in that horrible wheelchair? Do you want that for yourself? Or worse?"

"There can't be no worse than bein' lily-livered."

"Yes, there can. There can be not livin' to see your fifteenth birthday."

Lance's expression flickered with thought ever so briefly before he caught himself. "I don't care."

"Yes, you do. Besides, the army won't take you. You're too young. So just get that notion out of your head right now."

"I'll lie about my age."

Distressed, Barry noticed his brother's thin frame. "You may be strong, but you're skinny. They'll take one look at you and turn you down."

"I'll figure out a way."

Barry wished he hadn't mentioned it. He tried again. "They won't take you. I'm sure of it. And you know Ma doesn't want you to go. Don't you see her cryin' every day over Silas?"

"That's exactly why I want to go so bad. I want to kill the Johnny Reb that put Silas in a wheelchair." Lance's eyes narrowed.

"You can kill a thousand rebs but nothin' will make Silas walk again."

"Maybe not. But if I can make some rebs miserable, I will."

Barry could see that his brother was becoming overwrought. "You're tired and excited tonight. Things will look different tomorrow."

Chapter 6

Arabella didn't say anything to her parents on the way home. Father was furious, and her appealing to Mother wouldn't do any good. Why did Father have to make such a scene in front of the whole Birch family? If only Barry would elope with her, she'd go in a minute. She didn't care anymore that Mary Lou had already upset their parents with her elopement. In her eyes, Barry had more honor than the men who were fighting in the war. Where was the honor in killing? Many of them wanted adventure and hadn't even thought through what they were fighting for or what the war meant. Yet Father seemed unrelenting about Barry.

By the time they got home, Arabella had calmed herself enough to try to discuss the evening with them. As expected, Father went straight for his newspaper in the study. Arabella followed him. Mother followed as well, which didn't surprise her.

"Father, we need to talk."

Ignoring her until he sat in his brown leather chair, the look he finally did give her didn't leave her feeling confident the conversation would go her way. She had to try all the same. "I think you're being unfair to Barry. He's a good man."

Father straightened the newspaper. "Not if he won't defend our Union. You know I'm an ardent Unionist."

"Yes, Father, and I pray for our soldiers every night."

"Then you can understand how I feel. You can do better than to marry a coward." He looked at Arabella's mother. "Isn't that right, Melanie?"

Arabella noticed that her mother looked as though she wished she hadn't been drawn into the conversation. "I agree with what you say, my dear."

As usual with any edict from Father, Arabella was alone in trying to overturn it. "I'm sorry, Father, but I can't agree. Barry is not a coward. It takes more courage to take an unpopular stand than to fight in a war you don't believe in."

His face took on a paternal expression. "You're an innocent. I can't expect you to understand manly ideas such as honor, courage, and duty. Women are not called to serve in the same way we men are. You can be forgiven for not understanding."

"I know things seem dark now," Mother interjected, "but there are a lot of fish in the sea. As pretty as you are, you'll find someone else soon."

"Even if I wanted to go fishing—and I don't—where are they?" she couldn't resist asking. "The men are at war."

177

"They'll return," Father said, "and you can choose from any number of war heroes."

More likely, Father would choose one for her. Despite her frustration, Arabella decided not to say more lest she lose everything. At least he hadn't forbidden her from seeing Barry at church functions and elsewhere. She was determined to let Barry know she would never abandon him. Whatever war hero her father chose for her would never do. If she couldn't wed Barry, she would be an old maid.

The next day Barry shaved with care, even as he could think of nothing but the previous night. How could he let Arabella know that he would always love her? Maybe he shouldn't. If he let her go, she'd be free to marry another. Maybe that was best. She deserved better than to be hitched to a pacifist. While other men bravely fought, he remained behind. And now he could no longer hide behind his older brother. Everyone knew how he felt. There was no turning back.

Arabella. Images of her flowed through his head. If he couldn't have her, he'd be a confirmed bachelor.

Without warning, Barry heard his mother scream in agony. The sound came from Lance's room. He dropped his razor. What could it be? Terrible scenarios ran through Barry's mind as he rushed down the hall.

He ran through the door of his little brother's bedroom. "What's wrong, Ma?"

Her labored breathing made it hard for her to speak. "It's Lance. He—he's gone."

Barry looked at his brother's empty bed. "Gone?"

She nodded. Tears rolled down her cheeks. She handed him a note. "Read this."

Deer Ma:

Sorry to leeve without sayin goodby like I shuld hav, but if I had, you wuldn't hav let me go. I'm off to surve in the Army. Now, I know I'm not reelly old enough yet. I can lye about my age. Don't worry—it's for a gud cause, and like you always say, it's not a gud idea to tell a lye, but somtimes you hav to for a gud cause. Like that time you told Aunt Janet that her hat looked reel gud, but evrybody else made fun of her behind her back.

Now don't you worry, Ma. I won't be like Silas. I'll be all write. And Barry can help on the farm.

Your son,
Lance

Tears rolled down Ma's cheeks.

Barry tried to embrace her, but she pushed him away. "This is your fault. You should be going, not Lance."

He never thought his mother would be so angry with him. How much more would he have to lose over this war? "I tried to talk to Lance, but he wouldn't listen."

Pa came into the room. "What's all the commotion? I heard you two all the way in the kitchen."

"Lance ran off to join the army," Ma wailed.

"What?" Pa glowered at Barry. "This is all your doin'."

Barry felt helpless. "No, Pa. I tried to talk to him. But he wants revenge for what the rebs did to Silas. There wasn't no talkin' sense into him."

"Get out of my sight."

Seeing the rage-filled glint in Pa's eyes, Barry complied. No matter how rash Lance had been, no matter how much everyone wanted Silas to get well, no matter how much his parents hated him, Barry had to stand his ground. He couldn't change his mind.

But he could pray.

⁂

Tension ran high in the Birch household the next few days without relief. Barry could feel his family seething at him. Even Ma treated him almost like a houseguest she had to tolerate. To get away from them, he took as much refuge as he could in building his house. He prayed he could one day live in it with Arabella, but with or without her, he would have another place to go. The home of his childhood suddenly felt too small.

When he got low on nails, Barry went to the mercantile to buy more. The ring of the bell as he opened the door gave him a sense of familiarity and anticipation.

He eyed Bruce Nesbit and Cory Wilson playing a game of checkers in front of the pot-bellied stove. They had been distant neighbors of the Birch family for decades, but had never taken a special shine to Barry. Still, out of respect, he put on a cordial front when they met. "Mornin' Mr. Nesbit. Mr. Wilson."

Mr. Nesbit looked up with disinterest, then his eyeswidened. His mouth formed a crooked line that couldn't decide if it should be a grin or a smirk. "Lookee here, Cory."

Mr. Wilson nodded. "Lookee, lookee. Wonder what he wants?"

"Yeller thread, I'd say." Mr. Nesbit chortled. "And yeller cloth to make a uniform."

Barry flinched, though he tried to ignore the remark. He sought out the storekeeper behind the counter and resolved to complete his errand as quickly as possible. "Mornin', Zeke. I'll take a pound of iron nails."

Zeke nodded and shot a warning look to the older men. The storekeeper had always been a decent sort.

"I'm sorry to hear about your brother."

Barry nodded. "I'm really proud of him."

Reaching for the nails, Zeke seemed as eager to change the subject as Barry. "How's that house of yours comin' along?"

"Just fine. I think I'll be done by fall."

"Sure you're man enough to build a house?" Mr. Nesbit snickered.

"Or to do anything else?" Mr. Wilson muttered.

Barry felt his face grow hot and hoped he wasn't blushing, which would only add to his embarrassment and make him appear weaker. So Mr. Lambert must have said something to someone about the birthday party and the stand Barry had taken. At least Arabella didn't have to endure the taunts.

The bell on the door tinkled. As if summoned, Arabella entered, along with her mother.

Mr. Wilson rose and wiped the smirk from his face, tipping his hat to the ladies. "Good mornin', Mrs. Lambert. Miss Lambert."

Mr. Nesbit followed with a greeting.

"Good morning, Mr. Nesbit. And to you, too, Mr. Wilson." Arabella glanced at Barry long enough to realize his identity, and allowed her gaze to linger a little longer than necessary.

"Good mornin', Mrs. Lambert. Good mornin', Arabella." Barry kept his tone familiar, but not too familiar.

Arabella smiled. "Barry."

"Good morning, Barry." He felt relieved that Arabella's mother displayed warmth with her voice.

He surveyed the mercantile for Arabella's father. Arabella shot her gaze to the side and back to indicate he didn't have to worry—at least for the time being.

"How may I help you today, Mrs. Lambert?" Zeke asked.

Arabella touched her mother's sleeve. "Can I browse for fabric, Mother?"

Mrs. Lambert glanced at Barry, her gaze filled with sympathy. She nodded.

Barry sent her a quick smile. He was thankful to have an ally in Arabella's mother. He lingered around a set of tools on display, along with several pocketknives of fine quality. Then, after Arabella had a chance to browse a moment, he discreetly made his way to the fabric.

When she realized he was nearby, love shone in her eyes. He knew, at that moment, she would always love him. A lump formed in his throat. He had to think of a way to convince her father they could marry. He just had to.

She rubbed her hand against a bolt of cloth. "This yellow is a nice color. It would look good with your hair. I think this shade would pick up the gold highlights, especially as summer makes it blonder."

Yellow. Of all the colors in the world—sweet, oblivious Arabella had to choose yellow. Barry felt a sensation much like his heart falling into his stomach. He glanced around the store. He'd be eternally thankful that his taunters had made their exit.

"I—I think I'd prefer blue. In fact, I might take home a couple of yards so Ma can sew me a new shirt."

"I'd love to sew a new shirt for you, no matter what the color." Arabella's voice sounded soft.

"I'd love you to sew a shirt for me, too. And a pair of work pants." He touched a bolt of dark denim. Sturdy and serviceable, the fabric would hold up well against hard farm work. Still, as much as he'd like new clothes, they both knew they weren't really talking about fabric.

"This red would look nice on you." She held up a roll of chamois cloth near his face. Her gaze met his. "I wouldn't sew for any other man, you know."

"And I wouldn't take new clothes sewn by any other woman." Then he realized he had to make an exemption. "'Cept for Ma." He grinned.

He glanced around the store and saw that no one was paying attention to them. With a quick motion, he took her little hand in his and gave it a quick squeeze. Oh, to have the right to hold her hand, uninhibited, in public. And in private. But with Mr. Lambert's decree that they were not permitted to marry, he would never be allowed to hold her hand freely again. The thought of losing her was enough to make him wish he had the kind of constitution to make him run to the army. But he couldn't. All he could do was pray for God to show them a way to wed.

Chapter 7

"Wake up, Barry. I let you sleep as long as I could," Ma said. "You've got just enough time to milk the cows before you wash up to go to church."

Church. For the first time in memory, he didn't want to go. The men mocking him in the store rang in his mind. Did people in church know? Surely they wouldn't be so bold as to make snide remarks about Barry's stand in God's house. The idea of facing his congregation, now that his secret was out, upset Barry.

But there was one shining star he couldn't forget. Arabella worshipped with him. And she had committed to staying by his side. The thought of her urged him to ready himself for church.

Later that morning, shoulders squared as much as any soldier, he pushed Silas in his wheelchair and entered the white framed church with his family. Some of the church members turned to look at them. Silas clenched his jaw as a few stares went his way. But Barry also knew no small number of glares and curious looks were directed at him. As far as Barry knew, no one else in town had made a public proclamation of refusal to serve in the war. No one discussed those who paid immigrants to serve in their place. Judging from the looks Barry got, he was fodder for the local gossips. Maybe something else—something happy, he hoped—would happen soon so the busybodies would move on to other things.

Arabella sought him out and sat with him. He heard a couple of women whispering and hoped they weren't saying anything unsavory about her.

"Maybe you'd better move." As much as it pained Barry to make the suggestion, for Arabella's sake, he felt he had no other choice.

"You don't want to sit with me?"

"I want you to sit with me. Very much. But I don't want your life at home to be unhappy because of me. I know your father doesn't approve."

"Mother is softening him up for me. He's still mad, but he really can't keep us apart here at church without causing a stir. He doesn't want to call attention to our family that way." She smoothed her skirt.

"Well, we'd better not linger after church. I don't want to upset him."

Arabella nodded and handed him a letter. She was just in time, too, as her father called her away a moment later.

Even though he knew he shouldn't have, Barry read the letter quickly when he was supposed to be singing "When I Survey the Wondrous Cross" from the hymnal.

Courage of the Heart

Dear Barry:

    I don't care what they say about you—about us. You are the love of my life and you always will be. I don't want you to fight in this awful war, so don't back down. You are honorable and right to keep your word to your grandfather. God will show us what to do. I just know it.

Love always,
Arabella

Barry put the letter in his suit coat, in the pocket next to his heart. He would keep it, and Arabella, near his heart forever.

A few days later, Barry and Silas were sitting outdoors in the backyard, relaxing and enjoying the April sunshine, when the towheaded Stimple twins ran to the farm. He remembered Rachel running to tell them Silas had returned from the war. Judging from their serious expressions, the news the twins had to share couldn't be good.

Silas looked up from his novel. "What's wrong?"

The ten-year-old boys stopped and panted for breath. "It's Morgantown."

"What about it?" Barry folded his newspaper.

Robbie caught his breath long enough to answer. "The South. They're raidin' the town for supplies."

A shocked and concerned expression covered Silas's face. "How do you know?"

"Let me tell it." Bobby launched into the story. "Mr. Lambert told us, and said we needed to spread the word. Nobody knows where the rebs might head next."

"I hope they don't come out this far from town. But we've got to take precautions, get the cows up, and do our best to protect what little we have, lest they do decide to go on a rampage."

Barry cut his gaze to the boys. Robbie had stopped panting, and his cheeks, ruddy from his exertion, had softened. "We gotta keep goin'. After we spread the word to the Mannin' farm, we have to head back home."

The Manning farm was quite a distance. Barry wondered if the boys could make it that far. "Can I fetch you boys a cup of water?"

Robbie shook his head. "Nope. We need to get goin'."

The men bid the young messengers farewell and watched them depart. Silas barely let them get out of earshot before challenging Barry. "Whatcha goin' to do if they come out this far? You goin' to shoot? Or you just goin' to sit there like a bump on a log?"

Barry clenched his teeth.

Silas drummed his fingers on the book in his lap. "I've seen how people stare at you whenever you leave the house. And Pa don't have much respect for you no more, either. You know, you can redeem yourself if you go to

Morgantown and defend her. I'd do it myself if I wasn't in this chair." He hit the wheel with his fist.

Barry stared at his brother, so pitiful and paralyzed. If only things had been different. Then Silas wouldn't be broken for the rest of his life and his younger brother would be home, with no worry more cumbersome than what to expect for dinner. "It'll take me awhile to navigate the mountains, but I'll do it. I'll go there and defend the supplies."

Silas beamed, letting the book drop to the ground. "You really mean that?"

"I do."

"I'm so proud of you, Barry. I've never been more proud of you. Now get a move on."

After retrieving the book for his brother, Barry rolled Silas into the kitchen.

Silas couldn't contain his excitement. "Did you hear, Ma?"

"There you are. I was just about to call you in for lunch."

"But Ma," Silas persisted, "did you hear?"

"Hear what?"

"The South's raidin' Morgantown."

Ma dropped her spoon on the counter. "What?"

Silas repeated the news the twins shared. "Barry's goin' in to defend the town. Isn't that right, Barry?"

He nodded, but his stomach felt as though it had turned into a millstone.

"You are? But it'll take you forever to get there. It's so far away."

"But too close to ignore," Barry pointed out.

Ma rushed to him for an embrace. "Be careful, son. You should eat lunch before you go. And I'll pack you some food."

"I don't want lunch, but I could use the provisions. I'm not hungry now." Taking his leave of them, he went back upstairs to his room to retrieve a musket. He would have chosen the Henry rifle, but that belonged to Pa. In his lack of enthusiasm, he couldn't hurry his steps. The gun rack over his bed held his trusted musket. He knew how the weapon bucked, and how to aim it for accuracy. A collection of antlers testified to his skill.

The powder horn and ball case waited in their usual place in his top dresser drawer. He paused, looking around his boyhood room. The small iron bed he slept in, with its warm quilt made by his grandmother. The little multicolored braided rug handcrafted by his mother from rags. A pine cabinet that stored his clothes. Two windows framed by cotton curtains his mother had sewn when he was a child.

What type of rooms did Southerners leave? Did they look much like his? Did their mothers and sweethearts write to them every day? Did any of them take a stand against fighting—and feel the disdain and wrath of their fellow townsmen for it?

Rolling a loose musket ball between his fingers, he marveled at how something that appeared so innocent could become a lethal projectile. Could he kill a man? His marksmanship was good enough, but the thought of shooting to kill a human made his blood run cold.

He put the horn and case back into his drawer and placed his weapon back into its rack. With a slow pace, he returned to the kitchen.

Silas was the first to notice Barry was unarmed. "Where's your musket? What's the matter?"

"I'm not goin', Silas." Barry's voice sounded as a whisper.

Silas's eyes widened then narrowed. "You don't mean that."

Vexation clutched him. "I do mean it. I can't use my skills as a marksman to kill another human. I know that disappoints you, but I can't do it."

"Nobody wants to kill another human." Silas looked at his lap. "I might be paralyzed now, but I took out a few rebs myself before one got the best of me." Barry was taken aback by the mixture of pride and sorrow that filled his brother's voice.

"Wasn't that hard to do?"

"Of course it was hard to do. But I did it for my country. And I'd do it again. Our generation has been called to save this great nation, Barry. You've got to do your part. For me. For Lance."

Silas knew how to hit Barry where it hurt. "God has a plan for everybody's life. I don't think He has called me to fight. I don't feel that leanin' in my heart. I know I'm in this generation and a lot of people feel the same way you do, but I don't. I respect your feelin's, and I'd like to earn your pride and respect. But I can't. Not like this. I can't go. I won't go."

"Then you really are a lily-livered coward." The voice growling at him didn't sound like the brother Barry knew. "You'll never have my respect, and I doubt you'll ever have Pa's again, either. And do you think Lance will ever think the same of you? A boy is out there on the battlefield now, doing a man's job, and it's all your fault."

"I'm sorry Lance made such a foolish choice, but I didn't force him to do that. He wants revenge for what that reb did to you. Vengeance is the Lord's, but Lance doesn't want to believe that. He thinks he's bein' brave to seek revenge. What does that accomplish, Silas? If he kills a hundred rebs, will that make your legs better?"

A little frown touched Silas's lips before his expression hardened. "It would keep them from puttin' somebody else in a wheelchair—or worse."

Barry remained silent. His arguments were going nowhere with Silas, and he could see they never would.

"What about Arabella?"

Silas may as well have punched Barry in the gut. "What about her?"

"If you thought your chances of marryin' her were slim before, you can imagine what they'll be once her pa finds out you wouldn't even defend

Morgantown. Do you think Lambert will let you anywhere near his daughter if he finds out you didn't defend us against the rebs? He might not even let you see her at church anymore. He's not the only man who's lost all respect for you. Can you even live here if you don't go out there and fulfill your duty?"

"I don't care so much about the locals, but I can't deny what you say about Arabella gives me pause. You know how much I love her. I've loved her ever since we were children."

Silas seemed to be holding back a victorious grin. "I know it. Do you really want to sacrifice her now?"

Barry took in a breath.

"I can't do it. Not even for Arabella."

Chapter 8

Dusting in the parlor as Mother asked, Arabella's mood was pensive. With a loving motion, she swiped the top of a cherub figurine, a cherished heirloom from her maternal grandmother. She placed the ceramic piece back on the shelf. What would Granny think of the war, and about Barry's stand? The war had begun in April, and another April had arrived without a victory. How many more Aprils would the country be at war? Fighting had become wearisome. Everyone was ready to return to familiar routines. With the country unsettled, the future looked uncertain, and no one wanted to make plans. She longed for the days when she had nothing more to worry about than the color of her new spring frock. Would the world ever be such a carefree place again?

Arabella dusted her mother's collection of knickknacks without setting her mind to the task. She hadn't been herself since Barry had to declare his unwillingness to serve in the war. She didn't want to socialize—especially with Father's choices of company for her. The few bachelors not on the battlefield didn't appeal to her, in spite of his best efforts to make a new match. She couldn't find particular fault with any of the men he suggested. But they weren't her Barry.

Arabella's friends supported her, assuring her that refusing to court other suitors was the right thing to do. One of these friends, Sarah, worried each day about her brave Union soldier on the battlefield, and understood firsthand the pitfalls of being married to a fighter. She also understood Arabella's deep love for Barry, so deep that she could never leave him.

Bridget was another matter. Their relationship had become strained. Arabella never would understand how a woman could say she loved Silas, only to desert him when he was stricken as a consequence of duty. Arabella could see Silas's bitterness and Barry's concern. She wasn't sure what the future held for Silas but prayed God would guide him to promise.

Father had become distant since demanding she give up Barry. The love between father and daughter would always be strong, and in her heart, Arabella knew he wanted the best for her. To his way of thinking, marrying Barry was risky when the possibility of him fighting was imminent, but his declared cowardice—at least that's what Father called Barry's pacifism—made him an even worse choice for her. She could only pray to find a way to convince Father otherwise. But how? In the meantime, she lived for each Sunday, when she could see Barry at church.

Arabella shivered against the spring chill. The parlor didn't see heavy use and stayed shut off from the rest of the house most of the time. Maybe she should get her shawl.

Mother entered, scaring Arabella out of her daydream. "I have news. The Confederates are attacking Morgantown."

"What? This far north?" Her heart beat with fear. "Oh, Mother, what will happen to us?"

"I don't like it, but Morgantown is far enough away that maybe the rebels won't come here. But really, no one knows the future. All we can do is pray."

Arabella felt compelled to embrace her mother. The two women held each other. Arabella found comfort in her mother's understanding touch, sensing her empathy about Arabella's hopes and fears.

The women broke from each other and prayed together, holding hands. Mother led them in prayer.

"Heavenly Father, we pray for the safety of our region, and our own farm, and for our family. We pray for the men who feel called to fight in this terrible war, for their bravery and courage under fire. We pray for Thy will in the outcome of this war. Father, we pray it is Thy will for the loss of life to be small today, and for those who do lose their lives, that they will see Thy face and that their families find comfort in Thee. We pray for those here on the home front, for those who are whole, and those who are wounded, especially Silas. We pray for those who feel they cannot fight, especially for Barry. Keep us all in Thy care. In Jesus' name, amen."

The two women stood for a moment, not speaking.

"I—I'd better tend to things in the kitchen." Mother let go of her hand.

"I'll finish dusting and help you when I'm done." As Mother exited, Arabella wondered about Barry. She understood and admired his stand. But would this new attack make him see things differently? If he did, he'd defend Morgantown and earn the respect of his father and brother. If not, then he'd be standing, unrelenting, by his promise and his principles. Either decision earned him her respect.

She picked up a figurine without seeing it. The possibility of harsh news from the battlefield tormented her. The thought of him fighting left her frightened. What if he died?

Mother called from the kitchen. "Arabella!"

Still holding the dust rag, Arabella walked toward the kitchen until she reached her mother. "Yes? What is it?"

"Barry's here."

She looked no farther than by the kitchen table. Barry waited, standing.

"Barry!" She didn't bother to conceal her happiness upon seeing him.

To her disappointment, no smile crossed his lips. "Arabella."

Mother looked from Arabella to Barry. "Won't you have a cup of tea, Barry?"

"No thank you, ma'am."

Mother nodded. "I have some mending to tend to."

Arabella smiled. Her mother always showed tact. "Have a seat, Barry."

"No. I can't stay."

Anxiety clutched her midsection. Something wasn't right. "What's wrong?"

"A lot. I guess you heard about the attack."

"I did." She clutched at her midsection, but then with a deliberate motion, put her hands to her sides.

"You might imagine with the attack bein' so close by, Silas encouraged me to. I almost loaded my weapon and made ready to join the men defendin' our town's supplies from the rebs. But when I held my musket, ready to shoot a human—even if he is a reb, I couldn't bring myself to go and fight. All I could think about was Grandpappy, and the promise I made to him. I can't ask you to marry me, no matter how much I love you. All I can offer you is a life of disgrace, and upset for your pa. As my wife, you would never enjoy the popularity a pretty woman like you deserves. I'm settin' you free."

"No. Please don't. That's not what I want." She wanted to run into his arms, but his stiff demeanor stopped her.

"I want what's best for you. For your sake, I'll force myself to wish you well as you marry another man. I will pray nightly for your happiness. I know you will make some man very, very happy. I count myself lucky that I was able to share our love for a little while, and cherish my dream of making you my wife. I'll hold on to that memory forever." Barry's tone bespoke unmistakable sincerity.

"But what—what will happen to you?"

"From now on, I'll be a confirmed bachelor. It breaks my heart to pieces, but I want you to forget me. I'll never forget you."

"No! No!" She clenched her fists at her sides.

"I'm sorry, but that's the way it has to be." He turned and went out the back door.

Arabella sank to the floor and cried bitter tears.

Chapter 9

Seeming to understand Barry's sad disposition, Friday ambled down the country path toward the Birch farm instead of bouncing with his usual vigorous trot. Under normal conditions, Barry would have enjoyed breathing clean spring air, fragrant with budding trees and flowering plants. He would have relished fresh bursts of color found in nature this time of year. But today he wasn't even in the frame of mind to check on his strawberry patch, set to bear fruit in a couple of weeks. And a detour to the site of the new house was out of the question.

He'd planned to work on the house that day, but after the confrontation with his brother over the Morgantown raid, he felt in no humor to take on a project.

In light of what he'd told Arabella, he wondered if he should build the house smaller than planned. And why not? As a bachelor, with no intention of marrying, what would he do with a five-bedroom house?

One thing was certain. With his family's respect for him deteriorating every day, he couldn't remain in his childhood home much longer. The thought of moving before the house was finished crossed his mind. Then again, Pa would no doubt be glad to help him complete the house if it meant he would leave the Birch home sooner. Thank the Lord, his pa was a fair man. No matter how he felt about Barry's stand, he'd never go back on his word to let Barry have the plot of land for the house and, later, inherit the sixty adjacent acres.

When he entered the house, he could sense that tensions hadn't abated. He found his mother scrubbing the floor. "Oh, there you are. I was wondering where you were."

He didn't want to tell anybody about his visit to Arabella, but he had to confess sooner or later. "I went to see Arabella. I called off our engagement once and for all."

Mother dropped the wet rag on the floor and rose. "I wish you hadn't done that. Her pa will come around. Everybody's vexed right now over this war. Give him time."

"I'm not so sure about that. I'll always be made fun of. She deserves to be married to somebody popular. Somebody who can give her parties people will actually go to."

"Oh, Barry, I'm so sorry. Maybe you're doing the right thing. What did she say?"

"She was brave to tell me she didn't want to break it off. But I feel I have to."

"I pray things will change."

"If only they could."

~❦~

Later, Barry was washing up from milking the cows when Pa entered the kitchen. "The rebs set the suspension bridge at the Monongahela River crossing on fire."

Barry stopped lathering the soap. "What?"

"I heard it from Mannin'. He gets the story straight." Pa let out a labored sigh. "It's a good strategy. They want to disrupt communications and the B&O Railroad. It's enough to make the North come and fight 'em, so the pressure's off the South in the Shenandoah."

Barry dried his hands and let out a low whistle. "Brilliant."

"Yes, I'm sorry to say."

So things had changed. Barry had a thought. "I don't have to shoot anybody if I help put out the fire, do I?"

Pa brightened. "I reckon not."

Barry paused. His idea would put him at grave risk. "What would you say to me goin' and doin' that?"

Pa's expression darkened. "You've got to take your musket. Or maybe even my Henry rifle. You've got to be able to protect yourself, son."

Barry shuddered. If faced with a reb, wouldn't he instinctively try to defend himself? "I don't know. . ."

"Boy, it's the right thing to help put out the fires, but I won't allow you to go unless you take a weapon."

"All right, then. I'll take a weapon. My musket. I know how she works." Barry silently reminded himself that he didn't have to shoot just because he held a weapon.

"Agreed." Pa made his way over to Barry and put his hand on his shoulder. "I'm mighty proud of you, son."

Barry tried not to let his eyes mist. He hadn't heard those words in a long time from his pa.

~❦~

The mountainous terrain made the trip along Decker's Creek to Morgantown treacherous on the best of days, and Barry's dread increased the difficulty. Thankfully, Friday was a fine steed, steady on his feet.

What would Barry find once he got to the scene? Silas hadn't talked much about the war. Barry couldn't blame him. He could imagine the toll of death and destruction. Who'd want to relive such horror?

With Morgantown nowhere in sight, Barry was surprised to see two soldiers and a boy walking toward him on a lonely stretch of what passed for a road. The soldiers wore Union uniforms. Though emotions ran high and some people in the state sympathized with the Confederacy, Barry felt no danger since he sided with the Union. As he studied their approach, he noticed the boy walked with a familiar gait.

"Lance?" Taking in a breath, he urged Friday to move faster. He had to see if the soldier indeed was Lance. As he drew closer, he could see the boy's face light up with recognition. He broke out into a run.

"Barry!"

Barry stopped as soon as he was able and dismounted. Not caring what the other soldiers thought, he hugged his little brother. "You're safe and sound!"

Lance nodded. "But I'm sick. Dysentery, they tell me. Lots of the soldiers have it. Too bad nobody gets a medal for dysentery. I'm not much of a soldier, am I?"

"You don't have anything to be ashamed of." The tall soldier spoke with a clipped accent. He extended his hand to Barry. "I'm Mike." He tilted his head toward his companion. "That's Zig."

Zig nodded.

"So you're Lance's brother. I'm glad we ran into you."

"It's been a tough trip. I've had to stop a lot." Lance tightened his mouth in embarrassment.

Mike rubbed his fist in Lance's hair. "You've been a good little mascot all the same."

"Mascot?"

"That's right." Zig slouched, his hands in his pockets. "Nobody thought he was old enough to fight, but he tagged along with us and we couldn't say no."

"But he's had enough." Mike grinned, but not in a happy way. "Haven't you, squirt?"

Lance nodded. He slumped with defeat.

Barry didn't care. His little brother was safe, and once he got home, Ma could nurse him back to health. "Thanks for bringin' him this far. You're right; it's good you ran into me. I'm actually on my way to help put out the bridge fire."

"I think you're too late. It was out by the time we left," Mike said.

"Oh." Barry was surprised that he felt disappointment. "Looks as though I have an important mission all the same. Lance needs to go home."

"I wish we didn't have to go back." Zig looked in the direction of Morgantown.

"One day soon, maybe nobody will have to go back." Barry prayed his words would soon prove true. He wanted to thank the men, and he recalled he had packed some of Mother's delicious spoon bread and fried chicken for his own lunch. He reached for his satchel. "Here. At least take this food as a token of my family's thanks for takin' care of Lance."

Zig's eyes widened when he saw the food. "I ain't too proud to take it. Thanks!"

"Makes me miss my mother even more." Mike's eyes misted. "Thanks."

Barry wished he had more to share. At least by going home, no matter how tense the air, he'd be able to eat well. And now, so would Lance. "Come on, Lance. Let's go." He mounted Friday and waited for Lance to sit behind him. Lance's relief at not having to walk farther was palpable. He felt sorry for the soldiers on foot. "Didn't the army give you horses?"

"Rebs took ours," Zig admitted.

Barry shuddered. What if they came to the Birch farm and torched everything? He put such thoughts out of his mind. "I'll pray for your safety. Godspeed."

Lance held on as he and Barry rode back home. Barry prayed all the while and was relieved when they weren't confronted by any rebs during the trip or that Lance didn't ask to stop. Barry had so many questions he wanted to ask Lance, but he held back. As soon as the rest of the family saw that Lance had returned, they would be sure to fill the room with all sorts of queries before Ma would insist he go to bed. Barry could wait and hear the answers then.

Soon they were home. He could feel Lance's body tense with excitement when they were within short range of the house.

Unwilling to miss the moment of reunion, Barry hitched Friday temporarily to the post in the yard. They dismounted, and Barry followed Lance toward the house. Barry could sense his brother's anticipation and dread.

Barry put his arm around Lance's shoulders and walked with him to the house. Emotions roiled, but happiness at the thought of the reunion took precedence over the others.

When they entered the kitchen, Ma and Pa took no notice. "I don't want you to go, Horace." Ma tugged on his arm. "You're too old to play boys' games."

"It's my honor and duty to defend the Union, woman." He scowled.

"Ma! Pa!" Barry kept his voice sharp to cut into their conversation. "Look who's here."

Ma gasped. "Lance! My boy!" She ran toward Lance and hugged him.

"Ma." Tears ran down Lance's face.

"My boy." Pa embraced his prodigal son.

Ma urged Lance toward a chair. "What can I get you to eat? I have some spoon bread and chicken left over from dinner."

Lance rubbed his stomach. "Uh, I ain't so sure."

"He's not entirely well." Barry filled her in on the details of his interrupted mission. "Pa, I'm sorry I didn't make it all the way to town."

"You can be forgiven, all things considered." Pa's warm tone told Barry he spoke his true feelings.

Lance looked anxious. "Are you disappointed, Pa?"

Pa leaned toward him. "No. No, I'm not. It's a brave thing you did, goin' off to war. A mighty brave thing. But you ran away to do it, and you worried your poor ma."

Ma nodded. "You sure did. I'm glad you're home now."

"Me, too. Fightin' wasn't what I thought it would be. Not that I fought any. I was just along to keep the real men company." Lance looked up at Barry. "But even without fightin', I had to struggle with sickness, just like the others. And I didn't do a very good job of that. I can see why you feel the way you do."

Barry couldn't remember when he'd heard more encouraging words.

Arabella was stoking a fire in the stove when Father entered the house through the back door. "Lance is back. Or so I hear."

Arabella almost dropped the stove lid. "He is?"

"Yes. Barry brought him back."

She secured the lid. "What do you mean, Barry brought him back?"

"Believe it or not, he was on his way to Morgantown when he ran into him."

Arabella gasped. "So he decided to go!" Then the thought that he left without telling her bothered her. He must have meant it when he said he wanted her out of his life. She tried not to let her father know how much this new thought upset her. "We must go congratulate them." Then the thought that they might not have won overtook her. "We—we did win, didn't we?"

"The raid isn't over yet. Might go on for weeks." Father's face became grim. "According to what I hear, we lost three men trying to put out a bridge fire."

"How terrible! That makes me all the more grateful Barry and Lance are safe at home. And Barry was brave to go, wasn't he?"

Father scowled. "Don't think his brief show of duty means he's suitable for a daughter of mine."

"But Father. . ."

"You can see him in church and as your mother allows. Nothing more."

As your mother allows. Father didn't know just how much freedom her mother allowed.

Barry peered out the window and saw the Lambert buggy approach. He felt a mixture of ecstasy and embarrassment. Peering out from his room upstairs, he noticed Arabella looked glorious as always. Dark hair peeked from underneath her sunbonnet. She wore his favorite green dress. His heart beat faster upon seeing her, even though he had told her they had to part. In that moment, he knew he never wanted to part with her again.

What could he say to her that would make everything all right again?

Soon Ma called up the back stairs. "Barry!"

"Yes, ma'am?"

"We have company!"

"Yes, ma'am." He ran a comb through his hair and made sure his face looked clean and presentable before he walked down the stairs.

The women waited in the parlor. With her usual efficiency, Ma had already presented them with tea and cookies served on her good dessert plates. Seeing the magnificence that defined Arabella, he took in a breath in spite of himself before he greeted them.

"We came over to discuss our presentation for the next Women's Missionary Society meeting," Mrs. Lambert said.

"Yes, we did." Arabella stared at the floor and back. "And to say you were mighty brave to go defend the town, Barry, even if you did run into Lance first. How is he, by the way, Mrs. Birch?"

"Much better. Almost himself again."

From her position on the sofa, Ma made a show of looking out the window. "Oh, my, has Sugar gotten out?"

Following her lead, Barry noticed one of the cows had escaped. "Sure looks like it, Ma."

"Why don't you run along and get her put back before something happens."

Barry saw an opportunity and took it. He had a feeling his mother wouldn't mind. "Uh, care to come along, Arabella?"

Arabella looked to her mother for permission. "Is that all right, Mother?"

"Of course, child, run along." Ma smiled.

"I suppose it's all right," Mrs. Lambert agreed.

Barry waited until they passed the back stoop before he spoke. "I'm surprised you came by, after our last talk."

"I'm still hurting, but I couldn't stay away." She averted her eyes. "I don't reckon I should say something like that."

"I don't mind." Just being in her presence made him realize all the more how much he missed her. "I think about you every wakin' moment."

"And I think about you every day, too."

Spotting Sugar, unconcerned as she found new grass, Barry whistled and clapped. The cow eyed the couple but didn't move. Barry stopped and turned toward his love, taking her hands in his. "I'll always love you."

"And I'll always love you, too. In my eyes, you have shown your bravery."

He chuckled. "In your eyes, I've always been brave. But not in your father's eyes."

"I think I might convince him to come around. After all, I have Mother on my side."

"No, Arabella." His voice sounded harsher than he meant. "If our union makes your pa unhappy, I can't go through with it, no matter how much I love you. Your father has to be on my side, or I'll be a confirmed bachelor."

"A confirmed bachelor? But that's only for old, ugly men nobody wants. I want you for my husband, Barry."

"And I want you for my wife, Arabella. But not without your family's blessin'. This country has gone through enough turmoil without us makin' it worse right in our backyard. I'll be a bachelor forever before I'll see that happen."

Arabella cried unashamed tears. Wishing he were almost anywhere else, and anyone else, he gave her his plain white cotton handkerchief. Better to nurse a broken heart than to give in to selfish desires.

Chapter 10

A few days later, Barry had just washed up after milking the cows when he entered the study. He found Silas reading a Western novel.

Silas looked up from his book. "What do you think you're doin'?"

Though taken aback by Silas's prickly attitude, Barry grinned. Since he returned home from the war, almost any innocent action could set Silas off. The family had accommodated him by treading carefully. Barry hoped Silas's expectations changed soon. He was getting tired of having to be overly nice to his brother. "I was just lookin' for the newspaper. Pa asked me to fetch it for him. Have you seen it?"

"No. But I'm glad you came in. I don't want you to bother me this afternoon." Silas's tone mocked him. Silas seemed even more powerful and imposing in a wheelchair than he had when he could walk.

Barry kept his tone even. "I never try to bother you."

He sneered. "See that you don't. I'll be playing a man's game with my friends. They're all real men. We're celebratin' our victory in the raid."

Except for the fact that the Birch house and the surrounding homes had been spared, Barry didn't think it was much of a victory. The fighting had lasted well into May. The South had distracted the North from other fronts by taking troops to defend the area. They had taken prisoners and seized thousands of animals. True, Morgantown was safe, but according to what Barry heard, fire had destroyed bridges that would take time to rebuild. Yet the men wanted to celebrate that the B&O Rail line had been defended.

Barry knew what game Silas meant. He'd picked up the habit of playing poker during the war. Barry had a feeling Pa never would have allowed poker to be played in his house had Silas not been a wounded war vet. But to hear Silas tell the story, he had few pleasures left. He knew how to pull Pa's heartstrings to get his way. "I hope you enjoy yourself."

"I don't suppose you'd want to play, would you?"

"No."

"Good. Because you're not invited."

Barry knew he looked like a whipped little boy, but Silas's rudeness had come as such a shock he hadn't had time to compose himself.

"It's all for the best anyway. Mr. Lambert is one of the players tonight, and you two aren't gettin' along so well these days." Silas's voice sounded almost apologetic, but Barry knew better.

"That's all right. Poker isn't my game anyway." Though he was accustomed to Silas's barbs, they still hurt. He wanted to be included in his brother's life, but it seemed that was nothing but a dream.

Later, when the men arrived for the game, Barry made himself scarce. The horses needed grooming, and he took comfort in being among the gentle animals.

He started with one of his favorites, Lightning.

"Would you like to go for a ride after this, boy?" Barry petted the horse on the head. He whinnied, which Barry took as a signal that the animal wouldn't mind some exercise. Friday whinnied, too.

Barry looked down his nose at his horse. "Now don't you go gettin' jealous, boy. I'll ride you, too."

Suddenly Barry noticed the horses seemed restless. The sunny day indicated no chance of a thunderstorm, which would sometimes upset them. Had the weather taken an unexpected turn? He left the barn and realized what was happening. The smell of smoke permeated the air. The fire was coming from his house!

He watched as Bruce, Mr. Lambert, and Mr. Stewart ran out of the house. He'd never seen men run so fast. Flames were visible from inside the parlor. Clearly, the fire had become fierce and they were fleeing for their lives.

Barry remembered that Ma had served the men refreshments before the game. "Ma!"

"Over here, Barry!" She waved at him from the backyard and then ran toward the shed. Rachel followed her. He figured they planned to get buckets so they could try to put out the fire.

Pa and Lance had gone into town, so they were accounted for. But someone was missing.

Barry ran toward the poker players. "Where's Silas? He was playin' poker with you, wasn't he?"

"I reckon Bruce got him out." Mr. Lambert looked at the burning house. "He was smoking a cigar when a stray ash caught the curtain on fire. Went up just like that." He snapped his fingers.

Barry panicked. "No, Bruce didn't wheel him out. I saw him run out without anybody. Silas must still be in there. Somebody's got to save him!"

Mr. Lambert placed a hand on Barry's shoulder and looked toward the flames. "No, it's too late. Whoever does is signing his own death warrant."

"No. I'm goin' in."

Ma chose that moment to interrupt them. She handed him an empty bucket. "Why are you standin' there, son? Start puttin' out the fire."

"Not yet. I have to go in and save Silas."

She dropped her bucket and put her hands to her face. "He—he's still in there?"

"We think so. But I'll save him, Ma. Don't you worry."

Lord, keep me safe.

Seeing through the smoke was no easy task, but by staying close to the floor, Barry could discern his brother's whereabouts. Soon he discovered the card table and then felt the wheel of Silas's chair. The chair had landed on its side. Silas lay by the chair, trying to move himself forward with his hands. Every few inches he would have to stop and cough. Barry's eyes burned. He could tell that, though he made progress, it wouldn't be enough to save himself. Silas needed a man to drag him to safety.

"Hold on, Silas. I'm comin'."

Barely recognizable, thanks to a face blackened with soot, Silas coughed, then gagged. "Barry?"

"It's me." He extended his arm. "Take my hand."

Silas complied. Barry tried dragging him, but he could see that Silas, a dead weight because of his paralysis, was too heavy for him to make good progress. Fighting smoke, Barry threw Silas over his back. Staying as low as he could, Barry rushed out of the house. He crawl-stepped over the porch before the flames had time to do their damage. As soon as he got to a patch of ground, he laid Silas face up.

Silas coughed.

"Are you all right?"

Silas nodded. He tried to utter words but could only croak. Smoke had offended his vocal cords.

"Don't try to say anything now. Somebody will get a doctor, I'm sure."

Ma ran over to them. "Barry! Silas! You're both alive! Oh, praise be to God!"

"Yes, praise be to God." Barry looked at the heavens in thanks. The fire had been quenched, but the house was a loss.

For a few moments, all of them looked at the house, each absorbed in the grief of what they had lost.

Barry swallowed. "And praise Him that I've gotten far enough along on my house that you can live with me until we can rebuild here."

Ma's eyes misted. "Thank you, son."

❧

As usual when a life-threatening situation arose, their local doctor soon appeared on the scene. "How's the patient?"

Barry rose from his crouched position. "I'm fine but Silas needs help. How's everybody else?"

"No other injuries, thankfully."

The Lambert women must have heard about the fire, because soon Arabella ran to him. "Barry!" Her uninhibited embrace shocked him, especially considering his clothes reeked of smoke and were covered in soot.

"Don't ruin your pretty dress."

"This old thing?" She broke from him and brushed the dress with her hands. "I'm just thankful you made it out alive. You look a fright. Were you in the house when the fire started?"

Not wanting to answer, Barry surveyed the scene. Arabella's parents were standing with Ma. Judging from Ma's and Mr. Lambert's gestures, they were recounting the event. He spotted Rachel near them. Pa was in town on an errand. Barry wondered how long it would take Pa and Lance to realize their house had been the source of the fire.

"I think I'll let Ma tell it." Taking her by the elbow, he walked with her to the scene.

"And just look-a here." Ma swept her hand toward Barry. "The hero of the day."

"I'm no hero." Barry looked at the ground.

"Hero?" Arabella took in a breath. "Tell us what you mean, Mrs. Birch."

"Why, Silas wouldn't be alive right now if it weren't for Barry. He ran right in the middle of the house when it was burning and saved Silas. Nobody else would have done such a thing." Ma's eyes shone and her words ran together as her excitement grew.

Arabella touched Barry's forearm. "Is that right, Barry?"

Barry didn't want to brag, but he had to nod.

"You are ever so brave." Arabella squeezed his arm. "Were you scared?"

"Everybody's got a reason to be afraid at one time or another. I don't blame anyone for not wantin' to go through that fire." Glancing at the smoldering remains, he shuddered. "I don't mind tellin' you I was afraid myself. But with God's grace, all is well."

Ma looked at what once was her beautiful home. "Maybe 'well' is an exaggeration, but at least we're all safe."

"This is a cleansin' by fire. God has shown us what's important."

Mr. Lambert looked at Barry. "You were braver than I ever would have been."

"Did I just hear you say that Barry is braver than you are?" Arabella's voice was teasing, but Barry knew she was serious. "Does this mean he's worthy of my hand? Because I believe he is."

"Yes, it does, my dear. I'd be honored to have Barry Birch as my son-in-law."

Barry couldn't remember a time he felt more joyful. He dropped to one knee. "Arabella Lambert, may we resume our weddin' plans? Will you be my wife?"

"Yes, I will, a thousand times over! I'd marry you tomorrow if I could."

They kissed, and Barry heard cheers of approval.

Epilogue

Christmas Day 1863 turned out to be gorgeous and sunny, despite a winter chill permeating the air. The mood all around was as cheerful as the day. The Union had seen recent successes in Chattanooga, the South had been defeated at Gettysburg, and they had been unable to drive the Federal forces out of Virginia. All in all, the tide of the war seemed to be turning to victory. They were also citizens of the new state of West Virginia.

For the first time in years, the war didn't dominate Arabella's thoughts. She and her love, Barry, had just been joined in holy matrimony in the little white clapboard church they knew so well, where they were loved by the congregation. Finally, she was Mrs. Barry Birch. Her father's smile of approval made her day complete.

The wedding guests had been invited to a reception at the Lamberts' home following the ceremony. Mother had taken advantage of the Christmas season to decorate with beautiful winter greenery. The scent of cedar and pine gave the air a crisp, fresh feeling—as fresh as their new marriage. Cheerful red velvet ribbons used as accents reminded Arabella of the luxury of love.

Silas wheeled up to them. "May I kiss my new sister-in-law?"

"Of course." Barry patted her once between the shoulders, though she could barely feel his hand through the waist-length white cape she had chosen to wear over the dress as a bow to winter's chill.

She bent down to let Silas kiss her cheek and thought of Bridget. She would have been part of Arabella's bridal party had the wedding taken place only a few months ago. But Bridget had started courting another. Silas's bitterness—at least outwardly—lessened as time passed, but she suspected he might never find a wife. Silas didn't know it yet, but Arabella and Barry had an agreement with each other that they would take care of Silas once his parents were unable.

Silas looked up at Barry. "I wish you could wear the Union uniform."

Arabella took in a little breath and clasped her hands to her chest. Not so long ago, she couldn't imagine Silas saying such a thing to Barry.

Barry looked choked up and didn't speak.

"There's somethin' waitin' for you outside. Come on." He motioned for them to follow.

It wasn't until that moment that Arabella realized that the parlor was empty except for Silas and them. Everyone else had ventured onto the front lawn.

Silas rolled ahead of them. He positioned himself at the end of a line of men. Most of them wore the Union uniform, although those who hadn't because of age or infirmity appeared in their Sunday best. Twenty men stood in line. Silas was first, followed by Pa, Lance, Mr. Lambert, and sixteen other men they knew. Each held a weapon and fired on count, for a total of twenty.

Arabella watched the men, men she thought would never show Barry any respect, honoring him with such a show of pageantry. Barry wasn't one to cry but tears rolled unabated down his cheeks. She felt her eyes mist and tears fall down her own face. Most of the ladies retrieved lace handkerchiefs from their pocketbooks and sniffled. Her new mother-in-law cried the loudest.

After the show, Silas was the first to speak. "Barry, I'm terrible sorry for ever callin' you anything but brave. I wanted to do somethin' special for you on your big day, in front of everybody we know. We couldn't give you a twenty-one gun salute since you didn't serve in the armed forces, but I hope a twenty-gun salute will show you that I mean it."

"It was his idea," Pa noted.

Mr. Lambert was quick to add, "But we all agreed." The other men murmured acquiescence.

"I wish I could give you a medal myself." Silas's eyes misted.

"I don't need a medal. Your presence here today, and your respect, are honor enough for me." Barry bent down and embraced Silas. When Silas returned the gesture, the crowd applauded.

The salute had taken place near the end of the reception. Most of the food was gone, and some of the older guests made rustling motions showing their impatience to get home.

Barry seemed to read her thoughts, as he did so often. "I think it's time to go."

She nodded and took his hand.

They announced their departure amid more wishes for health and happiness from their guests. Arabella knew Barry loved her, but to have the support and love of friends and family meant the world to her, too.

The ride to their new home was a short journey down a country path. Viewing bare trees against the mountains, Arabella shivered and drew closer to Barry. He hadn't taken her to picnic in the yard lately because he wanted the house in its final form to be a surprise. Anticipation rose in her chest.

Soon their new home was in sight. Freshly painted in white, the home stood out among the gray trees. She imagined how gorgeous it would appear in summer once she planted pink and white flowers in front. "Barry, it's beautiful. Just as lovely as I imagined. And you gave me a veranda just as you promised."

"Of course I did." He pointed. "See the swing?"

"Just as I wanted."

"I'm glad I pleased you. I tried to listen to what you had to say."

She nodded. His sensitivity was one reason why she loved him so much.

"Are you ready to see the inside?"

"Yes, I am."

She started to walk through the door.

"Not so fast. Remember, I have to carry you over the threshold."

"That's a silly superstition, but a dear one." She held onto his neck as he picked her up.

"One more kiss before we go?"

"One more kiss."

The touch of his lips, so tender and sweet, melted away the world for her. Her dreams of being his wife, living with him in the beautiful home he built for her, were about to come true. For the rest of their lives.

The Snow Storm

by Lynn A. Coleman

Chapter 1

1875

Michael pulled the lapels of his thick woolen coat across his chest. The wind whistled in his ears. Small ice particles bit his nose and upper cheeks. His beard, heavily laden with ice, felt like it could snap off. The squall hit with such force, it sent the animals into hiding. Not that he'd noticed until it was too late. Thankfully, Noah and Sam were safely tucked away at the house. For once he'd insisted they finish cleaning their rooms before hunting. It would not have pleased Julie to see the house in such disarray. He had tried to keep up the place, but with two boys and a heap of chores, there wasn't much a man alone could do.

Michael ducked a branch leaning low across his path. Numbness settled in his right hand. The rifle he carried got colder and heavier by the moment. "I shouldn't have come out today," he mumbled and shifted the rifle to his left hand.

Christmas was a mere six days off, and a Christmas goose had been the boys' desire. He should have waited. He pushed his legs forward. The snowdrifts came up to his knees. He couldn't blame the boys for wanting something different for Christmas dinner. The thought of ham and beans on Christmas didn't appeal much to Michael, either. How he missed Julie's fine cooking. "Lord, I miss her. Why'd You have to take her?" he groaned his familiar prayer. For the past year he'd been asking, and there appeared to be no answer. At least not one he could settle with. "It ain't natural for a man to raise young 'uns alone."

Noah had become quite the young man. His gentle spirit came from his mother. Sam was a bit too much like his father. The poor boy couldn't sit still long enough for a flea to catch him. Noah took to books and learning just like Julie. Sam fought it from day one. Michael snickered. Past memories surfaced, when the roles had been reversed and his parents had tried so hard to get him to concentrate.

Crack.

A tree limb snapped above him. Michael dove out of the way. A snow bluff cushioned his fall. He turned back and looked at the fallen branch. It probably wouldn't have killed him, but it could have knocked him out. And in this weather, blacking out inevitably led to death. He felt his body temperature dropping. Pushing himself up, he brushed off his cloak of snow.

"Keep a steady eye," he cautioned himself. Talking to himself seemed to get more natural with each passing day. Julie had been his confidante and friend. No one else lived near them. They were miles from town; folks weren't all that inclined to come for a visit. Michael wasn't too inclined to invite anyone, either. He had enjoyed the solitary life until he met Julie. Oh, how she'd changed his world. His heart tightened in his chest. "Stop thinking about her now and get a move on."

He rounded a corner of the path and stopped dead in his tracks. "What is that?"

He dropped his rifle and ran to the lump of woolen clothing. He brushed off the snow. "A woman," he gasped. "What's a woman doing out here?"

What did it matter? She was either dead or pretty nearly so. Michael pulled off his gloves with his teeth and felt her bluish skin. "Cold." As if it would have been anything else.

He placed his fingers under her nose. A feather of a breath passed over the top of his forefinger. "Lord, she's still alive. Help me."

Michael scooped up the woman. Blond hair spilled out around the edges of her hat and scarf. *What is she doing out here, Lord?* he wondered.

"I don't know if you can hear me, Miss. But I'll get you warm." Michael kicked his rifle up with his foot and wedged it between her back and his arms.

Michael pumped his legs harder, running toward his house. Energy coursed through his veins and pushed him forward. Moments before, it had taken all his strength to keep pushing his own body. "Lord, help me," he panted.

His house came into view. He could smell the wood fire burning in the stove.

A slight moan tickled his ears. "You're going to be all right, Miss. I'll have you in the house soon."

She didn't respond. "Father, be with her. Help her warm up," he prayed as he stepped up the front stairs. The front door resisted his attempts to open it.

"Noah! Samuel! Open up," he barked. Of all the times for the boys to lock the front door. The howling winds screeched through the trees. *They must be scared,* he reasoned.

Noah opened the door. His eyes widened. "What's that?"

"A woman. I found her nearly frozen on the path. Help me." He placed his rifle by the door.

"What can I do?"

"Start heating some water. She'll need something warm to drink."

Sam bounced off the stairs. "Hi, Dad! Did you get us a— Who's that?"

"I don't know, Son. She was on the path. Go grab me your momma's quilt from my bed."

"Yes, Sir." Sam scurried down the hallway.

Michael laid the fragile woman in front of the woodstove. He pulled at the frozen buttons on her cloak and removed it. Next he worked on her boots. Her toes were pale and blue. Frostbite could be a real problem.

Sam ran in with his brown curls bouncing. The boy definitely needed a haircut. "Here, Dad."

"Can you get me a couple pairs of wool socks?"

"Yes, Sir." Samuel stared down at the frozen figure. "Is she...?"

Dead. The poor boy had seen his mother after she'd passed on. Michael reached over and held his son's hand. "No, Son, she'll be all right. We just have to get her warmed up."

Samuel nodded and ran back to the master bedroom.

"Water's on, Dad. What do you need now?"

"Help me take her dress off."

"But she's a girl, Dad," Noah protested.

Michael took in a deep breath. He didn't have time for modesty. On the other hand, what would this woman say once she came to and discovered he had removed her clothes? *Lord, I wish Julie were still here.* He turned to answer Noah. "I know, Son. But she needs to be dry."

"Can't we just wake her up and tell her to take off her dress?"

"If she could wake up, we wouldn't need to tell her. I'll take her dress off. You just help me hold her."

"Can I keep my eyes closed?"

Michael held down a grin. "Yes, you can keep your eyes closed." Michael was beginning to wonder if he could keep his eyes closed, too. Taking a deep breath, he reached out to the top buttons. The fact that they were on the collar of her neck was a blessing. "Why does women's clothing have to have such tiny buttons?" he mumbled.

"Dad, she's waking up," Noah called.

Michael's hands were mere inches from the woman's buttons when he saw the look of confusion change to horror. He pulled his hands away quickly. "I found you half-buried in the snow. You need to take off your wet dress. You need to get warm—and quickly. Can you stand?"

"I–I don't know." Her brilliant blue eyes beckoned for answers.

"Then you'll have to remove your clothing here by the fire. The boys and I will turn our backs and close our eyes. Your honor is safe with us, Miss."

She tried to reach her buttons. Her fingers were still too numb. Michael groaned. "I'll unbutton. Can you slip the dress off?"

She nodded.

Michael refused to look at the poor child. She didn't need to be embarrassed. He was embarrassed enough for the both of them.

Noah and Sam obediently turned away from the woman, and Michael didn't doubt that their eyes were closed as well.

"Who are you?" he asked, trying to ease the situation.

"Angela. Angela Harris."

≈≈≈

Angela trembled and pulled the covers closer. *How could I have gotten so confused and twisted around in the storm? And who is Michael Farley?* His two sons stared at her as if she had two heads. Of course, given that she was huddled in front of their woodstove in a cocoon of quilts and woolen blankets probably had something to do with it. She had been shaking for hours. Her teeth had chattered long enough, she wondered if they would break.

Michael Farley had left to tend to the animals in the barn after setting a pot of beans and ham to warm on the stove. Somehow the smell of food helped ease her worries. Angela rubbed her arms vigorously, her eyes scanning her surroundings. The house suffered from the lack of a woman's touch; it was relatively clean but cluttered. The soot on the walls from the stove hadn't been cleaned off in a long time. *Why is it that men don't notice these things? Did God give them less than perfect eyesight?*

"Are you feeling better?" the older of the two boys asked.

"Some. Noah, right?"

"Yes." A smile erupted on his young face, a handsome boy with a thin frame, dark hair, and blue eyes like his father.

"Why were you in the snow?" the younger boy, Samuel, asked.

"It wasn't snowing when I left my house."

"This storm sure did move in fast." Samuel sat with his legs crossed beside her. "Why were you walking alone?"

"I had some thinking I needed to do."

"Grown-ups," Noah huffed, then settled down next to Samuel. "Dad's been doing lots of thinking since Ma died."

"I don't like to think. I like to play." Samuel smiled. His cheeks were lightly peppered with brown freckles, his head crowned with a massive amount of curls. Some of her girlfriends would die to have hair like that; and to think, it was on a boy. Sometimes she really wondered why God favored some men with items women would love, like curls and really long eyelashes.

"Playing is good, but thinking is important, too. I wager you do more thinking than you think."

"Huh?"

"Tell me, what's your favorite type of play?" Angela inquired. It helped get her mind off her frozen body.

"He's always building things," Noah answered.

"Yeah, I built a boat in August."

"A boat. That's quite a task. Tell me, how did you build it?"

"I took a hunk of wood and whittled it."

"So you looked over the piece of wood and decided which end would be the bow and which would be the stern?"

"Yeah." The boy beamed.

"Sorry to say, but you were thinking. You had to decide the best way to proceed with the task. Once you did, you set out to do it. All of that is thinking."

"Never thought of that." Samuel's grin slipped.

Angela chuckled, then coughed.

Noah jumped up and got the mug of tea. "Here, drink this."

"Thank you."

"Where do you live?" Samuel asked.

"In town."

"How come we've never seen you before?"

"I'm usually busy working inside my house. My father counts on me to take care of it."

"Dad does that for us," Noah offered.

"Wish I had a big sister like you who could take care of us. Dad doesn't know how to cook anything besides ham and beans."

"No sir," Noah defended. "He cooks bacon and eggs."

"That doesn't count, Noah. That's breakfast. I miss Mom's cooking."

"Whoa, boys, no need to fuss."

The front door slammed open. A cold blast of air ran across her warm nose. Angela shook at the sight of Michael Farley. Something was wrong. She reached for her dress and found it dry. "May I use a private room to change back into my own clothes?"

She had on a pair of men's thick undergarments, but they didn't seem quite big enough for Michael. She'd guessed they'd belonged to his wife. *What was her name? Ja, Jen, Ju. . .Julie. Yes, that was it, Julie.* Angela didn't want to return to the cold, but she couldn't see herself staying here. If he'd give her directions, she'd be on her way.

"You may use my room." Michael shook off his coat and hung it on the peg near the front door. "How's the beans, Noah?"

"Ready to eat."

"Good, I'm starved. We'll eat when you've changed, Miss Harris." Michael waved her off.

Immediately she jumped up, held her quilt wrap around herself, and scurried off to the back bedroom. She gasped seeing the unmade bed, clothes piled in the corner—or were they on a chair? Who could tell? At least the front room had some order to it. This room had none. Angela tossed the quilt on the bed. She slipped off the men's underwear and wished she had left them on. Dancing from foot to foot, she hurriedly clothed herself in her feminine garments. The dress needed a good pressing, but it was dry and it was decent. Something she could wear in public. Although that quilt felt mighty warm and comfy. She glanced back over to the crazy quilt. She'd seen a similar one before, but this one had been made with silk cigar wrappers. She wondered who had smoked all those cigars. Had Michael? There had to be a story behind that quilt. But why was she interested? It wasn't hers, and she was simply passing through. She reached the doorknob and placed her hand on the iron thumb rest, then looked back at the bed and the quilt. Angela released the door and marched back to the bed and made it.

Upon entering the kitchen a few minutes later, she grinned at the solemn faces of Noah and Samuel. Beans and ham every night would get old on her, too. She could relate. "Dinner smells wonderful." She grinned. "Thank you."

"Set yourself over there." Michael pointed to a chair beside Samuel.

The heavy cast-iron frying pan seemed to weigh but a feather in Michael's hands.

"I'll leave after dinner. Can you give me directions back to town?"

He plopped the pan down in the center of the table and narrowed his gaze. "You ain't leaving."

Chapter 2

Wait?"

Michael didn't realize he had raised his voice. "Storm's still blowing; you can't leave."

"But. . ." Her hands trembled. Upon further examination, he noticed her entire body shook.

"You're still cold. Don't you know you can catch consumption? Get back in my room and put those undergarments back on and both pairs of woolen socks. You need to get warm." What was she thinking? *Why aren't women more practical about their clothing, Lord? It just doesn't make sense.*

Angela dropped her fork back to the table and timidly walked past him.

Alone in a strange house with strange men, she has reason to be nervous, he figured. *Especially with a man who has forgotten just how sensitive a woman can be,* Michael silently rebuked himself. Noah and Samuel scooped their beans and stared at their plates. He'd been too gruff. *Why'd she have to be a woman, Lord?* He could handle men. His knack for soft speech had died with Julie, and a beautiful blond with flawless skin wasn't going to get him to open up that area again. She'd just have to accept his ways. After all, it was his house, and he was in charge.

Angela reappeared with the woolen socks on her feet. Her dress seemed tighter around the waist. She'd put the long underwear on as well. *At least she listens.* He scooped up more of his beans and took his eyes off the alluring creature. Even dressed like that, she appealed to his senses.

"After dinner you can go through my wife's belongings. They're in a chest in my room. Take what you need." He didn't need to be sweet, but he could be polite.

"Thank you." She spread the linen napkin on her lap. "How long do you think this storm will last?"

"Hard to say." Michael forked his dinner. Beans just about every night was getting old, extremely old. Perhaps he should consider hiring a woman to come in and cook and clean a couple of times a week. Noah and Sam would love it. So would his own gut.

Angela clasped her hands and bowed her head in prayer. Michael stopped chewing. Prayers before dinner were occasional at best, though he still did evening prayers with the boys before they went to bed.

"I apologize for being an imposition. I do thank you for rescuing me." She picked up her fork and scooped up some beans. Her mouth stopped chewing instantly. Then, as if checking her responses, she swallowed the tasteless beans. Angela dabbed her mouth with the napkin and replaced it on her lap. "May I cook for you while I'm here?"

Michael bit his inner cheek to keep from grinning. He'd be a fool to turn down a woman's cooking. Even the worst cook in the world would manage better than he. Hadn't the boys complained enough in the past few days about their constant meal of ham and beans? "I won't pass it up. As you can tell, I'm not much of a cook."

She nodded, but refused to speak her thoughts. *Angela Harris must have been raised by a refined woman,* he mused. The town was bringing in new folks every day, but Michael had kept to himself. *How long has she lived in the area?* he wondered.

An awkward silence filled the room.

Noah reached over and touched Angela. "I can't wait to eat your cooking." His grin was infectious.

"The boys and I have been hard-pressed for a good meal for a long time."

"I'd be happy to help. Do you have some molasses?" Angela put down her fork.

"Yeah, on that shelf over there."

She scooped up the frying pan and returned the contents of her plate to the pan. The boys did the same.

"Do you mind?" she asked.

"Of course not." What else could he say? Admittedly he wanted to return his plate to the frying pan as well. But he held back. He couldn't appear too eager, could he?

Michael watched as she worked her magic with the beans. The fresh aroma that filled the room had his stomach gurgling. Maybe, just maybe, Angela was an angel from heaven sent to help his household. He'd been thinking about hiring someone. Perhaps she was up to the task. She couldn't live too far away if she'd gotten twisted around in the woods.

"Where do you live?" Michael asked.

"In town. My dad owns the feed and grain store."

Harris. Of course. He should have put the names together. Frank Harris was a fine man, an honest man. He'd never had any problems doing business with him. Which meant she'd been living in the area for years. Why hadn't he seen her before? Where did she keep herself? Surely he would have noticed Angela before, wouldn't he?

"I know your father."

Angela turned and smiled. "He's a good man." She removed the hot pan from the woodstove and set it on the table. She served the boys, then herself. Her gaze caught his, silently asking if he would like some. He wanted to accept, no question, but there was more than enough on his plate to feed his belly. He blinked his negative response.

"Hmm, good." Noah smacked his lips. "You gotta have some, Dad."

"It's wonderful," Sam mumbled.

"Samuel, don't speak with your mouth full. And, Noah, I'm sure it's wonderful, but I have plenty on my plate."

"It's your stomach," Noah quipped as he dove his fork in for another hearty scoop. "Thank you, Miss Harris. This is great."

"Perhaps you can tell me what you added to the beans to make the change in them?" Michael asked.

"Just a little bit of molasses and a small spoonful of your brown sugar."

Michael nodded. He could do that. Maybe he didn't need to hire someone, just get someone to teach him how. No, he didn't have time to learn how to cook, plus care for the land and livestock. He scooped another forkful, dreading the next bite. His appetite gone, he pushed himself from the table and went outside to bring in some extra wood for the night and first thing in the morning. The wind howled, driving the snow in swirls around him. The trees bent before the onslaught, groaning in protest. The storm was a bad one.

～❈～

Angela didn't know what to make of Michael Farley. He obviously wasn't happy that she was there, but he was too decent a Christian to put her out into the storm. Her father must be worried sick with her being gone so long. *Father, God, give Papa peace. Let him know I'm all right.*

She made herself useful and started cleaning up the dishes. Unfortunately, as she began to clean, she couldn't keep herself from also washing down several shelves. Dust and grime were piled thick upon them. *How long ago did he lose his wife?* she wondered.

A blast of cold air filled the room. Michael Farley stood with his arms full of wood. "Boys, get the door," he hollered.

Angela resisted the urge to assist him. He seemed to be a gentle bear of a man who had a growl that could send folks running. Was it the anger over his loss? What did it matter? *This is temporary until the storm lets up enough for me to go back home. Home.* Her heart sank. She'd have to inform her father that she couldn't marry Kevin Mason. He was too old, anyway. Her twenty-one to his thirty years worked for some, but. . . She shook the thought away.

He was a kind enough man, she supposed. But shouldn't a woman have feelings for her husband? Some sort of attraction? She brought the images of Kevin back to her mind. Nothing. . . not one stir of emotion, good or bad, came from his image. And certainly not like the stir of her emotions over Michael Farley. She was drawn to him in an irrational manner. She should be frightened but instead felt secure in his home. She wanted to bury herself in his chest and feel the security of his embrace, as if she'd already experienced it. The image, sense, whatever, seemed so real, yet she'd never met the man before today. Angela worried her lower lip. This didn't make sense. She'd known Kevin for years. Never, not even once, had she wanted to be in his embrace.

Samuel broke into her thoughts. "Miss Harris, do you wanna play?"

"What would you like to do?"

"Parcheesi. It's a new game. Daddy bought it for us." Samuel held the boxed game in his hand.

"I'd love to. I don't know how to play it, so you'll have to teach me."

"It's easy. I'll teach you." Sam's chest swelled with pride. He was cute. He seemed to have his father's eyes, but it was hard to tell under all those brown curls.

"Can I play?" Noah asked.

"Everybody can play," Sam announced. "Dad, will you play, too? We can have four players."

Michael dusted off his shirt and woolen pants, cracking the first smile she'd seen on his lips since she'd met him. "It'll be a good way to spend the evening."

Accenting his point, the wind howled and whistled through the cracks in the door and window casings. Angela rubbed her arms at the mere thought of the cold blasts of arctic air. She should have known by the absence of birds in the trees that a serious storm was coming. Thoughts of Kevin and a pending engagement had driven her deeper into the woods than she'd ever gone before. Getting turned around in an unfamiliar area wasn't good. She knew better.

Angela sat down at the table where Samuel had placed the interesting board game.

"Ya need a five to get out of your spot." Sam pointed to the area closest to Angela and handed her four red wooden pegs.

"You need to get all four pieces in here, but you have to go the long way around," Noah added.

It seemed relatively simple. Angela relaxed and tossed the dice that had been handed to her. She had to stay put, no fives. Perhaps this game would take longer than she expected.

The game progressed until Michael landed on the space where her piece was and sent her back to her base. "Hey."

He gave a disarming grin. "Sorry, those are the rules. If you land on a spot where someone else is, you send him back to the beginning. If he has two pieces on the same space, you're blocked and can't move forward."

"No one told me that." Angela looked over the board to see if she was in striking distance of anyone. This could be fun. Michael had a piece not too many spaces in front of hers. Angela blew on the dice and rolled again.

"Gotcha." The room erupted in laughter.

Angela's heart pounded seeing the love and compassion Michael had for his sons. The way he took time with them was a rare gift. She scanned his features. His coal-black hair seemed such a rich crown, with his dark eyebrows accenting blue-gray eyes that crinkled slightly at the edges when he smiled. His full beard required a good trim.

His gaze caught hers. Angela shivered. A glimpse of his soul seemed to appear in his eyes. She broke the connection and looked back down at the board game. Noah was leading with three pieces in home.

"I got you, Noah." Sam smiled.

"I'll still beat you," Noah said proudly, but the disappointment of having to bring that one piece all the way around the board again showed in his face.

Angela peeked up at Michael again, his eyes hooded and guarded. Strangely, disappointment settled over her. What was compelling her to want to know this man? Why did she feel so close to him, even though they'd never met?

Sam passed her the dice. She shook and tossed them. A three and a four. She counted out the spaces forward and removed her hand.

"Why didn't you knock Sam back to his base?" Noah demanded.

Angela scanned the board. "Oh dear, I missed that."

"I don't mind." Sam gave her a big toothy grin.

"Now, Noah, it's just a game, Son," Michael admonished.

"I know."

"And this is Miss Harris's first time playing. She's bound to miss a few things."

Especially if my mind is on silly things. She'd never been one to swoon over a man. Even in school when the girls would giggle and wiggle because a boy walked by. It never bothered her. They were just boys, nothing special. Why was Michael Farley bringing up all these silly thoughts and feelings? He'd done nothing to show he was interested. *You'd best get a handle on these emotions, or you're in for a real heartache.* Angela caught a glimpse of Michael's wink. Heat rose in her cheeks.

⚬⚬⚬

Later that evening Michael found himself in his bedroom unable to rid his mind of Angela's tempting image. It didn't mean a thing. She was a stranger, a mere child. A grown child but way too young for him. Not that he was interested in pursuing a relationship. Julie, his true love, could never be replaced. But there was something about Angela's mannerisms that drew his attention. The house lacked the womanly touch. The boys were totally enamored with her. Perhaps it was time to give serious consideration to hiring someone to come and clean his house and cook the meals. Michael rubbed his beard. It was thick, just the way he liked it for winter—giving him good protection from the cold. He caught a glimpse of himself in the mirror. The ends of his beard were ragged. He needed a good trim to be more presentable.

Presentable—for whom? Angela's golden hair, rich and full, again flooded his mind. The strands seemed to be spun with golden rays from the sun. Pure sunshine, and oh, how this house had lacked sunshine for so long. Michael's heart ached. He turned toward his bed. Memories of Julie's emaciated body lying there flooded him. He dropped to his knees. "Oh, God, why? Why did you have to take her? I know death was better than the life she lived that last year, but why illness, Lord? Why Julie? Lord, I'm trying to do right by the boys, but I can't do it alone."

A gentle knock on his door caused him to jump from his penitent posture. He walked over.

"Mr. Farley," Angela whispered.

He cracked the door open a couple of inches.

"What is the matter?" he asked.

"I hate to ask, but I'm having trouble falling asleep in these. . .these. . . Well, you know. And I was wondering if maybe your wife had some flannel nightgowns."

Julie's things? No. On the other hand, he had given her permission to wear Julie's dresses. Michael cleared his throat. "Yes, there are some in her trunk. Just a minute and I'll get one."

Why, oh why did he offer her Julie's clothing? Because he knew she wouldn't be comfortable in her own soiled dress. *You were being practical,* he reminded himself. Michael opened the chest and fought back the images of his wife wearing the various articles. Briskly, he ruffled through the clothing and pulled out two flannel nightgowns. With a couple quick steps, he stood by the door and thrust the gowns toward his unexpected houseguest.

"Thank you. I'm sorry to impose."

"No imposition; you're welcome." He couldn't close the door fast enough. Her soft blue eyes, the color of wild cornflowers, drew him. He wasn't looking to replace Julie. Attraction was for younger men. He had enough to think about without fighting an attraction to Miss Harris. Yes, he'd have to remind himself to call her Miss Harris, to think of her as Miss Harris. That would help.

He hoped.

He flopped on the bed. An image of Julie lying beside him warmed him. Yes, Julie, his beloved, his friend. Michael closed his eyes and savored the moment. "I don't want to be bitter, Lord. I do miss my wife." He shifted the covers and found himself hugging Julie's pillow. More evenings than not he found himself reaching out for it, for some form of comfort. When would he get over his loss?

He methodically counted down tomorrow's chores. This storm would change some of his daily routines. He'd make oatmeal for breakfast. The boys weren't all that partial to it, but it would warm their bellies and keep them full until lunch.

A flash of Angela working in the kitchen earlier that evening raked over his frayed nerves. The sweet aroma of the beans after she'd altered them. . .her angelic face. . . .

Michael jumped from the bed and paced. How would he survive having such a tempest in his midst for another day?

Chapter 3

A cool draft licked at Angela's nose. She scampered over to the wood-stove. Wrapped in a woolen blanket, she tossed in some additional logs. Angela shivered and pulled the covers closer. Before the rest of the household woke, she dressed in her stiff, soiled clothes and the men's undergarments. She had to admit they were warm. Last night, asking Michael Farley for a nightgown had been embarrassing but necessary. He couldn't expect her to live and sleep in the same clothes for days.

She lit a lamp in the kitchen and gathered the necessary ingredients to make biscuits. Hopefully she'd have enough time in the kitchen before the others woke up. Angela eagerly went to work. Helping was the least she could do for saving her life and giving her warm shelter during the storm. She'd awakened a couple of times during the night when she'd heard the shutters rattling against the house.

She checked the bread oven attached to the side of the woodstove; its temperature was perfect. In a large frying pan, she fixed generous slabs of bacon. She placed the tray of biscuits in the bread oven and set the table. A small bowl of honey, a small mound of butter, and the table was ready. Hearing footfalls upstairs, she scrambled eggs in the frying pan and put it on the stove. The coffee's rich aroma filled the room as the hot water seeped through the coffee grains.

"What smells so good?" Noah asked as he bounced down the stairs.

"Breakfast."

"Smells great." Samuel's smile reached to the corners of his eyes.

Michael's bedroom door creaked open. "You didn't have to cook for us."

"I wanted to. Come, sit down, and I'll serve." She knew she was being forward in the man's house, but all night she couldn't stop thinking about Michael.

The boys jumped into their seats. Michael stared over at them. "Boys, you're forgetting your manners. Wash up."

"Yes, Sir," they said in unison.

"Thank you." Michael's gaze softened. A flutter worked its way down Angela's spine, and she knew it had nothing to do with the cold. *Why'd I put on that long underwear? Step outside for a minute; that will cool you down,* she chastised herself.

Michael took two giant steps toward the door. "Feed the boys. I'll eat when I finish in the barn."

"But—" The door slammed shut. She wanted to protest his leaving without eating, but she also knew their exchange had been one of mutual attraction. He wasn't ready. After all, he loved his wife. The best she could figure from what the boys had said and didn't say, their mom had died a year ago and had been sick for a long time before she passed away.

"Homemade biscuits!" Samuel grinned.

"We haven't had homemade biscuits in a long time." Noah tucked his napkin under his chin.

"I hope you like them. They aren't as light and fluffy as I like to make them, but there wasn't a lot of time to sift the flour and allow them to rise."

Noah reached across the table and took two biscuits. *Good thing I made the whole batch*, she mused.

"Dad must be real worried about the animals. Ain't fit for someone to be out in that wind." Noah chomped down on his biscuit as bits of crumbs fell from his full mouth.

"Slow down, Noah, there's plenty for everyone."

He closed his lips. "Sorry, Miss Harris."

"You're forgiven. Did you say your prayers?"

Samuel bowed his head. "We forget sometimes. Momma wouldn't like us forgetting our prayers."

"Well, let's say them and then enjoy the wonderful breakfast the Lord is allowing us to have."

The boys nodded their heads and clasped their hands, waiting for her to lead them. *Lord, help me not to overstep my boundaries here.* "Dear Jesus. . ."

She led the morning prayer and the boys concluded with a hearty "Amen."

"How'd you learn to cook so well?" Samuel asked.

"My mother taught me. But she passed on a few years back, so I've been taking care of my father and brothers for several years. Thankfully, my brothers have married, so I only take care of Papa now." Angela began to wonder how long Michael would be in the barn.

"It ain't fun, losing your momma," Samuel sniffed.

A wave of compassion washed over Angela. She remembered her own moments of anguish after her mother passed. "No, it isn't. But after awhile you get used to it, and you remember all the good times you had with her."

"I wish I'd spent more time with her, knowing she was dying." Noah held his fork in midair, staring off in no direction in particular.

"I remember those same feelings. You feel guilty that you should have done more. Fact is, we probably couldn't have. Takes awhile to get rid of those guilt feelings and replace them with anticipation of seeing her again in heaven."

Noah gazed into her eyes. Tears threatened to fall, but the brave young man held his own. Angela's own eyes filled partly for her own loss and partly for the pain she saw in the boy's eyes. "I miss my mother, too," she barely whispered.

The room fell silent as she and the boys took a moment to reflect on their losses. *Great, just great.* She was responsible for this downward turn of emotions. *Lord, help me say the right thing here.* "What are you boys doing for Christmas?"

Samuel grinned. "Dad said he'd try to get us a Christmas goose. That's when he found you."

"Oh dear, he brought home a lady instead of a goose. Just don't call me a goose lady."

The boys erupted in laughter.

"Seriously, how do you prepare the house for Christmas?"

"Mom would set the house up real fancy-like. But men don't need fancy things," Noah stated and went back to his eggs.

"Oh, I suppose ribbons and such are too feminine."

"I like the way Momma made the house pretty," Samuel mumbled with his mouth full.

"Yeah, it was special," Noah added softly.

Ah, so this is why she was here. Well, besides the fact that Michael had saved her life. But the Lord wanted her here to make their Christmas special. Angela scanned the room. How could she dress up the place?

❧❧❧

"If this storm keeps up, I'm going to lose some livestock," Michael muttered as he fussed with the bales of hay. He'd lined every wall with hay to keep more heat in the building. His stomach ached for the tasty food that waited for him in the house. But he couldn't stay in there. Not now. Not until he got control of his emotions. Why he'd ever agreed to letting that woman help with the cooking was beyond him. Wasn't the old saying lesson enough—a way to a man's stomach, and all that? Michael groaned. He wasn't going to allow his stomach to dictate his emotions. He'd starve for the next couple of days if he had to.

Finished in the barn and with the wind howling, he had little choice but to make his way back to the house and face this new temptation in his life. After all, he wasn't really attracted to her, he reasoned. Loneliness and not having Julie around simply had gotten the better of him.

"The biscuits are great, Dad." Samuel smiled and sat up. He was working on something, and Michael sneaked a glance to find out what. Looking for a clue, he surveyed the room and stopped at Angela.

"I've put your breakfast in a pie tin and set it on the stove. Hopefully it's still warm."

"Thank you." Michael hung up his winter coat and hat and headed for the stove. He found a pie tin wrapped in a towel with a mound of food under it. Temporarily putting his plan of starving out the window, he sat down at the table. The first mouthful—pure nectar. His stomach rumbled in agreement.

The kitchen appeared brighter. Michael scanned the cupboards and shelves. They sparkled. Angela stood at the sink with her hands buried in sudsy water. Michael cleared his throat. "I appreciate the warm breakfast, but you really don't have to clean."

She turned to him and slowly raised her gaze to meet his. Azure eyes warmed his heart. *God, help me. I'm. . .*

"No trouble at all. I'm glad to help."

Michael looked down at his plate. *Much safer.*

"Dad?"

"Yes, Noah." The biscuit melted in his mouth. How long had it been since he'd had a decent meal?

"Sam and I are working on something for Christmas and—well, we were wondering if you wouldn't mind staying in your room."

A grin slid up his cheek. "Not a problem, Son. I have a thing or two I need to work on myself."

Noah's grin widened.

"Whatcha making, Dad?" Samuel dropped his charcoal stick and came over toward the table.

"Now, Son, it wouldn't be a surprise iffin I told you."

"I suppose, but did you build me a sled?"

Deepening his voice, Michael said, "Samuel."

"Sorry, Sir." Samuel's shoulders slumped.

Michael reached out and brought his youngest son to his lap. "You wouldn't want the joy of the surprise ruined by me telling you, would you?"

"No, but if it was a sled, I could use it now."

Michael laughed. "If, and I do mean if, it is a sled, you couldn't use it until this storm passes."

Michael's heart drummed as Samuel leaned against him. "Daddy, Angela says that after some time you feel better about losing Mommy. Is that true?"

What on earth was the woman telling his sons? "Yes, I believe it is." *But how long would it take?* Michael couldn't conceive an end to this misery.

"Angela said it was hard at first when her mom died."

Michael pushed down the knot in his stomach. Angela knew what she was talking about after all.

Angela came up beside them. "Sam, why don't you let your papa finish his breakfast?"

Samuel pulled away, and Michael looked toward the half-full plate. Eating was the last thing on his mind at the moment. "You can sit beside me while I finish, Son."

Samuel wiggled down and sat on a chair. "What are you making, Son?" Michael plunged his fork deeply into the hash brown potatoes.

"Dad!" Samuel groaned. "You just said I couldn't know."

"Oh, well, I'm a grown-up. You can tell me."

"Nah uh! Angela, do I have to tell Dad what I'm making him for Christmas?"

"Nope. Your papa will just have to wait, same as you."

"Aw, shucks. Hey, Noah, what are you working on?"

Noah laughed. "Not gonna get it from me, Dad. Good try, though. Come on, Sam, let's take this upstairs so Dad can't see."

Michael laughed and noticed Angela smiling. "What did you put my sons up to?"

"Pardon, Monsieur. You must have me confused with another," she feigned, placing a hand to her chest.

"And the woman speaks French as well."

"Not really. You don't mind that I helped the boys, do you?" She sat down beside him.

Lord, why am I so attracted to her? "No, not at all. It will help them with this long day."

"What are you working on for the boys?"

He leaned closer and whispered. "I'm just about through whittling some toys for them." He glanced at the stairway. "And I did make that sled for Samuel."

"I love Christmas. It's such a rich opportunity to share God's grace with others."

"It reminds me of when I was a child. I was a lot like Samuel." Michael eased back from her and returned to his breakfast. She smelled heavenly, cooked wonderfully, and she was way too appealing on the eyes. *Lord, help me.*

"That doesn't surprise me." Angela smiled.

"Oh?"

"You've barely sat still since I entered your home."

Am I that obvious, Lord? "Sorry."

"No apology necessary. The boys and I have talked." She placed her silky smooth hand upon his. "I understand their loss, and I'm sorry for yours. I can't imagine how hard it must be to raise a family on your own. At least my father had me to help. And all four of us were older."

He lifted his thumb to caress her hand, then stopped. What was he doing? He pulled his hand back. "I'd best get to work before the boys come down. Make yourself at home."

The chair scraped the floor. He put his dirty plate beside the sink. "I'll be in my room if you need anything."

⊷✷⊶

Angela blinked. *What were you thinking?* she asked herself. She went to the sink and cleaned Michael's plate. How dared she reach out and touch the man? Where was her common sense? Her mother had raised her well. She knew better. Or at least she thought she knew better. She'd never reached out and touched a man like that before. Well, no one but her father. But fathers didn't count. They weren't men, just fathers. *Oh, that sounds highly intelligent.*

One thing was certain, she couldn't marry Kevin, not if she could be so attracted to another man. The fact that Rosemary Cloutier had been visiting her father more often hadn't escaped her notice, either. Had her father found another woman but refused to marry her as long as Angela was in the house? Was that the sudden rush to get her married to Kevin?

Angela tore into the mounds of debris in the family area. Piles of old clothing, shoes. . .her hands stopped at a picture. *Julie,* she thought. *So that's where Sam gets his curls.*

"Let me have that." Michael's harsh tone startled her.

"She's very pretty."

"Yes, she was." Michael collapsed in a chair. "You don't need to be cleaning my house."

"Sorry. You said to make myself at home and, well, since my mother died, that's what I do. I clean, I cook, I sew. . .whatever is needed."

Michael nodded.

Angela sat down on the bench opposite him.

"I'm sorry," he said. "I guess I've let the place get. . ." He turned the picture face down on his right thigh.

"How can you possibly keep up with running the farm, the boys, and the house?"

"I've been thinking about hiring someone to come in a couple times a week to cook and clean. Would you be interested?"

"I don't know; I'd have to pray on it and. . ." She paused. Should she tell him about Kevin and her father's attempts to marry her off? "I'm not sure what my future holds at the moment."

Michael's eyes stayed fixed on his wife's upside-down picture. "One should pray," he mumbled.

What was he thinking? Had he slipped into a world of old memories with his wife? And why does it bother me if he has? Am I. . .no, I can't be, there's nothing there to suggest such a foolish thing. Other than the hammering of her own heart when Michael came close. *This is too strange, Lord. How can a reasonably intelligent woman fall in—* No, she wasn't in love, she was in lust. No, it wasn't lust, it was attraction. *How can I be so attracted to this man, drawn to him? Want to help him. Want to help his sons. It seriously doesn't make sense, at least not logical sense.*

She'd heard about love at first sight but had never experienced such a thing and thought it rather foolish. A woman took time to develop an acquaintance with a man before she opened her heart to him. That was the proper order of things. Not the misguided emotions she felt at the moment.

"What's going on in your pretty little head?" Michael asked.

Her cheeks flamed.

"Dad," Noah called out.

Chapter 4

It didn't hurt nearly as bad when he looked at Julie's radiant image. Michael set the picture on the small table by the divan. "Excuse me," he said, getting up to answer his son's call.

He caught a glimpse of Angela hiding her embarrassment. She was a beautiful woman. Could he keep his attraction to her from growing if she were to accept his offer to clean and cook for them?

He hiked up the stairs two at a time.

Why'd you have to offer her the job? he wondered. *Because you know she's not afraid of hard work. Just look at the way she tackled this place.*

Noah stood behind his partially opened door. "Dad," he whispered.

Michael leaned closer.

"Sam and I want to make something for Miss Harris for Christmas."

"That's a fine idea, Son." He prayed the boys weren't getting too close to the angel downstairs. "What do you have in mind?"

Samuel came up behind him. "Well, she's a girl, and we aren't sure what girls like. We thought we'd better ask you since you were married to a girl."

Michael held down his grin and scratched his beard. "Seems to me girls like fancy things. Like hat boxes and jewelry and stuff."

"We ain't got none of that stuff." Sam sighed.

"Ah, but in your momma's trunk there is some lace and fancy woman's fabric she'd bought before she got sick."

"Do you think Mom would mind us using it?" Noah released his grip on the door.

"I think your momma would be pleased that you used it as a gift." He prayed Julie would understand. Pleasing Angela was no longer something the boys alone wanted to do, but a desire stirred deep within him to do something special for her.

"Give me a minute and you can come join me in my room. We can go through your momma's things."

His sons' eyes twinkled with excitement, and it didn't surprise him to find a grin spreading across his own face.

A heavenly scent caused his nostrils to flare.

"What's Miss Harris making now?" Noah asked, rubbing his stomach.

"I don't know, boys, but I think we're in for a real treat."

"She's a good cook," Samuel declared.

"Yes, she is. Too good," he muttered, turning his back on the boys. Bit by bit, every tasty morsel that passed his lips fueled his desire to get to know her.

Downstairs, he found Angela in the kitchen. The table was littered with flour, bowls, and a variety of other things, her movements quick and fluid between the stove and the table. "What are you doing?"

"Baking. Sorry about the mess, but I'll clean it up."

"I mean, what are you baking?"

"Oh, just a few things I thought the boys might enjoy."

Michael's shoulders slumped. *She's cooking for the boys. Of course she is. She isn't. . .* No, he wouldn't finish that thought. He didn't want to be reminded about the angelic temptation taking over his kitchen and his heart. It was better this way. More pure, more right. God had sent her, their own Christmas angel, to furnish them with a wonderful holiday.

"Michael," she whispered.

"Yes?" His pulse quickened.

"If it's all right, I'd like to make up some special things for your Christmas dinner. The boys said you were hunting for a Christmas goose, and there are some things I can bake to make the meal special for all of you."

At least he was included in her "all of you."

"I won't stop you if it's what you'd like to do. The good Lord knows our stomachs could use some tasty meals."

"Thank you. And, Michael?"

He stepped closer. She smelled of cinnamon. Who'd have thought the smell would be so appealing? Her gaze met his—the warmth of her blue eyes, the widening of her pupils. Desire lurked beneath the surface. He saw it. She couldn't deny it. He couldn't deny it.

He reached for her hand. "Angela." Her name struggled to the surface and tumbled over his lips.

Noah and Sam's footfalls assaulted his ears. He released her hand and quickly stepped back. What had come over him?

"Dad, can we go in your room now?"

He cleared his throat and tore his gaze from Angela's. "Give me a minute, boys."

❦

Angela swallowed hard when Michael left her side. What had come over her? Over him? *Lord, stop the storm outside before this one inside of me brews into a tempest,* she prayed.

"What ya making?" Samuel asked, scurrying up on to the bench next to the table.

"I thought I'd make you a surprise."

"For me?" Samuel beamed.

"Yes, for you." She tapped his nose with her floured finger.

Noah laughed. "Your nose is covered with flour."

Samuel brushed off the white covering.

She might have desires for the boys' father, Angela admitted ruefully, but she definitely had fallen in love with the boys.

Michael called them from his room.

Samuel dipped his finger in the cookie batter. "Hmm, good. I like cookies."

She gave him a playful swat on his backside as he scurried off to join his father. She heard some whispering and turned just in time to find Noah getting a finger full of the cookie batter. "If you keep that up, there'll be none left to cook."

Noah smiled and ran off to his father's room.

What she didn't expect was to find Michael's finger in the bowl a few minutes later.

"Stop that." She swatted her dishtowel at him.

"But the boys bragged about it so much I just had to taste it for myself." Michael winked.

"You're the parent. You should show by example," she chastened.

"Do you mean to tell me your father never dipped his finger in your mother's cookie dough?"

Angela grinned. Her father had been caught on more than one occasion stealing a taste. "I didn't say that."

"I rest my case."

"Oh, you, go do something." She shooed him off.

"In a minute." Michael reached in and took another scoop.

"You're worse than the boys."

Michael grinned and scurried back toward his room.

"Men." She smiled. "They're just little boys in a larger frame, Lord."

"I heard that," Michael called back to her.

Joy washed over her, hearing the laughter in his voice. God might be using her to help bring healing into this house, but she'd have to watch the ever-growing attraction between them. If she didn't know better, she'd think they'd nearly kissed.

Impossible.

Was it? Angela flopped down on a chair. How was she going to tell her father she couldn't marry Kevin without telling him how attracted she'd become to a stranger? But was Michael Farley still a stranger? Angela nibbled her lower lip.

The wind howled. "And when is that storm going to end?" she muttered. *I need to get home. I need to get some sanity back into my life.* She turned and faced Michael's closed bedroom door. Did she really want to leave this haven? Here people weren't telling her what to do. She wasn't their slave. She did the chores because she wanted to. She was appreciated. She'd gotten more thank-yous and praises for her cooking from these three than she had in the past year with her father.

Kevin didn't mind her cooking, but he didn't compliment it, either. In reality, Kevin wanted a house servant more than he wanted a wife. Oh, she supposed he loved her on some level. Why, she couldn't imagine. Apart from his obvious appreciation of her looks, they had nothing in common. He liked the things she didn't, and she liked the things he had no interest in. No, she couldn't marry Kevin.

Michael's huge frame, dark hair, and wild blue-gray eyes came back into focus in her mind's eye. "Oh my." She fanned herself. "Work, I need to work."

Angela went back to making the cookies, stew, various breads, and some sweet jam to put on the Christmas goose. Yes, they would have a Christmas feast fit for a king. They deserved it. Desire meshed with reality. She wanted to participate in the meal with them. Perhaps the storm would continue for five more days. Reality weighed heavily on her shoulders. She should be home with her father, in her own home, in her rightful place, not enjoying some winter fantasy her mind had concocted.

Five more days.

She'd never survive it. After all, hadn't it been only twenty-four hours since she woke up in front of the Farleys' woodstove?

"Stop the storm, Lord. I need to go home."

Michael worked with the boys. He prayed Angela would accept the boys' hard work as precious gifts, even though they weren't something a refined woman like herself would purchase in a store. They had taken an old hat box of Julie's and covered it with new fabric. Gluing and pinning the lace around the border had given him fits. His fingers were more punctured than after several days of working with wire fencing. *How do women sew with these things?*

"Do you think she'll like it?" Noah asked.

"I'm sure she will."

"What is she going to do with it?" Samuel scrunched up his nose.

"I imagine she'll put precious things in there or perhaps a hat."

"But our hats hang on a peg by the door." Noah wrinkled his forehead.

"True, but ladies' hats are more delicate."

"Why?" Samuel's innocent question made Michael more aware of how isolated he'd kept the boys since Julie's death. He needed to change that. He needed to take a trip and visit her parents and perhaps his own.

"God made women more delicate, like a lady's hat."

"But why?" Noah leaned back on his elbows. "Female barn animals do as much as the male animals, sometimes more."

"True, but even there, look at the size of a cow compared to the bull."

Noah's eyebrows rose.

Michael continued. "With people, God made it that man would work and provide for his family, but that the woman would help take care of the house, raise the kids, feed us delicious meals, and stuff like that. They are still just as busy, but it's different work."

"Can Miss Harris be the woman for our house?"

Michael's gut twisted. "It doesn't quite work that way, Son. A man and a woman have to fall in love and know that God has a plan for them to marry. Like your mother and me."

"But. . ."

Noah interrupted. "Dad would have to kiss her."

"Oh." Samuel pulled his knees up to his chin. "Like Billy kisses the girls at school?"

"Sort of."

Michael wondered just what Billy was doing in school and why the teacher wasn't aware of it.

"Dad, I don't think you ought to chase Miss Harris like Billy does. The girls scream and run away from him."

Michael chuckled. "Trust me, Son, I'm not going to be chasing Miss Harris for a kiss. And before you get any more foolish ideas in your head, a man can hire someone to come into his home to do the cooking and cleaning. And I'm in a mind to do just that."

"Can you hire Miss Harris?" Noah beamed. "She cooks real well."

"I'll mention it to her, but she has other responsibilities at her home."

"I like Miss Harris, Dad. I hope she can work for you, too."

The question was, Did Michael want to hire Miss Harris, given the obvious physical attraction between them? She was too young to be an old maid, so trying to hook her claws into him didn't figure. But he couldn't for the life of him think of one good reason why she'd be attracted to him. His beard and his hair were wild and woolly. His house was unkempt. *Must be a reaction to me saving her life.*

He rubbed his beard. *Why am I attracted to her?* No, he couldn't allow that attraction to grow.

"Julie," he sighed, putting her things back in the trunk.

He came across her sewing kit and some warm, plaid, flannel fabric. He clutched the material to his chest. She'd purchased this shortly before she became ill. She'd planned on making new shirts for him and the boys.

No, he couldn't let his attraction to Angela grow. Too much would be lost.

Chapter 5

Angela fought her thoughts all afternoon and into the evening. The boys had loved their supper, and so had Michael, although he failed to give her more than a simple thank-you. Having him work in his room was a welcomed relief from the tension building between them all day.

The evening wasn't a total loss. Reading to the boys before they went to bed had been a blessing. Hearing Michael read the Christmas account from the Gospel of Luke blessed her as well. He had a deep, rich voice, and hearing him read the Word of God drew her closer to the Lord—almost as if He were right there in the room telling the story Himself.

The front room, dining area, and kitchen were finally clean. She hadn't worked this hard in a long time. Angela leaned back and stretched her spine. Even fall cleaning hadn't been this difficult. Fresh laundry hung in the living area. They wouldn't smell as fresh and clean as if they were hung outside, but the constant howl of the wind reminded her there was little chance of laundry doing anything but freezing outside.

"Miss Harris," Michael called out to her. At some point during the day, he'd regressed to using her formal name. "What are you doing now? Can't you sit still for a moment?" Michael huffed as he made his way through the hanging clothes.

Angela looked down at her toes. "I'm sorry. I didn't mean to upset you."

"Look, you're not here to be my slave. You may have to work day and night for your father, but in my house—"

"I'm not my father's slave."

"You could have fooled me. You can't rest, can you?"

"I can. I just feel I'm more useful helping you out." Her eyes began to water. Try as she might to stop them from overflowing, she couldn't. *He is trying to be nice,* she reasoned, but his words stung.

"Miss Harris." Michael lowered his voice. "Angela, you don't have to do all this."

"I want to. I feel useful."

"I appreciate your help, truly I do, but you must stop and rest. You're pale and weak. Don't forget you almost died out there." He raised his hand to her forehead. "You've got a fever. Please sit down and relax."

Angela sat down on the divan. Exhaustion swept over her.

"Now, it's my turn to serve you."

Angela sat up.

Michael gently pushed her back down. "Hush now. I'm going to make us some tea. I'm quite capable of that."

Angela leaned against the small feather pillow on the divan. She shouldn't have pushed herself so hard. With the inside of her wrist, she felt her forehead. Her temperature was elevated. A draft hissed through the window. A shiver swept over her. She grabbed the quilt she'd draped over the divan earlier and covered herself.

"Glad to see you're being reasonable. I don't need you falling ill. It's bad enough your father's going to be worried sick over you. He won't be pleased if I don't take the best care of his daughter." Michael handed her a piping hot mug of tea.

Angela wrapped her hands around the mug and let the heat warm her. "I wish there was some way to contact him."

"The wind appears to be settling down some. Hopefully the storm will end during the night."

Angela glanced at Julie's picture. "How did she die? If you don't mind me asking."

"Lung sickness or consumption. The doctor wasn't certain which. She withered away before my eyes. It's a horrible way to go."

"I'm sorry. My mother got some infection, and it just poisoned her entire body. Perhaps that is why I feel the need to keep everything so clean."

"Perhaps."

Angela sipped her tea. Michael gently rocked back and forth in the chair. What could she say? They were both lost in the memories of death and dying. Heaven was looking better every day.

For the first time in over a year, Michael allowed himself to think about others in this world who suffered. He and his sons were not alone.

He combed his beard with his hand and cleared his throat. "Angela, thank you for helping. I know I've let the house go. Have you thought about coming to work for me?"

"Do you think it wise?"

"I don't understand. Because I'm a widower and you're single?"

"No, but that is a point to consider." She pulled the quilt higher up to her chin. "I'm thinking more in terms. . ." She paused and looked away. "In terms of what happened earlier."

"Nothing happened." Only because sanity had entered his clouded brain just in the nick of time.

"Fine, believe what you will. But you and I both know what we saw in each other's eyes."

Heat filled his cheeks. The temperature on his neck rose a notch or two. "Nothing happened and nothing will. I love my wife."

"I see." She closed her eyes and bowed her head.

Was she praying? He could control his emotions. Foolish thoughts would not, could not, rule his actions. "I'm—"

"Please don't say it. You'll only make things worse. I don't understand what happened earlier any more than you do. But whatever this is, it is more real than the past two years with Kevin."

"Who's Kevin?" The words slipped from his lips.

"Kevin Mason has been attempting to court me for two years. He and Father have decided we should get married. I can't marry him. I won't marry him. A woman has to feel something for her husband. Something akin to what I felt earlier, I daresay. I won't marry a man I don't love."

"No one should marry someone without love." Michael clasped his hands together, fighting the desire to reach out and hold her hand. Marriage was hard work. He'd been stretched in more ways than a team pulling a plow during his marriage to Julie. He couldn't imagine tackling a life with someone he didn't care for.

"Thank you. Father will just have to understand."

"Would you like me to talk with him?"

"Would you like him to force you to marry me?"

"What?"

"Face it, we've been alone together for two days. How do you think he'll be feeling about my honor?"

"For pity's sake, Woman, was he raised in the Dark Ages? I merely rescued you from death. Am I supposed to marry you because of that?"

Angela giggled. "No. I'm just saying that if you speak of private matters with my father, he will be concerned about my honor."

"Oh. I get your point." He leaned forward, placing his elbows on his knees.

"Papa will be fine with your rescuing me."

"Let's not get your papa riled then. I don't need any more trouble."

Angela chuckled.

"I still could use a housekeeper."

"I'll pray about it, Michael."

"That's all I ask." Michael stood up. "Do you need anything?"

"No, I'm fine, thank you."

"Then I'll say good night. I'm certain I have a lot of work cut out for me in the morning."

"Good night."

He placed his hand upon her shoulder and gave it a gentle squeeze. "Rest, Angela; you've worked too hard."

"I will. I promise."

"Good night." Before another wave of emotion took over, he thrust his feet forward and worked his way through the maze of clean laundry. *Were there really that many clothes I had piled around the house?* he wondered.

Opening his bedroom door, he glanced at the piles of clean and unfolded clothing—the piles of only-worn-once-and-could-be-worn-again clothes and the mound of filthy clothing that needed immediate attention. He closed the door. Angela didn't need to see this mess.

Michael groaned. She'd been in his room the day before. She had seen it. Buying a new pair of pants instead of washing the old was ridiculous. But he'd found himself doing that on more than one occasion when he was in town. "Lord, I need a maid. I wouldn't mind Angela, but she is temptation like I've not experienced in a very long time. Heal her, Lord. Keep her from getting sick. In Jesus' name, amen."

Michael found himself snuggled in bed and for the first time since Julie's death not reaching for her pillow. His eyelids closed. His nightly prayer changed. He hadn't asked the Lord to give Julie a message from him. Instead, the image dancing through his mind was of Angela.

He punched his pillow and buried his face deep within it, stifling a scream. "God, help me. I can't give in to this. It's too soon. Forget too soon, it's impossible. I can't open my heart to lose it again. Please end this storm before I do something foolish."

᳅

Angela's chest felt heavy, tight, making it hard to breathe. "No, God, please help me." She jumped up and felt dizzy.

"Are you all right?" Michael called from her left.

"I—I need some tea."

"Sit, I'll fix some up for you. How's that fever?"

She felt her forehead. "I think it's gone." If that was the case, then she wasn't as sick as she thought. Her back ached. Her legs ached. It hurt to even lift her arms. *What's wrong with me?*

He came up beside her and gently felt her forehead. "You're going back to bed." He lifted her and carried her to the divan. "I'll remake my bed with fresh sheets. You're spending the rest of the day in bed."

"No, I—" Angela cleared her throat, abating the threat of a cough.

"This is not up for debate, Angela. You're going to do exactly as I say, understand?"

Angela couldn't argue; she had no strength. She'd overdone it yesterday. She knew it, he knew it, and now her body was fighting it.

"Give me a couple minutes. Drink your tea."

She reached out and clasped his hand. "Thank you."

"Just get better," he said through clenched teeth.

She leaned her head back down on the pillow and closed her eyes. She took in a deep breath. *Praise You, Lord, I didn't cough,* she prayed, then allowed sleep to take over. She was tired; she just needed to rest. She'd be all right. If only she could convince Michael of that.

Pleasant dreams cascaded over her. She drifted off. Her spirit soared, it was spring, flowers bloomed, birds sang in the trees. "Oh, Michael." She found herself embraced in his arms. "How can I love you so?"

❧❧❧

"Women," Michael mumbled as he fought to keep his temper. "What was she thinking?"

He pulled the sheets off his bed. The open windows would cleanse the air while he kicked up the dust and cleaned his room. "If she sees this dirty laundry, she'll force herself out of bed and work again. She's got a death wish, God. What is she trying to prove, anyway? That I'm a lousy housekeeper? I know that. Noah and Sam know it."

Michael shoved the dirty linen in a sack, then stuffed his filthy clothes in the armoire. While she rested, he would finish the laundry and do his clothes and any of the boys' that needed doing. He opened the cherry armoire he'd made for Julie when they were first married and piled the not-so-dirty clothes inside.

He spun around in a circle. "Not too bad." He put on fresh sheets, lit the small stove, and closed the window. "God, heal her. I don't need her father coming after me."

"Who did laundry?" Sam asked, following his brother down the stairs.

"Miss Harris. Noah, please get a kettle full of water and put it on the woodstove in my room."

"Sure." Noah headed into the kitchen.

Sam pushed himself up on his toes to try to look over the laundry. When that didn't work, he bent down and looked under them. "Where's Miss Harris?"

"On the divan, but I'm putting her in my room. She needs more rest."

Sam stood ramrod straight. Michael knew the child was thinking of his mother. The slight twitch of his right eye was a sure sign. A tick caused, the doctor said, by strong emotions. Michael hadn't seen it for months. *God, please don't let her get seriously ill.* "She's going to be fine, Son. She just worked too hard and needs more sleep."

Sam bent his head down. "Oh. Guess we'll have ham and beans tonight, huh?"

"Maybe. I think she made some beef stew yesterday."

"Really?" The boy beamed.

"Yes. Now, I must get her to my room. Excuse me."

Sam pulled back a plaid flannel shirt and followed his progress through the laundry jungle. *Lord, don't let these boys suffer another loss. It's too soon.*

The golden mane of hair cascaded over her pillow. Her skin seemed pale, but a slight blush of color painted her cheeks. Rather than disturb her, he lifted her and carried her to his room. Gently he placed her on his bed and covered her in a cocoon of quilts and pillows.

In her sleep she pulled the covers up over her shoulder and rolled to her side.

Michael left her, and Noah placed the kettle on the woodstove. "She going to be all right, Dad?"

"I believe so, Son." Michael placed his hand on his son's shoulder. "Are you hungry?"

"Starving. She made biscuits and sweet rolls, I think."

"Sounds wonderful. Come and help me by taking down the dry laundry while I fix up some flapjacks and bacon."

Noah patted his stomach. "Storms can be a blessing."

Michael gave a light chuckle as he closed his bedroom door.

"Who cleaned your room, Dad?" Noah asked.

"I did."

"You cleaned, Dad?" Sam asked, tugging on two shirts hanging on the line.

"I can clean; I just don't have much time for it."

"Mom used ta say you didn't clean, you just stuffed the furniture full of the dirty laundry."

Michael cleared his throat and looked at his feet. "Well, don't you go telling Miss Harris that. She's done too much. She was weakened from that storm."

Noah smiled. "Your secret is safe with us, Dad."

Michael managed to get six good flapjacks for the boys. The other half dozen were slightly charred. "Grows hair on a man's chest," his father used to say. Personally, he'd rather have a hairless chest and a belly full of good food.

The wind seemed to have calmed down. "Boys, I'm going to head out to the barn and check on the animals. Don't go waking up Miss Harris, now."

"No, Sir." He watched the boys climb the stairs. Perhaps they were still working on their Christmas gifts.

Christmas! The goose he'd promised for the boys. Michael bundled into his wool coat and headed out the front door. The blast of cold air caused him to pause. He pulled up his collar and tried to work his way through the deep piles of snow. *Noah and Sam will love playing in this.*

He retreated to his porch and took his shovel. The only way he'd get to that barn today would be to make a path.

Michael had no idea how long he'd been out in the cold, but his hands were numb and his back stiff. He'd fed the livestock and walked easily back to the house along the path he'd carved out. He'd need to reweave his snowshoes if he hoped to hunt with this much snow.

Stepping inside the house, he found the heat stung his body. He'd been out too long. Snow was still falling, but the flakes were larger. Soon the storm would end, and he could bring Miss Harris back to her home.

The door to his room stood wide open.

He stepped closer.

Sam stood beside his bed. "Are you still sleepy?"

Angela rolled over and held Sam's hand. "I'm feeling pretty rested. You up for another game of Parcheesi?"

"No, I need help making Daddy his present."

Michael stepped back.

"How can I help you?"

Sam leaned over and cupped his hand to Angela's ear.

"I think that's a splendid idea." Angela smiled.

Samuel stood up straighter and puffed out his chest. "He'll be so surprised."

"Yes, he will."

Michael stepped back farther, deeper into the family room. He hurried back to the front door and opened and closed it loudly. "Hey, everyone, I'm back."

"Daddy." Sam came running from the bedroom.

Michael saw Noah in the kitchen wagging his head. Michael winked at him. Noah held back his grin. The joy of being a family was warming this house again, and all because of a golden-haired Christmas angel. *Thank You, Lord.*

Chapter 6

By evening the storm had cleared, and the sky turned a brilliant blue before the sun set. "I need to get home." Angela sat down beside Michael at the kitchen table and held a hot mug of tea between her hands. "My family must be worried sick."

"I'd take you home, but are you strong enough to be out in that cold?"

"If I bundle up enough, I'm sure I'll be fine."

"Noah, Sam, I'm going to take Miss Harris home. I'll be gone for awhile. You boys promise me you'll stay inside while I'm gone." Michael turned to her. "Have you ever worn snowshoes?"

"Afraid not."

"I'd take you with the wagon, but the snow's too deep for my oxen. We need to leave right away if I'm to get back before dark."

"I'll be ready in two minutes." She rushed into Michael's room, put on her own clothing, keeping the long undergarments on. Lacing up her boots seemed futile. They were delicate in-town boots designed for style, not for tramping around in the woods. What had she been thinking when she left home? Finished, she jumped to her feet and greeted the family.

Samuel hugged her first. "You'll come and visit sometime, won't you?"

"I'll try, but I'm certain it will be after Christmas."

He nodded his head of curls and stepped back, swiping his eyes with the back of his hand. Angela took in a deep breath. She loved the child and would miss him, too.

Noah extended his hand. "Thank you, Miss Harris."

Such a little man, she thought. Angela pulled him into her embrace and kissed the top of his head. "You're welcome, Noah."

Michael grabbed the woolen lap blanket from the back of the stuffed chair and draped it over his shoulder.

"Time's a-wasting, Miss Harris." He opened the door and a blast of cold air instantly flooded the house.

"Bye, boys, I'll miss you." Angela waved.

"Bye." Noah looked down at his feet.

"Bye." Samuel sniffled. Noah put a protective arm around his brother's shoulders.

Tears threatened Angela's eyes. She turned and left the two precious boys she'd grown so attached to. How was it possible in only forty-eight hours?

"Here, put this around your shoulders. I'll hook the snowshoes up for you." Michael bent down and grasped her right foot. She eased it up slightly for him to attach the large, funny-looking contraption. She knew they worked. She'd just never needed to wear them. Her father's work always kept them in town. If she wasn't inside, she walked the streets after they were cleared.

"You ought to purchase a pair of real boots. These things aren't good for anything except to look at."

"Yes, I should. I don't do much walking around in the woods."

He fastened the other snowshoe to her left foot.

"Now when you walk with these, the trick is to lift your foot straight up and then set it straight down. We tend to drag our toes when we walk. With snowshoes, it's more like walking like a soldier on a march."

"Okay."

"Go ahead. Try them out." Michael sat down on a barrel and put his on.

Angela worked the awkward contraptions, lifting her legs straight up then down, just as he'd instructed. She turned back to see the boys looking out the window and grinning at her. *If nothing else, I've provided some entertainment for the family,* she snickered to herself.

Michael reached out his hand and helped her work her way down the path to the front gate of his property. It seemed to take forever to get that far. Walking in snowshoes would take practice.

"Angela, I know this will sound forward, but I need to carry you, at least until we get close to town. I'll never make it back to the boys before sunrise, let alone sunset."

Should she let him? He'd carried her once before, but that was different. She'd been numb from the cold. Now she would have to give her consent. She thought back on Noah and Samuel alone in the house. They'd been alone before, but she didn't like it. "All right, Michael. I'm sorry I don't know how to walk in these things."

"Takes some practice. Unfortunately, we don't have time."

He hoisted her up into his arms, and she wrapped hers around his neck. "You'll stay warmer this way," he mumbled.

Warmer was one thing. Holding him, or rather being held by him, sent waves of desire as well as comfort over her. How could that be? Why would she feel desire one moment and security and comfort as if she belonged in his arms the next? She focused on his blue-gray eyes. "Michael?"

He caught a glimpse of desire in her cornflower blue eyes. He held her tighter, then released her slowly. "No, Angela. I can't."

"I'm sorry," she mumbled.

Why'd the woman have to be so desirable? Not to mention her cooking abilities. It wasn't fair. Life wasn't fair. Hadn't he learned that last year when Julie died?

She turned her head and watched the path before them. He'd taken a shortcut through the woods rather than following the road to town. They traveled in silence.

Dogs barked in the distance. "Who's out there hunting, now?" Michael asked.

"Possibly someone looking for that Christmas goose," she quipped.

"Don't remind me."

"Oh, Michael, I'm sorry I've caused you so much trouble."

"You haven't." He shifted her in his arms. She tightened her grasp around his neck. "Sorry, I'll warn you next time."

"Thank you. Do you think you'll be able to get a goose for the boys in time for Christmas?"

"I'm going to try." *Good, talking about the boys and Christmas is a safe subject,* he reasoned.

"They're really excited about the things they've made for you."

Michael smiled. "I'm excited, too. They need joy in their lives."

"Yes, they do."

"It hasn't been easy since Julie died. At first her family came and helped for awhile, but once they saw I was determined to stay in the area and build the farm, they moved back home. I think they thought I'd have to send the boys to them. Truthfully, there were days I thought about it. I'm not sure having them live with me is best."

"Oh, don't even think that way. Of course it's best. You just need some extra help."

"Which brings us back to the question I asked you the other night. Will you come work for me, Angela?"

He could see the edge of town in the distance. The barking of the dogs was getting closer. Odd that someone should hunt so close to town.

"No, Michael, I can't."

"Why not?"

"You know as well as I." Their gazes locked. Who would break away first? Her hands fumbled behind his neck.

"Michael," she whispered. Her warm, delicate hand stroked his cheek and beard.

He dropped her. "I'm sorry," he said, feeling his face warm.

"Well, I've heard of cooling a person off, but. . ."

"Sorry, Angela, I didn't mean to drop you. I just didn't. . ." How could he explain it? That her hand touching his face so startled him he lost his composure?

"Help me up," she ordered and stretched out her hand.

"Sorry." He helped her to her feet and started to brush the fresh snow off her. But when he came close to her hands, he pulled back. He felt like he was eight years old again and having his first serious crush. Of course that girl, Vivian, had never known anything about it. She'd sit down beside him, and he'd be unable to move, unable to breathe.

"Michael Farley, you are the most ridiculous man I've ever met!" Angela's voice interrupted his thoughts. "If I'd given Kevin a quarter of the interest I've shown in you, he'd have persuaded my father to have us married years ago."

His face flamed. "I can't."

"Hmph. You can; you just don't want to. There is a difference."

"But—"

"Look, I know you loved your wife, and I know it still hurts to not have her a part of your life. But the way we feel for each other is real. That's why I can't work for you, Michael. It would never work."

The howling of the hounds closed in upon them.

<hr>

"Angela!" she heard someone calling.

"Angela!" someone called again.

"Over here," she screamed. The dogs stopped barking.

"They're looking for you," Michael offered.

And apparently you aren't, she silently observed. She turned to Michael. "Before they come, I have one more thing to say. God brought us together for a reason, Michael. I know it; and if you search your heart, you know it, too. You know where I live. If you ever decide to. . ."

"Angela!" her father's voice choked out her name. He came running toward her.

"Papa, I'm okay. Michael Farley found me in the woods and brought me home before the storm hit."

Her father extended his hand. "Thank you, Mr. Farley."

"Not a problem, Mr. Harris," Michael said as he shook the man's offered hand.

"Want to come to our house for some hot coffee before you head back home?" her father offered, holding Angela tightly.

"No, Sir, thank you anyway. The sun's getting ready to set, and Noah and Sam are waiting on me."

"Thanks again. I'll get all the details from Angela."

"Thank you, Mr. Farley," Angela said formally. "I appreciate everything you've done for me." She fought the desire to wink at him. Her father would surely catch that maneuver.

"You're welcome, Miss Harris."

He understood the subtle shift to the formal greeting. For a thickheaded man, he did have some sense every now and again.

"I love you, Papa. I'm so sorry. There was no way to connect with you sooner."

"Now, now, Dear. You're safe; that's all that matters. No one could go out in that storm. We just started searching for you about an hour ago."

Folks started gathering around, and Angela gave an abridged version of getting twisted around in the woods when the storm hit and getting so cold that sleep overtook her. Soon the crowd worked their way to town and dispersed to their homes, while she and her father made their way to the feed and grain store.

Being in her father's arms sent a wave of security over her. Angela waited until they were in the house and alone before she spoke.

The teakettle whistled. Her father removed it and poured the hot liquid into the teapot. "Why'd you go into the woods?" he asked, sitting down opposite her.

"Papa, I had to think about Kevin. I can't marry him, Papa, I just can't."

"Why, Dear?"

"I don't love him. He's nice and all, but there are no sparks, no desire. Shouldn't a woman have desires for the man she's going to marry?"

Her father looked down at the table.

"I know we don't talk about these matters," she persisted. "But Momma isn't around, and you have to know."

He coughed. "I understand. But what am I going to tell Kevin?"

"Tell him no. I'm sorry that sounds harsh but. . ." She poured the tea into the cups. "Papa, I'll tell him if I must, but he spoke to you."

"No, I'll speak to him. He's a good man; he'll understand. Besides, if he learns that your anguish over the decision to marry him sent you out into the woods, he'll never forgive himself."

"Please, don't tell him. I don't want to hurt him. He's not a bad man. He's just not my man." She sipped her tea to avoid telling her father who she felt her man was. She couldn't shake the certainty that she and Michael should be together. Perhaps it would just take more time. *Perhaps when he's over the death of Julie, he'll be able to see for himself.* But how long would that take? *Oh, Lord, don't let it take years.*

Chapter 7

Michael returned home before the sun fully set over the horizon. Its fiery display in the sky was no equal to Angela's lecture. The woman had passion and a boldness he'd not seen before in anyone of the opposite sex. Even if he could get past Julie, was he willing to explore living with a woman so bold? Nope, the tempest was gone. He was safe now.

"Hey, boys, I'm home."

"Hi, Dad, we're upstairs working. You can't come up," Noah called down.

"I'll be down here. When you're ready for bed, come on down." Michael moved into the kitchen. On the table sat a fine loaf of apple and raisin bread. He hacked off a large slab and topped it off with the whipped butter Angela had left in a small bowl on the table. His stomach grumbled with appreciation.

He went to the stove and heated up his pot of coffee. Everywhere he looked he saw traces of Angela. The decorative way she'd set up the house for Christmas. The breads, rolls, pies—the woman was a cooking machine. Of course, he and the boys were eating machines. If he could only convince her to come work for him.

Memories of her touch sent a shiver down his spine. No one had affected him like that, not since Julie. Perhaps she was right; the temptation would be too great. Besides, he wasn't ready for another relationship.

He poured himself a large mug of coffee and went into his room. The first thing he needed to do was unload his armoire of his dirty clothing. Inside the tall chest he found a packet wrapped in some of Julie's material with a note attached.

"Michael, please put these out Christmas Eve after the boys go to bed. Consider them a gift from Julie and myself."

He opened the packet and discovered the flannel shirts Julie had started to make for the boys with the material she'd purchased just before she'd taken ill.

His heart thumped. "Angela, Julie. . ." He held the shirts to his chest. "Lord, Angela is an angel sent from You."

In his mind he heard a whisper of a voice reply, "Not really."

The heavenly image of Angela's golden hair and cornflower blue eyes flooded his mind.

"Dad!" Samuel yelled.

"Saved by reality." Michael refolded the shirts and put them in the bundle. "In my room, Son. Give me a minute."

He placed the package in the armoire and closed the doors.

"Come in, Sam."

"Dad, I was thinking."

When Sam started thinking, it was time for Michael to put up his guard. "What about, Son?" Michael sat down on his bed, which he noticed was made with fresh linens. *That woman.* He wagged his head from side to side.

Samuel crawled up on the bed and sat beside him. "Well, Miss Harris, she helped us with your presents."

Michael nodded his head. He would wait to see where this was going.

"And well, you see, I was thinking. I was thinking that maybe we all ought to make something for her."

"Son, we already did that. We don't have much time for another gift."

"I know."

Noah entered the room. "But if we all worked together, Dad, don't you think we could do something more?"

"Possibly. What did you boys have in mind?" Michael tapped his knee for Noah to join them.

"She likes to cook, but we can't make pans, can we?" Noah asked.

"No, Son, I'm not a blacksmith. I'm afraid that's something we couldn't do."

Samuel scanned the room. Michael followed suit. "What about a sewing box like ya made Momma."

"Yeah, but bigger. Momma's sewing stuff was always all over the place."

"Hmm." Michael scratched his beard. "I have some cherry in the barn."

"Cherry?" Sam scrunched up his nose.

"It's a type of wood, a hardwood with a nice design in the grain. We'd have to work real hard to have it ready by Christmas. Of course, we wouldn't have it oiled by then."

"We need to give her a finished present, Dad." Samuel stood up on the bed and placed his hands on his hips.

"I suppose you're right."

Noah went over to his mother's sewing box. "Why don't we just fix up Mom's and give it to Miss Harris? I ain't gonna learn to sew, are you, Dad?"

"No, but—"

"Mom wouldn't mind, Dad. She doesn't need a sewing box in heaven 'cause she didn't take it with her," Sam surmised.

The boy was dangerously close to being too intelligent for his own good. "No, I suspect you're right."

"What do you have in mind, Noah?"

The three of them huddled over Julie's sewing box and planned.

On Christmas Eve, Angela realized she hadn't stopped baking and knitting for days. She had to make something more for the boys. The shirts were really from their mother. The question was how she would get the items to Michael's house without him noticing it until it was too late.

Kevin Mason took the news that they wouldn't be getting married rather nonchalantly. In some way she felt he seemed relieved. Like he'd asked for her hand out of duty or maybe just out of guilt for eating all those free meals. Whatever the case, he was now out of her life. He'd come over only once during the day and then simply visited her father in the store.

Dreams of Michael grew stronger each night. She prayed for him. She prayed for herself. She prayed for them. She prayed to get the images out of her mind. It was utter foolishness to fall so deeply for a man she barely knew. But having spent two full days with him and the boys, she felt she knew him better than she knew her own father, if that were possible. She groaned and went to the oven to check on her pumpkin pies.

"When are you going to stop baking, Angela?" her father asked as he entered their private living quarters.

"This is the last until tomorrow."

"Is there anything left to cook? There's just the two of us."

"I know, but. . ."

"All right, I can't take it another moment. What happened at the Farleys?"

"What?"

"Don't go giving me those innocent eyes. Tell me straight, Daughter. Did you fall in love with Mr. Farley?"

"Oh, Papa, I think so. I can't stop thinking about him. Day and night. Night and day. It's impossible." She sat down at the table.

Her father pulled out a chair for himself. "I see, and does he feel the same way about you?"

"No, he wants to hire me to clean his house and cook his meals."

His bushy eyebrows rose. "Why didn't you take him up on the offer?"

"Papa, I couldn't. What if. . ." She felt the heat of embarrassment rise on her cheeks.

"That bad, huh?"

She nodded. What could she say? And how was it her father understood such feelings? A fleeting thought that he was once a young man in love slipped through her mind.

"Look, I can't say that you should or shouldn't take the job. But Farley, he don't get out much. When do you think you'll see him again?"

"I don't know, Papa. I was kind of bold."

"What are you saying, Daughter? Please tell me you did nothing we should be ashamed of."

"No, Papa, nothing like that. I merely told him once he was over his wife, he should come see me."

"I see. You know it takes a man awhile."

"I know, but—"

Her father raised his hand. "Hush, Child, I have something to say.

The Snow Storm

I suppose you've probably figured out I've been seeing Rosemary Cloutier."

"Yes. Are you going to marry her?"

"Nothing like getting to the point of things, huh?" He grinned. "Well, she's told me to get serious or move on."

Angela laughed out loud. "Men, what is it about you? Papa, I know Mrs. Cloutier will never replace Momma, but if you love her. . ."

"That's just it, Child. It takes a man awhile to realize he can love another woman and not disrespect his first wife. You see, I love your mother very much, and the mere thought of thinking of another woman as my wife. . .let's just say it was none too comfortable."

"You're saying I should be patient?"

"Yes." He pushed his chair back and got up from the table. "It's only been, what, four days since you met him?"

"Five," she corrected.

"Five whole days, an eternity," he mocked and went to his room.

He did have a point, and patience didn't suit her well. "God, give me strength. I don't think I can wait two years like Mrs. Cloutier."

<hr>

Michael kissed Noah and Sam after finishing their prayers together. They'd had a delightful couple of days preparing for Christmas, everyone huddling in their own corners of the house, busily making gifts in secret and working together on Angela's gift. "Good night, boys. I'll see you in the morning."

"Night, Dad." Noah snuggled under the blanket up to his chin.

Michael pulled the covers up over Sam's chest and tucked the boy in.

"Daddy, is it really Jesus' birthday?"

"No one knows for sure, Son, but it seems as good a day as any, don't you think?"

"Yeah, but how come we don't know what His real birthday is?"

"Because they didn't write it down back then."

Samuel raised himself up on his elbows, undoing the tucked-in blankets. "Why didn't they write it in the family Bible, like we do now?"

Michael chuckled.

"Because Jesus was part of the Bible, Silly," Noah added with a hint of disgust in his voice.

"Noah."

"Sorry, Dad. Sorry, Sam." Noah rolled to his side.

Samuel wiped his nose with the cuff of his shirt. Michael thought of correcting him but couldn't afford the time. "Good night, boys," he said again, getting up from beside their bed.

"Dad," Samuel called out in his singsong voice.

"Do you want coal in your stocking, Son?"

"No, Sir."

"Then I suggest you get some sleep."

"Yes, Sir." Samuel scurried under the covers and squeezed his eyelids shut.

Michael thought he heard Noah say something about babies under his breath. Another thing he'd have to let pass if he was going to finish his gift for Angela.

He'd worked hard each night after the boys had gone to bed. At first it was difficult thinking about giving Julie's sewing box to Angela, but soon it seemed like a very practical thing to do. However, he didn't want Angela feeling like she was getting Julie's leftovers. Together with the boys, they had worked to refinish and also add a little bit to the box.

What he was working on would be an addition to the box or could be used as something entirely different. Carving the angel in the top of the small box he'd designed for pins and needles, or perhaps small pieces of jewelry, had been the hardest part. Putting the box together, while difficult because of the small size, wasn't anything compared to the intricate work on the angel.

Michael prayed as he worked the small chisel to carve the fine lines of the feathers within the wings. "Father, she definitely brought a change in this household, but I don't know if there should be anything more between us. I'm grateful, but I'm not sure if I'm ready for a wife. Angels are messengers, Lord, and I got the message."

A small voice rumbled around in his head. *"Did you?"*

Chapter 8

"Merry Christmas, Father." Angela hugged her father and gave him a gentle kiss on the cheek.

"Merry Christmas, Child. Did you sleep well?"

"Yes, Papa."

"What is our agenda today? I know you did not cook all this food for us. Where are we going?"

"I thought we could invite Mrs. Cloutier over for Christmas dinner."

"Did you think to extend an invitation at church last evening?"

"Yes." She winked.

"We are to have guests, then? Good, good, a house is merrier with more people. Are your brother and his wife invited to this special event?"

"Of course. Father, why do you think I wouldn't invite the entire family?"

"No reason, Child. I seem to be the last to know of your plans."

"I wanted to surprise you."

"And who else did you invite?"

"No one. Just the family and Mrs. Cloutier, of course. You will be making her part of the family shortly, won't you, Father?"

A deep rumble of a laugh filled the room. "In my own good time, Child. And I'll not fancy you pushing me one way or the other."

"Never, Papa."

He wagged his head and went back to his room, no doubt to dress for the guest. The one family she wanted to invite had been the Farleys, but Michael hadn't been in church last evening. She'd so hoped to see him and the boys. He should have been able to get his oxen and sled out by now. At least she had hoped he would have. It mattered little. She could not be forward and approach him. She'd already been far too forward than was proper for a woman of good breeding. Of course, she never did complete her studies at finishing school, not after her mother died.

Who was she kidding? She had reached out and touched Michael in a very forward manner. She knew it. He knew it. And he'd run from her faster than a fox with his tail on fire.

Well, if God has it in mind for the two of us to get together, it will take a major miracle. Something equivalent to getting a mule out of a pool of molasses, I daresay. She would pray and she would try to be patient, or she would be single the rest of her life. No man could have her heart, not after Michael Farley had put his brand on it, however unknowingly.

She placed a large pot on the coal stove and poured in a couple of gallons of fresh apple cider with several large cinnamon sticks and a few cloves, then let it simmer. She put the pork rib roast she'd prepared the night before in the oven, stuffing the meat with slices of apples and raisins.

Angela sat by the tree and waited for her father.

"Smells heavenly, Angela."

She inhaled deeply. The aroma of cider mixed with the scent of spices from the pork roast filled her nostrils, and her heart warmed with joy. It was a holiday of rejoicing. Today marked the day when God started the process to bring man back to Himself. It wouldn't be complete until Easter and the Resurrection, but each year it was a good reminder of just how miraculous it had been to bring a Babe into the world to bridge the storm of sin. "Thank you, Father. Come, I have something for you."

"Don't you want to wait for the rest of the family?" Her father smiled, his bushy eyebrows rising up his forehead.

"No, Papa, I want to give this to you now. You'll understand once you've opened it."

"All right, Daughter. If you insist." She could tell by the gleam in his eyes that he, too, still had the heart of a child when opening gifts. "But first, we must pray and thank the Lord for this glorious day."

"Yes, Papa." She held out her hand, and his thick, rough hand grasped hers.

"Father," he began.

Her mind drifted to Michael, to Noah and Samuel. Did they appreciate the gifts she'd made for them? She prayed she hadn't overstepped her bounds by finishing those shirts. Admittedly, she had had to redo Noah's because he'd grown so much. Samuel would fit the one Julie had intended for Noah.

"And, Lord, we come before You on behalf of Mr. Farley and his family."

Angela's head shot up, then relaxed.

"He's a kind man," her father continued, "but he's had a mess of trouble with his wife takin' ill like that. It's hard on a man raising young ones on his own. We ask You to go before him in all he says and does."

Angela bit her inner cheek. Father did understand what it was to have children without a wife. But Michael had it worse. He didn't have a daughter, and both boys were still young, though Noah couldn't be told that.

"We praise You for all that You've done for us this past year. And we ask only that You give us a wonderful day with our family today. In Jesus' name, amen."

"Amen." Angela choked down her emotions. God had blessed them this year. Everyone was healthy. She wasn't engaged to Kevin—was she ever thankful for that. And Papa was getting ready to find himself a wife in Rosemary Cloutier. Yes, life was good. So why did she ache inside for Michael? For Noah? For Sam? And most of all for what could have been with Michael and herself? *Oh, God, You know my heart. I give it to You. Tread lightly, Lord,* she prayed.

❦

"Daddy, Daddy, wake up!" Samuel shook him until he opened his eyes.

"What, Son?"

"You've got to see, Daddy. The house, it's beautiful. Where'd all the presents come from?"

"I don't know; we'll have to check." Michael slung his feet over the side of the bed. If he figured right, he'd gotten about two hours' sleep. He'd spent the night cleaning and putting up the remaining Christmas bows and decorations that he and Julie had collected over the years. He'd even chopped some sprigs of pine to put the bows on. If he did say so himself, he'd done a pretty fine job of it. Of course, he'd be dragging the rest of the day.

"Come on, Dad." Samuel tugged on his pajama sleeve.

The rest of the morning was a blur. The boys were so excited, and Michael fought an exhaustion headache—or was it the constant reminder of his Christmas angel and her present sitting under the tree?

"Dad, can we take Miss Harris her present?" Noah asked.

"What about Christmas dinner?"

"I ain't hungry."

"Me, neither," Samuel added, jumping up and down. "Can we please take her her present? Please, Dad. Please."

"All right. But first I need a nap." Not to mention it wasn't even eight o'clock in the morning yet.

"All right, Dad." Noah slumped his shoulders.

"Just an hour, boys. Then we'll leave. I promise. You can wake me up. Will that be all right?"

Sam nodded his head. Michael retreated to his room. He needed just a tad bit more sleep if he was going to address Angela. The woman demanded all of a man's keen senses.

Michael collapsed on his bed. Visions of Angela's golden hair calmed yet revived him all at the same time.

A short while later, Michael jumped out of bed, put on his Sunday best, and found the boys playing with the toys he'd carved. "You boys, get dressed in your church clothes. I'll hook up the sleigh."

"Really?" Sam jumped up.

He grinned. "Really. Come on, get a move on."

The boys ran up the stairs faster than he'd seen them go in a long time. Michael carried the new and improved sewing kit for Angela. He'd decided that gift would come directly from the boys. His more personal gift would come from him, when the boys weren't looking, he hoped.

If anything was decided last night, he definitely didn't want Angela removed from his life. What that meant in terms of them and a future relationship, he didn't know. At least he'd consider the possibility.

He hitched up the sleigh with the oxen, and the boys came running out of the house. No boots, but they did have their winter coats semifastened. Michael chuckled. *If Angela were here. . .* Nope, he wouldn't think that far.

"Where are your boots, boys?"

"In the house," Samuel said innocently.

"Noah, go grab boots for you and your brother. Samuel, bring the woolen lap blanket from the back of the sofa. You never can tell if another storm will blow in."

"Yes, Sir." The boys spun around and reentered the house. Michael climbed up and waited for his sons. "Thank You, Lord. They're good boys. You've blessed us."

The sleigh ride made the trip into town much faster than the day when he'd walked Angela home. Still, it took a lot more time than he thought it would. "She's going to be surprised, huh, Daddy?" Samuel said for the ump-teenth time.

"Yes, she'll be surprised."

"I can't wait," Noah exclaimed. "We worked so hard. She's going to like it, isn't she, Dad?"

"I'm certain of it. You boys did an excellent job."

"Can she be our new momma, Dad?" Samuel asked.

Michael swallowed the ice ball in his throat, nearly dropping the reins. "That's in God's hands, Son."

Noah smiled and winked at Samuel. What did he say wrong there? The boys were up to something. What, he wasn't certain of, but he'd need to watch them like a hawk. No sense leading Angela on when he wasn't sure himself. Or was he?

⚜

Angela stirred the hot cider and inhaled deeply the warm, homey scent. Memories of Christmases past, her mother at the stove preparing the cider, filled her. No longer did she feel the heartache of the loss. Instead she experienced profound gratitude that her mother had been such a great example of a godly woman.

Angela ladled a mug full of the warm cider. The pork roast sizzled to the point of near perfection. All the guests had arrived and were sitting in the front parlor around the Christmas tree. For the first time in her life, she felt—

What do I feel? Strange, alone, as if I'm not really a part of the family. But that's not really it. I am a part, but just not fully connected. "Face it, Angela," she mumbled to herself. "Your mind is on another family."

She fussed with the decorative settings on the table. Part of her gift was the meal she'd prepared. Father sat beside Rosemary on the sofa, his arm resting across her shoulders. *Perhaps a spring wedding,* Angela mused.

Just then, she heard someone coming up the back stairs to the apartment.

She listened intently. More than one person was coming. She walked to the back door.

A small knock was followed by some muffled voices. *Who can it be?* She opened the door. "Noah, Samuel."

"Merry Christmas, Miss Harris," the boys chimed in, their cherub faces grinning from ear to ear.

"We brought you a Christmas present." Sam puffed up his little chest.

"We made it," Noah offered.

"Oh, my. Come in, boys, come in." She glanced at Michael standing behind his sons. Had he intentionally held the piece of furniture in front of his eyes, or was he lifting it over the boys' heads so they all fit on the landing?

"Who's here?" her father called from the front room.

"The Farleys."

Michael lowered the piece and smiled. Angela thought her heart would burst. Had he had a change of heart, or was he doing this for the boys? He was a good father, and no matter how hard it might be for him to see her, he'd still do what was best for his sons.

"Come, join the family in the front parlor. Have you eaten?"

"No, but it sure smells good in here." Samuel leaned toward the stove.

"We have plenty. Would you like to join us?" She glanced up to Michael.

"Can we, Dad?" Noah cried.

"We didn't mean to—"

She placed her hand on his arm. "Of course you didn't. You're welcome to join us, Michael."

"If you don't think we'll impose, we'd be honored." He winked.

He winked, Lord. Oh my. Does he—

Stop it, Angela, stop making things out to be more than they are.

After brief introductions, the boys presented their gift to her. She recognized the piece, but they'd added legs and another drawer. "See." Sam opened up a door on the side of the piece. "Momma always said she needed more space."

Noah interrupted. "We added this area for your spools of thread."

"Boys, this is wonderful, and to think you've made it. It's so special." She reached out and kissed them both. "Thank you, thank you very much."

A special gift and a sacrifice for Michael. Her heart was full.

Rosemary and Angela's sister-in-law, Cynthia, went to the kitchen to finish preparing the meal.

Papa made light conversation with Michael about next spring's planting. She looked at Michael while the boys played quietly on the floor with some toys her brother had brought out from his old room. Now she felt content, as if her world were falling into place. Michael had to know they were meant to be together. He had to feel it, too. Didn't he?

They shared the meal, and everyone complimented her cooking. Cynthia and Brad went home shortly afterward. Papa escorted Rosemary home. The boys played outside in the snow.

Finally she and Michael were alone.

"Angela." Michael's voice was barely above a whisper.

"Michael, thank you for the sewing box."

"That's from the boys. They wanted to give it to you."

"But—"

"Shh." He touched his finger to her lips. Her legs wobbled. "I have a gift for you, but I wanted it to be a surprise, and I guess I'm selfish. I wanted to share it with you privately."

"Oh?"

He reached into his pocket and pulled out a bundle wrapped in pink silk. He tenderly placed it in her open hand. "Open it, please."

"Michael, I–I. . ."

He gave a light chuckle. "Just open it."

She obeyed and pulled the scarlet ribbon tying the silk cloth together. Her hands trembled. "Michael, it's beautiful." She traced the delicate angel on top of the box. "You carved this?"

"Yes, it's a box for needles, pins, anything small."

She opened the lid.

"You do wonderful work, Michael."

"I had great inspiration." She caught his gaze. "Angela, I don't know how to say this so that it sounds right. I'm not a man given to great words, and on more than one occasion I sent my wife crying because of what I said."

She nodded for him to continue.

"I can't get you out of my mind. I'm not sure if I'm ready to open my heart, but I want to. I'm afraid, Angela. I don't know if I could go through the heartache of losing someone I love again. Does that make sense?"

"Yes. Father shared with me about his own struggle of not feeling he was dishonoring my mother by allowing himself to have feelings for another woman."

Michael's posture relaxed.

"I know the Lord sent you to us. You've turned my world upside down and helped me get my focus back. I want you in my life, Angela. I just don't know if that means I'm ready to ask you to be my wife."

Angela let out a nervous giggle. "Oh, Michael, why don't we just take it one day at a time? I believe we should court before we start talking marriage."

Michael laughed. "You may be right there." He wrapped her within his arms, pulling her closer. "I think I've fallen in love with an angel, a golden-haired angel."

Angela placed her hand upon his chest. "I know I've fallen in love with a grizzly bear."

Michael roared with laughter. "I can roar."

"Oh yes."

"Be patient with me, Angela. I don't want to hurt you, but. . ."

"You loved your wife, and you didn't think it was possible to fall in love again."

"Yes. How'd you know?"

"Like I said, I had a talk with my father."

"Oh, right. Why does a man feel like he's the only one who's ever had these feelings? I know others have lost beloved wives, but. . .I just don't get it."

"Michael, the storms of life affect us all. Yet we also experience the joys of life, and God gave us a unique gift in love. It's so personal we can't imagine how anyone else feels these things as we do. But we know in our own minds that others do. I think it's just one of those great mysteries of God."

He leaned back on the sofa and thought for a moment. "You're a wise woman, Angela. I think you might be right there." He pushed a wayward strand of her hair behind her ear. "May I kiss you?"

Please! she wanted to scream. Instead, she nodded slightly. *What would it be like to. . .*

Oh, Michael. She wrapped her arms around him. The tender kiss deepened.

"Daddy's kissing Miss Harris!" Samuel screamed.

Instantly she and Michael pulled apart from each other. Heat rushed to her cheeks.

Noah came running to the doorway. "Did you kiss a girl, Dad?"

"Yup, and I think I'm going to be doing more of it." Michael took Angela's hand tenderly in his own.

"Eww, Dad, you don't kiss girls." Sam's nose scrunched up.

"You do when you're older, Son. And if you love them." Michael winked.

Epilogue

Two years later

I'll be back as soon as I can." Michael grabbed Angela from behind, wrapping her in his arms.

Angela turned around within his embrace. She combed down his winter beard with her fingers. "I wish you didn't have to go."

"I know, but if we're going to have a little one, I need to have this wood milled."

Angela smiled. They'd been married for six months, and the Lord had granted them the blessing of a child due in another six months.

"Promise me you'll call on the boys if you need something lifted."

"I promise." Life couldn't get any better than this. The year and a half of waiting for Michael to know beyond the shadow of a doubt that she and he were meant to be together had been hard some days. But most of that time they had spent wisely, slowly developing their friendship. And she'd accepted his offer of a job. It had given her more time to be with him, time they desperately needed.

"Don't forget Father and Rosemary will be coming for Christmas dinner."

"I'm honored to have them in our home any time, you know that."

"Oh, and I have a surprise for you."

Michael held her tighter. "What else could you possibly surprise me with? I'm so excited about the baby, Honey."

Angela giggled. "I can tell. I told you last night about the baby coming, and here you are off to get the wood milled for the baby's crib. You do realize it will be a few months before the baby is born, don't you?" she teased.

He nibbled the nape of her neck. She squirmed to get away. He tightened his hold.

"I know how long it takes, Angela."

"You could have fooled me," she said with a wink.

"Keep it up," he threatened playfully.

"Mom, Dad, we're going outside," Noah called out from the living room.

Angela broke free from Michael's hold.

"Bundle up, boys," Michael called back, not breaking his gaze from Angela's.

"Daddy, can I go to the mill with you?" Sam asked.

"No, Son. I need you to help your mom while I'm gone. Besides, you get to stay and play in the snow."

The Snow Storm

"Oh yeah." Samuel ran to the front door.

"Button up, Sam."

"Yes, Ma'am."

The door flew open and the boys tumbled out with boots flopping and jackets half-buttoned.

"I'll get them to finish dressing before I leave." Michael chuckled.

"Thanks."

"Now, where were we? You said you had a surprise for me?"

Angela wiggled her eyebrows. "I believe I do, but if I tell you, it won't be a surprise, will it?"

"Now that's not fair. I told you I was painting the windows and doors of the house the color of your eyes."

"True, but you can't keep a surprise."

"When do I get to see this?" Michael demanded, hands on his hips.

"Soon, real soon."

"You keep this up and I'll have to take you over my knee."

"You and what army?" she teased, knowing those to be fighting words.

He lunged forward. Swiftly she avoided his capture.

"Angela. . ."

"Later, Dear. The boys are watching."

He turned and saw their mittened hands cupped on the windows, their faces glued to the action. He turned back to her. "You don't fight fair."

She pulled the dishcloth off the hook and swung it over her shoulder. "Life's not fair, Darling. It's what we make of the storms and whether we allow God's joy to come in after them."

"You're right. And before another one brews, I'm taking the logs to the mill. I'll be home as soon as possible."

"I'll keep your dinner warm."

"Thanks. By the way, if I haven't told you I loved you this morning, consider yourself told." He winked.

"Boys watching or not, you better tell me better than that," she challenged.

Michael groaned but embraced her just the same. "I love you, Angela."

"I love you, too, Michael. Come home quickly. I'll be missing you."

"And I you." He kissed her gently on the lips. "Thank you for being patient with me."

"Thank you for loving me. I don't know when I've been happier. Go now, and hurry home."

She waved at Michael as he left, leading the team of oxen that were pulling the sled loaded with logs. As Samuel waved to his father, Noah bent down and made a snowball. Angela chuckled. She knew Samuel would soon be attacked.

An Irish Bride for Christmas

by Vickie McDonough

Chapter 1

Prairie Flats, Illinois, 1880

Where's Mama and Poppy?" Rosie hugged her rag doll to her chest and stared up at Jackson with worried brown eyes.

Unshed tears blurred the view of his niece as Jackson knelt in front of her. He blinked them away for fear of scaring her. He could handle his own grief, but seeing his niece crying for her parents nearly gutted him. How could he make the four-year-old understand that they'd just buried her mom and dad—that they weren't coming back?

Help me explain it to her so she'll understand, Lord.

He picked up Rosie and hugged her tight, needing solace himself. "Remember when Bandit got bit by a snake and died?"

Rosie looked up at him and nodded. Her eyes shimmered with unshed tears.

Maybe she understood more than he gave her credit for.

"We had to bury him, and then you and your mama put flowers on his grave and your poppy made a cross for it. Remember that?"

Rosie's lower lip trembled, and she nodded. "He's in doggy heaven. Poppy said so."

"Well, that's what happened today. Your mama and poppy died in a stagecoach accident"—he didn't want her to know they were shot by robbers—"and now they're in heaven with Jesus."

"But *I* want them." Tears dripped down her cheeks.

Jackson hugged her tight. "So do I, sweet pea; so do I. But Jesus needed them in heaven with Him. I'm going to take care of you now."

Jackson swayed back and forth as Rosie clung to his neck, crying. Why couldn't it have been him who died instead of Ben. Instead of Amanda.

God, I have to say I don't understand this. I know You see all and know all, but why this? How am I supposed to run Lancaster Stage alone and raise a little girl? Rosie needs a mother and a father, not an uncle who knows next to nothing about caring for a child.

He raked his hand through his hair. He'd agreed to keep Rosie while Ben and Amanda went to a nearby town to celebrate their fifth anniversary, but he didn't know they wouldn't return. Now Rosie was the only family he had left in the world. He needed her as much as she did him.

Jackson looked around the small room where he lived behind the stage office. It smelled of leather and saddle soap from his evenings spent polishing harnesses and bridles. He hadn't had time to sweep the floor all week. The windows were so dingy he hadn't needed a shade to cover them, and there was only one bed. He hated all the reminders of his big brother and his sister-in-law in their house—a house left to him and Ben when their mother had died—but that was where Rosie should be.

He flipped the quilt back and laid Rosie on the bed, pushing back his emotions. He didn't understand why God hadn't protected Ben and Amanda during the stage robbery. It seemed a simple thing for the God who created the universe to deflect a few bullets.

But Jackson knew his brother wouldn't sit by and watch another of their stages being robbed. Most likely, Ben had tried to stop it—and now he and Amanda were dead.

Rosie was an orphan, and he had a two-man business to run alone.

He drew the carpetbag out from under his bed and blew the dust off. He'd pack his things while Rosie slept and then take them back to the neat two-bedroom home next door.

A few minutes later, he took a crate from off the back porch and packed up his coffee, sugar bowl, and cup and plate. He rarely ate there, preferring Amanda's fabulous cooking and open invitation to dine with them. What would he and Rosie eat now? He wasn't much of a cook.

Setting the crate by the door, he put the carpetbag on top of it. Rosie would miss her mama's homemade sugar cookies. Maybe one of the church ladies would let him chop wood in exchange for some.

Entering the door to the stage office, he stared at the map with pins in it marking the four places where their stagecoaches had been robbed in the past three months. Why had they been targeted? They were just a small-time operation, transporting people and freight that arrived in Prairie Flats, Illinois, by train to the small area towns where the train didn't go. They rarely carried anything of great value, although someone seemed to know whenever they had a payroll shipment on board. With a shaking hand, he picked up a pin and stuck it in the spot where Ben and Amanda had died.

He dropped into a chair. Lowering his head to his arm, he let the tears he'd held back for the past few days flow.

Jackson awoke to someone knocking on the stage office door. He glanced around, wondering why he'd fallen asleep at the desk. Suddenly everything rushed back to him.

The rapping increased.

Rosie! He dashed into his room, and his heart slowed when he saw his niece curled up on his bed, hugging her dolly.

Someone pounded again, and Rosie stirred. Jackson hurried through the office, wiped his damp eyes, and opened the door. Judge Smith, the mayor, and the mayor's wife stood on the boardwalk. They seemed an odd trio to offer condolences, but he hoped they would do it quickly.

The judge cleared his throat. "May we come in, Mr. Lancaster? It's warm for late November, but that wind is stiff."

"Of course." Jackson stepped back, allowing the three to enter. Rosie appeared at the door between the two rooms, hair tousled from sleep, and leaned against the jamb.

"How can I help you, Judge?"

He glanced around the office, and Jackson noted when the man's gaze landed on Rosie. "Perhaps it would be best if Mrs. O'Keefe took the child in the other room while we talk."

Rosie's eyes widened, and she raced toward him. Jackson scooped her up, concern mounting. What could these men have to say to him that they didn't want Rosie to hear? Had someone discovered the identity of the robbers?

Mrs. O'Keefe ambled to the back of the room and peeked through the door to his private quarters. Jackson narrowed his eyes at her rudeness.

"*Tsk tsk*. Would you look at this, Judge? You'll see for yourself what I've been talking about. This is no place for a child to live."

To Jackson's surprise, the judge and mayor joined Mrs. O'Keefe at the door of his room. With the news of the two deaths, a funeral to plan, and a precocious young one to care for, he hadn't gotten his normal chores accomplished. Sure, his place was a bit disorderly at the moment, but what did that matter to them?

"I don't see nothing all that much out of the ordinary here. He's a single man, Maura."

"But he can't raise a child in a place like this. That's my point." She eyed Jackson over the top of her glasses, pressed her lips together, and shook her head.

Jackson shifted Rosie to his other arm. "Just what is this all about?"

The judge sighed and turned to face him. "Mrs. O'Keefe has petitioned the courts to get custody of your niece."

"What?" Jackson backed up against the door, clinging to his niece. She wrinkled her brow and looked from him to the judge and back. "Now you listen here. Rosie is *my* niece. My flesh and blood. We belong together."

"You sure you want to be talking about this in front of the child?" The judge lifted his brows.

No, he didn't, but he wasn't about to let Mrs. O'Keefe get her paws on Rosie. "Not really, but there's no point discussing it. I'm all the family she has, Judge." Rosie must have sensed his distress, because she laid her head down on his shoulder and hugged his neck, nearly choking him.

"You're a single man, living in a—a hovel, for lack of a more decent word. A little girl has no business living here and being raised by an unmarried man. Isn't that right, Harvey?"

Harvey O'Keefe gave Jackson an almost apologetic glance before nodding at his wife. The man had yet to utter a single word. Maybe Jackson had one ally in the bunch.

"I've made my decision, Mr. Lancaster. Rosie is a young and impressionable child. You're a single man and shouldn't be tending a little girl. It isn't proper. I'm giving temporary custody to Mrs. O'Keefe."

Jackson's already-crumbling heart shattered in two. "You can't do that. We're family, and family stays together."

The judge laid a hand on Jackson's shoulder. "I know this is a difficult thing, son, especially after losing your—" He looked at Rosie. "Um. . .well, you know. You can see your niece regularly, but you've no business tending to her physical needs. If you know what I mean."

Jackson shook his head. This couldn't be happening. He wanted to run out the door with Rosie and leave town, but his business was here. He had people and clients who relied on his service. And if he left, he'd have no way to support Rosie and no home.

"This isn't right."

"Let me have the child." Mrs. O'Keefe held out her hands, a smug smile on her plump face.

Rosie whimpered. Jackson cast the judge a pleading glance. "There must be something I can do. She needs me. I'm the only familiar person left in her world."

"I'll give you the chance to get her back. If you marry in the next month—say, by Christmas—I'll grant you permanent custody of your niece. Otherwise, she'll stay with the O'Keefes." The judge put his hat on and buttoned his coat.

"Can't this wait—at least until tomorrow? We just buried Rosie's parents this morning." Jackson searched his mind. There had to be some way to fix this nightmare.

"Prolonging the matter won't make it easier. You have until Christmas." The judge reached for the door, and Jackson stepped aside. He turned the handle then stopped. "Hand over the child, Mr. Lancaster."

"No," Rosie cried.

The tightening in Jackson's throat had nothing to do with Rosie choking his neck. He'd never broken the law before, although he was highly tempted now. But if he ran with Rosie, what kind of life could he give her? As much as it pained him, he had to follow the judge's orders.

He untangled his niece's arm. "It will be okay, sweet pea. You go home with this nice man and lady; then I'll come see you every day until you can come back home."

"I have cookies and milk waiting for you." Maura O'Keefe smiled congenially for the first time and held out her arms.

"I like cookies. Can Uncle Jack have one?"

"Maybe when he visits tomorrow." Mrs. O'Keefe patted Rosie's head.

"Can Sally come?"

Mrs. O'Keefe wrinkled her brow. "Who is Sally? Not a dog, I hope."

Rosie shook her head. "No, she's my dolly."

Jackson's legs trembled and his head ached. Rosie had never known a stranger, and that alone could make this horrible situation bearable. He couldn't stand the thought of her crying for him and him unable to console her.

"I can come to your house and eat cookies." She wriggled, and Jackson reluctantly set her down. She took Mrs. O'Keefe's hand and waved at him.

"You'll bring her clothes to the house later?" Mrs. O'Keefe lifted her brows at him.

He nodded, too stunned to move. Silently Mr. O'Keefe followed his wife outside. Shutting the door, Jackson slid to the floor, unable to digest all that had happened.

He'd lost everything he held dear in one day. A frigid numbness made his limbs feel heavy, weighted.

Why is this happening, God? How will Rosie get along without me?

"And how in the world am I supposed to find a bride by Christmas?"

Chapter 2

Larkin Doyle stared with her mouth open as Maura O'Keefe strode into the house with a little girl in tow. What in the world had the woman done now?

"This is Rosie Lancaster, and she's going to live with us. Rosie is in need of cookies and milk." Maura eyed Larkin with her brows lifted, and Larkin understood the silent message.

The lass tugged at Larkin's skirt. "I like cookies." The brown-eyed urchin stared up at her.

Reaching out a hand, Larkin smiled. "Then, wee one, we must go find some."

Rosie took Larkin's hand without hesitation. "You talk funny."

"Aye, 'tis true. I come from Ireland, which is why I talk as I do." The charming child won Larkin's heart immediately.

Larkin put a shallow crate upside down on a chair and set the child at the table. She gave her two gingersnaps and a glass half filled with milk. As Rosie nibbled the snack, Larkin studied her. The girl's brown eyes were so dark Larkin could barely see her pupils, and her wavy hair was only a few shades lighter. What a lovely lass she was. "Is that good?"

Rosie nodded. "Mama makes sugar cookies."

How sad. Did the lass not understand that her mum was gone? Larkin brushed a strand of hair from Rosie's face and tucked it behind her ear.

Wilma, the O'Keefes' cook, entered with a bucket over her arm. She glanced at Rosie. "Well, what have we here?"

"This is Rosie. She'll be stayin' here awhile."

Wilma pursed her lips and set the bucket down. She leaned toward Larkin. "Not another attempt to replace the baby Maura lost?"

Larkin shrugged, hurt by Wilma's callous words. "Rosie, I must go talk to Mrs. O'Keefe for a moment. You stay with Wilma."

Rosie scowled but nodded. She dipped the corner of her remaining cookie in her milk then stuck it in her mouth.

Larkin gave her a third cookie then patted the lass's head. "I shall be back in a minute."

Rosie picked up another cookie and waved at her.

Larkin hurried through the dining room, past the elaborate table, and into the parlor. Mayor O'Keefe sat in his favorite chair, hiding behind his newspaper as he often did. She located Mrs. O'Keefe in the spare bedroom, tapping her index finger against her thick lips.

"I was going to give this room to the girl, but I simply can't have her destroying the décor. This furniture was far too costly to allow a child to live here. Too, if we have guests, I'll no longer have a place to put them."

Larkin didn't ask but knew that meant Rosie would be sharing her room. She didn't mind but would have liked to have been asked rather than having Mrs. O'Keefe instruct her as to how things would be. But wasn't that always the case?

You're a servant here, not a daughter—and you'd best remember that, Larkin Doyle.

As much as she'd hoped for a loving family to live with after her parents had died, that hadn't happened. The O'Keefes had taken her in and given her a nice place to live and decent clothes to wear, but she was not an adopted daughter. Perhaps Rosie would fill that coveted position.

"May I ask why the lass is here?"

"You may." Mrs. O'Keefe sidled a glance her way as she closed the curtains on the lone window. "Rosie's parents were buried today. A single man the likes of Jackson Lancaster isn't fit to raise a child—a girl, at that. Besides, he didn't want the responsibility, so I very graciously offered to take in the orphan."

" 'Tis a sad day when family refuses to care for family." Larkin's ire rose at the uncle who coldly turned his back on such a darling child. What a horrible ordeal Rosie must have been through.

"Give the girl a bath after she eats her cookies, and find something to put her in. Her uncle was supposed to deliver her clothes here, but with the lateness of the hour, he may not come until tomorrow."

"Aye, mum." Larkin hurried back to the kitchen. Wilma nodded toward the table. Larkin's heart stopped when she saw Rosie's head leaning against the table. Poor lass. Larkin lifted her up.

"I want Uncle Jack!" Rosie suddenly went rigid and struggled to get free. Larkin set her down for fear of dropping her. The lass slumped to the ground, tears pooling in her eyes. "I wanna go home."

Larkin clutched her chest as the memories of her parents' deaths came rushing back. She knew what it felt like to lose those she loved and to become an orphan.

Cuddling the girl, she patted her back. "There, there, 'twill be all right."

Uncle Jack. The poor child must be crying for the very man who'd refused to care for her. What a horrible beast he must be. Even though she was a Christian woman, if she ever got the chance, Larkin intended to give him a piece of her mind.

⊱⊰

The sun peeked over the horizon, sending its warming rays across Jackson's back. He knocked on the O'Keefes' door then rubbed his hand across his bristly jaw. He should have taken the time to shave this morning, but after another nearly sleepless night, he'd been anxious to see how Rosie had fared and to get her clothes to her so she'd have something fresh to wear. Shoving his hands in his coat pockets, he waited. Maybe he was too early.

A noise on the other side of the door indicated someone was coming. His gut tingled with excitement while at the same time he worried about Rosie's well-being. Had she cried last night? Had she asked for her mama? For him?

A pretty young woman with thick auburn hair opened the door. Her green eyes widened at the sight of him and then narrowed. "Might I help you?"

He brushed the dust from his jacket and smiled. "I'm Rosie's uncle. I've brought her clothes and have come to see her."

The woman's cinnamon-colored brows dipped. "She's not yet awake. The wee lass had trouble getting to sleep last night, so I thought it best not to awaken her this morning. I'll take her clothes."

Disappointed, Jackson handed the small satchel to her. "Could I come back and see her later?"

She scowled and stared at him as if he were a weevil in a flour sack. He glanced down at his clothes. Did he look that bad? Or had something else twisted her pretty mouth like a pretzel?

"You'd best come back after the family has had breakfast. Mrs. O'Keefe can talk with you then."

She started to shut the door, but he stuck out his foot, holding it open. "Wait. I don't need to talk to the mayor's wife. I just want to see my niece and make sure she's all right."

"The lass is fine, other than having a difficult time sleeping in a strange bed. I tended her meself. Really now, I've other duties to attend to. Come back later."

Jackson stared at the closed door, feeling empty and alone. He looked up to a window on the second story, wondering if Rosie might be there. Would she look out and see him?

Backing away, he stared at the big structure, one of the few brick houses in Prairie Flats. White columns holding up the porch roof gave it a Southern flair. The house was much nicer and probably warmer than Ben and Amanda's clapboard cottage. But strangers couldn't love Rosie like he did.

Please, Lord, show me how to get her back. Comfort Rosie, and help her not to fret.

Shoving his hands in pockets, he crossed the street to Pearl's Café. He'd get breakfast, check on today's stage, and then go back to see his niece.

At the café, he pulled out a chair and stared out the window. He could just make out one corner of the O'Keefes' home from here. He thought of the gal who'd opened the door. She was a pretty young woman, even with that pert nose scrunched up at him and her eyes flashing daggers. What had he done to upset her so?

Maybe she hadn't had her morning coffee yet. He remembered seeing her walking down the boardwalk and shopping at the mercantile on occasion but had never met her before. Her singsong accent was unexpected on the Illinois prairie, but it was lovely and intriguing.

Two hours later, Jackson knocked at the O'Keefes' fancy front door again. The wood-carver had done an excellent job on the twisted columns. Jackson tapped the dainty gold door knocker several times then pounded on the wood with his knuckles.

Finally, the Irish gal opened the door, her eyes widening again at the sight of him. He was glad he'd taken the time to shave and change clothes.

"Wait here and I shall get Mrs. O'Keefe." She closed the door in his face, not even allowing him to step into the parlor. Was she always so rude?

Jackson slumped against the jamb, anxious to see Rosie. The longer he waited, the more his anxiety grew. Were they purposefully avoiding him? He glanced at his pocket watch.

The door creaked and suddenly opened. The mayor's wife pulled a shawl around her shoulders and stepped outside, her lips pursed.

"What is it you need, Mr. Lancaster? Surely you must know that as the mayor's wife I'm a very busy woman. I can't have you disturbing me constantly."

Jackson lifted his brow. Two visits constituted constantly bothering her? "I'm here to see Rosie."

Mrs. O'Keefe let out a *tsk*. "It's not good to trouble the child. She's been through enough."

"Seeing me won't upset her. She loves me, as I do her."

"Yes, well, the judge gave me custody, and if she sees you, she'll just want to be with you—and not being able to do so will frustrate her. So, you see, it's better if she doesn't see you at all."

Jackson ground his back teeth together as his irritation rose. "The judge said I could see her every day. I want to see Rosie now."

Mrs. O'Keefe backed up a half step but glared over the top of her wire-rimmed glasses at him. "I simply can't have you interrupting things here at your leisure. We will go talk to the judge and get this matter settled now."

She disappeared back into the house. Jackson wanted to ram his fist through her glass window but knew that wouldn't accomplish anything other than proving that he wasn't fit to care for Rosie. He gazed up at the cloudy sky. "God, I need help here. I can't lose Rosie."

Moments later, he followed Mrs. O'Keefe as she marched toward Judge Smith's office. Jackson prayed the man wouldn't be in court so the matter could be settled quickly. He had his own work to do.

The mayor's wife stormed into the judge's offices, past the surprised clerk, and knocked on his private door.

"Now see here, madam, you can't—"At Mrs. O'Keefe's glare, the thin clerk slumped back into his chair. Mumbling under his breath, he yanked off his round wire glasses and polished them.

Mrs. O'Keefe knocked harder. Jackson had never been in the judge's offices and glanced around the opulent room. It smelled of beeswax and leather furniture. Two chairs sat on either side of a small round table, and a fine Turkish rug decorated the shiny wooden floor. The clerk's cherrywood desk was nicer than anything Jackson had seen in a long while.

"Come in, Andrew." The judge's deep voice resounded through the closed door.

Mrs. O'Keefe opened it and plowed right in. "It's not Andrew, Roy. It's Maura."

Jackson sighed and followed her. *That's just great. She's on a first-name basis with the judge.*

"Roy, Mr. Lancaster here was at my door this morning at a most inappropriate hour, demanding to see his niece. I simply can't have that man coming and going anytime he chooses. As the mayor's wife, I'm a very busy woman."

The judge lowered his spectacles and glanced at Jackson. "That true, Lancaster?"

Jackson shrugged and resisted the urge to fidget. "Yes, sir, but I thought Rosie would need a fresh change of clothes when she arose. That's why I went so early."

The judge turned his gaze on Maura. "Sounds reasonable. The child needs her clothes."

"Yes, but then he returned in a few hours."

"That's because I didn't get to see Rosie, and that helper of yours told me to come back. I was worried how she fared last night." Jackson crossed his arms, irritated that he had to explain why he wanted to see his own niece.

"You see, Roy, we have guests constantly, and I can't have this man coming in and upsetting the girl when I have a dinner party to prepare for."

Judge Smith sighed. "I can see your point, but you can't keep the child from her uncle."

Jackson's hopes rose for the first time.

"Lancaster, I'm guessing Sundays are slow for you. Am I right?"

He nodded, unsure what that had to do with anything.

"How about Wednesdays?" the judge asked.

"Sometimes busier than other days, sometimes not. Just depends." Jackson swallowed, not liking where his thoughts were taking him.

"All right. Maura, you let the man see his niece twice a week—on Sundays and Wednesdays."

"But—," Maura squeaked.

"That's not—" Jackson stepped forward.

Judge Smith raised his hand. "I've made my decision. Lancaster can see his niece for two hours every Sunday afternoon and Wednesday evening." He smacked his gavel down as if he'd made a court decision.

Jackson's heart plummeted as the sound echoed in his mind. He combed his fingers through his hair, holding them against his crown. He promised Rosie that he'd take care of her. She would think he'd lied to her—that he'd deserted her.

A ruckus sounded in the clerk's office. "Someone said Jackson Lancaster is in seeing the judge. That true?"

Jackson recognized the voice of Sheriff Kevin Steele and stepped into the other room. The sheriff's steady gaze turned his way. "Sorry to have to tell you, Lancaster, but your stage has been robbed again. The driver's been shot."

Chapter 3

Larkin squirmed in her chair as Frank Barrett leered at her over his cup of cider. She broke his gaze and pushed her carrots around on her plate, uncomfortable with his attention. Even though some might find the man of average height with sleek dark hair and pale gray eyes handsome, something about him gave her the shivers. She couldn't help comparing him to Jackson Lancaster's rugged, often disheveled appearance that made him look like a boy in need of a mother's care.

"It was very benevolent of you to take in the Lancaster orphan. Must have been quite a shock for her to lose both parents at once." Frank turned his attention to Maura. "How is she adapting to life here?"

"As well as can be expected. Although I do believe Judge Smith made a grievous error allowing that scoundrel uncle of hers to visit. He had the nerve to return her a half hour late, and then the child pitched a royal fit when it was time for him to leave. I simply don't understand what she sees in him. He didn't want to keep her, after all."

"I can see how his visits would be disruptive and not in the best interest of the girl."

Maura picked up her glass and lifted it as if in a toast. "Exactly how I feel. The child has enough worries without pining for the very uncle who gave her away and refused to care for her. His visits will only prolong her healing process."

Larkin narrowed her eyes but focused on her plate. Maura allowed her to attend the O'Keefes' dinner parties but made it clear that she was to remain silent unless directly asked a question. To Maura, Larkin represented a trophy of the woman's hospitality and generosity. Taking in an orphan somehow set her above her peers—at least in Maura's mind. And now she had two.

Larkin took a bite of mashed potatoes covered in Wilma's thick beef gravy, but its flavor was wasted on her. Why did Maura always refer to Rosie as "the child" or "the girl" but never by her name?

Had she done that when Larkin first arrived? Searching her mind, Larkin couldn't remember. She'd been a distraught twelve-year-old, having lost her parents to illness only a few years after they had arrived in New York. The deplorable conditions on the boat from Ireland had caused her mother to take sick, and she never recovered. Then her da caught the same sickness and died.

She didn't dislike living with the O'Keefes and was grateful to them for taking her in, but at nineteen, she longed for a home of her own—a family of her own.

Maura wanted Rosie so badly that she was willing to offer her a home when nobody else would, but one spilled glass of milk and Rosie had been relegated to eating in the kitchen. Thankfully, dinner tonight was later than normal to accommodate Frank Barrett's busy schedule, so she'd been able to sit with Rosie while she ate and had put her to bed before dinner.

"Don't you agree, Miss Doyle?"

Larkin's gaze darted up at Mr. Barrett's question. One she hadn't heard. "Um. . .'tis sorry I am, but I did not hear the question." She swallowed hard, irritated that her accent thickened whenever she was flustered.

"I said that the Lancaster girl is far better off here than with her uneducated uncle. Don't you agree?"

Maura stared at her as if awaiting her agreeable response. Larkin knew it was better to deflect her answer than step in that miry pit. "Why do you refer to Mr. Lancaster as uneducated? He speaks clearly and runs a successful business. I wouldn't think an uneducated man could do that."

Mr. Barrett's brows lifted at her defense of Jackson Lancaster. She wasn't even sure why she defended him, since she despised the way he had abandoned Rosie.

"You'd be surprised what a man can do when he sets his mind to it." Frank narrowed his eyes at her.

His interest in her was undeniable, but she did not return the attraction. A sinister air encircled the man, and even though he was a friend of the O'Keefes, Larkin intended to keep her distance.

"I'd best look in on Rosie and make sure she's sleeping soundly." Larkin pushed back from the table, and Mr. O'Keefe and Mr. Barrett both rose.

"There's no need for you to check on the child, Larkin. I'll have Wilma do it."

"Beggin' your pardon, mum, but you asked me to tend Rosie. I wouldn't want Wilma to be off helping in the bedrooms when you might have need of her here." She rushed out of the room before Maura forced her to stay, grateful to be away from Mr. Barrett's leering.

In her room, she found Rosie still asleep, with both hands under her cheek. Larkin brushed a lock of hair out of the girl's face. She was such a pretty child. And resilient, even after all that had happened. Larkin's heart warmed. Maybe someday she'd have a sweet daughter like Rosie.

❧❧❧

Rosie bounced on her toes and ran to the door. "Is he coming?"

Why was the lass so eager to see the uncle who didn't want her? Perhaps she was unaware that he had abandoned her. Larkin shook her head, finding it difficult to understand why the man wanted to spend time with Rosie now. Did it ease his guilt? She looked through the tall, narrow window at the front entrance. "Here he comes now."

She tied Rosie's cloak under her neck and opened the door. The lass raced outside. "Uncle Jack!"

He picked her up and tossed her into the air. Childish giggles echoed in the quiet of the late afternoon, warming Larkin's heart. She was so glad to see Rosie smiling.

"I sure missed you, sweet pea."

"I'm not a pea." Rosie locked her arms around his neck and hugged him tight.

"Ready to go?"

Larkin's heart skittered as he turned to walk away. "Mrs. O'Keefe needs a word with you, Mr. Lancaster."

His dark brows dipped down. A muscle ticked in his jaw. "Why?"

Larkin shrugged. "She didn't tell me. Only that I must inform her when you were here."

He sighed, and his broad shoulders drooped a bit. He shifted Rosie to his right arm. "All right. Let's get the inquisition over so Rosie and I can have our time together."

"We going home?" Rosie patted her uncle's clean-shaven cheek.

"We'll see, sweet pea."

Larkin ushered him into the parlor. "Please have a seat and excuse me while I find Mrs. O'Keefe."

Darting out the door, she swiped at the band of sweat on her brow. Odd that she would be perspiring in early December. She located Mrs. O'Keefe upstairs in the spare room where the woman was sorting her Christmas decorations.

"I'll have to order some new ornaments this year. Some of the old ones weren't packaged properly and got broken."

The look she cast in Larkin's direction told her that Maura blamed her for the damage. "Mr. Lancaster is here. He's anxious to be off with Rosie."

"Hmm. . .we'll just see about that."

Downstairs in the parlor, Rosie's uncle stood as they entered. "Good day, Mrs. O'Keefe."

"Humph. It's been a busy day." She glanced at the mantel clock. "Since Rosie was half an hour late returning last Wednesday, you may only keep her an hour and a half today."

Mr. Lancaster's eyes shot blue fire. Rosie cast worried glances from one person to the next and clung to his neck.

"Now see here, I was only late because one of my coaches cracked a wheel. I had to see about getting it repaired since it was due to go back out the next morning."

Maura waved her hand in the air. "No matter. I want the girl back by six o'clock so she can get her dinner."

"She can eat with me." He stood rigid, like a soldier, holding Rosie in one arm.

"That wasn't part of the judge's deal. Also, I want Miss Doyle to accompany the child on her excursions with you."

Jackson Lancaster looked as if he could have strangled Maura.

Larkin stared at her, stunned by her declaration. "But, mum—"

Maura zipped an angered glance her way. Larkin swallowed, remembering the times as a child that she'd been punished for her disobedience. "Aye, mum. As you wish."

"No! Rosie is my family, not yours." Mr. Lancaster headed for the door. "The judge made no conditions and said nothing about my visits being supervised."

"You can accept Miss Doyle's chaperoning or not see your niece at all."

"We're leaving." He slung open the door and stormed out.

"Go with the man. Make sure he returns the child on time tonight."

Hurrying to do Mrs. O'Keefe's bidding, Larkin donned her cloak and followed the pair outside, feeling like an unwanted stepchild. He didn't want her company, but she didn't dare refuse Mrs. O'Keefe's orders or she'd be out on the streets. Hurrying to keep up with his long-legged gait, Larkin took two steps to his one. Rosie peered over his shoulder and waved. Larkin smiled at her.

Mr. Lancaster stopped suddenly, and Larkin plowed into his solid back. He turned quickly, grabbing her arm and steadying her. "Sorry. Look, Miss Doyle, I don't need anyone watching over my shoulder during my time with Rosie."

Larkin studied the ground rather than his fierce blue eyes. "I don't doubt that a'tall, but you wouldna want me to get into trouble for not complying with Mrs. O'Keefe's wishes, would you, now?"

Indecision darkened his gaze. Finally, he heaved a sigh. "I guess not. Follow me, then."

She hurried to keep up, running a bit to draw even with him. He loosened Rosie's arms from his neck and tossed her in the air again, gaining a wide grin from his niece.

"Do it again, Uncle Jack."

"One more time." He tossed her high, this time catching her and cradling her in both arms as one would hold an infant. Leaning down, he pressed his lips against Rosie's cheek and blew, making a sputtering noise.

Melancholy washed over Larkin. His actions reminded her how her da had played with her as a child.

"That tickles." Rosie giggled and rubbed her cheek.

Jackson Lancaster chuckled for the first time, and it took her breath away. A dimple in his tanned cheek winked at her before it disappeared as his expression sobered. She found his ruggedness appealing, much to her dismay. She didn't want to like the man after what he'd done.

Something didn't add up. Was Maura wrong in her opinion of him? Who told her he didn't want his niece? From what Larkin had seen, the man was willing to fight to spend time with Rosie.

They approached a small clapboard house painted a cheery buttery shade. Rosie peered over her uncle's shoulder. "That's *my* house."

Larkin nearly stumbled. This was Rosie's home? There was nothing unsavory on the outside of the cute cottage, other than it being much smaller than the O'Keefes' overly large house. Mr. Lancaster opened the door, then stepped aside and allowed her to enter first.

The house had a slight musty smell, but it *had* probably been closed up since Rosie's parents' deaths. A stairway led up to the bedrooms, most likely. A simple kitchen was to her left, and on the right, the parlor was decorated with a pretty floral wallpaper and a colorful rag rug. A small settee looked abandoned under the front window. Two rockers sat turned toward the fireplace. Everything was neat and tidy. All it needed was a family.

Surprised at the emotion that swept over her, Larkin crossed to the parlor window and looked past the lacy curtains that were held back with a matching tie to the cozy front yard. This was just the kind of place she'd dreamed about whenever she thought of having a home of her own—something simple but cozy. She felt a tug on her hand and looked down.

"Come see my room." Rosie's wide gaze beseeched her to follow.

Larkin looked at Mr. Lancaster, and he shrugged. "Make yourself at home. I thought Rosie might like to get a few of her toys to, uh. . .take back with her."

Larkin didn't miss the huskiness in his voice when he thought of having to return his niece. Like the morning sun bursting over the horizon in all its glory, she realized the truth. This man dearly loved Rosie and was pained by their separation. So why didn't he keep her?

"C'mon, Larkin." Rosie leaned sideways and pulled her along. He followed them.

Upstairs, Rosie went into her room, but Larkin stood out on the stairway landing, looking in. The furniture in Rosie's small room consisted of a little bed and a chair. Three crates turned on their sides held her few toys and another pair of shoes that looked to be her Sunday best. A book of children's stories leaned sideways in one crate, and a ring-toss game sat across from it. Another crate was filled with more than two dozen blocks of various sizes. Three empty pegs were attached to the wall at a height that the girl could manage.

"Would you like to take a book, game, and blocks back to the O'Keefes'?" Mr. Lancaster asked.

Rosie shook her head, her braids swinging back and forth. "No. They need to be here for when I come home."

Larkin couldn't help glancing at Mr. Lancaster. The longing look in his blue eyes took her breath away.

If she comes home, Jackson couldn't help thinking. Miss Doyle looked uncomfortable in the doorway. He'd made it clear that he didn't want or appreciate her presence, but he hadn't thought what it meant for her. Mrs. O'Keefe sounded like an ogre, and he didn't doubt that she'd be quick to punish Miss Doyle if she refused to accompany him. Obviously she hadn't wanted to come with him any more than he'd wanted her to join them.

Ignoring her, he dropped to the floor and picked up one of Rosie's books. "Come here, sweet pea, and I'll read to you."

Rosie complied and sat on his lap. He couldn't help glancing at Miss Doyle. She stared at him with a surprised look. What? Did she think he couldn't read?

He tried to forget she was there as he read the story "The Three Bears" from *Aunt Mavor's Nursery Tales.*

Miss Doyle's soft floral scent drifted through the room when she untied her cloak and laid it over her arm. She leaned against the doorframe, watching him. Feeling guilty for being so rude to her, he looked up. "You can sit on Rosie's bed, if you like, or in the parlor."

Relief softened her pretty features, but she didn't enter the room. "If you're sure 'tis all right, I *would* like to sit in the parlor. . .and give you and Rosie some time alone."

Appreciating her consideration, he nodded and watched her leave.

Rosie nudged him in the belly with her elbow. "Read more, Uncle Jack."

After he read three stories from the children's book, she wanted to play with her blocks. He built several towers, and she knocked them down, laughing with delight.

Being with Rosie made him realize he'd missed her more than he thought. Staying busy with work had helped keep his mind off the situation, which angered him whenever he thought about it, but working sure hadn't helped him to find a bride. He simply had no time to court, not that there were many unmarried women *to* court.

"I'm gonna build a house." Rosie collected her blocks in a pile and started stacking them.

It bothered Jackson that she didn't seem to miss him nearly as much as he missed her. In fact, she seemed to be getting along quite well without him. He stared at a knothole on the wall. Children were adaptable. Not so with adults.

He stood, and Rosie looked up at him. "Go ahead and make a house. I need to talk to Miss Doyle for a few minutes."

"Her name is Larkin."

He smiled. "That's a pretty name."

With the tip of her tongue in the corner of her mouth, Rosie carefully set another block on her growing stack.

Jackson entered the parlor and found Miss Doyle in Amanda's rocker. He wanted to be irritated, but instead, he thought she looked as if she belonged there. He walked closer and noticed her eyes were shut. For the first time, he wondered how hard Mrs. O'Keefe worked the girl—and surely having an active four-year-old had only added to her burden. How had Larkin Doyle come to live with the O'Keefes?

Jackson stepped on a board that squeaked, and Miss Doyle jerked and opened her eyes. "Ach, sure now, you frightened me. I fear I must have dozed off." She sat up and ran her hand over her hair.

Jackson dropped into Ben's rocker. A shaft of longing and sadness speared him. He missed his brother so much. Not just because of the business, but because Ben was his best friend.

"Are you all right, Mr. Lancaster?" Miss Doyle leaned forward in her chair.

Jackson nodded, irritated that she'd witnessed his grief. He turned his face away from her, trying to force back the tears stinging his eyes. He lurched to his feet and went to stand by the window.

"I want you to know, I'm sorry for your loss."

He couldn't respond with his throat clogged as if someone had shoved a rag down it.

The rocker creaked as she stood. He could sense her standing behind him. "I lost both me folks in a short while, leaving me an orphan, like Rosie."

Jackson didn't want her comfort—didn't want her in Ben's home. She was a member of the enemy's camp. He whirled around so fast that Miss Doyle took a step backward, her eyes wide. "Rosie is not an orphan. She has me."

Miss Doyle blinked her big green eyes. "Then why did you give her to Mrs. O'Keefe?"

Jackson clutched his fists together. All the anguish and pain of the past week came rushing to the surface. He leaned into Miss Doyle's face. "I never gave Rosie up. She was stolen right out of my arms."

Confusion, and maybe even a little fear, swirled in her eyes and wrinkled her brow.

Guilt washed over him for taking his frustrations out on her. He glanced out the window again and noticed the sun had already set. Shadows darkened the room, and he turned at a shuffling in the doorway. "It's time to go, sweet pea."

Rosie's lip trembled in the waning light. "No. I want to stay here with you."

Jackson crossed the room and knelt in front of her. "That's what I want, too, but we can't. Not yet."

"Why?" Tears dripped down Rosie's cheeks.

"Because the judge said you have to stay at the O'Keefes' until. . ." He cast a glance at Miss Doyle. How much did she know?

"I don't wanna go." Rosie dashed back to her room.

Jackson sighed and stood. It was so hard to take her back when he wanted to keep her so badly. He found her on her bed and picked her up.

"No. . .I don't want to go." Rosie kicked at him and pushed against his chest. "Put me down."

Holding her tight with his jaw set, he carried her outside, not even checking to see if Miss Doyle followed. Another chunk of his heart broke off and lodged in his throat.

Chapter 4

The window in the stage office door rattled as the door opened. Mrs. Winningham entered, followed by three of her six boys, reminding him of a mother duck with her ducklings.

Jackson laid his pencil down and rubbed his forehead. Ben or Amanda always handled the bookwork. Trying to make all those numbers line up wasn't something he enjoyed, but it had to be done.

He stood and forced a smile in spite of the headache clawing his forehead.

The young widow Mabel Winningham had made her interest in him well known, at least to him. She wasn't especially pretty, with her hair all pinched tight in a bun and those too-big-for-her-face amber eyes and buck teeth, but she was friendly enough. "Good day, Mr. Lancaster." She smiled, batting her eyes, reminding him of an owl.

The first of her boys, a three-foot-tall blond, stopped beside her. The last two, identical twins with snow-white hair, plowed into the back of their brother.

"Hey! Stop it." The older boy spun around and shoved one of his brothers, knocking him backward into the other boy. Both landed on the floor, staring wide-eyed at their attacker. They turned in unison to look at each other, and as if they passed some silent code, both wailed at the same time.

Mrs. Winningham grabbed the shoulder of the oldest boy. "Bruce, you stop treating your brothers that way."

"They started it," he whined, sticking out his lip in a pout that would have swayed a weaker woman to his side. "They conked me in the back."

"Sit down over there." She pointed to the extra chair near the window. "Bobby, Billy, stop that caterwauling. I can't hear myself think."

Jackson pinched the bridge of his nose, thankful that the other three Winningham boys were at school and not here. How did their mother find the energy to deal with them all day after day? He couldn't help feeling sympathy for her.

"Sorry about that, Mr. Lancaster." Her lips turned up in an embarrassed smile. "But boys will be boys."

He was certain she knew all about boys. Bruce knelt in the chair, blowing steam rings on the window Jackson had just cleaned the day before. "What can I help you with, ma'am?"

She patted her head, not that a hair was out of place, what with it all being stuck down. Did women use hair oil?

"I wanted to make sure that you know my sister will be riding your stage from River Valley to here the week before Christmas. I'm concerned for her safety, what with all the robberies and, well. . .you know."

He sighed inwardly. She wasn't the first person to challenge him on a passenger's safety, and he of all people knew the danger. "I'm working on hiring an extra man to ride shotgun. Before the robberies started, we had no need for a guard."

"Well, you certainly need one now." She hiked her chin and looked at him with piercing tawny eyes.

Evidently she wasn't interested in winning his heart today. Thank goodness. He needed a wife, but he wasn't ready to take on a whole tribe. One little girl was enough for now.

Suddenly she softened her expression, and he swallowed hard.

"Ethel's not married. I was hoping you might come to dinner once she's here."

Uh-oh. Jackson glanced at the calendar on the wall. Just two weeks to find a bride. Was he that desperate? At least the sister most likely didn't have a half dozen boys.

Surely some other woman—one without six hooligan kids—would like to marry a man who owned his own business and a nice house.

"Uh. . .thanks for the invitation, but I'm pretty busy right now, running things here by myself."

Her gaze hardened. "Well, maybe after Christmas. Let's go, boys." She spun around and yanked the two toddlers up from where they were wrestling. Bruce marked a *B* inside one of the many fog circles he'd blown on the window. He pointed his finger like a gun and pretended to shoot Jackson and then jumped out of the chair.

Jackson closed the door the boy had left open and watched through the window as the Winningham tornado blew down the street. He wondered how the slight woman managed to feed and clothe all those boys, much less keep them in line. He made a mental note to go hunting and take her some meat. But maybe it would be better if he delivered it after dark, so she wouldn't know who'd brought it. He didn't want her getting the wrong idea.

Jackson sat at his desk and opened the center drawer. Mabel Winningham's name had been at the bottom of his list of prospective brides—a very short list. He licked the end of his pencil and drew a line through her name.

Elmer Limley, the town drunk, had a daughter who was a few years older than Jackson. The spinster had never married and hid herself away in her home, doing mending for a few of the town's wealthier people. He'd often felt sorry for Thelma Limley. She was as homely as a stray mutt, but she was kind. She'd be nice to Rosie, but he didn't want his niece exposed to the likes of Elmer Limley. For the time being, he left Thelma's name on the list.

He'd even penciled in Larkin Doyle's name, not that the quiet woman had ever shown any interest in him. But if he married her, he'd never be free of Mrs. O'Keefe's meddling.

He stared out the window, watching a wagon slowly move by. He'd never thought too much about getting married before but always figured he'd marry for love like Ben had. Amanda had come to town to visit a family that used to live in Prairie Flats. The first time Ben saw her, he'd acted like a schoolboy with his first crush. Jackson smiled, remembering.

Ben and Amanda had lived only five short years together, but they'd been years of love and laughter. That's what Jackson wanted. A home he looked forward all day to returning to. Not one where he'd have to hide out in the barn because he'd married a woman he had no feelings for.

But couldn't love grow out of such a situation?

For Rosie's sake, he had to do something. He had to find a bride in just two weeks.

Tapping his pencil on the desk, he thought of all the smaller towns that his stage visited. Was there a woman in one of those places willing to marry quickly—a woman who'd be good to Rosie? His needs didn't matter so much, just as long as Rosie was back with him.

Looking up at the ceiling, he sighed. "I need some help, Lord. How do I find a wife so fast? Guide me. Show me where to look.

"Please help, Father. I can't lose Rosie."

Jackson tied his two horses to the ornamental iron hitching post in front of the O'Keefes' large home. Arriving to pick up Rosie definitely felt better than returning her. Even after two weeks, she still cried and fussed when he had to leave. In fact, her fits seemed to be getting worse rather than better. He ran his hand down his duster, making sure he looked presentable, and knocked on the door.

"He's here. Uncle Jack's here." Rosie's muffled squeals on the other side of the door made him smile. Nobody called him Jack, but early on, his niece had shortened his name to that.

The door opened, and Rosie rushed past Miss Doyle, grabbing him around one leg. He brushed his hand over her dark hair and pressed her head against his thigh. "Evening, sweet pea."

She reached her hands up to him, and he picked her up, planting a kiss on her cheek. "We going home again?"

"Not today. The sun's out in full force and there's no wind, so I thought you might like to ride Horace."

"Oh boy!" Rosie clapped her hands together and looked at Miss Doyle. "We're gonna ride hossies."

Jackson wasn't certain, given the natural pale coloring of Miss Doyle's fair skin, but he felt certain that all the blood had just rushed out of her face.

She stepped outside, closing the door behind her, and peered wide-eyed past him to the horses. "Sure now, I've never been on a horse in me whole life."

Ah, so that was the problem. Jackson flashed a reassuring smile. "It's nothing to fear. We'll just walk them."

"C'mon, Larkin. Hossies is fun."

Miss Doyle looked down at her dress. "I can't ride a horse in me dress."

Rosie giggled. "Your dress won't fit on a hossie."

A shy grin tugged at her lips. " 'Twould be a funny thing to see, for sure. What I meant to say is that I can't ride since *I'm* wearing a dress."

With a smile on her face, the young woman was quite pretty. She was always so somber and quiet around him. He'd wondered if she didn't like him for some reason.

Jackson lifted Rosie onto Horace's saddle and then offered a hand to Miss Doyle. Would she stand her ground and refuse to go? He wouldn't mind time alone with Rosie but didn't want the young woman to get in trouble with her employer. "Look, if you'd rather not go, I understand. We're not leaving town, just walking around. Rosie loves horses, and I thought she'd enjoy a short ride."

Miss Doyle darted a glance at the closed door and shook her head. "Mrs. O'Keefe says I must go, or. . ."

Jackson hated putting the young woman in such an awkward position, but since Rosie was all ready to ride, he didn't want to disappoint her. "I'll help you mount the horse, and then you can fix your skirts so they're respectable."

Green eyes stared at him as if he were a loon. "Will you be riding or leading the horses?"

"Ride with me, Uncle Jack."

He shrugged. "Guess I'm riding. But I can lead your horse if you prefer."

He could tell she didn't want to ride, but she shuffled toward the horse, stopping four feet away. His heart went out to her. Here she was being forced into another situation she didn't desire, but she wasn't complaining, and for that, he admired her.

Before she could object, Jackson scooped her up and deposited her on Maudie's back.

"Oh!" she squealed as she struggled to hide her bare calves with her skirt and cloak. That done, she glared at him. " 'Twould have been kind of you to have given me warning, Mr. Lancaster."

He grinned, enjoying her lyrical accent. She looked as ruffled as a hen being chased by a fox. "Call me Jackson—since we're seeing so much of each other."

"You can call her Larkin." Rosie smiled. "That's her name."

Jackson lifted a brow at the young woman, and she nodded. "Aye, call me by me first name."

He mounted up behind Rosie. "It's a pretty name. What does it mean?"

Glancing over his shoulder, he noticed her cheeks had reddened. " 'Tis actually a man's name. Lorcan means fierce or silent."

Well, the silent part sure fit, but not the fierce. Sweet might be a better description.

"Me da liked the name. He said it reminded him of a lark. A bird." She shrugged, as if that wasn't an acceptable reason for giving a baby girl a male name.

"It's pretty and suits you." He guided the horses toward the edge of town, wanting to kick himself for complimenting her. He didn't need her to think he was happy to have her around. She was just an intruder, an interloper, distracting him from the short time he had with his niece.

Jackson tickled Rosie. She giggled and squirmed, making him forget about his silent shadow.

Larkin concentrated on holding on to the saddle horn and not falling off the big horse while Jackson led it behind his mount. She'd made the mistake of peering down to the ground and didn't want to do that again. She rocked to the horse's gentle gait, relieved they weren't going any faster.

Up ahead, Rosie giggled as Jackson tickled her. Larkin admired his broad shoulders and the loose way he sat in the saddle. Not at all like her all-tensed-up gotta-hold-on-tight-so-I-don't-fall rigidness. Maudie's walk was gentle, making Larkin sway side to side a bit. Still, she didn't trust animals and kept a tight grip on the horn in case the horse decided to run away.

Larkin rubbed her gritty eyes and yawned. She'd lain awake late the previous night trying to make sense of things. Against her wishes, she liked Jackson Lancaster. His nearly black hair was almost the same color as Rosie's, and his blue eyes reminded her of the vast ocean she crossed after leaving Ireland. The man had a rugged, shaggy look, kind of like a lost pup that needed someone to care for it.

She knew he ran the stage line with his brother, who'd been killed. Perhaps it was too difficult to care for an ornery four-year-old and a business, too.

Rosie let out a squeal, and Jackson chuckled, making his shoulders bounce.

Larkin smiled, glad to see Rosie happy again. The lass was becoming more withdrawn at the O'Keefes', as if she were afraid she'd get in trouble for touching things, which she had.

Mrs. O'Keefe had little patience for a rambunctious child, especially one who accidentally broke an antique vase from Ireland. She had ordered Larkin to take Rosie on daily walks to help the child run off some steam. They'd been to the Lancaster Stage office several times, but to Rosie's disappointment, her uncle hadn't been there.

Why had Maura wanted the child in the first place? Did she think it lifted her up in the eyes of the community to be generous to an orphan? Did it fill a hole in her heart from losing her own child so long ago?

A rogue gust of wind flipped her cloak behind her, revealing her bare calf. Two men on the boardwalk elbowed each other and grinned at her. Cheeks scorching, she hurried to grab the corner of her cloak and secured it under her leg.

Jackson had done nothing to indicate he didn't want his niece. In fact, he acted the opposite. She was beginning to think Mrs. O'Keefe had misled her. But why?

Larkin always tried to believe the best of people. But if Mrs. O'Keefe had lied about Mr. Lancaster just to get Rosie, then she'd done the man a horrible injustice.

Jackson looked over his shoulder at her. "You doing all right?"

She smiled and nodded, warmed by his concern for her. She had tried hard to remain aloof. To not like Jackson Lancaster.

But it was too late.

Looking toward heaven, she prayed, *Father God, if Mrs. O'Keefe lied to get custody of Rosie, I pray You'll make things right. Jackson loves his niece, I can tell. They're family and should be together. Please make it so.*

Chapter 5

Mrs. O'Keefe peered over the top of her spectacles at Larkin. "When do you plan to accept Frank's offer for dinner?"

Larkin's heart skipped a beat. She'd hoped the subject wouldn't come up. "I'm not particularly interested in dining with him, mum."

Maura's pale blue eyes widened. "Why ever not? He's a fine-looking man and is vice president of the bank. It's more than a girl in your position should hope to find."

Her words cut like a surgeon's scalpel. A servant—that was the position she meant. As much as Larkin had hoped to become the daughter Maura always said she wanted, she knew she never would be. Maura had taken her in as a way to get free labor, and Larkin wasn't about to be tied the rest of her life to someone else who didn't love her. She twisted her hands together. "Mr. Barrett makes me nervous."

"That's the silliest thing I've ever heard. Why, he's a perfect gentleman." Maura's lips twisted, reminding Larkin of a snarling dog. "If he asks you again, you will accept. Is that clear?"

Larkin nodded, but inside she was screaming. Oh, how she wished she could leave this house and find a place of her own, but she had little money, and nobody would hire her if the mayor's wife told them not to. And how could she leave Rosie with Mrs. O'Keefe? The little girl's life would be miserable.

Maura enjoyed dressing her up and strutting the little lass around in front of friends and acquaintances, showing how generous she was to take in the waif. But at home, Maura couldn't be bothered with Rosie. She was relegated to the kitchen and Larkin's room and not allowed access to the rest of the house for fear she'd break another of Maura's valuable decorations. At least now Larkin had a cause to live for. She would tend the child she'd come to love and make sure that Rosie never knew the loneliness that she had.

Hurrying back to her room, she found Rosie sitting on the bed rubbing her eyes, her nap over. With her braids loosened, hair tousled, and cheeks red, she was as darling as ever. "Is Uncle Jack coming today?"

"Aye." A flutter of excitement tickled her stomach at the thought of seeing Jackson again. She was only happy for Rosie's sake. The lass was a different person on the days her uncle came. She was happy and not quiet and moody, like she'd recently become.

Larkin picked up the brush, undid Rosie's braids, and in quick order rewove them. She was thankful Rosie had quit asking for her mum and da but didn't like how she was starting to withdraw. The poor child had been through so much recently. She didn't deserve to be stuck in this house where only Larkin and Wilma loved her.

"Shall we go see if Wilma baked some sugar cookies while you napped?"

Rosie smiled and nodded. Larkin helped her into her shoes and fastened them, then took her to the necessary and then into the kitchen, where they washed their hands. Rosie shinnied onto a chair and drank half the glass of milk Wilma had set out for her.

Larkin cringed when she wiped her milk mustache on her sleeve. "Use your napkin, lass, not your sleeve."

Rosie shrugged and picked up a cookie. As she ate, she stared off into space. Larkin wondered what she was thinking about as she helped herself to a cookie. After eating another cookie, Rosie took two more and wrapped them up in her cloth napkin.

Larkin lifted her brows. "What are you doin'? Have you not had enough cookies?"

"I'm saving them for Uncle Jack."

How sweet. Larkin glanced at the clock on the hearth. Jackson was later today than normal. She wondered if he was having a hard time running his business without his brother's assistance. Each time she saw Rosie's uncle, the bags under his eyes seemed larger and darker. Did he ever sleep? Was he eating properly?

"He'll be here soon," Wilma said as she added potatoes to the pot of boiling water.

Being separated from Rosie seemed to be more of a problem to Jackson than the fact that someone was watching her for him. He should be grateful for that, at least, as busy as he was.

Larkin shook her head. Why all the worry about Jackson Lancaster? He could have kept Rosie instead of giving her to Maura. But hadn't he mentioned something about Rosie being stolen from him?

It was all so confusing that Larkin's head was swirling like a weather vane in a windstorm. Who was right? And who was wrong?

A knock at the kitchen door pulled her from her worries. Wilma dusted her hands on her apron and opened the door. Jackson had started coming to the kitchen entrance to avoid seeing Mrs. O'Keefe. It seemed to Larkin that every time the two were together, Maura enforced some new rule that only irritated the man further. Was there bad blood between the two of them?

Jackson tipped his hat to Wilma and Larkin, but his lovely blue eyes lit up when he saw Rosie at the table.

She smiled and waved to him. "I saved you some cookies."

"Did you, now? You know I like cookies." Jackson lingered in the doorway as if afraid to come in.

A frigid breeze cooled the overly warm room, stirring up the scent of wood smoke and baking chicken. Larkin's stomach growled.

"Sure smells good in here." A shy grin tugged at Jackson's lips.

"Well, don't just stand there letting in the cold air—not that it doesn't feel wonderful to me after standing in front of this stove all day." Wilma waved her stirring spoon in the air. "Have a seat at the table and eat those cookies your niece saved for you."

He hesitated a moment and looked past them. Was he making sure Mrs. O'Keefe wasn't around? Finally, he stepped inside and shut the door, then sat at the table. Rosie shoved her napkin toward him. He unfolded it and smiled. Larkin's stomach twittered at the sight of his dimples.

"Thank you for sharing with me, sweet pea." He took a bite and closed his eyes, as if he'd never tasted anything so good.

Larkin was saddened to think of him living alone and working so hard after all he'd lost. As far as she knew, Rosie was the only family he had left. His dark hair hung down over his forehead, so different from that of the many businessmen who visited the O'Keefe house, who wore their hair slicked back with smelly tonic. His cheeks bore the tan of a man who was often outside, not the paleness of men who worked in an office all day.

He caught her staring and winked. She resisted gasping and turned to find something to do. She grabbed a glass, retrieved the milk, and poured him some. When she handed it to him, his warm smile tickled her insides as if an intruding moth were fluttering at a window, seeking escape.

"I brought you a surprise." He looked at Rosie, reached into his coat pocket, and pulled out a handkerchief. He slid the bundle across the table.

Rosie clapped her hands and rose to her knees. She opened the present, revealing four perfect wooden replicas of animals. "A hossie!"

Jackson's longing as he watched his niece confused Larkin as much as his warm smile had. He didn't seem like the kind of man to abandon a child. She never wanted to like him, but she did. A lot.

"Look, Larkin, a cow. Moooo. . ." Rosie walked the cow and horse across the table. "Oink, oink," she said, picking up the pig.

"I think she likes them." Larkin smiled at him.

Jackson nodded and stood.

Rosie cast a worried eye in his direction but picked up the fourth animal—a sheep.

He glanced at Wilma then turned to Larkin. "I, uh. . .brought you something, too."

Larkin reached out and accepted the small wooden figure, her hands trembling and heart pounding. She'd never received a gift from anyone except at Christmas or on her birthday, and those had dwindled to next to nothing.

"It's a bird." He cleared his raspy throat. "It's not a lark, but I thought you might like it since you said your name reminded your dad of a bird."

Her throat went dry at the thoughtfulness of the gift and the time involved in making it. Larkin could only nod. She turned away, lest he see the tears burning her eyes, and poured a glass of water.

Wilma's upraised brow caught her eye. The cook grinned, something she rarely did.

Larkin swallowed another drink, wiped her eyes, and turned back around. "Thank you. I've never had such a thoughtful gift."

A shy smile tugged at his lips; then he broke her gaze.

She turned to Rosie. "Shall we go and put our lovely animals in our room so you can spend time with your uncle?"

Rosie stuck out her lip.

"Maybe she could bring one with her?" Jackson asked.

"Aye, that is a grand idea."

Larkin escorted Rosie back to their room, all the while examining her own gift. The bird, carved from a light-colored wood, more resembled a sparrow than a lark, but the fine craftsmanship and detail made even a plain sparrow exquisite. She probably shouldn't have accepted the gift, being as it was from a man, but she clutched it to her heart, knowing it was already one of her most treasured possessions.

Fifteen minutes later, Larkin and Jackson walked down the boardwalk with Rosie between them, holding their hands. To someone who didn't know them, they could be a family on their way to the mercantile or somewhere else. But as much as Larkin longed for a family of her own, she didn't dare hope it could be this one.

She didn't have the freedom to choose her own family. She'd always be grateful to Mrs. O'Keefe for taking her in when she was orphaned, but hadn't she paid her debt by working hard these seven years? Even indentured servants were freed after that long.

"I'm cold." Rosie blinked away the flakes of snow that had landed on her eyelashes.

Jackson lifted her up and wrapped his duster around her. "We'll be home soon. I've already got the fire going, so it will be warm."

Pulling her cloak to her chest to block the biting wind, Larkin quickened her pace to keep up with the long-legged man.

Though many people loved the snow that had started falling this morning, it only reminded her of the times in New York when her family had been cold, living in a drafty shanty with little food or fuel. She longed for the warmth of the sun and beautiful wildflowers.

"Afternoon, Miss Doyle."

Larkin stopped suddenly to keep from colliding into Frank Barrett. "Good day, sir." She attempted to go around him, but he sidestepped, blocking her way. At least the wind was less severe with his body shielding her, but the look in his eyes chilled away any warmth she'd gathered from his presence.

"When can I expect the privilege of your company for dinner? I'd hoped we could dine together before now."

She shivered, remembering Maura's warning. If she refused Mr. Barrett, Maura might put her out on the street, with no home and no job. But she wasn't a slave. She didn't have to dine with this man if she didn't want to. Perhaps she could put him off until another means of escape provided itself.

"Mrs. O'Keefe took in the Lancaster girl, as you know." She attempted to look around him to see if Jackson had heard her or noticed her gone, but Mr. Barrett blocked her view. "I've been quite busy caring for Rosie. 'Twould not be proper for me to dine with you and neglect me other duties. Perhaps after Christmas. . ."

"I'll talk with Maura and make sure that you have some free time. I've waited long enough for you."

His mouth pursed, and something flickered in his steely gaze that sent chills down Larkin's back, as if someone had dumped snow down her shirtwaist. "No. Please do not do such a thing."

"Why? Do you not wish to enjoy my company? I'm quite wealthy, you know." His mouth twisted into an arrogant snarl.

Larkin searched for an answer, but her mind froze.

"Excuse me, but Miss Doyle is with me at the moment."

Relief melted the chills at the sound of Jackson's voice behind Mr. Barrett. The shorter man spun around to face him.

"No one asked for your advice, Lancaster."

"The mayor's wife has instructed Miss Doyle to escort me and my niece. Do you want me to inform her that you kept her ward from her duties?"

Larkin hurried past Mr. Barrett to stand beside Jackson. He handed Rosie to her then faced Mr. Barrett again.

"Uh. . .no, I didn't mean to keep Miss Doyle from her duties." He glanced at her. A muscle ticked in his jaw. His cold gaze could have frozen hot water. "Another time, then." He pivoted around and marched down the boardwalk.

Somehow Larkin felt sure she'd be the one to pay for his displeasure.

⚜

Jackson double-checked the ammunition in his Winchester. He set it on the desk, then grabbed another rifle and loaded the cartridges in it. He had a payroll for Carpenter Mills that had to get through. With Shorty driving, him riding shotgun, and Cody Webster, a sharpshooter disguised as a city slicker, riding inside the coach, Jackson hoped to deliver the payroll without incident. His customers were getting leery of traveling on the Lancaster Stage after all that had happened.

His boots echoed on the boardwalk and down the steps. The four horses fidgeted, anxious to be on their way. Jackson handed up his rifles to Shorty then passed him a canteen filled with coffee and a small satchel that held their lunch. He walked to the front of the stage, checking harnesses and talking to the horses.

"Uncle Jack!"

He pivoted at Rosie's call, his heart jumping. He'd never minded driving the stage, but going today would mean he wouldn't be back until Thursday and would miss Wednesday evening with Rosie. Mrs. O'Keefe had been stern and refused to allow him to visit his niece on another day. No amount of sweet talk or arguing could sway her. As much as he loved Rosie, he couldn't take care of her and provide for her without his business.

Rosie ran into his arms, and he tossed her in the air. Larkin followed a few yards behind, walking demurely, her cheeks brightened by the cold wind that tugged at her dark green cloak.

"We sneaked out."

Jackson raised a brow at Larkin, and she ducked her head for a moment. "Mrs. O'Keefe had a tea to attend with the banker's wife and some of her other friends, and Mr. O'Keefe was still sleeping. Since you'll be gone tomorrow, we thought to come and see you off." Larkin shrugged one shoulder, as if it were a small thing, but to Jackson, it meant a lot.

He smacked a kiss on Rosie's cheek, making her giggle and washing away his longing of not getting to see her. She turned her head, giving him access to the other side of her face, on which he happily planted another kiss.

"I wanna go with you." Rosie clung to his neck.

"I wish you could, sweet pea, but it's too dangerous." He wanted to say, "Maybe after we catch whoever's been robbing the stage," but didn't for fear it would make her think of her parents.

"Bring me a present."

Larkin stepped forward. "Now, Rosie, 'tisn't good manners to ask for gifts."

Jackson handed his niece to her and helped a female passenger into the coach. He checked his pocket watch as Cody winked at him and stepped inside. Jackson closed the door and looked at Shorty. "Ready to go?"

His driver nodded and turned up his collar. "Yep."

Jackson knelt in front of Rosie and hugged her. "Be good for Miss Doyle, all right?"

"Her name's Larkin."

"Be good for Larkin. . .and don't correct your elders." He hugged his niece tight, never wanting to let her go. But time was ticking. The stage needed to leave, and Christmas was drawing closer.

He stood and gazed at Larkin. She was so pretty in her dark green cloak and with her cheeks rosy from the cold air. He felt a sudden urge to pull her close and hug her but shook off that crazy thought. "Thank you."

She nodded and took Rosie's hand.

Jackson cleared the huskiness from his throat, jogged around to the far side of the stage, and climbed aboard.

Rosie waved.

"We'll be praying for your safety," Larkin called out. She caught his gaze then darted hers to the ground.

Shorty let off the brake and shouted a loud, "Heeyaw!"

Rosie jumped up and down from her safe spot by the office window. "Yaw. Yaw!"

Jackson grinned and waved, his heart warmed by their brief visit. He positioned his rifle on his lap, watching as they left town to see if he noticed anything out of the ordinary.

The snow had stopped, leaving a thin blanket of white all across the open prairie. His cheeks burned from the chilly wind, and he hunkered down, keeping a watchful eye. It would be hard for anyone to sneak up on them for the next five miles, since they were on open prairie.

His mind drifted to the quickly approaching Christmas Day. It was on a Saturday this year. Would he even get to see Rosie? Would he spend the day alone, remembering last year's happy Christmas with Ben and Amanda?

And how in the world was he going to find a wife in nine days? But he had to—or lose all that mattered to him in this world.

A pheasant darted upward from a nearby bush, making Jackson jump.

Shorty chuckled. "A little edgy, huh?"

"I was just thinking, that's all." Jackson refocused on his duty.

If all else failed, he could ask the Widow Winningham to marry him. He shuddered—and he knew it wasn't from the cold. The thought of being a stepfather to her six rowdy sons made him quiver as badly as being lost in a blizzard with no coat on.

And how would little Rosie fare with all those rough boys? There had to be a better answer.

He checked the landscape for intruders—anything that looked out of the ordinary—then turned his thoughts to God. *Help me, Lord. Show me what to do. I can't lose Rosie.*

Desperate, he turned to Shorty. "I don't reckon you know any women that want to get married."

Chapter 6

Larkin sat on the edge of her bed and rocked Rosie back and forth.

The girl sniffled and huddled against Larkin's chest. "I want Uncle Jack."

Larkin stroked her hair and murmured softly. "I know, lass. He's busy with work, I'm sure of it."

As Rosie sobbed, Larkin's ire grew. How could Jackson disappoint his niece like this? Why hadn't he warned her that he'd miss two nights with her instead of just the one? She'd stirred Rosie up, thinking he was coming today, only to severely disappoint her.

Larkin rocked and prayed, hoping business had kept Jackson away rather than injury. It had been a whole week since he'd come for Rosie, but at least the child had gotten a few moments with him when they'd visited him at the stage office.

Rosie's breathing rose and fell as sleep descended. Her little body grew heavy.

Larkin tucked her in bed then softly kissed her cheek.

Caring for Rosie made her heart ache with longing. Oh, how she wanted children of her own—and, of course, a husband. But no man other than Mr. Barrett had shown an interest in her, and she had no desire to get to know him better.

She faced a dilemma similar to those of the sharecroppers in Ireland who worked the soil of the wealthy landowners. They had to give a share of their crops to these landowners and thus had barely enough to feed their families. There was no hope of a better life.

At least Maura had seen that Larkin was educated and had allowed her to attend school through the eighth grade. But she paid her no wage, only providing food, shelter, and clothing. How could she move somewhere else when she had no money? What man would want to marry a woman who was nothing more than a servant?

Jackson's blue eyes invaded her thoughts. The charming way his coffee-colored hair hung over his forehead made her want to brush it back. Would it be soft to touch, or thick and wiry?

Larkin shook her head at the foolish thought. She would never know the answer to that. Jackson Lancaster tolerated her presence only because he had to.

Dropping to her knees on the cold floor, she folded her hands and prayed, asking God to soothe Rosie, to protect Jackson—for Rosie's sake—and to provide a way for her to start a new life, outside the O'Keefes' home.

The next morning, Maura left with Rosie in tow as she went to visit the Flemings, a family with two girls a bit older than Rosie. Larkin donned her cloak and left after they were out of view. She marched down the boardwalk, her boots pounding on the weathered wood.

She'd stewed last night until she'd finally fallen into a restless sleep and then had to listen to Maura's gloating at breakfast. Maura was certain they'd seen the last visit from Jackson Lancaster. On and on she'd told Larkin and Mr. O'Keefe how much better off the child was with them.

Larkin wasn't sure if she was truly angry because Jackson had disappointed Rosie or because she had to listen to Maura's self-righteous boasting. More likely, both situations had fueled her Irish temper, one she kept in check on most days.

She knocked on the stage office door but knew by the darkness inside that nobody was there. She tried the door handle, thinking to leave Jackson a note, but found it locked.

Swirling around, she studied the town of Prairie Flats. The place lived up to its name. Located on the Illinois prairie, the town was as flat as a sheet of paper. There were few trees to block the steady winds, which was a blessing in the summer but a curse in the winter.

There was work to be done at the O'Keefes', but rarely having time to herself, Larkin wandered toward the mercantile. On occasion, Maura allowed her to purchase an item or two and charge it to the O'Keefes' account. Of course, there would be extra chores required to pay for those necessities.

Christmas was quickly approaching, and Larkin wondered what she could give the people in her life. She could make Rosie a doll, but she didn't want a new one competing with the doll the child's mother had made. Perhaps she could sew a small quilt from the scraps she'd been saving. Larkin smiled at the pleasure such a gift would surely bring the lass.

But finding something for the O'Keefes was more difficult, and the fact that it was expected took the joy out of the giving. Larkin sighed. What could she give them that they didn't already have? For just being the mayor of a small town, Mr. O'Keefe was a superb provider and often worked long hours. The O'Keefes lacked nothing.

A woman a few years older than Larkin smiled at her husband as they squeezed past in the crowded aisle. Melancholy tugged at Larkin, and she couldn't resist watching them. The husband wrapped his arm around his wife and whispered in her ear. The woman giggled and looked at him with adoration.

Larkin had never felt so lonely. Staying busy at the O'Keefes' had kept her from developing friendships, and Mr. O'Keefe, Jackson Lancaster, and Frank Barrett were the only men who actually talked to her, except an occasional guest at the big house.

An Irish Bride for Christmas

The scents of spices and leather and the sweet odor of perfume that a man was testing out as a gift for his wife hung in the air. People chattered, and two children played hide-and-seek around their mother's skirt as she waited to have her purchases tallied up.

What would it be like to wake up each day next to a man you loved and to have children to tickle and hug and receive wet, sloppy kisses from?

She stopped in front of a box of colorful Christmas ornaments and picked one up. Never had she seen such elaborate decorations—or even a real Christmas tree—until she'd move in with the O'Keefes. She had vague memories of hanging holly and ivy in their small home in Ireland, and those times were the happiest she could remember. Hers was a home where a child was free to laugh and talk, not one where she had to be cautious and quiet. The faces of her parents had faded over time, but not the feeling of being loved and cherished. Would no one ever love her again?

Larkin pursed her lips. She ached for a home of her own, and at nineteen, she felt it was time to find a way to get it. Perhaps she could find a job with room and board and a small wage. It wouldn't be much more than she had now, but it would be hers and not Maura's.

Still. . .how could she leave Rosie? The child needed her.

Leaving the store and its cheery inhabitants, she plodded along the boardwalk. Her dilemma tugged at her. She crossed the street and dropped onto the empty bench in front of the stage office. Still no sign of Rosie's uncle.

In spite of her irritation with him for hurting Rosie, she couldn't help worrying about Jackson. She'd asked around and discovered he had an excellent reputation. Not at all what Maura had said. And she knew he loved Rosie.

Larkin's thoughts drifted to a vision of Jackson laughing and tossing Rosie in the air. She'd never wanted to like him—thought him an ogre for not keeping his niece. But instead of hating him, she feared the opposite was true. Her feelings had grown like the abundant wild ivy of her homeland. Did she love the man?

But what did that matter? He could never return her feelings when she worked for his enemy. Looking heavenward, she prayed, "Please, Lord, don't let me feel these things for Jackson. And please bring him home safely."

She glanced in both directions, hoping to hear the jingling of harnesses and the pounding of horses' hooves. "Jackson, where are you?"

※※※

Jackson brushed down the last of the horses and then put the tools away. Now that each horse had fresh hay and water and a measure of oats, he could go home. But where was home?

He'd tried living at the big house but hated the silence of the place. Amanda's knickknacks and utensils cried out for a woman to use them, but he was out of luck in that respect.

He'd even spent an extra two days scouring the small towns his stage stopped at to see if there was a kind woman who'd marry him. But none of the available women wanted to marry a man they didn't know so quickly, no matter that he owned his own business.

He sighed and scratched his bristly beard. He wanted to see Rosie, and it didn't matter one bit that today wasn't his day. Turning around, he headed for the O'Keefe house.

Just a hug from Rosie, and he'd know she was all right. Then maybe he could sleep.

Seeing Larkin would be a bonus. The auburn-haired sprite's name was still on his list, but he didn't dare ask her to marry him. If she said no, his visits to Rosie would be awkward and unbearable.

He'd never been friends with a woman before, except for Amanda, and she was family. Besides, though Larkin's stance toward him had softened, she'd never indicated having any affection for him. She'd been through enough in her life. She didn't need to marry a man she didn't love.

He stopped at front of the O'Keefes' kitchen door. Was he doing the right thing, coming here on a day he wasn't expected? Before he could knock, the door flew open.

Wilma stood there with a bucket of dirty water. She blinked and smiled. "Well, about time you got back. Here, save my old bones a chill and empty this on that shrub for me."

Jackson took the bucket and did as she bid, glad that she seemed happy to see him. Inside, he set the bucket by the door, taunted by the fragrant scent of baking bread and knowing there was nothing warm for him to eat at home. "I realize it isn't my day to be here, but do you think I could see Rosie?"

Wilma's lips pursed. "I wouldn't mind except that she's abed with a fever, and I don't think it's proper for you to visit her in Larkin's room."

Concern stabbed his chest. "How long has she been sick? Has the doctor seen her? Larkin's room?"

Wilma nodded and moved a pot of something to the back burner. "Rosie shares Larkin's room. Seems the madam didn't want to take a chance on her breaking something in the guest room."

Irritation battled concern. Mrs. O'Keefe had made a big deal about his place not being good enough for Rosie, but now she was living in the servants' quarters. They were probably much nicer than his room behind the office, but the thought that the mayor's wife had banned Rosie from a better room irked him. "I want to see her. Either take me to her or bring her to me."

Wilma gave him a scolding stare then softened. "I imagine it would help her to see you. Give me a minute."

Jackson removed his jacket and hung it on a chair and laid his hat on the table. He paced the kitchen, enjoying the cozy warmth but anxious to see his niece. After what seemed like hours, Larkin hurried into the room. "You're back. I was so worried."

He stopped pacing directly in front of her. "How is Rosie?"

Larkin shrugged and twisted her hands together. "She's had a fever for two days. 'Tis my fault, I fear."

"Why?" Jackson took her hands to keep them still.

Her lower lip quivered. "We built a snowman. Rosie's been wantin' to play outside, and I thought 'twould do her good to get some fresh air. I—I'm so sorry." Tears gushed from her eyes and down her cheeks.

Jackson pulled her close and patted her back, hoping to comfort her. "It's not your fault. Children catch colds and fevers."

"I shouldna have taken her outside." Larkin clung to his shirt.

She sniffled, and Jackson couldn't resist resting his head against hers, hoping she didn't mind that he was fresh off the trail.

After a moment, she seemed to gather her composure. Wilma entered the room, and Larkin stepped back. "Sorry."

"Don't be." He smiled and wiped a remnant tear from her cheek. "I know it's not a proper thing to ask, what with her being in your room, but may I please see Rosie? Just for a minute?"

"If you want to know what I think"—Wilma glanced at them over her spectacles—"you're just what that child needs to get her back on her feet. She's pined herself into a tizzy missing you. I don't know what Mrs. O'Keefe is doing keeping you two apart."

"C'mon. I'll take you to her." Larkin took his hand and tugged on it.

He enjoyed the soft feel of her small hand in his. They passed a big closet and then entered a room that was slightly bigger than his but sparsely adorned. His gaze landed on a small lump under a colorful quilt. His throat tightened.

"The doctor says she will be fine. He left some medicine for her and said not to let her outside until Christmas."

Jackson knelt beside the bed and reached out his shaking hand to brush the hair from Rosie's overly red cheeks. Clearing his throat, he forced some words out. "Sweet pea, it's Uncle Jack."

Rosie stirred, and her eyes opened. She blinked several times; then her mouth curved upward. "Hi."

Jackson glanced at Larkin. "Can I hold her?"

Her lips tilted upward, and she nodded.

Jackson lifted one corner of the quilt, but Rosie sat and climbed into his arms. Her hot cheek warmed his. *God, please touch her. Heal her.*

"I thought you'd gone to heaven. Like Mama and Poppy."

Jackson clutched her small form as tightly as he dared. "No, precious. I told you I'd take care of you, and I mean to do that."

"Good." She snuggled in his arms and was soon fast asleep.

Larkin motioned to a chair in the corner. He took Rosie and settled down. Larkin laid the quilt over them both.

"Just let me sit here and pray a few minutes; then I'll leave." Not that he knew how he'd be able to leave her.

"If you need anything, just call out." Larkin patted Rosie's head and left the room.

It held a single bed, making him wonder how both Larkin and Rosie managed to get any sleep. Besides the chair, there was a small desk and a crate that held a stack of clothes. Two pegs hung on the wall, holding a pair of dresses, both ones that he'd seen Larkin wear. There wasn't even a fireplace. The lack of amenities stunned him, considering how fancy the rest of the house was.

The bird he'd carved sat in the middle of the windowsill. There were no pictures, no decorations of any kind. He hugged Rosie closer, his irritation with Mrs. O'Keefe growing. Had Larkin lived in near poverty her whole life? Was that what Rosie was doomed to endure if he didn't get her back—to be the mistreated servant of a selfish, wealthy woman?

A racket sounded in the kitchen and moved his way. Maura O'Keefe stormed into the room, her pale eyes colder than the winter sky outside. "What is *he* doing here?"

Larkin wrung her hands together. "He learned Rosie was sick and wanted to sit with her a few minutes. Surely you can't deny him that."

"Oh yes, I can. The judge was clear in his orders. Put that child in her bed and leave my house this instant."

Rosie whimpered and cuddled closer. "Don't go, Uncle Jack."

Jackson clenched his jaw tight to keep from spewing out his anger on the woman. If Rosie hadn't been sick, he would have marched right out the door with her, but he couldn't risk her getting sicker. Against his wishes, he laid her on the bed.

Rosie tried to cling to him, but Larkin squeezed in between them. "No. . . don't go. . ." Rosie's wails followed him down the hall and into the kitchen.

Maura crossed her arms over her chest and frowned. "First thing in the morning, I'm going to the judge and tell him what you've done."

Jackson glared back at her and stepped closer.

Her ice blue eyes widened.

"And maybe I'll just tell the judge how you've relegated my niece to the servants' quarters, not even giving her a bed of her own. What do you think he'll say about that?"

Mrs. O'Keefe paled. "Get out and don't come back."

Jackson snatched up his jacket and stormed outside without even putting it on. How had things turned out so badly? The days were ticking away. He couldn't leave his niece in that woman's care. If he didn't find a wife soon, he'd leave his business and whisk Rosie away in the night. The two of them could start over somewhere else.

Even as his thoughts traveled that trail, he knew that wasn't the answer.

God wouldn't have him react in anger, but where was He in all of this? So far his prayers had gone unanswered.

Jackson grabbed a fistful of snow, wadded it into a ball, and threw it against a tree.

Could he just walk away from the house his parents had built? And the business he and Ben had worked so hard to make a success?

And what about Larkin? Could he leave her to live out her days in that little room with no hope of a future?

He slammed the door to the office, rattling the window, and strode back to his room. If he had any hopes of getting Rosie back, he had to move into the big house and put aside his hurts.

He glanced at the calendar. Only six days to Christmas.

Chapter 7

"How is your dinner, Miss Doyle?" Frank Barrett's charming smile would have won over most maidens.

"'Tis delicious. Wilma is a fine cook." Larkin avoided his gaze and glanced at Maura, who was watching them. Why did she want to push Mr. Barrett on her? Larkin had no fortune. He had nothing to gain by a union with her.

"Christmas will soon be past; then I will expect you to accept my dinner invitation." Mr. Barrett shoved a huge bite of veal into his mouth.

Larkin's heart pounded, her appetite disintegrating. She glanced across the table.

Miss Eleanor James, eldest daughter of the town's banker, glared at her. The woman had made her interest in Mr. Barrett clear, but he seemed oblivious to her wiles. Why didn't he pursue Eleanor instead of her?

On cue, Wilma touched her shoulder just before dessert was served. "Miss Rosie is ready for you to tuck her in, Miss Doyle."

Larkin dabbed her lips with her napkin. "Thank you, Wilma. I shall see to her right away."

Frank Barrett and the other men stood as she rose from her chair, but he along with Maura scowled as she left the table.

Her heart hammered, and she almost felt guilty for prearranging her escape, but the thought of spending the evening avoiding Mr. Barrett's advances and her employer's glares had set her nerves on edge. As she passed through the kitchen and entered the servants' quarters, her heart slowed and her breathing returned to normal.

Rosie sat at the kitchen table eating a late-night snack of bread with apple butter. She smiled when she saw Larkin, then yawned. Normally she was in bed an hour earlier, but Larkin had asked Wilma to keep her up as long as she didn't get in the cook's way.

"Ready for bed?"

Rosie stuffed a final bite into her mouth and nodded. She licked her fingers, then downed the last of her milk and yawned again.

"Best get that youngun to bed before she falls off that chair." Wilma sidled a glance at them as she sliced a peach pie and placed a serving on one of Maura's favorite china plates.

Larkin carried Rosie to their room and helped her into a nightgown, then tucked her in.

"Uncle Jack comes tomorrow." Rosie's eyelids rose and closed, getting heavier by the second.

"Yes, lass, tomorrow is his day to see you." Larkin hoped his work wouldn't keep him away again. There hadn't been any robberies in the past week, but with people coming to visit family for Christmas, as well as extra orders to be shipped because of the holiday, Jackson seemed busier than ever. *Please don't disappoint Rosie again.*

Larkin brushed the hair from Rosie's face, thankful for the natural warmth of her forehead and not the burning fever that had kept the child in bed the past three days. Donning her own gown, she wondered if Jackson was poring over the stage bookwork or eating a warm meal. She wasn't certain but thought that he'd lost weight since she had first gotten to know him.

Kneeling beside her bed, she shivered and prayed, "Heavenly Father, please make a way for Rosie and Jackson to be together. Also, if You could work things out so I could leave and get my own place, I'd be forever grateful. Bless Wilma and thank You for her friendship."

She scurried into bed as she murmured, "Amen," knowing she'd be both delighted if Rosie was returned to her uncle and sad to lose the little girl she'd grown to love. She'd even miss seeing Jackson regularly.

She scooted down in the covers and snuggled up next to Rosie's warm body, hoping Maura didn't come looking for her, demanding that she return to the dinner party. And how was she going to get out of dining with Mr. Barrett? Would Maura actually punish her or perhaps even turn her out if she continued avoiding the man?

Larkin nibbled the inside of her cheek, wishing she had the nerve to tell him she wasn't interested. "Lord, make me bolder."

She closed her eyes; her body relaxed. As the fog of sleep descended, it wasn't Mr. Barrett's dreary gray eyes she saw, but Jackson's somber blue ones. He carried more than his share of concerns. She longed to rub the crease from his brow—to kiss away his pain.

Larkin's eyes darted open, and she stared into the darkness. Why hadn't she noticed before? When had it happened?

Jackson Lancaster had sneaked in and stolen her heart.

≈≈≈

"D'you find a gal to marry yet?" Shorty peered out of the corner of his eyes at Jackson then refocused on the road in front of him, keeping the horses at a steady pace.

"Not yet." If no problems presented themselves, he'd be home by noon and have time to clean up and see Rosie this evening. Christmas was only three days away, and his hopes of finding a bride were diminishing.

"I talked with two women from neighboring towns. One was seven years older than me and had three children." It wasn't that he didn't like children, but he had Rosie to think about. Becoming an instant husband and father to one child was daunting enough.

"The other woman had an elderly mother who lives with her." Jackson's heart went out to them, but he just couldn't bring himself to ask the woman to marry him—not when a pair of moss green eyes kept invading his dreams. And that cinnamon hair. He longed to run his hand through it but tightened his grasp on his Winchester instead.

Suddenly a flame ignited, as if he'd been shot in his gut, making his whole body go limp. When had he developed feelings for Larkin? Why hadn't he noticed sooner?

Shorty chuckled. "Two women at once might be a bit to take on."

Numb with the realization that if Larkin were to accept his marriage proposal, he could have Rosie back by Christmas Eve and a wife he loved instead of some stranger, he turned to Shorty.

The driver shot several sideways glances at him and looked around. "What's wrong?"

The ricochet of rifle fire echoed across the barren landscape. The edge of the footboard in front of Jackson and Shorty shattered. Both men ducked.

"Heeyaw!" Shorty shook the reins and urged the team into a gallop as he hunkered down.

Jackson scoured the area, his heart thumping hard.

"There!" Shorty yelled and pointed with his stubbly chin.

Three riders charged out of the tree line, rifles aimed straight at the stage. Jackson fired, and one rider lurched backward out of his saddle. Below him, Cody shot from inside the stage.

How had anyone known about the payroll? He'd handled it personally. He fired again, knowing he had to live for Rosie's sake. The child couldn't lose another person she loved.

As if he'd been branded with a blazing hot iron, his left shoulder exploded with pain. Jackson didn't take time to look at his wound but raised his rifle to the other shoulder and shot another man.

The outlaw clutched his side but stayed in the saddle. He slowed and turned his horse around. With his two cohorts gone, the third thief swung around and raced back to the trees.

Even though the outlaw might have been responsible for Ben's death, Jackson couldn't shoot the man in the back, but Cody must have had no qualms about it. His weapon blasted, and the last man jerked and flew off his saddle.

Fighting intense pain, Jackson braced his feet and struggled to stay on the jarring seat as Shorty kept the team racing for Prairie Flats. Jackson yanked his kerchief out and shoved it under his shirt to stay the bleeding. Though only noontime, a foggy darkness descended, and Jackson felt himself falling.

Chapter 8

Larkin steadied Rosie's hand as she hung one of the older Christmas bulbs on the tree. Though it was still several days until Christmas, Maura had insisted the tree be up and decorated, as well as the parlor and dining rooms, before her annual December 23 dinner party. Larkin hoped the pine boughs scenting the room didn't wither before tomorrow evening.

Mistletoe hung in clumps over doorways, tied with colorful red bows. Unlit candles stood in the windows like soldiers on guard, waiting for night-time, when they would be lit to show visitors the way. Pine boughs and red bows decorated the stairs and fireplace mantel.

Everything looked festive, but Larkin shivered at the thought of another evening with Frank Barrett. Maura had made it clear that she'd accept no excuses this time. Larkin sighed. She was expected to remain at tomorrow's dinner until all the guests left; then she was to change clothes and help Wilma clean up.

"Did you have a tree when you were little?" Rosie reached for another of the colorful glass balls.

Larkin hurried to her side. "Let me help you. And no, I never had a Christmas tree until I came to live with the O'Keefes."

"How come?" Rosie's lower lip protruded as if she thought Larkin terribly unfortunate.

"I lived in Ireland until I was eight. There are few trees to be found there, so we decorated with holly and ivy. The holly has lovely red berries on it. At Christmas, me mother would fix bread sauce made from bread crumbs, milk, and an onion with cloves stuck in it for flavoring."

Rosie turned up her nose. "I don't like yunyuns."

Larkin smiled. She turned at the sound of quickly approaching steps.

Wilma hurried into the room, her gaze jumping from Rosie to Larkin. "I need to speak with you alone."

A fist clenched Larkin's heart at Wilma's worried expression. What was wrong? Could something have happened to Jackson? That thought made her want to crumble into a huddled mass of misery. What if he died without knowing how she felt?

Larkin took Rosie's hand, forcing the horrible thoughts from her mind. She was overreacting. Wilma's distress could be the result of a simple problem, not that she was prone to hysterics. Perhaps Mrs. O'Keefe's food order for her party hadn't arrived.

"I've made some Christmas cookies." Wilma smiled at Rosie. "I don't suppose anyone would like to help me sprinkle colored sugar on them?"

Rosie bounced up and down as they walked toward the kitchen. "Me! I can do it."

"Before you can work, you need a snack." Wilma placed a plate with three cookies in front of Rosie and then set a glass of milk on the table. "Stay here and eat while I talk to Larkin."

They hurried back to the parlor and sat on the settee together. Wilma took Larkin's hands; her brows dipped down, and her lips were pursed.

"Tell me what's wrong. You're scarin' me."

"There was a stage robbery attempt, and Mr. Lancaster has been shot."

Larkin surged to her feet. "Where is he? Oh, is he. . .alive?"

Wilma nodded. "He's at Doc Grant's and will be fine. Sit down. There's more."

Larkin hurried to obey, though all within her wanted to rush out the door and over to the doctor's office.

"It seems Mr. O'Keefe and that Frank Barrett were part of the outlaw gang that's been holding up the stages. Since Barrett worked at the bank, he was privy to information about payroll deliveries. Barrett is dead, but Mr. O'Keefe is in jail. He was shot and is singing like a songbird now."

Larkin's eyes widened. She pressed her hand against her chest. "Poor Mrs. O'Keefe. Is that why I haven't seen her all day? How is she taking the news?"

Wilma's lips twisted. "Gone. On the train this morning. She was probably neck deep in all of this. That's why she kept pushing Barrett on you. Wanted to keep things all in the family."

Larkin peered around the cheerful room, such a contrast to the horrible news she'd just heard. "What will happen to all of us?"

"We're to close up the house. I don't know after that."

Larkin wrung her hands. Where would they live?

With Mrs. O'Keefe gone and Mr. O'Keefe in jail, what would happen to Rosie? Surely the judge would allow her to go back to Jackson. He would take his niece home and have no reason to visit Larkin ever again.

Could she tell him how she felt? Was it too forward of her?

She jumped up. *Please, Father, let him live.* "I must see Jackson."

"I'll watch Rosie while you go." Wilma's expression warmed, her eyes twinkling.

⚓

As the haziness of sleep fled, Jackson glanced around. He wasn't in his own bed. Where was he?

He tried to sit up, but a sudden pain in his shoulder and a pair of strong arms pushed him back.

"Hold it, young man. You've been shot."

"Doc?"

"Yep. There was a stage holdup, but you got the rascals. They won't be bothering you anymore."

Jackson lay back, his foggy mind struggling to remember what had happened. "Shorty?"

"He's fine. Just got a few scratches."

"Gotta get out of here, Doc. Need to check on Rosie." He attempted to sit up again, but the doctor held him down.

"Lie still or I'll give you something that makes you sleep. Tomorrow will be soon enough. I've already sent word about your injury and told the folks keeping your niece that you'll be fine—providing you rest."

Jackson sighed but relaxed. Had Rosie heard about his injury? Would she be worried? Would Larkin? How was a man supposed to rest when he had all these concerns muddling his brain?

A door rattled and someone entered with a swish of skirts. He hoped the doctor would pull the curtain so nobody would see him down like he was.

The swishing moved closer, and he turned his head. Larkin!

Worry wrinkled her pretty brow, and she twisted her hands together. "H–how are you? We were so concerned."

"Rosie was?"

Larkin shook her head. "Rosie's fine. She doesn't know yet. 'Twas Wilma and meself that were worried. 'Tis a relief to know you'll be fine."

He smiled and held out his hand. She stared at it, then stepped forward and clasped it. "I'll come and see Rosie when I get out of here. Probably tomorrow. Don't tell her about me. She'll just fret."

Larkin nodded. "I suppose you'll get Rosie back now."

"Why do you say that?"

Her eyes widened. "You haven't heard?"

He shook his head, wondering what she meant.

She conveyed to him what she'd heard from Wilma, who'd been at the mercantile when the outlaws were brought in to town.

Jackson stared at the ceiling. Numb. The very people who tried to take Rosie from him had most likely been responsible for his brother's death. Had it all been some big plan to steal Rosie? Or had Ben and Amanda just been in the wrong place at the wrong time? He'd probably never know.

His heart skittered. With Mrs. O'Keefe gone and her husband in jail, the judge would have to give Rosie back to him. He smiled, but when he looked at Larkin, his grin faltered. "What's wrong?"

Larkin glanced at him then stared at the floor. "I'm sure the judge will give Rosie back to you now. I'm truly happy for you."

"You don't look happy." Love for this woman warmed his whole body. He wanted to take her in his arms and kiss away her troubles. Why had it taken him so long to realize that he loved her?

"It's just that I shall dearly miss. . .Rosie."

Jackson bit back a smile. Glory be, the woman had feelings for him. They were written all over her lovely face. "Just Rosie?"

"Well. . .I. . ."

"Doc!"

Larkin jumped at Jackson's shout.

"What's all the caterwauling?" The doctor strode in, wiping his spectacles on the edge of his shirt. "Are you in pain?"

"No, but I need to sit up." Jackson sent him a pleading gaze.

"Sorry. Not today." He turned to leave.

"Wait. C'mon, Doc. A man can't ask a woman to marry him while he's flat on his back."

Larkin's head spun toward him, her beautiful green eyes wide. A slow smile tilted the lips he longed to kiss.

Doctor Grant chuckled. "Well. . .I suppose I *could* make an exception for that."

Jackson gritted his teeth, pushing away the pain as the doctor helped him up. The man quickly left the room, a wide grin brightening his tired features.

Jackson reached for Larkin's hand and took a deep breath. She looked so vulnerable, almost afraid to hope. "Did you know the judge gave me until Christmas to find a bride or I'd lose Rosie for good?"

Larkin shook her head.

"I realized yesterday that I'd been searching in vain. The woman I love is right here. Will you marry me, Larkin? Help me raise Rosie?"

Her lower lip trembled, and tears made her eyes shine. She nodded.

He grinned.

"I love you, too, Jackson. 'Twould make me very happy to marry you."

That was all he needed to hear. With his good arm, he pulled her to his side and kissed her, showing her how he felt and making promises for the future—promises he was eager to fulfill.

⚜

"Don't the candles look beautiful?" Larkin tossed the kindling she used to light the parlor candles into the fireplace. "Tradition has it that they are a symbol of welcome to help Mary and Joseph find their way as they looked for shelter the night Jesus was born."

"They'll help Uncle Jack find his way." Rosie stared at the dancing shadows the flickering flames made on the walls.

" 'Tis true. He and Doc Grant should be here soon. Let's go help Wilma."

In the kitchen, Wilma took the goose out of the oven. Its fragrant odors had been making Larkin's stomach growl for hours. "Thank you for cooking that tonight. Smells truly delicious."

Larkin lifted Rosie onto a stool. "There's one quaint custom in Ireland where the groom is invited to his bride's house right before the wedding and they cook a goose in his honor. 'Tis called 'Aitin' the Gander.' "

Rosie grinned. "You're the bride."

Larkin felt her cheeks warm. . .or perhaps 'twas just the heat of the kitchen. "Aye. Tomorrow your uncle Jack and I shall marry."

The thought of being Jackson's wife brought twitters to her stomach that had nothing to do with hunger. A knock sounded at the door, and she jumped. Her beloved was here.

Rosie slid off the seat, but Larkin beat her to the door, pulling it open. Jackson stood there, his arm in a sling and his jacket around his shoulders, blue eyes smiling.

"Uncle Jack!" Rosie wrapped her arms around Jackson's leg. He patted her head, but his gaze never left Larkin's face.

Larkin's heart flip-flopped. Oh, how she loved this man. And tomorrow he'd be her husband.

Someone behind Jackson cleared his throat. "It's cold out here. Don't suppose we could go inside where it's warm so you two could stare at each other by the fire." Doc Grant peered around Jackson's shoulder, grinning.

They hurried inside, and Larkin helped Jackson with his jacket. Rosie and Doc sat at the table. Wilma set a bowl of applesauce on the table and smiled at the doctor.

"I need to talk to you in private a moment," Jackson whispered in Larkin's ear.

She nodded and led him to the parlor. He glanced around the room at all the pretty decorations. Maura's dinner party had been canceled, but the lovely room would make the perfect spot for a Christmas wedding. Their wedding.

Jackson's gaze landed on the mistletoe over the doorway. He grinned wickedly, dimples flashing, and tugged her to the parlor entrance. "In America, we have a tradition. If two people stand under mistletoe together, they have to kiss."

Larkin's whole body went limp, and if Jackson hadn't pulled her to his chest, she was sure she'd have melted into a puddle at his feet. How was it she could come to love this man so much, so fast? His lips melded against her, and all other thoughts fled. Too soon he pulled back.

"No doubts about tomorrow?"

She shook her head. "Not a one. I've prayed hard, and God has made it clear. You and Rosie are my future."

"I feel the same way. Tomorrow can't come soon enough." He stole another quick peck on her lips and led her back to the kitchen. Jackson seated her at the table and took the place next to Larkin, holding her hand.

"I'm gonna get Christmas presents like Baby Jesus did," Rosie declared to Doc Grant.

He waggled his eyebrows at Larkin and Jackson. "I heard you're getting something really special for Christmas."

Jackson chuckled and hugged her.

"I've been looking for a cook and housekeeper." Doc Grant smiled at Wilma. "Looks like I've found one."

Larkin breathed a prayer of thanks to God, knowing her friend would have a place to work. . .and maybe more, someday.

She glanced at the table, her stomach growling. Steam rose up from the mashed potatoes. Canned green beans with bits of ham awaited them, as did Wilma's shiny rolls. Only the goose was missing.

The room quieted as Wilma carried a silver platter covered with a fragrant golden brown goose to the table. She set it in front of Jackson and stared at him. "Well. . .I guess your goose is cooked."

Doc Grant's gaze darted toward Larkin and Jackson. He burst into laughter at the same moment Jackson did. "Ain't that the truth."

Larkin failed to see the humor in the situation but laughed anyway, happy that her beloved's face held lines of joy instead of sorrow.

Tomorrow she'd become Mrs. Jackson Lancaster. She uttered a silent prayer: *Thank You, Lord.*

Little Dutch Bride

by Kelly Eileen Hake

Dedication

For all of us who need to be reminded of God's promise
to care and provide for His children.

Chapter 1

Willowville, Kansas, 1883

Hopeless." Jerome Sanders shook his head as he surveyed the once-proud barn, now dilapidated with age. The doors sagged on beaten hinges, wood roughened by weather and bristling with splinters for those unwary enough to brush against it. Just one more thing to be overhauled on Gramps's farm. Just one more item on a list he already couldn't afford.

He could sand out the worst of the splinters and rehang the doors easily enough; then the structure might last through the winter. If not, he'd start losing cattle, which was the last stop before losing the farm.

"Not going to happen." Jerome spoke the words aloud as he strode back toward the wagon. Gramps had left the farm to him, and he'd do whatever was necessary to honor that legacy.

For now, that meant heading to the general store for nails, sandpaper, and varnish. He added leather oil to the list in hopes that some of the items left overlong in the barn could be restored.

The trip didn't take long, since the snow still held off. He and the mules only had to contend with wind carrying the sharp promise of a cold winter.

Jerome was grateful to enter the store, where a central stove kept the whole place toasty warm. He nodded at a few of the older men who'd set up a game of checkers nearby and helped himself to a cup of sludge. Abel's coffee was thick enough to use as mortar. Jerome eyed it for a minute before discounting the possibility.

"What'd you like?" Abel slid out from behind his long counter.

"Best get some of everythin'," one of the old-timers cautioned. "Snow's a-comin'."

"Your knees tell you that?" one of his friends scoffed.

"You know my knees don't lie!" With that, he made it to the other side of the checkerboard. "Now king me."

Jerome couldn't help but smile as he gathered the items he'd need. He tacked on some dry goods and kerosene. . .just in case Horace's knees were right.

After he'd paid for the goods, while Abel packaged everything in sturdy brown paper, a flyer posted on the counter caught Jerome's eye: "Town meeting tonight—urgent. Meet at the church no later than five o'clock!"

"What's the meeting about?" He tilted his head toward the notice.

"Can't rightly say, but better to be there and hear it firsthand." Abel lowered his voice. "The elders have something up their sleeves. Been whispering all day."

"I don't know whether to be interested or wary." Jerome pulled out his watch. If he grabbed a bite at Thelma's diner, he'd be just in time for the meeting.

"Don't matter much, long as you're there."

"Count on it." Jerome took his packages, walked back to the rickety town stable, and put the load in his wagon. He popped in to give the mules some supper before heading to Thelma's.

A hot meal later, he strode into the church just as the meeting began.

Clarence Ashton clanged a large cowbell to quiet the assembly. Jerome eyed the older man as he leaned back, hands folded over a healthy stomach, waiting for the undivided attention of everyone in the building. Yep. The rascally mayor was up to no good. Again.

"Good evening," Clarence boomed, the front legs of his chair crashing to the floor as he leaned forward. "The reverend will bless this town meeting, and then we will begin."

Jerome bowed his head as the reverend began a slightly long-winded and extremely enigmatic prayer. Referring to fruitfulness at the beginning of winter seemed incongruous to a farming community.

"Now. . ." Clarence rose to his feet and began to measure the length of the platform with his steps as he spoke. "I'd like everyone to take a look around. Go ahead, see the familiar faces of your neighbors and friends."

Jerome looked around, trying to shrug off thoughts that he was the new one. Not quite a stranger, since he'd spent many summers of his childhood here, but not quite a "friend," either. He nodded at a few of the men he'd grown to know through farm business and waited for Clarence to continue.

"I'd say we all know each other and that this here qualifies as a tight-knit community. Am I right?" The mayor paused as everyone agreed with chins up and smiles in place.

"You lot look pretty pleased about that." More smiles in response to Clarence's statement, but Jerome could sense a change in the wind.

"Maybe you shouldn't be." The words stunned the townspeople like a visible blow. Some blinked; some shifted in their seats; others just gaped.

Jerome paid closer attention. What could the wily old fellow be getting at?

"What I'm getting at here is that we need new blood in this community. Now there's no denying that the women of our town are some of the finest in the country." He took a pause while every man in the audience who knew what was good for him vehemently agreed. "But we need more of 'em! There are three men to every female, and that's not going to help the growth of Willowville."

One of the checker players, obviously prepped for his role, sprang to his feet to belt out the question, "What're we going to do about it?" He added a theatrical wave of his cane for good measure before plunking back down.

"I'm glad you asked. As mayor, I've come up with a plan to motivate the young men around here to find some wives and rejuvenate our community."

Jerome's gaze slid around the room, lighting on some interesting reactions. The few unmarried ladies sat straight and tall, shyly avoiding the avid stares of eager bachelors. Not-so-eager bachelors all but squirmed as they braced for the announcement to come.

"The town is offering a cash incentive to any man who brings a new woman to town and ties her to Willowville by marriage." Clarence had to stop because of the dismayed gasps of the ladies and the furor of questions from the men. He held up his hands and glowered until things settled back down.

Jerome, for his part, couldn't have said a thing even if he'd wanted to after Clarence named the sum. *That'd be enough to save the farm. More than enough.*

"I ain't finished yet," Clarence barked out. "There's one more thing you have to know: You only get the money if you get the woman by the town Christmas celebration."

⊰•❈•⊱

Idelia van der Zee reached out and raised the wick of her kerosene lamp to coax a little more light onto the garment she was mending. She refused to so much as glance at the large basket full of fallen hems and hole-ridden clothing also awaiting her needle.

"*Wat* ails you, *dotter*?"

"When winter comes, I think of home." Idelia smiled at her mother. "Tomorrow is *Sinterklaas Eve*, which makes me think of Da."

"Ah, and how he would dress as Zwarte Pieten to help Sinterklaas hand out gifts at the docks?" Mama smiled. "*Ja*, these are good memories."

"It is strange, still, to think Americans have no Black Peter to help Sinterklaas, who is called Saint Nicholas." Idelia bit off her thread and reached for another shirt. "Stranger still that he comes on *Kerstmis* here."

"The Americans do not separate Sinterklaas Eve and Kerstmis, Idelia. You know they celebrate them as one."

"Ja, though I miss the way the excitement stretched throughout the month, as Sinterklaas came twenty days before Kerstmis. Now it seems the season only lasts but a week or so."

"I, too, miss the horns at sundown, announcing the coming of Kerstmis, and the day we celebrate our Savior's birth." Mama settled her spectacles on her nose. "But we've not seen the tradition of Sinterklaas since you were but a tiny child, since we came to America."

"Ja." Idelia left unsaid the longing to share the traditions with her own children. Should she ever find a good man and loving marriage, she'd want her children to enjoy the full experience of *Kerstdagen*—as she had long ago.

Her thoughts turned to Jerome, as they had so often since the early winter storm had landed him in their boardinghouse. She'd cherished their week together, but he'd left to take over his grandfather's farm. She shut her eyes against the swell of sadness that he'd not asked her to be his wife, that he'd been able to leave her behind as he began a new life.

"You think of Jerome." Mama's voice sounded grim. "Many a man in town would offer for you should you give any sign of accepting."

"Yes, Mama." Idelia kept her answer noncommittal. Mama did not know how deeply she'd felt for Jerome, how she'd wanted a lifetime of working alongside him, seeing love in his caramel eyes as he looked at her. And it was as well she'd kept her hopes secret. Less pain when they were crushed.

"It has been two months, Idelia." Mama's hand came to rest on hers. "And still you have not let him go?"

"My heart felt a strange tug the day he came to town." Idelia pulled a handkerchief from her sleeve. "But he didn't feel the same. He made no advances, much less promises."

"Love awaits you, Idelia." Mama patted her hand once before leaning back. "It will come when you least expect it."

"Then it must be soon, ja? For no more do I expect it."

Chapter 2

The next morning came as any other, bearing no clue that the day before had been one of the most cherished holidays of Idelia's childhood. She hastened to the kitchen to begin breakfast before the two boarders awoke and found her mother already bustling about, the warm scent of cinnamon perfuming the air.

"*Goedemorgen.*" Mama didn't so much as look over her shoulder as she stoked the stove.

"Good morning to you, too, Mama. I must have overslept."

"*Nee*, the sun has scarce shown itself this day."

"Mama, are you making *pepernoten?*" She couldn't hide her excitement as she saw Mama add brown sugar to the flour in her mixing bowl. Cinnamon, nutmeg, and ginger sat beside it.

"When you woke up I wanted to have them ready." Mama cracked an egg into the bowl, added some water, and began to stir. "Your talk of Sinterklaas last night made me think of how you loved these."

The hard cookies, almost a crispy gingerbread candy, had always been her favorite. She reached out to draw her mother into a hug. "*Bedankt*, Mama."

"Ah, *welkom*, Idelia."

Without another word, she set to making the morning meal for their two boarders. Mrs. Irming and Mr. Rolf had taken the two rooms of the van der Zee's humble inn and would expect breakfast to be prepared when they left their rooms.

Idelia took a deep breath of appreciation as Mama slid a pan of pepernoten into the oven, the heat spreading the fragrance throughout the kitchen. Soon enough, the sulfur of the eggs she'd make would overpower the homey aroma of the cookies. Yesterday's extra biscuits already sat atop the stove, warming, so she'd not have to do much.

The morning chores passed in a familiar rhythm, breakfast made, water pumped and brought in, until the boarders came downstairs. Idelia took a few of the pepernoten and fanned them on a china plate, setting them on the table before she joined everyone to bless the meal.

Mr. Rolf reached for the biscuits and gravy, Mrs. Irming scooped eggs onto her plate, and Mama poured coffee for their guests. Idelia wasted no time sliding the plate of pepernoten toward her, placing two of the sweet treats on her own plate before passing it along.

She crunched into the first bite, relishing the tickle of gingerbread as the cookie melted on her tongue. It tasted like all the things she loved about winter—happy memories and warm fires and the sweetness of spending time with loved ones. A small sigh of contentment escaped her.

"What're these?" Mr. Rolf poked one of the pepernoten with a blunt finger, pushing it across the plate.

"A Dutch winter treat," Idelia explained. "Kind of a hard, crispy gingerbread."

"Never liked gingerbread." Mrs. Irming sniffed. "Cookies shouldn't be so. . .spicy."

"Yurgh." Mr. Rolf swallowed and tried again. "You're missing out, then. These're good."

Mama shot Idelia an amused glance as the pepernoten vanished in minutes. Idelia smiled back, sending up a prayer of gratitude that she'd thought to put some of the cookies in the bread box. Later that night, when they took up the mending again, she'd brew some tea and bring them out.

"Gotta go." Mr. Rolf slapped his hat on his head and stomped out the door.

"I'll be leaving, as well." Mrs. Irming pressed a napkin to her lips before rising. "My son-in-law should have made a great deal of progress, thanks to the good weather. I expect you'll have a room free rather soon."

If those roof repairs were finished, it could only be a blessing to a family sure to be struggling. A new baby needed constant care, and it was good of Mrs. Irming to come to her daughter's aid.

All the same, it would cost the van der Zees. Idelia closed her eyes and tabulated the money they'd lose if Mrs. Irming moved into her daughter's house a week early. If only there were some leeway in their budget.

As it was, Idelia and Mama shared a tiny room behind the kitchen, where the stove's warmth kept them cozy enough. They'd cut back to only one lamp at night as they mended, and the light was so insufficient they'd moved to the kitchen table to see what they worked on. The laundry they took in during the warmer months kept them afloat, but even that tapered off in winter.

"Stop fretting," Mama admonished as she began to clear the table. "The Lord has always provided for us, even if things have been more difficult since your father passed on."

"I know." Idelia forced a smile as she started to scrub the dishes. "And together, we'll find a way to make it through the winter ahead. God has a plan—it's up to us to find it."

⇐✦⇒

If only he could find another way—but the more Jerome thought it over, the fewer options he had. The railroad strike last spring had brought Grandpa's farm to its knees. He scarcely had enough seed corn and wheat to make a go of it the next year. Meanwhile, everything needed repairs, livestock to be butchered for winter should be replaced, and Jerome's pockets were empty.

Either he could sell half the farm, failing his legacy, or he could take a wife before Christmas came. Both choices made his mouth dry and his palms wet. Lose the farm or gain a wife. No wiggle room in sight as he sat at his desk and was confronted with the accounts once again.

The meticulously written numbers scarcely betrayed the shake of an old hand—Grandpa hadn't let anyone know he'd lost his partner to influenza a year ago. Had been too proud to ask for help as the farm fell down around his ears. This land meant everything to him. And if Jerome let his own pride keep him from living up to his grandfather's expectations, they both would have failed.

When he came right down to it, Jerome knew the truth. There wasn't even a choice. He'd have to find a bride from out of town—and fast. Now he just had to figure out what woman would say yes, work alongside him to revitalize the property, and not drive him crazy with endless chatter.

Idelia. The name of the boardinghouse beauty whispered through his mind. When a freak storm had stopped his progress to Willowville, he'd thought to wait out the fierce rain in boredom. Cooling his heels had held no appeal. . .until he'd met the mother-daughter duo who opened their home to travelers.

The van der Zees were tall Dutch women, warmhearted ladies to the core. They'd insisted he learn their names, laughing with him until he pronounced them perfectly. Lurleen seemed absurdly young to be Idelia's mother, but the two shared fine white-blond hair and clear gray eyes. More than that, the easy affection between them made their bond obvious.

For four days he'd sat at their table, eaten their wonderful food, and had some of the best discussions of his life. The van der Zee women were remarkably well-read, intelligent, hardworking, and lovely; thus, Jerome couldn't fathom why they were left to fend for themselves.

Were the men of their town blind? True, they'd just come out of mourning for Mr. van der Zee, but Idelia hadn't mentioned a sweetheart who waited for her hand. The only way Jerome could explain it was that the men thereabouts were too awestruck—or too intimidated by a woman who could support herself—to step forward. Fools—the whole lot of them.

But perhaps Jerome could reap the benefit of their inaction. Marriage to Idelia—now that was a choice a man would be glad to make! He sat up straighter, pulled a scrap of paper toward him, and uncapped his inkwell. Now all he had to do was figure out how to make her say yes.

Wait. A letter would take too long. Today was December sixth already. A week for the letter to arrive, a week for her to respond—by then the snows would have come, making it impossible for her to come by Christmas. His brow furrowed. It'd have to be a telegram, then. And Alastair Pitt would make certain everyone in town knew he'd proposed. If Idelia refused, he'd be a laughingstock.

But if she agreed, Jerome would be the envy of every man on the prairie. He wouldn't even mind if his mother-in-law came over for the holidays and the births of their children. Lurleen would make a wonderful grandmother, after all. And he wouldn't expect Idelia to abandon her mother—not when the two of them ran a boardinghouse and took in mending to make ends meet. When the farm was a going concern, he'd be sure to send Lurleen a monthly allowance. In fact, he should be sure to mention that in the telegram. Idelia would need to know he planned to provide for both of them, or she might not be willing to leave.

The scratch of pen against paper continued long into the night, until he was satisfied with the telegram. Perfect. That ought to prove to Idelia just how serious he was.

Chapter 3

What a horrid joke, Clarence Billings!" Idelia scowled at the gawky lad. "No one would propose via telegram!"

"I'm tellin' ya, Miss van der Zee—if you come down to the telegraph office, you'll find a message with your name on it," the child insisted. "True as I'm standing here!"

"It must have been mistranslated." Mama shrugged. "Wires are never to be trusted. You must see if it can be made correct. The boy came through the snow to fetch us."

"All right." Idelia swung her heavy pelisse over her shoulders as Mama bundled up. "I must admit to some curiosity. I've heard of mistakes like this, where a man asks for a bridle and ends up with a bride!"

"I bet he was happy with the switch"—Clarence beamed up at Idelia—"if his woman were half as pretty as you."

"*Bedankt*, Clarence." Mama ushered them all out the door. "My daughter is a woman any man would be proud to call his own."

Not any man. Idelia shook her head to clear away thoughts of Jerome Sanders. By now he'd probably forgotten her name, no matter how they'd laughed when he learned it.

Idelia's gaze caught on the word "wife" before she read the entire message. Then she read it once more, her mouth shaping the words silently, her pulse pounding in her ears.

"Well?" Clarence puffed out his chest. "What did I tell ya?"

Mama stood as still as a stone, her head tilted slightly as she waited for the news. It was one of the things Idelia had never understood about her mother—this ability to remain calm even in the face of crippling curiosity and anticipation.

Obviously the Billings men were cut from the same cloth, as both father and son avidly took in her reaction. As tactfully as possible, Idelia led Mama to the far corner of the small shop.

"It's Jerome," she breathed. "He asks me to be his wife in Willowville." She handed her mother the message and spoke more rapidly. "He invites you, too, Mama!"

Lurleen van der Zee scrunched her brow as she tried to make out both Mr. Billings's writing and what few written English words she knew. "Wife. . . mama." She bobbed her head. "Ja, is truth."

"He wants us to come right away." Idelia chewed the inside of her cheek.

315

"Would you want to go, Mama? Leave the inn and start a new life?"

"I would not send you to this place alone." Mama's brief glower softened. "We sell the house to Mr. Rolf and go together."

"But Papa built our house. All the memories of him—"

"Stay in us. I remember the love of my husband, dotter. Now is time for you to learn of yours."

"You got an answer for that fellow?" Mr. Billings shifted his weight from foot to foot. " 'Cause I'll send it right out."

"Yes." Idelia smiled.

"All right. What's the answer, then?"

"Yep!" Clarence whooped. "You can tell just by lookin' at 'em."

"Yes?" Mr. Billings ignored his son.

Idelia took a deep breath as Mama clasped both her hands.

"Yes."

❧❦

"No." The telegraph operator rolled his eyes as he scribbled down the letters of an incoming message. "This here's to say the stage is late again—busted an axle."

"When will she be in?" Jerome slapped his hat against his knee. Idelia was supposed to arrive on the weekly stagecoach—yesterday.

"I reckon it'll be about two hours." The man raised his brows. "Your bride'll get here in plenty of time."

Now. Jerome didn't voice the unreasonable demand. Instead, he gave a curt nod and pushed through the door. Hazy sunlight lit the main street, dimming and brightening as clouds passed. Good weather to greet Idelia.

What to do for two hours until she came? The saloon held no appeal, and he'd spent yesterday afternoon playing checkers with the old loafers at the general store. . .while the stage never came. And while he didn't begrudge them their jabs about the possibility that he didn't really have a fiancée coming to town, he wasn't about to invite another round of ribbing.

Especially when he was starting to wonder if the stage would ever make an appearance.

He wandered over to the mercantile, where Sadie Straphin did everything from make orders, ring sales, mend clothes, and create frilly fussies for. . .well, whatever women used them for.

The bell strapped to the door gave a cheery tinkle as he stepped inside. Now that he had time to think on it, having a gift for his bride was a fine idea. There had to be some little gewgaw in this place that would make Idelia smile.

A hat? He paused before a wall of headgear. Idelia wore a simple bonnet outside, so maybe she'd enjoy having something fancier for church?

He plucked a straw hat off the display, looking at the yellow ribbon threaded around the brim and dangling down to tie beneath a lady's chin. A

316

spray of fake flowers burst from the side. The yellow color wasn't as pretty as Idelia's hair, so he put it back and reached for another.

This one boasted a purple-checked ribbon ballooning around a clump of brambles. Jerome brushed at the thing, trying to dislodge it from the hat. *Must've blown in the shop and Sadie didn't notice.*

"Like the bird's nest, do you?" A voice beside him made him stop trying to brush the thing off.

"Bird's nest?" He looked closer.

"Yes." Sadie reached over to straighten the ribbon. "Very popular."

Women had been running around with birds' nests on their heads and he hadn't noticed. Jerome blinked. The mayor was right—Willowville needed more women. Preferably women with more sense.

He handed her the hat. "Not today." While she rehung the thing, he retreated to the back corner of the store. For sure he'd have to get something now since Sadie knew he didn't like her hat. No sense riling up someone who could make a good friend for Idelia. . .even if these purses were too tiny to hold anything worth toting around.

He glanced in a small bin full of thin, gauzy fabric then backed away. Stockings were undergarments—far too intimate to give his bride when she stepped off the stage.

He bumped into a spindly shelf of small jars and soaps. Soap? He shook off thoughts of Idelia rubbing it into her long hair. *Too personal.*

A few steps took him to a display of handkerchiefs. Pretty, but for sure he wasn't going to give her a present that said, "I know you're going to be crying a lot."

It was then he spotted it—the perfect gift. Something to say he'd been thinking of her, something that she could actually use, and, most important, something that wouldn't embarrass either of them.

"These." He plunked them down on Sadie's counter and asked her to wrap them in some pretty paper. Jerome pocketed the gift and left the store.

Idelia would come soon, and now he was ready.

Chapter 4

This is it!" Idelia peered through the stagecoach's murky windows as they pulled into town. "I hope Jerome got the message that we'd be late." *I hope he'll be as excited to see me as I am to see him.*

"Is nice to be out of this coach." Mama gestured to the hard seats they'd been bouncing on. She ducked through the open door first, grasping a man's hand as he helped her down.

"Mama Lurleen?" Jerome's voice sent a flutter to Idelia's heart, but she still noticed that he seemed surprised.

"*Hallo.*" Idelia put her hand in his as she stepped out of the coach. "So sorry there were troubles." She looked up into his warm brown gaze, her breath catching when she saw the thin lines crinkling the sides of his eyes. *Ja,* he was glad to see her.

"I'm just glad you're here." He offered her his arm and belatedly offered the other to Mama. "You're both here."

"Ja, it was good you knew I'd never send my Idelia alone." Mama beamed up at him, and Idelia suddenly remembered another reason she'd liked Jerome—he was one of the tallest men she'd ever met. Usually she stood at most men's eye levels, but her fiancé was the perfect height for her to lean her head on his shoulder.

"You're flushed." Jerome led them to a small bench and gestured for her to sit. "You rest a moment while I fetch your luggage."

Idelia offered a small smile and a big prayer of gratitude that he didn't know why she was blushing. The idea of being so close to a man, even one as strong and kind as Jerome, made her nervous. As he easily hefted her trunk, she revised that opinion. Jerome made her *especially* nervous. But in an exhilarating, hopeful way.

"Excuse me, ladies." A short man with broad shoulders took off his hat and made an awkward bow, his eyes fixed on Mama. "I was wonderin' if you were staying in Willowville or if you were both passing through with the stage."

"Staying." Idelia looked past the man, whom she judged to be about the same age as her mother, in hopes that Jerome would come back.

"Oh, good." A wide smile spread across his face. "I'm Mayor Ashton, and on behalf of all Willowville, I want to say you're a welcome addition to our town."

"*Dank u.*" Mama pursed her lips the way she did when biting back a smile.

"We are come for my dotter to wed."

"I wondered." The mayor rocked back on his heels. "Heard tell a Miss van der Zee would be coming soon to marry up with the Sanders boy."

"That's right." Jerome's form blocked the sun, so it was hard for Idelia to make out his expression. "And you should know better than to frighten off my bride and her mother." He shifted so he stood beside her, his arm resting along the back of the bench and brushing against her shoulders.

"Mother?" The mayor cast another admiring glance at Mama, who'd stopped trying to suppress her smile. "Surely you mis-spoke, Sanders. These two can only be sisters!"

"I'd accuse you of blatant flattery," Jerome said, "but I thought the same thing when I first met them."

"*Dank u.*" Mama's eyes sparkled as she drank in the attention.

"Van der Zee, eh? I suppose that means you're Dutch."

"*Ja.*" Idelia had relaxed when she realized that Jerome knew the man and that he'd made her mother smile.

"Well, you'll have to tell me about some of your Christmas traditions. We have a town celebration every year—unless there's a blizzard—and we're always looking for fresh ideas."

Idelia felt a slight pressure on her elbow and realized Jerome was helping her to her feet.

Mayor Ashton wasted no time offering his arm to Mama. Her smile flagged for a moment when she stood up and he only came to her chin.

Not again. Idelia closed her eyes for a swift prayer. Hopefully the mayor wouldn't disapprove of Mama's height. Some men, she knew, felt threatened by that.

"It keeps getting better and better," Ashton said to Jerome. "Two women come to town, both as beautiful as statues but with smiles to warm a man's heart."

Mama instantly obliged him with one of those smiles, and Idelia joined in. The mayor, it seemed, would be a great help in making Mama feel comfortable in the new town. The two fell into conversation while Jerome gently drew her a short distance away.

"Idelia, I'm so glad you came to be my wife." His words melted her heart as he reached into his pocket. Could he have a wedding band for her? "And I want to give you something to celebrate your arrival."

❧❧❧

Jerome watched her eyes widen and felt a rush of gratitude he'd thought to bring her a welcoming gift. "This is for you." He pulled the package from his coat pocket and gave it to her.

She made tiny sounds of surprise as she turned it over, carefully unfolding the paper around her gift. She went about it as though unearthing something precious. Idelia's face glowed as she finally eased the gift from its packing.

"Bootlaces?" Her brow furrowed as she held them up, the paper crumpling in her hand. She turned her gray eyes toward him, her gaze a question.

Should have gotten her the bird's nest. He kicked a rock across the road.

"What bird's nest?" Though he'd thought it impossible, she looked even more confused as she repeated the words he'd not meant to speak aloud.

"Didn't mean to say that," he hastily assured her. Bootlaces and birds' nests. He wouldn't blame the woman if she hightailed it right back to that stagecoach.

"About the laces," he said, reaching for them, "I thought maybe you could use them, but it was a bad idea."

"No!" She pulled them to her chest at his gesture. "It was kind of you to think of me. I'm glad to have these."

"Well, then..." He couldn't take back a stupid gesture now, not when she was being so sweet and trying to thank him. Jerome shrugged and led her back to her mother. *At least she saw the meaning behind it and is staying to be my wife.*

"Wat is this?" Mama Lurleen pointed at the laces, making Jerome give a silent groan.

"A welcome from my husband-to-be." Idelia displayed the laces proudly. "To show that he will provide for even the little things that most men forget."

He clenched his fists to keep from taking her in his arms. How God had blessed him in giving him this woman as his wife—not just because she would enable him to get the money he needed to save the farm, but because she had such a generous heart.

Mama Lurleen spoke in a spate of Dutch words, and Jerome saw Idelia give her a warning glance. *Now what can that be about?*

A few minutes later, when he helped his bride-to-be into the wagon, he caught a glimpse of her feet. A trim row of buttons marched down the line of her boot.

⚜

"It's a good-sized town." Idelia counted a feed store, a general store, and a mercantile as they rode down Main Street.

"Yep. Gets busy in better weather. Most folks have stocked up for the winter already and are taking care of late autumn chores." Jerome flicked the reins, redirecting a mule headed for a clump of late grass.

"Not many people now," Mama agreed, "but the mayor."

"Clarence can always be found. We'll see him at church if the good weather holds till Sunday." He turned toward Idelia. "Everyone will be there, and I hoped we could make it our wedding day."

"*Ja.*" Idelia stifled her blush. She didn't want to sound overeager, but she and Mama would be staying at Jerome's farm. It wouldn't be proper to wait, and the last thing she wanted was to have a bad reputation in a new town.

"Until then, I'll be bunking in the barn." His words mirrored her thoughts.

"I won't stay in the house until there's no question in anyone's mind that it's right."

"Nee!" The fervor in Mama's rejection of the idea let Idelia know how much she approved of Jerome's decision.

"I won't have anybody thinking you're less than the ladies you are." He turned the wagon down a worn path. "We'll be home in a minute."

Home. Idelia leaned forward on the bench, drinking in the sight as they approached the farm. December stripped the prairie of all but the hardiest—and driest—of tall grass, coloring the landscape in browns and yellows. Come spring, the earth would burst in shades of green, but first all would be covered under a white layer of snow.

Up ahead, a two-story farmhouse stood straight and solid, with fair-sized windows to welcome them. Yards away, a barn slumped, red paint weathered and peeling, a good-sized silo looming at the far end. Not far away stood another structure, this one in better repair. It looked to be a stable.

"For both horses and cows?"

"Yep. There are hogs and chickens, too." She read pride in the subtle straightening of his spine.

"I had not known if we'd have many animals or mostly crops." Idelia glanced to see his reaction to her use of "we."

He didn't disappoint, looking back at her and nodding. "We grow wheat and corn in the fields. My grandma had a garden long ago. There are signs of plants now, but we'll have to replant it for it to be of use."

"I'd like that." *He, too, sees us as a team.*

She put her hands on his shoulders after he pulled up before the stable and came to the side.

He swung her down but didn't take his hands from her waist immediately. "Welcome home, Idelia."

The warmth of his fingers lingered even after he moved to help her mother. She took the time to gather her thoughts and get a closer look at the farm.

From a distance, the buildings seemed solid, but as she stood near the house, Idelia recognized it wasn't only the cattle barn that needed repair.

Parched weeds pushed through slats on the porch, shutters hung at crooked angles, and the entire house could use a good scrubbing—and a few coats of whitewash. This place hadn't seen the loving touch of a woman for too long, and she'd guess Jerome's grandfather had some trouble caring for everything in his later years.

It was good there was much to do. She and Mama would start tomorrow and work to make Jerome's farm a home they could all be proud to call theirs.

Chapter 5

Jerome woke to the sound of his rooster, which came through much louder since he was in the stable. For such a scraggly little bird, it had lusty lungs and a strut to match.

Jerome splashed himself with icy water from the pail he'd brought inside the night before. Thanks to a heap of fresh hay, the blankets he'd brought from the house, and the heat of the horses, he'd stayed comfortable through the night. When winter came, the nights would be freezing.

But I'll be back in the house with my beautiful bride come Sunday. With that in mind, he set about his morning chores. First he pitched hay from the loft to the horse stalls below, leaving the mucking for later. Next he climbed the ladder on the side of the silo, sinking into the soft silage at the top and forking loads of it below. The cows feasted on the sweet-sour mash of corncobs while he grabbed bucketfuls and slopped the hogs.

That's when things became odd. The chickens, already pecking at strewn seed, had not a single egg in the coop. *Idelia and Mama Lurleen must be up and moving.* Jerome quickened his pace back to the barn. Once he finished the milking, he'd see if the women had started breakfast.

His stomach rumbled in anticipation as he entered the barn. Both cows turned drowsy eyes toward him. He went to Maisy, a cow who'd seen many years with his grandpa but still gave milk. Not this morning.

He frowned. It was still fall—early for the cows to stop milking. Maybe the old gal had finally dried up. Jerome moved on to Netta, the younger cow he'd bought shortly after returning to the farm. Nothing.

Two cats prowled along the edges of the walls, impatient for their morning share of cream. With two milking cows, Jerome had more milk and cream than he could consume, so the hogs and mousing cats reaped the benefit.

He returned the three-legged stool and pail to their places and noticed what he hadn't before—two pails were gone. Idelia had been busy working alongside him, even if he hadn't known it. He made his way toward the house with a light step. His bride-to-be was already pitching in. And once they were wed, Mama Lurleen would return to her inn. Then he and Idelia could truly begin their life together, funded by her unexpected dowry.

The barn and stables would be repaired, the house neat and clean. The tools in the barn stable would be replaced, the crops flourishing from the new implements and the time he could spend in the fields. He envisioned the garden bursting with vegetables, the kitchen fragrant with good cooking, and

Idelia smiling as he came through the door. And someday they'd have children romping around their feet.

He knocked on the kitchen door before wiping the mud from his boots and entering. The smell of frying bacon hit him before he heard the telltale sizzle of the pan on the stove. Mama Lurleen nodded to him but kept an eye on the meat while Idelia stooped to draw a pan out of the oven. It looked to be some kind of bread, the scent warm and sweet as she set it on the table.

"*Goedemorgen*, Jerome." She gestured for him to sit while she fetched the coffeepot from the stove.

"Good morning, Idelia. Mama Lurleen," he acknowledged as his future mother-in-law set a platter of hot, crispy bacon next to the pan of breakfast rolls. A pitcher of chilled fresh milk rested by his arm as they all took their seats.

He bowed his head and offered a prayer of thanks for the women's safe arrival and the food before them. Then breakfast began.

Lurleen heaped bacon onto his plate while Idelia poured drinks. A tall glass of milk sat next to a steaming cup of coffee just behind his plate. Then they passed around the breakfast rolls.

Unable to resist, Jerome picked up one of the flaky brown pastries and bit into it, warmth spreading to his stomach as he savored the flavor. Small lumps like golden raisins offered an unexpected sweetness. "These are great," he praised. "What are they called?"

"*Krentebolletjes*," Mama Lurleen told him.

"Currant buns," Idelia added, reaching for her own glass of milk. "We found a small box of the currants in your root cellar."

"I like krankyballets," he said, trying out the new word.

The women both giggled, Idelia trying again. "*Krentebol-letjes*," she repeated.

"Maybe I'll just stick with currant buns," he decided, crunching into a piece of bacon. "Doesn't matter what you call them"—he swiped another from the pan—"so long as I can eat them!"

━◆━

"You wouldn't want them every morning," Idelia teased as Jerome proved to have the healthy appetite she'd remembered.

"Don't be so sure about that." He took a swig of coffee. "But I wouldn't want to talk myself out of other treats!"

"It is Kerstmis season, so we usually make the traditional feast." Idelia realized she'd have more than one reason to celebrate this year. It would be her first Christmas in her own house, as a married woman.

"*Ja*." Mama began to plan out loud, "We have *speculaas, kerststol, poffertjes, pasteitje, rollade, kerstkrans,* and *oliebollen*."

"And pepernoten," Idelia added. She'd make a batch of it as soon as they'd settled in and serve it with warm spiced milk.

"I have no idea what any of that is, but I'm already looking forward to it." He slathered butter on another bun and shot a conspiratorial glance her way. Then he turned to Mama. "I'd say Mayor Ashton would love to hear about all of them. Maybe you'll help him plan this year's town celebration of. . . Curstmiss?"

"Kerstmis, yes." Mama patted the table for emphasis. "Tradition is much important."

"And here we'll have the chance to start a few of our own." The smile he sent her made Idelia's heart beat faster.

Tomorrow. Tomorrow this man will take me as his wife before God and the community. "And what is planned today?"

Chapter 6

Since you've looked around, is there anything you need from the general store?" His question made her think of his awkward gift. Jerome might believe he'd erred in his choice, but Idelia would treasure those laces forever.

"The larder is well stocked, and we brought a trunk of provisions in case we were caught in a blizzard. The only things we wondered about were if you have a springhouse and where you keep the eggs." She gestured to a basket against the wall where that morning's eggs lay waiting.

"I don't have a springhouse," he admitted. "The well is rigged with a basket so you can lower milk and such to keep it cool. The eggs I store in the root cellar."

"We didn't see them." Mama and she had explored the root cellar earlier and been delighted to find sacks of vegetables, barrels of dried apples, and even a few jars of preserves. Bushels of potatoes and sacks of walnuts rounded out the supplies.

"I'll show you." He walked over to the trapdoor, opened it, and grabbed a lantern. Once it was lit, he led them down the wooden slats serving as stairs.

"Here." He took them to the side, where they'd found the preserves, and pointed toward the stairwell. There someone had carved a low niche into the soil, and Jerome had put straw-filled crates in the space.

"We didn't look behind the stairs," Idelia confessed. "Such a clever place, too. Now we can add to the winter store until the hens stop laying."

"Right. I haven't had the time to make any butter, though there's a churn upstairs. The smokehouse is fairly well stocked, but I planned to butcher a hog this week, and soon I'll be able to go to the pond and fill the icehouse."

"We'll have ice year-round?" Idelia couldn't hide her grin. "And extra cream, it seems. I think we can plan to enjoy some ice cream next summer!"

"Mmm." Mama closed her eyes.

"If you bleed the hog, we can boil water for the scalding and then make butter while you scrape it. With the three of us, we can butcher it today, if you don't have other pressing chores."

"Sounds like a fine idea. You never know when a blizzard will blow in, so it's best to have everything ready as soon as possible. While you boil the water, I'll wrangle out the biggest hog and start things."

Not many women would be more than willing to slaughter a hog the day before their wedding, and Jerome knew it. But then, only a rare woman would appreciate the thought behind so simple and plain a gift as bootlaces—especially when her boots buttoned.

How blessed I am in my bride, he praised the Lord as he grabbed his butchering kit. *I wasn't sure when I telegraphed her but knew she wouldn't come if it wasn't Your will. When she said yes, I wondered whether we'd be a good match, if we could share a lifetime together. Idelia is a beautiful, intelligent woman and a hard worker, but beauty fades and there is more than work between a man and wife. How thankful I am that she already loves this place, and her presence makes it even better.*

He made his way toward the hog pen, his eye on the big boar who'd taken a liking to shoving sows away from the trough. Slaughtering was never pleasant, but by choosing this mean fellow, he'd bring meat to the table and eliminate the problem.

Jerome grabbed a pail of slop and lured the bully from the pen. The sows had learned to let him through when grub appeared, so it was easy to get the hog around the corner of the barn. Didn't take much time to do the deed and hang the greedy pig to bleed out.

When he returned to the house, he found the women out in the yard, tending a large fire. They'd rigged a travois to hold the scalding pot, and the water was heating. Idelia saw him approach and gave a small wave before disappearing into the house.

"Will boil soon," Mama Lurleen pronounced and proved to be right.

By the time Idelia emerged from the kitchen, bearing a pail of milk and the butter churn, they had the hog in the huge pot. When its hide softened, Jerome would scrape off the hair and the butchering would begin.

"Potatoes and onions are on the stove," Idelia reported as she spooned heavy cream from the top of the pail into the churn. "And this morning's eggs are oiled and stored in the cellar. If the hens keep laying for another week or so, we should have enough to last through winter."

"Potatoes?" Jerome wasn't sure what she was making—they'd just had breakfast and noon was hours away.

"Ja." Mama Lurleen settled herself on a log he hadn't chopped fully yet. "Boil sliced potatoes and onions, and bake with butter and cream." She pointed to the hog to make her point. "Eat with slices of fried ham for dinner."

"It takes awhile, so it's good to start now," Idelia told him as she started a second fire to boil and clean the meat. "But since we have fresh cream and ham, and we'll make the butter now, it will be delicious today."

"Sounds like it." Jerome's still-full stomach gave a small growl as he imagined it. The plan also explained why she'd only brought out one of the pails of milk—they needed both butter and cream.

And ham. He used a long stick to test the hide and found it coming along nicely. By the time they sat down to that dinner, they'd have earned something wonderful. After the past two months of brutal work followed by hardtack, cold biscuits, and old coffee, Jerome relished the prospect.

It made the hours fly by, and when the sun shone high above, Mama Lurleen had made the butter, and the potato dish baked in the stove. He'd scraped the hide and done the butchering while Idelia boiled the meat and prepared it for curing. She'd also cleansed the entrails and set them aside for later use.

After lunch they'd smoke the ribs, hocks, and sides of bacon before making sausages. But for now, the women were slicing ham and making it sizzle in the skillet. He couldn't actually hear the sound from where he stood, drawing water to wash up for the meal, but he knew that when he stepped inside, the meal would be ready.

They sank gratefully onto the chairs around the table before thanking God for His provision, the productive morning, and the food waiting to nourish them. Jerome kept his eyes shut a moment after the prayer ended, inhaling the savory fragrance of the potatoes, turned thick, golden, and bubbling from the oven.

Silence reigned as they filled their plates and dug in. Jerome speared one of the potatoes on his plate and popped it in his mouth, its rich, creamy texture and flavor melting in his mouth. He followed it up with some of the butter-fried ham, chewing slowly to enjoy it all.

Yes, Jerome decided, *God has blessed me more than I even imagined.*

Chapter 7

Idelia woke early the next morning and rolled out of bed, careful not to disturb Mama. There were beds in only two rooms, and Idelia couldn't bring herself to sleep in Jerome's bed. The thought that after today they'd spend the night together as man and wife brought heat to her cheeks.

She threw on the dress she'd worn the day before and crept down to the kitchen, where she started to heat water. She'd dragged an old metal tub from the barn yesterday morning and stowed it in the parlor, where the door shut and the curtains were thickest. While the water heated, she lit the parlor fire for warmth and sneaked upstairs. When Idelia came back, she laid out some towels, her soap and brush, and her best dress—a light blue wool warm enough for the weather and a color that flattered her eyes.

The stove heated two large pots—not nearly so large as the scalding cauldron—at a time. She emptied the first round into the tub and put more on to heat. Snagging her cloak from a peg by the door, she fed the hens and gathered the eggs as swiftly as possible in the dark. The crisp cold of approaching winter chilled her before she came back to add more hot water to her bath. The small tub wasn't even half full, which would be enough.

Next she hurried to the barn, gratified to see that Jerome hadn't filled the trough with silage yet—she still had time. When she came back to the house, the water was ready. One more load and she'd slide into the bath. In the meantime, she started coffee, mixed batter, and took out the waffle iron.

She bathed hastily, wishing she could luxuriate in the warm comfort of the bath but knowing Mama was stirring and would like a bath herself. Besides, she still had to dry her hair and make breakfast! Idelia slipped into her chemise and petticoats before settling by the fire to towel dry and brush her hair, which hung past her waist. Luckily, the fine strands dried quickly, and she was putting it up in a soft twist when Mama came down.

"So early this morning!" Mama looked longingly at the tub while Idelia finished dressing.

"Go ahead while it's still warm, Mama," she encouraged. "I've done the morning chores and will have breakfast going."

"You could not sleep for thoughts of your wedding?" Mama knew her well. "I could not when I was about to marry your father—so much excitement."

"I wanted to have a bath this morning, too," Idelia pointed out. "And make sure everything goes smoothly."

"My *dotter* will make a fine wife." Mama reached out and cupped her cheek. "Ready and loving, you are. It will be good marriage."

"I hope so, Mama. It seems an answer to prayer." The smell of burnt coffee wisped into the room, making her head for the kitchen. Sure enough, the coffee had sat too long and was strong enough to bring any man to his knees. She sloshed it outside and set about making another pot.

While Mama took her bath, Idelia fetched the syrup and cooked up stacks of waffles. The sweet, buttery aroma filled the kitchen, chasing away the last traces of burnt coffee. On a whim, she decided to chop up some of the ham left from the day before and mix it into scrambled eggs. The large skillet sizzled, adding to the smell of a hearty breakfast.

"*Stroopwafels!*" Mama entered the kitchen with pails of the wash water, which she took outside, emptied, and brought back.

"*Ja.* I thought Jerome would like them." Idelia finished up while Mama emptied the rest of the tub.

"Smells great." Jerome came inside just in time, freshly shaven and wearing what looked to be a new shirt. He'd even polished his boots.

"*Stroopwafels*," Mama repeated.

"Waffles I know." He settled into his seat at the head of the table. "What's the other part?"

"Syrup." Idelia poured a mug full of coffee.

"That's one I can remember." He forked several onto his plate. "Stroop waffles." A large bite found its way to his mouth. "Mmm. . ."

"Is not *krentebolletjes*," Mama teased. "But Idelia thought you would like them."

"And she's right." Jerome dug into some of the eggs and ham. "This is mighty good."

"Better than the *krentebolletjes*?" Idelia couldn't help pressing—Jerome seemed more than willing to eat whatever she placed before him, but it was good for a wife to know her husband's favorite dishes.

"Not better." He leaned back as he chewed another bite. "Not worse. Everything you've made is wonderful."

"*Dank u.*" Idelia poured some more syrup over her waffles, just the way she liked.

"And you look beautiful this morning." His next words almost made her choke. "The men of Willowville will all be green with envy when they see how fortunate I am. . .and they haven't tried your cooking!"

"I, too, am fortunate"—Idelia met his gaze despite the blush she felt—"to have found a good man who is also handsome and kind. I will be proud to stand with you and become your wife."

Jerome rushed to hitch the horses to the buckboard. Getting to church at the right moment required precise timing. Too early and men would flock around the women. That wasn't an option. Too late and they'd be embarrassed upon their first introduction to the community.

Jerome planned on a respectable entrance before the opening prayer but after everyone began settling in the pews. That way, nothing could make Idelia think twice about going through with the marriage. They'd be wedded before they left the church, and no one would be able to sweep her away.

And if he were a betting man, he'd stake everything he owned that an entire contingent of Willowville bachelors would make a play for Idelia. Though he couldn't blame them—even if there was no money attached, any man with two eyes and ears would be interested in her—he'd do everything in his power to stop them.

Of far less importance was the stir Mama Lurleen would cause. She'd obviously wed young and born Idelia soon thereafter, making his mother-in-law-to-be an attractive young widow in her own right. Keeping the men from buzzing around Lurleen van der Zee would be Clarence's problem—Mayor Ashton would have to move fast to stake his claim.

They were under way right on schedule, clipping toward the service at a comfortable pace. Jerome was so pleased by their timing he almost didn't notice Idelia fidgeting with the ribbons of her Sunday hat. Almost.

"Something wrong?"

"Just nervous," she admitted.

"About the wedding?" Cold fear clenched his gut. *What if she doesn't want to marry me?*

"Of course not." She waved away the concern as though it were no more than a pesky fly. "Meeting everyone in town."

"Oh, they're good folk for the most part." The tension in his shoulders eased. "You'll be more than welcome."

"Especially when they taste what we will make for the celebration of Kerstmis," Mama Lurleen added. "Mayor Ashton should be pleased."

"I think you could bake a brick and please the good mayor, Mama." Idelia stopped fidgeting to tease her mother.

"Nee, no man would eat a brick."

"A man can do worse if he's making his own meal." Jerome grimaced at the memory of a stew he'd attempted. "I once made a dinner of burnt stew with too many onions. Couldn't choke it down, and even the hogs wouldn't touch it when I added it to their slop."

"Tough choice,"—Idelia chuckled—"break your teeth on a brick or burn your belly with stew. But I meant that the mayor is so taken with Mama, it wouldn't matter what she put before him."

"He is nice man," Mama Lurleen insisted.

"Clarence can be right ornery at times, though." Jerome thought it only fair to give Mrs. van der Zee a warning. "When he gets a notion, it takes a team of mules to pull him off it."

"I like decisive man." Mama Lurleen's voice was firm as she put an end to the discussion. "And I will like this town."

Her pronouncement came just as they pulled up to the church. Sure enough, Clarence was by their side, ready to help Lurleen out of the buckboard as soon as she held out a gloved hand.

Once Jerome swung Idelia out of the wagon and onto the ground, he could sense the crowd of men gawking at his bride. It took a prayer to quell his urge to tell them to go about their business and leave him to his.

"See?" Alastair from the telegraph office pushed through to give him a sharp elbow in the side. "I told you she'd make it."

"Of course." Idelia's expression was soft as she looked at Jerome. "I wanted to come here."

"And here she is." Jerome offered her his arm, the air crisp as he filled his lungs. *And she's mine.* He gave the other men a warning glance to make sure they knew it.

"Lucky man." Alastair looked from him to Idelia, his face a portrait of mischief. "With two whole weeks before the deadline."

Jerome fought to keep his smile as Idelia turned toward him, confusion painting her features.

"What deadline?"

Chapter 8

Goose bumps raised along Idelia's arms as she saw Jerome's expression. Obviously something was wrong—which was not to be permitted on their wedding day.

"Idelia. . ." He placed one large, work-roughened hand over hers, his calluses rubbing her gloves as he spoke. "The mayor encouraged the bachelors of Willowville to go marry before Christmas came and winter snowed us in."

"Wise." Mama Lurleen beamed at Mayor Ashton, who hovered by her side.

"Didn't want them to wait till spring." Ashton's words confirmed Jerome's statement, but a small wrinkle of worry wavered between his brows.

"That's right." A man she hadn't met broke into the conversation. "And Jerome's a lucky rascal to have found such a pretty wife so quick."

The man who'd first approached Jerome raised his voice and gave her a meaningful look. "Especially since now he gets the wife *and* the money."

"Money?" She scooted closer to Jerome and farther away from the troublemaker.

"Yep." Yet another man she didn't know butted in. "Since he got you here and is marrying you before the Christmas shindig, he gets a nice wad of cash."

"Is this true, Jerome?" She gazed up into his eyes, begging him to deny this awful accusation. Her groom wasn't a man who would send for a wife just for money. *Jerome chose me because he felt as I do.*

"It is true that if I marry by Christmas, the town council will give us a marriage gift." His eyes didn't meet hers.

"On account of the town needing fine women like yourself and your mama," Ashton placated, patting Mama's hand.

Mama, however, was not to be placated. She withdrew her hand from Ashton's at the same moment Idelia pulled free from Jerome's grasp.

"You brought me here for money?" The hurt ringing in her voice sent rage coursing through her. How dare he make a fool of her and trap her in this town! "You will be sorely disappointed, Mr. Sanders."

She turned her back to him, linked arms with Mama, who was glowering fit to scare a buzzard from a gut bucket, and marched into the church. Thoughts churning, she scarcely noticed men crowding the pews beside and around them until Jerome wedged himself at her side, displacing another fellow.

Since the other man smelled strongly of onions, Idelia took a moment to debate whether she should ask Jerome to sit elsewhere. She settled for pivoting slightly, giving him her shoulder.

The opening prayer sounded like a faint drone buzzing in her ears, so she made a prayer of her own. *What am I to do now, Lord?* The words came from her heart to her lips over and over again, though she didn't give voice to them.

It was plain as day she wouldn't be marrying Jerome this afternoon. It would be a mockery of a sacred commitment between man and woman if he did not love her.

The thoughts repeated over and over as they sang hymns. Idelia stood with everyone but couldn't find her voice. Praise was the last thing she felt able to give when her dreams of love and family had wisped away in the morning mist. She was grateful to sit again and set herself to listening closely to the sermon. If ever there had been a time when she needed the guidance of the Lord, this was it.

"This morning I'm going to divert from our study of the book of Romans to address what I see as a danger lurking in our town." The reverend's words did nothing to ease the tumult in Idelia's heart, but he pressed onward.

"The town council put out an amazing proposition recently, despite my objection. Until now, no one has gotten to the point where it is an actual problem, but as of this morning, that bridge has been crossed."

Please, Lord, don't let him be talking about me! Idelia reached up and massaged the back of her neck.

"The Word tells us that whatever man finds a worthy wife finds favor with the Lord and that a virtuous woman is a treasure. So it stands to reason that any man who finds a wife he'd be proud to call his own is blessed."

Jerome was nodding so vehemently Idelia could feel the ribbons of her hat wave in the breeze he caused. Well, he could bob his head until kingdom come for all the difference it would make.

She thought he'd sent for her because he, too, felt a special warmth. Because he'd established his home and was ready to share it and his life with her. And she'd accepted his rushed proposal because starting a family with a man like Jerome had been the cry of her heart since before Da passed on. And with him gone, her need to gather love around her, to expand their family, had intensified.

Had she been so anxious for a family of her own that she'd imposed her wishes over the Lord's plan? Her throat went dry. The telegram had seemed a perfect opportunity, the long-awaited answer to prayer.

Oh Lord, forgive my haste. I thought the path was laid before me, but I didn't seek You when the opportunity came. And now, Lord, here I am, bound to a man I cannot marry. Wedding vows are sacred, and now that I know Jerome doesn't feel that love for me, I'm trapped. Where do I go from here?

Home. I just have to get her home and reason with her before all the men here descend on her like hounds after a fox.

The hairs on the back of Jerome's neck prickled. The envy in the eyes of every man in town had been replaced by speculation. There wasn't a single bachelor who didn't gape at Idelia and her mother, but until Alastair stirred up trouble, Jerome hadn't concerned himself about it.

Idelia was to be his wife, and he'd been clear about staking his claim. But now everything turned topsy-turvy as Idelia's hurt and anger simmered throughout the sermon.

Anger he understood. In fact, he was mad enough to admit she had cause to be miffed. *Why didn't I tell her about the cash in the telegram?*

The answer all but smacked him in the face. *I knew it might make her say no. At the very least I should have mentioned it once she arrived and I'd made it clear how glad I was to be marrying her. What a mess.*

He had to save Gramps's farm. To do that, he needed money. In order to get that money, he'd been told he just had to marry a woman from out of town. He'd prayed about it and it seemed the Lord placed Idelia on his mind, so why was he being villainized?

Yes, Jerome saw he should have told Idelia about her unexpected dowry so they could share the joy that they'd save the farm. Including Idelia in the planning would have been the smart thing to do, and even he could see that having some local clodpoll tell a woman on her wedding day that her groom only wanted the money would put any gal's nose out of joint. But how could he fix it?

Jerome directed his attention back to the reverend's sermon. Since he was talking about the wedding incentive, maybe the man of God would have a solution to the problem somewhere in his message.

"Now I'd like to take you to Proverbs 15:27, a verse I feel is very relevant to this situation." He began to read. " 'He that is greedy of gain troubleth his own house.' I'd say that's pretty self-explanatory."

The air left Jerome's lungs in a whoosh. The fact that the reverend was looking directly at him reinforced whom that verse was supposed to reach.

Greed? Jerome's hands clenched in denial. How could it be greedy to want to restore and preserve his family legacy—to honor his grandfather? That was a noble goal, biblical in its own right.

And yet. . .the second part certainly applied to his situation. Though things were fine when he woke up, trouble had since descended upon his household. Come to think of it, until they got this sorted out, he wouldn't even be living in his house. Until he and Idelia were wed, he'd be bunking in the barn. He could feel himself scowling at the realization and glanced at Idelia.

One look at the upset on Idelia's face gave him indigestion, which was a real shame after such a fine breakfast. Anger he could respect, but the idea that he'd hurt her. . .well, that he couldn't stomach. Jerome looked at her lovely face again and saw her blinking as though holding back tears.

And that's when he knew. In trying to fulfill his goal, worthy though it may be, he'd only thought of himself. Now his Idelia paid the price for it. And what was another word for "greed" if not *selfishness?*

Chapter 9

If anyone asked Idelia how she'd gotten back to Jerome's farm after church, she wouldn't be able to answer. Simple fact of the matter was that everything blurred together.

One moment she was a bride entering a church with her intended. The next, a fool who wasn't wanted. Jerome was taking her in exchange for the money, almost like a punishment! And then the sermon, bringing home to her how much she needed her husband to treasure her. After that she just remembered Mama ushering her back to the wagon, pointedly ignoring everyone who tried to speak with them. Idelia didn't say a word, just kept a smile pressed tightly on her face until the farm was in sight.

The moment she saw the house, her facade crumbled. Home. *This was supposed to be home—a place where I was wanted, where Jerome and I would make happy memories to share.*

"This isn't my home." She spoke the words aloud, the finality in them sinking her heart a notch lower.

"Yes, it is." Jerome swung her out of the wagon but didn't release her. His hands still encircling her waist, he said, "I want this to be your home, Idelia."

"I know." She squeezed her eyes shut and stepped backward, out of his grasp. "You want the money to restore this place, and you can only have it if I marry you within the next two weeks!"

"No." He reached for her, saw the glare she shot him, and shoved his hands in his pockets. "I want you here because you belong here. With me."

The honesty in his voice pulled her up short. "Why didn't you tell me about the money? That the reason you sent for me immediately wasn't because you couldn't stand to wait until spring but because you couldn't afford to?"

"I was afraid you wouldn't come." He swallowed hard. "And I was too selfish to consider what you'd think when you heard about the council's proposition."

"Proposition." Mama snorted. "Not proposal. One is love, one business. You chose business."

So true. Tears pricked behind her eyes, tiny darts whose discomfort paled in comparison to her remorse. *I chose you for love.* She wanted to fling the words at him but couldn't. Not when he'd so obviously made his choice. Not when he didn't care for her in the same way.

"I don't anymore." Jerome stepped around Mama to clasp Idelia's hands. His warmth wrapped around her fingers, his gaze penetrating her defenses.

"When you came, I thought about how God had blessed me with not only the means to save the farm, but a wife to enjoy it with for a lifetime. I want to marry you, Idelia. No one else."

For a moment she believed him, ready to fall into his arms and give up her last shreds of dignity. She held back though. "Why?"

"I just said why." His brow furrowed. "You're the woman I want to spend my life with."

"Even if you didn't get so much as a dime?" She crossed her arms and awaited his answer. At the moment, she didn't know what she'd do if he had the wrong answer, but she had to know.

"Idelia,"—he took a deep breath—"I don't see why we can't have both. But the answer is yes. I want to marry you—money or no money—because of who you are."

"In that case," Idelia replied, moving to clasp hands with Mama, "you don't have long to prove it."

As the two women walked into the house, Jerome resisted the urge to let loose a howl of frustration. As soon as the door shut, he snatched the hat from his head and slapped it on the ground to vent some steam.

Didn't help.

He reached down, picked up the trusty hat, patted the dust out of it, and plunked it back on his head. It wasn't his Stetson's fault he was in this mess. Jerome acknowledged that.

He turned his head at the sound of a horse riding fast and saw Clarence Ashton pounding up to the hitching post. Jerome took a savage satisfaction in blocking the mayor's path to his house. It didn't hurt that Ashton looked more than a mite disgruntled himself. Good. If he had to suffer for this whole thing, Ashton should be in the stocks alongside him.

"Mayor,"—he made a show of tipping his just-dusted hat—"what brings you here this fine afternoon?"

"Cut the garbage, Sanders." Ashton tried to sidestep him. When Jerome anticipated the move, the mayor scowled. "I told the other men in town that I'd fine 'em if they stopped by your place today, but I can't hold 'em off forever. After the stunt you pulled this mornin', Lurleen won't so much as look at me!"

"*Mrs. van der Zee*," he said, taking particular care to emphasize the proper form of address, "realizes that this whole situation is your fault. You deserve a cold shoulder for trying to rush men and women into hasty marriages like that."

"Ha!" Ashton hooked his thumbs through his suspenders. "I didn't try to rush any woman into marriage. Just encouraged you young bucks to get out there and do as the Bible says—be fruitful. The town needs women and children, and you bumps on a log weren't doin' anything about it!"

"First off, I've scarcely been here for two months," Jerome countered.

"Second, you dangled money in front of our noses when you knew full well that the railroad strike last spring devastated the farmers hereabouts. There's not a man in this town who can say that a sum of cash like that wouldn't be a balm to his household. It was manipulative."

"Now see here, Sanders, I and the council did what we thought was right to encourage town growth and help some of the farms most affected by the strike—like yours. The proposition was straightforward. Everyone knew the score." The mayor worked his jaw. "Until you brought in those wonderful women and didn't see fit to tell them. And this here conversation isn't getting either of us back in their good graces."

"I asked her to marry me. She said yes. It doesn't get much simpler than that." Jerome couldn't quite meet Ashton's gaze as he said it. "But I should have told her we'd have the farm and the money, too."

"Why didn't you?"

"She might not have come."

"I'm not a lackwit, son." Ashton rolled his eyes. "I meant. . .why didn't you mention it, casual-like, once they got here? Didn't you figure some smart-mouth like Alastair Pitt would put a spoke in that wheel?"

"Nope. I just figured we'd get married, and Idelia would be my wife, and we'd set about building a life together. Guess I didn't think much beyond that."

Ashton took a step back, his brows relaxing. "So that's the way of it. It's not just for the money."

" 'Course not!"

"Don't get all het up. You wouldn't have sent for her if the council hadn't offered the incentive, and you know it. Just think about how that looks to a young gal and her tender mother."

"How could I ask a woman to marry me when the farm was failing and I wasn't in a position to provide for her?"

"Good point. Have you apologized to her yet, started to make it all up to her?"

"I told her I'd marry her without the money." Jerome followed Ashton's gaze to the house, where a curtain twitched as though someone had been peeking out just a moment before. "And now I have to make her believe me."

"Then we're going to have to strategize." Ashton tilted his head toward the house and lowered his voice. "Because 'making' a woman do anything she isn't inclined to do is harder than coaxing a carrot from a starving mule."

Chapter 10

Did you catch that?" Idelia glanced at Mama, who'd copied her position at the window on the other side of the door. They'd opened them to encourage a fresh breeze. When they overheard the mayor and Jerome arguing about their situation, they pressed their ears close to hear every word.

"Nee. Just 'strategy' and then mumbles." Mama looked as put out as Idelia felt.

"They're going to the barn now." She didn't eavesdrop often, but when the topic of discussion would decide one's fate, so to speak, it was much more difficult to resist. Idelia straightened up. "But did you hear what they said?"

"*Ja*." Mama brightened. "They are wanting us to not be upset with them and will now court us."

"Yes, us." Idelia couldn't help but grin at Mama's enthusiasm. Obviously she returned the mayor's admiration. "Even better, Jerome knows he was wrong not to tell me and told Ashton that he'd marry me whether he got money or not. . .that he couldn't propose before he knew he could support his wife."

"Is better." Mama shoved up her sleeves. "Now we remind them why my *dotter* is reward enough alone. He has not proven worthy yet, but sweet helps to chase away the bitter."

Thank You, Lord, that Jerome isn't too stubborn to admit he erred and to try to fix things. Thank You that he cares enough to want *to fix things. I begin to believe that it's not just the money, that Jerome returns my feelings in some measure. If it is Your will, I ask that You show me he is the man for me.*

"We need something special. . .and quick to make." Idelia pondered for a moment. Mama's uncharacteristic silence made her raise her brows. "No ideas?"

Mama shrugged. "Is for you to choose."

"Fresh pork chops from the butchering yesterday, with crackling bread. I'll run and get the meat while you ready the dutch oven. We'll need it and the stove oven both." Idelia scarcely waited for the nod of approval. Fresh crackling bread was a treat available only after a recent slaughter. The crisp bits of pork left after rendering the lard weren't usually in ready supply.

They got down to work—heating the dutch oven, melting shortening, and laying the spiced chops within to bake. While the meat cooked, Idelia mixed cornmeal, flour, and baking soda in a large bowl. She stirred the batter constantly as she added the beaten eggs and buttermilk before folding in the cracklings. A few minutes later, a large roasting pan filled with the batter slid into the stove oven.

"Would you watch the ovens while I make butter?" Idelia swiped her forehead with the back of her hand.

"You made fresh butter yesterday." Mama waved toward the well, where the crock hung on a long rope to keep cool. Soon enough it would be so cold that anything put outside would freeze straight through.

"*Ja*. But cracklin' bread is best with sweet butter."

"Ah." She brushed the coals off the top of the dutch oven, checking the pork chops inside.

At this silent agreement, Idelia hurried to scoop the morning cream into the churn, adding salt before she pumped furiously. When it began to resist, she poured in a generous measure of honey and finished churning. A quick wash and a moment in the butter press and it was on the table as Mama pulled the crackling bread from the oven.

Idelia stepped outside to ring the dinner bell, gratified to see the men rush from the barn in their haste. In the blink of an eye, they sat at the table, a succulent chop steaming on each plate.

"Dear heavenly Father," Jerome prayed, "we ask that You bless the hands that made this food, and thank You that Idelia and Mama Lurleen came to Willowville. Let them know how grateful we are. Furthermore, we ask that You help us be deserving of such bounty. Amen."

She couldn't help but give him a small smile for his efforts as she dished up hearty slices of the bread and passed around her sweet butter. Idelia watched as Mayor Ashton murmured something to Mama.

While Ashton cut into the meat first, Jerome slathered his bread with the creamy butter and bit into it with relish. His eyes widened as the flavor hit his tongue. "Cracklin' bread?"

"*Ja*." Idelia wouldn't say more. It was up to him to make the conversation while Mama and Mayor Ashton were deep in discussion about the Christmas gathering.

"Cracklin' bread?" Ashton, apparently not as deep in conversation as it appeared, wasted no time spreading a hearty helping of butter on his own. "Mmm. . ."

Mama shot her an amused glance, and for a moment, they shared a woman's contentment at a dish well done and a plan carried through. Making a special dinner let the men know their ire wouldn't last forever and gave Jerome and Ashton an opportunity to appreciate their efforts. Fortunately, the men were making good on their part.

"This is wonderful," Jerome praised. "Every time you get in the kitchen, I'm sure the meal can't compare to the one before, but you always prove me wrong."

"It's been this good each day?" Ashton put down his fork in astonishment and picked it up again when Mama started slicing more wedges from the pan. He dug in with gusto to make up for lost time.

"Wait until you taste what we make to celebrate Kerstmis," Mama promised. "Then you will know true Dutch cooking."

"I can't wait." Jerome wiped his face with his napkin.

Neither can I. Idelia couldn't escape the smudge of doubt that clouded her thoughts. *Because it's the last day we can wed and still make the deadline.*

Three days after the scene at the church and Jerome wasn't much closer to figuring out how to prove to Idelia that he cared about her more than the money. If worse came to worst, he could just wait until after the Christmas celebration so she'd have no fears. Then Idelia would be secure, happy, and, most important, *his*.

Only problem with that was the money issue. He wanted his wife more than he wanted any sum of cash, but how would he be able to provide for her without it? If he were to be completely honest, he didn't like the notion of waiting that long until the wedding, either. A woman like his bride-to-be was temptation enough to ensure he stayed in the barn. Indefinitely.

But shouldn't he be able to think of some gesture now? Something so she didn't have to feel like this anymore? Memories of the bootlace debacle kept him rejecting whatever came to mind. Jerome warmed every time he thought of Idelia's kind understanding and honest gratitude for his efforts.

This time, it had to be special. Personal, even. And hang the potential for embarrassment. Maybe if he'd been more willing to risk his pride, he wouldn't have lost his bride. So what would Idelia like best? What would she love more than anything else?

He prayed for guidance and wracked his brain throughout the day, until he was chopping logs for winter fuel and he heard the supper bell. One last swing split the huge felled trunk he'd been working on into manageable pieces, but a smaller one stood ready for him later.

Jerome headed to the well, drew some water, and splashed it on his face. He used his bandanna to dry off and gave one last look at the woodpile. An idea started to tickle the back of his mind.

On that disastrous Sunday, hadn't Idelia and Mama Lurleen mentioned Kerstmis horns? Long, thinner logs hollowed out and rested on the lips of wells so the sound carried when someone blew into them. Idelia had grown a little wistful, saying she missed the loud welcome of Christ's birth.

He tromped back over to the woodpile and ran his hand along the smaller, thinner log he hadn't yet cut, judging its thickness to be about right. Jerome smiled and decided he'd start the project the next day. This was something meaningful that he could—and would—do for his bride.

Chapter 11

Saturday evening, Idelia and Mama made bacon-and-sausage gravy to be poured over warm biscuits. It was simple fare, but that night they had another focus. Mayor Ashton, enthusiastic about having a Dutch-influenced Kerstmis celebration, had met with some resistance at the town council meeting. It seemed the menfolk were hesitant to make the change since they'd never sampled Dutch baking.

"I have half a mind to say it's not that they're worried about the dishes being tasty enough; it's that they want to get extra treats." Idelia rolled another batch on a floured board. "*Speculaas* will either make them admit it's a good idea or make them decide further testing is required."

"With one week, the decision is made today." Mama popped another round into the dutch oven before checking the ones baking in the stove. "And is not the only choice."

"*Ja.*" Idelia started stamping the cookies from the rolled dough. "Jerome has been kind and attentive, but I'd hoped for a clearer sign that the marriage is God's will. But time runs short, and we cannot stay here if I do not become his wife."

"You do not have to marry him." Mama stopped what she was doing. "We will find other way. Remember this."

"I will." Idelia transferred the cookies to a baking pan. "But if only—"

The long, low moan of a great horn sounded over the farm. Silence fell for a moment as she and Mama stared at each other. Then another blast resonated through the evening air.

Idelia put down the pan and rushed to the door. The sting of cold air hit her face the moment she stepped outside, but she didn't go back for her cloak. There, in the last rays of the sunset, was the sign she'd been seeking.

Jerome stood a few feet behind the well, holding the end of a horn braced against the edge of the well. He waved in greeting before blowing into the horn again. The sound repeated until the sun sank completely, and he drew the long instrument away from the well and walked toward her.

"You remembered." The words sounded choked, forced from her suddenly dry throat. "To usher in Kerstmis. You found a horn."

"Couldn't find one, so I made it." He held it up, its length made for two men to carry. "I thought I might not finish in time to use it properly."

"It's perfect." She ran her hand along the smooth-sanded surface. "The start of a tradition." Idelia sniffed at the thought.

"Someday I'll hold it in place while our son blows," Jerome agreed. "But tonight we won't make any decisions about time."

"But—"

"*Nee, dotter.*" Mama stepped forward. "Jerome is in the right. His gift tonight is just for us to enjoy."

✦❦✦

"Mayor Ashton has asked the two of you to speak with the council about your ideas for the festivities next Saturday, and he'll bring you back to the farm afterward." Jerome mentioned the plan just after church ended. He stared down two men who were making their way up the aisle, looking at Idelia with an avaricious gleam in their eyes. Only after they backed away did he register Idelia's words.

"We need to talk." She'd put her gloved hand on his arm.

"Agreed." He bolted to his feet. She couldn't make her decision yet—not before his second proof that he cared for her! "I'll see you later this afternoon, and we'll talk then."

Jerome gave her a broad grin and, seeing Ashton shepherding Lurleen toward the front, nudged Idelia to follow. Once everyone but the council and the van der Zees had cleared out of the church, he went on his way.

He made it home in record time, ready to make the most of the two things in his favor. First, Mama Lurleen knew about his plan and would do her best to keep the meeting going. Second, she'd kindly translated the recipe to English. While Jerome wasn't half the cook Idelia was, surely he could whip up a batch of her favorite cookies—*pepernoten*.

Especially since they were supposed to be hard anyway.

It wasn't long before he'd situated the horses and stood in the kitchen, laying out the ingredients. Flour, sorghum, water, an egg, and five different spices. He headed for the spice rack, holding up the recipe to check against the labels. Cinnamon he knew. Salt was easy. He spotted nutmeg easily enough, but the anise seeds and cloves were harder.

Hmm. . .the recipe said *powdered* cloves. Jerome opened the container and inhaled the aromatic spice. Smelled good to him, and it couldn't matter too much. Cloves were cloves, and everything would mix together anyway.

He grabbed the largest bowl in the kitchen and dumped the ingredients into it, then looked again at the instructions. *Knead.* Funny, he always thought women made desserts and such by stirring with a spoon or whisk.

Maybe it's a Dutch word for the same thing? Deciding that was probably it, he grabbed a whisk. He gave it some good, solid stirs and watched as everything melded together. Jerome looked at the recipe again. Oops. One egg yolk. Well, it couldn't make much difference that he put in the whole egg.

In fact, it would probably improve the mix. Since he'd been stirring it, the whole batter had gotten very stiff. *Better put in a little more water.* And while he was improving things, he might as well keep going. Those cloves were looking pretty strange, streaked and mashed into everything. Maybe if he added more of the other spices, it would even out. Strange that a cookie called pepernoten didn't have pepper in it. He added a pinch for good measure.

It's thicker. He peered at the bowl's contents. *It smells good.* So he started taking lumps and rolling the dough into balls. They weren't all the same size and some came out a little lopsided, but the recipe said to flatten them on the pan.

He squashed each one down flat then slid the first batch into the oven. They were supposed to take about twenty minutes—plenty of time for him to make the next batch. And maybe a few minutes to go and work some oil into his saddle.

Jerome returned to the house to find the oven smoking. He grabbed a dishcloth and wrenched open the door, plucking a piping hot pan of smoldering crisps out and dumping them on the stovetop. He stared at the blackened wafers for a moment before sliding in the next batch.

Okay, so he should have paid more attention to the "about" part of the instructions. Not a problem. This next lot would come out better. He wouldn't leave the kitchen until they were ready. Except to dispose of the singed ones. He gathered them up and hustled out to the hog pen, dumping the bunch into the trough and rushing back to the house.

He opened the oven door to check on the cookies. Still doughy. Jerome plunked down in a chair to wait. An eternity later, his pocket watch said it had been another five minutes. He opened the door again. Not ready yet. Mama Lurleen said they were supposed to darken. They were still pretty light.

But what if it only took a minute between just right and burnt? He checked more frequently until he thought they looked about the right color. Jerome decided to ignore that they looked like crispy, brownish-orange splats instead of cookies.

With plenty of dough left, he rolled more lopsided, flattened lumps and put them in the oven. The cooked ones had cooled, so he figured he should test one. He grabbed the closest cookie and popped it into his mouth.

That pepper sure made itself known. He grimaced as the cloves wedged between his teeth. And was it supposed to taste so. . .strong? He crunched it into shards and gave a swallow, staring at the mixing bowl in accusation.

He was just starting to pick up and hide the evidence of his failure when the door opened.

Chapter 12

No matter how long she lived, Idelia was positive she'd never forget the look on Jerome's face when she caught him with those cookies. A streak of dried dough crusted his hair, flour dusted his Sunday shirt, and his face was the very expression of consternation as he shoved a platter of his creation behind his back.

"You're home." He sidestepped toward a wall, still concealing the fruits of his labor. Jerome gave her the distinct impression that if she weren't in the doorway, he'd scuttle out of there faster than she could say, "Stop."

"Looks like you've been busy." Mama was pressing her lips together again, but it was no use. Her shoulders jerked up and down, betraying her smothered giggles. "What've you got there?"

"Nothing to be shared with another human being." He gave a pained sigh and brought the dish out. A heap of thin, dark, misshapen crisps piled atop one another, the source of the pungent smell permeating the room. "It didn't work."

"What didn't work?" Idelia looked from Mama to Jerome and back again, as they obviously knew what was going on.

"Had hard time with the *pepernoten*, did you?" Mama's words released her laughter, as well. "What went wrong?"

"You were trying to bake?" Idelia raised her brows but didn't add on the last part of her thought. *Those are supposed to be pepernoten?*

"Mama Lurleen said they were your favorite." He gave a sheepish grin and tried to run his fingers through his hair. His hand caught on the dried gunk, and he pried it loose with a glower. "I wanted to surprise you."

"You did." Idelia bit the inside of her lip to keep her chuckles muffled. Jerome had tried so hard to be thoughtful and had gone to a good deal of trouble to make this mess.

"You're always making delicious things for me, and I wanted to do the same for you." He made a hapless gesture. "Seems like baking is more of a science than I knew. Even with a recipe."

"It's not so bad." Idelia wracked her brain for something that would make him feel better. "You didn't burn them."

"Yes, I did." His shoulders hunched, and he looked gloomily at the plate still in his hands. "The first batch is in the hog trough." The "cookies" looked stranger the more she stared.

"Well, I love *pepernoten*." She took a deep breath and reached for one of his creations. She didn't move fast enough, as he jerked the plate away, causing the top one to fly up and land on his collar.

"What are you thinking?" His voice rang with reprimand. "You can't *eat* them. I'm not sure the hogs can stomach them."

"Now, Jerome." She reached around and swiped one off the plate, only to have him try to snatch it back. They both wound up with half of the thing. "You made it for me, and I'm going to try it."

"No, you're not." He made a futile grab. "No wife of mine is going to put herself in harm's way like that."

"I'm not your wife." The words stopped him in his tracks, his expression so sad she clarified immediately. "But I will be later this week." She took a decisive bite of the cookie in her hand and crunched despite the pain in her teeth. After a swallow she added, "So long as you never bake again."

"Deal."

❧

"You look beautiful." Jerome set his jaw. "Now go change."

"What?" Idelia looked down. "Why?"

"That's the dress you wore on our first wedding day. And I've already told you I'm not marrying you tonight."

"Jerome!" She clenched her teeth and let out her breath in a hiss. "Stop being so stubborn. Tonight is the Kerstmis celebration, and you have to stop digging in your heels."

"Nope." He bit back a grin. She looked so cute when she was indignant. "You'll have to wait for me like I waited for you."

"But you know I love you," she wailed. "There's no reason to wait."

If I give in, this will be our wedding night. He tamped down the temptation. "Yes, there is. No one will ever say that I married you for the money, and you'll never have cause to wonder. There will be no wedding until tomorrow."

"But I don't wonder." She drew close, smelling clean and looking so soft he had to put his hands behind his back like a military captain to keep from holding her. "And I don't care if anyone else does. We and God know that we'll mean our vows."

"I want *everyone* to know it." He watched as she came still closer, linking her hands around the back of his neck. "You are more than I deserve as it stands."

"And if marrying tonight is another blessing?" She laid her head against his chest, her hair tickling his chin. "We can't let it go to waste."

"You've heard my reasons." He took her hands from around his neck and stepped back. "And you must honor my decision."

"I don't want to be the reason you lose the farm, Jerome." Tears sparkled in her eyes. "That, I couldn't bear. Not when we can settle everything tonight."

"God brought us together, and He'll provide for our needs." He stooped a bit to meet her gaze. "I sent for you for the wrong reasons, Idelia. But I'm

345

keeping you for the right ones."

"I'll honor your decision, as I would the decision of my husband." Idelia drew a shaky breath. "And I'll consider it practice for our marriage to come."

"So we understand each other? No more trying to change my mind?"

"Not as long as you don't make me change." She managed a small smile. "Mama will never forgive me if we make her late."

"That's right." Mama Lurleen bustled into the room. "Everything is in the wagon but us. Let us go!"

It took more time than usual to get to the church, where torches and tables had been set up for an evening party. Jerome took special care not to jostle all the food Idelia and Lurleen had baked for the occasion.

They'd told him all the names and what they were, but he couldn't keep it all straight. And even if he could, he wasn't sure he'd want to. A little bit of knowledge in the kitchen could cause a whole lot of trouble.

As soon as they pulled up, Ashton was there to help carry everything to the tables. Though the other townswomen had brought gracious plenty, one table stood empty just for the Dutch desserts. It took the four of them two trips to transfer everything, and then the evening really began.

"Attention!" Ashton stood in front of the food and bellowed until everyone minded him. "Tonight is our celebration of the birth of Christ, God's own Son born as man to bring us salvation. So before we get to eat all this wonderful food"—he cast a glance at the dessert table—"we're going to have two special events."

Murmurs overtook the crowd at this development.

"First, the reverend is going to read to us from the book of Luke so we can remember the joy of that night long ago. It's not actually Christmas Eve, but that's what we're celebrating and that should come before anything else."

"What's the other event?" Alastair demanded.

"That"—a smile spread across Ashton's face as he stared at Mama Lurleen, who beamed back—"is a wedding."

Chapter 13

Idelia's gaze flew to Jerome, but he looked as mystified as she. So he still hadn't come to his senses. She could have gotten lost in her upset over that, but she realized Mama was moving toward the mayor.

"Mrs. van der Zee has given me the honor of her hand in marriage," Ashton declared when Mama reached him. "And we'd like to have this celebration double as our wedding."

Cheers met this pronouncement, but Idelia stood stock-still. Mama was getting married tonight? But what about the deadline? She looked up at Ashton suspiciously. If he was taking advantage of her mother for the money, the man would pay dearly.

"I want to remind you all that, as the mayor, I'm not eligible for the bride-by-Christmas offer." His hand found her mother's and held it tight, easing the tension in Idelia's chest. "Lurleen and I are both of an age where we just don't see the sense in putting off the good things in life."

At that comment, Idelia gave Jerome a pointed glance, but he kept his gaze fixed forward. Ashton and Mama blended back into the crowd as the reverend gave thanks for all the people in attendance and proceeded to read from Luke.

The familiar words brought peace to her heart. Reading of how the Son of God had humbled Himself to be born as a man to later die for those who killed Him never failed to stir her. Easter was a mix of sadness and victory, but Kerstmis. . .ah, Kerstmis, as the beginning of any wonderful story, brought pure joy.

Just as Jerome's telegram had brought the excitement of possibilities and love, Christ's birth was a promise of God's provision. Look how He'd brought Mama a new husband and used a foolish plot by a wily mayor to show Idelia how much her husband cared for her.

As she stood beside her mother during the impromptu ceremony, Idelia released her worry. Mama would do well as the mayor's wife, and Idelia would begin a family of her own with Jerome. No one was leaving; no one was sacrificing.

Thank You for the goodness You've given us, Lord. I know now that Jerome made the right decision in postponing our wedding and trusting that You will provide. She watched as Mama and Ashton were proclaimed man and wife. *You always do.*

❧

"You were right." Idelia spoke so softly Jerome almost missed the words. "Waiting is not just a pledge to each other, but a mark of our faith in the Lord."

"I knew you'd understand." He reached out and cupped her cheek with his palm. "And that you were willing to honor my decision even before you agreed with it showed just how strong our union will be."

"Yes." She pulled away. "But for now, let's enjoy the food before it's all gone. Mama will be hurt if you don't try some of her *kerstkrans*."

"Cursed grans?" It didn't sound too good to him. Especially if it was anything like the *pepernoten*.

"No." Idelia laughed at his expression. It's a round cake with sweet almond paste. There's a hole in the middle where we light a candle to celebrate the birth of Christ. We made more than one this year so everyone could have some, but it's so delicious we can't wait too long."

"Sounds good to me." Jerome followed as she piled a plate full of meat, vegetables, and pastry for him before choosing smaller amounts for herself. They found a large stump where they sat and ate in comfortable silence until Mama Lurleen and Mayor Ashton found them.

"Why didn't you tell me, Mama?" Idelia couldn't quite hide her confusion. "I would have been happy for you."

"We didn't decide until this evening." Mama Lurleen smiled and tucked her hand into Ashton's.

"I'm glad you wed." Jerome picked up his piece of the rounded cake and took a bite. "May your marriage be as heavenly as this dessert."

"And nothing like Jerome's *pepernoten*," Idelia added.

"I won't move to Clarence's house until after your wedding tomorrow," Mama Lurleen assured them. "Not that I don't trust you to be a gentleman, Jerome, but we must be certain the proprieties are observed."

"Absolutely." His smile was genuine. With Mama Lurleen gone to Ashton's place after the wedding, he and Idelia would have the entire house to themselves.

"Yeah, yeah." Ashton seemed a good deal less happy about the delay, so Jerome wiped the grin from his face.

Reveling in his own good fortune was one thing; celebrating another man's sacrifice was another. And he wasn't about to cross his new father-in-law. Clarence Ashton and Mama Lurleen were a duo no sane man would care to cross.

The night flew by in a haze of laughter, celebration, and more good food than Jerome would have guessed his stomach could hold. When he fell into bed, he sent up a short prayer of thanks.

Tomorrow I'll wed Idelia.

❧❧❧

"Are you ready?" Jerome pulled Idelia aside the next morning. "Because if you've changed your mind, this is your last chance to tell me." He looked so earnest, she wanted to hug him. "Once we're in that church, I'm not letting you go."

"I wouldn't want you to." She leaned over and gave him a peck on the cheek, stifling a blush as she did it.

He helped her out of the wagon and left to take his place in front of the church, where he'd wait for her to come to him.

Idelia smoothed the skirt of Mama's wedding dress, smiling at the memory of how Jerome had been worried about her gown the night before. She didn't hold to any superstition about the groom seeing the bride on the day of the wedding. The Lord brought them here, and a yard or two of satin couldn't ruin it.

"It's time." Ashton offered her his arm, having graciously offered to give her away. He kept his gaze fixed on Mama, though, who proudly marched in ahead of them.

Idelia didn't really pay attention to the blur of faces turned toward her as she made her way down the aisle. She'd begun a few friendships in the short time since she'd come to Willowville, but her focus was all for the man who watched her every step as she moved toward him.

The moment Ashton laid her hand in Jerome's, her breath caught, and Idelia could have sworn her heart didn't beat again until they'd both pledged to love, honor, and cherish each other for a lifetime. Of course, just as she drew in a deep breath, Jerome kissed her, and she felt faint all over again.

"I love you." His words pulled her back from the pleasurable dizziness swirling in her head.

"I love you, too."

Together they made their way back up the aisle, only to be stopped when Mayor Ashton cleared his throat. . .loudly. Several times. "Before the happy couple gets on their way," he bellowed, "the town council has an announcement to make."

They both stopped then turned to listen. If there was one thing Idelia had been quick to learn about the way things worked in Willowville, it was that Mayor Ashton's announcements were never dull.

"Now we all know that Mr. and Mrs. Sanders didn't meet the deadline, so they won't be getting the cash incentive for their wedding." The words put a slight damper on Idelia's happiness until she shook it off.

"The Lord will provide," she whispered to Jerome, who squeezed her hand in acknowledgment.

"But the council and I talked it over this morning, and it seems to us that the bride-by-Christmas offer did result in one valid marriage before the end of last night's celebration."

"I thought you said you couldn't get the money 'cause you're the mayor!" Alastair sounded outraged, and Idelia wondered why the man so hated to see others happy.

"And I hold to that." Ashton gave a simmer-down glare and waited for everyone to be silent. "But the rules of the whole thing said that the money would go to any man who could bring a new woman to town and bind her here by marriage by the Christmas celebration."

"He can't mean—" Jerome sucked in a sharp breath.

"Yes, I do mean that Jerome Sanders brought Lurleen van der Zee to Willowville, and she was bound here by marriage by the deadline. And that means Mr. Sanders is eligible for the reward. If the second-happiest newlyweds in town would come back up here, we'd be happy to give you your wedding present."

An English Bride Goes West

by Therese Stenzel

Chapter 1

Katherine Wiltshire gazed at the bewildering number of horses, wagons, and cowboys besetting the Kansas town she had promised Papa to come to. Her mouth went dry. How would she choose a husband from among them?

An ear-piercing shriek filled the air. Katherine startled. Savage Indians? Her father had warned her they were everywhere in the American West. At the chug and the hiss of the train departing, she let out the breath she'd been holding.

A chill shook her body, and her teeth chattered. Was it the December air or the fever that had plagued her for the last two days? Her stomach churned, threatening to undo her peculiar breakfast of grits and fried beaver. She needed to find the sheriff.

A whiskered man in a sullied shirt and waistcoat pointed at her personal belongings. "Where'd you like your baggage delivered to, miss?"

She glanced around. Somewhere in this hamlet was the land Papa had purchased before he died, but where was the deed? If she could find the property, how did one build a house? "My baggage? Please take me to your nearest hotel."

"That's some accent." The whiskered man lifted his dented hat. "Where you from?"

"Cambridge, England."

"Boy howdy, I've never met anyone from way over yonder. Welcome to Kennedale."

Kennedale. The town that was meant to bring a new start for her and Papa. How wrong he had been. "Once I'm settled in a hotel, I would like to speak with the sheriff."

The man snatched up her bags. "I'm afraid there's no hotel. The Grisford brothers' gang burnt it to the ground."

A gang of outlaws? Kate shuddered. Sweltering underneath her warm wool dress and cape, she removed her gloves. On her fourth finger lay Papa's cross ring. A reminder of his strong faith and his belief that God's plan was for them to move to America. Now all was lost. That notion twisted over and over in her heart until a steel band formed.

God was not to be trusted.

She reached in her reticule to collect a coin, but the man carrying her bags had left her standing all alone. He was now across the street and tromping down a wooden walkway.

Woolsack. Swallowing hard, she lifted her skirts and paced after him, up a set of steep steps and down a boardwalk to the front of a brick building.

With a thump, he dropped her bags and peered in a window. "Sheriff's not here."

"I'll wait." Her breath came in gasps. "Thank you most kindly for your assistance."

As she wilted onto a wooden bench, her hat slipped off and fluttered to the ground. Folding her shaking hands, she hoped the sheriff would arrive before it was too late.

~❧~

Charlie Landing pinned his newly polished tin star back onto his vest before taking a warm loaf of bread from the preacher's wife.

"Now that I've cleaned your badge, you can wear it proudly." Mrs. Gleason nodded, her white hair as neat as her crisp dress. "I'm just so pleased that Judge Ridgley sent you, a young buck of twenty-five, to protect us from that frightful gang of outlaws."

Charlie picked up his well-worn Bible from the table and gripped it. *Lord, help me to be a good sheriff.* "Thank you, ma'am. I need to get back to the jail, but tell Rev. Gleason I enjoyed our talk." He nodded good-bye and slunk out of the parsonage into a blast of brisk December air. If she only knew the truth behind why his uncle, the judge, had sent him.

It was either Kennedale or jail.

"Sheriff!"

Charlie looked up to see blond-haired, gray-eyed Miss Ida Leemore running toward him at a full gallop, clutching her elaborate floral hat. "I'm so glad I found you."

With one hand, he steadied her, keeping her at arm's length before releasing her. Now a Christian, for the first time in his life, he wanted to keep tongues from wagging. "What's the problem?"

She batted her sparse eyelashes and giggled, seemingly anxious for his undivided attention. Her wide grin revealed the large gap in her front teeth. "Well, it appears there's an English lady asleep at your office door."

Pivoting around, he shot a glance down the long row of shops and offices. He could just make out a woman in a burgundy dress, sitting with her head resting against the wall. A few people waited beside her.

His mind flitted through his list of former clients. Had he ever sold his goods to an Englishman? Sometimes the womenfolk didn't take a liking to the source of his supplies. He straightened his posture, hoping it appeared sheriff-like.

Ida's lingering gaze unnerved him. He shoved the bread into her hands. "Thanks."

Ignoring her further chatter, he strode down the wooden walkway. Even from a distance, this lady appeared so ashen he feared the worst. *Lord, help me.*

A sizable crowd had gathered by the time he reached her. "Stand back."

Murmurs dropped off and the townsfolk immediately receded.

Unease coiled around Charlie. After only a month on the job, they respected his authority. Respect he didn't deserve. "Let me take a look at her."

The woman whimpered and gestured oddly.

A cold gust of air sliced through his unbuttoned jacket. Charlie handed his Bible and his keys to young Ben Watson, whipped off his coat, and laid it across her. She had the silkiest brown hair he'd ever seen.

"Unlock the jail. I need to get her out of this wind." Charlie lifted the woman into his arms. "Make way, make way."

The cell door creaked as Ben jerked it open.

Charlie laid her on a cot. His jacket fell off her, and he couldn't avoid noticing her trim figure and soft-looking skin.

The townspeople filled the stark chamber behind him.

"English girls are mighty pale."

"I wonder if she's ever seen the queen?"

"Such a young thing. Where's her family?"

Ben poked Charlie. "Word is she came in on the train from Topeka alone. Want me to send a telegram to the sheriff there?" At fifteen years of age, he had been Charlie's shadow since he'd arrived in Kennedale.

"Good idea." Charlie stood and glanced at the folks who stared back at him expectantly, as if he were some kind of hero. Determination gripped him. He'd prove to them he was a good man. And an upright lawman. Surely, in such a small town, the details of his former ways wouldn't come to light and he could maintain his respectable identity.

"Therefore if any man be in Christ, he is a new creature." He clung to that scripture like a drowning man to driftwood.

"That's all, ladies and gentleman." He waved his hand. "Go about your business."

Mrs. Gleason wiggled her way through the crowd. "Can I be of assistance?"

"Water?" the young woman mumbled.

The reverend's wife procured a tin cup and filled it with water from a pitcher on his desk. She offered the refreshment to the young woman then leaned toward Charlie. "You probably won't hear from Topeka today. Would you like the reverend and I to look after her? Surely jail is no place to keep a lady."

The tension that knotted his shoulders released its grip. He had no idea what to do with the lone gal. "You, my dear Mrs. Gleason, are a gift straight from heaven."

"Oh, I do declare," she protested, but there was a twinkle in her kind eyes.

He reached into his vest pocket and handed her the few coins he had left. "This'll cover any expenses."

"Oh no, I could never—"

"I know money's scarce. I insist."

The young lady passed the cup back to Charlie and struggled to sit up further. "I daresay I have created a w—wretched commotion."

A sympathetic ache pierced his guarded exterior. He was well acquainted with being alone in strange places. Perching on the edge of the cot, he slipped his hand under her arm to assist her to a more comfortable position. She averted her glazed eyes and smoothed back her brown hair streaked with ribbons of blond.

"What's your name, miss?"

"Katherine Wiltshire. . .I mean. . .please call me Kate." Her face was as white as a lone cloud against a Kansas sky.

A million questions sprang to his mind, but Mrs. Gleason was leaning over his shoulder. "From?"

"England." Her head dipped, and some of her curls escaped and trickled down her long, graceful neck. "Papa and I. . ." She fanned her flushed cheeks with her hand. "W—we stopped in Topeka. He was ill. I didn't know how to care for him." She leaned forward, as if to tell Charlie a secret, and collapsed into his arms.

He caught her and eased her back onto the bed. The heat coming off her frame told him clearly this lady might not make it to tomorrow.

⚹

A rumble of a clearing throat, followed by a polite cough, woke Charlie.

Rev. and Mrs. Gleason stood in his office doorway, the sunlight shimmering behind them as if they were a vision from heaven.

Charlie's breath slammed down his throat. He yanked his feet off his desk and stood. "Good morning."

Mrs. Gleason smiled as if she held a wonderful secret and nodded toward the bright midday sun. "I believe it is afternoon."

The reverend perched in a chair by Charlie's desk. "We've come to talk to you about the English lady, Miss Wiltshire."

"Is she better?" Charlie sat down, snatched his uncle's letter, and shoved it under his Bible. He rubbed the look of concern from his face and blinked hard, trying to wake up. All night he'd been cutting leather for his friend Diego Muntavo, best silver-decorated saddle maker in the West, to try to make a little money before payday.

"After a week of much prayer and Mrs. Gleason's tender care, she's much improved." The reverend removed his hat. "The Lord must have great plans for her because I've seen this ague before and people often don't recover."

"I should have stopped by. . ." Charlie's voice trailed off at the sight of Mrs. Gleason's white-knuckled grip on the back of Rev. Gleason's chair. Odd.

Charlie cleared his throat. "But I'm sure you've heard about the four drunken arrests, and then Mr. Heelin caught a petty thief in his shop, which was followed by a fistfight over a horse. And then the missing Daley boy who was later found sleeping in the rafters of the flour mill."

"You should—"

The reverend blew a "Shh" to silence his wife.

What were they up to? Charlie shot a glance between the two. "Like I said, I should have—"

"We wanted to come and speak to you today about a serious matter." The reverend twisted his hat in his hands.

"We have an idea regarding Miss Wiltshire." Mrs. Gleason's bright eyes glistened. "You should marry her."

A bolt of alarm whipped through Charlie. A gunshot would have been kinder. He snapped to his feet. "Surely sheriffs aren't required to marry for the sake of the town?"

"Not at all." Rev. Gleason waved his hand. "Now sit down and hear us out. Katherine—"

"Kate," his wife corrected. She leaned in toward Charlie. "The dear girl wants to be called by a more American-sounding name."

"Kate is all alone. Her father recently died and made her promise to settle the Kennedale land he'd bought while still in England. Most likely fearing for her safety, he urged her to find a good man who loved the Lord and wed by Christmas."

"And we don't want her marrying some sweet-talking, two-bit scoundrel." Mrs. Gleason clucked her tongue with disapproval. "She's such a pretty young thing and is in desperate need of the protection of a good man. An honest man like you."

Charlie froze at their pleading expressions. He needed time to redeem himself, to prove he was a good person. He cleared his throat. "I–I'm not the right man." *My sins are too great.* "There must be others—men who are well thought of—who could marry this lady."

The preacher leaned forward. "I'm certainly no matchmaker, but she is a docile, God-fearing girl. A good wife can bring comfort to a man." Insight glimmered from the pastor's old eyes, making him look like a shepherd who'd herded many a lost sheep back into the fold. "She might help you find your way. Furthermore, Kate believes the Kennedale land her father purchased is located near town and is most likely worth a lot of money. You might do all right with her."

The word *no* formed on Charlie's lips until the edge of the letter he'd hidden caught his eye. Judge Ridgley was coming in five days.

The morning Charlie had been caught stealing guns, a severe snowstorm hit. His uncle, a judge, took him into his home and, over the two-day blizzard, shared the gospel with Charlie. Instead of a jail sentence, his shrewd uncle gave his newly redeemed nephew a second chance. . .but with certain requirements. Charlie had to fill the vacant position as sheriff of Kennedale, a town plagued by gun-toting outlaws, and show he had settled down into a respectable life.

A genteel, Christian wife, who was, by her manner and dress, a cultured woman, would certainly prove to his uncle that he was a changed man. And it didn't hurt that she was an attractive gal who needed his help. "Marry her?" Charlie rubbed his day-old whiskers, trying not to appear too agreeable. "I might consider it."

Mrs. Gleason beamed with pleasure. "She's waiting for you in our guest room."

As Charlie stood, his legs wobbled. And when he went to put his guns in his holster, it only took him five tries.

"Oh, I really don't think you'll need a weapon to persuade her." Mrs. Gleason pressed her lips as if restraining her mirth.

"You don't know my history with women."

Chapter 2

The shock of icy air rushing in from the open window invigorated Kate's clouded mind as she shifted to sit up farther on her pillows. Of all the outlandish, preposterous, nonsensical situations to find herself in. Marriage to a stranger? What could Papa have been thinking to suggest such a thing?

A wave of weariness claimed her like a sultry day. This past week, lethargy had undermined her every move and thought. Because she was normally passionate and strong-minded, her father often called her his whirling dervish.

But when he knew he wouldn't live much longer, he warned her. "My dear Kate, the West can be appallingly uncivilized. Cutthroat Indians everywhere. Please, I implore you, find a good man who loves the Lord, and try to marry quickly. . .by Christmas."

By Christmas? The notion was as foolish then as it was now. If only her normal strength would return. She would leap up from this bed, dress in a mad dash, and take the first train back East, far away from any scalping Indians. Instead, here she sat with foolish tears welling in her eyes.

Rev. and Mrs. Gleason had tended to her and prayed with her regarding her circumstances. Such kindness had rekindled her childhood faith. Could God truly help her out of this dreadful muddle?

Following the Gleasons' counsel that the sheriff was a good man of strong faith, she agreed to consider marrying him. But how could she make such a decision in her weakened condition? She yanked off her nightcap. "Lord, if You truly care about me, please tell me what to do."

Once she recovered, she would find Papa's land and build a home in memory of him—of that she felt quite confident. Perhaps a husband could be of assistance. She didn't even know what supplies were needed. Whom did one hire?

She studied her trunks that had come in from Topeka. They were filled with her mother's handmade linens, draperies, and bits and pieces, which Kate planned to use in her new home one day. Hope billowed in her heart. *Home.* It had a nice ring to it. How she wished she could be settled by Christmas. Of course, sadness tinged her thoughts. There would be no gifts from her family this year.

"Katherine."

A deep baritone voice startled her, leaving her as weak as a giddy schoolgirl. She clutched the bed covers to her chin and stared at the man waiting in the doorway. With his hat in his hand, she could see that his wavy chestnut hair matched the depth and warmth of his dark coffee-colored eyes. Seeing that he was tall with wide shoulders, she imagined him to be a very strong man.

Her cheeks flamed. Words clogged in her throat. "I—I believe I owe you an enormous debt of gratitude for aiding me in my sickly state and bringing me to the Gleasons'."

He leaned on the doorframe and folded his arms. "Just doing my job, miss."

"They have advised me that you are a good man and a brave sheriff and that I should speak with you"—every inch of her respectable breeding protested the need to admit she knew why he was here—"regarding my situation."

His head dipped for a moment, as if bowed in prayer. "Rev. and Mrs. Gleason are two of the most God-fearing people I know." His gaze pierced her. "And I agree with their concerns."

The sound of a throat being cleared let her know her guardians waited on the other side of the wall, but this knowledge did not deter her heart from fluttering. Maybe this wasn't such a clever idea. Although the reverend had assured her of Charlie's salvation, she needed more time to consider his character. "Please call me Kate. My father thought it sounded more. . .American."

He took a chair from a corner of the room and set it down a discreet distance away from the bed. "They think you need a man's protection and his name."

"My father wanted me to. . . I mean to say, he thought it important that I—"

"Will you marry me, Kate?"

Her stomach flipped. Was it the fever, or did her insides quiver at the kindness in his voice? "Why do you wish to wed a stranger?"

The warmth in his mahogany eyes receded. "I have my reasons."

Her heart couldn't thump any harder. What would Papa say? Convinced she knew his answer, she replied, "Yes." It came out in a whisper.

"In about two weeks, a Christmas Eve wedding, then?"

Christmas? A rush of pleasure consumed her. Just what Papa wanted. Visions of a home decorated with fragrant ivy, garland laced with golden ornaments, cards, lavishly printed, set on a fireplace mantel—

Thunderous sounds of gunshots split the air.

Charlie leaped up and stuck his head out the window. "Not good."

"What is it?"

"The Grisford brothers' gang."

⚶⚶⚶

Charlie narrowed his gaze as he halted in the dead center of Main Street. The explosions of shots fired in the air and the gang's wild screeches only added to the tension in his gut.

With a burning resolve, Charlie stood tall, legs wide apart, hands next to his holstered guns, and watched the row of brothers on horses thundering his way.

When his uncle told him he'd have to become the sheriff of Kennedale if he wanted to stay out of jail, Charlie agreed and was determined to show how committed he was to the Lord. Now, staring death in the face, atoning for his sins this way didn't seem like such a smart notion.

The bitter wind sent a chill up Charlie's spine, but he continued his firm stand. Once they noticed him, the band of five brothers, Gage, Gary, Gilroy, Glen, and George, silenced their hooting and hollering.

Charlie flexed his hands on each side of his weapons. Although the brothers' brains were a few bottles short of a case, their unruly grins did not bode well for the townsfolk.

As they came to within a wagon's length of him, Charlie recognized Gage, the oldest brother of the gang. Over the last five years, Charlie had sold guns and ammunition he'd stolen from various forts around Kansas to the brothers and other outlaws. More slippery than a greased pig, Gage had once offered Charlie a box of just-born puppies in exchange for some pistols.

Charlie spat and wiped his hand across his mouth. "I'm ordering you boys," he shouted out in a low guttural voice, "to leave this town."

Gage slid from his horse. His exaggerated swagger and twirling gun read like a dime-store novel. "You're a lawman?" He laughed, revealing his yellowed teeth. "I can't believe Gun-Toting Charlie is wearing a badge."

Charlie shifted his stance. Could any of the townsfolk hear him?

George, the youngest of the brothers, called out, "Did they tell you what we did to the last tin star man that tried to stop us?"

Charlie's uncle had left out that bit of information. His stomach twisted. Miss Wiltshire's words, "brave sheriff," mocked him.

Gage leaned forward. "He ain't here no more. And if you get in our way, you won't be, neither."

"I thought you said he moved to Cleveland," Gilroy called out.

"Of all the flea-brained brothers—don't tell." Gage threw down his hat.

By Gage's odor, Charlie assumed the brothers had been drinking, the only way they could muster the courage to continually steal from innocent people. Despite Charlie's familiarity with them, his anger remained. The folks in this town had put their trust in him as sheriff, Kate among them, and he wasn't going to let them down.

He hoped.

Charlie's jaw clenched. He eased a gun from his holster and cocked it. "Leave or you'll face your Maker today."

Gilroy pushed his hat back and swiped his forehead. "Gage, didn't you say the Maker ain't too happy with us?"

"We're here for more of Diego's fancy saddles." Dirt filled the creases of Gage's swarthy face.

Charlie gripped his gun so hard his hand hurt. The town's economy had been struggling to make it. Diego's saddles were bringing in orders from all over the Midwest, but he could barely keep up with the work, much less afford to have them stolen.

"And if we don't get what we want," Gage said, gesturing around the town, "we're gonna burn another building down. Which will it be this time, *Sheriff*? The schoolhouse?"

"As the law, I'm telling you you're done here."

"We like this place." Gage grinned back at his brothers, who sat on a row of horses sporting silver-studded saddles. "It's been very. . .profitable."

"I said. . .get out now!"

"One day you sell us guns, and the next you tell us where and what we can do?" George laughed. "You ain't nothing but a two-bit gun thief."

❧❧❧

Kate edged over to the open window. At first, when she'd heard shooting guns and the odious yells, she feared Charlie was wrong and Indians had come. Now all was quiet.

Kneeling down, she peeked over the ledge of the window to see what Sheriff Landing was doing. Sure enough, there was a group of gun-laden men on horses. The sheriff stood in front of the swarthy-looking fellows with his gun drawn. His voice rose loudly, but the wind muffled the words. How courageous of him not to back down. But why didn't he simply ask them to leave? Wasn't the lawman in the American West the final authority?

A filthy raven-haired man yelled back at the sheriff. Curiosity compelled her forward—what was he saying?

The words "two-bit gun thief" floated up to her.

She jerked back. What an impertinent thing to say. Although she didn't know him well, Sheriff Charlie was certainly no outlaw.

She peeked again. The sheriff kept looking up and down the walkway at the storefronts, probably to make sure all the townsfolk were safe. What an admirable gentleman. Rev. Gleason must have been right—Charlie Landing was a good man.

Weakness overcame her limbs. Praying for his safety, she crawled back into bed.

❧❧❧

Charlie glanced from side to side. Would the townspeople, hidden behind closed doors, find out he knew the Grisford brothers?

His mind raced with possible options, but before he could speak, a little girl, about age three, toddled out just behind the brothers and headed toward them.

The sight tore at Charlie's insides. He shouted, "Go back."

Gary slipped from his horse, ran over, and snatched up the child by the arm. He flashed a triumphant grin that stood out against his dark beard.

"Whaddya think, Gage? She'd make good firewood?"

But when the little girl started to cry, Gary's smile dropped. He gave the girl a little shake. "Aw, now, don't do that."

Gage folded his arms. "I'll make you a deal, Sheriff. You trade me her life for more of them fancy saddles."

Bile rose in Charlie's throat. This was all his fault. The past he so desperately wanted to escape had followed him here. Now an innocent child would pay for his sins.

The screams of a hysterical mother only deepened his misery. "Bethany! Bethany!" Two men, one in an apron, the other with a drooping mustache, dragged the woman back into the mercantile.

Gage looked back at the scene and laughed.

A surge of fury bolted through Charlie. He lunged for Gage then seized him by the collar. He pressed his Colt .45 to the outlaw's head. "Let go of your gun. And tell your brother to release the child if you want to live."

Gage growled but soon dropped his shooter. He nodded toward his brother, who lowered the squirming toddler to the ground.

Still gripping the outlaw, Charlie signaled with a jerk of his head toward the faint figures peering through the mercantile windows to come and fetch the child. No one dared. The little blond girl plopped down in the street, howling.

Guilt churned in Charlie's gut. In his selfishness, he'd never thought about what those embezzled guns would do to defenseless people. His sin mocked his new life and his commitment to the Lord.

God, help me. Bolstered by hope, Charlie shifted his captive toward his brothers. "If you get outta here and never come back, I'll release him after sunset."

The men grumbled among themselves.

The child's crying reached an ear-splitting peak.

Sweat dripped down Charlie's back as he clenched Gage tighter.

Gage struggled for a moment then held up his hand. "Go on, ya hear?"

The brothers inched their horses around and headed out of town.

Within ten minutes, Charlie had the toddler returned to the tearful mother, the outlaw locked in jail, and the whole town patting him on the back.

Charlie felt lower than a rattlesnake being grilled on an open fire by the devil himself.

Chapter 3

*W*oolsack. What had she done? In the morning chill, Kate paced the boardwalk outside the sheriff's office. She'd slept on and off for the last five days and was finally feeling like herself—well enough to regret her hasty decision. And well enough to do something about it.

She simply could not marry a man she did not love. And what had possessed her to agree to make such an exceedingly important decision in her deplorable state? Her heart pounded in anticipation of her conversation with a man who obviously had no character. A man who would prey on her momentary weakness.

Although the Gleasons had encouraged the arrangement, this was all the sheriff's fault. How could he presume on their kind hearts and ask an ill woman to become his wife? Now that she had returned to her normal sensibilities, she'd simply have to set him straight.

A babble of conversation drew her gaze. Sheriff Landing was striding toward her down the wooden walkway surrounded by an appallingly large group of wide-eyed women. For a moment, Kate suppressed a laugh at his stiff mouth and sagging shoulders as he endured their high-pitched chatter.

"Ladies, I'll look into your concerns." He cast a desperate look at Kate. "Now please excuse me."

The prattling didn't stop.

He tipped his hat in Kate's direction. A slow grin tugged across his lips as he passed by. "Morning. . .darlin'."

The women ceased talking.

Darling? Kate bristled. If he expected her to cling to his side in adoration like these other prairie women just because he had deftly rescued the town from some gun-toting ruffians, he was in for a dire disappointment. "May I have a word with you?"

<hr>

Frigid air fanned across Charlie's face as they stepped into his chilled office and he shut the door. By Miss Wiltshire's determined stride, he knew the room's icy temperature was due to more than just the fact that the potbellied stove needed stoking.

She whirled around. "I have made a grave error in agreeing to wed you. I don't know you, and I'm sure I could never make you happy. Could we. . .I mean, would you. . .release me from this betrothal?"

A fierce punch hit him in the gut. He tossed his hat onto a rack a few feet away. He had written to his uncle about the engagement and he was arriving tonight. Charlie had to have a compliant fiancée.

The fact that she had a fancy way of talking and a real ladylike manner made his situation look even better. He folded his arms. She wasn't even twenty, a foreigner in a strange country, and she thought she could survive on her own? She needed him as much as a lost sheep needed a shepherd. "I thought you wanted my help."

She marched to his desk and picked up a book. "I was not myself when you proposed to me. And I think it's improper of you to take advantage of me in that way."

"Take advantage? You said your father wanted—"

"Do not bring my dear papa into this."

"Listen, lady"—he clenched his jaw—"I got a lot more on my mind than marriage to some flighty, pretentious English—"

"Flighty?"

He paced over and stood nose to nose with her. "I agreed to marry you to protect you."

"Protect me? So I'm some waif you've taken in?"

"Well, it wasn't because I won you in a card game."

She slammed the book down on his desk. "I wouldn't marry you if you were the last man in Kansas!"

Charlie rubbed his whiskers. Those blazing green eyes of hers and that pink flush on her cheeks sure made an appealing sight. *But right now, cowboy, you'd better win her back.* His head dipped. "I'm sorry. Forgive me. I thought you were all alone in the world. The Gleasons said that you needed my help and that it was your father's idea for you to marry."

Her shoulders wilted. "It was. I promised him I would wed by Christmas."

"Anyone else asking for your hand?"

"No, but I'm certain that—"

"Today is December thirteenth." Hope rising in his chest, he pointed toward a calendar.

She smoothed out the fitted bodice of her dark plum dress and gracefully tucked a loose curl behind her ear. "This has all been most overwhelming."

He shifted his gaze away from her to keep his thoughts upright. God had given him a new heart, and he planned to keep it that way.

Although he'd witnessed her determined personality, fear lurked in her eyes. She needed security and someone to watch over her. And the more he saw of her, the more he was growing used to the idea of being that man. "I can provide for you, lend a hand with finding your father's land, make a home for us."

She quieted down as if weighing his words. Was that a good sign?

He cocked his head. "I did ask nicely."

A tentative smile broke through her reserve. "Oh, I'm dreadfully sorry.

My temper does get the best of me at times." She pulled off her hat and twisted it round and round. "As it was what Papa wanted. . ." As if she suddenly smelled a skunk, her dainty nose tilted regally. "Of course, I would only consider this if it was a marriage in name only."

He ran his fingers through his hair. But at the sight of her slight shoulders and young face, he realized she probably wasn't being snooty—just likely scared. "Sure." *For now.*

"I suppose I must honor my promise. Shall we seal it with a handshake?"

He grinned at her formal nature, but when he allowed his grip to linger, she flushed and paced over to the calendar. Touching the thirteenth day circled in red, she asked, "Is today important?"

His heart thumped once. Hard. "My life depends on it."

Long after the sun had set over the Kansas prairie, Kate admired the parsonage table, with its soft glowing candles surrounded by fragrant pine boughs, and the glistening bone china. It reminded her of formal dinners at home in England. A life destroyed by false accusations against her father. If there was one thing she could not abide, it was untruth.

She glanced over at Charlie as he conversed with Rev. Gleason in the front room. Charlie sported a dark ruby waistcoat with a notched collar. A crisp white shirt, a black string tie, and his lack of holster and guns completed the engaging picture.

And yet her nerves were getting the best of her. The Gleasons were hosting the dinner so she could meet Charlie's uncle. Would Charlie be pleased by her manner and dress? Would she meet his uncle's approval?

With Charlie's dark chestnut hair neatly combed and his face freshly shaved, she found his rugged good looks very. . .compelling. Even if this wasn't a true marriage, at least he was pleasant to look upon.

Mrs. Gleason came into the dining room with her customary bright smile. "I have a surprise for you." She lifted a cover off a dish and held up a pastry. The tangy smell of ginger, cloves, and cinnamon filled the air.

Flush with delight, Kate hugged the older woman. "My mother made mincemeat pie every Christmas."

"One of my dear friends had the recipe. I thought you might like a taste of home."

Tears brimmed in Kate's eyes. It wasn't so much that she missed England but that she missed the feeling of family and security. And for some reason, the thought of no trifle, no small present from someone who truly loved her, dimmed her anticipation of the upcoming holy day. She chided herself for such nonsense and quickly dabbed her eyes lest she spoil Mrs. Gleason's thoughtfulness.

Just then, Charlie and his uncle walked into the dining room. Charlie's face looked flushed. Was he nervous, too?

"Judge Ridgley, I'd like you to have the pleasure of meeting my beautiful fiancée, Katherine Wiltshire."

Kate smiled at such gallant praise. Maybe marriage would be better than she hoped. She shook the silver-haired gentleman's hand. "Lovely to make your acquaintance. Please call me Kate."

"An English lady?" Judge Ridgley sneaked an approving glance at his nephew. "I am very glad to meet you. And yes, Charlie's mother was my sister, but everyone calls me Judge, *especially* Charlie."

Charlie swallowed hard and let his gaze flit to the table.

As Mrs. Gleason refilled the judge's glass and asked about friends who lived in his town, Charlie leaned in toward Kate. His warm breath fanned her neck, and the manly smells of pine, outdoors, and soap consumed her.

Optimism welled in her heart. Could she grow to have affection for this man someday? Looking up into his warm mahogany eyes, she rested her hand on his arm. Surely he wouldn't try to kiss her?

"I need you to appear as if we are in love in front of my uncle," Charlie whispered.

A pang of disappointment welled in her chest. Kate released her grip and adjusted her white, high-necked blouse. What daft notion had taken hold of her? How could his attentions so easily woo her? He was merely playing his part of the lovesick fiancé. With her cheeks flaming, she lifted her chin and resolved to better *his* performance. She'd act absolutely besotted by him. "Of course."

The judge looked between the both of them, his one brow arched as if scrutinizing every move. He glanced above their heads. "Well, would you look at that."

Kate flashed a peek upward at the ball of mistletoe trimmed with ever-green and ribbons hanging over her and Charlie. Heat crept into her face.

Mrs. Gleason clapped her hands. "Kate told me that in England it's called a kissing ball."

Nodding, Judge Ridgley gestured toward Charlie. "Well, aren't you going to kiss her?"

Kate's breath fluttered.

Charlie's eyes widened. "Kiss her?"

She stiffened. The man wasn't in love with her, but he didn't have to act as if kissing her was the last—

Charlie's strong arms wrapped her tight against him. His warm lips smothered her gasp.

It was, for a fleeting moment, as if the world had disappeared. Her heart soared. Her breathing escalated when she returned his embrace with an ardor she hadn't known she possessed.

When Charlie pulled back, her legs felt as weak as buttered toast. Her determination to appear infatuated with him had surely muddled her emotions.

A tender expression filled his gaze before he pulled away. She swallowed. Was it hope? Pining? Shock at her responsiveness? Dazed, she watched as he strutted over to the judge, acting as if he'd just passed some test. Why was the judge's approval so important?

A tinkle of music filled the next room. Mrs. Gleason peered over the piano. "I have another surprise for Kate before dinner."

The tune of "God Rest Ye Merry, Gentlemen" filled the air.

Kate smoothed out her favorite periwinkle blue bodice and nodded at the English carol.

"Kate, will you sing it for us?"

Her mouth dropped open. She couldn't hold a tune even if the Archbishop of Canterbury offered her a basket to carry it in. Her mother had a beautiful voice and had often participated in church choirs, but Kate had always bemoaned her tone deafness. A flaw she was anxious to hide from Charlie. "I–I'm not sure—"

"Oh, forgive me." Mrs. Gleason flipped through her sheet music. "I'm sure this is a difficult time for you. Let's sing an American carol, 'O Little Town of Bethlehem.' "

As Kate mouthed the words, she stole glances at Charlie. His rich tenor voice rang out above the others'. She had many things to learn about this man. At the end of the singing, Rev. Gleason led everyone back into the dining room.

Judge Ridgley gripped Kate's hand and smiled. "I'm mighty glad to meet you, Kath—Kitty—Karen—"

"Kate," Mrs. Gleason and Charlie simultaneously interjected.

The judge nodded. "Kate. The woman who is going to marry my nephew. I just can't believe you agreed to take this scoundrel on."

Kate blinked. *Scoundrel?*

Chapter 4

Charlie stiffened. His hands clenched. Would his uncle betray him? Just when he was sure the jig was up, the judge's roaring laughter filled the dining room. Heaving out a long sigh, Charlie tugged on his tight collar and glanced around the room. How long would he have to dread someone discovering his past? How could he keep Kate believing he was worthy of her hand?

The judge slapped Charlie on his back. "Actually, I very much admire Charlie's strong commitment to the Lord, and although his life hasn't always been easy, I'm sure he'll make an exceptional husband. And I hope, for his sake, those Grisford brothers never come back."

"A hearty amen to that. Now let's eat." Rev. Gleason pulled out a chair for his wife.

The dapper judge also moved out a seat for Kate before sitting beside her.

Sweat beaded Charlie's forehead. Dread still clutched at his insides, until Kate patted the empty seat next to her. "Charlie, dearest, will you sit by me?"

Her smile and twinkling spring green eyes were like a drink of cold water to a parched man. If they hadn't been surrounded by people, he would have been tempted to kiss her again.

"I think we've seen the last of those bumbling bandits," Charlie crowed as he sat, bolstered by Kate's attention.

All those gathered around the table murmured approval and bowed to give thanks for the bountiful table. Soon the aroma of baked chicken and the hum of pleasant conversation passed around.

Charlie leaned back in his chair and enjoyed the savory meal, the lively exchange, and the eye-catching woman next to him. As he had imagined, Rev. Gleason and Judge Ridgley launched into an in-depth biblical discussion. And Mrs. Gleason beamed as Kate threw sweet glances Charlie's way. Touched by Kate's efforts to act the part of an adoring wife-to-be, he held her hand under the table.

She didn't pull away.

After dinner, they all moved to the parlor, and Kate offered everyone a hot cup of her mother's age-old recipe for wassail. Charlie savored its spicy apple cider–like flavor.

A roaring fire heated the room, but what warmed him most was Kate's friendliness during dinner and while they sat on the couch together. She'd touch his hand or lean her shoulder against his. She laughed at everything he said and even complimented his deep red vest.

Judge Ridgley stood in front of the fireplace. "I heard your friend's saddle business has been quite a boon to the economy in Kennedale."

Charlie sipped his drink. "If only we could find more men willing to learn the craft of saddle making to keep up with the orders. Sure would help this town to grow."

"Now that you're the sheriff," Kate said, "surely a town with a reputation for peace and quiet will draw more families here."

Charlie's chest swelled with pride. Maybe the gang of brothers wouldn't come back. Maybe his past would stay in the past. "I've got Diego convinced to stay here for now, but if more craftsmen aren't trained, he may have to move to a larger town."

"You're a smart man, Charlie. You'll come up with a plan." The judge smiled at Kate. "Tell me, dear, what was it about my nephew that made you say yes so quickly to marrying him?"

Kate bit her lower lip as if searching for the right words. "Rev. and Mrs. Gleason told me of his character and what a faithful believer he was. And of course, he so bravely dismissed those dreadful outlaws, and"—she smiled into her cup—"I find him very handsome."

Charlie shifted in his seat. Did the parlor shrink, or had he grown in stature? Never had he heard a woman speak so kindheartedly of him. His mother had been a weak-willed woman, her life consumed by the bottle. He knew Kate was just pretending, but it pleased him that she tried so hard to act the part of a trusting sweetheart.

The judge nodded across the room. "And you, Charlie?"

His mouth went dry. Kate? Memories of her rolled through his mind. Her creamy skin, the brown curls that had slipped loose and lay around her slender neck, the pink flush of her cheeks when she scolded him for asking her to marry him, her trim figure in the prettiest dress he'd ever seen. . . His heart thumped as he realized what a prize she was. A prize that could be easily lost. He'd never tell her about his former life. She'd be so ashamed. "She'll do."

He squirmed in his seat. Was that the best he could come up with? Sneaking a glance at Kate, whose lips were parted in shock, he resisted the urge to punch something. Not good.

⚜

"She'll do?" Kate's throat tightened as she got up from her place next to Charlie and strode to the window, his words playing over in her mind. Her body erect, she stared out at the glittering stars against a sooty sky. Of course, this engagement was nothing more than a practical union of two believing strangers. Her eyes stung with tears. Why had she even considered that it could be something more? A marriage of convenience was all she needed to fulfill her promise to her father. She'd been addled to hope for more.

She took in a deep breath to control her displeasure and the urge to throttle Charlie Landing. Now that she was going to be a wife, she needed to rein in her unruly nature. Her mother had been the model of demure graciousness, but alas, Kate had inherited her grandfather's quick temper. Smoothing back her hair, she turned to face the hushed group and fixed a smile on her lips, determined not to reveal her injured feelings.

"When you get your deed, Kate, what will you and Charlie do?" Mrs. Gleason changed the subject as she handed Kate and Charlie plates of mincemeat pie.

Charlie rubbed the back of his neck. "We should get a return telegram from the land office in Boston tomorrow."

Kate took the plate and sat down, far from Charlie. A tingle of pleasure replaced her earlier disappointment. "I am most anxious to start building a home. Also, I am an avid gardener, and although I've never grown my own vegetables, I am sure flowers and vegetables like the same treatment. I also enjoy decorating, but I feel furniture should always be comfortable and not too formal. We will have horses and a stable and—" She pressed her hand to her lips. "Forgive my blathering."

Judge Ridgley slapped Charlie on the back. "How are you going to pay for these things for your new bride?"

Charlie cleared his throat. "I suppose I'll have to sell some of the land to raise the money."

Kate's fork clattered onto her plate. One thing she would not abide was *his* making decisions about Papa's land. "Sell? Oh no, I couldn't part with one blade of grass. I'm not sure how much property he bought, but it can't be a great deal. And I must have enough for a house and a barn and a paddock."

The room and its occupants fell silent. All that was heard was the ticking of a mantel clock and the crackling and hissing of the fire.

Charlie's eyes narrowed in warning. He set down his plate and pulled Kate to her feet. "If you don't mind, I want to show Kate the new hymnbooks that just arrived at the schoolhouse. I know how much you love to sing, don't you, my dear?"

His insult jabbed at her. Was he making fun of her inability to carry a tune? Her hand trembled as she placed her unfinished pie on the side table. By his insensitivity, obviously he didn't care one whit about her.

Her voice rang as sweet as sugar. "Why, I couldn't think of anything better." She snatched up her wool cloak and stormed outside. The fierce wind made it nearly impossible to open the door to the schoolhouse that also doubled as the church on Sundays. The icy air pierced her cloak, only adding to her cross temper, but once through its double doors and out of the biting current, she found the temperature tolerable.

A rattling shudder echoed throughout the vaulted ceiling. Kate looked upward, alarm heightening her senses. "What is that appalling noise?"

"It sounds rather ominous, but it's just the strong winds blowing through the rafters. I guess this school's pretty old." Charlie leaned back against the closed doors. "Kate, I've agreed to marry you, but I'll not be controlled by you."

She strode up toward the front by the teacher's desk and spun around with arms folded. How could she make him see her land was the last link she had with her family? And that finding it and building a house consumed her every thought? She needed roots, a place to call home. And she wanted to blend into her new country. Why couldn't he understand that? The light of a full moon cast a stark beam of light through a row of upper windows, illuminating his broad shoulders and the square cut of his jaw. What was he thinking? And why did she care?

A slow suspicion stole over her. Was that a guilty look on his face? She'd stake the Queen's bonnet this was all just a business arrangement to him. Most likely, he knew about her land and reasoned it could bring a tidy profit, and that was why he wanted to marry her. A choking sense of betrayal made her head throb. "That is my father's property and I plan on living on it as soon as a house is built."

"After we are married, we might have to leave town. Who knows what might come up? A–and then we might want to have cash on hand to. . ." He ran his fingers through his hair as if struggling to tell her something. "The property and what we do with it will be ours to decide."

Her breathing quickened. Was he threatening her? What would he do if she refused? Did she know him well enough to marry him? She grabbed a candlestick from a table, needing to grip something to control her growing frustration. "Ours? My father bequeathed that land to me before we even met, and I will not part with any of it."

Charlie paced in front of the doors as if wrestling with his conscience. In one breath, he spat out, "The—woman—I—marry—will—just—have—to—trust—me."

She muttered under her breath, "How could I have ever thought he would make a fine husband?" All her hopes and plans were unraveling before her eyes. Bitter disappointment swirled around her. How dare he demean Papa's hopes and dreams. "I am not your wife yet."

"According to your father's wishes, you soon will be."

Her temper flared. "Not if I can help it."

She lobbed the candlestick across the room, and an explosive crash resonated around them.

Kate's mouth opened. She cut a hard look at the other candlestick, still sitting on the table. "What are those made of?"

Suddenly the doors behind Charlie banged open, sending him crashing into the back of a wooden bench.

Five Grisford brothers burst into the room in a gust of wintry air, boots slamming on the planked floors, their guns held high.

Her heart hammering, Kate dashed behind the desk and peeked out.

The shortest of the five brothers strode over and jerked Charlie to his feet. "Sheriff, we got a bone to pick with you."

❧❦❧

Warm blood dripped from Charlie's nose. He swiped it with his sleeve and frantically searched for Kate. He had to protect her. He reached for his guns, only to realize he'd left them at the jail. Not good.

Hands balled into fists, he flew into Gary and knocked him to the ground. Even as he wrestled the outlaw, all he could think about was Kate's beautiful face. And if they laid a finger on her—

A gun fired behind him.

Kate's scream filled the room.

A guttural sound filled Charlie's throat. The need to shield her engulfed him. He threw Gary to the ground and charged toward her cry. Grabbing Kate by the waist, he pulled her into the safety of his arms. "Are you hurt?"

"No." Her hair spilled around her shoulders, and even now, its clean smell captured him. She clung to him and trembled.

"What do you men want?" Charlie panted to catch his breath.

Gage strolled toward them, casually gesturing with his weapon. His brothers must have broken into the jail to set him free. "I see Mr. Lawman's found a fine-looking woman."

Charlie's gut clenched. Kate would hear about his former life. *Don't say it. Don't say it.* "I thought I told you boys never to come back."

Gilroy nodded. "Gage, he did ask nicely."

"So that badge gives you courage?" Gage waved his gun. "You didn't used to be so upright and honest. You're nothing but a thief and an outlaw."

Dread grabbed Charlie by the throat. *Please, please, Kate, don't believe his words.* Kate's grip tightened. "Don't be afraid; I'll protect you," he whispered.

But to his astonishment, Kate squirmed loose, marched a few steps away, and shook her finger in Gage's face. "How dare you insult Sheriff Landing. He is one of the bravest, most honorable men I've become acquainted with. I'm sure you don't even know the meaning of the word *honor*. He is true, industrious, thoughtful, kind, and I'll not stand by and let you demean his character. He asked you to leave, and I suggest you obey or—"

Charlie grabbed Kate, pulling her behind his back. Sweat ran down the sides of his face. This woman would be the end of him.

Surprised by the tongue lashing they'd received from a female with a British accent, the band of brothers stood with guns drooping.

Suddenly a slam thundered though the building like the sound of boots pounding on the roof. Several of the brothers gasped, their jaws hanging open as they surveyed the shadows in the darkened room.

"I'm warning you." Charlie glanced up. "Sounds like the whole town is headed this way. You'd better leave while you have a chance."

Another series of shudders racked the air. Glen's Adam's apple bobbed several times in a row. "Maybe he's right. Maybe we'd better go—"

Gilroy pushed his way through the group. "Before we burn this place down, let's take that purty girl with us."

George leaned back against the far wall, arms folded. "That was my idea," he shouted. "No one ever listens to me."

Ignoring George's words, three of the brothers advanced toward Kate. Desperation spiraled inside of Charlie. His breath heaved in his chest. Suddenly Kate yanked away from his hold. What was that English wildcat up to now?

An inkwell flew through the air and headed straight for George. The smash reverberated off the vaulted ceiling. Black ink covered the gangly teen's head as he slid unconscious to the floor. A pewter pitcher was next, followed by a tumbler.

Without waiting to see what else Kate would do, Charlie snatched her by her hand, burst through the back door, and slammed it shut.

His boots slipped around on the ice, and the tip of his nose burned with cold as he dragged three wooden barrels in front of the door. Moving carefully, he peered around the edge of the building and watched the darkened shapes drape one of the brothers on a waiting horse. As he watched them climb onto their horses and race out of town, relief caused him to release the breath he'd been holding. They were gone. For now.

Kate slid to the ground.

He fell to his knees beside her, gripping her by her arms. "What were you thinking, woman?"

"Thinking?" Her breath blew white. "I was trying to protect you."

"Protect me? I was handling the situation just fine."

"That detestable man had a gun pointed at both of us." Her teeth chattered. "You call that fine?"

"Well, what were you doing?" He helped her to her feet.

"I was negotiating." She struggled to stand and stumbled forward.

He caught her and drew her close, burying his face in her soft hair. Her sweet scent and warm body stirred up feelings he knew he needed to rein in. "You call throwing things negotiating?"

She didn't move away. "Why did he call you a thief and an outlaw?" Her frame shivered as she laid her head on his chest. "I'm sure he was just trying to make you cross. Had you met him before?"

"No, yes. . ." Her nearness was making it hard to form words. His mind whirled. Was she as attracted to him as he was to her? "I've seen him and his brothers before, but that's all over now." His body tensed, hoping she wouldn't ask any more questions. He took her hands and warmed them in his. "The most important thing is that you're safe."

Her quizzical look disappeared, and her eyes filled with tears.

"I was so scared."

He took her into his arms again, savoring the satisfaction of protecting her. "That was scared? I'd hate to see you terrified."

"You were very brave." She wrapped her arms around him. "I just let my temper get away from me occasionally. You know, Papa used to call me his whirling dervish."

He grinned, enjoying the feel of her so close. "Sometimes that dervish side of you comes in handy."

"Oh, I'll have to make a very large donation to Rev. Gleason to pay for the things I've broken."

"I'm sure he'll be glad you saved the schoolhouse from that gang of thieves."

She looked up and smiled. "I think I like you, Charlie Landing."

A rush of affection for this English wildcat flooded his chest. *A gift from God.* The words hit him. God had arranged this marriage as a blessing. But as much as he could see himself falling hard for this lady, he'd have to break the news to her soon. With what the Grisford brothers knew about his past, Kennedale couldn't be home for long.

As soon as they were married, they'd have to leave town.

Chapter 5

Kate sat nestled on the church pew beside Mrs. Gleason and shared a hymnal with Charlie. She couldn't help but smile as his robust voice sounded in her ears. The words to her new favorite hymn, "'Tis So Sweet to Trust in Jesus," challenged her faith. She needed to do what the song said and trust in Jesus more.

Charlie's finger accidentally brushed against hers, and she lost her place in the hymnal. She found it again and continued mouthing the words to the song, as she didn't want her ill-toned voice to distract Charlie from his love of praising the Lord.

She managed a glance behind her and flinched at the ink stain on the wall. But last night, after bandaging Charlie's chin, Mrs. Gleason assured her that Rev. Gleason was not the least bit upset at the damage. In his view, Kate had rescued the building from being burned down by that dreadful gang. A small comfort to her guilty conscience when one of the candlesticks on the table next to the pulpit leaned to one side like a tree in a stiff wind.

The singing over, Rev. Gleason took the pulpit as the congregation sat. He opened his Bible and read, " 'They that trust in the Lord shall be as mount Zion, which cannot be removed, but abideth for ever.' " He closed the good book. "Many of you are not aware that the hymn we sang, ''Tis So Sweet to Trust in Jesus,' was written two years ago by an English-woman, Mrs. Louisa M. R. Stead."

Kate grinned. No wonder she loved that song so much.

"Mrs. Stead wrote it after she watched her husband drown."

Kate's throat clogged with sympathy; she understood the pain of losing someone dear. She pulled a handkerchief from her reticule and dabbed her eyes. Instead of relying on God more after Papa died, she had maintained a distance. And although observing the Gleasons living out their faith had encouraged hers, had she truly learned the meaning of trusting God with her life?

She stole a glance at Charlie. With his daily Bible reading, surely he relied on God to lead him. Charlie's handsome profile sent a tingle down her spine. He would be her husband in a mere week and a half. She swallowed hard. Of course, theirs would be a marriage in name only. Was that best?

She did desire to have children. Panic shot through her—did Charlie want children? She had never asked him that important question. And she still hadn't convinced him of her determination to stay in Kennedale. Anxiety gnawed at her peace until her nerves twisted into a ball of yarn.

Rev. Gleason's words permeated her dark thoughts, convicting her of not paying attention. "Trusting God is never easy, but when you do as scripture encourages you, with all your heart, you'll find He will direct your path."

Kate gripped her hands in her lap. Now that Papa was gone, she would need her heavenly Father's direction even more. *No matter what, Lord, I promise to trust in You with all my heart.*

The congregation stood to sing the final hymn. But just as the music of the piano filled the church, a back door banged opened.

"Fire!"

All heads swiveled to see Ben Watson gasping for air, his face blackened with soot. "My house. Help!" was all he managed before falling to his knees and surrendering to a flood of coughing.

Charlie shouted instructions as he made his way to the door. "Mr. Heelin, bring us some gunny sacks from your store. Mr. Larson, we'll need your iron-work tools to break the ice on Caper Pond. Miss Leemore, bring some of your mother's salve. We'll need it for burns. And everyone, please wear gloves to keep from frostbite."

As he tore out the door, all the menfolk in the church clamored behind him.

Mrs. Gleason clutched Kate's arm. "Has the Grisford Gang struck our town again?"

Kate's throat tightened. Would Charlie be all right?

God was already testing her resolve to trust Him.

❦❧❨

Charlie bit back frustration as yet another hole froze over and the gathering crowd had to wait a few anxious moments while Mr. Larson, the blacksmith, smashed a new opening in the ice. This was Charlie's chance to prove to the townsfolk and himself that he was a good man. In minutes, buckets of frigid water resumed passing from hand to hand, but to Charlie's horror, the blaze roared on.

The Watson homestead was larger than most, as Tim Watson had added many small additions to the original structure. Now raging flames engulfed the entire back of the house, all because of a grease fire.

Mrs. Watson tended to her three small daughters some distance away, their wailing undiminished by the pile of water-damaged goods piled at their feet. The oldest one's smock was covered in soot.

"It's gone." Ben slumped to the ground near Charlie.

The acrid taste of burning timber permeated Charlie's mouth as he passed the next bucket. Compassion caused a lump to form in his throat. "Just part of the house is damaged. Come on, we're still fighting the blaze. We won't give up."

"Sheriff, quick," Diego said.

Charlie handed off the pail of water and ran to the rear of the homestead. Pointing to the first tree in a row of towering pines, Diego shouted over the roar of the fire, "Sparks drifting upward from the back of the house must've lit the top of that tree. I'm worried. Sap can ignite like a powder keg."

Flames leaped into the air, giving off ominous blue-black smoke. Charlie's gaze searched through the tools lying on the ground that the men from the church had brought. He sorted through the pile of picks and shovels until he found an ax.

Gripping the hatchet in his hand, he swung at the base of the flaming pine. He had to get this tree down before the flames scurried like rats to the other ones. But even with gloves, his hands felt raw from the icy water that had soaked them. After a few minutes, he could hardly keep his painful grip steady.

Ben and the men who were helping gathered behind Charlie.

"Be careful where you send this tree," Albert Heelin called out. "Maybe I should—"

"I got it." Charlie shrugged off the warning. He'd run off the Grisford brothers. Now he would save this home, finally proving his worth. Heaving the ax, he kept one eye out for live embers as the tree burned brightly. Finally, a creak sounded.

"Timber!" someone shouted.

For a breathless moment, the tree swayed and then leaned away from the house. But another splintering of wood caused it to shift.

"Look out!" Charlie yanked Albert out of the way. With a *swoosh*, the forty-foot ponderosa pine fell in a shower of sparks. Not backward as Charlie had planned, but to the side, slamming against the earth.

A high-pitched scream split the air.

Charlie rushed toward the sound, with Ben on his heels, to find Ben's little sister, Molly, trapped by one of the yet unburned branches. Panic seized Charlie. Because of the gust of air from the fall, the tree now burned with a sinister intensity.

His heart thumping, Charlie and Ben tried to wrench the screaming child free, but her dress had snagged on a branch. The flames of fire licked the limbs nearest her.

Mrs. Watson seized Charlie's arm. "What've you done?" Her hysterical words were barely discernable. "Y–you must save her."

Guilt engulfed Charlie like a sudden rainstorm. He'd been a curse to this town ever since he'd come. And now another child was paying for his sins. Adrenaline surged though his body. He lifted the smoldering end of the tree. Hot pain scorched through his gloves. The taste of burning flesh filled his mouth.

Ben snatched Molly from a fiery death and returned her to the safety of her mother's arms.

Charlie let go and stumbled backward on legs as weak as twigs. He landed on the frozen ground, hot agony piercing his hands.

"You all right?" Ben called between panting breaths.

Charlie winced at the raw blisters covering his palms where the flames had eaten through his gloves. Maybe he wasn't the man he thought he was. "Not good."

⋙❈⋘

Kate paused her sewing to savor the heavenly scents of cinnamon, cranberry, and apple tarts filling the Gleasons' parlor. The last three days, Ida Leemore's twice-daily visits to Charlie had tempered her enjoyment of adding English touches to the holidays.

Ida's mother, known for her doctoring, had died, but Ida continued the tradition of using her mother's secret healing salve. A recipe she refused to share even with the town's doctor, Neal Hadley.

In the last couple of years, the title of town spinster had been given to Ida. Although somewhat manly and in possession of a rather forward nature, she wasn't dreadful to look upon. The mole on her chin wasn't that large, and the gap in her front teeth was not as wide as the Kansas River, even if Ben Watson claimed it to be true. Was it the look of desperation in Ida's eyes? Or her overt flirting, as if frantic for a husband, that had earned her the ruinous title?

Kate threaded her needle with another strand. How she'd like to write her name on Charlie's forehead so Miss Leemore could clearly see to whom he belonged. Another high-pitched giggle sounded from the Gleasons' dining room—the room that was hard to see from the parlor—where Ida brought her salve to use on Charlie.

Charlie's low voice rumbled back in friendly banter, but Kate couldn't quite make it out. Her efforts to ward off a jealous spirit melted like wax on a candle. She heaved out a sigh as she ripped out the stitches she'd just sewn across the table runner instead of along the edge.

"There, there, dear, pay no mind to her." Mrs. Gleason patted Kate's hand. "In a few days she'll be done with her doctoring and you'll be wed to Charlie."

A wave of trepidation rippled through Kate. Was she truly prepared to do this? Since Charlie had gotten hurt, all the conversations she'd planned to have with him had been put off, as he was in too much pain. She tried as hard as she could to commit to Rev. Gleason's sermon and trust God with all her heart. But now a handsome man was pulling on her emotions, straining her trust that God had everything neat and tidy.

"Kate," Charlie called from the other room.

A giddy sense of happiness filled her as she bounded up from her chair and flitted into the dining room. Her breath caught in her throat at the sight of his chiseled jaw and mahogany-colored eyes. His gaze seemed to swallow her. Was it just her, or had the room become overly warm?

Ida's gaze was riveted to Charlie's hands.

But Charlie held his arms stiffly out from his body. "Miss Leemore tells me—"

"Charlie, please call me Ida. We're friends now."

Kate swept her hands behind her back and made two fists. Her determination to leave her temper behind was already failing. *Lord, please help me hold my tongue.*

"Ida has offered to sing at our wedding." He turned his attention back to Kate as a slow grin spread across his lips.

Kate swallowed hard. His inspection of her made her cheeks flush.

"Ida sings like a bird," he said.

A wave of inadequacy stole Kate's felicity. Was he attracted to Ida? With her broad shoulders and square frame, she certainly was a hard worker.

"When he begged, I couldn't say no. Never have been able to resist the charms of a lawman." Ida's laugh trilled.

Kate's ire loomed.

As if to prove her worth, Ida sang a little song as she tied a cloth around Charlie's palms, leaving his fingers free. A touch that lingered too long as far as Kate could see.

"There, all better." Ida smiled with a gap as wide as the Kansas River.

Charlie stood up, holding his bandaged palms close to his chest. "Thanks, Ida. You sure have a way with hurting people."

A lump formed in Kate's throat. What about the cups of coffee, the baked treats, and the extra pillow tucked at his head she'd provided for him? Surely he was merely trying to behave gentlemanly toward Ida. But indeed, did he have to try so earnestly?

"Just don't know what I'd do without your help, Ida."

Kate bit back a retort. *I know what I'd do with her.* She winced at her unkind thought. *Sorry, God.*

The blond girl stood and took a longing glance at Charlie. She shoved her things in a satchel and, with a defiant glance in Kate's direction, dropped an extra bandage to the floor.

"Let me get that." He knelt to retrieve it.

Ida fell beside him, her shoulder brushing his. "Please allow me. I can't let you hurt yourself. Then I'd have to keep coming back, and I have many other fellows. . .oh, I mean *things* to occupy my time."

"I'm sure you do." As he walked Ida to the door, he gave Kate's arm a squeeze.

Kate paced the floor. By all that's royal, why had he called her in there except to wax eloquent over Ida's talents and abilities? Abilities she didn't have. She wrestled with wanting to share with Charlie how much she'd been drawn to him in deeper ways and yet wanting to storm out and refuse to marry him. But her wedding veil, resting on the buffet table, reminded her that soon she would be Charlie's wife.

The thought made her blush.

And gave her a brilliant idea.

She strode through the kitchen to the front door. Ida and Charlie were still talking. Ida's hand touched his arm.

Anger forced its way past all propriety, and Kate bristled. The nerve of that woman. As soon as Kate threaded her arm through Charlie's, Ida pulled her hand back and her chatter ceased.

Heat flooding her cheeks, Kate stood on tiptoe and planted a kiss on Charlie's warm cheek. "Thank you, Ida, for helping his hands heal in time for our wedding."

Charlie turned his head, but not before she saw him bite back a grin.

Kate set a smile on her lips. "Good day, Ida."

Ida scowled. "Good day, Charlie. Katherine."

"Kate," Kate said, holding her smile until it hurt.

Ida huffed and left, tromping down the road toward home.

With her heart pounding, Kate made her way back to the dining room, picked up her wedding veil, and studied the intricate detail. She heard footsteps behind her.

"What was all that about?" His manly voice sounded firm but amused.

She swung around and allowed her brows to rise. "Pardon?"

A smile played about his lips. "You know what I mean."

"I daresay I have no idea—oh, you mean the kiss?" Her face scorched hot. *Woolsack.* She had to learn to control her temper.

Chapter 6

Leave Kennedale?"

Charlie flinched at the disappointment in Kate's voice. He crinkled the wax paper that held the sandwich she had brought by his office. Sweet Kate. With each act of kindness, he realized more and more the blessing she would be as a wife.

He grinned at the memory of the way Kate reacted to Ida yesterday. Kate sure was a wildcat, but when it came to telling the truth, she'd injure herself before telling a lie. She'd been hurt enough by deceit. He had to get out of Kennedale. It was only a matter of time before the Grisford brothers came back, and who knew what they would reveal this time?

There were just too many reminders of his previous sins in Kansas. His stomach churned at the thought of Kate being disappointed in him. Did she know how much he couldn't stop thinking about her? He never tired of gazing at her green eyes, the lushness of her hair, or the soft skin on her throat.

"Tell me again, why do you want to leave?"

He stood up from his desk and paced the room. "Not until after we are wed, of course. But I've always wanted to see Texas, and if we got a good price for your father's land. . ."

Kate's expression fell.

He hated to see the color drain from her face. This was hard for her to hear, especially since they'd just got the deed in the mail and realized it was prime land just on the edge of town, but he had to protect her good opinion of him.

"I—I thought you agreed to my suggestion that we rent the rooms above Diego's workshop until our house was built," Kate said. "The people of this town admire you. You ran off the Grisford Gang. You helped save most of the Watson homestead. You've made this place peaceful and safe."

If she only knew. Charlie folded his arms as he stared out the barred window that overlooked Main Street and watched the townsfolk going about their business.

He'd never had a home. His mother lived her life for the next drink and often left her children to fend for themselves. By age twelve, he'd run away to Topeka where he did odd jobs, stole food, even spent a few nights in jail. It wasn't until he got in with a couple of men who had a contact at a military fort that he began stealing guns and ammunition. Turned out selling stolen guns was very profitable.

For once, he'd had a decent roof over his head, three hot meals a day, and occasionally was able to bring food to his younger siblings. Although guilt gnawed at him, at the time he was determined to do whatever it took to survive. Kate with her fine ways would never understand that. "I don't want to be a lawman my whole life."

"What do you want to do?"

"I'd like to open a mercantile. I'm good at selling things." He fought a smile at the irony of that statement.

"Why can't you open a store here?"

"Al Heelin. I can't compete with him."

"I'd stake the Queen's bonnet—"

"I think we need to move, and that's that."

"Who's moving?" Ida Leemore stuck her head in his office door.

Kate scowled.

He swallowed a grin at Kate's inability to hide her feelings.

As Ida closed the door, a flurry of white flew in behind her. "I hear down at the mercantile, because of the severe weather we've had, the train from Topeka is expected to be closed till after Christmas."

"Come by the stove and get warm." Charlie pulled out a chair with his foot.

"Oh, thank you." Ida swished her skirt and fiddled with her cloak tie. "Oh, I can't get it undone. Charlie, would you be willing to help a woman in distress?"

A laugh welled in his throat as he felt icy daggers shooting from Kate's gaze, and he didn't blame her. Ida sure was putting on quite a show. He grappled awkwardly with the frozen strings and they untangled within a second.

Kate rubbed her arms and looked out the window. "In England, we don't get this much snow. How long will it last?"

"A couple of months." Charlie sat in front of Ida.

Ida pulled out her salve and bandaging supplies from her reticule. "Kate, have you ever thought of moving back to England?"

Kate's lips went white, a sure sign her hackles were raised. "I'd love to bring Charlie and our children to England one day, but we have no plans to go back presently."

Children? A bolt of alarm rang through him. Sweat broke out on his forehead. He shoved his bandaged palms at Ida, desperate to shift his thoughts. "My hands are feeling much better."

"That's because hometown gals know how to take care of hometown men." The steely desperation in Ida's gray eyes unnerved him. "Oh, I nearly forgot." Ida dug in her satchel. "When I told Mr. Heelin I was headed this way, he asked me to bring you this letter." She squinted at the cursive writing. "Oh, it's for Katherine—Kate—from an Ernest Ridgley."

Kate took the missive and looked at Charlie.

Charlie stilled. Why would his uncle be writing to Kate? Surely he would never reveal any details about his past. A sense of foreboding swept over him. His mouth felt as dry as tumbleweed.

Both women stared at him.

A sudden chuckle flew out of his mouth. He snatched the letter from Kate's hand with his fingertips. "It's a wedding gift, of course." He ripped the envelope open and a piece of paper slid to the floor.

As Kate retrieved the sheet, it flipped open. The legal document had CHARGES DISMISSED stamped in red. Kate's brow furrowed.

The inquiring look Charlie had long dreaded passed over her face.

"What charges?" she finally asked.

He had to get her out of Kennedale. . .fast.

＊＊＊

Kate's punch glass dribbled a few scarlet drops onto the wooden floor at the church Christmas potluck dinner. Two days until the wedding, and she was as nervous as a fox in a foxhunt. Although the tempting aromas of fried chicken, biscuits, and peach cobbler filled the room, her nervousness would never allow her to eat. She dabbed the spill with her handkerchief as her gaze searched anxiously for Charlie.

He'd said very little to her after he'd opened that letter, except that he had some praying to do and that she shouldn't believe everything she read. Of course, the correspondence was from his uncle, Judge Ridgley, a good man, but what had Charlie so perturbed?

There were so many things to discuss before the wedding. Surely if they could talk tonight, she could make him see the benefits of staying in Kennedale, he could explain that document, and she could share with him that she didn't want this marriage to be in name only. Before she lost her nerve. Moisture broke out on her forehead just thinking about it.

After much prayer, she knew in her heart that marrying Charlie was the right decision. But these unresolved issues still nagged at her. She hummed a few bars of "'Tis So Sweet to Trust in Jesus." That was exactly what she needed to do—entrust her worries to the Lord.

If only Papa could have seen how well things had turned out. . . Her gaze drifted over to Mrs. Gleason, who was teaching a little girl how to play the piano. The tinkle of "Jingle Bells" rang through the church. Ben Watson chatted with one of the Heelin girls, and Rev. Gleason laid his hand on Tim Watson's shoulder as the two men prayed.

How could Charlie consider leaving these wonderful people? And where was he? She'd knitted him a scarf as a Christmas present and was anxious to give it to him.

A flash of blond caught her eye. Ida Leemore was pulling Charlie from the church entrance to a supply room. Charlie followed behind her, pulling off his hat and gloves.

Setting her punch down, Kate maneuvered in the direction of their voices. She pressed her back to the wall and leaned toward the open door. Eavesdropping wasn't exactly a ladylike pursuit, but if she was going to be Charlie's wife, wasn't it a good idea to know everything about him? Their low murmurs were hard to hear. What would Ida have to confide in Charlie? Or was it the other way round? Either way, she wasn't budging.

Ida set her candle down and took Charlie's hands in hers. "I just wanted to see my fine work."

Her touch felt like a firebrand. Charlie stepped back. "I don't think it's appropriate—"

"It's just that I had pinned my hopes on you."

Panic swirled in Charlie's gut. "Me? For what?"

"A husband."

The small room, not much more than a closet, felt as if it was closing in. He'd come here tonight to talk to Kate. While he wasn't ready to divulge his past to her—probably never would be—he needed to let her know he was falling in love with her. To him, this was no longer a marriage of convenience.

But now this poor ungainly girl, who had run off every man who showed the slightest interest in her by her brash disposition, had her sights set on him? Not good. "Look, you don't know what you're saying."

"Surely you're fond of me. I've seen how you gaze at me. How complimentary you've been about my treatments."

"I–I've praised your work. I appreciate how you've tended—"

"Exactly. I can look after your needs. That English girl doesn't understand life on the prairie. You need me."

A sick feeling twisted in his gut. He cut a glance at the open door, hoping no one overheard this awkward conversation. Millions of words defending his sweet Kate sprang to his lips, but what good would it do to throw them in Ida's face? "I'm glad you think so highly of me, but my mind's made up about her."

"It is? Well, how'd you like me to tell that English snippet the truth about who you really are?" She leaned in and whispered, "Gun-Toting Charlie."

Shock bolted through him. "How did you—"

"It doesn't matter." Her hands gripped his arms. "I've admired you for so long. I know I could be a good wife to you. I can sing and mend people and work real hard. That English missy won't have anything to do with you once she finds out you-know-what." She drew closer and lowered her voice. "I know how to keep secrets."

His mouth went dry. She was right about Kate. His stomach tightened, and his thoughts whirled. The closet had become so hot and stuffy he could hardly breathe. He had to get out of there. "I should go."

"I'm tired of waiting. I don't want to be known as the Spinster of Kennedale. I'm only thirty-two. Please, Charlie, I know I could make you happy."

He headed for the open door but whipped around. "Don't speak of this to anyone." *Especially Kate.*

"Will you. . .marry me?"

His heart pounded. "I'll think about it."

Chapter 7

What is there to think about? Kate's breath caught in her throat. She had been looking forward to telling Charlie how much she'd grown to care for him. Now she wanted to throttle the man.

Not wanting to hear more, she scurried away from the door, her body trembling with emotion. Confused more than ever, she needed to get away from the church gathering to pray. As she slipped on her cloak, the tears flooding her eyes made it difficult to fasten the buttons.

Hot betrayal prickled her scalp. How could Charlie do this to her? How could he even consider marrying another woman? Her head throbbed with turmoil. Charlie cared for her, didn't he? "Oh Lord, I thought You wanted me to marry him."

She stepped out into the frigid air, the cold cooling her racing thoughts. Her steps crunched on the heavy snow that had blown onto the wooden boardwalk. She had to seek the Lord so she could sort out what to do next. As she walked with only the moonlight for company, a dark shadow scurried across the street. Followed by another, then another. Must be the Heelin boys playing around.

As she stood in front of Doc Hadley's storefront, a freezing wind gusted past her. Shivering, she pulled up the collar on her wool cloak and shoved her hat farther down over her ears. A fuming heat flushed her face. If she could just get her hands on Charlie—

A scuffle of footsteps sounded behind her. If that was Charlie coming to apologize—

A leathery hand clamped over her mouth. Her heart raced. "It's the purty girl." A man lifted her off her feet and dragged her into a snow-filled alleyway. She'd bet the Queen's bonnet it was the Grisford brothers.

⊷⊷⊷

His palms sweaty, Charlie washed down another swig of teeth-jarring, oversweet punch. His gaze, hungry for the sight of Kate, roved over the folks gathered at the church. He'd grown to love his English wildcat. Where was she? He had to find her before she got wind of his failings.

Before he'd come to the party, he'd spoken again with Rev. Gleason, who assured him all men had pasts they were ashamed of but God buried their sins as far as the east is from the west. Never having been east, Charlie took comfort in how far away that was. But even after they prayed together, he couldn't shake the notion that he needed to redeem his mistakes before he could ask

God to completely forgive him.

He kept trying to shove down his remorse. He desperately wanted to please Kate. Live on her father's small parcel of land. Approach Mr. Heelin, who was getting on in years, and maybe buy out his store. But Ida's icy words came back to haunt him. *That English missy won't have anything to do with you.*

It was gut-twistingly true.

His jaw clenched, he set down his drink. Time to find Kate. Time to tell her the truth—even if it killed him. When she broke off their wedding plans, it surely would. Maybe then he could finally rid himself of this condemnation.

As he dug for his gloves in his pockets and found them missing, he noticed Ida Leemore surrounded by a passel of women in rabid conversation. In a desperate move to keep from hurting her, he'd told her he'd consider her proposal, but as quickly as he'd said it, he'd told her no. He wasn't a man to wed at gunpoint.

Had Ida already told the women his secrets?

The women giggled.

Ida returned his gaze with a triumphant glare.

The jig was up.

❈

Kate looked up at the four Grisford brothers. "If you hurt me, I'll scream."

The tall one leaned in and squinted at her. "Yup, she's the sheriff's woman."

Kate struggled to stand, her nerves tightening into a knot. Would they take out their hatred for Charlie on her? She was in a grievous situation. Her very life could be at stake. She pressed her eyes shut. *Lord, I know I'm not very good at trusting You, but if You help me—*

"Look, missy, we ain't here to pester you. You know who we are. I'm Gage, and this here is Gilroy, Glen, and George. We got a brother, Gary, who's been throwing up, and now he's fevered and acting confused-like. He needs fixin', and we don't know how to do that."

A bubble of hysterical laughter rose in her throat. She wanted to exclaim neither did she but thought better of it. Her mind raced. Surely if she delayed long enough, someone would come looking for her. "I'm Miss Katherine Wiltshire."

She wanted to tell them she was far from the sheriff's woman but pressed her lips shut. Perhaps not the best time to bring up his name. "You'll have to tell me your brother's symptoms in great detail."

Gilroy snatched off his hat and offered her a wide grin. "Well, ma'am, he's got sunken eyes and won't drink nothing."

George elbowed his way in front of his brother. "And he complains a lot."

The brothers groaned.

"What?" George stuck his thumbs in his gun holster. "She asked for his symptoms."

Kate glanced around to see if anyone was coming to her aid. "Oh yes," she stalled, "complaining can be a wretched problem. What does he complain about?"

"Well"—George blew on his hands—"his headaches, my cooking, and his cold hands and feet—"

"Shut your trap." Glen punched his brother's arm. "We're wasting our time. Let's mount up and get outta here."

"We don't get to burn no building? I like fire." Gilroy snickered.

Firm steps sounded down the walkway.

Hope lodged in Kate's throat. Charlie?

Gage pulled out his gun.

Before she could scream a warning, Glen clapped his hand on her mouth and dragged her through the snow and out the rear of the alley.

A row of five horses tied to a stand waited patiently. They forced her onto a horse and led her away, Kennedale disappearing behind her like a mist.

After about fifteen minutes of hard riding, they came upon a house made out of sod. Snowdrifts nearly covered one side. A glow from a fire inside revealed a long moaning form wrapped in a blanket.

Kate's toes curled up in her boots. Her nursing abilities were appalling. She couldn't even save her own papa.

Gage pointed a finger in her face. "Now get to fixin' him. If he dies, we'll have to kill you."

"Now, Gage"—Gilroy slapped his hat on his knee—"that ain't nice-like. This is a proper lady you're talking to."

Terror tightened her throat. She pulled back on the foul blanket wrapped around the sick man. His face lay as white as the snow on the ground outside, and the gray tinge about his lips hinted at the shadow of death. She pinched his cheek. The skin didn't go back in place. *Oh Lord, please don't let him die.*

With no idea what to do, she rummaged through their few stores of goods and sprinkled a bit of sugar and salt into a canteen of water, something her mother used to do when Kate had been ill. She took the flask and held it to the man's lips. At first he refused; then he drank greedily, until it dribbled down the sides of his cheeks. She waited a few minutes and gave him more.

The psalm she'd read this morning flitted through her mind. How did it end? *"Surely goodness and mercy shall follow me all the days of my life. . . ."*

Kate sighed as she offered the man more liquid. Charlie wished to marry another woman, and now her existence was in peril. *Lord, if You think this is goodness and mercy—*

"Aren't you gonna do something fancy for him?" George asked.

"Quiet, please, I'm praying." *Lord, I fear I may meet You soon if You do not aid me.* The words " 'Tis so sweet to trust in Jesus. . . ." rang in her spirit. Desperation balled her hands into fists. She set her hands on her hips. "I am trying to, Lord."

"You're trying to what?" Glen asked.

Kate startled. "I'm. . ." She snatched the canteen and leaned in to give the sick man more water. "I was asking God for help."

George's gaze fell. "He don't hear too well out here."

Gilroy nodded. "Gage says we've made Him too mad."

"Oh, God is always listening, and He loves you." Kate fixed the cap on the canteen.

Gage spit on the ground. "No one ain't loved us since our ma died."

"I'm sorry. But all you need is to get to know your heavenly Father. One just has to. . ." A light dawned in her mind. The words to her favorite hymn played in her head. "You have to 'rest upon His promise.' "

"What promise?" Gilroy asked.

What she had been missing all along. "That His grace, and not your own, will see you through." She stood.

"Huh?" Gilroy scratched his head.

Kate gazed at her captors. Each one appeared riveted to her words. The fear-etched lines on their faces, slumped shoulders, and dark circles under their eyes told of their desperate need for a Savior.

She took in a fortifying breath. "We will pray together. Repeat after me."

"Repeat after me," Gilroy said.

Gage hit him on the head. "Not yet. She ain't started yet. Continue on, miss."

"To know God, you must first ask Jesus into your heart."

"Our ma taught us that when we was children," Glen said.

They continued to stare. She nervously licked her dry lips. "Then it appears you need to repent of your wretched ways and ask Him to forgive you."

The brothers took off their cowboy hats and nodded for her to start.

Clutching her hands to keep them from shaking, Kate led them in a prayer of repentance.

Once they finished, Glen knelt down and checked on Gary. "He shore is sleeping peacefully. I guess the Lord did hear us."

Kate bent over, noticing that Gary's face looked brighter. A rush of gratitude flooded her heart. *Thank You, Lord. Now if You could work on that maddening Charlie Landing. . .*

Gilroy scratched his head and set his cowboy hat back in place. "I know we said we'd return her, but if she was agreeable, she could marry one of us."

Kate straightened up. By the childlike expressions on their faces, she knew she had to be careful with their fragile faith. She wagged a finger. "Thank you for your kind offer, but I must decline. Now that you're Christians, you lads must live in ways that please God. No more riding into town and shooting your guns."

The brothers groaned.

"No more burning down buildings."

A grumble rolled through the air.

"No more drinking."

"Our ma'd never let us drink," Gilroy said. "Gage just splashes it on himself to smell mean."

"Don't tell." Gage threw his hat on the ground.

"And you must become men of your word, which means you must take me back to town." She bit her lip, hoping her boldness would convince them.

"But what are we gonna do? Stealing guns and selling them to the Indians is all we've ever known." Gage snatched up his hat from the dirt-covered floor.

Kate's stomach clenched. "Indians? Around here?"

"Pawnee and Osage mostly." Glen shrugged. "Just over yonder beyond the ridge we passed on our way in. I stopped and asked Great Wolf to come to see if he could help Gary."

"I don't think we need Indians, really. I'm sure prayer and more water. . ." Her voice died at the sight of three savages standing in the opening to the sod house.

The light of the flickering fire revealed their partially shaved heads that boasted narrow ridges of hair down the middle. Their beaded earrings and some sort of quills weaved into their animal skin garments took on an ominous glow.

Kate's legs gave way, and she wilted neatly to the ground.

⸎

Charlie paced down the snow-covered walkway, his gut raw with emotion. He wiped off some snow on the bench outside the jail and folded onto it. The spot where he first laid eyes on Kate.

His breath came out in white puffs against the cold air. The bitter wind only added to his misery. He held his head in his hands. What was he doing thinking he could live an ordinary life? Marry such a fine girl? It was wrong. All wrong. He didn't deserve such happiness.

"Sheriff?"

Charlie looked up to see Ben Watson. Yet another person he'd let down. "What are you doing here?"

"I came by to tell you Miss Leemore's telling everyone at the church supper some mighty wild tales about you that I know aren't true."

"Well, how do you know they aren't?" His voice came out sharper than he'd intended. For the first time in a long time, moisture dampened his eyes.

Ben shifted his feet. "I just. . . My father says you can tell a lot about a man's character by the way he worships on a Sunday."

"Your father's wrong." Charlie stood, pulled off his badge, and pinned it on Ben. "Go back to the church and tell him they're all true."

With resignation like two sacks of wheat settling onto his shoulders, Charlie trudged into his dark office, lit a lamp, and quickly scribbled two notes. One to Rev. Gleason, explaining why he was leaving. And one to Kate, telling her the truth about his past. It was time he faced up to his charges. He would pin the notes to the church door and then go back to Topeka to turn himself in.

Chapter 8

"Thank you kindly." Kate took Gage's outstretched hand and slid off the horse in front of the church. Her numb fingers touched the rag tied around her forehead. "You were most kind to help stop the bleeding."

"Great Wolf shore was gentle with you when you fainted and clonked your head." Gage slid off his hat.

Kate swallowed hard and smoothed her hair once again, ensuring it was still there. Great Wolf's men had been exceedingly kind. And when she complimented their eardrops, she'd bet the Queen's bonnet they blushed. "Do continue to give Gary the special water I mixed up. God will pull him through." *Like He pulled me through. Thank You, Lord.*

The burden of facing Charlie and possibly calling off their wedding lay as heavy as a blanket of ice and snow. *Lord, now what do I do?* She closed her eyes as the presence of God comforted her with a reminder that His grace would see her through. When she opened her eyes, the Grisford brothers stood around her as if unsure what to do.

She blinked at the lights still streaming from the sanctuary windows. It was surely past eight o'clock, and the Christmas dinner was still going on? Her stomach fluttering, she hastened toward the church doors. "I'll see you next Sunday in church."

Gage stepped forward, his hat gripped in his hands. "You think the reverend will allow us to come?"

She paused. "There may need to be some restitution for the hotel you burnt down, but I'm sure Rev. Gleason and the whole town will welcome you to your new way of life."

"Well, thank you, ma'am. . .er, Miss Katherine."

"Now that we are friends, I prefer to be called Kate."

"Me and my brothers," George said, standing next to Gage, "we've talked about your idea about us learning the saddle-making trade, and we think it's a mighty fine notion."

"That will be lovely. I'll inform Mr. Muntavo to expect you on Monday morning."

The brothers climbed onto their horses and tipped their hats in a gentlemanly manner as they left. Pleased but exhausted, she yawned. She couldn't take one more misfortune. As she turned back toward the church and went through the first set of doors, two pieces of paper pinned to the door fluttered away in a gust of wind into the darkness. She pulled open the second door but halted at the sounds of shouting. In the middle of the room stood Rev. Gleason, Mr. Watson, Mr. Larson, Mr. and Mrs. Heelin, Ben Watson, and Ida Leemore, all speaking at the same time.

"Now we know the truth about why he came here." Mr. Larson's bushy white eyebrows furrowed in anger.

"I'm glad he left town. We don't need any outlaws hiding among us." Ida pulled on her wool cape.

"But he was a good sheriff." Ben stomped his boot.

"He helped save our home," Mr. Watson said.

Rev. Gleason held up his hand to silence the room. "All I know is Charlie Landing is a forgiven man. Let him who is without sin cast the first stone."

Kate pushed her way through the gathering. "What do you mean? What has Charlie done?"

Ben scurried up to her. "Miss Katherine—"

"Kate," the church members chimed in.

"Oh dear, no need to do that," Kate protested.

Rev. Gleason stood beside her. "You're one of us now, and we'll call you by your American name."

Ben nodded. "Kate, what happened to your head?"

"It's nothing. What happened to Charlie?" Kate pulled off the cloth wrapped around her forehead.

Ida's lips puckered with satisfaction. "He's gone back to Topeka. Concerned about the safety of our town, I told everyone what I'd learned—that he used to steal guns and sell them to the Grisford brothers. That's why they kept coming back here."

"No, it can't be." Kate's thoughts spun. The words "two-bit gun thief" floated back to her. But Charlie would never hide the truth from her. Untruths had destroyed her and her father's lives. A bitter sense of treachery welled in her throat.

Ida sniffed with a look of smug satisfaction.

Kate stared back at her. "You wanted Charlie to marry you. You begged him to. I heard you ask him in the church closet."

Ida's face blanched. "I—I didn't know. . .You were there?"

Mrs. Gleason patted Kate's arm. "My dear, understandably you're upset."

Kate shot a glance between Ida and Mrs. Gleason. "No, I heard her ask him, and he agreed to consider it."

"Agreed? That two-faced scoundrel changed his mind as soon as he said it." Ida flushed. "I mean—"

"Charlie's gone to turn himself in." Mrs. Gleason's gaze fell. "I'm afraid the charges on that document from Judge Ridgley were true."

Kate's jaw dropped open. "And he left without telling me?"

Mrs. Gleason leaned in. "You'll just have to make your home with us."

Home. The word still filled Kate with longing. But a longing for what?

Her father's land? Four walls? Without Charlie, it meant nothing.

"Perhaps we'd better head back to the parsonage, dear." Rev. Gleason gestured toward the door.

Mr. Heelin stopped in front of Kate. "Now I know why he was so anxious for me to buy your father's land. He wanted money to get out of town. 'Course, I couldn't buy it. I'm retiring soon."

Kate's mind clicked with revelations faster than a telegraph machine. Papa's land. Charlie wanting to leave Kennedale. His dedication to reading his Bible. His love of hymn singing. His love of her. She stepped away from the group, wanting to sort out her thoughts.

Charlie was a redeemed man still burdened by his past.

She spun around. "While he may not have revealed all of his history to me, I know that he is a good man." A glimpse of the Bible resting on the pulpit caught Kate's eye. "Reverend, you said, in your sermon this Sunday past, " 'They that trust in the Lord shall be as mount Zion, which cannot be removed, but abideth for ever.'"

He nodded.

"I'll not be moved. My place is with Charlie." A warm glow filled her. *I love him.*

Ben rubbed his hand over his mouth. "But the train. . .snow's closed the rails to Topeka. They'll not open till next week."

"Then I'll have to find someone who can take me," Kate said.

Mrs. Gleason touched her shoulder. "Be reasonable, dear."

Ida folded her arms. "Someone would have to be a fool to travel in this weather."

Lifting her chin, Kate replied, "I know just who to ask."

Chapter 9

"You want to go where?" Gilroy Grisford's morning mug of coffee tumbled out of his hand and nearly put out the campfire.

"Topeka. Now please rouse some of your brothers and take me." She stood outside the sod house and gestured behind her. "I have a wagon and fresh horses. It can't be that far."

Gilroy scratched his head. "In heavy snow it's near impossible to find the trail."

"Maybe Great Wolf can lend a hand." Gary stood behind his brother and pulled his blanket around his shoulders.

"Gary, you're better." A warm sense of relief eased the tension in her shoulders.

"Yes, ma'am." A slow smile spread across his face. "Better in body and soul. Now about my Indian friend. . ."

"Indians? Again?" Kate swallowed, her nerves returning.

"They're the only ones who can follow a route in this weather."

"Woolsack."

Charlie paced in front of the smoky fireplace in his uncle's guest room. "I don't understand. How can the court claim insufficient evidence? I'll give them all the evidence they need."

His uncle grinned. "It's the way the law works. I'm sorry, Charlie, but you're a free man. That's why I sent that document to your wife-to-be. All along, I assumed you'd told her. I thought it would be a relief to her."

Charlie swallowed the bitter taste of smoldering wood in his mouth. Sweet Kate. What would she do now? Who would protect her? Even the thought of another man standing beside her sent daggers of pain into his chest. He slammed his fist on the table. "You don't understand how my sin weighs on me."

"We're all sinners."

"Innocent people have been hurt by my deeds."

"God has given you a free gift of forgiveness. Accept it."

Misery stole over Charlie like a cold draft. He understood what his uncle was saying, but he couldn't let go. The swindling, the stealing, the lying, the greed that loomed over him like a shadow. . . "I can't."

"You mean won't."

"Won't?"

"Jesus paid an awfully high price for you to toss it aside." His uncle opened the door. "You'd better think on that, son."

An opening and shutting of doors and raised voices sounded downstairs. Uncle Ridgley had sent a message to his pastor to come, but Charlie wasn't in the mood for more words. Steps alerted him to someone coming up the stairs.

He stared at his clenched fists. "Go away."

"If you think I'm leaving, Charlie Landing, you have yet to understand British women."

Kate. Feelings of hope, joy, and relief fought for space in his chest. His mouth opened, but no words came out. He shot to his feet and flung open the door. "What are you doing here?"

"We have a wedding to attend to."

"A wedding?" For a moment, his mind went blank.

"Our wedding? Christmas Eve? My promise to my father?"

Guilt snatched his fleeting happiness away. "He didn't want you to marry an outlaw."

Kate strode into the room. "According to your uncle, the court has declared you innocent."

"I'm not innocent." Charlie ran a hand over his lips. "And I no longer have a job or a town to call home."

"But the people of Kennedale love you."

"Hah. I couldn't save the Watsons' home. Diego was counting on me to find more men to learn saddle making, and now you know why the Grisford brothers kept coming back, and they will continue until—"

"It's all taken care of."

"What's taken care of?"

"Mr. Heelin is retiring so you can open your store, and I've spent time with the Grisford brothers and they are new men."

This woman would be the end of him. "If those bandits hurt you in any way—"

"They've repented and accepted God's forgiveness, and they want to learn the saddle-making trade—all five of them. Now if I could just get them to bathe."

Charlie ran his fingers through his hair. "You told the Grisford brothers about God? Did they come into town?"

"No, they kidnapped me."

He startled. "Kidnapped?"

"Their brother was very ill, and they wanted my help. So I mixed up a special drink for Gary and told them all about their need for repentance. They readily accepted God's grace."

Grace. A light seeped into his being. God had redeemed the five brothers. Why couldn't he accept it, too? "They didn't hurt you?"

"No, and they brought me here along with Rev. and Mrs. Gleason and three of their Indian friends."

"I thought you were terrified of Indians."

"I was until I decided to trust in Jesus. Did you know there is a large group of people downstairs waiting for us?"

"For what?"

"To get married."

His condemned heart lay heavy with guilt. He shook his head. Although not wanted by the law, he was an outlaw and a thief, and he'd not ruin her life by giving her his name. "I've changed my mind."

She flinched. "Deplorable situation you've gotten yourself into, but you've promised to marry me."

Dread weighed his gut. "I'm no good for you."

Her quivering lower lip betrayed her ramrod-straight posture. "But, Charlie. . ."

"Please leave." He led her to the door and shut it behind her. Desolation clutched at his insides as he rested his head on the door. Tears welled. He'd just closed the door on the most wonderful woman. His gift from God. But he wasn't worthy enough to receive it.

My grace. The words floated across his mind. He ran his trembling hand over his mouth, trying to swallow back his engulfing emotions.

Suddenly a warbling sound, akin to two cats fighting, rang out behind his door.

> *'Tis so sweet to trust in Jesus,*
> *Just to take Him at His word.*

The voice screeched and squawked, fluctuating up and down.

> *Just to rest upon His promise*
> *And to know, "Thus saith the Lord."*

Who was making that awful noise? He jerked open the door.

Kate's eyes were clamped shut, her head thrown back, her mouth wide open.

> *Jesus, Jesus, how I trust Him!*
> *How I've proved Him o'er and o'er.*
> *Jesus, Jesus, precious Jesus!*
> *Oh, for grace to trust Him more!*

Grace. The word tugged again at his heart. His love for Kate overwhelmed him, and he pulled her into his arms as sobs racked his body. "I want to, sweet Kate. I want to."

She wrapped her arms around him. "Can't you accept God's unearned favor like the Grisford brothers have?"

Charlie crumpled to the floor, his face buried in his hands with Kate beside him. "I don't deserve it."

"None of us do. It's a gift." She laid her cheek against his arm.

Hope flickered in his heart. "Lord, I need You," was all he could manage. He sat up and held Kate's face. Several moments passed in silence as he worked to collect himself. "It's His grace, isn't it," he said, his voice trembling, "that helps a man forgive himself?"

"Yes."

He kissed her lips. Her broad smile warmed his heart.

Lord, I've been a fool. Thank You for Your grace that throws my sins as far as the east is from the west. And thank You for Kate, my sweet Kate.

"Does this mean you'll marry me before the sun sets?" Kate blurted out.

He studied the messy curls sprung loose from her bun and the look of tired excitement in her green eyes. He loved her. His English wildcat. "Yes, my sweet Kate."

⁂

Christmas Eve night had come, and through the parlor window, stars flickered like candles in the night sky. Light snow fell like clumps of soft sugar, and the pleasant harmony of carolers walking the streets rang in the air.

Kate smiled with warmth at those who gathered in the room, witnessing her and Charlie's vows. Rev. and Mrs. Gleason, four swarthy brothers, one still pale brother who had insisted on coming, three Indians, a local pastor and his wife, and one uncle.

Charlie leaned in. His eyes shone vibrantly as only a redeemed man's can. "I guess this means we're staying in Kennedale."

Joy welled in her throat. She glanced at Uncle Ridgley, who'd just finished preaching the wedding sermon. She couldn't believe all that God had done for her. More than just finding a husband, she had found a home.

Charlie nudged her.

"Oh, I do," she said.

The judge smiled. "I pronounce you man and wife. Charlie, you may kiss Katherine—"

Charlie held up his hand. "If you don't mind, I'd like to kiss Kate, my bride and now my wife."

He pressed his lips to hers.

Her heart welling with joy, Kate responded, delighted with her Christmas gift from God.

Angels in the Snow

by Colleen L. Reece

When I consider thy heavens, the work of thy fingers, the moon and the stars, which thou hast ordained; What is man, that thou art mindful of him? and the son of man, that thou visitest him? For thou hast made him a little lower than the angels, and hast crowned him with glory and honour.
PSALM 8:3–5

Prologue

. . .a bird of the air shall carry the voice,
and that which hath wings shall tell the matter.
ECCLESIASTES 10:20

Wyoming Territory in the late 1880s

No one knew where it started. Some said the mysterious stranger who rode into Jubilee and quickly passed on through brought the news. Others believed it came from the East, passed person-to-person over the shining, silver Union Pacific Railroad tracks from Cheyenne to Rock Springs that turned blood-red in the sweltering sun, then traveled northwest to the Teton Valley by stagecoach. The more fanciful maintained hundreds of golden-leafed cottonwoods and aspens avidly whispered the news to one another each time the autumn wind blew.

No one knew where it started, but young and old agreed: it was one of the most important messages the town had received since learning of the Little Bighorn Massacre in 1876. Before nightfall, every Jubilee inhabitant, except those sleeping in the cemetery next to the town's only church, had heard the news: Matthew Coulter was coming home.

Matt Coulter: unsurpassed in western Wyoming at riding, roping, shooting.

Matt Coulter: driven from Jubilee in disgrace seven years earlier.

Matt Coulter: bright-haired cowboy with a smile like an angel.

The young man had not been smiling that long-ago day. Blue hatred flashed from his eyes at his accuser, Jedediah Talbot, before Matt fixed his piercing gaze on the judge who had been imported for the trial. The wizened man pounded a gavel on a small table in the saloon-turned-courtroom, then gestured out the window to the towering Teton Mountains.

"See those shadows?" he barked. "Take a good look. If any man of you has the slightest shadow of doubt that Matthew Coulter rustled this man's cattle from the Lazy T, there will be no hanging." He slammed the gavel down again.

His charge had an effect. In spite of some fairly convincing evidence, the twelve men were either unable or unwilling to convict Matt. They returned a startling verdict, especially since the accused said nothing in his own defense except for the single quiet statement, "I never stole a head of cattle in my life."

"More than I can say for some in this room," Sheriff McVeigh, the

401

grizzled, long-term keeper of the peace in Jubilee and Matt's best friend, called.

Guffaws and titters greeted his remark. They were quickly silenced by a third heavy thud of the gavel and a sheriff-directed glare from the judge.

An hour later, the jury shuffled in from a back room where they had been deliberating. "We ain't sure whether he's guilty or not," the foreman flatly stated. He carefully avoided looking at Matt. "Because of that, we ain't goin' to hang Matt Coulter." He scratched his head and sighed. "However, things bein' what they are, we'd like to suggest for him to mosey on."

"Since you haven't found him guilty, he can do as he pleases," the judge snapped. "Case dismissed." He lifted his creaking bones from his chair and strode from the room. A loudly protesting Jed Talbot tailed him.

After a few awkward moments, Matt followed. The curious crowd surged through the swinging doors and watched him mount his magnificent black stallion, King. McVeigh laid a detaining hand on King's neck. "No need for you to leave, Matt," he said, loudly enough for all to hear. "Like the judge says, you can do as you please about following advice that don't hold water. I say, stay."

Coulter stared into the sheriff's eyes. A muscle twitched in his set jaw. His lips thinned to a seam. "Thanks, but I don't stay where I'm not wanted." He swept the crowd a contemptuous glance and touched his heels to King's flanks. Head high, shoulders as stiff as if he had a rifle strapped to his spine beneath his buckskin jacket, Matt slowly urged King down the dusty street. He didn't look back, not even when a girl's clear voice called, "I believe in you, Matthew Coulter. Go with God. Prove your innocence. Then come home to. . ."

The ringing affirmation of faith broke in midsentence. A few bystanders later insisted Matt checked King for the space of a heartbeat before urging him into a dead run. Others said, "No such thing." In any event, the poignancy of the moment stilled the jeers common to someone being run out of town. The crowd watched until King and the man with whom many had shared grub and campfires melted into the lengthening afternoon shadows cast by the frowning Tetons.

No one spoke then or later of two hidden factors everyone, except perhaps the judge, knew played a part in the jurors' decision, good men though they were.

First, fifty-year-old Jed Talbot, owner of the Lazy T cattle ranch in the foothills, was the most hated man in Wyoming Territory. On the rare occasions he appeared on the dusty or snow-clogged streets of Jubilee, inhabitants wisely kept out of his way. The raging demon born and nurtured by Jed's years of hard drinking would hold full, triumphant sway until satisfied.

The stern discipline Jed normally exercised over himself, and always over the cowhands who hired on with him—most of whom quit and rode away in a few weeks or months—vanished like August snow with Jed's first drink.

Jubilee knew from past experience that once the rancher "gave his devil a run," Talbot would sober up and return to what most folks derisively called the "Tipsy T."

The second reason was Jed's seventeen-year-old daughter, Lass, noble and truthful as her given name, Alicia. Lass was admired and respected even more than her father was despised. Milk-and-water maidens pleased their mamas with pretended horror at Lass Talbot's antics, but they secretly longed to be like the strong young woman who many believed actually ran the Lazy T.

Tales of her courage and daring provided fodder for campfire and town gossip, and Lass Talbot's fame spread through the often harsh, unforgiving land. It increased a hundred, nay, a thousandfold, after the trial. Let those who would, prate of vanished heroines. When the courageous girl publicly challenged her father's iron authority and pledged unswerving loyalty to her friend Matt Coulter, she became dearer to Jubilee than Joan of Arc or Helen of Troy.

Young and not-so-young cowboys, ranchers, even merchants, rode miles out of their way to catch sight of Lass on her favorite horse, Diogenes. No hairpins could keep her thick, wildly flying braid beneath a hat. It gleamed in the sun and matched to a tint the chestnut stallion's glossy coat. Her superb figure bent forward when she called into his ear—a picture to linger long in the beholder's mind.

Yet two obstacles blocked the dozens of would-be suitors longing to camp on the girl's doorstep and win her hand. Both appeared insurmountable.

Chapter 1

But they that wait upon the LORD shall renew their strength;
they shall mount up with wings as eagles; they shall run,
and not be weary; and they shall walk, and not faint.
ISAIAH 40:31

Two obstacles blocked those who yearned to win Lass Talbot. Both loomed higher than Grand Teton, the 13,770-foot monarch of the mountain range that reared above the valley and Jubilee. Dried leaves and rolling tumbleweeds whispered Jed's threat to run off any man foolhardy enough to come courting his daughter. True and exaggerated stories told of those who dared the Lazy T owner's wrath, only to find themselves staring into Talbot's surly face and the business end of a rifle barrel. Such tales effectively dampened most of the intrepid swains' ardor. One by one, they reluctantly gave up their pursuit of Lass. While they might continue to admire her from afar, common sense prevailed; so most settled for other girls with less fire but with more reasonable fathers.

A few bold enough to persist readily admitted Jed wasn't the only problem. "How come you ain't interested in any of us cowpokes?" a new hand asked Lass after being smilingly turned down when he offered to saddle her chestnut stallion. "We ain't a bad lot. Well, no worse than most." He grinned and shoved his disreputable sombrero farther back on his curly head. "We'd shore admire to ride with you," he said in a droll voice. "S'posin' of course we could keep up with Di–Di—what's his name again?"

Lass threw her head back. A rare trill of laughter rang out in the sunny air. She stroked her horse's beautifully curried mane. "His name is Diogenes (*Di-ah-jen-knees*), and you're absolutely right." A bewitching dimple showed in her left cheek. "You can't keep up with him. Only one horse ever could." A shadow crossed her face.

A familiar pang went through her.

An icy voice cut into the conversation. "What's carrying on out here?"

Lass caught sight of her glowering father marching toward the corral. Her heart sank, knowing all too well what lay ahead. How little he resembled the father she had adored, the broad-shouldered hero of her little-girl days! Lass couldn't remember seeing her father smile in the eight years since they laid gentle Alice Talbot to rest in the cottonwood grove she loved. On that

404

long-ago afternoon, Jed's twinkling blue eyes dulled to slate; his laughing mouth became a seam that held in all but the harshest words.

Undeniable evidence of years of dissipation marred his once-handsome countenance. Broad bands of white streaked Jed's chestnut hair. He appeared at least ten years older than his actual age. He seldom shaved and held his bristly chin higher every day. Now he strode toward Lass and the friendly cowboy like some avenging Nemesis. "Get off my ranch," he ordered the cowboy.

Dull red stained the young rider's face. "Why? I didn't do anything."

"I'll not have the likes of you hanging around my daughter. Pick up your pay and go, before I lose my temper and throw you off." Talbot turned his glare toward Lass. "Either go riding—alone—or get in the house. I've told you before to stay away from the hands." He spun on his heel and headed back toward the sprawling log ranch house that had once been not just a house, but a warm and welcoming home.

The discharged cowboy took a step forward, muttering under his breath. Fire leaped to his eyes. "He ain't got no call to talk to you that way," he protested.

"He's my father." Lass managed a smile of thanks. She could see from his reaction that her soft words changed his anger to sympathy, so she finished saddling Diogenes and rode away. From a rise beyond the ranch, she watched still another in the long line of hands driven off the Lazy T disappear into the bunkhouse, then come out carrying rifle and bedroll. A little later, he mounted the horse on which he had ridden in looking for a job less than a month before.

No real regret filled Lass, but the memory of his innocent complaint, *"How come you ain't interested in any of us cowpokes,"* pricked like a burr under a saddle blanket. To escape her thoughts, she impulsively leaned forward and called in Diogenes's ear. He responded with a magnificent leap forward. The rush of air created by his long strides stung and reddened the girl's smooth cheeks and brought tears to her eyes.

Although she allowed Diogenes to run until the ranchhouse was lost behind a low hill, Lass could not outrun her churning thoughts. "Whoa, boy!" The chestnut changed from gallop to canter, slowed to a trot, and in answer to his rider's pressure with knees and reins, halted well back from the edge of a rise that afforded a splendid view of the valley and mountains. Lass dismounted and tossed the reins to the ground so her horse would stand, as trained. He was barely winded and soon began munching a patch of grass while Lass seated herself on a sun-warmed rock and stared at the world around her.

Why must the cowboy's innocent question buzz in her brain like a pesky fly? Was fear of her father's anger the real reason she couldn't get interested in one of the boys or men eager to win her approval, or was she simply using him for an excuse? It wasn't the first time she had pondered the questions. "It probably won't be the last, either," she told Diogenes, her only confidant except for God. Lass sighed and wrinkled her forehead, then grinned. When she was a small girl and told secrets to her first pony, she had looked around to make sure no one heard. People would surely laugh at a girl who talked to horses. Now it didn't faze her. Diogenes was a better companion than most folks she knew.

"It's because you understand," she praised him. He whinnied in response.

Lass flung herself flat on her back and gazed into the inverted blue bowl above her. Her keen, range-trained eyes discovered a tiny speck. She watched it grow until it became recognizable: a graceful eagle, making wagon-wheel circles in the sky. Love for God and the land filled her and temporarily blotted out the persistent questions she knew needed answering.

At last she sat up, took a cross-legged position, and settled down for a heart-to-heart talk with her horse. The dimple in her left cheek came and went as she remembered her father saying, "You talk *to* horses, *with* other people. You can't carry on a conversation with something that has no way of responding."

Lass had indignantly replied, "Diogenes responds, just not in words." She didn't add that a toss of her horse's fine head, a low nicker, or a gentle nudge with his nose said volumes. So did the way he surveyed her with intelligent brown eyes when she spoke.

"How come you ain't interested in any of us cowpokes?"

Lass broke off a bit of sage, crushed it so its pungent scent filled her nostrils, and addressed the nagging questions she knew would not go away until she did.

"I always hated those namby-pamby storybook girls who fluttered and flirted and waited for a knight to come riding up on a white horse," she told Diogenes. A mischievous grin tilted her lips upward. "If I'd lived then, I could have outridden any of them, especially if I'd had you."

Diogenes inched nearer and snorted. Lass took it for agreement. She absently patted his smooth neck and stared unseeingly across the cattle-dotted grazing lands to the sloping foothills. "I don't know how much horses remember, but you should know by now where your name came from. I've told you often enough!" She sternly eyed him. "In case you've forgotten, Diogenes was a Greek philosopher. According to legend, he walked the streets with a lantern. When people asked why, Diogenes supposedly said, 'I am searching the world, looking for an honest man.'"

Lass thrilled to the story, as she had done a hundred times. "No chivalrous dandy in a tin suit for me," she told her horse. "Someday, God and father willing, I may find a truly honest man."

You thought you had, her rebellious heart reminded. *Where are they now? The black stallion King and the man whose honor you upheld before the whole town? In all this time, why didn't Matthew at least write. . . .*

A few tears seeped from behind her eyelids. Lass forced them back and proudly lifted her head to again face the sky. The eagle had returned, soaring above the earth and its problems and heartache. A favorite scripture came to mind: Isaiah 40:31. Lass softly quoted, ". . .they that wait upon the Lord shall renew their strength; they shall mount up with wings as eagles; they shall run, and not be weary; and they shall walk, and not faint." A great longing to be free as the noble bird above her possessed the troubled girl. Would she ever be free, to live and to love?

Unable to bear the exquisite pain of too long a silence, too many uncertainties, Lass slowly slid into the saddle and turned toward home. Again she urged Diogenes into a run. Again the wind whipped her face. This time it dried her tears. Yet even as before, it could not silence the mocking voice that had haunted her since she was seventeen years old and watched the only man she ever truly loved and trusted ride away from Jubilee—and out of her life.

Late November brought more than snow to Jubilee and the Tetons. Rumors about Matt Coulter continued, increasing in intensity, but with no visible results.

"Just who is this Matt Coulter, anyway?" a pale-faced newcomer demanded of the local storekeeper. "How come everyone's talking about him?"

The succinct answer, "If you were Jedediah Talbot, I reckon you'd know," whetted the stranger's curiosity to razor sharpness, but the storekeeper's level-eyed stare and clamped lips warned the conversation was over. Not so the buzz and meaningful glances between Jubilee inhabitants whenever Matt Coulter's name came up—which it did constantly. The question, "What will Talbot do?" inevitably followed. Shrugged shoulders, raised eyebrows, and the significant shake of heads were the only responses. Talk hadn't run so rampant since the serious Indian fighting in Wyoming Territory stopped in the summer of 1876, bringing welcome peace to the settlers.

Sheriff Patrick McVeigh, weathered from his long years of keeping the peace in the frontier town, only grunted at the inquisitive newcomer who attempted to pry information out of him. "Sonny," he told the indignant young man, "around here it's healthy to keep your nose out of other folks' business unless you want to risk getting it cut off."

One snowy afternoon in early December, rumor became certainty. The stagecoach rolled into town behind a team of exhausted horses. A lone passenger stepped down.

"He doesn't look like much," the newcomer complained after a quick glance at the arrival.

"What were you expecting? Billy the Kid?" someone taunted, but no one laughed. Matt Coulter was a far cry from the ruined man who had left Jubilee seven years earlier. He still had the same glorious golden hair, forget-me-not blue eyes, and angelic face—if one overlooked the lines time had etched into a once carefree expression. Lithe, thirty years old, and "powerful as a mountain lion and twice as dangerous," someone whispered.

Matt gave one lightning-fast look at Jubilee's straggling main street, then looked neither right nor left but headed straight for the sheriff's office.

By nightfall, everyone for miles around knew Matt Coulter was back, wearing a US Marshal's badge and a grim expression. It struck fear into the hearts of all those who had ever been involved in questionable activities. Maybe Matt hadn't come back for Talbot, after all. Maybe he was tracking someone else. Certain secret, shady deals were hastily canceled. With a US Marshal in town, it was a good time to lie low.

Chapter 2

But the LORD said unto Samuel, Look not on his countenance, or on the
height of his stature. . .for the LORD seeth not as man seeth; for man looketh
on the outward appearance, but the LORD looketh on the heart.
1 SAMUEL 16:7

Matt Coulter, a US Marshal. Incredible. Questions followed, asked over drinks in the Sagebrush Saloon and teacups in the homes. Tongues wagged as if tied in the middle and loose at both ends. When had Matt become a lawman? Why? Where? Most important, why had Coulter really come back? Mutters of, "Glad I ain't in Talbot's shoes," raced like wildfire. So did anticipation. Would Talbot finally get what he deserved?

Sheriff McVeigh heard the talk along with everyone else in Jubilee. He glared and pulled down the corners of his mouth until he looked liked a prowling cat that had swallowed a sour mouse. "Good thing it ain't summer. Folks around here would have sunburned tongues from flapping them in the breeze."

Old memories die hard, especially when they concern possible injustice. So it was with Jubilee. Jury members shook in their shoes and gave serious thought to packing up in the dead of night and moving their families elsewhere. They grew until the foreman of the jury came out of the general store and nearly plowed into Matt Coulter.

Matt's smile didn't reach his steady blue eyes, but his quiet, "How have you been?" went a long way toward setting folks' minds at ease. So did the fact that he offered his hand to the man who had pronounced sentence on him.

"I never felt so downright skunky as when I shook Coulter's hand," the foreman later confessed to his cronies at the Sagebrush Saloon. "I mumbled somethin' about I wished things could have been different." He took a swig of beer and wiped foam from his mouth.

"What did Coulter say?" someone prodded. An impatient growl rose from the crowd of listeners. "Hurry it up, will you?"

The foreman set his mug down on the age-scarred bar. The solid thud rang loudly in the silent saloon. "I'll be jinxed if he didn't up and say, 'Seven years is a long time. You did what you felt you had to do. No hard feelings.' Then he shook my paw 'til it near broke my fingers." He flexed those callused members, and an awkward grin spread over his face. "Didn't have the gumption to ask how come Matt came back if he felt that way." The foreman sent a significant glance at the others. "Reckon none of us has to."

"Mighty tough on Lass," someone commented. "She and Coulter were always good friends." A murmur of sympathy set restless feet shuffling. "Wonder if she knows Matt's back?"

"I sure ain't going to be the one to tell her," someone said.

"*I* sure ain't going to be the one to tell her daddy," another voice chimed in. "I'd just as lief stay on top of the ground for a while, not under it."

A murmur of agreement swept through the gathered crowd. A bold young cowboy burst into an exaggerated rendition of "Bury Me Not on the Lone Prairie." He hung onto the last note until a burst of laughter drowned out his plaintive song, then grinned a devil-may-care grin and finished his drink.

"Pipe down, you lunkheads," the bartender ordered. "Jed Talbot's nothing to laugh about." His reminder sobered the rowdy crowd as nothing else could have. Every man present knew the bartender spoke the truth.

"Someone's gotta tell Jed," the foreman stated after a short silence. He grimaced. "When I was knee high to a bumblebee my mama used to tell me a story that reminds me of us. It was about a bunch of mice, and—"

"You had a mama?" jeered the singer. Mock awe settled over his now innocent-looking face. "All this time I thought they found you 'neath a cactus."

The foreman shot him a look that would have shriveled a less daring cowboy. "You want to hear the story, or don't you?"

"Shore. Me and the boys always did want to hear a story about a bunch of mice." The cowboy smirked and rolled his mischief-filled eyes.

The foreman ignored the sarcasm. "As I was sayin' before Big Mouth here interrupted, the mice had a bad problem. The family cat. Somethin' had to be done before he ate up any more of the mice's relatives. Those left came up with a bright idea: hang a bell on the cat's neck, and he couldn't creep up on 'em."

"Pretty smart," the interested bartender put in.

A smug smile crept over the foreman's face. "Not as smart as they thought. There was still a mighty important question. *Who would bell the cat?*"

A moment of letting the story sink in passed before the singing cowboy stood. "I ain't no mouse. I also ain't belling any cats." He sent a significant look around the circle of watching cowhands. "And I still ain't telling Jed Talbot who stepped down from the stagecoach." He jammed his worn Stetson down on his head and strode out of the deathly silent Sagebrush Saloon.

Because of the town's general agreement with the cowboy's sentiments, several days passed before news of Matt Coulter's return reached the Talbots. Sheriff McVeigh, Jubilee's unanimous choice of messenger to the Lazy T, had suddenly decided to take a long-delayed vacation.

"Now?" Matt demanded. "How come?" Suspicion leaped to his mind like an Indian to the bare back of a wild mustang. His eyebrows drew together in a forbidding line, and he cocked his head and slitted his eyes at his friend.

"Why not?" Pat McVeigh grinned. Every line in his unshaven face showed how much he was enjoying the interchange. He always had loved verbally sparring with Matt. "I've been putting off going to Denver to visit my dear old mother for many a day." His sorrowful tone didn't match the twinkle in his eyes.

"Your dear old mother is in better health than you are, you old fraud," Matt snapped. "Who's going to keep the peace in Jubilee while you're gone?"

The sheriff tilted his worn swivel chair back until Matt thought he'd go head over teakettle backward. The chair gave a loud squawk of protest. "I reckon a properly authorized US Marshal ought to be able to hold the town together for a couple of days. No more than a week, or maybe two, at the most." He cocked a shaggy eyebrow. "Wouldn't you say so?"

"In a pig's eye, if you mean this US Marshal," Matt rudely told him. "What would Jed Talbot say?" Yet even as he protested, a live coal of excitement ignited and set a fire raging inside him. What better way to show Jubilee Matt Coulter was not the man he had been seven years earlier? Not the careless rider who gave much thought to his wild, free life on the range and little to what lay beyond his mortal years? Was this the purpose for which he had felt called back to Jubilee?

Bang! McVeigh's chair came forward with a crash of its front legs. His eyes gleamed. "Talbot doesn't run this office. I do. Always have, always will, unless I get voted out, which ain't likely. No one else wants the job, not even Talbot."

The words, "He will rage," slipped from Matt's lips of their own volition.

A banner of triumph waved in the sheriff's face. "Let him." His sunbaked hand reached across the battered desk to the young man he had loved since childhood. "Well? Is it a deal?" He faked a hollow cough. "I do need a vacation."

Matt hesitated the same amount of time it took for a tiny vein in his tanned forehead to pulse a single time. His own hand shot out. "For better or worse."

McVeigh's grip threatened to paralyze Matt's strong fingers. After a moment, the sheriff released them and dryly commented, "Better or worse. Hmm. Seems to me I've heard those words before. In church, maybe, with a pretty girl walking down the aisle, wearing a white dress, and. . ."

Matt lost the rest of the sentence. A vision of a strong, seventeen-year-old girl who wished him Godspeed an eternity before danced in his mind. That girl had laughed up at him, teased, and cajoled him. Lass Talbot: a good comrade—and so much more! He had fallen in love with her when she still wore pigtails and was far too young to think of love and marriage.

"What's she like now?" he abruptly asked.

The sheriff didn't pretend to misunderstand. He stroked his stubbled chin and quietly said, "She ain't married or promised."

"I know. Otherwise, I wouldn't have come back." The meaningful look that passed between them showed the rare friendship they had always shared. "I suppose it's because of Jed." Matt held his breath, fearing the answer yet needing to ask the question that had haunted him ever since he rode away.

"Naw." The sheriff leaned forward and propped his massive forearms on his desk, threatening to topple the stack of papers next to them. "What I mean is, she's twenty-four years old. Her own boss. Or she could be if she left the Tipsy T." Admiration flooded his weather-beaten face. "Folks say Lass just about runs the ranch single-handed. Jed's drinking has been getting worse." Concern clouded the sheriff's countenance. "Used to be, he held it down to coming into town a few times a year and rampaging around. Now I hear he's also drinking at home."

"Why does she stay?" Matt burst out. Feelings he thought he had conquered swelled into his throat, bitter as gall. "A girl like that."

The sheriff ran his hand over his grizzled face again. It rasped like a buzz saw and set Matt's teeth on edge. "I asked her once." He leaned back in his chair again, hands clasped behind his head. "Never will forget her answer."

"Well?" The question cracked like a rifle in the hands of an expert marksman.

A poignant light stole into eyes that had seen it all: Indian fights and settlers; births; death by sickness, violence, and old age; peace and prosperity; trouble and lawlessness. "Lass said when she figured she couldn't bear things for even one more day, she remembered the meaning of her father's name. She told me surely a man who carries a name that means what Jedediah means cannot forever withstand his daughter's storming heaven on his behalf."

McVeigh pulled out a red handkerchief large enough to flag down a speeding train a mile away and vigorously blew his nose.

"So what *does* Jedediah mean?" Matt demanded.

"*Beloved of Jehovah.* Can you beat it?" The sheriff blew again. "Jed Talbot, running around with a moniker like that!"

Matt's heart pounded. If he hadn't already loved Lass, this new revelation of a heart bigger than the Territory of Wyoming would have done the trick. Yet why was he surprised? Her faith and belief in a loving God after Alice Talbot died had strengthened all around her, except her father. In Matt's years away from Jubilee, memories of gentle Alice lent understanding of what Jed had suffered. Suppose he, Matthew Coulter, were married to Lass. His heart jumped at the thought. Wouldn't he also turn bitter if she died? Yes. Hadn't he done the same thing when unfairly accused and driven from Jubilee seven years before?

Chapter 3

*...he that loveth not his brother whom he hath seen,
how can he love God whom he hath not seen?*
1 JOHN 4:20

J ubilee had reeled with shock when Matt Coulter stepped down from the stagecoach that dutifully carried passengers to Rock Springs and beyond. Before they fully recovered, a strangely altered Sheriff McVeigh climbed aboard the outgoing stagecoach early one frosty morning. Curious onlookers found themselves in danger of having their jaws permanently dislocated from shock, for the sheriff grinned and called, "Take good care of my town while I'm gone, Marshal. Don't take any guff. You hear?" His stentorian voice echoed over the sparsely populated street like heavy thunder in a rock-walled canyon.

Hear? Matt's ears burned. He felt heat surge into his face. Anyone within a mile radius couldn't help hearing! A gleem in the sheriff's keen eyes spoke more plainly than words. For reasons of his own, which Matt could pretty well figure out, the sheriff meant the inhabitants of Jubilee to know who was in charge.

The stagecoach driver cracked his whip over the backs of his team. "Giddap!" His horses responded. Wheels groaned and began to roll. Ten minutes later, coach and horses dwindled to moving black specks in the distance.

"Where's the sheriff off to?" the owner of the general store asked. "Must be trouble somewhere for the sheriff to head out so early." He wrapped his coat closer around his body and blew on his bare hands. "Cold, too."

A cowboy disagreed. "If there was trouble, the sheriff'd hightail it out of here on his horse, not that creaking stagecoach. Besides, he was all duded up."

The storekeeper looked worried. "Leaving like this isn't like Pat McVeigh." He turned to Matt for an explanation he was obviously unwilling to ask.

The new acting sheriff tore his gaze from the road leading out of town and looked into a sea of inquiring faces. "He's gone to Denver to visit his mother."

Astonishment rippled through the crowd and swelled when Matt added as casually as he could, "I'm filling in for him while he's gone."

"Well, I swan!" The storekeeper scratched his head. "If that don't beat all!"

Laughter bubbled up inside Matt and spilled into the quiet morning. "Well, boys? Think you can put up with me for a few days? A week? Two at the most?"

The little group exchanged glances before the storekeeper grinned and said, "Looks like we don't have much choice. McVeigh told you not to take any guff. He'll skin us alive if we try and make trouble while he's gone."

"That's for certain!" A grinning rancher cocked his head to one side and spat a stream of tobacco juice into the street, then warily eyed the acting sheriff. "You ain't going to run me in for spitting in the street, are you?"

"Not this time," Matt retorted. "Just watch yourself."

A round of laughter greeted his sally and the small crowd dispersed. As they walked away, the rancher's voice floated back to Matt, "Talbot's going to have seventeen kinds of fits when he finds out what's going on here in Jubilee."

Matt silently agreed. He sighed and wrinkled his forehead. The last thing he wanted right now was a confrontation with Jed Talbot, yet how could he avoid it? He turned on his boot heel and ambled back toward the sheriff's office and jail, puzzling over the position McVeigh had put him in by leaving. If there were only a way to avoid further trouble! He sighed again. "I'm afraid there will be a lot more 'worse' to this job than 'better,'" he muttered.

Matt reached his destination and lifted a hand to open the sturdy door. He halted. Froze with his hand in midair. What if he—

"No." He shook his head. "It would never work!" Matt gave the door such a hard push that it slammed open and banged against the wall from the force of his attack. The action catapulted him into the room. He righted himself and closed the door behind him, feeling foolish and thankful the two cells beyond the open inner door sat bare and empty of occupants. Doubts about his harebrained idea gathered like thunderclouds preparing to assault the earth. Still, he couldn't quite banish or forsake the idea that had come to him. Bold, daring, a long chance.

Matt sat down in the sheriff's chair, folded his hands, and bowed his head. Should he follow through on the idea that had sprung full-blown into his churning brain? Common sense shouted, "No." The cold, hard reality was: if the plan failed, everything at stake would be lost. Probably forever.

Yet in spite of the terrible odds against success, the instinct Matt had learned to respect and follow in order to survive long, hard years tantalized him with the thought: *Suppose the plan works? It would solve everything. Forever.*

Head still bowed, Matt Coulter forced his dilemma from his mind. The quiet morning offered time and privacy to remember, to recall things he often shoved aside in the interest of more urgent problems. He closed his eyes, forced himself to relax, and let the past sweep into the silent room.

❧

"*I believe in you, Matthew Coulter. Go with God. Prove your innocence. Then come home to. . .*"

Lass Talbot's voice broke before she finished the sentence. Was the missing word *me*, Matt asked himself a thousand times as he drifted down the broad and easy tumbleweed trail that led so many cowboys to perdition. Pangs of regret mingled with hatred and bitterness. He railed against the God who allowed blameless men to be punished. Prove himself innocent? He could not. Would not. Doing so meant inflicting pain greater than the loss to Jubilee of a single cowboy, a range rider who had dared dream of happiness beyond his reach.

A year passed. Two. Three. Matt wandered the length and breadth of the West, from the Panhandle of Texas to the Dakotas and Canadian Border. His riding, roping, shooting skills meant no lack of jobs. He and his black stallion, King, won prize money at rodeos. Time dulled his anger against the jury who had neither condemned nor exonerated him, but his hatred of Jed Talbot and love for Lass burned brighter with each passing day.

Four years. Five. Riding on when the restlessness within him became too strong to resist. Whooping it up with the best—nay, the worst—of his companions, with a single exception. He steered clear of women, especially those who worked in saloons. Several times, it meant riding away when a jealous swain resented the attention girls paid the indifferent cowboy. Lass Talbot might never know of his loyalty, but he would.

The sixth year of exile brought change. A mean steer Matt and King were chasing on a Texas ranch suddenly reversed directions and charged. Powerful horns plunged deep into the stallion's side. King fell, carrying Matt to the sun-baked earth. Matt tried to spring clear, but one foot lay trapped beneath his dying horse. With a terrible roar, the steer went for Matt. By the time help came, Matthew Coulter lay bleeding and broken.

Kind ranch hands and a grave-faced doctor cared for him, but they held out little hope. "If he weren't such a magnificent specimen, I'd give him no chance at all." Doc shook his graying head. "Little enough chance, even though he is."

In the midst of pain and delirium, a powerful hand gripped Matt's right hand. "Don't give up," a man's deep voice ordered. "God will see you through."

Matt tried to tell the speaker God had abandoned him long ago. The words became an unintelligible croak. Matt was too weary to try again. The voice called again. The grip on the injured man's hand increased in intensity; a frail lifeline to cling to in the ebb and flow of agony that left Matt exhausted. Time became indistinct in that raging river. During one lucid moment, Matt wondered: Did the stranger stay beside him night and day? Each time the pain receded, he felt strength flowing into his body from his unknown companion. It gave him endurance to face the next wave of pain.

A week or an eternity later, Matt opened his eyes and wonderingly looked around. His mind cleared and he examined the room in which he lay. Whitewashed log walls. The smell of medicine. Sunlight half-heartedly poking through clear glass between calico curtains. A merry fire blazed in the open fireplace.

He languidly turned his head toward his right hand. It lay limp on a brightly colored patchwork quilt. It also felt strangely naked. No longer was it clasped in another's. Matt raised his gaze from the bed and surveyed the tall figure hunched in a hand-hewn rocker. The twin to Matt's quilt covered the unknown, sleeping man. Silver hair topped a deeply lined face, bearing evidence that its owner had kept constant vigil for a long, long time.

Matt's body involuntarily twitched. The man opened his eyes. For a moment, Matt thought he would drown in the steady gray gaze. He started to ask who the man was, why he had stayed with him, but the stranger forestalled him.

"I am Pastor Andrew," the deep voice Matt knew so well quietly said. "I am so glad you are better! God is good."

Matt could only stare. He had seen a thousand glorious sunrises and thrilled to each, but never had he seen such radiance in a human face. He swallowed hard and weakly forced out a few words, "Why do you care?"

"My Lord loves His children. So do I." He laid a hand over Matt's lips to still further speech. "When you are better, we will speak of many things."

It was the beginning of friendship—and much more. Matt learned that Pastor Andrew's wife had died a few years earlier, leaving him alone. He had insisted Matt be brought to his home after the accident. During the long convalescence that followed, Matt discovered another with the faith and trust he had only found in Lass and her mother. Pastor Andrew led Matt to Christ step by step, more by what he was than what he preached. Weeks later, Matt brokenly said, "I reckon it's time for me to ask Jesus to be my Trailmate. What do I do?"

Joy shone on the old pastor's face. "You know the way, Matt. Confess your sins. Ask Jesus to forgive you and invite Jesus to live in your heart."

"Is that all? It doesn't seem like enough." Doubt filled Matt's heart.

The steady, gray gaze grew concerned. Matt felt Pastor Andrew could see into his very soul. "Jesus cannot live in a heart that carries hatred and bitterness."

Matt felt as if he'd been hit by an avalanche. "You mean. . ." He choked and couldn't go on. Six years of raw emotion boiled up inside him.

Pastor Andrew reached for his worn Bible. "First John 4:20 asks, 'how can a man love God whom he hasn't seen if he doesn't love his brother whom he has seen.' Matthew, you have to love God more than you hate Jedediah Talbot."

A geyser of anger exploded. "That rotten skunk cheated me once. Now he's going to do it again?" Matt jerked open the door and started out.

Pastor Andrew's quiet voice stopped him on the threshold. "Only if you let him." He paused, then spoke words the troubled cowboy knew he would never forget. "You had no choice before. This time, you do."

Chapter 4

L ass Talbot stood at her bedroom window and watched the softly falling snow with blurred eyes. How quickly and beautifully it camouflaged the leafless cottonwoods and aspens, wrapping their naked branches in a blanket of white! She took a deep breath then slowly released it. If only she could be wrapped in warmth, protected and sheltered against storms far worse than those that swept down from the north and gripped Jubilee in their wintry clutch.

Lass sadly turned from the window. She wrinkled her forehead in silent protest against the sound of her father's voice raging in the sitting room of the log ranchhouse. Jed's voice grated on, desecrating the holy hush just outside her window. Lass caught her lower lip between her teeth. The contrast between the landscape's purity and her father's profanity sent a blizzard of pain straight to her hurting heart. Until today, even in his worst moments, Jed had never before sworn inside their home. Was this the end? Could she continue as she had from day to day, passionately hoping and praying for her father's redemption? "Please, God, give me strength and guidance," she prayed. "I need You so."

Hot tears scorched the inside of her eyelids, but Lass refused to let them fall. Her father despised any sign of weakness in himself or others. Once he had been compassionate, understanding. The Lazy T had been a joyous place, ruled by Alice Talbot's rod of love. After she died, Jed had hardened. Now Lass sometimes felt her father's heart had turned to pure granite. He paid grudging respect only to those as strong as he.

She glanced back out her window, desperately seeking peace from the gentle, falling snow. "That's why Father hates Matt Coulter so much," she whispered. "Matthew is strong." She traced the outline of a snow angel on the frosty glass.

It's why you love him. You always have. You always will, an inner voice said.

The troubled girl's heartbeat quickened. She felt blood rush to her head. "I?"

Yes, you, the little voice accused.

"That is absurd! We were childhood friends, nothing more."

Oh? her heart mocked. *Then why did you call after him that day, begging him to come back to you?*

Lass covered her ears, trying to still the taunting voice. Too honest to attempt to deceive herself longer, she faced the suspicion she had refused to face a hundred times before. "Lord, it's foolish," she brokenly said. "It's been seven years." She thought of the heartache that had plagued her all that time. "Seven years grieving over a man who rode away without looking back."

A scripture sprang to mind. Lass had thrilled over it when her mother read it to her many times during their years together before Alice answered the final call.

"And Jacob loved Rachel; and said, I will serve thee seven years for Rachel thy younger daughter," Genesis 29:18.

Another well-loved verse followed, bringing fire to the girl's cheeks.

"And Jacob served seven years for Rachel; and they seemed unto him but a few days, for the love he had to her," Genesis 29:20.

Lass whirled from the window and threw herself onto the patchwork coverlet she had fashioned for her narrow bed. Could hearts break from pain? "At least Rachel knew Jacob loved her! I don't even have that, Lord. You know as well as I do, Matt Coulter hasn't seen fit to send a single word in all these long years!" She laughed bitterly. She had no need for caution. The thick, heavily chinked log walls both held in and kept out voices, unless they were raised in anger like her father's.

"I'm no Rachel, to wait and wait and wait. What if seven more years pass, as they did for her?" She beat her fists into her pillow. "Lord, why must life be so hard? Sometimes it is so unbearable, I don't know how long I can hold on here."

Heavy footsteps and a loud thump on her door brought Lass to her feet, hands still clenched. "Who is it?"

"Your father. Come out this instant," Jed bellowed.

Lass hesitated. The last few months had taught her the wisdom of riding off on Diogenes or taking refuge in her room to escape her father's profane ravings. She knew from experience there was no reasoning with him when he drank. For years Jed had restricted his sprees to town, but lately he avoided going into town and did his drinking at home. Strong as Lass was, she could not withstand the change in his personality triggered by a bottle.

"Come out, I say!" The heavy door creaked on its hinges.

Lass considered climbing out the window and thought better of it. It would be no easier facing him later than now. She flung wide the door. "Yes?"

"Did you know he's come back?" Jed roared. He resembled an angry bull Lass had once seen charging a rodeo rider. The Lazy T foreman, Dusty, only remaining hand from before Alice Talbot died, stood a few feet behind Jed. He awkwardly twisted his work-stained hat and dug the toe of his worn boot into the braided rug at which he stared.

"Who?" It came out in a whisper. Only one person's return could bring such fury to her father's face. Lass tried to quell the voice shouting inside her, *He's here. Matthew Coulter has come back.* She must not betray by word or look the joy she felt leap into her veins with every beat of her tumultuous heart. Now was the time to dissemble, for her sake, Matt's, and her father's.

Jed frothed at the mouth and stared at her from red-rimmed eyes. "Matthew Coulter, that's who! That stinking cattle thief should have been hanged. Would have been if the jury'd had any gumption." A string of profanity followed.

Lass couldn't stand it any longer. "How dare you use such language to me, Father?" She planted her fists on her hips and whipped up scorn to still her trembling knees. "You would horsewhip any man who spoke so in my presence. Now you bring these vile words into our home! What would Mother think, knowing you have so little respect for your daughter—*and hers?*"

Jed's jaw dropped. His face paled.

Lass took quick advantage of his stunned silence. "I didn't know Matt Coulter returned. How could I?" she demanded. "I haven't been to town in ages." She looked at Dusty. "When did he come?"

"Coupla days ago," the obviously embarrassed foreman replied. He took a deep breath. "That ain't all."

Jed snapped out of his temporary shock and spun on one heel. "What?"

Dusty kept his gaze fixed over Jed's shoulder and on Lass. "Coulter's wearing a US Marshal's badge and—"

"Get out!" Jed thundered. His right hand hovered above his hip where a gun belt hung low. His fingers changed to a claw, ready and waiting.

Lass had seen him angry and belligerent before, but never like this. *Dear God, don't let him shoot Dusty!* She pushed past her father and stood between the two men. "You'd better go," she told Dusty over her shoulder.

"Leave you here with him like this? Not in a hundred years!" The foreman caught her wrist and swung her aside. He stuck his face into the maddened man's countenance and shouted, "Jed Talbot I've put up with a lot in the last eight years, but I ain't standing for this. You've no call to take your madness out on Lass!"

"I said for you to get out," Jed hissed. He touched his gun significantly.

"If I do, I'll tell the acting sheriff you pulled a gun on me and send him out to pack Lass off somewheres so she'll be safe from you," Dusty threatened.

One word appeared to penetrate the sodden brain. *"Acting* sheriff?"

"Yeah." Dusty paused, then grinned again. "McVeigh's taking a vacation."

Lass felt her mouth drop open. An icy chill sped up and down her spine. She gripped the foreman's sleeve. "Wh–who is taking his place?"

"Matt Coulter." Satisfaction oozed from every pore of the weatherbeaten face.

For a long, terrible moment Jed stood frozen to the floor. His face sagged.

Lass felt he aged a good ten years in that moment. She started toward him from force of habit. He waved her off and reeled backward until he reached his bedroom, which was next to hers. The heavy door couldn't quite deaden the rasp of a seldom-used lock after he slammed the door shut.

"Sorry you had to be in on that." Sweat beaded Dusty's kindly face when he turned to Lass. "I never saw a man so eaten up with hate." He mopped his forehead with an oversize kerchief. "Do you want me to take you to town?" Hope showed in his eyes. "Or you could ride in on Diogenes and stay a spell with someone." He worried the rug again with his toe until it lay in a crumpled mess. "Just until Jed settles down. He always does."

The temptation to walk away and never return faded. "I'll stay," Lass replied.

"If you ain't an angel, then I never heard tell of anyone who is," her long-term friend burst out. "I'll just mosey over to the bunkhouse, get my bedroll, and come back for the night." He nodded at a couch. "Looks like a good place to bed down, just in case. I mean, it's a lot softer than my bunk."

Lass recognized his attempt to lighten the situation. She started to tell Dusty it wasn't necessary for him to stay and keep watch. Memories of the ugly scene they had just witnessed stopped her. "Thank you," she quietly said.

"No trouble at all." He grinned, put on his hat, and started for the front door. "You'll be all right while I'm gone, won't you?"

She held her breath and listened for sounds from her father's room. None came. "I'll be fine." She searched for a smile and tremulously put it on. "I'll go in my room and lock the door."

"Stay there," Dusty commanded. "It ain't smart to take chances when your daddy's letting his dark nature loose. Trust me, Lass. I know what he's like."

Lass fled to her room and locked the door, as much against the tears that threatened to gush because of the faithful foreman's caring for her as against possible intrusion by her father. How good to know she had an earthly protector in place of the father who should have been her comfort and stronghold!

A few minutes later, Dusty tapped on her door. She opened it and assured him she was all right, then relocked the door. Curled into a ball of misery, she tried to concentrate on happier times. In a few weeks, it would be Christmas. Her spirits sank, as they had each Christmas since her mother died. The Talbot annual observance of Christmas for the past eight years had been a travesty.

"Lord, as far back as I can remember before Mother died, Christmas was such a time of wonder," Lass told her Friend, Jesus. She closed her eyes and let her mind wander on paths to the past, trails that led back to happier times when Jed Talbot laughed and joined wholeheartedly in celebrating the birth of Christ.

Were those days gone forever? Would life continue its sameness? No, she decided. Not with US Marshal-Acting Sheriff Matt Coulter back in Jubilee.

Chapter 5

I will remember my covenant with thee in the days of thy youth,
and I will establish unto thee an everlasting covenant.
EZEKIEL 16:60

In addition to a heart filled with love, gentle Alice brought to her marriage with Jedediah Talbot a rich dowry from doting parents who adored their only child. She also brought three traditions, begun in the mountains of Virginia by her great-grandfather and solemnly observed by all who came after.

First, no one in Alice's family ever opened presents on Christmas Eve. "It is a time to celebrate the birth of Jesus," Great-grandfather had announced to his bride generations earlier. "A time to read the scriptures and ponder on what the world would be like if God had not loved his rebellious children enough to send His only Son. A time to keep holy and fill the air with song and praises."

From babyhood, Great-grandfather's children knew better than to ask for presents from under the brightly decorated tree that adorned their home on Christmas Eve. They piped out carols of old from the time they could lisp, then grew up and taught their own small, round-eyed children the tradition, that it might not be lost to future generations.

The second tradition was less holy but equally important. Every year when snow lay in the yard on Christmas Eve afternoon, all who were young and young at heart bundled up, threw snowballs, and made snow angels. Great-grandfather's usually stern, bearded face filled with mischief as he lightly packed snowballs that broke apart in flight and showered his family. Smiling Great-grandmother wore a cloak and scarf of her own weaving. She taught the rosy-cheeked, excited children how to make snow angels. The family praised God with Christmas laughter and the simple joy of being together.

The question, "Will it snow?" hovered in the crisp air annually and repeated itself a hundred times following Thanksgiving. The weather seldom brought disappointment. Passing years engraved memories of "Christmas Eve snow" on hearts so deeply, they helped ensure the ritual would be observed long after Great-grandfather and Great-grandmother had passed on to their heavenly home.

While the first tradition fostered worship and the second family fun, the final tradition was the most cherished. It offered the opportunity for the youngest and the oldest alike to experience the real meaning of Christmas.

"Consider how it was when Jesus was born," Great-grandfather told his family. "The Wise Men brought rich gifts; the shepherds, only themselves. What we give is not so important. What counts is for us to give our best to Jesus."

"Will Jesus come get presents from under the tree?" the oldest child asked.

"No, my son. He takes His presents from our hearts." Great-grandfather smiled. "Jesus tells us in Matthew, chapter 25, that any time we feed the hungry, take in strangers, give clothing to those in need, or visit the sick or those in prison, it is the same as if we were doing all those things for Him."

"He did?" the saucer-eyed boy asked.

"He did?" his equally impressed sisters and brothers echoed.

"Yes. Jesus also says those who do these things will inherit the kingdom He has prepared for us." Great-grandfather smiled again. "But we must do our good deeds secretly. Jesus tells us in Matthew 6:4, He will see those secret deeds and reward us openly."

He pointed out the window to the row of snow angels etched into the smooth white surface. "Those are snow angels. You can be 'secret angels,' by doing good and unselfishly giving to others of your time, your treasure, and your love."

From Great-grandfather's simple words, the final tradition sprang. Each family member sought ways to be "secret angels." They performed private, unexpected deeds of kindness to one another. Food baskets mysteriously appeared on needy families' doorsteps. Bits of money or treasured possessions quietly passed from person to person with no fanfare, no recognition expected. If the recipients suspected the source of the gifts, they remained silent, unwilling to deprive the givers of hugging to their hearts the joy of true and selfless giving.

Over the years, those who delighted in being "secret angels," discovered something unusual. They remembered their often-sacrificial gifts long after the memories of the brightly wrapped "tree gifts" they joyously unwrapped on Christmas morn faded. This, too, they passed down to their children.

Alice Talbot was among those of the fourth generation who faithfully kept the three cherished traditions, even though Wyoming Territory lay miles and a lifetime away from her Virginia home. She inducted her adoring husband, and later, their only child, into her childhood customs. The Lazy T family continued Alice's heritage for sixteen happy Christmas seasons. Jedediah Talbot only laughed when a gaping Dusty once caught his rancher boss making angels in the snow with Lass and his beloved wife.

"Want to join us?" Jed called.

Dusty gulped. "Naw, not me. I—uh—gotta mend some harness." He strode away as fast as his bowlegged gait could carry his range-hardened frame, mumbling to himself while peals of laughter rang out behind him.

Angels in the Snow

It was the last Christmas laughter rang out at the Lazy T. The following year, snow fell on the quiet mound where Alice Talbot had been laid to rest.

～✿～

Lass stirred from her reverie and shivered. A quick tug on her patchwork coverlet brought its welcome softness over her body. She snuggled into its familiar depths and gradually felt herself warm, at least on the outside. She still felt as icy and barren inside as the glaciers on Grand Teton. "If only Mother had lived," she murmured. Icicles of pain poked into her heart. After eight long years she still hadn't recovered from the loss of her mother. Perhaps it wouldn't have been so hard if Father had been different, if he had turned to her seeking mutual comfort instead of blaming God for his wife's death.

From her prone position, Lass could see out the top of her window. Dusk had settled, but enough light still touched the earth to show it was still snowing. It had been much the same on the day eight years before when Jed announced, "If you want to stick up a tree for Christmas, put it in your own room." He had paused. The misery in his face caused Lass to take an involuntary step toward him. His outflung hand held her off. Bitterness replaced the grief in his face.

"We'll not be indulging in all that angel foolishness, either." His words fell like hailstones, bruising his daughter's soul. "No need, now that Alice is gone."

The echo of his heavy steps as he crossed the living room and slammed out the front door resounded in the sixteen-year-old girl's heart. She wanted to cry out, to protest they must not break the precious family traditions. She could not.

She knew only too well that when her father spoke like that, she need not argue.

Now she slid down under her coverlet even farther. Her twenty-four-year-old heart protested as strongly and silently as it had done long ago and every Christmas since. After a moment, a tremulous smile softened her lips. She could only remember a few times when she refused to obey her father. That Christmas eight years ago was one of them. Even after her father's edict, Lass knew she could not and would not break the unbroken chain of family tradition. She would respect and continue as much of her Christmas heritage as possible without openly rebelling. Father might bar her from doing so outwardly. He had no control over what she silently and privately did. Besides, he would never know unless he one day returned to the faith of his ancestors and she could tell him.

Lass closed her eyes. Her smile spread, lifting her spirits by remembering the past and looking toward the present and future. Every Christmas Eve afternoon since her mother died, she had managed to slip away long enough to make a snow angel. It didn't matter how bad the weather was or that she must quickly obliterate every trace of her angel in the snow. Flinging herself on the snowy ground and moving her heavily clad arms and legs up and down until she left an imprint brought a wealth of memories of her mother and better times. It also renewed hope that coming years might be different and better.

Lass followed her solitary rite by a private time on Christmas Eve. She quietly read aloud the story of the birth of Christ from the Gospel of Luke. She repeated her daily plea for her father to repent. She sang praises in a true, sweet voice. Lass had little fear of interruption, but she performed her worship in the shelter of her own room. Even though Jed Talbot chose to absent himself from the Lazy T on both Christmas Eve and Christmas Day, there was always the chance he might return. Lass wanted no confrontations to mar Jesus' birthday.

Sometime between Christmas and New Year's Eve, a goodly sum of money appeared on her pillow. The first year this happened, Lass tried to thank her father for the impersonal gift. What she really wanted was for him to put his arms around her and hold her close, the way he used to do.

Jed gave her a stony stare and said nothing. Neither did he acknowledge the hand-sewn shirts and the socks she faithfully knitted and left in his room that year and in the years that followed. It became a tradition Lass secretly hated.

She again roused from her musings. Her unsteady fingers lit a candle and placed it so it would shine on the time-worn sheets of paper she took from their hiding place in a box beneath her bed. Each page held only a short prayer. They all said substantially the same thing. The girl's heart swelled when she read words she wished with all her heart it had never been necessary to write.

Heavenly Father, perhaps someday I will again be able to openly observe the three priceless traditions. They must not be lost, especially the "secret angel" giving. I have no gold or frankincense or myrrh. Even if I possessed them, I wouldn't be allowed to bestow them. I do have a gift for my earthly father, something far greater than any of those the Wise Men brought: the gift of prayer. This I vow to give, not only at Christmas but every day of the year. Great-grandfather admonished his family to always give their best. This is my best, Father. May it be acceptable unto You.

Lass slowly folded the sheets and returned them to their hiding place. In a short time she would write another such message, unless God, Himself, intervened with a miracle to change her father. Goodness knew she had done everything she could, to no avail. It hadn't been easy not to reproach him, but for the most part, Lass had held her tongue, telling herself surely things must get better.

Now they had grown infinitely worse. It had been bad enough to be the target of range gossip, even though Lass knew most of it was kindly toward her. Today the unbelievable had entered the log ranchhouse: language so vile, it surely must be an affront to the God who had once been Head of the Talbot household.

A cry for help and release rose from Lass, an appeal first uttered by David. *"Lord, how long wilt thou look on? rescue my soul. . ."* Psalm 35:17.

Chapter 6

Then said I, Woe is me! for I am undone;
because I am a man of unclean lips. . . .
ISAIAH 6:5

*W*hat would Mother think, knowing you have so little respect for your
daughter—and hers?"

Throughout the endless night following the showdown with
Lass, her stinging indictment resounded in her father's brain until he thought
he would go mad. After he buried Alice, he had painstakingly built a wall of
defense against pain, using bricks of anger, bitterness, and drink. It effectively
kept others out and his torment within, where no one could see. Not even
God. Especially not God. Had He not betrayed Jed by taking Alice? Agony
gradually subsided into numbness.

Now Jed's carefully constructed wall lay in shards beneath his dusty boots.
His numbness fled like shadows at noon. He had never felt such exquisite pain
as the flood of almost-forgotten feelings flowing from his exposed heart—not
even when Alice left him. His daughter's words had swept aside every pre-
tense. For the space of a heartbeat, Jed had seen in her eyes the man he had
become. Nay, the beast. A drunken sot who turned away from Lass when she
most needed him, too concerned with his own feelings to consider hers.

Fully clothed, Jed lay in the clutches of the whiskey; yet inside his still
body, a spark he hadn't known still existed began its work. It flickered, subsided,
flickered again and caught like match to pine kindling, scorching upward until
Jed wondered if he would die. He thought he had known the depths while
drinking. They were nothing compared to the flame within Jed that continued
to rage. Higher and higher, until he could stand it no longer. "Please, let me
die," he screamed, unable to recognize his plea was but a whisper no one but
the God he had despised could hear. "I cannot go on living this way."

Sleep from sheer exhaustion claimed him, interrupted by a herd of night-
mares. Jed awoke at last, amazed that his mind felt clear. He wrinkled his nose
at the heavy odor of sweat and whiskey that permeated the room. He rose
from the bed where he had flung himself after locking the door the previous
night and peered through the window. Jed normally found himself murky as
the growing dawn after a drinking spree, crouched like a living thing outside
the log house.

No sound came from his daughter's room. Jed shuddered. Would Lass ever forgive him? Could she, when she learned what he knew he must tell her? He longed for liquor to fortify him for the ordeal that lay ahead. No. If he once succumbed to temptation, there would be no turning back. There never was.

The dim reflection in the glass showed a haggard face that rightly belonged on a hundred-year-old. Or a dead man. Jed fell back. So that was what people saw when they looked at him! He had brought it on himself. He staggered to his bed, sank to its edge, and buried his face in his hands. "Alice, oh, Alice!"

An hour or a lifetime later, Jed couldn't be sure which, he stood and quietly began preparing for what he knew was the only way out. He changed into warm clothes, packed a few other things, and buckled on his gun belt. "I won't need much where I'm going," he muttered grimly.

Like a midnight prowler, Jed worked the noisy lock until it gave way. He inched his door open and waited to see if the noise had disturbed Lass. She must not know what he planned to do. Her door remained closed. Jed rejoiced. He stepped into the living room, grabbed his rifle, and stealthily crossed the room. A quick forage in the well-stocked pantry provided the scanty stores he wanted.

Lamplight from the bunkhouse sent a sickly yellow stream into the early morning air and fear into Jed's heart. If Dusty saw him, his game was up. Luck held until Jed finished saddling Duke, the most powerful horse on the Lazy T. He swung into the saddle. Another few minutes and he'd be gone. Snow had begun falling. By the time he was missed, not a ranch hand could track and find him.

Matt Coulter could.

Jed flinched. Now was not the time to think of Matt Coulter. A man fleeing for the reasons Jed had created needed to be clearheaded and "unstampedable."

"Hey, Boss, how come you're riding out so early? Lass ain't sick, is she?"

Jed froze. What rotten luck! He glanced toward Dusty, who was hurrying toward him from the bunkhouse. Even the faint light couldn't hide the concern in the foreman's face. "Lass is fine. Still asleep, far as I know." Did his voice appear as unnatural to Dusty as to himself? "Thought I'd check the line shack."

"What for and why now? A storm's brewing." Dusty sounded amazed. "No one's likely to use it in the dead of winter." He cast a suspicious look at Jed. "Besides, last time any of our boys were there it was fine and dandy."

Jed's nerves stretched to the breaking point and gave way. "Mind your own business, you old buzzard! If you say anything to Lass, you're fired." He ignored Dusty's inarticulate protest, spurred Duke, and turned to face the west.

"When will you be back?" the undaunted foreman yelled after him.

"Maybe never." Jed leaned forward and felt the sting of snow pellets on his face, pellets no colder than the possible implications of his answer.

Angels in the Snow

Lass awakened earlier than usual, filled with foreboding and heaviness of spirit. In spite of her warm blankets and coverlet, she felt cold. More than the chill of winter had entered her heart. She hated to leave the security of her room. What would Father be like this morning? What would they say to one another? She had been too mentally fatigued the night before to even consider a new day.

At last she rose and made ready for whatever lay ahead. She paused to offer thanks to God for keeping her through the night, then earnestly prayed for strength to face the hours before her. Forcing a smile to her lips, she unlocked her door and stepped from her room. Lass strained to hear sounds from her father's room. Silence prevailed, and she gave a sigh of relief. She needn't start breakfast just yet but would let her father sleep until their usual hour.

Freed from routine, she bundled up and stepped outside. Snow whirled to the ground in its maddest winter dance. Lass sank ankle deep in the soft stuff when she noticed Dusty standing by the corral and plodded over to join him.

"Morning, Dusty. Wonder if the snow's going to keep up."

"More like keep down," he said sourly, although he touched his hat to her. "It's been doing this since dawn."

Astonished at his tone, Lass demanded, "What were you doing up so early?"

She smiled and added, "I thought with most of the hands off the ranch until time for spring roundup you'd be catching up on your sleep."

Dusty avoided her gaze. Not even a trace of his usual fond smile for her crossed his sober countenance. "Not today." He respectfully touched the brim of his hat again. "If you'll be excusing me, I have work to do." He stalked off, leaving her to stare at his retreating back and wonder what on earth ailed him.

"Is anything wrong, Dusty?" Lass called.

He stopped abruptly and hesitated just a mite too long to be convincing, then he turned and gave her a grin that definitely looked pasted-on. "Now, what could be wrong? Ain't it a beautiful winter day?" He rambled on, acting more evasive with every sentence. "Don't worry your pretty head over it."

"Over *what*?" she flashed back at him.

Chagrin erased traces of innocence, but Dusty again tried to throw her off the track of what obviously gnawed at him. "Don't mind me. I'm just mumbling."

Lass rushed to him as rapidly as boots sinking in the snow allowed. Her heart pounded with fear. She grabbed the foreman's coat lapels and hung on for dear life. "All right, Dusty, let's have it. Is something wrong with Father?" She knew by the look that crept into the foreman's face she had hit dead center.

"I—he—" Dusty's stammering fell on deaf ears. Lass turned and struggled back to the house. She didn't even wait to kick off her snowy boots but stumbled to Jed's bedroom door and beat on it with both fists. "Father?"

Not a sound came from within.

Lass beat again with one hand, turned the knob with the other. To her relief, the catch released. She pushed the heavy door inward and lunged through it. The room lay empty. Mussed sheets and blankets showed someone had slept in the bed. Some of the girl's fear lessened, but when she checked the room further, it rose again. Enough clothing was missing to raise an alarm. "Dusty?"

"I'm here, Lass." Nothing remained of the foreman's surliness. "You weren't supposed to know." He shuffled his snowy boots and looked down at them. "Your daddy said he'd fire me if I told you he rode out early this morning. Said he was going to the line shack." Wild horses couldn't have dragged out of him Jed Talbot's final words about maybe never coming back.

"The line shack? In this weather?" Lass stared disbelievingly. "Why?"

"He wouldn't say." Dusty heaved a sigh that sounded like it started in the toes of his boots and worked its way upward. "I couldn't help wondering if it had something to do with his learning yesterday that Matt Coulter's now a US Marshall and acting sheriff of Jubilee." His steady gaze never wavered.

Lass weakly sank to the edge of the mussed bed. Why must this new trouble come upon them when they already had plenty? "It must be pretty bad for him to ride out in the dead of winter," she brokenly said. The suffering Jed had put her through paled in comparison with the love beating strong in her heart now that her father could be in grave danger. "Was he drunk?"

"No!" Dusty yanked himself up to full height. "Far as I could tell, he hadn't been drinking at all this morning. Funny thing." He scratched his head. "There was something different about him. Even when he yelled at me, he seemed kinda like the Jed Talbot he was before your mama died. Beats me, but he did."

Her mind flew to the line shack she had often visited, but never in winter. Were there supplies to last her father if a blizzard trapped him? Neighbors who were just as experienced with the rugged terrain of western Wyoming in the dead of winter as Father had died trying to outride storms. Could he conquer and survive?

She sprang to her feet. "Why are we standing here? We need to go after him."

"We couldn't make it a mile from the ranch without getting lost. Don't worry. Your daddy's bound to be at the line shack by now. By the way, if you ain't had breakfast, I could go for a second one." Lass quickly prepared ham, eggs, and biscuits, more to please him than from hunger. She poked down some food because she must eat, while Dusty tried to cheer her with funny range stories.

Two hours later the snow stopped. A knock on the door sent Lass flying to see who had come.

Matt Coulter stood outside, leaner of jaw than when he left. Yet the blinding light in his eyes Lass remembered so well steadily shone. In the split second before she flung herself into his arms, Lass knew what her heart had been trying to tell her for seven long years. That poignant blue light was for her.

Chapter 7

Teach me thy way, O LORD, and lead me in a plain path, because of mine enemies.
PSALM 27:11

Lass Talbot buried her face in Matt Coulter's sheepskin-lined coat. Her tears mingled with the snowflakes melting on the sturdy garment and cooled her burning cheeks. A moment later, powerful arms surrounded her. If only they would never let her go! For the first time in years Lass felt safe, protected against every storm that raged. She lifted her face to the one above her as naturally as a sunflower turning to the sun. Matt's winter-chilled lips curved into a smile of incredible sweetness, then found her own. Time, place, and the clump of Dusty's boots carrying him to the open ranchhouse door melted into unimportance. Nothing mattered except the fact that Matthew Coulter had returned—to her.

"Well, now. If this ain't a sight for sore eyes!" The Lazy T foreman's drawl recalled Lass to the present. She gasped and broke free from Matt's arms and the spell cast by his kiss. The single teasing kiss he had stolen when she was a girl belonged to long ago. This was a man's kiss. It paid homage to the woman Lass had become. Without a single word, Matt Coulter had claimed his mate and bound them together with eternal vows Lass knew nothing could ever break.

"Are you two going to stand out there all day?" Dusty complained. "You're letting a whole lot of cold air into this nice warm room."

Matt's eyes gleamed and a joyous laugh erupted. "So we are. Getting an unexpected greeting like this chased everything else out of my mind."

Lass felt her face heat. She hastily backed into the living room with Matt right behind her. What must he think of her, throwing herself at him that way? *I don't care,* her heart sang. *He came. He's here. He's mine. I've waited seven years. I'm not going to let anything take this or Matt, away from me. Ever.*

"I reckon you just put your brand on her," Dusty dryly observed. "Good for you, son, and welcome home." He held out a rough paw and shook Coulter's hand. "Never did believe you were mixed up in that cattle stealing business."

Lass saw the warning look that passed from Matt to Dusty, the hard grip of hands before Matt quietly said, "Thanks. I always knew where you stood." He slipped out of his wet coat and hung it on the outside doorknob, then closed the heavy door behind him. His body took on a certain stillness but his voice remained steady when he glanced around the room and casually asked, "Is Jed here? There are a few things I need to talk over with him."

Something in the set of his jaw shattered the veil of happiness enveloping Lass. She wordlessly stared at Matt. The US Marshal's badge on his heavy shirt gleamed brightly. Lass couldn't tear her gaze away from the symbol of authority. So he hadn't come just to see her. Hopes for a rosy future dimmed. How could she have forgotten the trouble between Father and the man she loved most, next to God? Must she again become a wishbone, torn two ways?

And if you do? a mocking inner voice taunted. *What then?*

In the hush that followed Matt's question, Lass silently prayed for help. Part of her mind heard the scrape of Dusty's boot and his quick explanation of Jed Talbot's absence. The other remembered a verse learned at her mother's knee. "*Teach me thy way, O LORD, and lead me in a plain path, because of mine enemies,*" Psalm 27:11.

Lass fought against the unhappiness rising like floodwaters within her. If ever anyone needed to know the ways of the Lord and to find a plain path, she was that person! She closed her eyes, feeling she walked a narrow trail between yawning canyons of love and duty, each threatening to swallow her up if she faltered or stumbled on even one step of the path. Her determination to allow nothing to stand in the way or destroy her future happiness seemed childish; a cardboard sword defiantly held up in the face of insurmountable obstacles.

Matt Coulter's sharp, "He went out in this storm? Is he insane?" yanked Lass out of her miserable reflections and back into the present.

"Lass wanted to go after him, but I told her it would be worse than insane," Dusty said. A wrinkle grew between his eyebrows. Lass could tell he was trying to keep up a cheerful expression for her sake, for he added, "I'm pretty sure Jed had more than enough time to make the line shack before the worst of the storm. He wasn't drinking, and he was riding Duke. Biggest and best horse on the Lazy T, far as I'm concerned." He smiled at Lass but his eyes remained anxious.

She made a little sound of protest, and Matt turned to her. "Dusty's right," he thoughtfully said. "It won't do your father any good for us to go hightailing after him and get caught halfway between here and the line shack." He pointed out the window. "The snow's thickening, and it was hard enough going when I rode out from town. All we can do for now is to wait and take for granted all is well."

"Jed Talbot's mighty good at looking out for himself," Dusty put in. "What I mean is, he knows the country and the weather signs. Chances are, he's long since at the shack, all holed up by himself and aiming to stay there until he's able to head for home. The temperature's dropping, which means the snow will freeze hard enough for folks to travel a lot easier if they have to."

What the men said certainly made sense, but the prospect of sitting around doing nothing sickened Lass. On the other hand, she felt relieved the inevitable showdown between Matt Coulter and her father was temporarily postponed. Who knew what would happen between them? Memories of her father's rage and whitened face from the night before when he learned Matt was not only back, but an official of the law on two counts danced in the girl's mind. So did the inscrutable looks between Matt and Dusty.

"What do you know that you aren't telling me?" she demanded of them.

"Wha—at?" Dusty's eyes popped wide open. "Lass Talbot, you're too suspicious for your own good!" His lips shut in a tight, unyielding line.

The foreman's accusation didn't fool her even a little bit, but Lass subsided. Nothing she could do or say would convince Matt Coulter to tell her whatever secret he and Dusty shared unless or until he was good and ready. She had battled his stubbornness for years and learned it was like two rams butting heads. As for Dusty. . .she grimaced. If a long-standing secret lodged beneath his worn Stetson, she had little chance of learning what it was now. This morning's slip of the tongue would not be repeated, especially after the warning look she had intercepted while it sped from Matt's eyes to Dusty's.

His eyes crinkled at the corners. "I can't imagine anyone dumb enough to step outside his own home in weather like this, let alone miss an acting sheriff."

Lass felt her heart turn somersaults. To hide her confusion, she quickly said, "I'll whip up supper when it's time. You and Dusty may as well eat with me."

"That's an invite I don't pass up," the foreman chortled. "I'm plumb tired of my own fixings, since Cookie lit out for greener pastures." He pulled the corners of his mouth down. "At that, I'd rather eat my own cooking than the messes the boys who stayed on for the winter cook. They should be thrown out to the prairie dogs." He smirked and every line in his leathery face deepened. "Except I'll bet no self-respecting varmint would touch the stuff!"

Lass couldn't help laughing in spite of her worries. "I promise you won't toss my cooking to the prairie dogs, Dusty. Mother started teaching me to cook as soon as my hands were big enough to hold a spoon." She blinked back the mist that accompanied a vision of herself: a happy, bright-haired child who loved to trot from kitchen to pantry to root cellar after her mother.

"I remember your apple pie." Matt looked longingly toward the kitchen. "I don't suppose you have apples on hand, do you?"

"Barrels of them! We—I stock up in the fall to be sure we will have enough."

Several hours later, Dusty shoved his chair back from the depleted store of vittles on the table and with obvious reluctance shook his head when offered a third piece of pie. "I just can't eat like I used to," he mourned.

Lass giggled and caught Matt's look of disbelief. She had lost track of how many times she had passed the venison roast, mashed potatoes and gravy, home-canned vegetables, hot biscuits, and three kinds of jelly. Matt hadn't been far behind Dusty when it came to packing it away. She furtively observed him when he blinked his eyes and glanced at the foreman's empty plate. He could use a little more meat on his bones. He'd always been tough as whipcord, but the years had fine-tuned him down until he resembled a winter-starved mountain lion.

For a few moments, Lass was able to lay aside her concern for her father. She let the blanket of her love wrap itself around her heart and fill its emptiness. She needed no mirror to know her feelings shone in her telltale face. She didn't care and gloried in her love. Matthew Coulter deserved to see the change from childhood bud to love in full bloom, born the day he rode away and sheltered deep in a heart that for years refused to acknowledge it remained.

Shortly after supper, Dusty gave an incredibly fake yawn and excused himself, leaving Lass and Matt to sit close to one another in front of a blazing fire. Their love was too fresh and sweet to linger on the past. "We have the rest of our lives, sweetheart," Matt whispered into her chestnut hair. "I wonder what Jubilee will say when US Marshall-Acting Sheriff Matthew Coulter takes a wife?"

Lass felt herself blush. "They'll shake their heads and say they knew it all along."

She mimicked a village gossip. " 'Land sakes, how else would it be, what with Lass Talbot boldly calling after a man being run out of town!' " She bit her lip. How could she have been so stupid as to bring up the past?

Some of her joy dimmed. Tacitly consenting to be Matt's wife placed her in the dreaded position of being unequally yoked. Lass pressed her fingers to her temples. She could not, would not, think about it now. For this brief time, she would revel in Matt's love. If tomorrow brought separation, at least she would have tonight—and remember its sweetness all the days of her life.

Matt stayed silent for a moment, then said, "Someday when we have more time, I'll tell you about a man I met while I was gone. He helped change my life. It's too long a story for now." He kissed the tip of her nose. "I will tell you one thing." A soft and reminiscent smile curved his lips. "When he learned I came from a town called Jubilee, he told me what it meant. Hundreds of years ago, every seventh year was a year of rest. Fields and vineyards were not to be planted or harvested. Every fifty years was a Year of Jubilee, a hallowed year of proclaiming liberty to all the inhabitants of the land."

He stroked her cheek with a strong hand. "I wandered more than six years. The seventh offered rest. Even though it isn't officially a Year of Jubilee, I can't help feeling it brought me liberty and freedom. You see, Lass. . ."

Matt didn't have a chance to finish. Dusty burst through the door without knocking. "There's the devil to pay," he panted. "Duke just limped in." He paused and gulped for breath. Lass wanted to scream but no sound came.

Matt's face turned bleak. "Well?" His question cracked like a whip.

Dusty's reply rang a death knell in the girl's heart. "Jed ain't with him."

Chapter 8

*For the Son of man is come to save that which was lost. How think ye? if a man
have an hundred sheep, and one of them be gone astray, doth he not leave
the ninety and nine, and goeth into the mountains,
and seeketh that which is gone astray?*
MATTHEW 18:11–12

The fickle winds of public opinion had shifted mightily in the few
weeks since Matthew Coulter returned from parts unknown. His
quiet presence and lack of ill-will toward those who once suggested
he leave town made a great and lasting impression on the inhabitants of
Jubilee. Many of those who had condemned him the loudest now proclaimed
even more loudly that they, "never had put much stock in Jed Talbot's tale of
cattle being rustled from the Tipsy T."

The settlement's change of heart brought an even deeper resentment of
Jed. Men growled to their cronies in the Sagebrush Saloon that the wrong
person had been run out of town. Others whispered a tar-and-feather party
might be in order. Yet because of Lass, not even the most bitter among them
would even consider lifting a hand against the father they despised but knew
she loved.

Into this volatile atmosphere rode grim-faced Matthew Coulter and an
equally disturbed Dusty on a cheerless morning. They blew into the Sagebrush
Saloon like a norther from Canada and wasted no time stating why they'd come.
"Lass Talbot needs our help," the acting sheriff said tersely. "Who's with us?"

Riders and townsfolk, alike, sent their chairs crashing to the floor. A call
for help on behalf of the girl they revered brought them to their feet, to a man.

Matt Coulter dared to hope they'd actually help. He heard Dusty draw in
a quick breath, then froze when the bartender called, "What's the trouble,
Sheriff?"

"Her daddy rode out to the line shack early yesterday morning," Matt said
heavily. "Last night Duke came back limping, wearing an empty saddle."

Jaws dropped in amazement. The air chilled. For seconds, or an eternity,
no one spoke. Finally, the young cowboy who had been summarily dismissed
from the Lazy T for the crime of talking with Lass earlier that month uttered
a mirthless laugh. "So Jed Talbot needs himself a rescue party in the dead of
winter." He shrugged and shoved his Stetson farther back on his head.

"Reckon I'll pass." He dropped back into his chair and propped his worn boots up against the edge of the table.

Approval whispered through the crowd. "Where's your Tipsy T riders?" someone called. "I hear tell there's still a few Jed ain't run off." Rude laughter greeted his sally and several more men parked themselves back on their chairs.

Matt started to speak, but Dusty beat him to it. Face purple as twilight over the Tetons, he bellowed, "No-good bunch of skunks up and refused to go."

"How come?" the man demanded. A growl of support rose from the crowd.

Matt saw Dusty clench his big hands. "Oh, they all had their reasons. One was plumb wore out and couldn't think of leaving the bunkhouse," he sneered. "Another said he was coming down with the 'creeping awfuls,' whatever that's supposed to be. That set off the rest of them. They all decided they were feeling mighty poorly." He paused. "None of the hands have been on the ranch long enough to appreciate and be loyal to Lass." His voice broke on the last word.

Matt thumped his fist on the nearest table. Liquor splashed from partly filled glasses. Midnight silence fell over the room. "Look, boys. I've got as much or more reason to hate Jed Talbot than anyone here, but a mighty fine girl—no, woman—needs help. Far as I know, it's the first time she's ever asked for it." Matt caught a few shamefaced nods of agreement.

Encouraged, he continued, "She agreed to wait at the ranch to see if any of you would come." He let his gaze travel from face to face. "You all know Lass Talbot and how much she thinks of her daddy, whether he deserves it or not. You all know she will head for that line shack to find Jed even if she has to go alone, which she won't. She won't. Lass will have Dusty, me, and I'm hoping some of you."

Again he scanned the men's faces. His heart sank. Few of them still looked him in the eye. Those who did wore defiant expressions. Some of those gathered shuffled their feet. How could he reach them? He must! Three searchers in a Wyoming Territory winter had little hope of finding Jed Talbot.

Words from months earlier sprang to mind, altered to fit the occasion. Matt felt his heart pound. He lowered his voice, but it rang in every corner of the silent saloon. "As acting sheriff, I could order you to go. I won't." His level gaze shifted from man to man. "What it comes down to is this: you have to decide whether you love and respect Lass more than you hate her father. If so, you'll ride out with us. Not for Jed Talbot's sake. For hers."

Matt waited long enough for what he said to sink in. "Dusty and I'll give you fifteen minutes before heading back to the Lazy T. We'll be at the store if any of you come looking for us." He turned sharply on his boot heel and strode out with the foreman at his heels. Had his impassioned plea been of any use?

Heat from the store's potbellied stove warmed Matt's hands but not his heart. From his vantage point, he could see out the window and across the street to the saloon. Dusty crowded close, silent for once. Five minutes passed. Ten. Twelve.

The saloon doors quivered and swung open. Dusty gripped Matt's arm with the force of eagle talons and hoarsely said, "Someone's coming out!" A man emerged from the saloon and hesitated just outside.

"Jury foreman from your trial," Dusty hissed. His cruel grip tightened.

Matt's icy heart leaped like an antelope in full flight. He stared at the motionless figure just outside the saloon doors. The jury foreman glanced toward the store. He took two slow steps in its direction, halted, and turned back toward the saloon, as if unsure of his next move.

"Come over here," Dusty pleaded in what sounded suspiciously like a prayer.

The uncertain man wheeled and glanced at the store once more. Then he scuttled off down the street as if pursued by a thousand howling demons.

Matt hadn't realized he was holding his breath until his lungs felt they would burst if they didn't get air. "Well, that's that. Let's ride."

"How can we tell Lass?" Dusty brokenly asked. "Not a man here will put aside his feelings long enough to help one of the finest women God ever made!" The heartbreaking question rode sidesaddle all the way to the Lazy T.

Dusty need not have been concerned over telling Lass. She knew it the moment the men rode in unaccompanied by anyone from town. "All of one accord, they began to make excuses," she told Matt and Dusty when they stepped inside. "I can't remember where I heard that saying, but it fits. Well, no use crying over what can't be helped. I'm ready to ride when you are."

"I'd like to mop up the earth with all of them," her foreman blurted out.

Lass put her hand on his arm. "Don't blame them too much," she sadly said. "Father has created bad feeling with almost everyone in Jubilee. It's natural they aren't willing to risk their lives for his sake." She searched for a smile and glued it to the lips she knew would tremble with fear and anxiety if she permitted it. "I'm just glad I have you and Matt."

Dusty turned away, but not quickly enough to hide the wetness in his eyes. "We're wasting time chinning," he gruffly said. "We need to hit the trail. Not that there will be much to follow, what with the snow and all."

"Dusty's right," Matt agreed. "Lass, won't you reconsider and let us go without you? We'll do everything we can to find your father. I promise."

Lass shook her head. "Thanks, Matt. I couldn't bear the waiting."

His jaw set in the line she knew so well. "All right, then. It's boots and saddles for all of us." He broke into the semblance of a smile that curled inside the girl's heart like a bird with its head beneath its wing to shut out storms.

❦

Lass lost track of time long before they reached the vicinity of the line shack. Sometimes she felt they had been riding for days, endless time periods fighting the elements. Despite her frantic prayers, the weather worsened. The trek changed and intensified with every hour. Although searching for Jed remained important, the blasting wind soon challenged the riders to a battle for their own survival. Lass had been in tough places during her lifetime on the range, but none had ever threatened her life and that of her companions so violently as this December day. Speech between them was impossible. Lass turned to her Father and Friend for help. Her tired brain refused to form the plea of her heart, but she knew One heard and understood. He always had. He always would.

Light snow swirled around her. It stung her face with icy slaps but kept her from sinking into apathy. At times she wondered why they were there, what they were doing out in the storm. Oh, yes. They were seeking that which was lost. The words triggered off another of the beloved Bible stories learned in the long-ago days before Mother died and Father withdrew from her and the world. Lass could almost hear her mother's voice reading the beautiful words of the story, even above the howl and whine of the storm.

"How think ye? if a man have an hundred sheep, and one of them be gone astray, doth he not leave the ninety and nine, and goeth into the mountains, and seeketh that which is gone astray?" Matthew 18:12.

In the midst of the storm, Lass again became a child. A child who pelted her mother with questions. "Were the mountains tall and rocky, like the Tetons? Were there deep canyons and rushing streams? Was the shepherd afraid to go? Did he wonder if something would hurt the ninety and nine he had to leave?"

"We don't know exactly what it was like in the country where the shepherd lived," her mother had replied. "I'm sure it was not easy. The shepherd may have been in danger and very frightened. He would, of course, have made sure the ninety and nine were safe before leaving them."

Lass had wanted to know other things in order to understand the story. "How did the shepherd know one of his sheep went astray? Did he count all the sheep in his flock every day? He had so many! Why was the lost one so important?"

"Remember what Jesus said when He began the story," Alice reminded. "He said, 'For the Son of man is come to save that which was lost.' That's why God sent His only Son. He doesn't want anyone in the whole world to ever be lost."

"Mother, if I were a lost sheep, would you and Father come find me?"

"Oh, yes!" Alice Talbot's radiant smile shone down through the years and set her daughter's heart aglow. "We love you too much to let you stay lost. So does God. Alicia, my darling, always remember this one thing: if you had been the only person who ever lived, or who ever would live, God would still have sent Jesus so someday you can live in heaven with Him. He loves you that much."

Lass squared her shoulders and rode on, comforted by the thought not three, but four, searched for the soul who went astray—in life, as well as in the storm.

Chapter 9

How think ye? if a man have an hundred sheep, and one of them
be gone astray, doth he not. . .seeketh that which is gone astray?
And if so be that he find it, verily I say unto you, he rejoiceth more of
that sheep, than of the ninety and nine which went not astray.
MATTHEW 18:12–13

Just when Lass Talbot knew she could go no farther, a muffled shout from Dusty roused her to full consciousness. "We're there. Thank God!"

Lass lifted heavy eyelids and started at the snow-shrouded line shack, faintly visible through the thick stand of trees surrounding it. Fear clogged her throat, real and heavy as the drifts that nearly obliterated the crude shack. Would Father be inside? If not, she knew he was doomed. A man without a horse or shelter in this kind of weather had no hope.

The white downpour lessened for a moment. She blinked and stared harder. Was that—yes! A thin curl of smoke rose from the chimney of the line shack. Relief poured into her, so strong it left her weak and slumped in the saddle. She turned toward Matt to share her joy. The set of his jaw silenced the words crowding into her throat and demanding release. New fear sprang full blown. For a craven moment, Lass longed to cry out, to demand they turn back into the storm and away from the shelter they had struggled so hard to attain.

Don't be a fool, part of her mind chided. *Turning back means certain death for all of you. Warmth and safety lie inside those storm-beaten walls.*

So does the possibility of tragedy, whispered another part of her mind. Lass shuddered. What might happen in this lonely place between the two men she loved? If Father had been drinking—and it seemed inconceivable he had not—the simple sight of Matt Coulter would be more than enough to send him into a rage. Once it happened, there would be no stopping whatever retribution Jed Talbot might take against the sworn enemy he felt had gone scot-free.

I must go in first, Lass told herself. *I'll stand between Father and Matt. Neither will be able to get to the other as long as I remain between them.* Her lips twisted. Was the moment she had dreaded so long racing toward her with the speed of a cyclone? The time when she must choose between Father and Matt? *Please, God, not now,* she prayed. *Not here in this isolated shack with only me and a weary Dusty to intervene.* The very thought made her shiver.

"I'll take care of the horses," Dusty volunteered.

"Come, Lass." Matt held out his hand, gaze steady but unreadable.

She slid from the saddle and clumped through the snow to the door of the line shack. Now was no time to falter. The next few minutes would irrevocably determine her future, her father's, and Matt Coulter's.

Lass pounded on the door, vaguely aware of the tang of woodsmoke and wet clothing. "Father, are you here? It's Lass." She pushed the weathered door open and stepped across the threshold into a dim and strangely silent room. A sullen fire in the open fireplace provided the only light. Lass blinked until her eyes adjusted to the gloom. A huddled form lay on one of the crude bunks built to house riders caught far from home. "Father?" she repeated.

A soft moan sent her flying to the bunk. An unshaven face burning with fever looked up from the tangled blankets. Lass found no recognition in her father's eyes. She lightly shook his shoulder. "Father," she pleaded in a voice so filled with love it should have brought Jedediah Talbot back from the grave. It didn't. He pulled away from her touch and writhed in delirium.

A strong hand gently pushed her aside. "Let me, Lass. He doesn't know you."

She numbly stepped away but came fully alive when Matt muttered something unintelligible even to her keen ears. "What is it? Is he drunk?" She sniffed the air for betraying fumes of whiskey but found none. "Matt, *what is it?*"

He ignored her except to say shortly, "He's sick, not drunk. Find a candle or lamp and get it lighted so I can examine him," he barked. "Build up that fire and heat water. Melt snow if there's no water inside. I have a hunch. . . ."

Lass didn't wait to hear what the hunch might be but flew to fetch a light.

Within minutes the line shack changed from forbidding to snug, a shelter against the storm for both searchers and the lost sheep.

It didn't take Matt long to discover the source of Jed's fever. While water heated, light from the lamp Lass held high revealed Jed's right shirt sleeve had been ripped away to form a crude bandage for a head wound. Lass gasped when Matt removed the badly stained piece of cloth. Once the compressing bandage was taken away, fresh blood leaked from a deep and angry-looking cut on the side of Jed's forehead. Dull red streaks splayed from it, an indication infection had already begun its deadly work.

"This appears to be the culprit," Matt said. He frowned. "I can't think why Jed didn't wash it out with whiskey. He had to be conscious after it happened or he couldn't have torn off his shirt sleeve and put on the bandage. Or built a fire."

"I know why," Dusty—who had come in from caring for the horses—triumphantly told him. "Far as I can tell, there ain't a speck of whiskey in this shack and hasn't been since who knows when."

Lass whirled to face the grinning foreman. "You mean. . ." Her voice died. Dusty scratched his head and looked puzzled. "I don't exactly know what

I do mean! It's just surprising that anyone, 'specially Jed Talbot, would ride out with a blizzard coming on and no whiskey in his saddlebags."

"How do you know there wasn't?" Lass demanded. Hope for something she could not explain or identify fluttered fragile wings and beat against reason.

"We had to unsaddle Duke, didn't we?" Dusty shot back. Lass caught his quick glance toward Matt. "We didn't say anything because, uh, you know what your daddy's like. Besides, we figured since we didn't find whiskey in the saddlebags, Jed probably had a bottle stashed in his shirt."

"Forget all that for now," Matt commanded in a stand-and-deliver voice. "We've got a fight on our hands. Jed needs a doctor. There's no way under heaven for us to get him one. That means each of has to do our dead level best to save him. This cut needs stitching. Can you do it, Lass? Dusty, what about you?"

Lass stared in horror and shook her head. Dusty gulped and looked sick. "I never did, but if it means saving Jed's life, I'll try. Can't you do it, Matt?"

The question hovered in stillness broken only by the now unconscious man's raspy breathing. Matt turned and gazed deep into the eyes of the girl he loved. The poignant blue light she knew and loved slowly came into his eyes. "Lass, my darling, after all that's gone before, can you trust me? Enough to put your father's life in my hands? And God's?"

The last two words didn't register. So it had come. The wishbone moment she prayed would never happen and had always known was inevitable. Memories from the past ran through her head like crown fire among summer-dried pines. So did her choices. If she refused to trust Matt, her father might die. Doing so would also mean the death of Matt's love. On the other hand, if he harbored revenge, what a perfect place to get it! Her father was so sick with fever he might well die no matter what choice she made. No one would ever be able to prove whether fever or a bungled attempt to care for him took his life.

Lass searched Matt's face for the slightest hint of triumph. She found nothing but concern, compassion, and love in the eyes of the man she cherished. So be it. Father's life lay in her choice. Right or wrong, she must follow the instincts and feelings of her heart; they had served her well all the days of her life. Lass pulled herself to full height and spoke in a clear, ringing voice. "I trust you."

Dusty made a choking sound and mumbled something about heating more water, but Matt opened his arms. Lass flew inside. Again she felt the hard beating of his heart beneath her cheek and felt she had come home. After an all too short, precious time, Matt gently put her away. "There will be time for us later. Your father needs us now." He strode across the room, rolling up his sleeves as he went. Five minutes later, he returned to the bunk, the skin of his hands shriveled from soaking in hot water. With incredible gentleness, he began the task necessary to save Jed's life.

The following hours came and went in a meaningless blur. Dusty packed in great stacks of wood and kept the fire blazing. Lass prepared simple food and prayed. Matt sat by Jed's bunk, alert to every restless move. For three days and nights, they watched and waited for the fever to run its course and subside. When it did not, Matt told his companions, "We can try packing him in snow. There's the danger of pneumonia, but. . . ."

Lass licked fear-parched lips. "Go ahead. The threat's no worse than this."

The drastic measure paid off. After the snow bath, Dusty and Matt rubbed Jed's body until his skin glowed, then wrapped him in hot blankets. The next morning, he opened glazed eyes—and looked straight into his sworn enemy's face! With a wild cry, he raised himself up, then went limp and fell back.

"Are we going to lose him now, after all our hard work?" Lass cried.

"Not if I can help it!" Matt said grimly. "Please, God, let this only be a setback. I was a fool to let him see me before I could explain I didn't come back to get him!"

"You didn't!" Dusty exclaimed.

Lass froze. Enlightenment penetrated the dim recesses of her mind. "You just said, 'Please, God.'" Words that had made no impression at the time swept in and brushed the cobwebs from her weary brain. "I remember. The day you stitched Father's head, you asked if I could trust you. You said, 'Enough to put your father's life in my hands? *And God's.*' Matthew Coulter, are you a Christian?" She caught at his sleeve. "Have you forgiven my father?"

"I am. I have. I started to tell you the night Duke came in without Jed. There's been no opportunity since." He lifted her hand from his arm and sighed. "Again, this is no time to discuss it. Buck up, Lass. Your father still needs us."

All that day and night, the three faithful friends hovered like ministering angels over the man who had wronged them. "More like angels in the snow," Dusty succinctly said when the bad weather continued. Their efforts were rewarded. The following day Jed again opened his eyes. This time a slight stirring of his body warned the others. Matt immediately stepped to the far side of the line shack. Jed wouldn't be able to see him from the bunk.

"Lass?" her father whispered. "Dusty." He shook his head as if to clear it.

"Don't try to talk," the foreman warned, after Lass nodded. She suspected Dusty knew she couldn't have spoken if an avalanche threatened the line shack!

A faint trace of the smile his daughter once knew and loved crossed Jed Talbot's haggard face. "Who's the boss around here, anyway?" he asked.

"Lass and me," Dusty promptly told him. "Get some shut-eye. You can talk when you're stronger."

Jed moved his head from side to side. "I can't rest until I talk. Just in case. . ." His voice trailed off, and he stared at the ceiling with anguished eyes.

Chapter 10

And it shall come to pass, that before they call,
I will answer; and while they are yet speaking, I will hear.
ISAIAH 65:24

Lass clasped the hand plucking at the blankets. "Speak quickly, if you must."

Jed's words fell like pebbles in a pond, sending waves of shock. "The night you showed me what I'd become, I prayed God would let me die."

Lass gasped, but her father relentlessly continued. "I knew I couldn't go on as I'd done since Alice died, one of the living dead. I could no longer stand the man I'd become. I believe that recognition was God's last warning."

Lass blinked. *Her father*, mentioning God other than in bitterness and blame? Matt appeared to have turned to stone. Dusty coughed and shifted position.

Jed didn't seem to notice. "I left my whiskey at the Lazy T. If I couldn't survive without it, I'd at least die sober." A mirthless grin brightened his stern face. "Fate—no, God—had other plans. Duke and I made it to within a half mile of the shack before he stepped on a rotten, snow-covered log. It broke. He fell. So did I. Something smashed against my head, and everything went black."

Jed licked dry lips. "Dusty, get me some water, will you?" His faithful foreman nodded and obeyed. The injured man drank it and continued. "I came to, wondering where I was and what had happened to my horse."

"Duke made it back," Dusty put in. "A little lame, but he will be all right."

"Good. Anyway, I don't remember much after that. I know I ripped a sleeve from my shirt and wrapped my head to stop the bleeding. I remember stumbling into the shack and reaching the bunk before blacking out. I woke up cold, got a fire going, then hit the bunk again. After that, nothing." Jed's face shadowed and he half turned from Lass. "That's the easy part."

She tightened her grip on his hand. Her nerves twanged. She sent a warning glance toward the corner where Matt hunkered down out of her father's sight.

"Why don't you wait?" she whispered to Jed. "You don't have to go on now."

"I've waited too long as it is," he said harshly. "I suspect Dusty knows but is too loyal to say so. Maybe for Alice's sake." Jed turned back to his daughter.

"Matt Coulter never rustled a single Lazy T steer. I framed him. You were all I had left after Alice died, Lass. I couldn't stand the idea of anyone taking you away from me." A dull flush suffused his worn face. "I never worried until Matt came along. Then I saw in your eyes the same expression Alice used to wear."

Lass felt her face flame. She gave an inarticulate cry and started to pull away.

Jed refused to let her go. "Hear me out. Please." His eyes reminded the girl of a child pleading for love and forgiveness. "I don't have any excuse, except I was so bitter at God for taking Alice, I went loco." He lay quietly for a moment.

A change stole over his features. His eyes grew bright. His voice strengthened. "If I make it back to the Lazy T, I want you to send for Matt Coulter and Sheriff McVeigh. If I don't get out of here, it's up to you and Dusty. I don't expect Matt or the town to forgive me, but Jubilee needs to know the truth. God and I had it out the night I learned Matt had come back wearing a US Marshall's badge and could put me away if he spoke up. Jail couldn't be worse than the prison of my own making I've lived in for years."

A wistful note crept into Jed's voice. "Lass, if no one—even you—ever forgives me, I think maybe God will. I wish I could be sure." Color flooded his stubbled face. "I want you to know it's not just because I'm scared and ashamed to face Him and Alice. If I'm going to cash in, I'd like it to be knowing Matt Coulter understands I tried to square things."

The sudden grating of heavy boots on the hard floor sounded loud in the small room. A tall figure stepped to the edge of the bunk. Backlighted by flames in the fireplace and the dull, yellow glow from a lamp on the crude table, Matt Coulter cast an ominous, looming shadow. Lass held her breath and waited.

Jed tilted his head back and looked at the dark form above him. *"You!"* He raised himself to a sitting position. "You were here all the time?"

"Yes." The affirmation left no room for compromise.

Jed's eyes burned from the shadows with a look Lass felt must scorch anyone in its path. "You helped Dusty and Lass care for me." Not a question, but a statement. "Were you the one who patched my head?"

"I was."

Why must Matt sound colder than the highest peak on Grand Teton? Lass wondered. Had her ears deceived her into thinking he'd proclaimed himself a Christian and had forgiven her father? The wonderful hope that sprang to life with Matt's declaration struggled to survive then chilled. So did the joy that surged through her when her father unburdened himself of his long-held wrong, recognizing there was little hope of forgiveness unless by God.

Jed fell back against the pillow. "In the name of all that's holy, *why?*"

Matt stepped aside until fire and lamplight shone directly on Jed. "A man called Pastor Andrew brought me back from the dead. When I was ready to ask Jesus to be my Trailmate, he told me I couldn't do it with hate in my heart."

Jed gasped, but the steady voice went on. "Pastor Andrew said I had to love God more than I hated you. That I had no choice when you cheated me of my good name, but you couldn't cheat me out of my salvation unless I let you."

"You had a choice the first time!" Jed muttered. "You knew I railroaded you. Why did you say nothing except that you were innocent? It's stuck in my craw ever since. Couldn't you prove I was lying?"

Matt didn't answer.

Not so Dusty. "He did it for Lass, you long-legged donkey," the foreman blazed. "Begging your pardon, Boss, but I've had a lot of time to figure. The way I see it, Matt reckoned it was better to take the blame and ride out than show you up as a mean, ornery skunk. He couldn't stand having Lass lose her daddy less than a year after her mama was took."

Lass reeled from the truth. She stared at Dusty. At Jed. Finally, at Matt, who had kept the faith. Hot tears came. She turned from her father and blindly rushed into Matt's arms. "Why didn't you tell me? You could at least have written!"

She felt his arms twitch. "I did, Lass. The letters all came back."

All her anger and the hurt of thinking herself forgotten spilled out. "Father?"

His words sounded muffled. "Yes. I told myself it was for the best."

Matt's arm tightened over her shoulders, and he said to the man in the bunk, "Jedediah Talbot, you're a miserable sinner. So am I. There's one difference. It took a long time for me to admit it, but I did. God's forgiven me because of what His Son did a long time ago. You said you wished you could be sure God would forgive you. You confessed your sins before Him and before us, not knowing I was here." Laughter eased the tension in Matt's rich voice. "I'm glad you didn't know. It makes it a lot easier for me to believe you mean it. That's what it's all about: being sorry; receiving forgiveness; riding new trails, with Him."

"You really believe God will forgive me?" Jed whispered. Lass wanted to weep at the uncertain hope in the question. How far Father had fallen from the joyous Christian man who was once head of the Talbot household!

"He already has, Jed." Matt's words rang with truth. "The Bible says so.

"Pastor Andrew showed me the promise in Isaiah where the Lord says He will answer before we call and that He hears us while we're still speaking."

Matt stopped. His voice dropped to little more than a whisper, yet sounded louder than a shout to Lass Talbot's heart when he said, "I also know God will forgive you *because I have*, and He's a lot more willing to pardon than I am."

Great tears coursed down Jed's leathery time-worn face. He made no effort to wipe them away. He had come to the line shack expecting to die. By the grace of God, he would leave a new man. He nodded and a few minutes later, his even breathing told Lass he had fallen into the sleep his body needed to heal.

Dusty cleared his throat and stepped to the window. "Storm's over."

Matt smiled down at the girl in his arms. The wonderful blue light Lass knew shone for her came back into his eyes. "In more ways than one."

Lass rested her tired head against his chest. "Yes. Oh, Matt. . ." She couldn't go on. For seven long years they had waited. Now their jubilee beckoned, more joyful than Christmas hymns. More fragrant than crushed hemlock branches. More golden than the ring Matt would soon place on her finger to make her his. More precious than the Christmas Eve snow angels they would make.

What "secret angel" gifts could she bestow this year? Anticipation sent a thrill through her. Dared she give her father the little store of Christmas letters that vowed to pray for him every day of the year?

Perhaps, even though it would break tradition by being given openly. Great-grandfather had told his family to always give their best. How little gold, frankincense, and myrrh meant compared with the gift of prayer!

"What are you thinking, my darling?" Matt whispered. The light in his eyes intensified until Lass felt she would drown in their blueness.

"About Christmas and the best gifts."

"What happened here today is all I need or want," he said quietly.

"And I."

Someday she would learn the full story of Matt's long years of searching. Someday he would know the pain she had felt when she believed he had deserted her. For now, it was enough to hold him close and silently thank God.

About the Authors

Irene B. Brand is a lifelong resident of West Virginia, where she lives with her husband, Rod. Irene's first inspirational romance was published in 1984, and since that time she has had multiple books published. Many of her books have been inspired while traveling to 49 of the United States and 24 foreign countries.

Kristin Billerbeck makes her home in the Silicon Valley with her engineering director husband and their four children. In addition to writing, Kristin enjoys painting, reading, and conversing online.

Lauralee Bliss has always liked to dream big dreams. Part of that dream was writing, and after several years of hard work, her dream of publishing was realized in 1997 with the publication of her first romance novel, *Mountaintop*, through Barbour Publishing. Since then she's had twenty books published, both historical and contemporary. Lauralee is also an avid hiker, completing the entire length of the Appalachian Trail both north and south. Lauralee makes her home in Virginia in the foothills of the Blue Ridge Mountains with her family.

Tamela Hancock Murray lives in northern Virginia with her two daughters and her husband of over twenty years. She keeps busy with church and school activities, but in her spare time she's written seven Bible trivia books and twenty Christian romance novels and novellas.

Lynn A. Coleman is an award-winning and bestselling author of *Key West* and other books. Lynn is also the founder of American Christian Fiction Writers. One of her primary reasons for starting ACFW was to help writers to develop their writing skills and to encourage others to go deeper in their relationship with God. She makes her home in Keystone Heights, Florida, where her husband of thirty-six years serves as pastor of Friendship Bible Church. Together they are blessed with three children and eight grandchildren.

Bestselling author **Vickie McDonough** grew up wanting to marry a rancher, but instead, she married a computer geek who is scared of horses. She now lives out her dreams in her fictional stories. Vickie is the award-winning author of over thirty published books and novellas. Vickie is a wife of thirty-eight years, mother of four grown sons and one daughter-in-law, and grandma to a feisty eight-year-old girl. When she's not writing, Vickie enjoys reading, antiquing, watching movies, and traveling.

Kelly Eileen Hake received her first writing contract at the tender age of seventeen and arranged to wait three months until she was able to legally sign it. Writing for Barbour combines two of Kelly's great loves—history and reading. A CBA bestselling author and member of American Christian Fiction Writers, she's been privileged to earn numerous Heartsong Presents Reader's Choice Awards and is known for her witty, heartwarming historical romances. A newlywed, she and her gourmet-chef husband live in Southern California with their golden lab mix, Midas!

Therese Stenzel enjoys staying home with her children in Oklahoma, where she and her husband making their home. Obsessed with English history, English tea, and reading historical novels, she writes historical novels full-time.

Colleen L. Reece was born and raised in a small western Washington logging town. She learned to read by kerosene lamplight and dreamed of someday writing a book. God has multiplied Colleen's "someday" book into more than 140 titles that have sold six million copies. Colleen was twice voted Heartsong Presents' Favorite Author and later inducted into Heartsong's Hall of Fame. Several of her books have appeared on the CBA Bestseller list.